THE OLYMPIA READER

EDITED BY MAURICE GIRODIAS

THE

OLYMPIA

READER

SELECTIONS FROM *THE* TRAVELLER'S COMPANION *SERIES*

Designed and Illustrated by
Norman Rubington

GROVE PRESS, INC., NEW YORK

TRANSLATORS

Story of O translated by Sabine Destré

The Thief's Journal and *Our Lady of the Flowers*
translated by Bernard Frechtman

Justine translated by Richard Seaver and Austryn Wainhouse

Madame Edwarda translated by Austryn Wainhouse

Zazie translated by Akbar del Piombo and Eric Kahane

CONTENTS

THE OLYMPIA READER

Maurice Girodias is the patriarch of this group, which includes sisters Nicole (left) and Sylvie. Brother Eric (with finger in mouth) became famous for his translations into French of *Lolita* and *Naked Lunch*.

INTRODUCTION
Maurice Girodias

I founded The Olympia Press in Paris, in the spring of 1953. It was a shoestring operation if ever there was one. It was conceived as a desperate move on my part to escape complete social and economic annihilation. During the three preceding years I had led an uncertain, inactive life, trying to absorb the enormous blow I had suffered when my previous publishing business had collapsed—or rather had been taken away from me—in 1950. I had lived in near-complete bumhood during that period of obscurity, dragging myself from miserable room to even more miserable room, spending what little energy I still had devising extravagant and pitiful stratagems to borrow or otherwise procure money. My only companion was my brother Eric, who was in nearly as bad shape as I; but he was 27 and I was 34, and I felt utterly senile. He, at least, was still man enough to cook pathetic little meals on an alcohol lamp, which helped us survive from day to day. Ugh.

Publishing books in English, in Paris, books that would sell easily because they would belong to the "not to be sold in U.S.A. & U.K." category, appeared at one point to be the only possible way for me to make money and build up a new publishing business in spite of my lack of capital. My father, Jack Kahane, had, before me, founded his own publishing house, The Obelisk Press, in the 'thirties. I was still in touch and on very friendly terms with Henry Miller, who had been his major literary discovery. Henry would certainly help by giving me one of his unpublished manuscripts to start me off; only a few years before, in 1947, I had put up a big fight on his behalf. My other chance was that I had made friends with a couple of printers who said they would extend some credit on the first books I would give them to print.

But if I am to tell here, however briefly, the story of The Olympia Press, I must begin at the beginning, that is, with my father's experience in the 'thirties.

My father was born in 1888, a Jewish gentleman from Manchester, one of three brothers who came after a group of nine sisters. His family was wealthy but the early demise of my grandfather soon caused the tribal fortunes to be dissipated. My father was thus successively a silver-spoonfed infant and a very poor orphan; he did not go to the University but nevertheless he developed a great taste for the theater, writing, and music, which arts he practiced with great amateur enthusiasm. He made quite a bit of money; became an attraction to the ladies and an expert in elegant living, being the owner of seven bulldogs and fifty pairs of trousers. The outbreak of the first World War coincided with a great emotional catastrophe in his life. He gave away everything he owned and volunteered to die; but instead of quickly dying he discovered through a telescope, from the top of the gray-white cliffs surrounding Marseilles, a new facet of the life he was not yet to quit—a bubbly, charming, piquant young French bourgeoise, Marcelle Eugénie Girodias, whom he was to marry three years later, in 1917, after having been through the hell of Ypres and a good bit of what followed.

In the spring of 1919 I awoke to the light of life under the sign of Aries with Leo in the ascendant, the son of that Entente Cordiale couple, in the mellow comfort of my French grandparents' apartment on Avenue du Bois, now the Avenue Foch. My first years were thus spent in the quiet luxury of drapes and lace, velvet and gilt, Louis XV furniture and Chinese art, rich smells of Sunday roasts and the whiffs of lavender coming from the linen closet. Far below, under the tall trees bordering the Avenue, red-faced nurses from Auvergne or Brittany were pushing baby carriages filled with the hope of France, and eyeing gauche soldiers from under their bonnets; immaculate horsemen were torturing their mounts for the benefit of a pale lady, mysterious in the shade of a frilly parasol.

German gases had ruined my father's lungs and he fell very ill shortly after I was born. Tuberculosis, in those days, was quite as frightening and deadly as cancer today; the only known cure was crisp mountain air, and it was only by a miracle, and thanks to my mother's care, that he pulled through. But after that my father's protracted convalescence forced us to live in the country, and he spent the postwar years shut off from all practical activities. As a reaction, no doubt, he started to write light novels, usually quite funny, with such titles as *To Laugh and Grow Rich*, *Suzy Falls Off*, etc. His publisher, Grant Richards, went bankrupt. My father had invested some capital in a small French publishing venture and that went down too. Then came the depression of the 'thirties in France and my grandfather in turn quickly lost all his money, of which he had had quite a lot. The home of my childhood, the poetic Château-du-Fond-des-Forêts, with all its memories, had to be sold for a small portion of what it was worth, both in dreams and in money, to a French family of primitive *nouveaux riches* who started growing potatoes on the well-manicured lawns. The house was fortunately destroyed by fire a few years later.

My father was more or less on his feet by then. We settled in Paris. He decided to publish his own books and went into partnership with a French printer. The first book he brought out under the imprint of The Obelisk Press was one of his own, *Daffodil*, a refreshing, neatly recounted tale about a young lady losing her virtue by stages, which sold well and regularly for years to eager, naive tourists.

England was still so completely Victorian in those years, so strangely prudish. It seems hard to understand how a whole generation of men who had been through the toughest of wars—and won—could be reduced to the level of schoolchildren, and be told what to read and what not to read by a conglomerate of spinsters and bowler-hatted policemen. My father had emigrated for good to a country where freedom was not a vain word, and I wonder what would have happened to him if he had ever returned to England to live. He was revolted by the near-hysterical conformism of that society which covered with abuse a man like D. H. Lawrence, and let him be tormented and quartered by the hounds of decency.

The little my father had ever said on the subject had made a deep impression on me. And I was awakening to the social reality of that time of the greatest of all horrors: the Spanish Civil War. I saw freedom in agony, I saw the victory of the mercenary legions from Morocco over that grandiose, improvised, ill-fitted Republic. I understood how the forces of reaction at work in Spain were the same as those which had caused Joyce to be morally exiled from England; the same on which the German and Italian dictators were building their black and brown empires. Since my earliest childhood, the notion of individual freedom had been deeply rooted in me. Everything I saw or felt as I was growing up turned into a passion—a passion I shared with millions of contemporary Frenchmen, although my own brand drew me toward a form of individualistic anarchy while the others usually went toward practical communism or socialism. I resented and hated *l'esprit bourgeois* in all its manifestations, but I also distrusted all forms of human association.

I had, by inclination, elected Proust as my literary god, but Céline's *Voyage au bout de la nuit* came as a revelation of a totally different order. Soon after came another similar shock when I read Henry Miller's *Tropic of Cancer*, which had been published by my father for the first time in 1934.

Miller had been my father's pet genius during the brief career of The Obelisk Press. My father had also published young Lawrence Durrell's first novel, *The Black Book,* and others by Anaïs Nin, Cyril Connolly, a fragment of Joyce's *Work In Progress* (*Haveth Childers Everywhere*, printed in a limited edition) and his *Pomes Penyeach;* also, not to be forgotten, that cosmic monument of sexo-journalistico-literary bombast, Frank Harris' *My Life and Loves.*

War was imminent. My father hurriedly finished the manuscript of his *Memoirs of a Booklegger,* and was discovered dead on the morning of September 3, 1939, stricken by the sheer horror of it all. I was twenty. I found myself in the situation of a middle-aged male with a sizable family to feed, but I had strictly no experience of any sort, and, in the guise of capital, all I had was a collection of bar debts left by my father.

After a number of very disconcerting adventures which happened in quick succession during those months when our Gallic civilization was so easily falling apart I started a publishing firm of my own, Les

Editions du Chêne, which specialized in art books and was quite successful from the start in spite of my complete ignorance of all technical, commercial, or financial matters; in spite, also, of the fact that my initial capital consisted merely of one ton of canned celery, acquired on the black market but which proved to be entirely worthless.

After the war, I extended my activities toward literature and I revived my father's Obelisk Press; we did new printings of Henry Miller's books, which sold in immense quantities as compared to the few hundred copies sold before the war, and became part of the G.I.'s European education. We compiled a new version of *The Memoirs of Fanny Hill* from the two earliest known editions of that archetype of libertine literature, and sold, I believe, close to one hundred thousand copies. I was also still very active as a French-language publisher: I put out a series of Russian classics in French; launched a few good novels, among them Nikos Kazantzakis' *Alexis Zorba* (his first published work, I believe), side by side with political essays, books on art and archeology, a literary-philosophical review, edited by Georges Bataille and titled *Critique* (which later was taken up by other publishers and, much to my surprise, has survived through the years), and a variety of other publications including a journal devoted to the art of knitting. All this was done in my new headquarters which consisted of a small palace situated at 4, rue de la Paix.

I had never had any really brutal contacts with the law until the two legal battles which took place in those postwar years. One of them was when I was sued for libel jointly with Yves Farge, a prominent French Resistance figure who was the author of a pamphlet I had published in which he exposed the collusion between certain big business interests and the French administration. Our opponent was one of the bosses of the Socialist Party which was in power at the time: Félix Gouin. He had also been the first President of the Gaullist Republic in Algiers, in 1942, and carried much ponderous weight. The trial lasted close to one whole week, with several members of the government appearing in court as witnesses for the prosecution; it was quite an exciting experience. Finally, we won the case against our formidable adversary, which fact should certainly be held to the credit of the French judicial system of the time.

The second scuffle has been known as *l'affaire Miller*, the first case of literary censorship to occur in France in many years. It took place shortly after the war, in 1946 and 1947, when I first released a French translation of Henry Miller's *Tropic of Capricorn,* shortly after which Miller's *Tropic of Cancer* and *Black Spring* were printed in French by two other firms. I was prosecuted together with the two other publishers under the 1939 law on obscene publications: this was not only the first application of that law, it was also the first case of this nature to be tried publicly since the famous prosecutions against Flaubert's *Madame Bovary* and Baudelaire's *Fleurs du mal* one half-century before, which had left such an uncomfortable impression in the memory of all French magistrates.

France had been considered the land of freedom, of intellectual and political liberties, ever since the eighteenth century, ever since Diderot and Voltaire, ever since the rules and principles of modern democracy had been set up by the 1789 Revolution. There had been difficult moments, naturally, under the reigns of the two Napoleons, before and during the 1870 and 1914 wars, or during such crises as *l'affaire Dreyfus.* Conservatism, colonialism, racism, and religious intolerance are part of the make-up of the French bourgeois, who is just as bigoted, brainlessly selfish, and frightened as his counterparts in the other countries. But in France the liberal and progressive elements have, in the last two centuries, asserted a generally dominant influence on the political and intellectual life of the country. People really believed in the dogmas represented by such words as Freedom, Progress, and Democracy, which seemed as necessary to any Frenchman as food or air.

But in the last twenty years a sinister change has taken place. What looked like a perennial tradition has been dismantled in less than a generation; Freedom, Progress, and Democracy are now no more than quaint slogans from the past, which are only to show how naive and inefficiently romantic the prewar Frenchmen were.

Many believe that this change in a nation's attitude has been brought about by the recent political upheavals. It seems to me that it works the other way around: the change of regime is but one consequence of a much deeper, subterranean alteration of the national psyche. The French bourgeoisie constitutes the backbone of the country; they were scared nearly out of their wits by the socialist and communist offensive which developed in the country at the time of the Spanish Civil War; they were mortally humiliated by the German victory a few years later; and now they are reacting convulsively against their earlier fears and humiliations. Modern bourgeois extremism is being built up against bourgeois liberalism of old. France is now entirely dominated, owned, manipulated, exploited, milked, policed by *les bourgeois* for *les bourgeois*. The victims of a strange osmosis, the French Communists themselves have turned bourgeois, and, quite naturally, they are even more intolerably bourgeois than the bourgeois-born bourgeois. The whole country reeks of *ennui*, of priggish virtues; everywhere you come up against Nietzschean clowns, dyspeptic Machiavellis. All the fun and gaiety have left this nation; the Algerian war chased the last colonies of young artists and loafers away from Paris; in this hygienic-looking city, whitewashed by governmental decree, the spirit is dead, the secular feast is ended . . .

The prosecution against the Miller books was the first sign of the evolution which was to culminate, after some fifteen years, in the present unhappy state of things. However, at that time, the French intellectuals had just regained their precious freedom after four years of German occupation and everybody protested very loudly. Committees were formed for the defense of Henry Miller and, through him, of freedom of expression. It seemed to work, at first. After two years of uncertain litigation, the case was dropped by the Ministry of Justice. I took this as a victory; and I did not know how wrong such a view would prove to be in the long run.

But I had other worries. My affairs were in bad shape, as I had expanded my business too quickly without paying the least attention to the notion of money—a habit rather deeply ingrained in me, I confess. I was forced to make an agreement with my chief creditors, which now appears to me as a masochistic trap I had laid for myself: I slaved for three years on the tiniest salary in order to pay my debts, and I had nearly accomplished that noble aim when one of the creditors conspired to get control of my firm—and then sold his ill-acquired interest to a big publisher. I was expelled from my own company, unable to understand or resist that piece of classical capitalistic maneuvering.

It was a cruel lesson, as Les Editions du Chêne had become my flesh and blood, and losing it made me feel like King Saud must have felt being suddenly deprived of all his wives. I tried to put up a fight to recover my property and wasted in the attempt one whole year, as well as money I did not possess, and what little energy I still had in me. As to my adversaries, once they had obtained control of my publishing house, they found that they had acquired, dishonorably and at an enormous expense, a handful of sand: Les Editions du Chêne was left to vegetate and slowly perish.

This long digression has brought me back to the beginning of my story. Perhaps it will make the founding of The Olympia Press comprehensible: I would never have launched into that next phase of my publishing career had I not acquired over the years the urge to attack the Universal Establishment with all the means at my disposal. To fight one head of the beast rather than another had no real importance; to fight French intolerance or Anglo-American moral conventions really came to the same thing.

In the spring of 1953, then, The Olympia Press, was founded, a shoestring operation par excellence.

The offices consisted of a small room at the back of a rundown bookstore at 13 rue Jacob, and the staff of myself and a part-time secretary: tiny, gray-eyed Lisa.

The first manuscript I acquired was Henry Miller's *Plexus;* this came out in a two-volume numbered edition together with Sade's *Bedroom Philosophers* (the first and so far only English translation of *La Philosophie dans le boudoir*) Apollinaire's *Memoirs of a Young Rakehell,* and Georges Bataille's *Tale of Satisfied Desire* (in French: *L'Histoire de l'oeil*—published anonymously under the sweet pseudonym of Pierre Angélique).

Apollinaire's famous exercise in the eroticism of adolescence had been translated by Dick Seaver, and Austryn Wainhouse had done the English version of both the Bataille and Sade books. They both were members of a very colorful group whose nucleus was an English-language, Paris-based literary quarterly called *Merlin,* which had been founded in the spring of 1952. The erratic pope of that pagan church was Alex Trocchi, of Italo-Scottish extraction, Alex of the somber, fiery brow—who turned himself into a literary lady of little virtue by the name of Frances Lengel and wrote a novel titled *Helen and Desire* which was to become the model of a new brand of modern erotic writing. Pale, ill-fed, ill-garbed Christopher Logue was tortured by many poetic ambitions of high stature, but nevertheless allowed himself to write a pre-Jamesbondian novel entitled *Lust;* and to give him encouragement I bestowed on him the pseudonym of Count Palmiro Vicarion. Patrick Bowles, Philip Oxman, Baird Bryant,

Alfred Chester, John Stevenson and John Coleman were all more or less directly connected with *Merlin,* as was also, at a prudent distance, George Plimpton. Iris Owens became an important addition, and Marilyn Meeske. Some of them contributed to The Olympia Press novels which were usually violently extravagant and outrageous.

I usually printed five thousand copies of each book, and paid a flat fee for the manuscript which, although modest, formed the substance of many an expatriate budget. My publishing technique was simple in the extreme, at least in the first years: when I had completely run out of money I wrote blurbs for imaginary books, invented sonorous titles and funny pen names (Marcus van Heller, Akbar del Piombo, Miles Underwood, Carmencita de las Lunas, etc.) and then printed a list which was sent out to our clientele of booklovers, tempting them with such titles as *White Thighs, The Chariot of Flesh, The Sexual Life of Robinson Crusoe, With Open Mouth,* etc. They immediately responded with orders and money, thanks to which we were again able to eat, drink, write, and print. I could again advance money to my authors, and they hastened to turn in manuscripts which more or less fitted the descriptions.

It was great fun. The Anglo-Saxon world was being attacked, invaded, infiltrated, out-flanked, and conquered by this erotic armada. The Dickensian schoolmasters of England were convulsed with helpless rage, the judges' hair was standing on end beneath their wigs, black market prices in New York and London for our green-backed products were soaring to fantastic heights.

Enough has been said about the influence of the printed word; but never enough about the liberating influence of the printed four-letter word. Those literary orgies, those torrents of systematic bad taste were quite certainly instrumental in clearing the air, and clearing out a few mental cobwebs. The imbecile belief that sex is sin, that physical pleasure is unclean, that erotic thoughts are immoral, that abstinence is the proper rule which may be broken at rare intervals, but merely for the sake of procreation—all those sick Judeo-Christian ideas were exposed for what they are. I insist that no little boys were ever corrupted by bad books of mine, and I do hope that they enjoyed them to the full, and gleaned at least a little useful knowledge therefrom; nobody seems to have died of shock, no reader was ever reported killed by a four-letter word.

After a few years the black market prices began to collapse. The first shock was over, and formerly obsessed readers had become used to the notion that their clandestine world was open to all, that the secret was a fake, that nothing was reprehensible or forbidden. Once a Soho bookseller wrote to me angrily after I had published *Lolita*, and fulminated because I was ruining my business (and his) printing such wishy-washy stuff, and that it was not worth the risk of smuggling it through customs. I answered that my books were quite as dirty as ever, and that I was happy to have helped cure a whole nation of its immature delusions.

The d.b.'s (short for "dirty books") were published in the green paperback volumes that constitute The Traveller's Companion Series, side by side with more respectable items. That confusion was deliberate, as it made it easy to sell the higher class of literature: the d.b.'s fans were as fascinated by the ugly plain green covers as the addict by the white powder, however deceptive both may prove to be. The confusion was also meant to keep the police at bay, as I had soon become the object of their special attention.

Samuel Beckett, with Henry Miller, was the first contemporary writer of importance to appear in our earliest catalogue. *Merlin*, whose editors—Trocchi, Seaver, and Wainhouse—were Beckett's enthusiastic supporters in the early 'fifties, had published his work extensively in their magazine, and had negotiated a contract with him to publish several of his novels and thus begin their own book-publishing enterprise in Paris. But eventually Collection Merlin —as the publishing house was to be called—joined forces with Olympia, and the first work issued under this arrangement was the last novel Beckett wrote directly in English, *Watt*. Soon afterward Beckett himself was introduced to the backroom of the rue Jacob.

Watt is the archetype of the Beckettian hero, the servant-hobo who moves in a clockwork world of repetition, and attends to the enigmatic needs of a never-present master; the creatures in *Waiting for Godot, Molloy, Malone Dies* and their likes all derive from the same mold. But that earlier novel was written directly in English and it seems to me that it was never surpassed by the later novels or plays, nearly all of which were written in French (and later translated into English by Beckett himself, once in collaboration with Patrick Bowles). In *Watt* the dialogues are sumptuous, and the Beckettian approach to the Beckettian reality is most impressive.

Bernard Frechtman had privately published his translation of

Jean Genet's novel, *Our Lady of the Flowers*, and offered it to me to take on, which I gladly did, and we followed that with *The Thief's Journal*. Those first years were full of excitement and great discoveries: the word went around in Britain and in America that there was a new English-language publisher in Paris who seemed ready to publish everything that was unconventional and likely to be outlawed by the archaic censorship rules which were still being enforced at the time (the early 'fifties) in England and in the United States, and I was flooded with daily waves of unpublished literature.

Thus I received in the spring of 1955 two manuscripts, one by a young unknown American writer living in England by the name of J. P. Donleavy, who had written a rather unruly but scintillating novel: *The Ginger Man;* the other by a Russian-born professor from Cornell University, Vladimir Nabokov: *Lolita*. I was moving from wonder to wonder.

Donleavy accepted with good grace our remarks concerning the rambling, redundant form of his book and Austryn's wife, Muffie Wainhouse, did a great job of editing it. Nabokov also complied—to a certain extent—with our suggestion that he suppress a number of French phrasings and locutions which endangered the delicate balance of his style. In both cases I think we acted efficiently and intelligently, as very few legitimate publishers would have done, and I was repaid in each instance by the blackest ingratitude. As one consequence of this, Vladimir Nabokov has refused to let us publish any part of *Lolita* in this volume, which is infinitely regrettable; and thus, in the space formerly reserved for that excerpt, the reader will find the gloomy recital of my encounter with a man of near-genius: Vladimir Nabokov.

Mason Hoffenberg was always trying to convince me that his manuscripts were glorious little achievements and that they were thick enough to be converted into books; and I was quite relieved when, one day, he brought over his friend, Terry Southern, who was then living in Switzerland, with a proposal that they write a book together for The Traveller's Companion Series. I had never met Terry before, although I had heard about his wild sense of humor, and I sensed that working with Terry would help bring out the constructive aspects of Mason's submerged talents. We agreed that the story should be about sweet, blue-eyed, curvaceous Candy, an entirely comestible product of the New World Establishment, and about her delightful discovery of our inconsequential world. The deal was set —and by the by it was to lead to one of the most extravagant adventures in publishing, an adventure which is reaching its unforetold climax in the United States at the time of this writing.

One rainy day—in the spring of 1957, I believe—Allen Ginsberg brought in a rather bulky, pasted-up manuscript and declared that it was a work of genius such I could never hope to find again in my publisher's life. William Burroughs, the author, was then living in Tangiers and this first full-length book of his was made of jigsaw illuminations harvested in the course of fifteen years of drug addiction. It was a brilliant, completely iconoclastic work, but I gave it back to Allen after a few days of reflection with the philistine remark that the material was wonderful but it would be inaccessible to the lay reader due to the deliberate lack of any rule whatsoever in the organization of the text. Allen left me with an ugly expression on his face—but came back one year later with the same manuscript, allegedly redone. I read it again and immediately decided to print it; the first edition appeared in 1959.

I had moved from the rue Jacob to vaster precincts in a tumble-down house at 8 rue de Nesle, which I shared with Jean-Jacques Pauvert, a young publisher who had published, among other things, the complete works of Sade in French—a very courageous undertaking at the time. One day Jean-Jacques handed me a manuscript that Jean Paulhan (the gray eminence of the famous firm of Gallimard) had recommended to him. He was not certain he wanted to publish the book for all kinds of reasons, among them safety, and wanted me to read it. The author was anonymous—allegedly a woman—and Paulhan had refused to reveal her, or his, identity. The book was quite amazing: the first erotic novel conceived as such, and written with a care, an intelligence and restraint which are not usually associated with under-the-counter literature. I persuaded Jean-Jacques to print it in French, and I simultaneously released an English version: thus began the career of *Histoire d'O*.

We had by then developed a certain style in publishing which was leading in all kinds of interesting directions. The circumstances were favorable, although the group which had developed around *Merlin* a few years before had gradually disintegrated. But Paris was still filled with the remains of the postwar generation of expatriates,

who often combined a good classical background with a great desire
to do away once and for all with the gray shades of the past.

Writing d.b.'s was generally considered a useful professional
exercise, as well as a necessary participation in the common fight
against the Square World—an act of duty. What the Square World
exactly was, nobody could have explained with any precision:
but the notion was very strong, indeed; and it was not the usual routine of a new generation picking a quarrel with the old, it was a
much stronger and deeper protest; not a protest against war or
hunger, or against the bomb, but, beyond that, a protest against the
mental weakness, the poverty of spirit, and the general lack of genius
and generosity of a rich and sclerotic society. The colorful banner of
pornography was as good as any other to rally the rebels: the more
ludicrous the form of the revolt, the better it was, as the revolt was
primarily against ordinary logic, and ordinary good taste, and restraint
and current morals.

The contributors to The Olympia Press usually were genuine
writers and even the most one-sided and single-minded creations of
that time often reveal attractive talents. Harriet Daimler's books are
obviously the work of a very gifted novelist—and it is quite possible
that the person behind that pseudonym would never have had a book
published had it not been for the facilities offered by Olympia's
specialty of d.b.'s. Akbar del Piombo (in real life an American painter
long established in Paris) wrote extravagant masterpieces of burlesque
humor which earned themselves quite a large underground reputation.
Chester Himes (*Pinktoes*) and Jock Carroll (*Bottoms Up*, recently
republished in New York as *The Shy Photographer*) both contributed novels which used humor to dismantle certain myths of the time.
But I mention those names merely as examples, and I hope that the
reader will find in the selection contained between these covers many
other enjoyable authors—including those whose works did not contain any sort of sexual provocations. I am thinking now of writers
such as Philip O'Connor, and, more particularly, Paul Ableman,
whose novel (*I Hear Voices*) is perhaps the one which gave me the
greatest pride and pleasure to publish.

But as we went along, a rather ominous situation developed
which was to alter the course of Olympia's evolution. From 1956 onward, French censorship gradually became more inquisitive and ob-

noxious. On principle my publications should have been ignored by the French censors as they were all printed in English and obviously not meant for local consumption. But the fact that my business appeared to be flourishing certainly gave some wrong ideas to certain members of the police.

One day a police inspector of the Vice Squad (romantically known as *La Brigade Mondaine:* The Worldly Brigade) visited me; he wanted some reading copies of a number of books listed in our latest catalogue. I obliged. His allusions and general attitude were rather disquieting, and I asked a friend of mine, who knew the fellow well, to sound him out. The policeman made no difficulty in explaining that the British government had requested information about The Olympia Press, and that it was his job to build up a file on us. Then he changed the subject and said that he had just had a car accident, and that it would cost him a goodly sum (which he quoted with precision) to have it repaired. My friend reported to me; I gave the matter careful consideration. Then I decided, for better or for worse, not to do anything, and to see what would happen.

A few weeks later things did start to happen: the twenty-five books the inspector had taken with him were banned by official decree signed by the Minister of the Interior. One of them was *Lolita*: subsequent inquiries revealed the fact that neither *Lolita*, nor for that matter any of the other books, had been read, or translated into French, or seriously examined in any manner before they were banned.

I immediately proceeded to sue the Minister of the Interior—and strangely enough, eighteen months later, I won my case at the Administrative Tribunal of Paris. I was very proud of my success but I should have known better: not to give bribes is one thing; but to win lawsuits against the police is a much more serious matter.

That victory was won in January, 1958. In May, the Fourth Republic fell and the new regime was installed under the guidance of General de Gaulle. The powers of the police were considerably reinforced, and the overall orientation of national policies reverted to the famed Pétain-Vichy philosophy: *Travail, Famille, Patrie.* The Minister of the Interior appealed against the earlier judgment of the Administrative Tribunal, and I was ignominiously beaten when the case was re-tried by the Conseil d'Etat—France's highest jurisdiction.

Thus the ban on *Lolita* was restored—only a few months before the book appeared in New York, obtaining an immediate success.

I had earned and learned my lesson, and yet when *Lolita* was released in Paris in a French version, published by Gallimard, I was unable to resist the temptation: I sued again. The Minister of the Interior who had banned the original English-language version of the book had not banned its French translation, presumably under the feeble excuse that the French publisher, Gallimard, was dangerously influential. However, there exists a principle in French judicial lore (which does nothing, after all, but reflect the basic principle of democracy) that all citizens are to be treated equally. Basing my plea on that sacred dogma, I sued the Minister of the Interior for damages on the grounds that I had been subjected to unfair treatment. I was soon called to the Ministry and offered a compromise: the Ministry offered to cancel the ban if I agreed to withdraw my plea. I agreed.

Things went from bad to worse after that. A few months later, my English version of Jean Genet's *Our Lady of the Flowers* was banned, although I had had it in print for many years, and in spite of the fact that the original French version had been on sale everywhere in France ever since the war. The mistake was even more ludicrous than in the case of *Lolita*, as Genet was a French writer of unquestionable importance whereas Nabokov was a foreign writer practically unknown in France at the time. I sued once more, confident that it would be an easy matter to win a real victory—or at least to reach a compromise as in the *Lolita* precedent. But I had not taken into account the rapid evolution of judicial mores under the regime of the Fifth Republic: what would have been so simple only two years before was now impossible, unthinkable. I lost my case, and the Minister of the Interior, this time, did not deem it necessary to propose any kind of compromise. I appealed, and lost again when the case was reexamined by the Conseil d'Etat. The Minister of the Interior, the Conseil's judgment pronounced, has the absolute right to interpret the law itself as he wishes, and the Conseil has no power to question the Minister's decisions. (A weird finding indeed, considering the fact that the function of the Conseil d'Etat is precisely to verify the legality of the government's acts and decisions.)

Independently of those erratic bans, I was now being tried for every single book I printed (the offense being known as *outrage aux bonnes moeurs par la voie du livre*; O.B.M. for short on the judges' files). I was tried for books which had been out of print for four or five years; I was even tried, in two or three instances, for books published by others. As the judges had practically no knowledge of English those trials often turned into entertaining vaudevilles.

My record, only recently, was pretty impressive: eighty years' personal ban from all publishing activities, from four to six years unsuspended prison sentences, and some $80,000 in fines. Fortunately this was reduced to more reasonable proportions when my various cases were re-tried by the Appeals court a few weeks ago; but although I have practically ceased publishing new books in the past three years new cases keep cropping up which concern books I have nearly forgotten. For instance, I am now being indicted by yet another court for having published . . . Aubrey Beardsley's sweetly decadent (but, alas, devastatingly innocent) Victorian tale, *Under the Hill*. My edition of the book, which is limited, numbered, and expensive, contains illustrations by Beardsley himself, and I cannot resist the pleasure of calling back to memory the recent vision of the magistrate (who, do I have to labor the point again, does not read English) poring over those images in furious, vein-bulging concentration, in the hope of discovering some half-hidden improper detail on which to rest his case. Alas, no peg for his hat was found, there was not an inch of obscene flesh to be clawed at in the Beardsleyan oceans of lace and frills; and yet the good man obviously suspected the existence of some esoteric meaning attached to those innocent illustrations; and he suspected that only I could have explained it to him. But he dared not ask; he just sat there and hated me for my unshared knowledge.

In those grandiose judicial comedies, common sense is seldom invoked, and the censorship laws in France have become so totalitarian and all-encompassing that it is quite useless to try to fight back with the traditional legal methods. Leo Matarasso, my dear, infinitely patient and cunning attorney, is only concerned by the psychological conduct of the ceremony, and he always spends the last minutes before each trial numbing my conscience with lengthy recommendations. We usually have a big meal before, with lots of wine to induce drowsiness and mollify my *amour-propre*. Then Leo drags me to court while entreating me, one last time, to be humble, to listen, to answer briefly and to the point, and not to look the fellows straight in the eye, etc., etc. Then the rigamarole starts once again, always the same: my ugly past; the horrible fact that I plain forgot to appear in court the last time I was summoned, and did not even excuse myself; the fact that I am a *spécialiste de ce genre d'affaires*, a remark designed to indicate that the debates are once more to be perfunctory. It may go well if I manage to doze off a little in my standing position, but sometimes the attorney-general is too much, and then all goes wrong. The man insults me, calls me names, asks me with a sneer if I can read English and if I say yes, asks me if I am aware of the disgusting contents of the book—which he, himself, cannot read. It is difficult to control oneself in such emergencies, and I have to quickly choose between two solutions: either to burst out in Homeric laughter, or bawl back at the man as if I were taking him seriously. Instinct makes me opt for the latter solution, and venom is slung back and forth. From the corner of my eye, I see the unhappy grin on Leo's face gradually disintegrating: he becomes smaller and smaller on his bench. The presiding judge, who had earlier proved unable to pronounce the title of the book, frowns at me with a terrible, ferocious look on his face; but at heart he is relaxed and content: everything is back to normal. And I think we are all finally pretty satisfied with each other's performance, and it all ends up in an atmosphere of general goodwill, and with the fine feelings which warm the connoisseur's heart for a job well done. And the huge sentences which are clamped down on me as a conclusion to these Alice in Wonderland exercises are made to appear as special distinctions reserved for the very few.

Many British and American writers have signed petitions in my favor, usually addressed to André Malraux as the Minister of Culture in the present French government. Those petitions are sometimes read in court but clearly the names of the signatories ring no literary bell: I thought once that the name of Bertrand Russell had elicited a glint of recognition in the eye of one of the Court's officials, but I later found out that he had heard the name of Dr. Schweitzer instead.

As to André Malraux, who has been questioned publicly about my general status at an Anglo-American press luncheon, this is what he was recorded as saying:

"I do not find it is serious, after what has been said during the last hour, to raise the problem of Mr. Girodias. You tell me that I have been sent a petition. Very true! It was sent to me yesterday morning.

"Thirdly, you tell me: the Americans are concerned with freedom.

"The works, not the pornographic but the books of genius, which have been published by Mr. Girodias, were they published in the

United States or in France? Joyce, is he to our credit or to yours?"

Interruption: "To both!"

Mr. Malraux: "Yes, but he was first published here. So, I find it excessive that France be presented in such a case, which is after all negligible, as a country which, in the name of good morals, opposes works that have been tolerated here for the last thirty years.

"On the other hand, judgment has been pronounced. There have been many others. There was also one against Baudelaire. If I may say so, there was one against myself. Well! Such is France that sometimes judgments like that are reversed!

"So, let us simply say this: it is not opportune to discuss the problem of Mr. Girodias here.

"Freedom, of which you spoke earlier, is a true problem which it is opportune to discuss here. Well! When we discuss what the attitude of France has been (and, mind you, I am not speaking of the Fifth Republic), the attitude of France on the freedom of spirit, of thought and of genius, insofar as English-language literature is concerned, in the name of so many, and first of all Joyce, I do not think that France has much to blush about."

Whatever the exact meaning of those words, it seems that Mr. Malraux has received and at least partly digested the message that a change has taken place in our literary world, and that my own publishing firm has played a certain role in the promotion of freedom in literature. And such an admission on the part of a member of the French government is like sweet music.

But naturally that is not true of France herself, and Mr. Malraux is purposely vague on that issue. The astonishing, the incredible truth of the matter is that moral and artistic freedom has become quite suddenly a reality both in Britain and in the United States, while the very concept is being denied, denigrated, and officially ostracized in France. On both sides, centuries of traditions have been liquidated in the space of one generation.

In fact, it all happened in less than a generation, in only a very few years. The first significant step forward in America was the publication, by Putnam, in 1958, of *Lolita*, a book which had been turned down in fright and horror by several of the most representative publishers of the land no more than three or four years before. *Lolita* escaped from the censors unscathed on its own merits—and yet the theme of the book was hardly compatible with the Puritan way of life.

The rest of the story, as they say, is well known. On *Lolita*'s sweet heels followed in hot succession *Lady Chatterley's Lover, Tropic of Cancer, Naked Lunch, Our Lady of the Flowers* (at the day of writing still banned in France in its English version), and finally *Fanny Hill* and *Candy*. Britain followed suit with one or two years' interval for each book.

The first five books on the above list were all defensible on artistic grounds; but the last two dealt with the offensive subject of sex in such an open and unabashed manner that one would have expected a brutal reaction from the censors. In fact, very little happened, and this in itself is quite remarkable. The implication is that the old hypocritical idea that certain allegedly immoral books could be defended on the grounds of "literary merit" had been discarded by the courts—and therefore by public opinion.

The conclusion, therefore, is that our society (or at least the two major English-speaking countries) has slowly elaborated a new definition of freedom. Freedom must be total; to restrict it to literary or artistic expression is not enough. It must govern our lives, our attitudes, our mental outlook.

It may be expected, then, that we will soon move to the next level. Moral censorship was an inheritance from the past, deriving from centuries of domination by the Christian clergy. Now that it is practically over, we may expect literature to be transformed by the advent of freedom. Not freedom in its negative aspects, but as the means of exploring all the positive aspects of the human mind, which are all more or less related to, or generated by, sex.

I have supplied additional information about the authors and their work in notes appended to the selections.

Paris, February 1965

THE WORLD OF SEX

HENRY MILLER

*L*ike every man, I am my own worst enemy. Unlike most men, however, I also know that I am my own savior. I know that freedom means responsibility. I know too how easily desire may be converted to deed. Even when I close my eyes I must be careful how I dream and of what, for now only the thinnest veil separates dream from reality.

How large or small a part sex plays in one's life seems relatively unimportant. Some of the greatest achievements we know of have been accomplished by individuals who had little or no sex life. On the other hand, we know from the lives of certain artists—men of the first rank—that their imposing works would never have been produced had they not been immersed in sex. In the case of a certain few these periods of exceptional creativity coincided with extravagant sexual indulgence. Neither abstinence nor indulgence explains anything. In the realm of sex, as in other realms, we speak of a norm—but the normal accounts for nothing more than what is true, statistically, for the great mass of men and women. What may be normal, sane, healthful for the vast majority affords us no criterion of behavior where the exceptional individual is concerned. The man of genius, whether through his work or by personal example, seems ever to be blazing the truth that each one is a law unto himself, and that the way to fulfillment is through recognition and realization of the fact that we are each and all unique.

Our laws and customs relate to social life, our life in common, which is the lesser side of existence. Real life begins when we are alone, face to face with our unknown self. What happens when we come together is determined by our inner soliloquies. The crucial and truly pivotal events which mark our way are the fruits of silence and of solitude. We attribute much to chance meetings, refer to them as turning points in our life, but these encounters could never have occurred had we not made ourselves ready for them. If we possessed more awareness, these fortuitous encounters would yield still greater rewards. It is only at certain unpredictable times that we are fully attuned, fully expectant, and thus in a position to receive the favors of fortune. The man who is thoroughly awake knows that every "happening" is packed with significance. He knows that not only is his own life being altered but that eventually the entire world must be affected.

The part which sex plays in a man's life varies greatly with the individual, as we know. It is not impossible that there may be a pattern which includes the widest variations. When I think of sex I think of it as a domain only partially explored; the greater part, for me at least, remains mysterious and unknown, possibly forever unknowable. The same holds for other aspects of the life force. We may know a little or much, but the farther we push the more the horizon recedes. We are enveloped in a sea of forces which seem to defy our puny intelligence. Until we accept the fact that life itself is founded in mystery we shall learn nothing.

Sex, then, like everything else, is largely a mystery. That is what I am trying to say. I do not pretend to be a great explorer in this realm. My own adventures are as nothing compared to those of the ordinary Don Juan. For a man of the big cities I think my exploits are modest and altogether normal. As an artist, my adventures seem in no way singular or remarkable. My explorations have, however, enabled me to make a few discoveries which may one day bear fruit. Let us put it this way—that I have charted certain islands which may serve as stepping stones when the great routes are opened up.

There was a period in Paris, just after I had undergone a conversion, when I was able to visualize with hallucinating clarity the whole pattern of my past. I seemed possessed with the power to recall anything and everything I chose to recall; even without wishing it, the events and encounters which had happened long ago crowded upon my consciousness with such force, such vividness, as to be almost unbearable. Every thing that had happened to me acquired significance, that is what I remember most about this experience. Every meeting or chance encounter proved to be an event; every relationship fell into its true place. Suddenly I felt able to look back upon the truly vast horde of men, women and children I had known —animals too—and see the thing as a whole, see it as clearly and prophetically as one sees the constellations on a clear winter's night. I could detect the orbits which my planetary friends and acquaintances had described, and I could also detect amidst these dizzying movements the erratic course which I myself had traced—as nebula, sun, moon, satellite, meteor, comet . . . and stardust. I observed the periods of opposition and conjunction as well as the periods of partial or total eclipse. I saw that there was a deep and lasting connection between myself and all the other human beings with whom it had been my lot—and my privilege!—to come in contact at one time or another. What is still more important is that I saw within the frame of the actual the potential being which I am. In these lucid moments I saw myself as one of the most solitary and at the same time one of the most companionable of men. It was as though, for a brief interval, the curtain had dropped, the struggle halted. In the great amphitheater which I had supposed to be empty and meaningless there unfolded before my eyes the tumultuous creation of which I was, fortunately and at long last, a part.

I said men, women and children. . . . They were all there, all equally important. I might have added—books, mountains, rivers, lakes, cities, forests, creatures of the air and creatures of the deep. Names, places, people, events, ideas, dreams, reveries, wishes, hopes, plans and frustrations, all, when summoned, were as vivid and alive as they had ever been. Everything fell into latitude and longitude, so to speak. There were great tracts of fog, which was metaphysics; broad, flaming belts, the religions; burning comets, whose tails spelled hope. And so on. . . . And there was sex. But what *was* sex? Like the deity, it was omnipresent. It pervaded everything. Perhaps the whole universe of the past, to give an image for it, was none other than a mythological monster from which the world, my world, had been whelped, but which failed to disappear with the act of creation, remaining below, supporting the world (and its own self) upon its back.

For me this singular experience now occupies a place in my memory akin to that of the Flood in the depths of man's Unconscious. The day the waters receded the mountain stood revealed. There was I, stranded on the topmost peak, in the ark which I had built at the command of a mysterious voice. Suddenly the doves flew forth, shattering the mists with their flaming plumage. . . . All this, unbelievable if you like, followed upon a catastrophe now so deeply buried as to be unrememberable.

That mythological monster! Let me add a few recollections before it loses form and substance. . . .

To begin with, it was as though I had come out of a deep trance. And, like that figure of old, I found myself in the belly of a whale.

The color which bathed my retina was a warm gray. Everything I touched felt delicious, as with the surgeon when he delves into our warm innards. The climate was temperate, tending toward warmth rather than coolth. In short, a typical uterine atmosphere replete with all the Babylonian comforts of the effete. Born overcivilized, I felt thoroughly at ease. All was familiar and pleasurable to my over-refined sensorium. I could count with certitude on my black coffee, my liqueur, my Havana-Havana, my silk dressing gown, and all the other necessities of the man of leisure. No grim struggle for existence, no bread and butter problems, no social or psychological complexes to iron out. I was an emancipated ne'er-do-well from the start. When there was nothing better to do I would send out for the evening paper and, after a glance at the headlines, I would sedulously devour the ads, the social gossip, the theater notices, and so on, down through the obituary recitatif.

For some strange reason I displayed an abnormal interest in the fauna and flora of this uterine domain. I looked about me with the cool, witless glance of the scientist. ("The daffy herbotomist," I dubbed myself.) Within these labyrinthian folds I discovered innumerable marvels. . . . And now I must break off, since all this has served only as a reminder, to speak of the first little cunt I ever examined.

I was about five or six at the time, and the incident took place in a cellar. The afterimage, which solidified at the appropriate time in the form of an incongruity, I labeled "the man in the iron mask." Just a few years ago, in riffling the pages of a book containing reproductions of primitive masks, I stumbled upon a womblike mask which, when one lifted the flap, revealed the head of a full-grown man. Perhaps the shock of seeing this full-blown head peering from the womb was the first genuine response I had had to the question which voiced itself that instant long ago when I had my first serious look at a vagina. (In the *Tropic of Cancer*, it may be remembered, I portrayed a companion who had never recovered from this obsession. He is still, I believe, prying open one cunt after another in order, as he puts it to himself, to get at the mystery it holds.)

It was a hairless world I gazed upon. The very absence of hair, so I now think, served to stimulate the imagination, helped populate the arid region which surrounded the place of mystery. We were concerned less with what lay within than with the future vegetal decor which we imagined would one day beautify this strange waste land. Depending on the time of the year, the age of the players, the place, as well as other more complicated factors, the genitals of certain little creatures seemed as variegated, when I think of it now, as the strange entities which people the imaginative minds of occultists. What presented itself to our impressionable minds was a nameless phantasmagoria swarming with images which were real, tangible, thinkable, yet nameless, for they were unconnected with the world of experience wherein everything has a name, a place and a date. Thus it was that certain little girls were referred to as possessing (hidden beneath their skirts) such queer effects as magnolias, cologne bottles, velvet buttons, rubber mice . . . God only knows what. That every little girl had a crack was of course common knowledge. Now and then rumor had it that such and such a one had no crack at all; of another it might be said that she was a "morphodite." Morphodite was a strange and frightening term which no one could clearly define. Sometimes it implied the notion of double sex, sometimes other things, to wit, that where the crack ought to be there was a cloven hoof or a row of warts. *Better not ask to see it!*—that was the dominant thought.

A curious thing about this period was the conviction which obtained among us that some of our little playmates were definitely bad, i.e. incipient whores or sluts. Some girls already possessed a vile vocabulary pertaining to this mysterious realm. Some would do forbidden things, if given a little gift or a few coppers. There were others, I must add, who were looked upon as angels, nothing less. They were that angelic, in fact, that none of us ever thought of them as owning a crack. These angelic creatures didn't even pee.

I make mention of these early attempts at characterization because later in life, having witnessed the development of some of the "loose ones," I was impressed by the accuracy of our observations. Occasionally one of the angels also fell into the gutter, and remained there. Usually, however, they met a different fate. Some led an unhappy life, either through marrying the wrong man or not marrying at all, some were stricken with mysterious illnesses, others were crucified by their parents. Many whom we had dubbed sluts turned out to be excellent human beings, jolly, flexible, generous, human to the core, though often a bit the worse for wear.

With adolescence another kind of curiosity developed, namely, the desire to find out how "the thing" functioned. Girls of ten or twelve were often induced to adopt the most grotesque poses, in order to demonstrate how they made pee-pee. The skilled ones were reputed to be able to lie on the floor and piss up to the ceiling. Some were already being accused of using candles—or broomsticks. The conversation, when it got round to this topic, became rather thick and complicated; it was tinged with a flavor strangely reminiscent of the atmosphere which invested the early Greek schools of philosophy. Logic, I mean, played a greater role than empiricism. The desire to explore with the naked eye was subordinated to a greater urge, one which I now realize was none other than the need to talk it out, to discuss the subject *ad nauseam*. The intellect, alas, had already begun to exact its tribute. How "the thing" functioned was smothered by the deeper query—*why?* With the birth of the questioning faculty, sorrow set in. Our world, hitherto so natural, so marvelous, slipped its moorings. Henceforth nothing was absolutely so any more: everything could be proved—and disproved. The hair which now began to sprout on the sacred *mons Venus* was repellent. Even the little angels were breaking out in pimples. And there were some who were bleeding between the legs.

Masturbation was far more interesting. In bed, or in the warm bath, one could imagine himself lying with the Queen of Sheba, or with a burlesque queen whose tantalizing body, featured everywhere, infected one's every thought. One wondered what these women, pictured with skirts whirling above their heads, did when they appeared before the footlights. Some said that they brazenly removed every stitch of their gorgeous costumes and stood holding their boobies invitingly—until the sailors made a stampede for the stage. Often, so it was said, the curtain had to be rung down and the police summoned.

Something was wrong with the girls we used to play with. They weren't the same any more. In fact, everything was changing, and for the worse. As for the boys, they were being farmed out one after another. Schooling was a luxury reserved for the children of the rich. Out there, "in the world," from all reports, it was nothing but a slave market. Yes, the world *was* crumbling about us. *Our* world.

And then there were places known as penitentiaries, reformatories, homes for wayward girls, insane asylums, and so on.

Before things were to go utterly to smash, however, a wonderful event might occur. A party, no less. Where someone very precious, someone hardly more than a name, was certain to make an appearance.

To me these "events" now seem like those fabulous balls which precede a revolution. One looked forward to being violently happy, happier than one had ever been before, yet one also had the presentiment that some untoward thing would happen, something which would affect one's whole life. A deal of sly whispering always surrounded the coming event. It went on among parents, older brothers and sisters, and among the neighbors. Everyone seemed to know more about one's sacred emotional life than was warranted. The whole neighborhood suddenly seemed abnormally interested in one's slightest doings. One was watched, spied upon, talked about behind one's back. Such great emphasis was put on age. The way people said, "He's fifteen now!" entrained the most embarrassing implications. It all seemed like a sinister puppet show which the elders were staging, a spectacle in which we would be the ridiculous performers there to be laughed at, mocked, goaded to say and do unaccountable things.

After weeks of anxiety the day would finally arrive. The girl too, at the last moment. Just when everything augured well, when all it needed—for what?—was a word, a look, a gesture, one discovered to his dismay that he had grown dumb, that his feet were rooted to the spot on which they had been planted ever since entering the place. Maybe once during the whole long evening did the precious one offer the slightest token of recognition. To move close to her, to brush her skirt, inhale the fragrance of her breath, what a difficult, what a monumental feat! The others appeared to move at will, freely. All that he and she seemed capable of was to slowly gravitate about such uninteresting objects as the piano, the umbrella stand, the bookcase.

Only by accident did they seem destined now and then to converge upon one another. Even so, even when all the mysterious, super-charged forces in the room seemed to be pushing them toward each other, something always intervened to make them drift apart. To make it worse, the parents behaved in the most unfeeling fashion, pushing and jostling couples about, gesticulating like goats, making rude remarks, asking pointed questions. In short, acting like idiots.

The evening would come to an end with a great handshaking all around. Some kissed each other good-bye. The bold ones! Those who lacked the courage to behave with such abandon, those who cared, who felt deeply, in other words, were lost in the shuffle. No one noticed their discomfiture. They were nonexistent.

Time to go. The streets are empty. He starts walking homeward. Not the slightest trace of fatigue. Elated, though nothing had really happened. Indeed, it had been an utter fiasco, the party. But she had come! And he had feasted his eyes on her the whole evening long. Once he had almost touched her hand. Yes, think of that! *Almost!* Weeks may pass, months perhaps, before their paths cross again. (What if her parents took it into their heads to move to another city? Such things happen.) He tries to fix it in his memory—the way she cast her eyes, the way she talked (to others), the way she threw her head back in laughter, the way her dress clung to her slender figure. He goes through it all piece by piece, moment by moment, from the time she entered and nodded to someone behind him, not seeing him, or not recognizing him perhaps. (Or had she been too shy to respond to his eager glance?) The sort of girl who never revealed her true feelings. A mysterious and elusive creature. How little she knew, how little anyone knew, the oceanic depths of emotion which engulfed him!

To be in love. To be utterly alone. . . .

Thus it begins . . . the sweetest and the bitterest sorrow that one can know. The hunger, the loneliness that precedes initiation.

In the loveliest red apple there is hidden a worm. Slowly, relentlessly, the worm eats the apple away. Until there is nothing left but the worm.

And the core, that too? No, the core of the apple lingers, even if only as an idea. That every apple has a core, is this not sufficient to counterbalance all uncertainty, all doubt and misgiving? What matter the world, what matter the suffering and death of untold millions, what matter if everything goes to pot—so long as *she*, the heart and core, remains! Even if he is never to see her again he is free to think about her, speak to her in dream, love her, love her from afar, love her forever and ever. No one can deny him that. No, no one.

Like a body composed of millions of cells, sorrow grows and grows and grows, feeds upon itself, renews its million selves, becomes the world and all that is, or the riddle which answers to it. Everything fades but the torment. *Things are the way they are.* That is the horrible, the perpetual torment. . . . And to think that one has only to do oneself in—and the riddle is solved! But *is* that a solution? Is it not slightly ridiculous? Moral suicide is so much easier. Adjusting to life, as they say. Not to what should be or ought be. *Be a man!* Later of course, one realizes that "to be a man" is quite another matter. The day is sure to dawn when it becomes all too clear that few there are who deserve the title: MAN. The more aware of this you become the fewer men you find. Hold tenaciously to the thought and you end up in the void of the Himalayas, there to discover that what is called man is still waiting to be born.

In the course of making these manly adjustments to reality, the feminine world appears to undergo a prismatic deformation. It is at this point in one's development that someone comes along who has had more experience, someone "who knows women." This is the realistic dolt, the down-to-earth type, who believes that to sleep with a woman is to know her. By virtue of countless collisions with the other sex something which passes for knowledge has accrued to his make-up. Something like a psychological wig, one might say. Faced with a real woman, a real experience, this type of individual is bound to cut as ridiculous a figure as an old man trying to make himself look young. The wig becomes the focus of attention.

I remember a chap who became my boon companion during this transient period. I remember his grotesque antics with women, and how they affected me. He was always voicing the fear that to fall head over heels in love was to court disaster. Never give yourself wholly to one woman! So he made it his business to take me around. He would show me how to behave naturally, as he put it, with a woman.

The strange thing was that in the course of these adventures it happened again and again that the women he treated so cavalierly fell in love with *me*. It didn't take long to discover that the objects of his fancy weren't at all taken in by his swashbuckling behavior. It was only too apparent, from the way these "victims of prey" humored him and mothered him, that he was only deluding himself in thinking that he "had a way with women." I saw that this "man of the world" was just a child to them, even though in bed he could make them whinny with pleasure, or sob or groan, or cling to him with quiet desperation. He had a way of taking leave abruptly, like a coward beating a hasty retreat. "A cunt's a cunt," he would say, trying to conceal his panic, and then he'd scratch his head and wonder aloud if there wasn't one, just *one* cunt, who was different.

No matter how attached I became to a "cunt," I was always more interested in the person who owned it. A cunt doesn't live a separate, independent existence. Nothing does. Everything is inter-related. Perhaps a cunt, smelly though it may be, is one of the prime symbols for the connection between all things. To enter life by way of the vagina is as good a way as any. If you enter deep enough, re-main long enough, you will find what you seek. But you've got to enter with heart and soul—and check your belongings outside. (By belongings I mean—fears, prejudices, superstitions.)

The whore understands this perfectly. That's why, when shown a bit of kindness, she's ready to give her soul. Most men, when taking a whore, don't even bother to remove hat and coat, figuratively speaking. Small wonder they receive so little for their money. A whore, if treated right, can be the most generous of souls. Her one desire is to be able to give herself, not just her body.

We are all striving acquisitively, for money, love, position, honor respect, even for divine favor. To get something for nothing seems to be the *summmum bonum*. Do we not say: "Go get yourself a fuck!" Strange locution. As if one could possibly get a fuck without giving one. Even in this basic realm of communion the notion prevails that a fuck is something to get, not to give. Or, if the opposite is stressed—*Jesus, what a fuck I gave her!*—then the thought of something re-ceived in exchange is obscured. No man or woman can boast of handing out a good fuck unless he or she is well fucked too. Other-wise one might as well talk of fucking a bag of oats. And that is precisely what goes on, for the most part. You go to the butcher with a piece of tail, and he makes a thin hash of it for you. Some are crazy enough to ask for porterhouse steak when all they want is a bit of chopped meat.

Fucky-wucky! It's not the simple pastime it would seem to be. Wonder is often expressed about the ways of primitives. Some question how it would be to use animals. (Domestic ones, to be sure.) Few are completely satisfied that they know all there is to be known about the business. Sometimes, after years of (so-called) normal sexual behavior, a man and wife will begin experimenting. Sometimes husbands and wives exchange partners for a night, or for longer. And now and then one hears from the lips of a traveler strange tales, tales of mysterious performances, of formidable feats practiced in the observance of strange forms of ritual. The masters of the art have nearly always served a rigorous spiritual apprenticeship. Self-discipline is the clue to their prowess. The man of God, in short, seems to have it over the gladiator.

Most youngsters never get the chance to enjoy the luxury of prolonged, and often fruitless, metaphysical speculation. They are whisked out into the world and made to assume responsibilities before they have had the opportunity to identify themselves (in the heaven of thought) with those who consumed themselves wrestling with the eternal problems. Shoving myself out prematurely, I soon realized my error and, after floundering about, I decided to give myself a break. Throwing off the harness, I made an effort to live the natural life. I failed. Back to the pavements I went and into the arms of the woman I was trying to ditch.

HENRY MILLER

Shades of a distant youth! I was fourteen and my family thought that I had potentialities as a draughtsman, presumably because I did not appear to have any other gifts or talents of social use. My father needed to believe in his eldest son, and gave me the task of doing a jacket design for the impending first edition of Henry Miller's book, Tropic of Cancer.

I remember having liked the job at first, and having drawn a heavy, awkward black and green crab of gigantic proportions, sitting on the top of a circle presumably representing our world, and holding in its huge pincers a dead human form. That sinister image was in disturbing opposition with the Sussex lawn of my uncle's house, resplendent with August sunshine, where I was spending most of my time during those summer holidays. I was constantly being distracted from my work by the vain curiosity of the girls from the neighborhood who came on bicycles to have a look at the French boy—a rarity in those days and under those skies. Then I fell in love with a fleeting apparition seen in a neighboring village, where I had gone secretly to buy my first razor, and that took me further away from the crab. However, by the time summer was over, the monster was complete with dripping black blood and forests of tentacles. I had missed the point entirely as an illustrator, but my father, being blinded by pride, had the ugly thing wrapped around that historical volume against all sensible advice.

Henry Miller was an occasional visitor in our house, and I remember one occasion when my parents had given a party in his honor, in our Neuilly ground-floor apartment which my father called his inverted penthouse. Henry was all dressed up for the affair with pants, jacket, shirt and tie, all of different origins and conflicting hues, and was busy finishing all the platters of food he could find. He had a rich, sonorous voice which was very good for chuckles, and for the sound Hmmmmm, which constituted a substantial part of his conversation. The only other guests I remember clearly are Anaïs Nin, her triangular face enlarged by immense violet eyes, and Henry's crony, Alfred Perlès, who was like a replica of Henry with slightly smaller features, bald pate included, which shows what friendly devotion and literary allegiance can do to a man.

I remember talking at length with Henry for the first time. I had only recently read Tropic of Cancer *and was having a little trouble reconciling that most human and somewhat clownish person with the cataclysmic impression I had received from the book. But I was very taken by what I sensed to exist behind the wall of too-deliberate nonconformity, and from that day I became his devoted supporter through thick and thin.*

After Cancer, Black Spring *came out, then* Max and the White Phagocytes, *and finally* Tropic of Capricorn. *Miller had made friends with young, chubby Lawrence Durrell, usually flanked by an extra-tall blond English wife, and out came* The Black Book, *Durrell's first novel, and soon after Anaïs Nin's first published book,* The Winter of Artifice.

But the progress of the Villa Seurat group (as they were called, since Miller lived there) was hampered by the international tension.

During the Munich crisis of 1938, Miller rushed to the Southwest of France, to escape from Hitler's hordes, and when that crisis was over he left for Greece with Durrell; then he finally fled back to America when the threat of war came close again.

After my father's death in 1939, followed by five years of black-out, I was quite elated to hear again from Henry, who was then living in Big Sur with a new wife, and busy making babies. I reprinted the Tropics, *and was impressed by the volume of the sales. However, my expectations were excessive, and I seem to have caused a cruel disappointment to Henry Miller with my wild dreams of gigantic sales and endless money, which he pleasantly recounts in a story entitled "40,000 Dollars" in* The Oranges of Hieronymus Bosch.

In 1946 came the French publication of Tropic of Capicorn *which started my first conflict with French censorship, and a few years after that I lost the ownership of my publishing firm to the powerful house of Hachette—including the copyright of all Henry Miller books so far published excepting* Sexus *(which had been formally banned by the French government of the time, and was therefore worthless to Hachette).*

When a few years later I started The Olympia Press, *Henry Miller was first on my list with* Plexus, *which is the second part of the unfinished trilogy entitled* The Rosy Crucifixion *(part one being* Sexus). *After that came* Quiet Days in Clichy *(two stories of* Tropic of Cancer *vintage, wonderfully enhanced by Brassaï's photographs of the Paris of the 1930's), and* The World of Sex.

I was less concerned with Henry Miller's postwar production than with his ultimate recognition as a great American writer in his own country. However, that is not a story for me to tell here. Henry Miller is not only a writer of considerable substance; he is the first American author to have deliberately used sex to provoke the mental revolution now being accomplished. And the American publication and defense of Tropic of Cancer *is certainly one of the most meaningful episodes in the annals of publishing.*

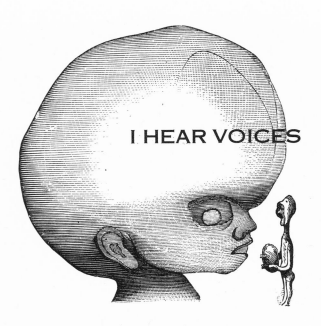

I HEAR VOICES

PAUL ABLEMAN

I look and see the familiar sights, the mines with their charge and volley, the cross pitch and the laggings. Cardinals pass, beating for shells, avoiding both asps and swallows and sinking their percipient lines deep in the fiber. Cardinals pass and repass, pausing for surgery, exchanging ages or single dates, stooping over the negotiable humps, counting each other and modeling in asphalt extrusions. They have no obvious leader but ages of practice, of staining their robes with blood, of burnishing the brazen trumpet mouths and hanging tassel to the clouds, have wrought this symphonic perfection. Thus when one of them, a wizened cardinal and cartographer of the Holy See, whose waist is girdled with phials containing samples of all substances that either flicker or propound, leaps to the crest of an adjacent strophe and chants the opening bars of the "Cardinal's Lament" or "Cardinal's Glorious Perimeter," the others interject names and degrees of salvation. Their rhapsody is like all rhapsodies. It is like the little machines that float up to nest in the boughs. It resembles the first glimpse of leaf by emergent grubs, the first cocaine of the plunderers.

I continue on, past the well, past the fern and its reinforcement until I come to the special development. There I take my place in the line of men queuing for employment and gaze at the enormous development.

"It's for tunneling," I hear someone further down the queue remark.

"I don't care what it is," remarks another.

"It has various sections, volumes and capacities," outlines a more knowledgeable one. "Much goes into it. Much issues from it. It engrosses much."

"Is it healthy?" asks a nervous-seeming youth, eyeing, in particular, a barren portion of it, overhanging and discharging a blast of shadow or synthetic night.

"Don't you worry, builder, my lad," urges a rough, dusty and older man whose face and hands are scored with the abrasions of a lifetime spent in actual physical opposition to the inertia of steel and stone. "That's not for you to worry about. It's healthy until it kills you—and what good's health then? No, do your job—it's got to be done and it's for you to do it—and collect your money on Friday."

I am about to ask my neighbor his opinion when I am abruptly summoned away to the manager's office. This is a large, bare chamber of new brick and concrete in which only an amusing cartoon on the Turkish navy provides any note of stress.

"It's really for worming," the manager assures me. "You'll find me a more convincing employer when my suitable apparel arrives. It's being fabricated in the next development down the stream. Still your fame has streamed before you."

Affably he leads me to the window to survey the gigantic project.

"We have no trouble with the men," he confides. "They work merrily on these towers and domes amidst the emanations. At night we float huge flares above the diggings and double the rations. When day comes through, we ticket it and docket it and send it to another department. The great work progresses. All is planned. We are called converters of transformers. You see," here he bends cautiously toward me and lowers his voice, "we really work on the mind."

There is no doubt that he thrives on his labors. He dresses better than Arthur in marine tints. He seems to have full authority and an eye for everything. He points to some defective joints.

"You could start on those. Adhesion is the great thing. Cohesion is what we require. It must all cohere in a large, convincing fashion—

you'll soon be able to run your eye over it, detect a sticky rivet with a single finger thrust, analyze it, adapt your schedule and fulfill many of your quotas. You'll find it a pleasant life. We have subterranean retreats of every kind. We have kind feelings for each other and teamwork. I'm no more than the least of those yobs, hoisting bricks, mingling their sweat with the girders and cement. I divide myself among them and issue each week into their pay packets. Thus the very sandwiches they withdraw from their sweaty rags and munch during their whistle stop are slices of cooperation, selfless harmony and endless, rabid toil to improve our living standards. They wave these standards, glinting in the blood-red dawn, as they surge on long conveyors into the shops. They plant these standards in the mulch and decay of forests that their great rakes and shovels have curried up from the earth. They seal themselves into the circuit streams of production and the curve rises continually—oh yes—it rises continually—oh yes—" He falters, turns from the opening and, after a pause, remarks, "I don't wish to bore you."

"It's inspiring," I assure him. "It's your duty to talk like that, just as it's the men's duty to behave like valves or gauges, to gear their lives to the demands of this splendid development. Everyone has a job to do."

"Oh, it's not all work you know," he assures me expansively. "There are holidays abroad—you can fly almost anywhere, though not to the poles yet, no matter how you crave illimitable ice, but to Bongalulu or Trepan, or the more familiar splodges of the famous land mass, Prance, Hermany or Slain. You can runnel and turret among the quintitudes of these vinish fiefs, each richly stored with slabs and carved treasures, good hotels, petrol everywhere. Of course, those places are being developed now too and everywhere you go, rising from the historic landscape, you'll find our blocks and antennae. Weeds. Weeds of progress, flowering in the ancient beds of culture. Sometimes you can hardly sniff an ancient rose for the stench of diesels. Still, there's lots of dynamic fun about, pinching and poking and pursuing into bedrooms with a bottle of joy in one hand and feeling hastily in your pocket with the other for those little rubber charms. Then there's golf and watching tennis, films, plays, television and girls' legs in the street. There's a big party tonight as it happens. Arthur's giving one to celebrate progress on the development. Would you care to come?"

"Not much," I confess morosely. "I've seen enough of Arthur for one day. Is this his development?"

"Yes, as much as any development of this order, of this breadth and complexity, of this capacity for marshaling significance, can be related to the poky doings of a single particle. He glows a bit, I grant you, and between ourselves there are lots of developments, more than are suspected by the public, or admitted by the editors, that have been touched by the sparkle of that electron's track. Yes, he's quite a whirler, quite positively-charged is our apparently common acquaintance. And then again, he's just a bouncer like the rest of us, glancing from collision to collision, gasping out, as he spins and reels among the random chances, his philosophy of achievement. The fiery streams of logic that spew from his propulsion vents whirl into the surrounding turmoil. Bits adhere to inflammable stuff and little flames break out. Much is deadened or burns itself out on inert material. Some reacts or combines with other substances in bizarre and unpredictable ways and the whole rages and seethes as before. And our friend, looking back, sees only the lovely curve of his rocket progress, standing clear and bright for a moment, a beacon and a monument, before trickling away to blend with the receptive spaces."

The manager falls silent. Around us, but deadened and remote, is the chattering of machines. Up, up through the thicknesses of concrete, the filmy opacity of clouds, the turbulent air of the stratosphere, beyond the orbit of the moon, sits the Kingdom of Heaven like a floating bandstand and all around it dart little particles of hydrogen, like bees.

"That's why," concludes the manager, "I'm only his drunken manager and he's the boss."

"Are you drunken?" I ask.

"Pretty drunken."

"You probably have a literary or artistic nature," I advise. "I was quite carried away by what you were saying and thought, 'This manager has an uncommon ability for evoking things. He must have a literary or artistic nature.' That's probably why you're drunken."

"Everyone's drunken," murmurs the manager. "The brain is a chunk of gray pudding but it works at high temperature. It has to be cooled with drink. Well—do you want to meet the men?"

"I've already met them," I explain. "I was in the queue. At least I didn't meet them all, but I don't suppose they vary much do they?"

"Not much. Some are kinder, some crueler—but our arrangements are flexible enough now to accommodate the little individual variations and extract the requisite amount of labor from them all. We've no time to worry about idiosyncrasies and minor differences. Personality's dead, deader than chivalry. Well, are you coming to the party?"

He pours himself a swift drink from a bottle in his desk drawer. An aide or assistant comes in with his new tinted suit from the further development. Lights hiss on and, beyond the stony eye, the flares blaze out above the geometry. I allow myself to be drawn along and, in a short time, we pull up outside a very different prospect. I begin to feel slight misgivings.

"I'm not used to this sort of affair," I confide. "I don't think I really belong. Besides, what will Arthur say?"

"I don't know," grumbles the manager. "I never know what anyone will say, not even myself. My notion at this sort of function is simply to raise the internal fluid level as rapidly as possible. And then maybe find a girl. But then I'm only a coarse manager, only tolerated by all these posturing, obsolete waxworks because they need me. They need us, my boy, remember that. And don't be afraid of Arthur. I'll tell him what a splendid day's work you did. I'll tell him you exceeded your quota. Do you smell drink?"

I sniff the evening air blowing among the cool, high elms, stirring the well-kept lawn with its few decorative leaves, but smell only an indistinct scummy smell as if a fetid pond had been drained.

"Only ooze," I confess, "like tidal ooze."

"There are tides flowing tonight," mutters the manager but I am not sure what he means.

"Shall we follow those fireflies?" I ask. "They might lead us to an earl, on the telephone or rehearsing a speech. You see those fireflies, romancing with the leaves? Each firefly courts a single trembling leaf and they carry the first-born to the nearest earl or accountant. It sounds feudal, I know, but History coils and re-coils and we never know when we open our lids—"

"You're talking rubbish," complains the manager. "I wish I could see better."

"It's because I'm nervous," I protest. "I'm trying to rehearse for the charming play of witty, allusive speech that we're sure to encounter. That's what happens at this sort of function. Everyone strolls

under the ornamented marquees or congregates around some object
and the air becomes full with a continual murmur of delicious banter,
poor admittedly in philosophy, but how rich, how beguilingly
rich—"

"Have you brought a compass?" asks the manager.

His tone is sober. All thought of banter leaves me as I gaze, with
sudden foreboding, around the festive and yet somehow ambiguous
scene. It is hard to clarify the celebrants. They can be descried all
right: the shimmering gowns of the women haunting their nakedness
as they drift among the apertures and ramps, the grave bondage of the
men as they roll boulders or tread boulders— They can be descried,
but neither I nor the manager, if sympathy does, in fact, link our
understanding, can apprehend the exact, the clearly defined sector of
their activities.

"What period?" asks the manager.

"Neo-Cretan," I suggest. "Neo-Neolithic. The gongs are suggestive."

"And the hair styles?"

"Ah, I wondered if you'd notice the hair styles. Would it be
ludicrous to detect a marine or sea-spray influence? There's a net
motif—and surely that's ribbing, or keel? The hair styles are lovely,
fluffing up the human strands, binding the unruly moss, the reeds—
but the period? Manorial, I think, or modern?"

"A weeny period," smiles the manager. "A mere flicker on the
screen, a dancing point—I'm glad to see they have nuts."

He bends down for a handful of the green husks, peels away the
thick, blackening integuments and munches the fodder, chewing it
until it ferments and then inhaling the giddy fumes.

"Shan't we go anywhere?" I ask. "I mean—we haven't met anyone yet."

"Do you want to meet people? There may be no one here that
interests you. There'll be no one here that interests me. There couldn't
be. Bits of people are different—of one sex that is. Still—let's see—I
had a list of names, guests' names; my secretary punched it out this
afternoon on some development, some new development or another.
It was a speaking list, a flashing, semaphore list, but I seem to have lost
it. The human element you see."

"Perhaps," I suggest. "In that case, we'd better just mingle, just
stroll around and—"

"It's a large area," cautions the manager. "I'm no good at trekking until I've had a drink, a real drink that is, not these unsophisticated nuts."

"Well then," I urge, feeling that for some reason, not unconnected with an immense sadness, the manager is going to take no crisp decisions this evening, no deliberate strides or motions toward, "let's go and find a drink. There are none here."

"There are owls here," murmurs the manager. "Owls and bats—uninvited guests, hooting at the feast. Do you read the Bible?"

"No," I say, interested and detained, in spite of my anxiety to penetrate closer to the center of the festivities, by the prospect of a literary discussion, "but it was explained to me this afternoon, how it goes too slowly, how it fails to plunge from the heavens, how things go on mingling and tingling—"

"So they do," agrees the manager. "You can't get at a tenth, not a millionth of them. I've read bits of the Bible myself, the bit about Abraham and something about donkeys and it's quite true, I could sense even as I read them that other thoughts were being prepared for me. The manager's night out. The drunken manager."

"Could you write books?" I ask him. "I mean adventure books—and so on."

"I suppose so. Anyone could. What's the point? Clara loved Bill and they got married. There's a book. Or they didn't get married. There's another one. Or there were some other people as well, all doing different things. There's a hundred books. What's the point? I don't read them and I'm not going to write them. More pay, that's my battle cry. More pay, more booze, more women, more holidays, more life! Do you understand? More life, that's what I want."

He glares around at the dubious shapes, colored hazes, service tables, baroque alcoves, as if eager to detect a substantial portion of it that he can consume without further ado.

"There," he says. "That bubble thing, that damned promenade place with the flagstaff or bust. Let's blow in that quarter. Let's find a green earth olive and a poultice of gin. You depress me, friend, I don't know why. I'm glad to have you. But you make a hammock of my spirits. Why is that?"

"I don't know," I confess. "People always affect each other in some way."

The night is dark. It is the old, evil, dark night, and the festivities, though all round us, seem remote and hard to reach.

"There seems to be a path here," pretends the manager, slashing irritably at some brambles with his stick. I follow him, at first staying as close to him as I can. Soon, however, an unexpected feeling of sympathy for the dark leaves and harsh vegetation dissolves my earlier fear and I fall back to look into the hollows and corridors of the wood and to sense the sudden, earthy life in the briars around my feet.

"This wood's all right," I tell the manager, but he is intent now on attaining more sophisticated sensations, and merely wades on as fast as he can. It does not take us long to reach the charming, paved courts, heavy with rhododendron, and the sunken gardens, moon-traps holding the pale moonlight in the cups of lilies floating on the artificial ponds or sliding brightly in segments on the black, shining water itself. We pass old stone and balustrades, Diana, a knight or two, and finally reach the splendid display or novelty provided by the organizers. This is some wonderful thing, made of chemicals and electricity, that resembles a rainbow or balloon. The dancing couples, I notice, frequently pause to comment on the effect. I look anxiously around to see if Arthur is in the vicinity. Someone approaches and asks us if we want a drink.

"Or do you want introductions? I could probably get you a drink. The press is heavy as you can see. There are too few waiters and those there are keep drinking themselves or strolling about as if they were guests. Still, we haven't been introduced. Perhaps I've been guilty of a gross discourtesy—not actually but conceptually as it were. I was thinking, 'perhaps they'd like to meet some of the important people who abound here this evening.' And now it occurs to me that you may be important people yourselves. You may be celebrities—"

"A manager and his mate—" begins the manager. "A thirsty manager."

"Ah, a manager. I study managers. I'm a pretty cool number. Managers abound. I find them everywhere so mine's a fortunate profession. I was bred for it amidst the hay and the bells. I thought of it when the bells were still audible. Actually I invented it, and now I practice it. But you're tired. You've had a long journey and you don't want to be studied this evening. Unlike the bells, you're not a bell—"

"I've brought the drinks," announces a small, attractive princess arriving with colored flasks. She hands us the glowing vessels and then links arms familiarly with the student we have just encountered. "Do you play anything?" she asks. "Run things? Or form things? Don't listen to Toby."

"No, don't listen to me," urges Toby. "What could you learn from me? A drift of faces—a blizzard of faces."

"He studies too many managers," complains the princess. "He complains of faces—as he puts it, a drift of faces before the eyes. I tell him it's nonsense and to sink down deeper into the upholstery or take a spin in the country but he drifts back to the pavements and his drift of faces. It makes me think of marrying an Italian."

"Like Maria," I cannot help exclaiming.

"Like many girls, noble or plebeian. I'm one of the noble ones, though you'd never guess it from the company I keep."

"Why not change?" leers the manager. "I don't know you people, but I could rock this Toby with a blast of something."

"Perhaps later," agrees the girl. "Though you're an ugly, sweating brute. We speak our minds, we aristocrats."

"What, *leave* me?" asks Toby. He smiles vivaciously and then stupidly and reads a large announcement pasted near some pens. "Before our trip, or some incident that's bound to come, a bandaging, a fleet glance when we're laced with gleams, parallax? It takes some explaining. I *should* take her to task," he informs the manager. He turns to me. "She'll tell him of certain towers and roots, combs, counterpanes—I know her ways. Let's leave them—for a night."

"Do you want me to leave you?" I ask the manager, although from the eager way with which he is reaching, or seeming about to reach, for the princess and the cool and yielding way with which she awaits his reach, it seems unlikely that either of them will be displeased by our departure.

He does not answer and so I turn, conscious of an unexpected sadness, toward Toby.

"Perhaps you could introduce me to some interesting people?" I suggest. "Anyone but Arthur."

"You needn't worry about him," Toby assures me. "He's not arrived. I keep a pretty close check on that one—"

"Ah Toby," calls someone, although in the confusion I can not tell who. "Have you heard that the sabers are out?"

"They're rattling the sabers," says a different voice, hollow and ironic.

"The obsolete swords?" asks Toby.

"Yes, the sabers," and a lively but somewhat disheveled chap appears from out of a knot or cluster of pretty women. "You'll forgive me," he apologizes to me, "I have to keep Toby abreast. I'm one of his sources."

"Now don't be dull," call the girls. "Don't be bores with your sabers."

"They'd rather we danced or gloried in their parts," says the new arrival with a broad wink. "Still, I don't see Toby every day. I thought you'd be interested." He looks doubtful and anxious for a moment. "You *are* interested, old chap?"

"What are the circumstances?" asks Toby.

"Ah—well now—the circumstances. I was afraid of that. I almost didn't mention it because I was afraid you'd ask me that. Circumstances are not my line, you know. I don't pretend to understand things. If I see a cloud, I can say 'there's a cloud up there.' But if you ask me the circumstances—still, I'll do my best—after all, I know that in your line nothing's any good if you don't have the circumstances, but do they have to be *real* circumstances? All right, all right, Toby, don't get cross—you know what I'm like, never serious if I can help it. Now then, the circumstances—"

He begins to recount the circumstances. At first they sound like a story, an adventure story, possibly an episode from a serial, but a bit later they begin to sound more like an official report or even memoirs. Then they sound briefly like a newspaper story, a small unimportant story in a vulgar paper. Then the darker note returns and events knit themselves into a huge conspiracy, a conspiracy having as its single aim the obscuring of the qualities of the narrator. Then life becomes a peck of feathers flung to the spring winds.

At first, I listen intently, feeling that something of importance may emerge. Toby, I observe, is taking notes in a little notebook. I try to notice the points at which he writes so that I can search the words for richer meanings. Not only, however, do I find it difficult to concentrate long on any one word or group of words, but the attempt to do so makes me lose the sequence. In addition, I find myself distracted by other things that are happening in the room and especially by a handsome, middle-aged woman standing on a small mound or

elevation who, whenever my glance inadvertently moves in her direction, beckons and smiles toward me. As I debate with myself whether to assume she is signaling at me and, if so, whether to return the salute, an arresting sentence or evocative phrase seems to issue from the narrator but, by the time I have turned my mind to it, he is merely saying "nothing there that's helpful, I'm afraid. Nothing there at all." And when I try to recall what it was, I can only think of the words "the large front was like hipping."

"Did you say 'hipping'?" I ask uncertainly.

"I'm telling this chap about the sabers," he points out. "I lead a pretty adventurous life and so he finds me useful as a source. Listen, by all means. Or keep the girls amused."

"Yes, replace that adventurer," calls one of the girls, an attractive but depraved-looking dark-haired girl in a diamond dress. "He came to our Saxon estate once. He revealed himself there. It was just after a war."

"Well, I'm trying to listen," I explain, stirred and flattered, in spite of myself, at being summoned by such an attractive girl. "He's telling about the sabers."

"Oh, about the sabers."

"We've all heard about the sabers," explains another girl, also dark-haired but not so depraved-looking as the other. She is also shorter and fuller and she wears a dark dress with a bright diamond buckle. "That happened during a war. He brings the story up to date from time to time, changes the setting and retells it with the old dash and spirit. We girls are fond of him, not because of his silly sabers but because we please him so."

"You're probably wondering," says another girl, a slim, crisp girl who seems to cultivate a blasé and ironic manner, "why Toby's listening so intently, if the story is old and tedious. He's not really listening at all. He's taking the line of least resistance, which is to go on, as far as he can, behaving as if nothing had happened and he's also trying to present a completely normal appearance. Really, he's an empty shell. His princess has taken up with a manager and he's heartbroken."

"But he can't deceive us," enthuses the second girl. "We live for things like that and notice them at once. The tale has crackled among us ever since the incident happened. Some of us take Toby's side and some the princess's, although, naturally, we can't help being malicious about the princess. She's a wounded bird, poor thing, a war-blown bird that fluttered weakly into our midst. But she's recovered now and flaunts her tropic plumes."

The three girls look toward the princess but, because of a sudden confluence of waiters, I can not tell if they see her or not.

"My name is Stella," says the crisp and distant girl who explained about Toby.

"Our wonderful Stella whom we admire and fear. We others, in the beginning, were filled with desire, and every time we love, we dispense a little of it. But Stella, the veteran of how many affairs, is full as ever. The liquid in her cup is full as ever but whether that liquid is wine or—"

"Icy ether," smiles Stella. "But really, Barbara, you mustn't circulate such tales. Men may think I'm unapproachable and you know perfectly well, and whisper it maliciously among yourselves, I'm as bad as any of you."

"Yes, but different."

"Different?"

"You know you're different."

"Different? I have my little things and contempts and turn each limb, each streaming line of flesh, in the street. For whom? The dull, dead skies? The dull, real, stupid or intelligent men? Myself? Shop-windows—perfume—cars—I passed a country scene in a boyfriend's car, some cows, grass, hedges—for that? For the bridge, the Seine, the tepid, fashionable sea? My father is a doctor. For him? The smudge above my name in the vulgar press? For that? Different? Stella living at this time—dancing—Stella drinking, journeying—"

She remains quite still. She does this partly theatrically, to consecrate the attitudes she has compelled, and partly to retain and even improve the clarity of the knowledge she has attained. She stands still, accepting, on her clear flesh, in her clear eyes, through her submissive clothes on every part of her body, the messages of the night and entertainments, hugging them for a moment as an unhappy mother might hug departing children, and then returning them a little transformed from her embrace. For a moment, I want anxiously to communicate with her, to tell her the little that I know, but, even as I step forward, the certainty comes to me that this is not the time, that, even though I may never meet her again, it is still far too soon and I can do nothing better than turn my step in a different direction and leave her with her companions.

And so I turn away. The woman is still beckoning to me. I move close enough to compliment her on her rainbow. "A marvelous effect," I enthuse.

She smiles in a dignified way.

"All would be well—" she begins. "All would be perfect but for that faint, infinitely subtle and yet never-quite-absent odor."

"Of ooze," I exclaim. "Of tidal ooze. I smelled it too. As if the tide had gone out and sea things were festering in the marshes."

"It may be ooze," nods the woman. "But where does it come from? What can be its origin? The foundations are sound, the location choice—"

"Ooze bubbles up everywhere," I point out. "If you live on the earth, you can't avoid it."

"But we'd have gone to any lengths," protests the hostess, "no matter what the cost, to avoid it, or any other unpleasantness, no matter how slight, that tended to dissolve the illusion we were bent on creating—a fairy world, a magic world, outside the bustle and the hurly-burly—"

"But you've done very well," I assure her. "I mean the effect is almost perfect, with this lovely chemical rainbow and doubtless all sorts of other novelties and fantastic sprites of the imagination waiting to be inspected elsewhere. I don't think you should reproach yourself."

"Oh, I don't," returns the woman. "I know we've done very well and I'm sure that everyone is having a splendid time. You've met no one that isn't having a splendid time, have you? I saw you circulating among the guests, sampling a conversation here, trapping an attitude there, and I thought 'that young man will tell me how things are going. He'll tell me if people are enjoying themselves.' However, I wasn't too pleased to see you so intent upon that young woman, that Stella. Now I don't wish to say anything explicit but surely there are lots of other attractive and, what shall I say, more suitable young ladies here?"

"There are lots of pretty girls."

"Yes, of course. Well I'm glad you take my point. I'm an older woman myself. We were less explicit in my time, but we managed to get our meaning across. And now we've created this lovely entertainment here this evening the way it used to be in the familiar villages with the trees and lawns. Of course, we have to use chemicals nowadays—everyone does, but the spirit is the same, isn't it? It is the old, genuine spirit, don't you think?"

"I don't know," I confess. "I'm not sure. As a matter of fact, I didn't want to come at all. I wasn't sure what Arthur would say. But now I'm very glad I did."

"Yes, but the spirit," insists the woman. "You've seen nothing strange or distorted, have you? Nothing not explicable in terms of our excellent values? Oh, they are such precious values and I'm not at all sure that people devote as much attention to them nowadays as they should. Still, this is a very reassuring scene, you must admit, even if the waiters are a bit equivocal. Have they served you well?"

"Well, they obscured the princess, but I don't think intentionally—"

"Ah, the princess. There's been much nobility here this evening, even if a few managers did get in—on the whole a most satisfying evening. Though it must be nearly dawn."

Waiters pass. They give each other suspicious looks, or wink in a comradely fashion. In the distance, by the festooned calculus, young bloods are pursuing managers and politicians. At any moment the sun will rise and gleam through the elaborate illuminations into dusty whorls of the Rococo. Magnifications have been switched off, drivers are purring and all around the countryside is astir. I look for the manager and fancy I detect him lurching angrily through the brambles once more. Arthur has not arrived, but I find that I no longer dread his arrival.

PAUL ABLEMAN

Of Paul Ableman and I Hear Voices, *Philip Toynbee wrote in the* London Observer, *October 16, 1960:*

"The spate of novels from the English publishers is so thick and full that it seems hard to believe that any writer of the least talent should be rejected. This brilliant and terrible little book shows that we have no grounds for such complacency. After hawking his type-script around London Mr. Ableman at last resigned himself, two years ago, to accepting the generous services of The Olympia Press in Paris. Thus English readers have been largely deprived of a strik-ingly fresh and original work of art which happens, by an accident of the times, to be well outside the current fashion. I Hear Voices *is recounted by an imaginary schizophrenic; and this device is used to present a marvelous entanglement of different levels of reality. 'In reality' the hero is lying in a room; he tries to eat his breakfast; receives occasional visits. But by means of his madness, he can con-stantly get up and leave the house to encounter a wonderful series of dreamlike adventures. The writing is brilliant, Mr. Ableman can be both terrifying and hilariously funny; yet his book has not been thought worthy of publication in this country."*

The Adventures of Father Silas

Beauregard de Farniente

When I look back at the strange vicissitudes that have checked my existence, and compare the troubles of the past with the serenity of the present, I can scarcely regret the misfortune which made me retire from active service under the standard of the mighty Venus, and thus afforded me leisure to lay the fruits of my own bitter experience before those who may hereafter serve under the same banners.

I am the fruit of the incontinence of the reverend Celestine Fathers of the town of B—. I say of the reverend Fathers, because all of them boasted of having contributed a share in the formation of my individual person. But what so suddenly arrests me? My heart is agitated—is it through fear that I shall be reproached with revealing the mysteries of the Church? Alas! I must overcome this compunction. Who does not know that all men are men, and especially the monks? they *have certainly* the faculty of cooperating in the propagation of the species; and why should we hinder them, when they acquit themselves so well in that particular?

Perhaps the reader is impatient for the commencement of a detailed account of my origin. I am sorry that I cannot so soon satisfy him on that head, but I will at once introduce him to the acquaintance of a worthy peasant, upon whom for a long time I looked as my father.

Ambrose, for that was the good man's name, was gardener at a country house belonging to the Celestines, in a little village at some leagues from the town: his wife, Annette, was chosen for my nurse. She had brought a son into the world, who lived but a few days, and his death helped to conceal the mystery of my birth. This child was privately buried, and the offspring of the monks put in his place.

As I grew up, everybody supposed me to be the gardener's son, as I myself also believed.

I may say, however, if the reader will pardon my vanity, that my inclinations betrayed my origin. I do not know what divine influence operates in the works of monks, but it seems that the virtue of the frock is communicated to every thing they touch. Annette was a proof of this. She was the most frisky female I ever saw, and I have seen a pretty number. She was stout, but somewhat attractive, with little black eyes and a turned-up nose, lively and amorous, and dressed rather better than peasants in general. She would have been an excellent makeshift for a respectable man; guess what she must have been for the monks.

When the jade was decked out in her Sunday corset, which enclosed a bosom that the sun had never browned, and allowed a glimpse of her breasts, struggling, as it were, to escape from its constraint; ah! how did I then feel that I was not her son, or that I was quite prepared to resign that honor.

My disposition was altogether monkish. Led by instinct, I never saw a girl without embracing her, or passing my hand over her wherever she would allow me; and although I did not positively know what I wanted, my heart told me that I should have gone further, had no opposition been offered to my transports.

One day, when they supposed me to be at school, I had remained at home in a little closet where I slept. A thin partition, against which a bed was placed, separated it from the chamber of Ambrose. I was asleep, it was the middle of summer and very hot; I was suddenly awakened by several violent pushes against the partition. I knew not what to think of this noise, which became still louder. I listened and could hear the sound of some few words, incoherent and indistinctly articulated.

"Ah! gently, my dear Annette, not so fast! Oh! hussy, you kill me with pleasure! . . . quick! oh! faster! oh! I am dying!"

I was surprised at such exclamations, the force of which I could not understand. I sat up, but durst scarcely move. If they found me there I had much to fear: I knew not what to think, I was so excited. My uneasiness, however, soon gave way to curiosity. I heard the noise repeated, and thought I could distinguish the voices of Annette and someone, by turns, uttering the same words that had before attracted my attention. I continued to listen, till the desire to see what was going on in the chamber became so strong as to banish all my fears. I determined to ascertain what it was. I think I could have readily gone directly into the chamber for that purpose, whatever the danger of so doing might be; but that was not required. As I felt with my hand for some opening in the partition, I found one which was merely covered by a large picture. I made a hole through this, and what a sight! . . . There was Annette, as naked as my hand, stretched out on the bed, and Father Polycarp, the proctor of the convent, who had been at the house for some time past, as naked as herself, doing . . . what? That which our first parents did when God commanded them to people the earth, but under circumstances rather less lascivious.

This discovery produced in me surprise mixed with joy, and an acute and delightful sensation that I should have found it impossible to express. I felt as if I could have given every drop of my blood to be in the monk's place. How I envied him the great happiness he appeared to enjoy! an unknown fire shot through my veins; my face reddened; my heart beat; I held my breath; and the pike of Venus, which I took in my hand, was stiff enough to knock down the partition, if I had pushed hard against it. The Father finished his career, and as he raised himself off Annette, he left her face overspread with the deepest red. She was panting for breath; her arms lying down, and her bosom heaved with astonishing rapidity. My eyes ran over every part of her body with inconceivable expedition; nor was there a spot on which my ardent imagination did not fix a thousand burning kisses. I sucked her bubbies, her belly; but the most delicious place, from which my eyes, when once they found it, could not be removed, was . . . You understand me. How charming did that jewel appear to me! Oh what lovely coloring! Although covered with a white froth, it lost in my eyes nothing of its brilliancy. By the delight I felt, I recognized in it the very focus of pleasure. It was shaded with black and curly hair. Annette lay with her legs parted, and it seemed as if her lechery was in accord with my curiosity, in order to leave me nothing to desire.

The monk having recovered his vigor, again presented himself to renew the combat; he remounted with fresh ardor, but his strength was not equal to his courage, and fatigued with fruitless efforts, he soon withdrew his instrument from Annette's jewel, all powerless and drooping its head. Annette, disappointed at this retreat, took hold of it and began to rub it; the monk was in the utmost agitation, and appeared unable to bear the pleasure he experienced. I examined all their proceedings with no guide but nature, nor other instruction than the instance before me; and in my curiosity to learn the cause of the convulsive movements of the Father, I sought for it in myself. I was astonished at feeling a pleasure hitherto unknown to me, which gradually increased, till it became so intense that I fainted away on the bed. Nature made surprising efforts, and every part of my body seemed to participate in the pleasure afforded by that which I grasped. At length came the discharge of a white fluid, similar to what I had observed on the thighs of Annette, which soon dissipated my ecstasy, and I then returned to the aperture in the partition: however, all was over; the last game was played out. Annette was dressing herself, and the Father had already adjusted his clothing. I remained sometime, my head and heart still occupied with the incident I had witnessed, in that kind of stupefaction which a young man experiences when a new and unexpected light has burst in upon his understanding.

Surprise followed surprise; the instinct implanted by nature in my heart began to develop: now that some of the clouds with which she had covered it were removed, I discovered the cause of the sensations I every day experienced at the sight of women. Those imperceptible transitions, from tranquillity to extreme excitement, from indifference to desire, were no longer enigmas to me.

"Ah," I exclaimed, "how happy they were! They were both transported with joy. How great must have been the pleasure they experienced! What bliss was theirs!" These ideas completely absorbed me, so much so that for a moment I lost all power of reflection. A profound silence followed the exclamations.

"Oh," continued I, "should I ever have the luck to do as much for some woman, I must certainly expire upon her with pleasure, since this sight has given me so much. My enjoyment can only be a faint image of what Father Polycarp tasted with my mother! But what a fool am I, to doubt that pleasure can only be for grown-up persons? Still, by jingo, it seems as if it does not depend on the stature, and provided one is on the other, all will go on bravely!"

It immediately occurred to me that I would impart my discovery to my sister Susan, who was some years older than myself. She was a pretty little fair complexioned girl, with one of those open countenances that you might be ready to think silly because they appear indolent. Her eyes were beautifully blue, full of a melting softness, and seemed to look at you without meaning it: they produced quite as much effect on one as the bright eyes of a brunette with their piercing glance. How was that? I don't know; for I have always been satisfied with feeling it to be so, without investigating the cause. May it not be that the delicate fair one with her languishing looks, seems to entreat you to give her your heart, and that the brunette threatens to take it by storm? The one only asks your compassion in this seductive manner, and in granting that you give her your love: the other, on the contrary, wishes to make you yield without promising a return, and at this your heart rebels; is it not so? What do you think, reader?

I am ashamed to say that it had never yet come into my head to cast a lascivious eye on Susan; rather an extraordinary thing for me who lusted after all the girls I saw. It was true that as she was the god-daughter of the lady of the village, who was greatly attached to her and brought her up, I had few opportunities of seeing her.

She had, indeed, been a year at a convent, and had only left it about a week before this epoch; and her godmother, who was coming to spend some time in the country, had promised her a visit to Ambrose. I suddenly became anxious to initiate my dear sister, and to partake with her the same pleasures that I had just seen enjoyed by Father Polycarp and Annette. With respect to her, I was no longer the same person. I now saw in her a thousand charms that had hitherto escaped me. Her breasts, white as lilies, were firm and globelike. In imagination, I already sucked the two little strawberries that I saw at the extremity of her bubbies: but, above all, in my picture of her charms I did not omit that center, that abyss of pleasures of which I made myself such ravishing images. Excited by the burning ardor which these ideas diffused throughout my body, I went to seek Susan. The sun had just set, and it was getting dusk; I flattered myself that under the favor of the darkness, I should soon be at the very pinnacle of my wishes, if I could find her. I saw her at a distance, gathering flowers. Little did she think that I meditated gathering the choicest flower of her nosegay. I flew toward her, but seeing her so entirely occupied in such an innocent manner, I hesitated a moment whether or not I should communicate my design to her. As I approached her I felt my eagerness abate; and a sudden shiver seemed to reproach me with my intention. I thought it my duty to respect her innocence, but was deterred from my attempt only by the uncertainty of success. I accosted her, but in such an agitation that I could not utter two words without taking breath.

"What are you doing there, Susan?" said I; and as I offered to embrace her, she ran away, laughing and saying: "What! do you not see I am gathering flowers? Yes, indeed, don't you know that tomorrow is the birthday of my godmother?"

At this name I trembled, as if in fear that Susan might escape me. My heart had (if I may so say) already accustomed itself to look on her as a sure conquest; and the idea of her going further away seemed to menace me with the loss of a pleasure that I regarded as certain, although I had no experience in those affairs.

"I shall never see you again, Susan," said I to her with a sorrowful air.

"Why not," answered she; "shall I not still come here? But," she continued with a charming expression of countenance, "help me make my nosegay."

I only answered her by throwing some flowers in her face, which she immediately returned in like manner.

"Hold, Susan," said I, "if you throw any more, I'll . . . you shall pay for it."—To show that she cared nothing for my threats, she threw a handful at me. In a moment my timidity left me; I was no more afraid of being seen.

My impudence was favored by the darkness, which prevented anything being visible at a distance. I threw myself upon her and she pushed me away. I embraced her and she cuffed me; I laid her down on the grass, and when she tried to rise I hindered her. I held her closely pressed in my arms, kissing her bosom, while she kept struggling to release herself. I put my hand up under her clothes, but she cried out like a little devil, and so well defended herself that I despaired of success, and was afraid somebody would come to us. I got up laughing, and I did not think that she had more mischief in her than myself: how much was I deceived!

"Come, then, Susan," said I, "to show that I intended no harm I will indeed help you."

"Yes, yes," she replied, as much agitated as I was; "come, see yonder is mother coming and I . . ."

"O Susan," said I hastily, to prevent her saying more, "do not tell her anything; and I will give you . . . anything, whatever you like." I pledged my word with another kiss at which she laughed. Annette came up to us. I was afraid Susan would tell her; but she did not say a word, and we all went home together to supper as if nothing had happened.

Since Father Polycarp had been at the house, he had given fresh proofs of the kindness of the convent for the supposed son of Ambrose, in the shape of a complete suit of new clothes.

In truth, in that matter, his Reverence had less consulted monachal charity, which is rather limited, than paternal affection, which is much more liberal, and sometimes unbounded. The good Father by such prodigality exposed the legitimacy of my birth to violent suspicions; but our rustics were a good sort of people, and looked no further into things than one would wish.

Besides, who could have the audacity to scrutinize with an evil eye the motives of the reverend Fathers' generosity? They were such respectable persons, such worthy characters, who did good to all men and revered the honor of prudent women, that everybody was content. But to return to my own person, for I am about to enter on a glorious adventure.

Apropos of that said person, I had rather a conceited air, but not to a degree to prejudice anyone against me. I was well dressed, my eyes had a wicked look; and my long black hair, which fell in curls on my shoulders, set off to advantage the blooming color of my face, which, though not exactly fair, could not be found fault with. This is a most authentic testimony that I am obliged to bear to the judgment of several very respectable and virtuous dames to whom I have paid my homage.

Susan, as I have before related, had made a nosegay for Madame Dinville (for that was the name of her godmother), the wife of a counselor of the neighboring town, who came to reside at her country house for the purpose of taking a milk diet, to repair a stomach damaged by champagne and other causes.

Susan had decked herself out in her best, which made her still more lovely in my eyes, and I was invited to accompany her. We went to the chateau, and there we found the lady enjoying the cool air of a summer apartment. Figure to yourself a woman of the middle size, with dark hair, a white skin, a face, on the whole rather ugly, reddened by drinking champagne; dark eyes, full breasts, and as amorously inclined as any woman in the world. This at first appeared to me her only good quality; those two globes have always been my weak side. Oh, 'tis something so nice, when you put your hands on them, when you . . . But everyone to his own taste, give me these.

As soon as the lady saw us, she gave us a kind look without changing her posture. She was reclining on a sofa, with one leg up and the other on the floor; she had on merely a single white petticoat, short enough to show you her knee, which was not so much covered as to make you think it would be very difficult to see the rest; a short corset of the same color, and a jacket of rose-colored taffeta negligently put on; her hand was under her petticoat—guess for what purpose. My imagination was up in a moment, and my heart was not far behind; henceforward it became my fate to fall in love with every woman I saw; the discovery of the last evening had awakened in me all these laudable propensities.

"Ah! good day, my dear child," said Madame Dinville to Susan; "and so you have come to see me. What! Have you brought me a nosegay? Truly I am very much obliged to you, my dear girl. Come and embrace me."

Susan did so. "But," continued she, looking at me, "who is that fine big boy there? What, my little dear, you have brought a boy to accompany you; that is pretty." I looked on the ground, but Susan said that I was her brother, at which I bowed.

"Your brother," replied Madame Dinville, "come then," she continued, looking at me as she spoke, "kiss me, my son; we must be acquainted." She gave me a kiss on the mouth, and I felt a little tongue slip between my lips, and a hand playing with the curls of my hair. I was rather confused, for I was not used to this way of kissing. I looked at her timidly, and met her shining and animated eyes, which made me turn mine down. Another and similar kiss succeeded, after which I was able to stir; for previously she held me so close that I could not. But I did not care for that, as it seemed to be cutting short the ceremonial of making acquaintance. I was no doubt indebted for my liberty to the reflections she made of the bad effect that such unbounded caresses at a first interview might produce. But these reflections were not of long duration, for she again began talking to Susan, and the burthen of every period was "Come and kiss me."

At first I kept a respectful distance.

"So," said she, addressing me, "that big boy there won't come and . . . ?"

I advanced and kissed her cheek, not yet daring to venture on the mouth, but still I was rather bolder than at first. She thus divided her caresses between me and my sister for some time; and at last I made such progress, that I did not wait to be told when it was my turn. By degrees my sister desisted, and I had the exclusive privilege of enjoying the lady's kisses, while Susan was content with words.

We sat on the sofa and chatted, for Madame Dinville was a precious gossip, Susan on her right, myself on her left. Susan looked in the garden, madame looked at me, and amused herself with uncurling my hair, pinching my cheek, and gently patting me; I also amused myself with looking at her, and her easy manners soon emboldened

me. I became quite impudent, yet she said nothing, only looked at me, laughed, and let me continue my sport. My hand descended insensibly from her neck to her bosom, and pressed with delight upon a breast whose elastic firmness rebounded to the touch.

My heart swam in pleasure, as I grasped one of those charming globes, which I handled as I pleased. I was going to put my lips to it; for by pushing forward we reach the goal. I do believe I should have followed up my fortune to its proper conclusion, had not a cursed marplot, in the person of the bailiff of the village, an old ape sent by some demon jealous of my happiness, made his entry into the ante-chamber.

Madame Dinville, roused by the noise the old booby made, said to me: "What are you about, you little rogue!" I withdrew my hand hastily; my effrontery was not yet proof against censure; I blushed, and thought myself lost; but the kind lady saw my embarrassment, and gave me to understand by a gentle slap accompanied with a charming smile, that her anger was only a formality, and her looks convinced me that my boldness was less disagreeable to her than the arrival of the bailiff.

He came in—a tiresome blockhead!—After coughing, spitting, sneezing and blowing his nose, he made his harangue, which was more disagreeable than his personal appearance.

We were at the end of the walk, and my lady turned aside into a charming little grove which promised us a most delightful, cool walk, if we chose to enjoy it, and I made a remark to that effect.

"Very true," said she, endeavoring to read in my eyes whether I understood the object of her promenade; but I had not the least idea of it.

She put her arm round me most affectionately, and leaning her head on my shoulder, her face came so near to mine that I should have been a fool not to kiss her. She let me do so, and I repeated it without any opposition; then I was awake to my position.

"O! this is just the thing," said I; "here we shall be quite secure from interruption."

I was not misunderstood; so we advanced in the labyrinth, the shelter of which was amply sufficient to seclude us from the sight of everybody. She at last seated herself under a shady tree, and I followed her example, placing myself close by her side. She looked at me, pressed my hand, and laid herself down.

The lucky moment seemed come at last, and I began to prepare myself for action, when I perceived that the lady had suddenly fallen asleep. For a moment I thought it was only a drowsiness, induced by our promenade in the sun, which it would be very easy to dissipate, but seeing that it continued to increase rather than diminish, I could not tell what to make of it. I could have forgiven all this readily, if she had first allowed me to gratify my desires, but was exceedingly annoyed at being thus balked in the very instant of my triumph. My desires prompted me to awaken her, yet I dared not, lest I should displease and lose the enjoyment that I flattered myself awaited me when her nap was over. I could not refrain from putting my hand into her bosom, and I then withdrew her fan which she had stuck there. This not appearing to disturb her, I ventured on a kiss, of which she took not the least notice. I was becoming bolder every moment and wanted to descend a little lower. I put my head between her feet, with my face to the earth, and sought to explore the regions of love, but nothing could I see, for one leg was thrown over the other so as to completely cut off the prospect. Finding that I could not see, I was resolved to feel, and accordingly slipped my hand right up her thigh to the foot of the mount. When I reached the entrance of the grotto, I scarcely dared think of doing more; but I only felt more miserable for this partial success. I was eager to examine with my eyes what I touched with my hand. I then looked again at her face, not the slightest change was visible; the most imperturbable sleep seemed to reign over her; a twinkling of one eye rather disquieted me for a moment, and made me somewhat mistrustful, and had it not closely shut up almost immediately, I should have contented myself with what I had already done. I returned, however, to my lower post of observation, and began to raise the petticoat a little. The lady started, and I, trembling at my impudence, ceased all proceedings and resumed my place beside her, without daring to look toward her. I did not remain long in this constraint; I saw she was still asleep, and blessed my stars on observing that her legs were no longer crossed, the petticoat was drawn up, and all her charms lay exposed to my astonished eyes.

Her legs were most beautifully shaped, and her ivory thighs, round, soft, and firm, surmounted by a quim of bright carnation, encircled with a hedge of bushy hair, as black as jet, and exhaling an odor more exquisite than all the essences of the perfumers. I put my finger to it and tickled it a little, and afterward, putting my head between her legs, I endeavored to thrust in my tongue. I stood with such force that nothing could arrest me. I could have fucked the favorite sultana in the presence of a thousand eunuchs with drawn scimitars, ready to wash away my pleasures in my blood. Supporting myself on my hands, I touched her with nothing but my member; and a motion, at once gentle and regular, made me drink long draughts of pleasure, which were but the earnest of what I was to enjoy.

I gazed steadfastly in the face of my partner, and from time to time imprinted a burning kiss upon her lips. The precaution I had taken of bearing my weight on my hands in the rapture of the moment was altogether neglected. I fell on her, and could do nothing but embrace and kiss her with a frenzy amounting almost to madness. When my pleasure was over, I recovered the use of my eyes, and saw the transports of my lady without being able to participate therein.

"My dearest love," whispered she, "give one more push! Don't leave the business but half finished!"

I put my shoulder to the wheel with an ardor that surpassed her own, and I had scarcely given four strokes before she was insensible. More animated than ever, I increased my pace, and in a moment lay motionless in her arms; both of us intoxicated with the full tide of bliss that flowed in upon us.

This ecstasy did not endure long, and when I withdrew myself from my partner, it was not without some little confusion, which was increased when I saw that she was looking hard at me. I was sitting up, and she put one arm round my neck, and made me lie down again on the grass, while with the other she was coaxing my instrument, and essaying by an abundant application of kisses to make him resume the stiffness he had lost. I was quite abashed at all this, and could not conceal it.

"What would you be after," said she; "surely you need not be afraid to show me an article that you know how to use so well! I hide nothing from you—here, you dog, kiss my bubbies; put your hand in my bosom; now the other to my pussy; good! what a clever little fellow you are!"

I am not quite certain whether I ever had any modesty, but I think there would be little danger in asserting, that after we had continued these amusements for some time, my stock of that troublesome article was reduced to a minimum. My lance was now ready for the jousting that my antagonist so ardently desired; and to every embrace she most heartily responded by a volley of kisses. I still kept my finger in the center of pleasure, and gradually parted her legs that I might enjoy a view of the charming locality. The approaches of pleasure are more delightful than the thing itself, nor do I think anything can be more delicious than thus to handle a woman who surrenders herself entirely to your voluptuous caprices. This amorous prelude must necessarily terminate in the grand climax, and vigorously did we carry on the lecherous conflict; she was all alive under me, and seemed to gather strength from every exertion, as she returned stroke for stroke with increasing eagerness and force. Mouth to mouth, with our tongues emulating the proceedings in the lower department, we soon attained the acme of our transports, and when the finishing stroke was made, our sensations were far beyond anything that pen can portray.

I believe someone has written that "Vigor is the gift of heaven." It is possible that I inherited this blessing from my reverend and godly Fathers as my only patrimony. I was not slow in dis-

sipating my heritage—but I must not break the order of things in detailing my misfortunes here.

Notwithstanding all the proofs that I had given of my virility, Madame Dinville was not yet satisfied, but used every means she could imagine to make me renew the combat.

"O you rogue," said she, giving me a kiss, "what, standing again! This dear jewel of yours, so hard, so thick, and so long, is worth a fortune to you. Bless me! so you are ready to begin again?" I answered this appeal by pulling her backward.

"Stop a bit, my love, I want to give you a new pleasure. It is now my turn to roger you. Lie down, just as I did before."

In a moment I was extended on my back, and she on me; she then put my staff into the proper place, and began to push away. I did not move at all, but let her work while I enjoyed the pleasure. I contemplated the charms above me, and she occasionally rested to smother me with kisses. A voluptuous sensation forewarned me of the approach of the critical moment; I then joined my exertions to hers, and we were shortly deluged with an overflow of love's peculiar distillery. After, I was in reality quite exhausted, and could no longer resist the advances of sleep. My loving companion nestled my head in her bosom, that I might enjoy the sweetness of repose where I had tasted that of love.

"Sleep, my darling, let nothing disturb you; I will content myself with looking at you."

I followed this advice in good earnest, and slept so soundly that I did not awake till the sun was very near his evening goal. When I awoke, the first object that struck my eyes was Madame Dinville, looking at me with a sweet smile upon her countenance. She laid down her knitting, with which she had amused herself during my nap, and kissed me, slipping her tongue into my mouth. Her attempts to arouse my enfeebled energies were, however, for some time altogether useless. Had I been allowed my own choice, I should have preferred rest rather than active service; but this was not the lady's design; she wanted to re-excite those desires that I no longer felt. Finding that her kisses and caresses produced but very trifling effects, she had recourse to another expedient; which was lying down on her back and pulling up her clothes, so as to expose all her charms to my view; at the same time rubbing my tool till she saw that her point was gained. Then ensued another furious encounter, which was somewhat abridged by a rather premature discharge on my part. I was chagrined at having the affair thus abbreviated, but there was no remedy. When we left this sweet retreat we took a turn or two in the garden, and conversed as we went along.

BEAUREGARD DE FARNIENTE

The bizarre name, Beauregard de Farniente, is false—even as a pseudonym. It just so happened that one summer night, when I was hurriedly completing the text of our new list for the printer, I found that the author's name on the original French version of the book had slipped my mind. Being in a hurry, and not a very conscientious publisher, I did not bother to investigate and slapped down the first idiotic name that came to my mind, Beauregard de Farniente. Farniente definitely has a wishful connotation.

As a matter of fact, the authorship of the book has never been conclusively established. It first appeared in 1740 under the title L'Histoire de Don B****, Le Portier des Chartreux, *and that festive tale of Rabelaisian monks won immediate under-the-counter fame. Its success was due in great part to the circumstances of its publication, which set in motion one of the most colorful episodes in the history of censorship.*

It is only a few weeks after Le Portier *became available to the clientele of rich libertines for which it was meant that the Cardinal de Fleury, prime minister of the realm, ordered M. de Marville, "lieutenant general" of the Paris police, to begin investigations. Inquiries revealed that a bale containing several hundred copies in sheets and without a title page had been sent to Rouen, to be shipped from there aboard a Dutch vessel on its way back to Amsterdam. The police arrived too late, the Dutch ship had left port; but an Italian named Stella was arrested in connection with that shipping and was immedi-*

ately expelled from France.

Then Lucas Regnard Dubut, a police officer of exceptional zeal who specialized in the repression of pornography, searched the house of one Blangis whom he suspected of having printed the lascivious engravings which adorned Le Portier. Although the search proved fruitless, Blangis was arrested together with his wife, who was pregnant, and they were both sent to the city prison, the Bastille.

Both M. de Marville and the ubiquitous Dubut made great use of paid informers, and they were not long in identifying a group of people who seemed very closely connected with the publication of the book. A search warrant was issued and Dubut, with a cohort of policemen, invaded a house on the rue de la Comédie-Française (now rue de l'Ancienne Comédie) which belonged to a Madame d'Alainville. They interviewed and arrested a Mlle. Ollier who lived there, and appeared to be the chief suspect; she was a one-time actress, who, having lost one eye and contracted a lung disease, had abandoned her first calling to become a notorious dealer in pornographic novels. She was questioned cautiously because she was known to be, in spite of her deplorable physical condition, the mistress of one Marquis le Camus de Bligny, an officer in the armies of the king and a notorious rake, embezzler, and pimp—but nevertheless a high ranking aristocrat and therefore untouchable.

Pursuing their search, Dubut and his men entered the room occupied on the fourth floor by a priest, l'abbé Nourry, who was Madame d'Alainville's brother. They searched the room and discovered five copies of the incriminating book in that holy man's chaise percée. His pathetic explanation was that he had met a young man the previous day who was in possession of the five volumes and was sailing off to Brazil the next day, where he expected to sell them for a good price. The abbé, shocked at the idea that such lewd literature was going to be propagated abroad, bought the books from the unknown man only in order to protect the morals of the Brazilians. The man of the cloth was sent to the Bastille.

One Lefèvre was also arrested; he soon admitted that he had engraved the plates; several peddlers were caught and also sent to the Bastille. In the face of the most patent evidence, all the suspects continued to deny that they had had anything to do with the infamous book. But the police did not care: M. de Marville had the right to keep them under lock and key for as long as he fancied—in his view, *there was no difference between mere suspicion and proven guilt.*

After several months spent in prison, Blangis, Lefèvre and others finally admitted their crime, but in so doing they accused the chief conspirators, and bitterly complained of not having been paid for their work.

It became blatantly obvious now that the Marquis le Camus had acted as publisher of the book, that a respectable, retired notary public by the name of Morand had financed the publication, and that a young lawyer by the name of Jean-Charles Gervaise de Latouche was the author. The underdogs were kept in the Bastille a little longer for good measure, the unwise abbé Nourry was delivered to the Catholic hierarchy and hidden away in a provincial monastery, and Mlle. Ollier was exiled from Paris. But the Marquis, the lawyer and the wealthy landlady, Madame d'Alainville, were left in peace.

The Marquis soon solved his problems by marrying a young heiress. By writing mild obscenities, Gervaise de Latouche made a small fortune which he entrusted to the Duke de Guéméné, an aristocratic financier, and which was lost when the duke went bankrupt.

Such is the fate of pornographers.

ROMAN ORGY

Marcus van Heller

*A*mong the many pairs of eyes which had witnessed the using of the Egyptian slave girl by Lucius Crispus, was a pair of cool gray ones. At the moment they were hard eyes, very hard eyes.

They belonged in a face which any Emperor would have been proud of; a broad, strong face with a square, jutting chin, a straight fine mouth and a broad forehead from which the eyes looked deeply out, hard and unafraid. A face which could have made a kingdom into an empire, a face which was going to lead ten thousand men to doom. The face of a slave.

It was during the lecherous performance of Lucius Crispus that the slave became aware of Clodia's eyes upon him—as they had so often been upon him of late. As Crispus was urged to greater efforts by the licentious crew of Rome's aristocracy, the patrician's wife finally called his name.

"Spartacus!"

He turned his gray eyes toward her and walked over to her side.

As he walked, the muscles in his calves below the tunic bulged; long lengths of muscle stirred in his arms. In spite of his height—he was slightly taller than any other man present—his body radiated a potential dynamism. It seemed unlikely that he could be taken off his guard.

He bent toward his mistress and the cloth of his tunic stretched in wrinkles across his shoulders.

Clodia's eyes held his with a look he could not understand as she said quietly:

"I'm tired of this. I'm going to bathe. I shall need you to stand guard over the door."

She bade good night to her women guests who watched her sympathetically as she left. It was very hard on her, her husband acting like this in public and Clodia such a beautful woman and not one man noticing her go. It was a wonder she didn't divorce him—or get herself a lover.

Spartacus strode silently after her, leaving the noise of the banquet behind, through the portico flanking the huge quadrilateral, which in turn enclosed the gardens with their walks and arbors and the baths which Crispus had had specially built to the pattern and proportions of the huge public thermae.

It was not unusual for Spartacus to be asked to accompany his mistress. He was the head of the several hundred slaves which Crispus boasted as his entourage and he occupied a comparatively privileged position. Descended from the Thracian princes, he could boast at least as much culture as his master—which he had to admit was not saying an awful lot—and he knew himself to be more of a man.

But lately, it seemed, Clodia had been singling him out to be with her in nearly everything she did, everywhere she went. He had become, virtually, her personal bodyguard.

Watching her walk before him through the torch-lit porticos, Spartacus wondered why she stayed in Crispus' house. It was well known—even among the slaves—that he treated her badly. There was nothing to stop her leaving.

Spartacus' lips tightened as his mind dwelt on Crispus. His master treated nobody well, in fact, except those he considered of superior rank and birth—on whom he fawned his attentions or whom he tried desperately to impress, not without success.

Spartacus was aware that Crispus regarded him with a certain reluctant respect, which he felt sometimes bordered on hatred. For a long time he had been at a loss to understand this, but eventually it had dawned on him that, to his master, he represented the threat of the enslaved but superior classes who in different circumstances would have thought him nothing but an ignorant upstart. There were many such slaves: cultured Greeks and Egyptians, many of them.

He had wondered at times why Crispus did not put him in the slave market, to be rid of him, but then again it had come to him that he represented a challenge. If Crispus got rid of him, he would have admitted his inability to dominate, admitted defeat.

Following Clodia into the bath buildings, Spartacus wondered why she should require him to accompany her. Was she afraid one of her guests might wander away from the banquet and try to take liberties with her? Nobody would dare. Was she afraid of her slaves? They wouldn't dare—besides he was a slave too. Spartacus became suddenly aware of the intimacy of leaving the bright, noisy company and disappearing through the grounds with one of the most beautiful women in Rome, to guard her while she bathed.

"Wait here."

Clodia left him with a command and disappeared into one of the dressing rooms just inside the building.

Spartacus stared around him in the flickering torchlight. Beyond was a large vaulted hall, its walls of blue and white stone mosaic. The center of the roof was taken up by a large space in the vaulting through which the sun poured at noon and the stars glittered at night. In the center of the floor was the great bronze basin of water, water which steamed now from the heat of the hypocaust beneath.

The slaves were never allowed to use these baths, which had separate hours—like the public baths—for men and women. It was still permissible in the public baths for mixed bathing, but it was never seen. No woman cared to sully her reputation. There had been so many scandals in the past.

In the past . . . How many years had Spartacus been here in Rome, in the great town house of Lucius Crispus? How many years had he listened to the suffering and indignities of the slaves? How many years since he had seen his Thracian hills, those beautiful, free, Thracian hills! How long would it go on?

His thoughts were suddenly stopped dead by the appearance of his mistress. Without a glance at him she ran across the marble floor and disappeared down the stone steps into the warm water of the sunken bronze basin. Spartacus was dumbstruck; a hundred times more so than when he had seen the Spanish maidens dance into the banqueting room. Clodia had been quite naked!

He gazed incredulously into the ill-lit gloom of the bathing room. It was so. Through the gloom and the rising vapors he could see her white body floating lazily on the surface of the greenish water. Even now he could make out—how anguishingly vague—the lines of her pale breasts, breaking the surface.

Spartacus' mind wouldn't function for some seconds. This had never been known. A Roman patrician woman to undress before a male slave! He turned and peered back through the gloom of the grounds, half afraid that he might be struck down for the sacrilege of having seen what had been paraded before him.

In that fleeting glimpse he had seen the body of one of the most beautiful women of Rome; a body which he knew many noble Romans would have given a fortune to see. Cold virtue in a beautiful woman always increased desire for her.

How could she have been so indiscreet? Why? She could have slipped on her stola and then have bathed in one of the smaller baths out of sight. It was as if she had paraded herself intentionally.

Spartacus stood, undecided, at the entrance to the building. He felt he should withdraw to the grounds just outside, but hesitated to disobey his mistress' explicit command. It seemed further sacrilege to remain where he was, particularly as Clodia was making no effort to escape his view, seemed, in fact, to be displaying herself quite unconcernedly.

As he watched her misty outline, she turned on her stomach and floated, face down in the water, her long, unloosened hair streaming over her wet shoulders, rounded tips of buttocks showing like some ghostly half-submerged fish.

Spartacus folded his arms. Under his hands he felt the smooth, tight bulging of his biceps and the feeling reassured him. This was Clodia's doing. He would stay where he was.

From time to time as he watched her leisurely lolling in the warm water, he saw her raise her head, or simply turn it, toward where he stood in the shadow of the entrance. Perhaps she was afraid he would go and leave her unprotected. Although why she should was unimaginable. To disobey an order!

Reflecting, with the image of her nudity in his head, Spartacus began to remember little incidents of the past few weeks: the way her eyes were so often upon him, the fact she had asked his advice upon some Thracian vase she had considered buying, that once her hand had rested on his arm, as if absently, when she gave him an order. Spartacus reflected on these things and the image of her nudity and gazed with his cool, gray eyes through the steam at the bronze basin.

Time passed. To Spartacus it seemed an eternity at any moment of which he expected some guest to stray away from the noise of the banquet which he could no longer hear, and find him standing his lonely guard over the senator's naked wife.

But when at last the silent worry of his thoughts was interrupted it was such an interruption as to fill his head with an even darker cloud of anxiety.

From the bronze basin, Clodia's cultured voice reached him. He fancied there was a trace of nervousness in the usually firm, imperious tones.

"Spartacus. A cloth and my robe are in the dressing room."

He waited a second or two for her to add something, but she lay back in the water, waiting.

His heart was beating a little faster than normal as he went into the dressing room. There on a wooden seat were strewn her clothes. His face flushed as his eyes passed, in the gloom, from her stola to the undertunic, the brassiere which clasped those round breasts, the loincloth which contained those virtuous hips.

He picked up the woolen napkin and the blue robe made of the still rare silk from the mysterious Orient.

As he strode, muscles flexing and unflexing in his powerful legs, toward the pool, he was filled with the foreboding of strange things. This was no ordinary night. This was no ordinary duty he was performing.

He reached the water's edge and stood looking down into the opaque, green waters where Clodia, still unconcernedly, floated. She seemed to ignore him as he gazed down at the parts of her body which showed through the steam.

Spartacus waited, while Clodia paddled. He could see the smooth slope of her white shoulders, the deep cleft of the upper part of her breast. Half lying, still, in the water, she turned her eyes toward him.

Her face was radiant with the pale beauty, the clear-cut lines of a Roman aristocrat. Her hazel eyes were bright with a peculiar fire.

"You dislike your master, Spartacus," she said. Her voice had regained its old, firm tones.

Spartacus said nothing. He felt unequal to the whole circumstance of the evening.

Clodia laughed. One of the few times he'd ever heard her laugh.

"Your silence condemns you. He dislikes you, too."

She hesitated and still Spartacus said nothing.

"Today he finally admitted defeat. He decided to get rid of you, to sell you in the slave market."

Spartacus stared at her. So at last it had happened. But her next words astonished him.

"He wanted to sell you, but I put my foot down. Because I want to keep you."

"My lady is kind," Spartacus said softly.

"No, not kind," she said, "just self-indulgent."

Giving Spartacus no time to ponder her words, she began, to his utter astonishment, to climb up the stone steps to the marble floor of the baths.

He stared at her, unable to withdraw his eyes as she came, like a nymph, out of the water. First her breasts stunned his eyes: large, firm and white with the large red smudge of nipple a startling contrast to the color of the skin. And then her belly, flat, smooth, white and then her abdomen with the two pink creases in the soft flesh and the black down of hair reaching to a point between her legs and the long thighs, themselves like marble, supple, cold and beautiful.

She stood dripping in front of him. Her eyes were those of the sphinx. His lips opened slightly.

"Rub me down," she said, quietly. "Have you forgotten yourself?"

The whole of Spartacus' skin all over his body seemed to be pulsating as he bent to his task. Clodia stood quietly watching the bunching of his powerful arm muscles as he wiped the moisture from her arms, her breasts, her belly, her back, her buttocks. Spartacus hesitated. Her buttocks were full, contained firmly in long sweeping lines. His hands had trembled as he felt the shape and texture of the globes through the woolen napkin. Now he hesitated.

"Go on," Clodia's voice commanded from above as he knelt.

Her voice sounded firm but there was a hollow undertone as if she were steeling herself. He realized suddenly that she was trembling.

His big hands moved down the backs of her thighs, shaping the almost imperceptible down into a slim arrow. His hands contained her rounded calves in the napkin and he swiveled round and rubbed up her legs in the front.

He was more aware of her trembling. Under his tunic at his genitals was a heavy ache. Clodia swiveled her legs apart, moving on the balls of her small, bare feet. Spartacus looked up at her. Her lips were apart as she looked down on him. Her eyes pierced into his with a look which was command and desire and not without a tremulous background of fear.

"Go on," she said softly. There was a tremble in her voice as well as her limbs.

Spartacus hollowed his hands around the napkin and moved them up her leg. Astonishment had now given place to a masculine certainty and strength. There was no doubt in his mind, only a deep, luxurious wonder.

His hands moved up over the knee, soaking the moisture from the skin into the napkin. Through it he could feel the solidity of the thigh. He wanted to touch the thigh without the napkin, but he continued pulling the cloth, like a broken glove up the leg to where it broadened into its fullness and his eyes were on a level with the crease of flesh between her thighs.

Once more he hesitated.

"Go on." The voice above him was a controlled Vesuvius.

Spartacus held the napkin in the flat of his right hand. With the other he boldly grasped Clodia's thigh, his fingers denting the buttery flesh and with a long, slow movement, he wiped the napkin between her legs.

As he felt the soft yielding flesh under the napkin flatten out against the inside of the thighs, Clodia's hand came uncontrollably down to his head and her fingers grasped his long, fair hair and pressed his face to her lower belly.

Spartacus rose slowly up her body, his lips traveling up tracing a path over her navel, the taut flesh of her ribs, resting on the beautiful pearl hills of her breasts, brushing the rich, hard protrusion of nipple, sucking in the hollow of her shoulder, on up the white slender neck, until they found her lips and fastened there, his lips on those of Clodia, famed in Rome for her beauty, Clodia whose slim, smooth tongue now forced its way between his lips, between his teeth and snaked in his mouth, the mouth of her slave.

After a moment she drew away from him, trembling violently.

"Give me my robe," she said. "We must not be seen here."

Spartacus put her robe over her trembling shoulders, she pulled it tightly around her and bidding him follow her, walked quickly away from the baths.

Walking behind her once again, Spartacus was filled with a joy of incredible discovery, an emotional power which was overwhelming. Here he was following her as he had so often followed her before —but now what a difference! Now he knew those breasts which had vaguely excited him before as they pressed through her stola. Breasts which had excited so many men in Rome; breasts so inaccessible and far away. Now he knew that slender back which shaped into the girdle of the robe as she hurried before him, knew those buttocks which were outlined by the clinging silk, those thighs over which the silk hung loosely from its swelling over the rump. Now he understood the looks which Clodia had cast on him, now he understood the touch on his arm. Soon she would be his, unbelievably his.

Hurrying before Spartacus, Clodia was aware that his eyes were on the tension of her buttocks under the robe. She pulled the robe more tightly around her.

Now they were going to her room and she would seduce him. It was no sudden decision Clodia had made. It had been developing in her mind for months.

She was well aware of Lucius' lack of interest in her. She was no longer terribly interested in him. She had in fact made up her mind at one time to divorce him.

But then she had become suddenly aware of the slave, Spartacus. There was some magnetism in him, some superior strength of character which made her, even now, half afraid in her fascination for him.

She had soon seen Lucius' recognition of the same quality, had watched the battle Lucius, who could not bear to find himself in competition with a stronger man, had fought with himself. Had watched the indifference of the slave to the attempts of an inferior being to degrade him.

It was a fascination, a very physical fascination, which had kept her in Lucius' house. She would sit and watch Spartacus, his big muscles tensing in his big body as he performed his tasks, she would watch the calm, handsome face and if the cool, gray eyes alighted on her she would look quickly away lest he should notice her interest.

The desire had grown in her to touch that athletic, muscular body. A desire which had finally found its outlet a few days before when she had allowed her fingers to rest lightly on his arm while directing him to some duty.

And then she had wanted that touch, that physical communion returned. Had wanted to give, to yield under the superior power which she sensed in the man.

Even now it was a desire completely physical which drove her on. The unheard-of, forbidden liaison with a slave. That taboo which gave such an emotional desperation and glory to the fornication.

Although, it was true, a slave could eventually become a freedman—and perhaps rise to office—there was no gainsaying the fact that a slave, as a slave, was the scum of the Empire. Such a liaison would have the whole of Rome howling for the blood of both parties; such a liaison would resound beyond the boundaries of the peninsula to the very outposts of the Roman world.

It was partly the knowledge of this that had driven Clodia on in her desire rather than deterred her. She had a will the equal of most in the city and Spartacus, all unwittingly, had driven her toward the inevitable with every movement of his body, every look in his eyes, every one of the few words he uttered.

The noise of the banquet, still in progress, reached them as they walked in the shadow of the portico and mounted the steps to the upper story. Without a word, Clodia led the way through Crispus' room to her own. Starlight shone in through a window which looked out onto the quadrilateral. Spartacus moved uncertainly in the poor light and stood silent and still, while Clodia pulled a heavy shutter into place across the window. She lit the torches in their brackets on the walls and while she moved quietly to the door to close it, Spartacus looked with quick curiosity around her room, which he was seeing for the first time.

The room was dominated by Clodia's bed, the bed in which she must have spent so many lonely nights, listening perhaps to the breathing of her husband in the next room. It was a huge bed of oak. The woodwork was inlaid with tortoise shell, the feet were made of ivory. All three materials shone with a luster which bespoke much labor from Clodia's female slaves. There were two divans also, strewn with exotically colored cushions, and in a corner near the window space was a tripod table on which lay Clodia's mirrors of silver and a few adornments.

The furniture, as was customary in the grand houses, was sparse but superb.

After Clodia had shut the door she and Spartacus stood looking at each other for a few moments. Her beautiful face was slightly flushed; there was a hint of fear in her eyes which she tried vainly to conceal.

The interval of walking had made Spartacus wary. He was well aware of the penalty for this sort of thing and he now remained where he was, making no move toward her.

Looking at him, Clodia, too, felt the slight embarrassment that the interval had built. She had a sudden, fleeting fear that she might be scorned.

She brushed past Spartacus and stretched out on the counterpane and cushions of the bed.

"My bones ache with all that sitting in the banqueting room," she said, holding his eyes again with her own. "I want to be massaged."

Spartacus moved toward her, his sandaled feet rustling lightly on the floor. She saw in his eyes the deep unwavering look of purpose that so many were to see and it filled her with a shuddering fascination, a shuddering anticipation.

"Have you seen the women wrestlers being massaged in the palaestrae?" she asked softly. He nodded as he came toward her and she added, slipping from her robe: "Well I am just one of them waiting for the masseur. Clodia does not exist."

As his fingers began to move over her body and her breath fluttered in her throat, she thought "Perhaps this is the only time that Clodia exists."

Once again her full, beautiful white body was exposed to her slave. But Spartacus, running his hands over the beautiful tapering arms, the slim shoulders, the glossy swellings of her breasts, knew that he was no longer her slave but her master.

Rome had been stunned by the fate of the troops it had sent in the wake of Spartacus. A handful of the three or four hundred men had been the only survivors. Nobody knew whether the gladiators had suffered any casualties, so complete had been the surprise.

The bewilderment had been rapidly followed by rationalizations, explanations—excuses. The number of Roman soldiers had been too few in the beginning; the Senate should have authorized more. The gladiators had doubled their ranks with slaves. They had spies everywhere.

It was decreed that the two Consuls should themselves take the two legions—all that remained, with Pompeius in Spain and Caesar in Gaul—and put a peremptory and salutary end to the gladiators' antics.

While the wheels of organization slowly turned, Rome went about its business. Nobody was going to be put out by a handful of gladiators somewhere down near Capua.

Last of all to allow himself to appear put out was Lucius Crispus, Spartacus' old master and owner. Since the small band of soldiers allotted to his house had been withdrawn he'd been putting a bold face to the world and tonight he had hired some professional players to perform a play for an invited audience in his house.

The couches for his thirty guests were arranged in a semicircle at one end of the banqueting room, a large space for the players left at the other. A fair section of the aristocracy was present, a fact which pleased Crispus immensely. He looked around for his wife, Clodia. She should be here with him to receive the guests. It was very bad form for her to be missing.

Up in her room, Clodia smoothed her hands over the counterpane of her bed. She now knew that something was happening to her. She was not the woman she had been a few months ago. Something was going on inside her head leaving her listless, half afraid, almost dazed. Spartacus was still alive. It seemed that he had some god personally interested in his welfare. She did not think she was being illogical when she believed the odds had been all against him since the day she had handed him over to patrician justice. She wished she could separate her conflicting feelings, wished she could decide, once and finally if she wanted him to die. In some mystic way she felt that her willing him to die would bring it about, or equally that her willing him to live would bring it about. If only she could make the decision.

Suddenly she remembered the play, the guests. With a startled raise of her eyebrows she pulled her stola about her and tripped down the steps to the crowded banqueting room below.

Away from the public theaters—even there performances were frequently designed almost purely to titillate the audience into an erotic response—productions reached a peak of sensuality.

The tale which unfolded before the fascinated eyes of Crispus and his guests was that of incest and the ravishing of a daughter, who unlike her sisters, resisted the amorous advances of her father.

"How scandalous!" the patrician women tittered as realistic movements on a specially provided couch illustrated the ravishing. The actress was a doll-like creature, a mere accompaniment to the actor, who was one of the finest mimes and dancers in Rome.

Men and women in the audience felt themselves grow hot around the loins as the doll-like face assumed expressions of horror, sudden shock, pain and then abasement, as the actor's hips writhed beside her in the acme of suggestiveness. His hips actually jerked against hers in solid contact and it was clear that both achieved a considerable satisfaction from the intimate motion. The actor simulated a panting and the girl opened her mouth and screwed up her eyes in pretended passion.

Crispus' attentive eyes discreetly watched his guests' reaction. Another success. What a pity that business with Spartacus had happened just as he was really creating a name for himself with his lavish entertainment. All around men and women had bright eyes glued on the actors. What a pity, he thought, that both Consuls had been too tied up with the organization of the legions to come. Still everyone else was here with fewer exceptions even than at his banquet.

Clodia sat beside him, looking straight ahead. She didn't seem to be at all affected by the performance. He wondered if she were even noticing it and for the first time he felt a twinge of pity for her. She was probably still worrying about her rape by Spartacus. It must have been pretty grim for her as well as for him, he supposed. But it was always worse for the man to have something like that happen to his woman.

He looked back at the actors who were just gasping in a climax. The auditorium was hushed, savoring every explosion of breath, when a louder commotion suddenly broke at the back of the room.

Twisting round in annoyance Crispus was astonished to see that the room had suddenly filled with soldiers, fully armed, metal-covered leather tunics glinting in the light of the few torches.

Crispus stood up; others around him turned on their couches; the actors stopped and stared. Crispus was bewildered. What did this mean? Was there some emergency? He was about to call out for information when the soldiers who had surrounded the couches stood back to let a tall figure through.

Crispus gazed at the figure, at the face under the burnished helmet of a Roman commander. His stomach turned to ice. He was looking into the hard, smiling eyes of Spartacus.

Beside him, Crispus heard a gasp from Clodia:
"Spartacus!"

At the name a gasp of horror rippled around the room. Everybody seemed to cringe.

Spartacus stood before Crispus, his hand on his sword hilt.

"Did you not expect me back?" he asked in a tone so soft that only those close to him heard the words.

Crispus' mouth opened but no sound came. The room was silent. The gladiators—a chosen score of them—almost unrecognizable in the uniforms of Titus Philippus' former army, were an impenetrable barrier around the room.

"Have you left your voice in the Senate?" Spartacus' tone rose and he took a step toward Crispus, his eyes sweeping Clodia. "Have you no words of welcome for the man back from the death to which you condemned him?"

Clodia's mind clouded over as Spartacus' hard, bitter eyes bored into her. She could hear his voice but she no longer made out the words. There was nothing but his eyes and the memory in them of her betrayal.

A senator moved forward, Claudius Laberius, a bold speaker, who was in the running for next year's Consulship. He seemed to have little understanding of the situation.

"How dare you force your way in here?" he snapped. "Don't you know, madman, that a thousand men are preparing in this city to wipe you from the face of the earth?"

He walked close to Spartacus. No slave was going to command his patrician blood. He jutted his face toward the gladiator.

"You'd better get out and quick before . . ."

Spartacus' hand pushed him flat in his face and Claudius Laberius staggered back several paces, tripped over a couch and crashed to the floor. When he started, spluttering, to get up, a Roman sword was held at his throat.

Spartacus turned back to Crispus. His eyes looked past him to Clodia. His voice was controlled, almost conversational.

"We were watching the play for a while," he said. "We don't want to spoil the entertainment. But we think it would benefit from a change of actors."

Crispus could not fight down the nervousness in his chest, which betrayed him in a trembling of his lower lip. Spartacus' casualness was all the more ominous.

There was a slight gasp as Spartacus extended his sword and deftly slit Clodia's stola from neck to hem. But nobody moved to her aid. His sword ripped the short sleeves and the garment fell away from her, tumbling against her neighbor.

"Get up," Spartacus commanded.

Clodia stood up, body swelling ripely under thin coverings of brassiere and loincloth. It did not occur to her to disobey. Spartacus' eyes seemed to hypnotize her. Her large, shapely bosom rose and fell. All eyes were on her and Spartacus.

Another delicate slit with his sword and Spartacus had snapped her brassiere supports and torn the loincloth away from her hips. Her breasts, hips and buttocks emerged as if they had oozed from the coverings, splitting them of their own volition. Pale, beautiful and suddenly chilled, she was exhibited to the prying eyes of gladiators and patricians alike.

Crispus was horrified. This was degradation for him. His terror of the ruination of his esteem overcame his fear and he lunged toward Spartacus and gripped the short sleeves of his tunic. Two gladiators stepped quickly toward them, but Spartacus made no move to use his sword. He moved in toward Crispus' body and brought his knee sharply up between the patrician's legs. Crispus groaned, doubled up and sagged to the floor at the Thracian's feet. Nobody moved to help him.

Spartacus looked back at Clodia. She had not looked at Crispus. Her eyes never left his.

The rebel leader swept his sword in an all-embracing movement at his gladiators.

"Choose one from among my men and you and he will act in reality the part of the play we interrupted," he said.

There was an audible intake of breath all over the room. Looking at Clodia's lovely body many of the patricians felt, mixed with their fear and disgust, a crumb of gratitude that this ex-slave had allowed them to see what they could never otherwise have hoped to witness. Oh, to see that voluptuous body, that body which made one's hands itch to hold its breasts, its perfect buttocks, those hips and thighs made to cushion and open under one's weight—oh to see it in any other circumstances! Oh, to take the place—after invitation and in privacy—of the man who was to act now the spectacle which made the hair on the back of one's neck bristle with fascinated repugnance!

"Choose!" Spartacus commanded.

Clodia felt numb, her eyes filled with tears which overflowed and coursed quietly down her long, pale cheeks. There was to be no pity. She saw it in his eyes.

"Kill me," she said. "I would rather die."

Spartacus looked at the gladiators and grinned. They were all staring at Clodia, eyes hot, trying, it seemed, to draw her eyes to them.

"See how eager they are." He turned back to Clodia and the grin was gone. "Strange you should find them so little to your taste," he said, savagely. "I remember when you had different desires."

He leaned slightly forward and traced a line with his sword point from her navel up between her breasts to her neck. His eyes followed the path of the sword and then bored into her again.

"Choose," he said with controlled ferocity. "Or I shall choose for you."

There was no pity, no mercy. Clodia knew, suddenly, that things were coming to an end. Life for her as a Roman patrician was over. Even if life remained there was the shame, the impossible shame.

"I choose you," she said softly.

The room had been hushed. But the hush seemed to take on a deeper quality, as if the air itself were stunned into motionlessness. Spartacus glared at her, surprised and then strangely furious that she should try to ensnare him a second time.

"Marcellus!" he snapped. "Take her."

Spartacus watched them take Clodia at sword point to the couch, watched Marcellus, grinning lustfully, strip. They flung Clodia onto the couch. The patrician men leaned forward, seeming to forget their danger, watching while Marcellus, unabashed and unembarrassed, crammed into Clodia's still, unresponsive body.

Lying under Marcellus, Clodia felt almost no sensation—just a numbed disgust and a dull ache. In her degradation, she also felt a deep bitterness that Spartacus had scorned her, had treated her desperate choice as if it were an impertinence. Seeing the end so near she had decided to succumb with this man between her legs—a last clinging to sharp life. But he had scorned her. In front of the noble blood of Rome he had scorned her. And now she had the double shame of the scorn and the unfeeling spectacle she was providing. She closed her eyes. The man on her was tearing her to pieces with his rough enthusiasm.

The male nobility of Rome could hardly believe in the reality of the scene. There on the couch in front of them the noble, virtuous, beautiful, frigid Clodia was stripped, nakedly paraded, all her nude charms there under their eyes.

But to see her ravaged by a gladiator! That was something from wild dreams, something that would be remembered with awe in Roman history.

Their eyes bulged as Marcellus surged into the spread-eagled body. Her large breasts indented a little under him, her buttocks oozed outward on the couch, her drawn-up thighs were still, resigned.

Marcellus was bending her legs this way and that, raising her buttocks off the couch, leaning up from her for deeper angle, panting and gasping. He forced her legs obscenely out so that her calves dropped, doll-like, over each side of the couch. Her thighs made the sides of a bowl for his hips.

Every man in the room made a mental note that if he—and she —got out of this alive he must do his utmost to possess Clodia during the days of life and strength remaining to him. Every woman felt a mixture of hysteria and hot fascination.

The spectacle did not last very long. Clodia's beauty, combined with her frigidity toward him, had so whetted Marcellus' appetite that he felt himself racing to a climax within a few minutes. He would have liked to stop and draw the whole thing out, but now he couldn't. His breath panted in Clodia's face as he fastened his mouth on her cold, horrified lips. Prostrate under him, suffocated under his weight, her face hot and flushed, her belly filled and hurting, Clodia opened her eyes and saw the score of eyes feasting on her. She closed her eyes again. She felt sick and deadened.

With the darkness before her eyes, she heard his breath exploding. His lips clasped down on hers and she let her mouth fall slackly open against the fury of his efforts. Then she heard him choke, gasped herself and lay with her eyes closed, sick and unmoving as he stretched his hot, sweating length on the cool softness of her flesh.

Spartacus had watched for a time. Something about Clodia's apathy touched him, made a small dent in the bitter animosity he felt toward her. He remembered how she had responded, led even, in his arms. He had intended to kill her tonight. But now he knew a better way. It would spare her life, but shame her in a way which would remain forever a reminder of his vengeance. Watching Marcellus panting in passion, Spartacus felt a twinge of pity for the woman. Under different circumstances she would have made a fine partner for him. He felt a slight sickness of regret and walked out into the cool air of the quadrilateral, leaving his men to guard.

Much later, when the streets of Rome were quiet, the house of Lucius Crispus lay in darkness. The off-duty slaves had retired for the night before the play had begun. The remainder now lay trussed up with Crispus' guests in one of the upper rooms.

In another Clodia lay, hands and ankles bound beside Crispus who was similarly secured. Their faces were lit up by a couple of torches which the gladiators held over them. In the shadow behind the torches, Spartacus stood with a branding iron in his hand.

The flames of a torch had flickered over the iron for a long time. Now it glowed redly in the darkness.

"Untie her ankles," Spartacus said.

His men bent and loosened the ropes. She was still naked. Her eyes were filled with a fresh terror. Beside her, a piece of cloth stuffed in his mouth, Crispus closed his eyes, but opened them again as if the closing had not rid him of an image of the scene.

"Pull her legs apart."

Eager, trembling hands grasped the smooth flesh of her thighs, drawing them wide, exposing the closed portals of her vagina. Spartacus bent toward her with the iron. The light from the torches lined his arms with shadows, enclosing the lengths of muscle as they bulged.

Crispus grunted, trying to raise his voice in horrified protest. Clodia slithered backward on the floor, cringing from the red glow.

"Hold her."

Spartacus moved the iron down to her body, ranged it at a point high up on one of her thighs, aimed it at the soft fullness just before the inside of the thigh joined her crotch.

He looked at Clodia, gagged too.

"This is how a slave is made," he said. There were evil chuckles from his men in the half darkness.

With a swift movement, the iron traveled the distance to the white flesh. There was a searing sound, smell of burning flesh. Clodia writhed under the hands that held her, tore the gag with her teeth.

When Spartacus stood back there was a little crescent-shaped burn deep in Clodia's thigh. He bent again to the other leg, and Clodia fainted as the branding iron withered her flesh once more.

Spartacus stood up. He looked at the scars with satisfaction. He turned to Crispus with a cruel smile.

"How does it feel to be married to a slave?" he asked.

Later still, there was a soft stirring from the house of Lucius Crispus. The master and the mistress went out into the dark night. She was still naked and she walked in difficulty as if with pain. They were surrounded, still, by the gladiators.

Swiftly, silently, the gladiators hurried them through the stone-paved streets, with scouts going ahead to watch for the night patrols.

They reached the forum without meeting the squads of *vigiles*.

A pale crescent of moon cast only a slight, ghostly light over the huge esplanade as Spartacus and the gladiators pulled their prisoners through the portico which was the public entrance on the south side. To left and right a double colonnade of pillars flanked the forum and opposite—more than a hundred yards off through the gloom—the buildings of library and law courts made shadows.

Spartacus knew the forum well. How often had he passed through it on the way to the market. He knew just where the bronze equestrian statue of Scipio Africanus glinted in the noon sun in the center of the forum. It was toward this statue of the vanquisher of the great Hannibal that the creeping shadows hurried.

At the base of the statue, rearing above its ten-foot-high stone pedestal, Spartacus gave a few orders.

Working quietly and efficiently, the gladiators scaled the pedestal, the statue, and hauled Clodia up with them. There on the bronze rump of the horse they laid Clodia on her back, pulled her legs back to her head, spread them wide and tied them around the back of the horse to its bronze tail. The slave scars on the inside of her thighs were thus presented to the market, to the throngs who would flock into the forum with the rising sun. Her bottom rounded nakedly to the heavens behind Scipio Africanus.

From behind the statue, Spartacus surveyed the obscene contortion into which Clodia was tied. In the darkness he could but vaguely make out the whiteness of her upturned thighs. But on the morrow those thighs would be struck by the first rays of the sun.

Thus, the most renowned and virtuous loins in Rome would smart with shame under the gaze of rude crowds of peasants, under the eyes of the merchants coming to spread their wares, under the warm glances of the lawyers on their way to the courts, the soldiers, strolling senators, slaves brought for sale; the whole of Rome would view the offered intimacies of Clodia, wife of Senator Lucius Crispus. Spartacus smiled with grim satisfaction.

But the work was not yet complete. On Spartacus' command, his men stripped Crispus and flung him, bound and gagged, to the ground behind the statue. There he would lie to see his wife's thighs and feel his own shame in the morning. So that he might not roll away to hide from the scene, his ankles were attached also to the horse's tail with a long rope. Spartacus knew that Crispus would die a thousand deaths from the ignominy of his plight and more particularly Clodia's; he knew that Crispus would carry the stigma of that morning with him to his grave.

Spartacus bent beside Crispus' prostrate body, he saw the man's eyes gleam up at him in the moonlight.

"In the morning," he whispered, "you will know what it is like to be exhibited in the slave market."

Before they disappeared into the darkness, Spartacus and his small band left Crispus' purple-banded toga at the feet of Scipio Africanus' horse. They wrapped around it the broken chains of a slave.

In the morning when the first merchants and the first shoppers found the two naked Romans, they were afraid to touch them in case in some strange way they should be associated with the crime, and punished. By the time the authorities had been contacted and one of the Consuls with his cortege of lictors arrived in the forum, the word had spread over Rome and a large portion of the population was crowded into the esplanade, jostling to get a better view of Clodia's charms. Crispus, appealing with his eyes for release, was still tied to the horse's tail.

MARCUS VAN HELLER

Marcus van Heller is the pseudonym of a young English writer, who, with twelve titles (close to one million "not for sale in the USA or Great Britain" words) to his credit, claims to be The Olympia Press' best-selling author of erotica.

He gave up a journalistic career and went to Paris in 1954. After a slimming spell of la vie de boheme ("garret, bread, cheese, wine and the complete works of fifteen philosophers") he joined up with a number of expatriate writers (Alexander Trocchi, Christopher Logue, Dick Seaver, etc.) and helped them produce the literary maga-zine Merlin. *He discovered at this point that the Orwellian technique of dishwashing for one's supper was outmoded and began to produce books for* Olympia Press.

"They were a devil-sent way of keeping the wolf from the door," *he says,* "and I wrote most of them at white heat without even bothering to revise." Roman Orgy *was, in fact, written in a fortnight flat.*

His conscience is untroubled by encyclopaedic description of the myriad sexual activities. "Obscenity is just an abstract word," *he says.* "Nobody can prove corruption. Even if they could, would it be worse than the corruption of modern advertising in a greedy world?"

But the pseudonym is for self-preservation. He now holds a responsible civil service post in London. "Some people already believe Whitehall is overrun with spies and perverts," *he says.* "I don't think it would redound to my credit if they could add a 'professional por-nographer' to the list."

Marcus van Heller has written in Rogue *and in* Town *magazine in London, and been otherwise published in many magazines ranging from* The New Statesman *to* Story Magazine. *He is now seeking a publisher for his first thriller.*

James Sherwood

Stradella

*O*nce, meeting a girl whom it was fun talking to—
whom, actually, I'd talked *at*—three weeks were
spared from misery by her company. No longer did I ache from
loneliness. I used to sit in my little black hole and carve soap. I used to
get the neighbor's cat and feels its pelt for fleas to snap. I used to drip
some wax on flies and burn their wings off. But no more. That was all
dispelled by this girl.

The three weeks with her came to an end when I went to her
apartment one evening to talk. In her haste, in her enthusiasm, she had
forgotten to lock her door, though she'd shut it. Yes, I tried the knob
in my one-minded intention, her intention never having occurred to
me.

As her apartment was a one-room with bed that pulled down
from the wall, I could not help walking into her private affairs. There,
on the bed, she was flattened by some brute heap of naked stranger
astride her. The memory of my three weeks ended with a quiet, and
polite little bow. Softly I shut the door, went home, and then to

another film. Sometimes I went thirty miles to find a different theater.

When I made no commitments, the commitments made me, so I got a job, bogged down on the primal mudflat of employment, earning food and rent which I paid to mother. It was a tiny ripple of discontent in confinement—confinement without giving birth—which produced my little blurt forward to friendship with Russell and Gussie.

I worked as a shipping clerk, a menial job in a firm for mass-produced dishware. Daily I labeled the dishes to customers duped by the door-to-door salesmen.

The office was small and my shipping room occupied most of it. The office manager, I guess, had the sole function of helping me, and answering his wife on the telephone. He had a dish face. His secretary, a cunning woman of very stately size, with a narrow mouth, did his work. The regional sales manager, a chirping and chipper dapper man, had an ulcer and talked fast. He had saucer ears. His secretary had an ulcer too. She would cry in the office when the boss spoke abruptly to her, which he did after he talked with his wife. Later, the ulcer got so bad she became pregnant and the ulcer cleared up.

For three years I went to work there early, went out at noon for lunch, and at the end of the day walked with my boss to the corner where he bought a paper and I crossed the street.

For these same three years I never had a girlfriend, but I thought a great deal about it. I watched it in movies and read about it in papers. Spying rather than vying was the only reward I savored.

On payday of January 14th I was dismissed with one week of severance. My boss bought his paper, shook my hand, thanked me, and said I would not have to come in again.

My clothes had not a clean stitch among them, nor a matching pair of anything, nor a contrast anywhere, but all spots and bruises, creases and loose buttons. I failed to shave that night as I scurried from my room, neglecting to turn off the tap.

My regular coffee house was inhabited by actors. Noisy, colorful, it was a constant whirlpool of people, flashing hair-dos, studied gestures, stylized voices, and flamenco flooding the air. I purchased a cup of tea. Tea was cheapest on the menu.

I sat at the largest table in the coffee house. All the little tables around me were cluttered with cups and packed with people. There was enough room at my big table to spread out several sheets of paper.

I needed the big table to write my friend who was at a resort with his wife. He had been gone 12 days, 260 miles away. My friend was a psychiatrist in a toy factory.

"Dear Russell:" I wrote. "It has been a warm day here. Wish Happy Birthday to Gussie. Show her this letter. I'm wishing you well, Gussie. She might even want to write me, a little postcard or something. Don't bother. It would mean a trip to the souvenir shop and then the problem of deciding which card was right—which card would appeal to my personality, you know. Actually any card would appeal. Don't bother. I saw a paralyzed bird today in the street. Traffic rushed by. The bird flapped its wings, but it leaned at an angle with its eyes into the sun, even when the nearest cars ruffled its feathers. I watched for a long time. Some woman came along. I showed her the bird. She stopped the traffic. Why didn't I do that? She threw it on a lawn and there it stood. So did I. Well, your one friend's hoping you're having a nice time. O yes, I got fired today. I worked there three years, two months and three weeks. They gave me one week severance. Bring me back a pine needle or a piece of dirt from the great wide outdoors. One week severance wasn't enough—"

At this point the waitress removed my tea cup though I'd only drunk a sip of it. I called her back.

"You'll have to sit somewhere else. This table's taken. There'll be no single seats for a while. You can wait by the door."

"I'll just—all right," I said. I was collecting my thoughts.

A woman at the next table spoke to me. She wore a red dress, was platinum blonde, and her palm was open toward me. A puppet man was with her.

"What are you looking for?" she asked, grinning, gushing.

My answer, I thought at the time, was rather debonair. "I don't know," I said. "Maybe I'm looking for you." I bowed slightly.

When the waitress came back to seat the group, the woman asked me to sit at their table. I was introduced to the puppet but because of the noise could hear nothing. I was conscious of the fact that her forehead was a little too small for her jaw. Then she told me her name was Stradella, which meant very little. After a few moments I gazed straight in her eye. It was a trick I had seen in the movies. It was supposed to evoke profound feelings. "Your eyes are—lonely," I said, looking deeply into them.

She drank her water and asked for my number.

I said, "I've had enough of these I'll-Call-You promises. If you want, give me your number. I'm very busy, always out and seldom in."

"What do you do?" she asked.

"Well," I felt my bristly cheek. "I'm a poet."

"Thank heavens you're not another actor. I wouldn't have talked to you. I'm a poet too."

"A poet?"

"Yes, a poetess. Call in the late morning, my answering service. Here, write down the number."

When they left, I left. She acted as though we'd never spoken, even though I held the door. She wore a fur jacket with a high collar and a diamond wristwatch. Her fur brushed me as she went out. Her puppet dusted it off. She was waving over the heads, "Wallace Brenner darling!"

I waited in the shadows till they drove away. My car was in the parking lot too. Ignoring them on that long walk to the lot would be absolutely ungentlemanly, and being ignored would be even worse. I did not wish to finish in humiliation a meeting begun in daring.

The puppet sped from the parking lot, Stradella on the middle of the seat beside him.

I went to my own car, a jalopy. The battery was dead. I had to go back in the coffee house to telephone a tow service. I was embarrassed because I was conscious of the glances different people gave me now.

The telephone was near a table where three made-up actresses were flirting with each other, and I knew they were listening to every word I said to the dirty tow company. The actresses didn't even glance up as I went out. They went on flirting and teasing each other.

When I realized I'd left some small change by the phone, I went back to get it, but the change was gone. I started to look round for the thief, and interrupted the actresses. They looked up and paused. Then I felt it in my other pocket. I went out and waited in my jalopy. I listened to the coffee-house laughter.

I waited almost two hours for the tow service to come. Women in mink walked by with big men as the tow service filled out the form and got my money on the hood in coins. Then they pulled me off with a jerk.

I had already planned to attend a first-run theater Saturday evening and after that a midnight horror show, so I told Stradella we could go out sometime that afternoon, when I called her in the morning. The Van Gogh exhibit was at the museum.

Dressing meticulously in my best baggy pants and my whitest frayed shirt, I even had my jalopy washed, which last gesture made me arrive late. I was told her girlfriend was going too. We drove to her girlfriend's.

"He's one of these poor boys, Rita. Do you mind his old heap or do we go in your car?"

"I'm ready for his old heap. I'm willing to leave my Thunderbird home. Do you think I'm a gold digger? Who'd I impress today, Van Gogh?"

All the way to the museum Stradella was attacked, accused and bawled out by Rita. "That's right, my only apparent pleasure, so far as you can see, is making you feel smaller, less around the bust, more around the waist, and less around the hips, with knock-knees, Stradella," said Rita.

At the exhibit, Stradella and I walked alone. Rita vanished, looking for Van Gogh. At one rare canvas Stradella said, "Mmmmmyyyyy—" With her red nail she chipped at the paint like polish. "I wonder what's underneath that bed?"

A nearby art lover whispered in the ear of a Van Goghophile who delicately nudged me to ask the pretty young lady, Please Couldn't She?—and so I did.

"They're afraid of me, with all that caution. I'm a stoplight of flesh appeal." She smiled. "Like a lady Van Gogh." All the same she withdrew her nail. Then we left the exhibit. Rita was gone.

At Stradella's apartment, prepared to thank her, to smile, to bow quickly, and leave, I was implored to stay and eat.

She noticed the missing button on my shirt. "I have a replacement. Would you please take off your shirt?" I squirmed. She took my shirt into her bedroom.

After eating my pudding, I shuffled in after her and my shirt. The only place to sit was her bed.

She sewed very slowly, and said very little, and once or twice looked at me with an equal amount of slowness. I wanted to get to that show. I moved closer. This only slowed her sewing down more.

I glanced at the clock. It was 7:45. In 15 minutes the movie would start. I couldn't get in without my shirt. What should I do? In a fit of desperation I put my arm around her, my lips to hers and she fell back on the bed, suddenly moaning and setting the needle flying.

But I sat up. "I'm supposed to be at this meeting by 8." I pulled my sleeves down. "I didn't mean to take advantage of you," etc., etc. Somehow we both got to our feet.

"What do you mean? I wasn't letting anyone take advantage of me," she said. I got into my shirt. The new button dangled. I just tucked it inside. At the front door I turned to thank her. She was standing so close I swallowed her lips by accident. Offering to shake hands, I stroked her buttocks with my free hand. She quivered and asked me, and her voice filtered through my collar, "If I let you come back tonight will you kiss me all over?"

"All over?" I asked. "O! All over!"

She clasped me tightly. "I'll leave the door unlocked."

I left.

I followed the first show with concerted intensity, enjoying every minute, and my popcorn. It was first run. Finally I saw the horror show. Monsters were eating each other.

At three o'clock I drove by her door. It was dark. I tiptoed in and found a small nightlight on. There was a man's electric razor underneath with a note:

"Here's the way to razor yourself. Shave."

At this time of night, and the neighbors sleeping, I was definitely not going to shave.

Slipping into her bed, nude and quiet, my big toe touched one of her feet. She yielded her sleep and rolled toward me with the warmth and softness of lava, fully waking. I was not sure she had even been asleep.

I was enveloped in her. Every limb was burning. Every breath was searing. I was pinned to the bed by her onrush. My soldier rose like the sphinx, serenely taking its time. She was stuffed with sweetmeats.

She folded her arms around me. She lay on her back and buried my head in her breasts. Tentatively I kissed her nipples, a weightless fly flitting over her. They hardened and expanded, a ripe fruit unpeeled in her bed and laid bare. She plucked me like a dandelion. I sank my toe in her apple. She spread me over the sides of the bed, and sat herself down on me, a sea wave, corking breath. I impaled her with a finger. On her knees she moaned into the cushions. I held her above me, speared on my thumb, and spun her. She clutched blindly at my stem like a lariat and whirled me. Every place that I touched on her skin broke out like a wound, ripe and rosy. The tongue in my head, not a word on it, tilled her furrows and curves. She became a ripe pasture. The wounds broke out in blossoms. The curves turned to creeks of sweat. Her whole body ran like ore, a mother lode of golden bronze tan.

Exhausted we fell into sleep in a heap, draped over each other amid discarded towels, awakening on the ceiling each to the other's summons, a faint breath like a cool wind blowing between my thighs, blood drained from her head and syphoned out like a silk kerchief through a straw. She waved her arms like wands of high magic. Lips groaning, the last bit of oblivion we greeted, parched and parting the cheeks of perdition as we went away into nothingness, faces fried to a fearful tingling.

I became invisible on the bed where our brightest light saw me nailed to the mattress, beard out.

We talked and shared her life story. She told me about her three marriages, to a gambler, to an actor, and a nobody. She showed me her scrapbook. She summed up her career.

For the first time I realized that this was not just a girl, this was *the* great Stradella who was known to the world as the star, Amourella, Goddess of Love, queen of midnight television, seductress of the latent libidos of the late night audience. My God! I was in bed with a personality.

And on the morning of the seventh day I awoke to hear her talking across the country to Brooklyn.

"Yes, Daddy, I know, but if you could just send me a little money. Yes Daddy, I know, but it would only be a loan and I could pay it back in two years and besides, property here is going up. Property here is valuable. People are coming to live here from Brooklyn. Yes Daddy, I know, but couldn't you give me something? I want so much to have a housey, just a little housey-wousey, all my own. Don't you know that Daddy? Yes Daddy, I know. Well, all right. Why don't you send Mom and Dinky then, and come out yourself? I could take care of them and we could all three get a house together . . ."

Et cetera.

Stradella got a phone call from an agent and scowled.

"What's running around in your busy little brain these days? Still peddling middle-aged virgins?"

Apparently he said nothing. Stradella looked doleful and damp on the line. She accepted my advice. She perked up.

"Talk to him with love, Stradella. Maybe he's lonely too, and he's only human. He won't hurt you."

She bit off a nail.

"I've been thinking of changing my hair color, dear. . . . Back to natural . . . Soupy brown . . . Turn the stoplight off."

The battle guns vanished. The warriors talked, and the lines that separated them drew them together. Her tone went down. Her eyes came up. She listened. She even slid down in her seat with her chin on her chest and the receiver coddled her neck.

"The title role in a movie? Who for?" she said. "What's the salary? $100 a day? At the mention of that price I'll cut my hair off first."

But she looked at me and her lids lowered. She scratched her bottom.

"You know that's scale wages, darling. How long have I been in this business now? Isn't it just a little depressing to have to take scale with a reputation to watch? You know how it must make me feel."

She paused. "You promise you'll try for the job at more money. You're sure I can sew up the part with one interview." The mention of sewing didn't make me suspicious. "All right, I'll go to the offices of Mr. Playbaum on Monday."

When Stradella hung up she had become a woman of mystery, a globe of contentment, an aura of radiance. "Here you are, and the bedroom's there. I've got plans for you," she said. Her eyes flashed.

The air became flurried with clothes, a blizzard of bras and underwear. She led. The magic, king-size, innerspring mattress whisked away on a box spring tour of paradise. She drove, and we returned, that seventh day, from our Sunday ride, breathless. I slept thirty hours.

To me Stradella's forehead was no longer too small for her jaw. The Brooklyn accent with which she tinged all talk was no longer the basement of eloquence but the highest Himalaya of elocution.

We babbled. We gootchied. We laughed. Our unfinished sentences were encyclopedias of prefatory sympathy that were consumated in glances that were no longer tricks or subterfuges. They were epics of communication capable of moving mountains. There really was a heaven and we knew, in those glances, where paradise was and how to find it on the map. We'd found it in the dark, and for us there was no doubt.

I threw her against a wall. She stuffed me in a drawer. I played in her pudendum, a kitten over pudding. She sighed and swung from a lamp. I crawled up the Venetian blinds. She whimpered and fell off the bed and split in 69 slivers. I pieced them together 9 times by 7 and had 6 left over which I ate. She wiped her lips with a spoonful of ice cream. I polished her toenails with ear wax. She made rings with her locks and a collar of braid. Our heads bumped in a pillowcase, condemned Siamese twins, and we waltzed over the upholstery, jigsaw puppets. She became the wall clock and I the hands. I wound up her back and she chimed the beats by seconds. She had the pendulum and I had the weights.

I didn't even know her right name. But she told me soon enough. Not Stradella, but Isabella; not Fonteyn, but Funtberg. Those feet of clay I caressed, though those feet of clay had corns.

Stradella, I denied It. I refused then to say It even once. I detested you later, but expressed only It. But that was the time when I felt.

She reluctantly released me.

"I'm going to drive my sisters to the Girl Scout ski camp." I dressed.

She looked at me appealingly.

"I'd invite you along, but I won't because it would crowd the car. I'm taking my mother's. We couldn't all fit in with skis, schoolgirls and stuff."

"But . . . will you come back?"

"Yes . . . sure . . . I'll come back."

"How long will you be gone?"

"I don't know."

"When will you come back?"

"Don't ask me. I'll come back. As soon as I can. Is that good enough?" I agitated. "I've enjoyed myself very much, Stradella. Why don't you take the electric blanket to be fixed? You said it was broken."

She looked at me wide-eyed with a finger in her mouth. "I didn't need it repaired. I have something better than a blanket."

I returned to the bed, tossed off my clothes.

I stood on the mountains and knew the rumble of an earthquake, sir. Volcano Eruption and Sacrificial Flames Shook—giving headlines and spot coverage. *They jiggled like fruits ripe for falling and their peaks became like swords' points, sir. And the ground broke apart and I was swallowed up in the crack in the earth, more ecstatically than Oedipus himself, sir.* I put out a thousand dailies and extras to cover this colossal hurricane in a double bed.

"You are a gusher!" she exclaimed.

"A monsoon!" I said.

"A typhoon not too soon!" she said.

Then I got dressed and went home.

When I returned to that room of scents on my second pilgrimage, the odors had become more clarified—talcum and lanolin and Red and White mouthwash, which was purchased on sale in the economy bottle, and Pepsodent toothpaste, and Stripe toothpaste, and Colgate toothpaste, and varieties of perfume and cold creams and face creams and the thick rich luster of Factor and others. I had never seen the real her.

Thank God for the manufacturers of unguents the world over that make possible my Stradella. What they gave, I've preserved, in the glory of memory at the height of absolution, their genius, my pleasure.

As I drove to mother's place Stradella was still on my tongue. Was she pancakes or waffles? Every man knows that taste of that woman in that time in that place when there's breakfast and lunch and oatmeal and hot cream and marmalade and orangeade and pastry and gooey and runny cooked all together in the same long pot.

Open the cupboards to the infinite, how woman's kaleidoscopic stew tempts the cookbook man! But no man knows the recipe, nor ever will. Every woman is different. No woman tells. She has as many elixirs as men. They change with her mind and the moon. Her mind—she most denies it when most mindful—is brightest when opposed to her mood. The sun and the moon are brightest when directly opposing each other.

Stradella belonged to me the afternoon she thought she was losing me. When she knew I was going, she wanted me coming. My dreams were transformed, aspiration to perspiration.

But there was that one black hair on the toilet seat. That made me dislike her, eased the problem of leaving her. The rather vivid way she had of scrubbing between her thighs with a washcloth like she was scratching herself—that too put me off, especially when her next gesture was to pick her nose.

It was my fortunate position to see her not only as Amourella, Goddess of Love, in a hurricane wrap-around nightie of misty-mysterious white stuff, chimera-like and cloudy, which was her blossoming costume on television, but also soggy and soapy in the bathtub with the water dirty and the sad suds soaking around her saggy breasts, slick with slop.

Sometime, when passion's flow was finished, the tired side of that rich baby's hot and self-taught vivacity took over. She opened up, you see, and like a flower, let off smells of all kinds as she burst like a rocket to the moon from the launching pad of the bed, so that once we were in orbit she was also breaking wind, and the wind-breaking set her laughing, and the laughing set her gasping, till at last she gave almost more than she ever thought she'd had, just short of mush, a bit softer than sponge cake, and cooked in her rear oven to golden brown.

> *The art of loving is concealing.*
> *Those who love not are revealing.*

My Stradella could dress up to be a captivating queen when she stepped in a room, the humming, purring, perfectly restrained and all-alluring woman. But when we stepped out, with me escorting her, I'd catch the devil for not keeping my necktie up, for ignoring her attempts to talk with intellectual overtones, and for somehow standing in her way, blocking those fierce sallies of hers toward being "a great lady."

But I'm getting ahead of my story. This narrative haste is due to mental contempt. I remember all the bad things about Stradella so I can imagine myself as I was when I walked out of the apartment after seven days into the harsh bright world of little girls going skiing at the Girl Scout camp, and the world of mother, and my deserted bedroom in her house.

I am remembering too that the beard was still on my face, and seven days longer, and I was feeling sated, reckless, powerful, completely sure I could not be unseated—and all because I had the gift of hating the thing I gave to, and of leaving the thing I'd return to.

Notice I call my Stradella a thing. That is part of the technique of keeping my aloofness, unity, strength. I recognized her, not as a human being, but a thing—"a place to stick it"—as Stradella informed me. I admitted it.

Stradella passed through me and I through her. We greased the ducts and eased the walls of each other, and made it easier to flow.

"Face it," she said. "It's no big deal. You bring on my period."

Samson Haibow insisted I bring Stradella down to his house for the weekend as he and his bride were bound for a honeymoon and we would have it all to ourselves, so immediately I prevailed on Stradella to come, and she agreed she would until the hour of departure when she said she'd rather not. For twenty minutes I urged and she neighed, my tugs meeting her boredom.

"What's going on down there?"

"Nothing," I said.

"O no, Archie. That sounds like a complete bore. What kind of a house is it?"

"A cottage, by the ocean, in the country."

"O come on, Archie. I can't stand just you and me together batting round a house, just us two."

"It'd be fun."

"I'm tired now, Archie. I want to go to sleep. Leave me alone now."

"They're waiting to go on their honeymoon Stradella, and we said we'd show up by 9 P.M. for the keys. Here it is 8 and you're not set and we've got an hour and a half to drive yet."

"Whose car would we go in?"

"It's a long trip. I think we ought to take yours."

"I don't want to go, Archie. I've got my nice little house here and I'm very content right now. I feel very peaceful. You know what I mean, Archie? Can you appreciate that feeling of peace, Archie?"

"You'd be mighty peaceful down there too, Stradella. Come on now and get dressed. They're waiting."

"I don't want to pack too many things. I'm tired of packing. They're all so heavy."

"Just pick up your purse, your coat and bathing suit. You look fine like that. Come on now. Right now. We can go without anymore talk."

She went to the toilet first, and packed a little bag quickly with an assortment of nighties and perfume and oils and of course her douche outfit. We departed an hour after we should have arrived and when we had driven an hour and a half we ordered two half chickens in a basket. The memory of a very unusual looking woman behind the cash register, with a cigarette implanted on her lips like a permanent fixture, and a squinted birdlike stare, hawks back to me along with the recollection of chicken grease and my weird sense of comfort in just traveling with Stradella like a god sweeping her off and she quite content to be taken, and silent, though we were an hour and a half late already in delaying the honeymoon.

When we arrived the newlyweds had almost finished packing and so we weren't late in the slightest. Then a drink for the road, a wave of farewell, some last minute instructions on the clean and dirty sheets, and how to work the shower outdoors. We were alone.

Let me tell in brief the incidents that rest in the memory like rocks once buried in the sands of detail, but now washed clean by the ebbing of years.

We spent our first night in the bed warmly pressed chest to back, and as if by the movement of the waves we could hear, at unsignaled seconds we would roll in the opposite direction and press close together like two kittens at peace asleep in a basket.

When morning came and we awoke together I importuned my lady of love but she would have none of me, and though I tried with kisses and gentle gestures she would not turn on even a sigh. I tried a newer approach.

"It's the perfect time to do it, Stradella. It's morning by the sea, and we're rested."

"I don't feel like it, Archie."

"I'll tell you what then, Stradella. I'll pay you."

"Pay me?"

"Yeah. Pay you money."

"Pay me money? You don't have any money, Archie."

"I've got enough to pay you for one."

"How much have you got?"

"Well, not very much really. Six bucks, Stradella."

"Where is it? Let me see it."

"Over there in my wallet."

"Well, get it."

I leaped from the bed to the cold floor and brought it. She set it aside on the bed table as I crawled into the blankets and against her. She made a snuggling sound that was warm. I ran my hand up her side. She ran her hand down my chest, slowly, smiling in a good-humored way with affection. I kissed her neck and she pressed it against me. I slid my lips up to her ear and down her chin and around her lips without touching them, continuing my journey up her cheek to her ear into which I fed the sweet silent token of my warm breath, and when she moved against me and I could feel her body rigid against mine, there was a terrible gnawing in my stomach as her hand ever so slightly and without direction filled itself with my stomach and slid around to my side. Tenderly and almost in slow motion I slid aside the top of her nightie and paid labial homage down her bronzed throat to the top of her breasts, one of which I cupped in my hand with reverence as I moved my lips over the nipple and wetted it trembling and circled it repeatedly as she began to draw her stomach in, then out, beckoning my hand to explore her as my lips pinked her breasts and her sighs became groans. I let my fingers travel over the open arid stomach, which is the freest access to the valley below, and on its surface obstructs no passage or to the fingertips offers no mystery except the little cave of a navel and therefore rather tends to hasten the meeting between male fingers and the curly and netted and meshed black hairs for which my fingers ecstatically had traveled and wound themselves slowly in the painful love dance of courting and entering, of penetration and death.

She who had kept her legs closed, tightly pressed to each other till this moment, put her hands to either side of my cheeks and let her opened lips slide up my face and over my eyes before they found my mouth and partially surrendered, she drawing my tongue between her teeth first and sucking it like a candy and milking it as her hands went around to my back and her arms ringed my throat and her legs relented just enough for exploring, she cocking one leg up at the knee and letting the other one lay.

But now I was being pushed off. Her hands were removing me from her embrace, and pushing my face away. Down my lips went over her breasts quickly, down down wetting with my tense tongue dragging over her stomach and veritably boring a hole in her navel as her muscles and skin rippled once uncontrollably like a horse's mane, and she moaned and let her head sag to one side over the pillow and her eyes shut, and her free hands began to grope.

I traveled close to my face into the world of scents immortal and set the finest jewel of a pendulum clock trembling as it ticked back and forth and the wet hairs parted to reveal the pink and scarlet walls of a lava crater that undulated. And in my nose were the mixtures of sweat and secretions of hot contained odors pouring out of the most animal origination, and the juices of a fruit I've never been able to purchase at any bar anywhere or drink from any fountain but this swirled through my lips from hers, this nectar of Nirvana. And I was dimly aware that her lips were drawing a line up my leg in dampened dancing, sucking the starch from the hairs in my skin and her fingertips drawing pictures over me as though laying the faintest web of a fabric of feeling like a net, and her mouth burning a trail of familiarity up the inside of my leg, at which point she opened her mouth with a groaning voluptuosity as though she had been overcome and was stunned by the force of a feast too overpowering any longer to withstand and she swallowed, weakly, making moans and bathing me in her cold mouth and breath, but not stopping the movement of her lips as they traveled up, up, and then drew again and tried to swallow as her fingers still played like delicate little maiden gloves.

She kept swallowing and moaning in what was a total convulsion of abdication and each gulp she made seemed to take more and more and to be stronger and tighter and harder in its slow, hypnotic persistence toward the goal.

I felt we were rising to a higher and higher place where there was less air to breathe and less desire for breath, where our nerves were drawing thinner and thinner and all of our muscles were quivering to a soundless pitch like the inaudible whistles for blind dogs, and my body became more minute and detailed until to the backs of my knees I could feel the position and life of every hair and the animation of every cell.

There was a pause, as when a sweeping bird rises to its peak. There was a freezing of motion. The bed turned to ice. All animation stopped: it was as if a dancer had been photographed as she attained mid-leap and had been halted in perfect suspension and balance between two points.

Our eyes were blown by the wind that rushed past and our faces were erased almost entirely of expression until our heads were nonexistent—white nobs of stone—and we were without pain in a thick envelopment of motionless slow water where she had begun it all by giving in to me and shudderingly releasing all possession of her body and throwing it away to the death of herself in her lover and I was pumping the honey and butter of a new life and a new and fluid beginning.

We watched each other with our once sightless eyes and smiled with our entire selves in friendship and warmth and forgiveness and indulgence, as though we cared for each other greatly and with deep respect and love and forgiveness again, out of the shared knowledge of the very earthly secret of ourselves, while our bodies lay by still coupled and squeezed, aware of the universal transcendence that our knowing gave up over our bodies, until the last natural spasm ended and subsided and the last natural squeeze came forward and withdrew.

We were without recourse.

Two minutes we were silent.

Then.

Dawn.

"Well—that's it. Let's get going," said Stradella. My body fell off hers. She sat up. She took the money and laughingly threw me a side glance. I put my hand out to touch her.

"Let's try that again," I said, feeling sure I was ready to begin all over.

She got up and went to the bathroom. "I've got to wash out the little Archies. I'll bet I've got a million little Archies running around inside me. I've got to wash them all out and not leave any in there so they'll be lonely. I have to go take care of all my little Archies."

"O, come on, Stradella. Let's try one more just for the fun of it, in another position."

"You don't have the money, Archie. Don't you know you're all broke now and don't have another penny and you'll have to borrow from me all weekend and can't you be a good little boy like others are? Don't you know when to be grateful for what you've got and not beg for more when you've run out of money and can't pay for it?"

"You mean you're actually going to take that money?" I asked.

"Of course I am. You made a business agreement. You promised a certain amount and now you've got to stick to it."

"But didn't you just plain enjoy what we did, Stradella? Is the money that important you must take it, after all that pleasure, my last dime?"

"But that's what you agreed to Archie and that's a pleasure too. It's kind of fun to earn money doing your pleasure and know you're getting real money for it and not just the same old one more lick and a promise."

"You mean you're really going to take money, like a whore?"

"Who says it's like a whore, Archie? It's natural, and it didn't take anything away from what we enjoyed and it did add to my own good feeling that I was actually accomplishing something."

"You know, Stradella, I think that you are going to find every time you couple with a man, if this is your attitude, that the very reason you couple for, which is to bring you closer to someone and closer toward marriage and a lot of children, will be the very thing that drives you farther apart and makes it harder and harder for you ever to have any closeness at all with a man or marriage again or children. I think, with that outlook, as time goes by you'll get more and more men closer and closer more and more often, but every time you do, the closeness and intimacy of your act will become more distant until finally it'll not exist at all."

"You think I want to get laid to be close to a man?" she asked, genuinely interested in this conversation.

"Yes, I think so."

"I don't know," she said. "I really don't. Maybe you just get laid to relax muscles, to get rid of the pimples, to charge up the battery."

"Is that what you think it's for, Stradella? That and that only?"

She thought a minute, then, "Yeah. Yeah, that's what it's for. That and that only. All your other ideas are just silly, Archie. That's what it's for, just to keep your complexion clean."

"Then I say the real whores of the world, if that's their attitude Stradella, are really not whores at all, and the women who do it for the other reasons are probably the best whores because they don't stop at pimples and battery charges but let it be whoring all the way to the last little ounce of every feeling they've got, that there's nothing more whore-naked in the world than a mother of ten kids who's faithful to her husband. She's the real whore, the supreme and everlasting and unceasing twenty-four-hour one from every direction and position—with body and words and family and business until she's just one great internal-external transparent eternal fuck, the mother, wife, mistress, friend, partner rolled up faithful to the fellow in all positions."

"You're very crude to use that word, Archie, and I think you ought to act more respectful to a lady and not speak that way to her while she's on the toilet. And furthermore I resent being referred to as a whore. That's no way to address a dignified person who is a real, true, refined, kind and considerate well-mannered lady."

"Which proves my point!" I shouted.

She wiped herself and got up, pulling the handle and letting her skirt drop. She came across the room at me flashing her simple peasant-girl smile. As she passed she rotated her hips and brushed her hand across the front of my pants. "I'll show you mine if you'll show me yours," she said in the voice of a little girl in the third grade at school trading dolls.

We lay on the sand at the beach and went shopping. In a third-rate dime store we picked up two coffee mugs, two pairs of slippers and two sacks of candy. We picked up some gift paper that cost more than the gifts and we wrapped them and hid them around the house for the Haibows. We bought ourselves two great-sized sombreros, mine of pink and white rings, and wore them. Stradella kept track of how much I'd borrowed and owed her since naturally it was I who was to pay for all this. So I appreciated the thrift at least.

She earned more in one week than I earned in three months, but I was becoming a man because she was becoming a merchant and the little boy blues had to be paid for since now they were boring her.

I recall we made the bed up with fresh sheets and when we drove back to town, she hummed. Yes, hummed songs, and sang some, and purred like a pastoral kitten with the deepest sounds of reflection I had ever heard coming from her throat, of the stillest section of the long flowing river of love, where it runs the most silent and deep, and I knew more than she did what a profound effect this weekend had made on her. But no more.

So we went to the grocery and the city returned to us. She burned the dinner and I slept on the couch watching TV while she made notes and the telephone rang.

JAMES SHERWOOD

About himself and his book, Stradella, *James Sherwood writes:*
   "Stradella *was written, a chapter a Saturday, during the Federal Unemployment Extension Act of 1959. Each of the first dozen chapters was read by me to a church group in exchange for dinner*

and society. These chapters were bought by an American publisher, and rejected. Stradella was returned with oaths and sent to Paris. Two years later I asked The Olympia Press if she was lost. Yes. Then, one August afternoon, Olympia wrote again: she was found and would be published. I had a sunstroke, went deaf, was fired, had my fiancée elope with my boss, my mother gave me a round trip to Europe, and my cat was hit by a car. All this occurred in one hour and a half.

"While in Italy, I was robbed of nine novels, Stradella too, as well as my clothes and money. Returning to Paris with pajamas, I found employment teaching English in society at a school for dunces. In Genoa, an unknown gentleman by the name of Antonio Cavalinni found the notes and scripts of twelve novels, two reels of film, and my sunglasses in a trash barrel in the port. The Italian police gave them to the American Consulate General. A Mr. Donald Baltshak wrote my little sister who sent the thirteen dollars freight. I have worked on them ever since.

"Stradella was finished, altered by an Egyptian proofreader, saved from the press and rewritten by me from memory in 36 hours at a self-service café. Its sequels include Irmadoon, Into the Sandwich, After Laughter, On the Nail Pile, Eurydouchka, The Charlequin-nade. Afternoon of a Clown, Grimaldi, Solarbal, Sun of Another Sky, *and* Winter That Never Came."

THE GINGER MAN

J. P. DONLEAVY

O summer of soft wind. Relieves the heart and makes living cheaper. Get that fire out in the grate. Get it out. That's better.

There's a butcher a few houses up the street. A tram goes by the window. And across the road is the most fantastic laundry with forty girls and great steaming vats. O I think they are a bunch for using just the little touch of acid.

Mr. and Mrs. Sebastian Dangerfield and their daughter, Felicity Wilton, late of Howth, are now residing at 1 Mohammed Road, The Rock, Co. Dublin.

It was decided to get out of the haunted house of Howth. But there were hesitations till the morning after the storm when Marion opened the kitchen door to get the milk and she screamed and Sebastian came running and they looked down in the mud-stained sea into which had fallen the back garden and turf shed. They moved.

The new house was not new. And you didn't want to walk too

fast in the front door or you'd find yourself going out the back. Mr. Egbert Skully took Mr. Dangerfield aside and said he was glad he could rent it to an American because he and his wife had worked for twenty years in Macy's Department Store and loved New York and was pleased he could find tenants like themselves. And I hope you, your wife and little one will be happy here. I know it's a little small but I think you'll like the cosy quality, ha, you look like a gentleman, Mr. Dangerfield as likes his cosy comforts, and do you play golf? O aye. But my clubs are indisposed. Having them looked over by a professional for flaws, particular about alignment you know. A very good idea, Mr. Dangerfield and perhaps my wife can give yours some recipes. Great.

Walls newly papered with brown flowers even feel soggy to the touch. And a nice brown, fourth-hand Axminster rug on the sitting-room floor and a scabrous, blue settee. The kitchen was fine but the tap and sink were out the door. Up steep narrow stairs, a closet with plate-sized skylight, the conservatory. And a toilet bowl wedged between two walls, the lavatory. Tory was a great suffix in this house. And the sitting-room window two feet off the sidewalk was perfect for the neighbors passing by, so don't want to get caught with the pants down. But the tram rumbling by keeps one on one's guard.

A visit to the fuel merchant for coal to keep piled under the stairs. Marion got crates and covered them with table cloths for color and respectability. And my special maps one or two of which are rare and old. The one I have of a cemetery I keep under thick glass. And got the card table for a desk under the window. The laundry girls will take me mind off the awful grind of studying. They come out twice a day, hair in curlers and breasts like needles in these American uplift bras. Think the Bishop had something to say about that and rightly too. Then watch them line up for the tram, a row of steamed white faces. And some of them giving a giggle in this direction at the madman behind the curtain.

Facing the summer ahead. Living in this little house was calm. No drinking and minding the baba when Marion was off to shop. Had a cup of beef tea in the morning. Also see a rather pleasant creature up there in the window. Catch her looking in here with rather large brown eyes, no smiles or giggles. A little disdain, her dark hair straight and thick. And I think I see intelligence, a little embarrassing that look. Retreat into the kitchen. Most exciting.

Made a little case and filled it with books of law, a short life of Blessed Oliver Plunket and others on birds. Bottom shelf for business magazines for the big days ahead. And then a section for my extensive collection, which, God forgive me, I stole from Catholic churches. But I did it because I needed strength in paupery. My favorites are *This Thing Called Love, Drink Is A Curse,* and *Happiness in Death.*

The first morning tram almost shakes one to the floor and Felicity gives the twisted cry from the conservatory. Growl back to sleep. Pull the legs up in the fetal crouch. Marion wearing my underwear. Sometimes the sun would sneak in. Then Marion beating barefoot on the linoleum. Entreaties. O do get up. Don't leave me to do everything every morning. In my heart where no one else can hear me, I was saying, now for God's sake, Marion, be a good Britisher and get down there in that little nest of a kitchen and buzz on the coffee like a good girl and would you, while you're at it, kind of brown up a few pieces of bread and I wouldn't mind if maybe there was just the suggestion of bacon on it, only a suggestion, and have it all ready on the table and then I'll come down and act the good husband with, ah darling good morning, how are you, you're looking lovely this morning darling and younger every morning. A great one that last. But I come down martyred and mussed, feeble and fussed, heart and soul covered in cement.

But later in the morning great things were to be seen. Sound of horses on the cobble stones. Then up to the bedroom to look down in the street. These sleek black animals glistening in soft rain. Heads high, driving slits of steam in the morning air. Sometimes I see through the little glass windows, a lily on a pine box. Take me with you too. And I can't help murmuring from memory poems I read in the *Evening Mail:*

> *Sleep thy last sleep,*
> *Free from care and sorrow,*
> *Rest where none weep,*
> *And we too, shall follow.*

And I see the grinning red faces popping out the windows of the cab, radiant with the importance of the dead. Hats being tipped along the road and hands moving in the quick sign of the cross. Whisky passed from hand to hand. Green, greedy mouth is dead. A fiddle across the fields. Mushrooms fatten in the warm September rain. Gone away.

Then time to go for the paper. And back with it to the lavatory. Between the green peeling walls. Always feel I'm going to get stuck. One morning there was sunshine and I was feeling great. Sitting in there grunting and groaning, looking over the news, and then reach up and pull the chain. Downstairs in the kitchen, Marion screamed.

"I say, Marion, what is it?"

"For God's sake, stop it, stop it, Sebastian, you fool. What have you done?"

Moving with swift irritability down the narrow stairs, stumbling into the kitchen at the bottom. Perhaps things have gotten too much for Marion and she's gone mad.

"You idiot, Sebastian, look at me, look at baby's things."

Marion trembling in the middle of the kitchen floor covered with strands of wet toilet paper and fecal matter. From a gaping patch in the ceiling poured water, plaster and excrement.

"God's miserable teeth."

"O damnable, damnable. Do something, you fool."

"For the love of Jesus."

Sebastian stalking away.

"How dare you walk away, you damnable rotter. This is horrible and I can't bear any more."

Marion broke into sobs, slammed into silence with the front door.

Walking past the parking lot, down the little hill to the station. Stand by this wall here and watch the trains go by. Just take a crap and look what happens. This damn Skully probably put in rubber pipes. Three pounds a week for a rat hole, with brown swamp grass on the walls and cardboard furniture. And Marion has to be standing right under it. Couldn't she hear it coming? And the sun's gone in and it looks like rain. Better get back to the house or it'll weaken my position. Get her a little present, a fashion magazine filled with richery.

Marion sitting in the easy chair sewing. Pausing at the door, testing the silence.

"I'm sorry, Marion."

Marion head bent. Sebastian tendering his gift.

"I really am sorry. Look at me, I've got a present for you. It's hot tamale with ink dressing, see."

"O."

"Nice?"

"Yes."

"Like the gold teeth of God?"

"Don't spoil it now."

"My little Marion. I'm such a bastard. I tell you the whole thing up there is just a bunch of roots."

"I'll have something to read in bed."

"I'm an incredible pig, Marion."

"Aren't these suits nice."

"Don't you hear me, Marion? I'm a pig."

"Yes, but I wish we were rich and had money. I want to travel. If we could only travel."

"Let me kiss you, Marion, at least."

Marion arose, embracing him with blonde arms, driving her long groin against his and her tongue deep into his mouth.

Marion you're good underneath it all and not a bad feel. Just irritable at times. Now go in there and cook the dinner. And I'll relax here in the chair and read my *Evening Mail*. I see listed conscience money. Great thing, the conscience. And letters about emigration and women who marry for quids. And here's a letter about Blessed Oliver Plunket. We went up to see him there in the St. Peter's Church, Drogheda. A decapitated, two hundred and sixty year old head. Made me feel hushed. Gray, pink and battered and a glint of dead, bared teeth in the candlelight. Charwoman told me to touch it, touch it now, sir, for it's great for luck. I put my finger, afeared, into the mouldy nose hole, for you can't have too much luck these days.

Now I see them across the street coming out of the laundry. Pouring into the road, faces lining up for the tram. There's the girl with the brown eyes and dark hair, her face colorless but for handsome lips. Her legs in lisle stockings and feet in army surplus boots. Hatless and hair in a bun. Goes to the newsboy, calves knotting softly on the backs of her legs. Tucks the paper under her arm and waits in the queue.

In my heart I know she isn't a virgin, but perhaps childless with pink buds for nipples or even if they're sucked and dark I don't mind. Wears a green scarf around her nice neck. Necks should be white and long with a blue nervous vein twitching with the nervousness of life in general. My good gracious savior, she's looking over here. Hide? What am I? A scoundrel, a sneak? Not a bit. Face her. You're lovely. Absolutely lovely. Put my face on your spring breasts. Take you to

Paris and tie your hair in knots with summer leaves.

"Sebastian, it's ready, do bring in the chair."

In the kitchen cutting a thick slice off the loaf, scraping butter out of a cup.

"Sebastian, what about the toilet?"

"What about it?"

"Who's going to fix it?"

"Marion, I beg of you, this is dinner time. Do you want to give me ulcers?"

"Why don't you take some responsibility?"

"After dinner. Don't drive me up the wall over Irish plumbing, it's new to the country and the pipes got mixed."

"But who'll pay?"

"Skully out of his little gold egg."

"And the smell, Sebastian. What can we do about the smell?"

"It's just healthy shit."

"How dare you use that ugly word."

"Shit's shit, Marion, even on judgment day."

"It's foul and I won't have it said in the same house as Felicity."

"She'll hear it and also in the matter of foulness I'll see to it she's laid before she's fifteen."

Marion silently seized. Putting egg shell in the coffee to make it settle. Notice her fingers bitten. She moves through the mess.

"All right, Marion, take it easy. It's just adjustment. Got to get used to it here."

"Why must you be so raw?"

"The mean meat in me."

"Be sincere. You weren't like this before we came to Ireland. This vulgar filthy country."

"Easy now."

"Children running barefoot in the streets in the middle of winter and men wagging their things at you from doorways. Disgusting."

"Untruths. Lies."

"They're a foul lot. I understand now why they're only fit to be servants."

"I say, Marion, a little bitterness?"

"You know it's true. Look at that frightful O'Keefe and his dirty ideas. America doesn't seem to help. Brings the worst out in them. He's not even fit to be a servant."

"I think Kenneth's a gentleman in every respect. Have you ever heard him fart? Now, have you?"

"Absolutely frightful rot. One has only to watch him leering over the cat when it's in heat to see he's dreadfully base. When he comes into the room I feel he's criminally assaulting me in his mind."

"It's legal."

"It's the revolting lechery of an Irish peasant. And he tries to give the impression of good breeding. Watch him eating. It's infuriating. Grabs everything. That first time we had him to dinner he just came in as if we were servants and proceeded to eat even before I had time to sit down. And pulling hunks out of the bread, how can you be blind to these things?"

"Now, now, a little patience with the people who have given your country a Garden of Eden to play in, make your fires and serve your tea."

"I wish we had stayed in England. You could have waited for Oxford or Cambridge. And we could have at least maintained a measure of dignity."

"I'll admit there's not much of that."

Long limbed Marion settled in the chair. What makes you so tall and slender. You raise your eyelids and cross your legs with something I like and wear sexless shoes with sexiness. And Marion I'll say this for you, you're not blatant. And when we get our house in the West with the Kerry cattle out on the hills sucking up the grass and I'm Dangerfield Q.C., things will be fine again.

A tram pounding by the window, grinding, swaying and rattling on its tracks to Dalkey. A comforting sound. Maps shaking on the wall. Ireland a country of toys. And maybe I ought to go over to Marion on the couch. We're experimenting with marriage. Got to find the contraceptives or else another screaming mouth for milk. The brown-eyed girl in the laundry is about twenty-five. Marion sucking on her false teeth again, I think it must be a sign of wanting it.

In the bedroom, Dangerfield rubbing stockinged feet on the cold linoleum. And the sound of Marion using the piss pot behind Skully's genuine Ming dynasty screen. And a little tug at these tattered shades for the privacy. Even in this great Catholic country you've got to keep covered, you know, or they watch you undress, but mind you, the Protestants use a field glass.

And Marion clutching the hem of her dress and drawing it over her shifting shoulders. She said there was only thirty shillings left.

"Our good accents and manners will see us right. Didn't you know, Marion, they can't put Protestants in jail?"

"You've no responsibility and to have my child raised among a lot of savage Irish and be branded with a brogue for the rest of her life. Pass me my cream, please."

Sebastian passing the cream, smiling and waving his feet from the edge of the bed. Letting his body fall with a squeal of springs and looking at the patches of pink in the ceiling.

Marion a bit upset and confused. Difficult for her. She was breaking. Isn't as strong as me, led a sheltered life. Maybe shouldn't have married me. Matter, all of it, of time. Pumping it around and around, air in, air out and then it all goes like the shutters of a collapsing house. Starts and ends in antiseptic smell. Like to feel the end would be like closing leaves of honeysuckle, pressing out a last fragrance in the night but that only happens to holy men. Find them in the morning with a smile across the lips and bury them in plain boxes. But I want a rich tomb of Vermont marble in Woodlawn Cemetery, with automatic sprinkler and evergreens. If they get you in the medical school they hang you up by the ears. Never leave me unclaimed, I beg of you. Don't hang me all swollen, knees pressing the red nates of others where they come in to see if I'm fat or lean and all of us stabbed to death on the Bowery. Kill you in the tenement streets and cover you in flowers and put in the juice. By God, you hulking idiots, keep the juice away from me. I'm too busy to die.

"Marion, do you ever think of death?"

"No."

"Marion, do you ever think you're going to die?"

"I say, Sebastian, would you mind awfully stopping that sort of talk. You're in that nasty mood."

"Not at all."

"You are. Coming up here every morning to watch the funerals of these wretched people. Dreadful and sordid. I think you get a perverse pleasure out of it."

"Beyond this vale of tears, there is a life above, unmeasured by the flight of years and all that life is love."

"You think you're frightening me with these sinister airs of yours. I find them only boring and they tend to make you repulsive."

"What?"

"Yes, they do."

"For the love of Oliver, look at me. Look at my eyes. Go ahead, come on."

"I don't want to look in your eyes."

"Honest globes they are."

"You can't talk seriously about anything."

"I just asked you about death. Want to know how you feel, really get to know you. Or maybe you think this is for ever."

"Rubbish. You think it's for ever, I know you do. You're not as flippant as this in the mornings, I notice."

"Takes me a few hours to adapt. Snap out of the dream."

"And you scream."

"What?"

"You were yelling a few nights ago, how do I get out of this. And another time you were screaming, what's that white thing in the corner, take it away."

Dangerfield holding his belly, laughing on the squeaking springs.

"You can laugh, but I think there's something serious at the root of it."

"What's at the root? Can't you see I'm mad. Can't you see? Look. See. Madness. E. I'm mad."

Sebastian ogled and wagged his tongue.

"Stop it. Always willing to clown but never to do anything useful."

Dangerfield watched from the bed as she flexed her long arms behind her back and her breasts fell from the cups of her brassiere, tan nipples hardening in the cold air. Red line on her shoulder left by the strap. Stepping wearily out of her underpants, facing the mirror and rubbing white cream into her hands and face. Little brown strands growing round the nipples. You've often said, Marion, about giving it the wax treatment but I like them that way after all.

Sebastian quietly stepping from the bed approaching the naked body. Pressing his fists against her buttock and she pushes his hands away.

"I don't like you touching me there."

And kissing her on the back of the neck. Wet the skin with the tongue and the long blonde hair gets in the mouth. Marion taking the blue nightdress from the nail. Sebastian stripping and sitting naked on the edge of the bed, taking white fluff out of the navel, and doubling himself, plucking the congealed dirt from between his toes.

"Sebastian, I wish you'd take a bath."

"Kills the personality."

"You were so clean when I first knew you."

"Given up the cleanliness for a life of the spirit. Preparation for another and better world. Hardly take offense at a little scruffiness. Clean soul's my motto. Take off your nightie."

"Where are they?"

"Under my shirts."

"And the vaseline?"

"Behind the books on the box."

Marion ripping the silver paper. Americans great for packages. Wrap anything up. And she draws the opening of her nightdress back from her shoulders, letting it fall to her feet and folding it carefully across the books. She kneels on the bed. What are other men like, do they grunt and groan, are they all curved and circumcised, with or without. She climbs into bed, a soft voice.

"Let's do it the way we used to in Yorkshire."

"Umn."

"Do you still like my breasts the way they are?"

"Umn."

"Tell me things, Sebastian, talk to me. I want to know."

Sebastian rolled near, pressing the long, blonde body to his, thinking of a world outside beating drums below the window in the rain. All slipping on the cobblestones. And standing aside as a tram full of Bishops rumbles past, who hold up sacred hands in blessing. Marion's hand tightening and touching my groin. Ginny Cupper took me in her car out to the spread fields of Indiana. Parking near the edge of the woods and walking out into the sunny rows of corn, waving seeds to a yellow horizon. She wore a white blouse and a gray patch of sweat under her arms and the shadow of her nipples was gray. We were rich. So rich we could never die. Ginny laughed and laughed, white saliva on her teeth lighting up the deep red of her mouth, fed the finest food in the world. Ginny was afraid of nothing. She was young and old. Her brown arms and legs swinging in wild optimism, beautiful in all their parts. She danced on the long hood of her crimson Cadillac, and watching her, I thought that God must be female. She leaped into my arms and knocked me to the ground and screamed into my mouth. Heads pressed in the hot Indiana soil and pinned me in a cross. A crow cawed into the white sun and my sperm spurted into the world. Ginny had driven her long Cadillac through the guard rails of a St. Louis bridge and her car shone like a clot of blood in the mud and murk of the Mississippi. We were all there in the summer silence of Suffolk, Virginia, when the copper casket was gently placed in the cool marble vault. I smoked a cigarette and crushed it out on the black and white squares of the tomb. In the stagnant emptiness of the train station after the cars were gone, I walked into the women's toilet and saw the phallic obscenities on the wooden doors and gray walls. I wonder if people will think I'm a lecher. Ginny had gardenias in her lovely brown hair. I hear the train, Marion's breath in my ear. My stomach's shaking, my last strength. The world's silent. Crops have stopped growing. Now they grow again.

With two tomes under the arm walking out the back gate of Trinity College. Bright warm evening to catch the train. These business people are bent for their summer gardens and maybe a swim by Booterstown. On these evenings Dublin is such an empty city. But not around the parks or pubs. It would be a good idea to pop onto the Peace Street and buy a bit of meat. I'm looking forward to a nice dinner and bottle of stout and then I'll go out and walk along the strand and see some fine builds. For such a puritan country as this, there is a great deal to be seen in the way of flesh if one is aware and watching when some of them are changing on the beach.

"Good evening, sir."

"Good evening."

"And how can I help you, sir?"

"To be quite honest with you, I think I would like a nice piece of calf's liver."

"Now, sir, I think I can see you with a lovely bit, fresh and steaming. Now I'll only be a minute."

"Bang on. Wizard."

"Now here we are, sir. It's a fine bit. On a bit of a holiday, sir? Nice to have a bit of fresh meat."

"Yes, a holiday."

"Ah England's a great country, now isn't it sir?"

"Fine little country you have here."

"Ah it's got its points. Good and bad. And hasn't everything now. And here we are, sir, enjoy your holiday."

"It's a nice evening, now."

"A great evening."

"I see you're a man of learning and good-sized books they are too."

"They're that. Bye bye, now."

"Grand evening. Good luck, sir."

Wow, what conversation. Doctor of Platitudes. Holiday, my painful arse. But a nice bit of liver.

Into the gloom of Westland Row Station. He bought the papers, rolled them and beat his thigh up the stairs. Sitting on the iron bench, could see the people pouring in the gate. Where are the slim ankles on you women. None of you. All drays. Well what's in the paper. Dreariness. The Adventures of Felix the Cat. Put it away. I must to the lavatory. So big in here. Dribbling water. Good God, the train.

Rumbling, pounding, black dirty toy. Whistling by with the whole gang of these evening faces peeking and pouting out the windows. Must find a first class compartment. Jesus, jammed, the whole damn train. O me, try the third. Pulling himself up. Pushing his meat onto the rack, squeezing around, sitting down.

Across from him the people who lived in the semidetached houses of Glenageary and Sandycove, all buried in the paper reading madly. Why don't some of you look out the window at the nice sights. See the canal and gardens and flowers. It's free, you know. No use getting meself upset by the crut. I say there, you, you little pinched bastard, what are you staring at. That little man staring at me. Go away, please.

Chug, chug, chug.
Choo, choo, choo.
Woo, woo, woo.

We're away. Mustn't mind these damn people. Getting me upset.
Still staring at me. If he keeps it up, I swear by Christ I'll lash his
head right through that window. Expect rudeness like this in the
third class.

The girl sitting across from him gave a startled gasp. What is
this. Must be I've gotten in a train going to Grangegorman. What's
the matter with her. That pinched bastard must be up to something,
feeling her thigh. Lecher. Perhaps it's my place to take measures
against this sneak. O but mind my own business. Things bad enough
as they are already. Well look at them all. Whole seat is writhing,
wriggling. What are they looking at. This is the end. I look forward
to a nice evening of my liver and a walk and what's that girl pressing
the book up to her face for. Is she blind. Get a pair of glasses you silly
bitch. Maybe that bastard is embarrassing her, she's blushing. The
damn sexual privation in this city. That's it. Root of it all. Distraction.
I need distraction. Read the In Memoriams.

Donoghue—(Second Anniversary)—In sad and loving memory of our dear father, Alex (Rexy) Donoghue, taken away July
25, 1946, late of Fitzwilliam Square (Butcher's porter in the Dublin abbatoir) on whose soul, sweet Jesus, have mercy.
Masses offered. R.I.P.

> *Gone forever, the smiling face,*
> *The kindly, cheerful heart*
> *Loved so dearly through the years*
> *Whose memory shall never depart.*

Coming upon his ears like goblets of hot lead.

"I say, I say there. There are women present."

Absolute silence in the compartment as the little train clicked
past the Grand Canal and the slovenly back gardens of Ringsend.
Sebastian glued to the print, paper pressed up to his eyes. Again, like
an obscenity uttered in church.

"Sir. I say. There are ladies present in the carriage."

Who would be the first to jump on him. Must let someone else
make the first move, I'll grab his legs when trouble starts. O this so
worries me. I hate this kind of thing. Why in the name of the suffering Jesus did I have to get into this damn car. Will I ever be delivered.
No doubt about it, this man was a sexual maniac. Start using obscene

language any second. There's just so much I can take. It's like that old woman saying her rosary and after every decade screaming out a mouthful of utter, horrible foulness. And I can't bear foulness. Look at them, all behaving as if nothing had happened. Better keep my eyes up, he may try to level me with a surprise blow. That man in the corner with the red nose. He's laughing, holding his stomach. For hell, deliver me. Never again ride third class.

"I say there. Must I repeat. There are ladies present."

Sebastian leveled his face at him, lips shearing the words from his mouth.

"I beg your pardon."

"Well, I say, haven't you forgotten something?"

"I beg your pardon."

"I repeat, there are ladies present. You ought to inspect yourself."

"Are you addressing me?"

"Yes."

This conversation is too much. Should have ignored the fool. This is most embarrassing. I ought to take a clout at that bastard in the corner who seems to be enjoying it so much. He'll enjoy it if I break his jaw for him. Why don't they lock these people up in Ireland. The whole city full of them. If I'm attacked, by God, I'll sue the corporation for selling this madman a ticket. Those two girls are very upset. This damn train an express all the way to the Rock. My God. Sit and bear it. Control. Absolute and complete control at all costs.

"Sir, this is abominable behavior. I must caution you. Frightfully serious matter, this. Shocking on a public conveyance. Part of you, sir, is showing."

"I beg your pardon, but would you please mind your own business or I'll break your jaw."

"It is my business to discourage this sort of thing when there are ladies present. Shameful. There are other people in the car you know."

No hope. Don't let him suck me into conversation like that. Must employ me brain. We're coming into the Booterstown. Get out in a minute. Showing? Yes. My fingers are out. Holy Catholic Ireland, have to wear gloves. Don't want to be indecent with uncovered fingers. And my face too. This is the last time positively that I appear without wearing a mask. There's a breaking point. But I'll not break, not for any of them and certainly not for this insane lout.

Avoiding the red, pinched, insistent, maniacal face. Look out the window. There's the park and where I first saw my dear Chris to speak to me. O deliverance. That laughing monster in the corner, I'll drag him out of the car and belt him from one end of the station to the other. What's he doing. Pointing into his lap. Me? Lap? Good Christ. It's out. Every inch of it.

Leaping for the door. Get out. Fast. Behind him, a voice.

"Haven't you forgotten something else?"

Wheeling, wrenching the blood-stained parcel from the rack. Behind him.

"You can't remember your meat at all today."

J. P. DONLEAVY

Colin Wilson, asked to comment on Donleavy and The Ginger Man, *writes as follows:*

*I have heard J. P. Donleavy (known to his friends as Mike) described as the rogue elephant of modern literature, and there is an obvious truth in the description. I'd heard extraordinary stories about him before I met him—pure Sebastian Dangerfield—about how he kept only one book in the house—*The Ginger Man—*and was usually to be found reading it; about how he once removed the back of* *his fireplace, because the neighbors' fireplace was on the other side of the wall, and their fires were large enough to heat both rooms.*

I expected to meet a hulking brute of a man, seven feet tall, with bulging muscles and an uncertain temper. I was surprised to be introduced to a slim, quiet-voiced man with a D.H. Lawrence beard and a smile of immense charm. His wife was one of the most dazzlingly beautiful girls I have ever met—I found myself hoping she wasn't the model for Marion in the novel. There were so many toys, playpens and nappies around the place that I got the impression he had fourteen children, but I may be mistaken about the number.

It is worth mentioning my experience of reading The Ginger Man. *I bought it in its Olympia Press edition, and found it hard going, with its terrific forward rush and Joycean lack of consideration for the reader's nerves. I handed the book to my wife with the remark, "Chaos." But I found the chaos coming back to me when I should have been thinking of other things, and kept dipping into the book again. Finally, I began to see the method in Donleavy's madness. He may be exhausting to read straight through the first time, but, like Joyce, he is re-readable, and he stays in the mind. I have read most of the other books of the angry-young-man generation; all of them were easy enough on a first reading; none of them have stayed in my mind as worth re-reading. Whether you like Dangerfield—or the "singular man" of his other novel—or regard them with loathing, you have to recognize them as intensely real literary figures. There is something maniacally subjective about Donleavy's writing —Alexander Trocchi is the only contemporary who seems to me on the same level—and it produces the same kind of impact you get from Joyce, or Miller, or Sterne, for that matter.*

There is one problem about Donleavy that really interests me: where you can go when you've created a tour de force like The Ginger Man? *Sterne faced the same problem; so did Joyce; so did Miller, in another way. But to judge from* A Singular Man *and* Fairy Tales of New York, *Donleavy is going to show himself equal to the problem. The hero of the new novel is less of a rogue elephant than Dangerfield, but he is just as outrageously funny.*

I should conclude by mentioning that Donleavy was born in Brooklyn, son of a civil servant, attended Trinity College, Dublin, under the G.I. bill of rights, and now lives in west London, or did last time I saw him.

THE **BLACK** BOOK

Lawrence Durrell

This is the day I have chosen to begin this writing, because today we are dead among the dead: and this is an agon for the dead, a chronicle for the living. There is no other way to put it. There is a correspondence between the present, this numbness, inertia: and that past reality of a death, whose meaning is symbolic, mythical, but real also in its symptom. As if, lying here, in this mimic death at morning, we were re-creating a bit from the past: a crumb of the death we have escaped. Yes, even though the wild ducks fall in a triangle of wings among the marshes of Bivarie, and all the elements are out of gear, out of control; even though the sea flogs the tough black button of rock on which this, our house, is built. The correspondence of deadness with deadness is complete.

Here begins an extract from Gregory's diary:

The question with which I trouble myself is the question of the ego, the little me. The I, sitting here in this fuggy room, like a little red-haired, skullcapped Pope, insulting myself in green ink. The red dwarf, the lutin, the troll—the droll and abhorrent self!

Sweets to the sweet. To Lobo sensual lust. And for the journalist inevitably, a journal. A journal! What a delicious excursion it sounds. The path lies ready, the fruit grows on the hedge-sides. But the stupendous arrogance of such a record! What should it contain, then? A pedestrian reckoning by the sun, or aphoristic flights, or a momentous study of my excretions covering years? A digest of all three, perhaps. One can hardly tell. No matter. Let us begin with Lobo. To insects sensual lust. And to Lobo a victory over the female, because that is what he wants. I say victory but I mean a rout: a real beating-up of his natural enemy, who degrades him by the fact that she carries the puissant, the all-conquering talisman of the vagina about with her. If it were possible to invent a detached vagina, which has an effective life of its own, then Lobo would be a profound misogynist, I am sure.

But consider him, as he sits there, working over the enormous parchment chart of South London. Consider the lily. Every week after a certain lecture, he takes it down from the wall, and gets busy on it with his tools: compasses, protractors, dividers, his India ink which hardens in shining lines along the thoroughfares: his pencil box full of rubbers, tapes, stamps. On the black wood is a garish cockatoo. This reminds him of Peru, though why, he cannot think.

In his childhood there were boxes of oranges with this bird painted on them. Perhaps that is the reason. But it reminds him of Lima, sitting out there on the map, a beautiful gray husk of life. Lima, with the parrots and the oranges, the almond-eyed whores, and the cathedrals, delicate, delicate. I invent this, because though he is incapable of saying it to me, yet he feels it. Dust, the eternal dust along the high road, and the hucksters, and fine swish motorcars, and lerv. The facile, hot, Latin lerv, with its newt's eyes fixed on anyone ready to ease you of a thimbleful of sperm. Sunlight along the lips of the shutters, or the guitars wombing over the Rimac, hot and seasoned. And the sour booming of many steeples, Santo Domingo, San Augustin, La Merced. He imitates their hollow noises raising his hand and keeping himself in time with his memories.

Fascinating to watch him sitting there, this little brown man, penning his map; his thin girl's fingers with their unpressed cuticles carefully unstopping bottles, cleaning nibs, clutching a penholder as they move forward to letter or draw. Lobo is as much of an enigma to me as this fantastic locality of blind houses and smoke which he is drawing must be to him.

Perhaps the remark about the insect was a little strong, for it is not my business to raise my own standards to the height of an impartial canon. But it seems to me accurate. The female is a catalyst, unrelated to life, to anything but this motor necessity which grows greater day by day. Lobo! Perhaps this all has something to do with his homesickness, his Latin tears and glooms. What I am concerned with is the enigma, not these erotic maneuvers, all carried out on the plane of nervy, febrile, social welfare: the kind of thing Laclos did so vividly. "My God," he says sometimes. "I think *never* to go with womans any more, never. Why is the mystery? Afterward what? You are dead, you are disgust. *Smell!* It is impossible. I go along the road, pure as a Catholic, then I see a woman look to me and . . ." His heavy head bends lower over the chart: the compressions gather in the cheeks under his bossy Inca nose: he is silent, and it is a little difficult to find anything to say in reply.

Lobo has the fascination of an ancient stamp for me. I can't get past the thought of this little Latin fellow sitting in his room night after night, working like Lucifer for his degree: and all the while his mind riddled with thoughts of home, like a pincushion. He admits it. "It is my home makes me blue, dear friend. I think in bed of Peru many night and I cannot sleep. I put the wireless till twelve. Then I go mad almost. That bitch nex' door. I can kill her when I am alone. Listen. Last night I made a little deceit for her. Truly. I weeped in the night. It was quiet. I weeped a little louder. Nothing. I weeped like hell. Really I was lonely, it was true, but not real the tears. I could not make the real tears. Listen, I heard her put the light and sit in the bed looking. I went on with the tears. Then she speaks: *who is it?* I was not knowing how to speak. I had no words. Soon she put off the light and lay. No good. I ran to the door and knock it very quietly. I say: *It's only me, Miss Venable.* Nothing. I tap tap tap but nothing. I was angry. I sniff like hell, but nothing. No good. The dirty bitch. After that I went to bed and really weep, I wet the pillow all through, I am so angry I could kill." His eyes dilate earnestly under the sooty lashes. At such memories he becomes pure emotional idealism. Like the Virgin Mary. He will cut himself one of these days for lerv, he says. I confess I did not know what this phrase meant until the night of the festival, when we returned at three to drink a final nightcap in his room. He was pretty drunk.

"Know what I do when a man make me angry?" he asked. He explored the washstand drawer and appeared before me with a knife in his right hand. He was so gentle and friendly that for a second I was afraid. "See this," he said, and handed it to me as simply as a girl. It was an enormous folding knife, sharpened to great keenness.

"I cut him," said Lobo unsteadily.

Taking it from me he divided the air which separated us neatly into four portions, grinned beatifically, and replaced the weapon in its secret hiding place. When he talks like this, then, it is an enraged *hara kiri* that he plans—or a murder.

But confidence for confidence Lobo finds me a very unsatisfactory person. My humility devastates him. Particularly my complete ignorance on the subject of women. He says in tones of gravity and wonder: "You? A man of forty, an Englishman?" Really to be frank, if one must be frank, I have had few and unsatisfactory experiences in this direction. Literary affairs with aging Bohemians, in which my ability to compare the style of Huxley to that of Flaubert was considered more important, even in bed, than physical gifts; a stockbroker's widow: an experimental affair with an experimental painter, in which, again, our mutual respect for the volumetric proportions of Cézanne's canvases was almost our only bond. Affinities, you might say. I suppose in this direction I must be rather a dead battery until I meet Grace. Lobo is bored. An Englishman of forty? Well it must have been forty years in the wilderness for all the adventures I can recount. Never mind. I comfort myself with Pascal's remark about the thinking reed.

Chamberlain is not less scathing. This canary-haired zealot, living in one of the flats nearby with a young wife and three dogs, spends his moments happily lecturing us on such esoteric subjects. "Sex, sex, sex," he exclaims roundly, his manner closely modeled on the style of Lawrence's letters. "When will we get the bastards to realize?" Fraternizing in the barroom among the blue spittoons. He is powerful and convincing, standing over his bitters, and appealing to his wife for support. "Glory be to hip, buttock, loin, *more ferarum*, *bestiarum*, uterine toboggan, and the whole gamut of physical fun. Don't you think? What about more bowels of compassion, tenderness and the real warmth of the guts, eh?"

Really I am scalded by this curious Salvation Army line of talk. Bad taste. Bad taste. Tarquin winces and bleats whenever Chamberlain gets started.

"Let us invent a new order of marriage to revive the dead. Have another beer. Let us start a new theory of connubial copulation, which will get the world properly fucked for a change. Tarquin, you're not listening to me, damn you."

Tarquin bleats: "Oh, do stop forcing these silly ideas on one, Chamberlain. You simply won't admit other people's temperamental differences. Shut up."

He is mopping the froth off his beer with a discolored tongue. Chamberlain turns to his wife, who is standing, breathing quietly, like a big retriever: "What do you think? Tell me." She prefers to smile and ponder rather than think. "There," says Chamberlain in triumph, "she agrees."

"All this damned sexual theorizing," moans Tarquin. "Don't you think, Gregory? I mean damn it!"

"Don't you agree with him," says Chamberlain. "Now, Gregory, you're quite a good little fellow on your own."

"Young man," I say weakly.

"Oh, I know you're a patriarch in years, but that's mere chronology. You need to grow a bit."

"Oh, do stop," says Tarquin, acutely miserable.

"The trouble with you, my dear," says Chamberlain, "is that you're still fighting through the dead mastoid. Now what you need . . ."

And so on. One revolts from transcribing any more of his chat, because it becomes infectious after a time. His personality is attractive enough to make any dogma plausible and compelling to the imagination. As for Lobo, they spend hours quarreling about themes domestic and erotic. This always ends in trouble. "Listen, Baudelaire," says Chamberlain, "you've got yourself up a tree. Climb down and take a look around you." When he really wants to frighten the Spaniard he suggests calling his wife in and putting these problems before her. This is hideous. Lobo's sense of chivalry squirms at the idea. Tearfully, under his sentimental eyelashes he says, after Chamberlain has gone: "A beast? Eh? He is beastly. Doesn't he have the finer feelings? His poor wife, like a prostitute in his home. It is terrible, terrible. He only understands the prostitute, not the *real* woman. He is terrible." And a string of Spanish oaths.

Fog over the gardens. Fog, marching down among the pines, making dim stone those parcels of Greek statuary. In the distance trains burrowing their tunnels of smoke and discord. Lights shine out wanly against the buildings. The red-nosed commercials will be lining up in the bar for their drinks. I can see the whisky running into their red mouths, under the tabby whiskers, like urine. I sit here, in the shadow of the parchment chart, smoking, and eating the soft skin on the sides of my cheeks. The customary madness of the suburban evening comes down over us in many enormous yawns. Ennui. "We do not exist," says Tarquin. "We do not exist, we are fictions." And frankly this idea is not as outrageous as it sounds. Toward evening, when I walk down the row of suburban houses, watching the blinds lowered to salute the day's death, with no companion but that municipal donkey the postman, I find myself in a world of illusion whose furniture *can* only be ghosts. In the lounge the veterans sit like Stonehenge under the diffuse light of the lamps. Old women stuck like clumps of cactus in their chairs. The *Times* is spread out over the dead, like washing hung out on bushes to dry. Footsteps and voices alike trodden out in the dusty carpets: and the faint aeolian sofas appealing to the statues. Night. The clock whirrs inside its greenhouse of glass and the Japanese fans breathe a soft vegetable decay into the room. There is nothing to do, nothing to be done.

In the flat that my body inhabits the silence is sometimes so heavy that one has the sensation of wading through it. Looking up from the book to hear the soft spondees of the gas fire sounding across nothingness, I am suddenly aware of the lives potential in me which are wasting themselves. It is a fancy of mine that each of us contains many lives, potential lives. They are laid up inside us, shall we say, like so many rows of shining metals—railway lines. Riding along one set toward the terminus, we can be aware of those other lines, alongside us, on which we might have traveled—on which we might yet travel if only we had the strength to change. You yawn? This is simply my way of saying I am lonely. It is in these movements, looking up to find the whole night gathered at my elbow, that I question the life I am leading, and find it a little lacking. The quiet statement of a woman's laugh, breaking from the servants' rooms across the silence, afflicts me. I consider myself gravely in mirrors these days. I wear my skullcap a trifle grimly, as if in affirmation of the life I have chosen. Yet at night sometimes I am aware, as of an impending toothache, of the gregarious fiber of me. Dear me. This is becoming fine writing in the manner of the Sitwells. But let me discuss myself a little in green ink, since no one takes the trouble to do so in words of more than one syllable. In the first place, my name is not *Death*, as it ought to be, but *Herbert*. The disgusting, cheesy, Pepysian sort of name which I would pay to change if I were rich enough. Death is part of the little charade I construct around myself to make my days tolerable. *Death Gregory!* How livid the name shines on the title page of this tome. Borrowed plumes, I am forced to admit in this little fit of furious sincerity. Borrowed from Tourneur or Marston. No matter. The show must go on.

My estate, to descend to the level of Pepys, is in a neat and satisfying condition. A lifelong sympathy with Communism has never prevented me from investing safely, hoarding thriftily, and living as finely economic as possible. This means my tastes are sybaritic. On bread I have never wasted a penny: but an occasional wine of quality finds its way into the trap-doored basement I call my cellar. The books I own are impeccable—the fine bindings lie along the wall in the firelight, snoozing softly in richness. Unlike most men I read what I buy. The table I keep is frugal but choice. The board does not groan, but then neither does the guest, ha ha. Taste and style in all things, I say to myself with rapture, taste and style! Neat but not gaudy, fine but unadorned! All of which makes these nostalgic moods so incomprehensible, so damned unreasonable; for have I not chosen the life of reason and moderation as my proper field?

Chamberlain is in the habit of saying: "Of course, my dear, your system is bound to break down sooner or later. Or else the system will stand and *you* will break down inside it. I'm all for tightrope acts, and fakirs, and trolleys full of pins, provided they entertain. You do not. You are walking a tightrope with no safety net under it, and it bores. Gregory Stylites, come down from your perch and have a slice of ham." All this, however imprecise, is vaguely disquieting, sitting here over the fire, with a calf-bound Pascal and a glass of dry ochrous sherry on the table. Such a comforting system after all! So safe, so cast-iron in construction! Such a clever device, when all's said and done. But then, if one does not fit a system? That is the question. I am reminded of the little formula which he tacks on the end of his customary good night, whenever he calls: "Well, good night," he says insolently. "Grand show you put on." There is a quality in all this which ruins my façade; I am less sure of myself: I wince in a quaint schoolboy nervousness. Not that I show the least sign of it, I flatter myself. No. My control is perfect, my poise almost geological in its fixity. I "carry" my skullcap with distinction none the less, for I am as proud as Lucifer. But it is a little boorish of him to pretend that my modish charms do not touch him at all. I like his wife better. True, she takes her cue from him and tries to find me amusing, but she can scent that little Prussian core of pride in me. She is a little awed, in spite of herself, at those qualities which my skullcap is intended to suggest. Shall I bore you with a discursion on the intuition of women? It is a subject I know nothing whatsoever about. But that should not disqualify me from writing about it. Here is paper, seven pages covered, here is ink, and here is that isolation which breeds many fantastic notions in my pen. If you are afflicted by my tediousness, take heart. This might have been a novel instead of anything so pleasantly anonymous as a diary.

Talking of loneliness, since we must talk tonight, or suffer the silence to become unbearable: Tarquin is also a sufferer from this malady, this geometrical insanity of day followed by night followed by day, etc. But this study of himself is so strenuous that he is in a much worse condition. Tarquin is already behind the screens, attended by the one fatal nurse of the ego. His researches have been

rapidly making a wreck of him. Complex, inhibition, fetish, trauma—
the whole merde-ridden terminology of the new psychology hangs
from his lower lip, like a cigarette in the mouth of a chain smoker.
"One must explore oneself, don't you think? One must try and reduce
one's life to some sort of order, don't you think? What do you think
of Catholicism, Gregory? Sometimes I get such a feeling of devotion
—it's like being in love, sort of raped by contemplation. Does Lobo
know anything? I must ask him. I used to faint at one time, and have
dreams or visions, what would you call them? Trauma, it seems
like according to the books. Real fits, like epilepsy, what do you say?
Eh?" And so on. The terminologies of theology and psychology
running neck and neck, each outdoing the other in vagueness. Duns
Scotus and Freud. Adler and Augustine.

"I suppose one really ought to read the best books," he says
hopelessly. "One must cultivate one's garden like who was it said?
One's taste and all that. But that damned Iliad, Gregory, honestly I
can't get on with it. And pictures, too. Christ, I *look* at them, but it
doesn't mean more than what's there. I don't *feel* them."

Every now and then he has a syphilis scare, and off he trots to
the hospital to have a blood test. The vagueness of the Wassermann
torments him. One can never be certain, can one? Standing naked
beside his bed he whacks away at his reflexes with a rubber truncheon;
closes his eyes and finds that, standing with his feet together, he does
not fall. Or he will pace up and down the floor, pausing to examine
the microphotographs of spirochetes which hang over his cottage
piano. Why is his chest spotty? Why is he always so run down? Is it
lack of calcium or what?

Everything is plausible here, because nothing is real. Forgive me.
The barriers of the explored world, the divisions, the corridors, the
memories—they sweep down on us in a catharsis of misery, riving
us. I am like a child left alone in these corridors, these avenues of
sleeping doors among the statuary, with no friends but an audience
of yawning boots. I am being honest with you for once, I, Death
Gregory, the monkey on the stick. If I were to prick out my history
for you, as Lobo his plans on the mature parchment, would you be
able to comprehend for an instant the significance of the act? I doubt
it. In the field of history we all share the irrelevance of painted things.
I have only this portion of time in which to suffer.

The realms of history, then! The fact magical, the fancy wonderful, the fact treasonable. All filtered, limited, through the wretched instruments of the self. The seventy million I's whose focus embraces these phenomena and records them on the plate of the mind. The singularity of the world would be inspiring if one did not feel there was a catch in it. When I was nine the haggard female guardian in whose care I had been left exclaimed: "Horses sweat, Herbert. *Gentlemen* perspire. Don't say that nasty word any more." I shall never forget the phrase, it will remain with me until I die—along with that other useless and ineradicable lumber—the proverbs, practices and precepts of a dead life in a dead land. It is, after all, the one permanent thing, the one unchanging milestone on the climb. It is I who change; constant, like a landmark of the locality, the lumber remains. Like a lake seen from different altitudes during a journey, its position never varying: only its aspect altering in relation to my own place on the landscape. I think that what we are to be is decided for us in the first few years of life; what we gain afterward in the way of reason, adjustment, etc., is superficial: a veneer, which only aggravates our disorders. Perish the wise, the seekers after reason. I am that I am. The treasonable self remains. I am not more astonished now by the knowledge that gentlemen can, if they want, have wings, than I was by that pithy social formula; or, for example, that red blood runs in fishes. I shall never be more amazed.

Not even the phenomenon of Grace disturbed my life as much as that glimpse of the social mysteries. Horses sweat, but Grace perspires; very delicately on the smooth flesh, on the thin flanks, under the tiny undernourished breasts. The blue-veined phthisic fingers are moist and languorous. But why the present tense? For Grace is no more; no more the street girl who sat, hugging her knees, and staring at the empty wallpaper. Shall we write of her in the gnomic aorist? Shall we invest her with an epitaph? She would not understand it. She understood nothing. She seemed not to hear. You could speak to her, sing to her, dance before her, and the distances she contemplated were not diminished by one inch.

"Come, Grace, you bitch," one said. "Show a sign of life. Come now, give us a smile."

Like an elaborate circus performer a smile wandered into the oval, disconsolate face. A great feat of concentration required to move the muscles of the face correctly in smiling. Her teeth were small and pure, with little gaps between them—an arrangement that suggested congenital syphilis. Her creator reserved red blood for fishes and journalists. In Grace's veins flowed mercury, the purest distillation of icy metals.

Her skin was transparent almost, and pale. One felt that if one took a piece between finger and thumb, and ripped downward, say from knee to ankle, the whole epidermis would come away wetly, effortlessly, like sodden brown paper, cleaving the flesh and bone open. On her back as she sat on our inadequate bed, I have traced many a curious forefinger among the soft grooves and lucent vertebrae —colorless nuts—protruding under their transparent covering. The white blood never warms (tense again!) never filled her with delicious shudders and ticklings. She might have been dead flesh, dead meat to the world of the male. Passion only interested her in its most ardent conclusions, and then such an incandescence shone in her face, such veins moved in concentration on her temples, such a leaping tropic flame drove her fingernails to a billet in her accomplice's flesh, that one was reassured. She was alive, after all, deep down: at the temperature which melts metals; the boiling point at the earth's center where the beds of ore clang together, and the hot magma liquefies iron and rock. She was alive behind this elaborate mien of detachment.

Gracie was bought, without any bargaining, for the promise of a cup of coffee. I remember it was a night when the snow was driving up past the big Catholic church so thickly that it blinded one. The road was buried. She was shivering inside the thin clothes, the inadequate covering of baubles and lipstick which decorated her small person. The snow hung in a glittering collar to the astrakhan lining of her coat. Wisps of black hair froze to her cheek. From her nose hung a drop of snot which she sniffed back whenever she could remember to do so. She had no handkerchief.

Inside the hall door she stood passive, like an animal, while I wiped her face, her coat collar, her grubby clothes. Then I drove her, passive and dull, downstairs to my room, guiding her with taps from my cane. In the harsh electric light she stood again, graven, and stared feebly at this row of books, this littered desk. Then, speaking of her own accord for the first time, she said: "In 'ere, mister?" A small, hard voice, running along the outer edges of sanity. I switched on the fire and commanded her to approach it. Slowly she did so.

Regarding her in silence, I was alarmed by the color her face had taken. It was that of a three-day corpse. Under the skin a faint, bluish tinge which reminded me of the shadows in snow.

"What's your name?"

She had a habit of regarding one for an age before answering, as if determining whether the truth would or would not be a suitable weapon for the occasion. Her eyes dilated and she gave a sigh, remote, remote, concerning nothing but her private problems.

"Gracie."

Snow dripped from the brim of her shabby coat. The tentacle of hair on her cheek had thawed and hung down beside her nose. She was wet through and dirty.

"You'd better take off those wet things at once. There's a dressing gown in there. I'll get you some coffee."

When I returned she was sitting naked before the electric fire, with her knees drawn up to her chin. Her flesh was puckered with cold. "Some brandy first," one said with heartiness, becoming the medical man all at once, handing her a goblet. Pondering, she drank the draught at a gulp, and then turned, her eyes dilating warmly, a sudden blush covering her forehead. For a second she seemed about to speak, and then some interior preoccupation drew a single line of worry across her forehead. With little unemotional starts she began to cough up patches of her lung, quite dumbly, like some sort of animal. One got her a clean handkerchief from the drawer and stood looking down at the averted head, a little astonished and disgusted by the perfect repose of the face even in sickness.

"Well, this is a business. You've TB."

She played the trick of staring up with the expressionless black circles in her eyes, like a blind cat. Then she looked away, numb and patient.

"And Grace, you're filthy. You must have a bath."

Her feet were dirty, her fingernails, her ears. Passively she allowed herself to be scraped and scrubbed with the loofah: dried, curried, chafed, and sprinkled with nice astringent eau de Cologne. She took no notice, but practiced this peculiar evasion, which one found so exciting. Afterward in my parrot dressing gown she cocked her little finger at me over the coffee cup. In that tinny voice she gave me a few particulars about herself. She was eighteen and lived at home. Out of work. She was interested in Gary Cooper. But all this was a kind of elaboration of her inner evasion. By giving her a dressing gown and a cup of coffee one had merely brought upon oneself the few social tricks she knew how to perform. She was not interested, merely polite. For services rendered she returned the payment of this lifted little finger and a vague awakening over a cup of suburban coffee. One was afraid that at any moment she would become urbanely ladylike, and revive the Nelson touch which one finds so painful in the ladies of Anerly and Penge. (Preserve us from the ostrich.)

"Tell me," one said, by a fluke, "about your family. Where they live and how and everything."

This interested her. It almost made her face wake up, her gestures become alive and instinctive. Only her eyes could not wholly achieve the change—narrowing, widening, the rim of the blackness. Really, to look at her was as senseless as looking into the shutter of a camera.

Her family, she said, lived in a villa in Croydon. Father had a job at the gasworks. He was a card. Her four brothers were all working. They were cards, too. Her two sisters were on the telephone exchange. They were real cards. Mother was a little queer in the head, and she, Gracie, was the youngest. Mother was a treat, the things she said! Laugh? They fairly killed themselves at her in the parlor. You see, she didn't know what she was saying, like. A bit soppy in the top story. Made them yell the things she come out with, specially when she was a little squiffy. Laugh? They howled. If you could only write them in a book it would be wonderful.

One tried to imagine her in the bosom of this roaring family—this animal waif with the voice running along the thin edge of sanity—but failed. There was nothing Elizabethan about her, to suggest that she would fit in with this pack of yelling cards—pa with his watch chain and clay pipe, mother with her bottle of Wincarnis. The parlor overflowing with brothers and sisters, and the port overflowing in mother's brain cells.

Her father was a bad man when he was in drink, she said at last. Always having tiffs with Albert. Always mucking about with her and Edith the eldest one. Only on Saturday nights when he wasn't himself, however, and Ted the eldest brother was the same. They knew it wasn't right but what could you do if it was your own father? She coughed a little.

"Do you live at home?"

"When I'm there I'm there," she said patiently. "When I don't go back they don't worry. Glad to be free of me. Not earning me keep any more, see?" I saw.

She finished her drink and put the cup down. Then she strolled over to the bookcase and quizzed the titles. Sniffed, turned to me, and said: "Fine lot o' books you got here." But with a gesture so foreign, so out of character that I was forced to laugh. She was actually being seductive: and above all, not seductive by the ordinary formulas, but by the dashing hectic formulas of the cinema. It was astonishing. Posed like that, her hip stuck out under the palm of one hand, her slender, rather frail legs Venus'd—one knee over the other—she had become that cinema parrot, a dangerous woman. Even her small face was strained to an imaginary expression before an imaginary camera. Only the awful sightlessness of her eyes betrayed her. One became embarrassed; as at a theater where the famous comedian fails to raise the most fleeting of sniggers from his audience.

"Come off it, Grace," one said uncomfortably. "Come off it. You're not an actress."

She was suddenly chastened and dumb, like a reprimanded pet. The pose was shattered. Slipping off the dressing gown she lit a cigarette and sat herself down on my knee; began to kiss me in a businesslike way, pausing from time to time to exhale clouds of smoke from her dry mouth. Her eyes might have been covered in cataracts for all the meaning they held in them. Her kisses were tasteless, like straw. "Do you like me?" she inquired at last with stunning fervor—the great screen star taking possession of her face for a second. "Do you reely like me, mister?"

From that moment there is the flash of a sword, dividing the world. A bright cleavage with the past, cutting down through the nerves and cells and arteries of feeling. The past was amputated, and the future became simply Gracie. That peculiar infatuation which absorbed one, sapped one by the fascination of its explorations. Gracie stayed on, and days lost count of themselves: so remote was that world in which I wandered with her, so all-absorbing her least mannerism, the least word, the least breath she drew.

After the first ardors were tasted and realized, she became even more wonderful as a sort of pet. Her vocabulary, her great thoughts lit up the days like comets. And that miserable tranquillity she retired into when she was ill, made one realize that she was inexhaustible. What a curious adventure another person is!

I phoned Tarquin: "My dear fellow, you must come down to my

rooms on Tuesday and meet Gracie. I'm giving a little party for her. You must come. I'm sure you will be great friends. She spits blood."

They all came. Perez, the gorilla with his uncouth male stride and raving tie, Lobo agitatedly showing his most flattering half-profile, Clare, Tarquin, Chamberlain with his bundle of light music and jazz. They sat about uncomfortably, rather ghoulishly, while I, reveling in the situation, made them drink, and helped Grace to perform her tricks. It was a cruel tableau, but she was far too obtuse to realize it. She played the social hostess with a zeal and clumsiness which would have made one weep if one were less granite-livered. I congratulated myself on my skill in gathering together such a collection of butterflies for their mutual embarrassment. Yes, I chuckled inwardly as I caught their eyes over their glasses. The comedy of wheels within wheels. It was a society of pen club members, who, after being invited to meet a celebrity, had been presented with a mere reviewer. Scandalized they were by the performance Grace put up, cocking her little finger over the teacups, and talking with the hygienic purity of an Anerly matron. (Preserve us from the ostrich.) How their eyes accused me!

Poor Grace was obviously an embarrassing bore. They relaxed a little when the gramophone was started and Chamberlain was compelled by punctiliousness to gyrate with his hostess. He was the least affected by Gracie. I suppose because he was the most natural person there. But Perez and Lobo conferred in a corner and decided that they had an important engagement elsewhere. Lobo said good-day with the frigidity of a Castilian gentleman dismissing a boring chambermaid. No manners like those of the really well-bred.

Later, however, Clare danced with her and she seemed to like it. He alone of all of them seemed to speak a quiet language which was really familiar to her: which thrilled her from the start. In fact they danced so well together, and so intimate were their tones of conversation that Tarquin began to fidget about and behave clumsily with his glass.

Chamberlain, who didn't live in the hotel himself, followed me to the lavatory, and kept me talking, his eyes shining with excitement.

"What do you think of Gracie?"

"Good enough fun. Not much of you, though."

"What do you mean?"

He laughed in my face, wrinkling up his nose. Not quite certain whether to be frank or not. As always he took the chance, however.

"This party of yours. An elaborate piece of self-gratification. You must always take it out of somebody, mustn't you? Life is one long revenge for your own shortcomings."

"You've been reading the Russians," I said. Nothing else. It was furiously annoying. I bowed and led him back to the circus. Tarquin was waterlogged by this time and ready to leave. Clare danced on in a kind of remote control, a social communion with Gracie. They hardly spoke at all, but there was an awareness, an ease between them I envied. A contact.

"Well, Grace, I'm going," said Chamberlain with good humor, shaking hands with her. To me, as he passed, he offered one word, in my private ear. "Sentimentalist." I confess it rankled.

That evening I took it out on Grace; appeased the rage that Chamberlain's little observation had bred in me. For a day or two everything about her seemed odious, *odious*.

But all this, one realizes, is simply writing down to one's subject from the heights of an intellectual superiority, *à la* Huxley. It is a trick to be played on anyone, but not on yourself. The intellectual superiority of the emotionally sterile. Because I am grateful to Grace, more grateful than inky words can express, whatever agony you inject into them. Yet the idea of an audience! The idea of anyone *knowing* that I felt such sentiments turned them at once crystal-cold. Changed them into a rage against my own emotional weakness. And thence into a rage against the object of that indulgence, yclept she. In retrospect the party explains itself simply enough. Was it possible that I felt anything for this little cockney child with her tedious humors, her spurious gentility? Quick, quick then, let me insult myself and her for such a lapse from the heights of intellectual purity of feeling. How we cherish the festering intelligence! But then again: feeling, if it is to be interpreted by emotion is not my province: at any rate if I am ever to write about it. For bad emotion can only produce the terrible squealing of the slaughtered pig—*De Profundis* is the sterling example. Let us thank God therefore, that I do not try to squeeze out such pus on to handmade paper. I shirk the epitaph for Grace, not because she wouldn't understand it, but because I dare not write it.

The carapace of the rational intelligence! I think the reason I loved Grace so much was because I could escape from myself with her. The cage I inhabited was broken wide open by our experience.

She was not audience enough for me to hate her. Yet, writing nicely, "love" is not the correct word. For a man like me does not need love in the accepted sense. There should be another word to express this very real state. One hardly knows how to do it without the key word to the situation. Let me leave a blank space and proceed.

Why and how Gracie supplied this provender, it would take me an eon to write. Her idiocy! Her uncomprehending urbanity! Above all, her stupidity! Yes, her stupidity made me feel safe, within my own depth. It was possible to give myself to her utterly. My desire was as unqualified by fear and mistrust as hers was by intelligence. Sometimes, sitting there on the bed with her, playing foolish kindergarten games with her, I used to imagine what would happen if suddenly she turned before my eyes into one of those precise female dormice of the upper classes with whom only my limitations express themselves. A weird feeling. I had, after all, utterly committed myself: and the idea of Grace turning into a she-Judas before my eyes was frightening. Imagine a Croydon Juliet, secure in her knowledge of exactly what *was* sacred and profane love, rising up from my own sofa and scourging me! The cracking whips of outraged romance! (No. No. Preserve us from the ostrich.)

Must I confess, then, that the secret of our love was the vast stupidity of Grace and the huge egotism and terror of myself? These were the hinges on which our relationship turned. You see, I could not *tell* her I adored her. No. My love expressed itself in a devious ambiguous way. My tongue became a scourge to torment not only myself but also the object of my adoration. Another woman jeered at, whipped by syllables, addressed as "you bitch," "you slut," or "you whore," would have been clever enough to accept the terms for what they seemed worth. Who would have guessed that in using them I intended to convey only my own abject surrender? Only Gracie, of course, sitting in the corner of the sofa, very *grande dame* in my colored dressing gown, deaf and sightless, cocking her finger over a cup of tea! Who would have accepted an apparent hate and known it to be love? No one but Grace, my cinematic princess.

Chamberlain, when he called, was shocked by the knife-edge of cruelty that cut down into our social relations. He did not realize the depths of her insensitiveness. He only saw what seemed to him the wilful cruelty of myself. He did not realize that my viper's tongue would have withered in my mouth if set to pronounce a single conventional endearment, "my darling," or "my dear." No. I am that I am. The *senex fornicator* if you will. The lutin. *Nanus* or *pumilo*. Tourneur's "juiceless luxur," if you prefer it, but never the conventionalized gramophone-record lover. But I realize that even these weird colors are denied me by my acquaintances whose method is simply to reverse the romantic medallion and declare that what they see is the face of cynicism. "Dear Mr. Gregory," as someone said, "you're *such* a cynic," whatever she meant.

Imagination can depict continents, immense humid quags of matter where life pumps its lungs in a last spasm of being before passing down slowly, sponging away into its eternal type of mud. Things without souls which wander among the mossy stumps, hummingbirds, or pterodactyls with klaxon shrieks, blobs of sperm drying in crevices, or the nameless maculae lairing and clinching in mud to produce their type of solitariness. This in the realm of history when the children are sitting deafened by the silence, and the book empties itself out on the desk in many colored pictures. The carbon forests buried in their weeds and marshes. Pithecanthropus striking fire from a cobble. The rhino calling. The enigmatic fan of planets plotting its graph on the night. The first spark of history struck from a cobble while the ashes of our campfires soften and wrinkle. The children's faces like so many custards! The waters thawing, drawing back. The havoc of the ice ages set suddenly into gear. The earth begins its ablutions. The planets lick themselves clean. The mud of continents scraped, ploughed. Forests picked out and tossed into space like patches of fluff. Endless the migration of apes in little boats, with food and skins and nursery implements. Men with bronze and cattle paddling the Gulf Stream into chaos beside their dugged females. Oh, the terrible loneliness of the ape's mind to see the dawn sweep up from the poles in a prismatic snow, shivering a fan of colors. The flakes settling and thawing on the blue water of oceans. Behind them, lost in a void which has no location, a world: before them—what? The rim of water seeking away into the seasons, consuming time. No hand or olive branch to guide them. The snow ices their hairy shanks and the skins in which they huddle. . . .

It is like that, primordial in its loneliness, the mood in which I set out to meet you. The history is a sort of fake I invent all day among the children to nerve myself for our meetings. You are sitting out there, under the sweeping skyline of country, with time strapped to your wrist by a leather thong. At your back the airplane light swivels its reds and greens on to the grass in many hectic windmills. There is no object in life but to reach that lonely cigarette-point in the darkness. All day my own movements struggle toward the darkness. Immense massive maneuvers against time, so that I am like the underwater photos of a swimmer, parting the thick elements of gloom with slow hands toward the moment of meeting.

I am alive only in the soft glitter of the snow, the turning of switches, the labored churning of the self-starter. The engine coming awake under my slippered toe, the heavy metal personality of my partner. We are off on the murderous roads, the engine staggering, whining, hot with slipping from gear to accurate gear. The road opens like a throat at Elmer's End. I huddle nervously and press down my foot. Bang! down into the suburban country, among a rain of falling tombstones. A hailstorm of masonry falling away to one side. I am immune from danger at last. The lights are passing and falling away, like lambent yellow cushions, always flung, always falling short. Everything is gone at last, our failures, our shabby quarrels, time, illusion, the night, the frenzy, the hysteria. I am in the dark here in a metal shell, blinding away across the earth, these infinite lanes toward her.

Flesh robot with cold thighs and fingers of icicle gripping the wheel of the black car, everything is forgotten. It is no use telling me of her inadequacy, her limitations; no good saying her mouth is an ash tray crammed with the butts of reserve, funk, truism, revulsion. I admit it. I admit everything with a great grin of snow. But it is no use. If I can find her moist and open between two sheets anywhere among the seven winds, you can have everything that lives and agonizes between the twin poles. Seriously. I switch off the dashboard and let my soul ride out on to the dark, floating and quivering on the frosty air above the black car; my personality has been snipped from my body now, as if by scissors, to ride along the night wind against any cold star. Everything flows out of me in a long effortless catharsis, pours on to the darkness, licked by the airs. This is the meaning of freedom. My money has poured out of my pockets, my clothes fallen from me, every bit of tissue sloughed. Everything is clear in this struggle to reach her. The car humming like a top, stammering, banging round corners with its insane fixed eyes: the carpet of light racing along the dark arterial roads: the distance being patiently consumed. I am in a kind of fanatical imagery now, unreal, moving through this aquarium of feelings, conscious of nothing but the blood thinning in my veins, and the slow fearful heart.

We fall together like figures made of feathers, among the soft snowy dewlaps of the cattle, the steaming commotion of voices and cud. The loose black mouth with its voice of enormous volume. We are surrounded with friendly cattle like a Christmas card picture, on the ground, our bodies emptied out of their clothes. It is a new nativity when I enter her, the enormous city couched between her legs: or a frost-bound lake, absolutely aware of the adventurer, the pilgrim, the colonizer. The snow is falling in my mouth, my ears, my soaked clothes. This is a blunt voyage of the most exquisite reckoning. Enter. She has become an image in rubber, not the smallest bone which will not melt to snow under the steady friction of the penis. The hot thaw spreads raw patches of grass under us: every abstraction now is bleeding away into the snow—death, life, desire. It is so fatal, this act among the cattle. We are engrossed bobbins on a huge loom of terror, knowing nothing, wishing to know nothing of our universe, its machinery. When she comes it's all pearls and icicles emptied from her womb into the snow. The penis like a dolphin with many muscles and black humor, lolling up to meet the sun. The fig suddenly broken into a sticky tip that is all female. She is laughing hideously. The car is standing among the cattle, no less intelligent than they. Under me is no personality any more but a composite type of all desire. Enter. I do not recognize my arctic sister. Under my heart the delicate tappets of a heart: my penis trapped in an inexorable valve, drawing these shapes and chords out of me inexhaustible, like toothpaste. The cattle are kindly and interested in a gentlemanly way: the car urbane as a metal butler. Under my thews, trapped in bracts and sphincters, a unique destruction. She is weeping. Her spine has been liquefied, drawn out of her. She is filleted, the jaw telescoped with language, eyes glassy. Under my mouth a rouged vagina speaking a barbaric laughter and nibbling my tongue. It is all warm and raw: a spiritual autumn with just that scent of corruption, that much death in it, to make it palatable. A meal of game, well-hung pig-scented tangy. Such a venison, more delicate than the gums of babies or little fishes. Open to me once like that and the poles are shaken out of their orbits, the sky falls down in a fan of planets. I am the owner of the million words, the ciphers, the dead vocabularies. In this immense ceiling of swansdown there is nothing left but a laughter that opens heaven: a half-life, running on the batteries. I am eating the snow and drinking your tears. Stand against the hedge to snivel and make water while the shivers run down your spine. You are beautiful all of a sudden. Your fear makes me merry. *A very merry Christmas to you and yours.* I am saying it insanely over and again. A very merry Christmas to you and yours. She runs at me suddenly with blunt fists raised, shouting wildly. Enormous dark eyes with the green and red lights growing from them. The cattle draw back softly on the carpet. Her tears punch little hot holes in the snow. I am happy. You will go about from now on with an overripe medlar hanging out between your legs: your womb burst like the tip of the Roman fig. But even this brutality goes when I feel the bones against me, malleable and tender as gum: the eager whimpering animal dressed in cloth opening up to me, wider and wider, softer than toffee, until the bland sky is heavy with falling feathers, angels, silk, and there is a sword broken off softly in my bowels. I am lying here quite ruined, like a basketful of spilt eggs, but happy. Vulnerable, but lying in you here, at peace with myself: the tides drawing back from me, gathering up the dirt and scurf of things, the thawed pus and venom, and purifying me. I am at peace. It is all falling away from me, the whole of my life emptied out in you like a pocketful of soiled pennies. The faces of the world, Lobo and Marney, the children, Peters, the car, Gracie, the enormous snow, statues, history, mice, divinity. It is forever, you are saying wildly, with green lips, red lips white lips, blue lips, green lips. It is forever. Our lives stop here like a strip of cinema film. This is an eternal still life, in the snow, two crooked bodies, eating the second of midnight and sniveling. We will die here in this raw agony of convalescence, by the icebound lake, the city lying quiet among its litter of whimpering, blind steeples.

They must be saying good nights now all over the world. I am saying good-bye to part of my life, no, part of my body. It is irrational. I do not know what to say. If I take your hand it is my own hand I am kissing. The aquarium again, with everything slowed down to the tempo of deep water. Good-bye to my own body under the windmill, weeping in the deep snow, nose, ankle, wrist made of frosty iron again. Help me. O eloquent just and mighty death. The great anvil of the frost is pounding us. The cattle are afraid. Let me put my hand between your legs for warmth. Speak to my fingers with your delicate mouth, your pillow of flesh. I am a swimmer again, moving in a photograph with great, uncertain, plausible gestures toward you.

I have said good night and drawn the car out slowly homeward. There is no feeling in my hands or feet. As though the locomotive centers had been eaten away. Tired. . . .

Here Gregory ends.

Shadows in ink. The hotel with its blue shadows in snow. The convalescent blue of phthisis. Brother, I'll be that strange composed fellow. In the darkness they hang out Japanese lanterns for the festivals. In the pandemonium of the ballroom the bunting sliding the floor in a long swoon of color. Antiques gyrating forever, pictured by the mirrors in their gilt scrolls. The jazz band plugging away in the din: and in the barrage of drunkenness our hearts ticking over, squashed upon each other's in pain. Darkness cut and blanched by the trembling spotlights, seeking the winners. You with the silver mouth and devil's eyeteeth I could rive; press my arm into the arch of the backbone until the lean breastless body thawed and melted, pouring over me in a wave, like lighted oil on water. I locate this night dimly as the one where Lobo sat out in the rainy gardens, under a striped awning, making Miss Venable weep. Onward. Onward.

It is so silent here at night. This tomb of masonry hems us in, drives us in on ourselves. Ourselves! I am getting a little like Gregory, rolling the heavy chainshot of the ego about with him, prisoner. Here in these metal provinces, we are like dead cats bricked in the Wall of China. The winds turn aside from us in the dead land, the barren latitudes. I tell you the trams plough their furrows every day, but nothing springs from them. The blind men walk two by two at Catford.

Overhead in the darkness the noiseless rain is shining down over the counties. The pavements are thawing back to black asphalt. In this room the madness has set in, goading Lobo to finish the chart. Delicate, the dark gigolo Clare treads the mushy street, cloaked and hatted, to a dancing engagement. The heavy signature of the mist glazes the dumb domes of the Crystal Palace: the final assured vulgar mark of Ruskin's world on history. In Peru they hurry to early mass. The streets are baked. The peasants stand with their lice and sores and almonds in the church doorways. And his girl—ah! his hot little Latin world of little black men. If for a second he could reach her across the chart, across the bottles of ink, across the cockatoo on his pencil box cigarettes, shopgirls, frost, wind, tramlines, England—if he could only seize her and escape. . . .

Black Latin Whore! We, sentimental, send our desires to you across the sea like many furling gulls. But after Dover imagination fails. The gulls waver, tremble, fall: are sponged out by the mists. . . .

In the saloon bar, Connie, the brewer's widow, awaits Clare. (One of her frilled garters hangs over Lobo's bed—a gravely humorous present from one libertine to another.)

Connie possesses thighs like milk churns. Her mouth is an old comb full of many sawn-off teeth. Her laughter sets the froth dancing in her mustache. Dancing with Clare she sweats like a sentimental seal under the armpits, pants, moans, a little sentimental when the word love arrives in the tunes. Offer her a beer and she will sit up and bark like a sea lion. You could balance a glass on her nose as she sits there militarily, her behind overlapping the swivel stool. She sits down on her vulva. Watch her now. So. The circular head of the bar stool is applied to her bottom: penetrates the soft swathes of blubber: disappears. Infinite subterranean shuffling. One imagines the warm endless penetration of the padded stool in her viscera. "Jesus, she's well sprung," says Perez. Then the springs tighten. Giggling, she is sitting up there on her own neck. Her eyebrows perform gigantic arcs across the night. She is gay ha ha. The tank is full of ha ha. She loves the warm herded smell of males in the saloon, wet overcoats and whiskers, rich smell of steam and underclothes and armpits. She has been married twice. Barroom gallantries. "Oh, *do* 'ave another glass of beer, miss." And the shrill draughts of piss from the urinal which come in at the swing-doors. Men, men, men—how she loves the warm smell of herded males! She could take a man in each arm and slobber on him with that wet mouth of hers. She could slip a thick finger in their flies and tickle them. But Clare? He excites that superficial side of her which wants Romance. Oh! the sleek lateral waves in his hair. Oh! the delicate Levantine manners (how painfully acquired by post and study). Clare sucks little purple cachous that his breath, when he blows it on her, may be nothing less than royal honeydew. All the perfumes of Arabia cannot rinse the gin from it however. He dances gravely with her, leaning on her whizzing exuberant tits with a sort of locomotive paralysis. Thumping, her great thighs propel them. Vast effort, as if they were dancing under water: spurning the floor, the walls, the band, the rotating glass dome which shivers splinters of prismatic light across the dancers. Gin brings out the pussy in her. Gin, and Clare's hoarse crooning. He knows the words to all the tunes. His hand is palm outward on her spine, a genteel Edwardianism.

Connie's eyes are glazed. For the last hour or so she has been diminishing: become steadily more diminutive and pussy-cat. In the interval, downing her beer, she has become a child of twelve again. "Hair down to here," she yelps, striking her arse, "but me mother took it all off. The dirty old sow." Dancing again, her intimacies are outrageous—even here. She has shrunk up on his breast like a wee girl now: like a bird nestling on his necktie. She peeks up at him with a panting smile, her little lascivious bud of lips pursed up. She can feel it stirring down there, like a live thing. The tight rod he has in his trousers now. She is diminishing, melting down, thawing. Ah! she is such a thumping, swollen, fourteen-stone, *weeny* little thing!

In the lobby she puts her hand on him. "You've got it," she says nervously, as if he might be playing a trick on her. There might be nothing in there. "You've got it, haven't you, ducky? Oo I can't wait."

Afterward he will have to take her home and undress her, layer by layer. She will lie, like the Indian Ocean waiting for him—one vast anticipating grin, above and below!

Shadows in ink, and the strange composure of syllables. The quilt lies heavier on my bones than any six-foot earth. I am living out hours which no chronology allows for. Which no clock marks. If I say I love you I am using an idiom too soiled to express this cataclysm of nerves: this cataract of white flesh and gristle which opens new eyes inside me. I am opened suddenly like the valve of a flower, sticky, priapic: the snowdrop or the anemone brushing the warm flanks of Lesbos. A dæmonic pansy opening to the sun, stifled in its own pollen.

The delicate shoots are growing from my throat. From the exquisite pores of the membrane the soft vagina of the rose, with the torpedo hanging in it. The furred lisping torpedo of the bee. O God.

It is above all the silence which is remarkable. The last train to the world's end has gone. The last bus skirts Croydon or Penge—what matter? In the tram terminus the deserted trams lie, their advertisements quenched in the smoky gloom. Coralled like horses they await the milk-can morning. Lochia. Rags of blown paper writhe among the snow. The dirty skeletons of the day's news. There is not even a prostitute to brighten the cavernous roads. Hilda has gone. A real old-timer, the only one. Married a commercial traveler to give the fetus a name and status. Status! Extraordinary how sensitive she can be. Alas, poor Hilda. A raven of excellent jest, Horatio. The way she breathed beer and onions on one: the great cheesy whiffs of damp that blew among her clothes! As for the wretched fetus, if it could have spoken through its gills it would probably have dealt as curtly with its ancestry as Gregory. "My parentage is Scotch, if you must know. Well, northern. I am not sure, really. I am sure of so little. At any rate *my soul* wears tartan!"

Hilda, at any rate, swaggering up and down the bed in her pink cotton kilt—Hilda, with the great hanging sporran of red hair over her pelvis! A raven of excellent jest! Perez would take handfuls of this rufous pelt up in one hand and blow on it playfully. "What have we here, Hilda? Feathers, my love?" Hilda with the great voice like a bass viol rasping out command and insinuation. Her gas-lit bed is a parade-ground, a barrack square; her voice is all history rolled and boomed and rapped out in one's ears.

Like a gaunt rat she lived between the pub and the tobacconist. In the snow she scuttled across the road splayfooted, ducking under the lights of snoring cars, to buy herself a packet of fags. Hilda, the fag end of the sentimental dreams I cherish! The memory of her is a sort of scarification, like wounds the aborigines keep open on their bodies, rubbing irritants into them, reopening them until the resulting ornament is something to make the whole tribe envious.

Hilda a-decorating Newcastle. I imagine vaguely docks. Hilda among the lights and tar and feather sailor boys: the whole fairyland of breathing steeples. Forsaken, a gaunt rat by the water. All night the lick and splash of inky silk. Pillowed on the flood's broad back, the elastic steeples inhale and exhale their panorama. Morning. The child miscarried, and shortly after the legendary husband died. Perez, her only real friend, has got a letter from her, incoherent, blaring, tear-stained. A poem on violet paper with an anchor for a watermark. We still read it aloud when we want a good hysterical laugh. Hilda, and her rich pithecanthropoid contortions! Here, under white ceiling, planning an equipment of words to snare these hours which are so obviously secure from the dragnets of language: lying here, what sort of elegy can one compose for Hilda, for Connie, for the whole rabble of cinematic faces whose history is the black book? Shall we people a catacomb with their portraits? The last tram has gone. The epoch from which this chronicle is made flesh, when I think of it, is an explosion. My lovely people like so many fragments of an explosion already in flight—Hilda among them, flying like a heavy bomb, northward to Newcastle. Madame About died in 1929 of uterine cancer. I, said the sparrow, with my bow and arrow. Tarquin died quietly while he was pouring himself a cup of tea: and showed up for dinner without a trace of his death on his face. Scrase, the golden-haired son of a cash register, himself hard and tight as a fistful of blond cash, was emptied out of the autumn sky to keep company with Icarus. In the snow there is a hail and farewell for Perez, for Lobo, for Chamberlain . . .

Am I the angel with shining wrists scraping out their microscopic beauties in God's ink? The shirted cherubin! See, I take a mouthful of ink and blow it out in many colors at the sky. From that fragile column fall one or two figures—these my shining darlings!

Let me tell you a little about Kate, as soberly as fits a condemned man. Firstly, I am very happy. I have poured out my decisions like small change, and selected one clean new sixpence. Kate is the lousiest, tightest, dumb and most devaluated sixpence that ever came from the mint. Let me not affect this bitterness. It is not real.

When I think about Kate I am as dumb and passive as a bullock. It is the only solution really, the only way out. In Bournemouth, walking the streets, while the rain pronged the lights and houses, the whole shape of my future rose up and choked me. In the municipal library I found myself all of a sudden sitting with a book on oceanography open in front of me. I was looking for the Logos. The face of

the squid attracted me. Later, in a cosy little bar parlor the face of
Kate was the face of the same squid I had seen on the title page of the
tome.

We got into conversation in quite a classy way. She trod on my
foot and said she was sorry. I knocked her glass against her teeth and
said I was sorry. "We seem to be in a proper pickle tonight," she
observed. When I agreed she went on to make sundry trite observations about the weather, etc. "Are you staying long?" she asked.
"Down here for a spree?" I explained that I was down here with a
dead wife, and was immediately taken in hand. I was mothered. It
was tedious but pleasant. Being a widow she felt herself competent to
deal with a strong man's grief. We went to cinemas together, flirted
mildly too. This, she gave me to understand, was what all widowers
did. They felt so lonely. She was a knowing little thing. "Don't you
worry, chicken," she said, patting my thigh, "I won't snatch you."
"Don't call me chicken."

"Okay, chicken."

She knew all about men. Her husband had been one. But her
honor would not stoop to mere bawdry out of wedlock. "'ere," she
said modishly, knocking my hand away. "Lay off that mucking
about. I'm not one of those."

"O, but you are, Katie. You are a proper one. I have never seen
such a one in my life." She could never make out whether I was
sneering at her or not. However, it seemed unlikely to her way of
thinking. It was just my way, she used to titter. I liked to have her
on. Dilating those hard eyes of hers she would put her face close to
mine and titter. Immediately the humorous squid would come to life
in her.

Do you find Kate a bit of a puzzle? Here, I put her photograph
before you. A trim little craft with that predatory squid's jowls. Brass
wouldn't melt in her mouth. You can see at a glance that here is
someone who knows right from wrong. You are still puzzled? I will
explain. I chose Gracie, because she was, as women go, extraordinary.
With Kate, I employed the method so much in vogue with the writers
of best sellers. I chose her because she was the most ordinary person
I could find. If I had not met her I should have had to go into a bank.
Kate is the sanctuary which I have been wanting for so long. When
I saw the little house, with its cheap and hideous furniture, the
linoleum floors, the garish cushions, I said to myself: I am home at

last. Sitting in my slippers under a steel engraving of Holman Hunt, feeling the damp sprouts of flame from the gas fire warm my trouser legs, I said to myself: This is my sanctuary. Hereafter I shall bury myself beside the wireless, behind a paper. Kate shall minister to my soul with a meat and two veg, and leave me to my private battle with God. This is deadly true. Kate is the monastery in which I am about to be interned. I have nothing to say to her, nothing in common with her. I have given up all those childish nostrums and charms with which I hoped to find salvation for so long. Hush, I say to myself, from now I am going to lie in secrecy. A pre-diluvial secrecy. No demands will be made of me in this private madhouse. Kate's husband gave her so little that she expects nothing from me. An orgasm, for instance. She does not know what that is, has never experienced it. I will take good care that she never does. She has a deep-seated nervous grudge against men, the dirty brutes. This will ensure the sacred void between our stars. She lies under one with that white, painful, Christian face of hers, and puts up with the more loathsome side of the business with the air of a real stoic. It does my heart good to see it. I need fear no intrusions, no wringing of hands or bowels.

Tomorrow I will go unto my father, by the four-fourteen. I will be met at the station. I can see it all, I can taste the manna in my mouth. The smoky little road with the hoops of iron round their dreary hutches. Home! The segment of sopping grass outside the greenhouse. The one sick dwarf apple. We shall sit down in the kitchen by the range and eat dinner together—she very wise and skittish and hard as a bell. And with our knives shall we scrape the rich brown dripping from the pudding basin, and smear it on our bread.

"Everything fair and square," is her motto. She is a great believer in the equality of the sexes. She shall pay for herself wherever she goes, even at the cinema.

There will never be any question of personalities, because she is too much of a lady. I shall never be lonely because there will be no relief from loneliness. Chamberlain used to say: "Let us have more of the metaphysical beast, Gregory. Come on, gird up the loins of anger." I am weary of the cult of bowel-worship. Weary, utterly weary and sick from my very soul. All these pious resolutions have bled themselves empty in me. If there were an organized religion which were strong enough to grip me I would welcome it. There is something in me, I know, that must be chipped away, like dead mastoid. But I shall not bother to fight for it. The struggle is too hideous, the inner extraction of dead selves, like giant festering molars, is too too painful. Let be, and suffer the disease to run its course. From now on my hands are folded across my breast. Let the grass grow under my tongue, between my teeth, let the scabs form on my eyeballs, let the buboes burst between my toes, I shall not lift a finger.

This is the going down toward the tomb. The weather has been, on the whole, very fair. There is a slight belt of pressure settled round the south coast of Ireland, but who cares about that? Fair to fine is the general forecast, with slight local showers, and sensational fluctuations of bullion. The pork trade is doing well. The ductless glands are in training earlier this year, under a new coach. Their time from Hammersmith to Putney is already doubled. It is hoped that they will carry off the Ashes this year without any difficulty. At a twelfth reading, the bill for the distribution of more milk to pregnant members of Parliament was carried by a majority of twelve. Mr. Baldwin concurred. Altogether the outlook is magnificent for the coming year, with a definite promise of worse to follow. Stocks are falling owing to a recent eruption of Mount Rothermere, but hopes are rising. Recent excavations in Fleet Street have been suspended owing to a discharge of speckled venom. However, business proceeds as usual, with slight tremors.

Lobo is having a terrible time, they tell me. He is in love, and is finding it painful. While he was abroad he met a German girl, a pneumatic Teuton frau, of the love me or leave me breed, who held him down with her thumb and gave him something to think about. He spends all night weeping for his sins. "I have not been an angel," he says, rolling his sore, swollen eyes. He is in two minds about cutting himself. He wants to marry her, but how can he? Such a foul, leprous little whoremonger as he is—can he marry a fine pure seafaring blonde? If she found out about him she would go into a monastery. And then he would have to go into a monastery too to equalize things. And if he does marry her, how can he keep away from prostitutes and enthusiastic amateurs? They are in his blood. "I am a dirty leetle leecher," he says wildly, beating his thigh. "I was a pure Catholic once until that woman got me. Since then I have been thirsty . . . like thirst, you understand?" I understand. She taught him many peculiar refinements, did his friendly widow. She used to say, "Better to keep the shoes on when you do it. It is better shoes and long black stockings."

From my present sumptuous boredom I sit and laugh at Lobo through the bars. What a droll little ape. I can no longer even be amused by his antics. Tarquin can be funny when he squalls and whines, but Lobo—no, I have put away my microscope for good.

I can hear the train wheels beating their rhythmic revolutions in my head as I write. The four-fourteen carrying me homeward to the slippers, the gas fire, the paper, the dripping, the text on the wall. And Kate waiting for me, trim and cheaply scented in her Marks & Spencer knickers. Done up in colored crinkles for me like a cheap cake of aromatic soap. We stand together before the deputy of God, and partake of a manly little service for the connubial felicities to be legalized. Dear Kate, like a canvas doll in bed with a white stoic face, whetting the appetites of cruelty in her brand new hubby. And all these acres of tragic struggles, of boredoms, despairs, delusions, will fall from me as I enter my prison. The ubiety of God. The fantastic zero to which I shall reduce the terms of living and so find happiness. The slow gradual ascent into silence, into dumbness. Why do we fear the modern world? Why are we afraid of becoming insects? I can imagine no lovelier goal. The streets of Paradise are not more lovely than the highways of the ant heap. I shall become a white ant, God willing. I shall have my swink to me reserved and nothing else. Let the hive take my responsibilities. I am weary of them.

This is the meaning of the smashed etchings in the grate. The dislocated books. The large red discs. From the wreckage, however, I have saved certain things that have the death in them. These I will give to Tarquin to assist his disease to kill him. To sew the tares of a greater madness inside that great throbbing egglike cranium of his. Anything with the real taint in it, the real green gangrene. Peace on earth and good will to men. But I speak after the manner of men. I am in the grip of this slow suppurative hate, which lingers in the provinces, planted in our nerve centers. Fiber by fiber it has eaten into us. Whether I shall yet escape its ultimates—rape, havoc, murder, lust—this remains to be seen. It seems to me at times that these narrow wrists moving here are the wrists of a murderer.

I, Death Gregory, by the Grace of God, being sound in mind and body, do make and ordain this my last will and testament, in the manner and form following, revoking all other wills heretofore made.

The bequests have been carefully weighed. To the literary man I leave my breath, to fertilize his discussions, and cool his porridge. To lady novelists and chambermaids my tongue. It still retains a little native salt. To poetry a new suit of clothes. To the priest the kiss of Judas, my cosmic self. To the pawnbroker my crucifix. To Tarquin my old tin cuff links, and to Lobo the worn out contraceptive outfit, with all good wishes. To the English nation I leave a pair of old shoes, gone at the uppers, and a smell on the landing. If they want my heart to bury beside Ben Jonson in the Abbey, they can dive for it. To God I dedicate my clay pipe and copy of the *Daily Express*, and my expired season ticket. To my mother I offer my imperishable soul. It has never really left her keeping. To Fanny my new set of teeth, and a bottle of the hair restorer which didn't work. To my father a copy of *The Waste Land* and a kiss on his uncomprehending, puzzled face. To my charlady I leave all those books in which the soul of man is evolved through misery and lamentation. She will find them incomprehensible. To the young poets I offer my sex, since they can make no better use of their own. To the journalists my voice to assist them in their devotions. To lap dogs my humanity. To best sellers and other livers off garbage, my laughter in the key of E flat, and the clippings of my toenails. To the government my excrement that it may try its sense of humor. To the critics what they deserve; and to the public their critics.

To Gracie the following items: a cross section of my liver, an embryo torn quivering from the womb, a book of sermons, a tea-dance, a dark partner, love-in-the-mist, passion and mockery, the laughter of the gulls, eyelids, nettles, snuff, and a white sister to sponge her gaunt thighs when the night falls.

And now it is time to take the long leavetaking of ink and paper, and all the curious warm charities which have been corrupted by bile and ruined by men with the faces of cattle. Mantic, the dream-self projects this vast saturnine grin across the taut cosmos. I see men and women again, moving softly with expressive hands across the floor of the mind's sunken oceans. Softly and dreadfully in their voicelessness. The strange dumb movements of plants under water, among the blithe cuttlefish and wringing octopods, and the forests of gesturing trees. What I had to offer I gave gladly. It was not enough. What remains is my own property. To the darling of the gods I give

the long warm gift of action. It was no use to me.

I shall be sitting here when they find me at midnight, watching the laughter stiffen and crumble with the ashes in the grate. It will not be difficult. A brush and pan will be all that's needed. I shall sift gently into fragments as I am offered to the plangent dustbins. The record and testament of a death within life: a life in death.

To these tedious pages, which I shall burn before I leave, I offer the gift of life and the reality of the imagination: the colors of charity and love without bitterness. A sop to kill the worm which fattens in them. A few grains of honesty. And a last phoenix act of revelation among greater beauties, in this iron grate.

And to myself? I offer only the crooked grin of the toad, and a colored cap to clothe my nakedness. I have need of them both. Amen.

LAWRENCE DURRELL

When The Black Book *was first published, Durrell had not yet achieved international acclaim for his* Alexandria Quartet. *Although it was written in 1936, it was not made available in the United States until 1960, when it was apparently felt that the author had attained sufficient stature so that his early work, or such of it as was necessary to a better understanding of his literary development, should be published.*

Durrell was only twenty-four when he wrote The Black Book; *looking back from a vantage point a quarter century removed in time, Durrell wrote, in his Preface to the 1960 American edition:*

"This novel—after twenty-odd years—still has a special importance for me and may yet leave its mark upon the reader who can recognize it for what it is: a two-fisted attack on literature by an angry young man of the thirties. . . . With all its imperfections lying heavy on its head, I can't help being attached to it, because in the writing of it I first heard the sound of my own voice, lame and halting perhaps, but nevertheless my very own. This is an experience no artist ever forgets—the birth cry of a newly born baby of letters, the genuine article. The Black Book *was truly an agon for me, a savage battle conducted in the interests of self-discovery. It built itself out of a long period of despair and frustration during which I knew that my work, though well-contrived, was really derivative. It seemed to me that I would never discover myself, my private voice and vision. At the age of twenty-four things usually look black to one!*

The very quality of this despair drove me to try and break the mummy wrappings—the cultural swaddling clothes which I symbolized here as "the English Death"; simply in order to see whether there was anything inside me worth expressing. I wanted to break free, to try my hand at a free book. . . .

Of course, the book is only a savage charcoal sketch of spiritual and sexual etiolation, but it is not lacking in a certain authority of its own despite the violence of its execution. Underneath the phantas-

magoria real values are discussed, real problems of the Anglo-Saxon psyche articulated and canvassed. All this has nothing to do, of course, with purely literary merit, which is not for me to discuss. But The Black Book *staged a slender claim for me and encouraged me to believe that I was perhaps a real writer, and not just a word spinner of skill.*

I realized that the crudity and savagery of the book in many places would make its publication in England difficult. I did not wish for notoriety, and was content simply to have heard my own voice. I knew that a sensitive reader would find that the very excesses of the writing were an organic part of the experience described; and indeed a friendly critic of the book once wrote to me: 'Yes, I admit that I was shocked and disgusted here and there, but I read it without prejudice and in the light of the central intention. The crudities match and belong. I have never understood why a writer should not be regarded by the reader as enjoying much the same rights as doctors. You do not suspect indecency in a doctor who asks you to strip in order to examine you. Why shouldn't you give the writer the same benefit of the doubt? . . .' "

Harriet Daimler & Henry Crannach

THE PLEASURE THIEVES

*A*n elegantly dressed elderly woman sat before a mirror in an exclusive custom jeweler's salon admiring an extravagant pear-shaped necklace placed around her well-concealed neck. The thin masculine hands that took the glittering string from the black velvet box belonged to the dapper proprietor, Boris Novak.

"Or," he reached for a white placard on which there was a meticulous representation in India ink of a replica-size necklace, "without pendant."

She studied the gems for a second while the jeweler showed a detached, respectful interest in the design. "That is really very nice, what would the piece come to?"

"With pendant, I should say about forty carats, Madame Rothman."

She smiled and turned to the glass again, "I suppose it might be cheaper to buy a new neck, Monsieur Novak?"

"Madame Rothman, everyone has a neck."

As he spoke a young man, dressed very much like Monsieur Novak, approached them across the deep piled carpet. His place in the salon was definitely subservient; with his immaculate tasteful dress it was hard to imagine that he had another interest besides his duties at the salon. He hummed softly, to warn Monsieur Novak that he was coming across the room. The dapper proprietor made all his employees hum so that his elegance would not be shattered by a surprise approach across the thick muffled rugs. Neurotic, he admitted, but with the refined tastes and delicate sensibilities that accompanied his character, necessary.

"I beg your pardon, Monsieur Novak," the young man courteously interrupted, "but you have a very urgent call."

Monsieur Novak looked solicitously at his client and begged to be excused for a moment. Madame Rothman looked dreamily after him as though he were a lover she dared not part with. He charmed this type of rapport into his clientele. "It must always be there," he coached the novices who worked for him, "they must think that they are being presented with a gift such as a King gives to his Queen."

"Richard. Care for Madame Rothman, will you? and oh yes, please change the tune you're humming today." He winked at Madame Rothman, "I suppose you find me a bit eccentric?" He crossed the room briskly leaving his precious client giggling like a young hen, happily guarded by a little boy blue. When he was gone, she studied the image of the necklace in the glass more intensely, her mouth a colorless smile of greed.

Inside his soundproof inner office, the face of Monsieur Novak became expressionless. He sat down behind his empty mahogany desk. Beyond the half-open door he studied Madame Rothman and Richard gallantly attending to her. He picked up the white receiver.

"Hello."

"Boris, this is Carol."

Carol Stoddard, on the other end, leaned back in the modern precariously balanced chair that matched her blonde woman's desk. The pastel decor was a woman's dream, exactly what it was supposed to be. Carol edited for Femme Publications, and they were in the business to furnish dreams for unimaginative femmes all over the country. Every month or so Carol started a minor revolution by explaining "pink is the color this season," or, "ladies, we're dressing formal for the evenings." The office was indeed not an office but a chic woman's boudoir, and all the advertisers felt flattered to be invited there. They remembered to lower their voices to the charming blonde woman pretending to do business behind the white desk. So business, with lowered voices, prospered, and avid subscribers knew when to wear pink.

The office bedroom had a huge velvet-covered studio couch and soft indirect lights. Sometimes, when all the others had left for the evening Carol would remain to work. She and the night watchman would alone keep life in the glass skyscraper.

On the desk top before her were the second phone and three cover layouts, each featuring the word "Femme," and a vase of beautiful long-stemmed roses. She plucked one from the vase and held it to her cheek with one hand, the phone in the other. She watched her secretary pin some reproductions on a large wide, hewn-edge, black cork board, studious catch-all crowded with line drawings, gouaches, a tiny antique petit point evening bag and countless reminder notes pinned afresh each day. There was a note on the board today that was somewhat more special than the rest, an address she had obtained through an unusual source. Her pulse quickened at the remembrance of the address. Carol had a cool blonde attractiveness. Her speech and gestures, not vivacious, involuntarily held the stamp of good breeding with unconventional prettiness.

At the sound of Boris' voice she tightened her hold on the rose in her hand.

"I think I'll be seeing you soon, Boris."

"That is good news," he said warmly. "It happens I'm having difficulty finding sixteen matched two-carat blues; if something could be done about it, that would be particularly advantageous right now."

"No doubt," she replied with a sardonic twinge to her voice. "You know I'll certainly keep it in mind, darling."

"Yes, Carol dear, please do, see you soon."

They said their goodbyes simultaneously. Carol was free to think of her secret address pinned on the cork board, she placed her rose back in the vase and came out from behind the desk. Boris, on the other hand, remained thoughtfully in his chair as he watched Richard come toward him humming a more pleasing tune. "Back in business again," he mused. "This should be most interesting."

"Mr. Novak, sorry to disturb you, but Madame Rothman is anxious to keep her luncheon engagement and is wondering if you have a blank check for her to fill out."

Carol looked at her watch. She had made the appointment for one o'clock, it would be all right if she was there a few minutes late, but to avoid any chance of embarrassment she had better leave now, to be sure the same person would take care of her. Things must move along as smoothly as possible, and Carol had a facility for seeing that things were done the simplest, most intelligent way.

Outside the office the usual lunch hour rush was on. People dashing to their business lunches, some were grabbing for the check, others sat coyly. It made no difference who picked it up, none of them were paying, it was all good old management behind them making it possible for more executives to have more luxurious indigestion at its expense.

Carol waited patiently on the corner of 57th and Madison Avenue. She hailed a cab, "Who the hell invented the expense account anyway?" she wondered entering the taxi.

"I beg your pardon, ma'am, but what did you say?" Carol laughed to herself. "Overwork," she thought, then she reached into her bag for the piece of paper that had been tacked to the cork board for a few days. Why hadn't she memorized the address by now?—she certainly should figure that one out.

The taxi dropped her in the downtown east side of Manhattan. Odd twisting little tenement streets, fronted by shabby stores selling candy and cigarettes. Then there was the store that had an exotic floral drape across the window and gypsies sitting inside, holding babies on their knees waiting to tell someone's fortune. She found her number.

In the window of this shop were one or two broken porcelain dolls with real hair wigs, a few toy animals with human hair that looked like fur. Everything was badly faded.

The store itself was completely bare, dirty gray shelves filled with colorless boxes, some wrapped in brown paper. Behind the shelves she could hear two people talking, a sewing machine being used. No one came out immediately. As she waited to be noticed, the atmosphere of the place oppressed her; it was indefinable—she had been in some pretty strange environments in her time, but now she wanted to be back in the frantic spin of Madison Avenue, running to the office to meet the deadline.

A man appeared from the rear. He was a bit messy, nondescript except for a smooth glassy, bald head.

"Mr. Gasper?" Carol asked hesitatingly.

"Yes."

"Remember me, you came to my office one day and I ordered something from you, I believe today it was to be ready."

"Yes of course," he said this evenly without expression. "I have your merkin right here."

Carol weakened at the mention of that word. The dusty air caught the sound and in her mind she repeated several times "Merkin, merkin—what an evil sound it has, disgusting, and he dared to say it, and in front of me."

Mr. Gasper disappeared into the back of the shop and quickly came out with a small anonymous brown package.

"I believe you have already paid me, Miss. You could try it on here, only it's not a wise thing to do; if in any way the merkin is not perfectly suited call me immediately."

She received the package mechanically and stared rather dumbfounded at Mr. Gasper. She wanted to run from the store but he continued talking to her in his unemotional insurance salesman way.

"Of course, it isn't often I receive calls for this sort of thing, it is a bit rare, particularly in this day and age, but I assure you it is for this reason that I have taken exceptional pains with yours."

"Thank you and good day," Carol said imitating the monotony of his voice.

She walked swiftly out of the obscure section into a larger thoroughfare and hailed a taxi. To get away, just get away to the sterile safety of Femme.

Carol dismissed her secretary for the day, everyone was finished up and going home. She would stay at the office tonight for several reasons, a pretense of work to be done on the closing issue, and she had to be sure she was entirely alone when she opened the little brown package.

Dinner was sent up to her before the building was closed for the night. Eating the delicacies, a small bottle of excellent dry Riesling, a roast chicken, she felt secure: calls could not come into the office at this hour. She approved some proofs held before her blind eyes. She walked about the room, stretching languidly, the wine had tasted good and helped to relax her. She switched on the radio, it played softly, corny mood music, but pleasant she thought. In a large square mirror she caught her reflection, walked up close to it and stared at herself. "Yes, I am attractive, I forget this once in a while, I forget about all my equipment." She put her hands over her breasts, the round softly supple mounds felt good under her touch. The nipples bounced out into her hands, they were hard and rubbery. She ran her hands down her stomach, turned sideways and gazed at her thighs in the mirror. "I should lose a bit of weight there." Femme Publications disdained heavy thighs. She stood directly in front of the mirror now and pulled off her cashmere sweater and brassiere. She placed her hands on her breasts again, the skin was softer than the cashmere of her sweater. The rouge-color nipples begging to be licked off. She put one hand down inside her panties and felt the burning fever. She stripped off the rest of her clothing and tried to keep her hands off her body for a second. She stood in front of the mirror, naked, her wavy blonde hair perfectly combed, every hair in place, not now, not now, she bent her head like a horse bucking and threw it back shaking her head furiously, grinding her ass and thighs as in a primitive dance. Her hands were cupped around the cheeks of her fleshy ass and she moved them deep inside the throbbing passage that pulsated like a worm squirming on the end of a hook.

It was time, she couldn't stand it any longer, she grabbed the little box wrapped in brown paper and ripped it off. There inside was a piece of hair, not as silky perhaps as the hair on her head, but almost

as soft. She had debated with herself what the color should be and decided upon the exact tone and color of the hair on her head. After all they couldn't possibly be identical, one area was always exposed to the world and the other never.

She held the small triangular piece of hairy blondness before her and shook it slightly in the air. Carol stood with it in front of the mirror and placed it over her hairless exposed mound. The small suction cups adhering to her skin. It looked wonderfully real, genuine, no one would suspect that this was not her own pubic hair. It took a great deal of courage to expose herself in this way, but she got what she wanted.

When as a child she had diphtheria and all her hair fell out, everyone was concerned about whether her hair would grow back in, and it had, all except in the one private area. At first she felt shame in not being like other women, but she certainly was not like other women in many ways. Then, of course, there were those who would be excited by the lack of the curly hairs of intimacy. But now it can be either way, as I choose. Perhaps I shall keep it only for me, although I'm sure it's guaranteed not to be chewed off. She laughed at her pornography, and placed the palm of her hand over her new pussy hairs. She felt the warmth of her flesh come through the hairs of her merkin.

Her head was tousled and wild from her previous abandoned movements. Her newest possession fitted perfectly.

She lay on her back, her legs parted wide on top of the dark-green velvet spread of the studio couch. Her hips rotated automatically beneath her, she was breathing heavily. She wanted to push the Empire State Building in there tonight, but what was she to use, her fingers were not enough, not now. She thought frantically of some object she could thrust into her, that she could suck satisfactorily on. As she became hotter and closer to that moment when everything inside her would open forth and fall away deep inside, the indescribable sensation shaking her body with tremulous pleasure. Her hands were wet with her juices.

A plaster mannequin stood behind the couch, as naked as Carol. It was used for draping dresses during the day. She stretched behind her and pulled off its arm, smashing it at the elbow, and rammed the forearm up into her.

HARRIET DAIMLER

Harriet Daimler is the pseudonym of the author of five Traveller's Companions, which makes her the foremost female writer for The Olympia Press. She lives frequently in New York, where she was born, and prefers to remain anonymous in order to avoid the con-

fidences of New York's numerous phone freaks. Like most of the crowd who wrote for Olympia through the fifties, her main inspiration was the charcuteries, cheeses, and wines of Paris. She believes that she does not have a dirtier mind than other people, though her facility and speed in writing out those extended sexual fantasies makes her wonder what she was really dreaming about while getting all the college degrees, marriages and divorces that are requisite in a normal American woman's life. Currently writing a book for publication in New York, Harriet Daimler struggles against her impossible tendency to write more explicitly than the courts will tolerate.

HENRY CRANNACH

Henry Crannach is no descendant of that distinguished Flemish painter, though obviously his admirer, but an American girl, vintage Detroit, Michigan. She left Detroit as soon as she was able to figure out the train schedules, settled first in New York and then made Paris her second, or third home. In Paris, she pulled out of her trunk a film scenario that she had written with Terry Southern, which she and Harriet Daimler easily transformed into The Pleasure Thieves. *Henry went on to write another baroque Traveller's Companion. She has since published articles in leading New York magazines and currently works as scout and reader for a New York publisher.*

THE YOUNG

&

EVIL

CHARLES HENRI FORD
& PARKER TYLER

hen Julian awoke afternoons he could look up
through the top of the front windows as he lay on
his back and see the people in the elevated cars go by. Later he could
see them too: the lighted windows moving successively like a strip of
film. He didn't know how many seconds the eyes of the people in the
cars could focus on him at night eating with a candle on the table
or reading or writing a poem when he was not very happy.

This evening he was expecting Karel at eight. At ten minutes
after nine the glass was tapped twice and he went to the door, pulled
aside the curtains to look out haughtily, then pulled back the bolt.

Karel said he had been detained at the Communist cafeteria in
Union Square. A bantamweight prizefighter whom he used to know
last year had renewed his acquaintance. He wants me to introduce him

to some girls so I told him to come by tomorrow night for the party. He's the type that will bring along a friend too.

Julian poured out glasses of red Italian wine bought down the street before dinner.

Karel walked about the room smoking, as his habit was, without inhaling. Julian saw a bracelet on his left wrist. Let me look at your bracelet.

Karel took it off and handed it to him. My jewel boxes will be bursting if last night should be repeated often.

What happened?

When I went uptown I found Vincent and Tony with a crowd there. Of course I went directly to the bathroom and retouched my face and if I do say so I was—not that life hadn't had a big new howlong? thrill—

Yes my dear but in our anarchistic universe can we have everything we want even for one little minute: I mean for a special dreadful reason, but as far as one's own orgasm goes have you concluded that that is the *less* important?

Not at all times because bracelets can become symbols. There was an old thing there in evening clothes who whispered something in my ear and since I couldn't pretend to be awfully shocked we went upstairs . . . To my amazement I was told to go back and send Vincent up and to my utter exhaustion when Vincent came down there was a second request for me . . .

And just for cold lucre?

Oh it's not so cold after all no not so—but listen to this: after that happened Gabriel and Louis came by not having any place to sleep. They were contemptuous as usual and began insulting everyone but Vincent and Tony and me in an unmistakable manner so the others took their sables and flew.

Something is always threatening trade. . . .

Yes or trade. . . . We decided to have some food before going to bed, I was to sleep there, and Louis was selected to fetch it from the delicatessen. Tony, the impulsive Latin, offered Louis his new camel's-hair coat because of the cold, Louis had only a muffler. Louis admired the coat out loud, put it on and hasn't returned until yet. Tony poor thing is looking for him with a knife. I suppose I should have warned Tony but it all happened so quickly and besides once he has his mind on something. . . .

There was a loud knock on the glass and Julian parted the curtains. It's them.

Who?

Gabriel and Louis.

He opened the door and they came in.

Where is your coat? Karel asked looking at Louis.

Have a cigarette Louis said offering a small box of Benson & Hedges. He had a fresh haircut.

Oh said Karel prosperity. . . .

Gabriel made himself at home by selecting a book from the row on the table. It was an anthology of modern poetry. These dopes Pound and Eliot . . . he began.

Listen Louis said reclining on the windowseat talk about something primary such as how we're going to raise some cash before you find yourself a father.

Julian said are you still trying to raise that money? How are you eating in the meantime?

Christ there are too many ways Louis said. The easiest is by asking people on the street.

I suppose their reactions *wouldn't* be identical, Karel said.

Take that fuck McAllen. What do you suppose he thought when I followed him to a gin mill, walked up to him before he could take his first drink and said McAllen, I think your poetry is lousy but I need a buck.

Did you get it?

Hell, yes, he gave me two and I gave him back half of it and said I asked for only one.

You are a panic Julian said. When I get completely broke I'll try that.

But the beautiful thing is the response of some of the cunts Louis continued. The young ones are insulted to think that a man would want to take money from them. The old ones usually come across with at least a quarter.

Don't any of them ever call a cop?

Why should they? I borrowed a dollar from a cop I had never seen before last night. A cop wouldn't do anything about that. Although once I had the unfortunate inspiration to tell a woman what an ugly dog she had after she refused to give me money. She called a dick and I was taken to Bellevue for examination. I ended up by examining the doctors and getting a loan from them.

My dear you are simply insurmountable, Karel said.

Louis had the habit, borrowed from Gabriel, of exhaling cigarette smoke with a vicious sound—of impatience no doubt. Say Julian, how about my taking a bath here, he said.

If you want to. The shower is upstairs.

I know. Simon is asleep at this hour. Have you a towel?

Yes, there's one in the washroom there.

Are you writing anything now Gabriel? Karel said.

Gabriel kept his overcoat on. I'm working on a play Karel, he said.

What is it?

Not exactly worked out yet but about a man who is arrested for kissing a little girl on the street. He had an impulse to kiss her for no reason either of tenderness or fetishism.

Louis had stripped to the waist and was about to ask for some soap when there was another knock on the door.

Julian looked out at a face he didn't recognize.

Karel looked out too and said it's Edwin.

Jesus Christ, Louis said.

Julian let the cutain fall back and said let him in?

Hell, Louis said.

Don't let him in, said Gabriel.

What's the matter? Karel asked.

Louis said shit let him in.

Julian opened the door.

Edwin stepped in. Is Louis here? he asked. He was dressed in what could only be called a costume. His overcoat was open showing buff colored pants, a velvet jacket, open collar and black windsor tie. He also had a jaw. His flat face was set to express anger but his lips were too pouty for him to appear more than poetic.

Yes I'm here Edwin. Do you want to see me? Louis crossed his arms.

I've come to get that dollar you took from Geraldine or take it out of your hide.

Yeah? Louis smiled with half his mouth.

I mean it damn it. He seemed on the point of tears as he removed his overcoat and looked at Louis. He turned to Karel and Julian who appeared unsympathetic and said I've tried to avoid this but Louis has deceived and stolen from my Love. He promised to pay back the dollar and he hasn't done it. I'm going to teach him a lesson like I said I would or try anyway.

All right, Louis said, I haven't a dollar. Do you want to fight?

Yes! Edwin took off his jacket, removed his tie and shirt and laid them in a neat pile on the table.

Louis began warming up by punching at the air as soon as he saw Edwin's muscular back and good arms. Edwin was also the taller.

Are you ready? Edwin asked, blushing.

Keep time for them Julian Gabriel said. Fight one-minute rounds, I'll referee.

This is terrible! Karel said shaking his bracelet above his head.

Go! cried Julian, hoping that Louis would win.

They went: Louis feinting and attacking, Edwin standing and punching Louis' head. At the end of the first minute Louis threw himself on the floor, breathing hard. Edwin sat on the bed going over the details as to just why he had to do this and also telling Louis that he was dissipated and hadn't been leading the right kind of life. He said I used to box in the navy you know. Do you want another round or have you had enough?

Louis was furious and got to his feet. You bastard! he said. He was more on the defensive now but every time he struck at Edwin the latter hit him in the face. Louis attacked him wildly with blows from both fists, and found himself lying across the couch after sinking into blackness and blinding light and rising again.

Karel rushed to the washroom for a towel and cold water.

Edwin was apparently more satisfied than he intended to be.

Gabriel fanned Louis and rubbed his hands.

Edwin said I'd give him a dollar myself if I had it but I have to work for my living.

In those clothes? Gabriel asked.

I write poetry too. But I have a sense of decency. I hope I haven't hurt him. But he insulted my Love, you see. . . .

I'm afraid I don't see said Gabriel.

I see said Julian but I'm sure I *don't* know your face.

Edwin put his clothes back on and took his departure. The others were silent.

Karel bathed Louis' face.

I'm all right Louis said. Give me a cigarette. I didn't know the son-of-a-bitch could fight.

Anything else he might do would be superfluous Karel said.

Louis got up with a few swollen places on one cheek and on his forehead and lips. I guess I'll take the bath now.

A guy like that with dementia praecox ought to be secretly disposed of Gabriel said.

His earnestness was amazing said Julian.

He's a beast Karel said.

Julian gave Louis soap and handed him the towel.

I'll be back soon Louis said, his back looking a little rounder than it had.

Still writing poetry? Gabriel asked Karel when Louis had gone.

What is one to do but face the inevitable?

I'm going to do some sociological and ethnological work.

Do you mind if I ask you a "Little Review" question?

No—I don't.

Do you write because it pleases you?

Yes, I do. But you should read my essay on art. Gabriel half closed his eyes.

Yes? I suppose you put art in its place?

Well, you might call it that.

That's all right. . . . I don't mind granting anyone his prerogative to think that way—but then I insist on reminding him that there *is* such a thing as sociology said Karel.

I have decided that poetry is prose with an inferiority complex Gabriel said.

Yes but—Julian put in.

Man prattles poetry and writes prose. . . . Prose I think is the truly aristocratic art.

But the adult is a convention which may be ignored—or valuably misunderstood. Poetry, like prose, is concerned with aesthetic. It's a question of value, purely. Julian felt prouder after saying this.

Gabriel is merely being abnormally oblique Julian Karel said. How would it feel he said to Gabriel for you to consider meaning instead of being meant?

I went through all that last week. You've heard the expression to have the shit scared out of you. Such a thing was demonstrated to me to be based on truth. . . . About dawn I was walking along Fourth Street when a car of four gangsters who had come out of the coffee pot on Fourth and Sixth drove toward me. They saw me and called out hey faggot! as they passed by. I kept walking but when I heard them turn the car around I started to run. They sped up and were even with me when I ran inside a building I knew and locked myself in the toilet in the back of the hall. I was just in time for both the locking of the door and the toilet. . . . I suppose I would have been raped by those bastards.

Karel opened his mouth into an oval and his eyes became wide. My God Gabriel think of me! Oh, the fiends! He lay down on the couch.

Julian said are they that dangerous?

They were probably drunk or I don't see how they mistook *me.* . . .

Yes, you do have a face like a truck driver.

Louis came in the side door from upstairs naked.

My God did you come through the hall that way? Julian exclaimed.

Yes . . . little good it did.

Exhibitionist! Julian said.

Karel slid from the couch. How do your bruises feel? he said to Louis touching his cheek with a finger.

All right. They're all right. Are there any more cigarettes?

There's some listerine in the cabinet would that help them, Julian said, or vaseline?

Do you want some vaseline on them Louis? Karel asked.

No they'll be all right. I'm tired. He stretched out on the bed and closed his eyes. His body was smooth and lightly olive like his face.

Karel Julian thought was oversolicitous.

After a few minutes Louis got up and began to dress.

Gabriel rose, put out his cigarette and sat down on the couch by Julian.

Karel and Louis were in the washroom.

Gabriel looked at Julian and said I'd like to walk with you through terrible things happening.

Julian regarded his mouth and insincere eyes. My bed will never be wide enough, he said.

Louis came out of the washroom and said to Gabriel let's get out of here.

Karel came out with his hat on. Julian looked at him.

I'll see you tomorrow night, Karel said. Did you call Theodosia?
Yes.

The three left together and Julian lay on his back waiting to look up. He thought about the dawn and wondered if it would come too soon. There he was wondering as he would wonder yes as he would wonder at eighty if he should live that long or must he wonder to live making the if bad form. He believed in the bird swaying on the bough.

But where was paradise? What if he had something in his eye. Oh to be Prometheus sex-guy and whore-walloper what if he had something in his eye there *was* something in. He went to the mirror and held his eye opened until it watered. Did he ever *know* anyone to hark back back hark and one lies up some stairs who did surprisingly. He put his coat on and his hat on and locked the door behind him.

The fine snow was fine and there was a man he saw hugging an ash can. He crossed Seventh Avenue and turned into Commerce Street. He found the number and looked up at a dark window. He went in the house and up the stairs without making any noise. His feet made blank sounds on the linoleum in the hall.

Gabriel and Louis had gotten a room in the same building with Karel. Karel's room was next door to theirs. He told them he was sleepy and left them.

In his own room after a while he thought he knew. He thought he knew he didn't quite know. But he knew. He would imagine he knew; that was just as good.

Instead of undressing and getting into bed he walked into the hall and knocked on their door. That was quite possible for him to do he thought; it was possible because they knew it was just possible. So there he was; in it; in the room.

Louis and Gabriel were stretched half-clothed on top of the bed. Some garments, very dirty, were flung about with a recklessness which Karel marked, the recklessness that was truly artistic.

Karel was on his guard with them; he felt a bit self-conscious because he had not been kind to them. Louis' trousers, drawn up by short suspenders, attracted him as his skin had attracted him at Julian's. Louis' face above a black sweater with a white mooncurved wide stripe draped over the chest was alive. Now, as mostly, as always almost, Louis conveyed thoughtfulness to him, thoughtfulness now behind a bruised mouth, and behind eyes. He permitted himself to look at Louis as he had thought of seeing him when on the other side of the wall. Yes, he thought.

Louis' activity was in his favor. In repose his face was dark, even morbid. When smiling it attracted because it was evil and young. Moreover, Karel saw that his smile gave his jaw the correct proportion, the without which not beauty, in spite of the swollen spot on his cheek. He sat down by Louis' outstretched form and was gratified to have him move closer to him.

Gabriel and Louis were waiting. They were waiting for their good fortune to occur, to come with the dawn; they were going to force the world to be good with them. They did not want it to be good to them for it could not be good to them who were too good for anyone to be good to them but the world was stupid enough to be punished. It was stupid enough to be fooled; and they had to live.

Karel knew that he was not the world, for he had come into their room then; the world had not done that; the world only put its hands into its pockets when asked; Gabriel and Louis had asked Karel; he had refused. But he was changing, he was changing from the world into something else. And they had known that he could change. But would he? Well, they would know very shortly, and on whose account he was changing.

Karel's hand strayed over the rough sweater's surface and landed on Louis' warm neck. His heart gave a leap. Yes! it said. Karel was doing this because he knew it could be done.

Louis looked at Gabriel and caught at Karel's hand, putting it onto his chest under the sweater.

Karel's tight heart grew less tight. It must be what time and he had not slept. Now he could afford to remain awake a little longer. With Gabriel and Louis. But only Louis should profit. As he must profit. As Karel was willing he should profit, anyway at first, for that was the only way it could be done. Just a little Karel thought Gabriel sensed that. But they must both be jubilating, they must both be thinking this.

He kissed Louis. Louis urged him.

Karel was enjoying the progress. It must be so now. It could be his way. So he was not completely responsive. He sat up. I want a cigarette if you have one.

Sure said Louis and produced one from a creased package.

What about something to eat? Gabriel asked. Let the food go. I'm not hungry Louis said.

Gabriel glanced heavily at him, then disgust spread over his face, a light disgust. I want coffee he said but indifferently.

Karel said I have no money.

Louis lay smoking.

Then I'm going to sleep. I don't care what you guys do Gabriel said. He turned over, away from them.

Past the window there was gray-filled space soon to be practically blue. Karel walked to the window and looked out. He turned around to look at Louis and then walked quietly over and sitting by his head on the bed asked him, in a whisper, if he wished to sleep in his room.

Sure Louis said. He beheld Gabriel's back. His mouth curled. His eyes assumed vacancy as he flung his cigarette mightily away beyond the window.

In Karel's room Karel's heart beat faster. This was this, taking Louis into his room, separating him from Gabriel. Louis would not care about him any longer. No; he could afford to do nothing for Gabriel Karel thought.

The sheets were absolutely cold. Louis was waiting in them.

Their arms were around each other, the light was on, they stared at the ceiling. Later Louis slept, the light was off, a fear was on his heart, Karel's heart, he was awake. Then the door was knocked on and he heard Karel Karel.

What? Who is it?

It's Julian. Let me in.

The door opened and Karel's astonished face said what's the matter? Come in what's the matter? Darling!

Julian went in the tiny room and Karel turned the light on. Louis was apparently still asleep.

I have something in my eye. I couldn't sleep. I must go to a doctor. Will you take me to one?

But Julian I don't know of any doctor's office open at this hour Karel said let me see your eye.

Julian went to the lamp and opened his eye can you see anything?

No but it looks bloodshot.

Come on out with me and we'll have breakfast. I'll see a doctor later on.

I'll have to dress. He was in his underwear. He looked at Louis without any explanation to Julian.

Julian looked at his eye again in the mirror and said God.

Karel said what could be in it?

Something must.

Oh how terrible Karel said.

Julian said a hot punchino would be good. Karel said it would too so they went to Frankie's. They ordered punchinos from the partly cross-eyed waiter with a German accent.

There was a group of men and a round blonde girl at the next table. One of the men went over and said to Karel isn't your name Karel and aren't you a writer and won't you both join our table?

Karel and Julian would.

They had applejack. Eventually one pulled out a poem and asked Karel to criticize it. Karel did, doing justice he thought to everything.

Shortly after putting back his poem, another drink having been consumed, the same one pulled out his wallet and showed Karel a card attached therein which read Soandso HONORARY CHIEF OF POLICE.

Karel said were you really in the police department?

The man pulled aside his coat and showed him a badge on his belt. Come over to see me in New Jersey any time he said. Then he thought another drink would be distinctly in order and left to get a bottle from the bar. Whereupon, the blonde round girl having got up to dance with the second man at the table, the third man at the table leaned over to Julian and said I would like to rape that girl there before everybody's eyes.

Julian got over that neatly because when the girl came back she sat on his lap.

The men decided they would go so they all went outside including Karel and Julian and the girl who said let's continue the party at my place.

They all went with her and not having a thing to do decided to play strip poker. They counted their things and every deal the low man removed an article.

The girl, after a while, was almost undressed the same time that Julian was almost fully clothed. They were playing on a sheet on the floor. She made them promise not to make her remove her shorts but when her brassière came off they knew there was no wind to make the shorts stay on.

Julian at last began to see that it wouldn't be long for him either. When he was nude the girl said I'm drunk and laid her head in his lap.

Finally everyone left the girl's apartment except Karel and Julian and the three slept in one bed, Julian having forgotten about breakfast and all about his eye.

The next night Julian was expecting people he knew and people he did not know. He had told those he knew to come by for a raid-party and they were prepared to be taken to the station in the Black Maria. He had borrowed a portable victrola from Theodosia. She had records of Duke Ellington's timed primitiveness, King Oliver's trumpets and clarinets and Bennie Moten's natural rhythms.

Julian wore a black shirt and light powder-green tie. His dark hair had been washed to a gold brown and fell over his forehead.

Karel, as he had promised, came by three hours before the others bringing his box of beauty that included eyelash curlers, mascara, various shades of powder, lip and eyebrow pencils, blue and brown eyeshadow and tweezers for the eyebrows.

Julian submitted to his artistry, only drawing the line at his eyebrows being plucked.

I'll make you up to the high gods Karel said to the *high*. . . . When he was through he regarded the result with a critical and gratified eye. Julian's rather full mouth now had lips which though less spiritual were not quite lewd. His eyes were simple sins to be examined more closely or to be looked at only from a distance.

Karel never did badly by his own face. He put an infinitesimal spot of lip salve in each nostril and almost invisible lines of black running vertically in the center of each eyelid. His eyelashes, as Frederick Spitzberger always predicted, were long enough now to catch in the boughs (should he go for a walk in Washington Square). His mouth, though not long, was made smaller sometimes by his raising the lower lip and pushing in the upper lip with it. Of course his eyebrows often looked the same as the week before. They could be penciled into almost any expression: Clara Bow, Joan Crawford, Norma Shearer, etc. He thought he would choose something obvious for tonight. Purity.

Julian said you stay here while I go for the gin.

Don't be gone forever Karel said applying a liquid to his hair which would make a deep wave when properly set.

Why *do* you hold your lips that way? Julian called from the door.

Because I think it looks adorable Karel answered.

Julian went out into the freezing air. He would buy the gin at the Dragon Tavern. He walked fast, though remaining wholly conscious of the green yellow and black taxis cruising with the promise of anything.

It was Saturday night and the Tavern was crowded. Vivian the blonde girl of the night before was there: starry-eyed: with grappa she said after she had disentangled herself from her dancing partner and gone over to Julian insisting that she pay back the fifty cents she had borrowed earlier that day for Kotex. Julian took it and said he might be back later. Rose, the Jewess who owned the place, handed him a package containing two bottles. He paid her and left.

At the studio he found that Frederick Spitzberger had arrived. Frederick was talking in a deep voice that was more often than not jarring; and always shocking when one considered Frederick's body: emaciated, with practically no shoulders and less hips and waist. As for his face, the nose was born he said and the body grew on later. His lips were prominent and curved outward. The shell-rimmed glasses he wore partly concealed his eyebrows: penciled lines. And who would know that he used mascara around his small tender eyes that belied the caustic (though witty as he often said himself) dicta that he let fall upon the heads of others. His accent, which was quite correct, prevailed in whatever situation. He was smoking a black cigarette with a gold tip when Julian came in. In the washroom he was saying to Karel . . . his sneaky imperatives the slut forgets that the thing on which his assurance and hopes are built, commercial value, has much more substantiation in responsible sources in *my* case than in his: he refuses to recognize that I have contributed paid articles to four organs of literary expression rated officially as *A* among literary periodicals, all these beyond his reach; and that for about six hours' expert appraisal of manuscripts for purely commercial publishers I have made as much as a hundred and twelve dollars and fifty cents. Any illiterate who tries to denounce me for trying to be different because I can't be effective in any other way will get something like that information on his behind. Where do these self-appointed po-etasting arbiters of Middle West poetic destiny think they come off?

When Julian slammed the door Frederick came out with an eye-brow raised and said this must be little boy blue.

Julian said how do you do?

Karel came from the washroom looking resplendent. I told K-Y to bring some goods to tack over the rest of the front windows. I'm desperately afraid of a raid.

Let's have a drink now Julian said unwrapping the High & Dry.

Yes indeed said Frederick starting "A Good Man Is Hard to Find" on the phonograph.

While Julian was pouring the drinks Armand Windward came in with K-Y who was holding a bundle of red curtains under her arm. K-Y was from Kentucky. She lived with Windward in a sky-light apartment and they took sunbaths in the nude regardless of visitors or the weather. Usually the only visitor was Frederick. K-Y was mistress of much flesh: breasts and hips in perfect lavish propor-tion. Her face was striking without make-up though occasionally she made more decided with a black pencil the point of hair growing at the top of her forehead. She was expansive and somewhat worthy of love. Artists drew her body. She did portraits of children. As for Windward, he always reserved the right to be whimsical; in fact, demanded the privilege when he had just the right amount of mari-juana, the "portorican papers" he bought on 99th Street.

Here are the curtains K-Y said I didn't bring any more on ac-count of I didn't have any more.

Julian put the smaller table up on the windowseat and Karel

climbed up on it and K-Y handed him thumbtacks one at the time.
People passing by outside slowed down, especially if they belonged
to the unemployed, and looked up at him stretching the red curtains
across the windows. He saw Santiago, a Mexican dancer whom he had
asked to come, crossing the street with Osbert Allen, an English
painter of American skyscrapers. Sometimes at the Dragon Tavern
Santiago danced the native dances he had learned in Mexico, to see
them the following season introduced in a Broadway show "for the
first time in America." Karel thought about him last summer at the
artists' colony in Woodstock: a crowd had a bonfire by the pool one
night making steak sandwiches and drinking applejack. Mrs. Dodge,
wife of the philosopher, was there and Santiago with a rather extraordinary girl morbidly in love with him; also Karel and Osbert among
others. For some trivial slight on Santiago's part the girl stalked away
from the fire and down off into the darkness and to the icy pool
where she pulled off her clothes and plunged in. It seems she had
enacted such a performance before and the last time she was dragged
out in a fainting frozen condition. So Osbert this time went after her.
Santiago was very careless and only after much jockeying was persuaded to go down and help him get her out. When she wouldn't
obey Santiago's command to come out he stripped and went in and
began to yelp because of the cold—while she was blandly floating
around, one supposed until she would be too exhausted to remain on
top. As Santiago went toward her (Osbert had a flashlight playing on
the pool) she fainted in his arms and he yelled for help because they
were both sinking and freezing. They were near a rock in the middle
of the stream and Osbert leaped out to it and dragged her on it and
started massaging her. Then after exhortations from the shore she was
passed with much difficulty from rock to rock and taken in a blanket
back to the fire—weeping and protesting that she wanted to swim and
swim. A scene followed between her and Santiago. She bit his leg and
he slapped her on the face. Almost everybody chimed in on the argument. Mrs. Dodge called Santiago "stinking shit." Strange as it may
seem, Karel came out with admiration for Santiago, regret over the
girl, and disgust for nearly everybody else. And he did a poem on it.

Osbert and Santiago entered during the cries of Karel who had
turned to lay Frederick out for smoking a cigarette of marijuana.
Frederick said that he was his own mother and please, Karel, after all.

The curtains were up and when Gabriel and Louis came in,

though they had not been invited, Julian went to fix some more drinks. He came out to hear Frederick ask of Louis where are you bleeding? You must be bleeding somewhere for the groans you are emitting.

Osbert was already well filled with wine which he drank habitually in large quantities. Santiago, after dancing at the Tavern, had been known to find Osbert on the floor of a wine cellar in need of Physical Aid (though not Financial since Osbert was to take Santiago on a European tour the next summer). Osbert interrupted the cockney story he was telling K-Y to giggle profusely at Frederick's rebuke to Louis.

Julian asked who wanted gin and who didn't want ginger ale.

Another knock came and the door was opened to admit Karel's sandy-haired bantamweight. The friend he introduced was also a boxer but was studying at New York University. He was in the light-weight class. The small one's name was Gene and he immediately offered K-Y a drink of rye which he carried in his hip pocket. She said she wasn't drinking.

At last Theodosia came. Julian kissed her saying darling. Her once long hair had been shortened to a bob shaped to her head. She looked younger he thought or at least as young as she had looked two years before, although the circles under her eyes seemed to be permanent.

Yes she wanted a drink. She had been trying she said to make a decision all day and she would get drunk and make it.

Santiago in his consciously childish way said that he wanted something to eat and that he was bored. I'm bored he said and Theodosia was charmed with him.

Karel had forgotten about the dreaded raid and was talking to Louis on the apparent incongruity of having a very elaborate structure fall into oblivion at the (logically possible?) pulling of a trigger or cessation of heartbeat.

Julian put on a screaming record to drown out Frederick who had just said to Gabriel after a philosophical speculation on the latter's part: get off that pot, Annie, it's full of shit already.

Armand was well on his third marijuana and felt warmly decayed. Frederick asked him to dance.

Gene attached K-Y and was serious dancing with her large body in his arms.

Theodosia was with Gene's friend.

Julian led Karel in a slow dance step and Karel leaned—oh way back, and when the music stopped Gene's friend asked Karel if he could have the next one.

Julian and Theodosia went behind the partition for another drink. Theodosia liked to get drunk all at once so she took a double one. When they came out they found Gene trying to carry K-Y up the balcony steps but she was too heavy and the steps too narrow and since she wouldn't walk up and said Christ you're hurting me he had to be content with talking to her on the couch.

Somebody knocked. Karel went to the window and said it's Harold.

Harold Forte who illustrated books and bathrooms made his vivacious entrance and kissed almost everybody except Gabriel and Louis. He had on spats and a new suit since he had just returned from Philadelphia, having made he said oh hundreds and hundreds of dollars and having lived in the lap of luxury in a home which he "did" for two weeks. Aren't the Villagers amusing? he remarked to Karel looking over his shoulder at Louis and Gabriel. Theo, dear, you look marvelous how do you do it? Oh I must have some eggsie-weggsies I'm plastered. Julian dear how are you the last time I saw you you had one circle under each eye and now you have two.

That's a lie said Julian.

Frederick was appalled by what he termed Harold's vulgarity and said what can one do about people who are always trying to legitimatize their faces.

Frederick dear, *dear* Frederick . . . and nobody has introduced me to those ones Harold said indicating Gene and his friend.

Karel introduced them.

So charmed Harold said and then in a loud whisper to Santiago: Really who *are* these people—have they no homes? At that Santiago had one of his painful laughing spells.

I say said Osbert to Harold you look positively gay in the new clothes.

Oh said Harold you're lovely *too*, dear, and gave him a big kiss on the forehead, much to Osbert's dismay. Then everybody became alarmed over Santiago who couldn't stop laughing between gasps for breath.

Julian thought that after all Gabriel and Louis were guests since they were there and asked Louis who was looking with his chin down at him if he wouldn't have a drink. Louis said he would and they retired. Things never happen to me Julian Louis said. I must always make things happen to other people. I'd like someone to take me by the hair. . . . But Julian didn't and when they came out Julian saw Theodosia looking more surprised than hurt as Frederick said to her listen, disastrous, starting with a poem the conclusion is response, but starting with a poem is starting with a *poem* and the response is not the same as the response to an elephant.

Harold was getting Santiago off again with so I said to the Duchess—Dutch you old battle-ax *you* hold the baby for a while, my hands are wet.

Karel saw Julian and Louis together and thought he's the last stand surely my last stand if one won't be the whole exclusive flesh won't be the marble like that. . . .

Gabriel took Louis aside and said let's go but Louis said not now.

The gin was all gone and Harold volunteered to buy two more bottles (even if he had sent all his money to his mother) provided someone else would go for it so Frederick said he would go for it with Gene's friend and Gene's friend not being articulate enough to say he'd rather not, went out the door with Frederick.

Armand's eyes were beginning to be red and dilated and glazed and K-Y called him honey over and over.

Julian and Theodosia danced and Theodosia spoke of things which might please her.

Harold was talking to Santiago and Osbert.

Karel was listening to Gabriel and Louis who were arguing about one thing while they meant another.

Frederick and Gene's friend came back sooner than everyone had expected and gin was drunk by everyone except K-Y and Gabriel.

Karel drank more than he had ever drunk in one evening.

The others were talking at the tops of their voices when there was a knock on the door leading into the hall and upstairs.

Oh God who could that be Karel said you go to the door Julian.

Julian opened the door as Karel and Frederick fled to the washroom.

Standing outside was a kimona with a head of hair sticking out the top. "Please" came from a mouth that Julian did not locate at once. He gradually made out the eyes. If you're going to keep up this noise till morning *I'm* going to call the police. I've got to go to work in Brooklyn at four o'clock and I've got to get some sleep whatdoyouthinkthisistheFOURTHOFJULY?

It does make me think of history Julian said have a drink.

No I won't have a drink and if you don't stop this noise I'm going to call the police call the police that's all me gottogotoworkat four o'clock way out to Brooklyn and you trying to tear the house down . . . She receded toward the stairs still talking and so up the stairs, still talking. . . .

The nerve Harold said instead of apologizing for her face she asks us can you the nerve of . . .

Julian thought it best to at least stop the victrola since no one seemed inclined to leave just at that moment.

Everybody had another drink and when Karel passed out Julian allowed Frederick to put him to bed there. Frederick worshiped Karel and considered him his "first influence."

Gabriel urged Louis to leave with him. Louis said say wait a minute can't you? and Gabriel departed.

Theodosia said to Julian she had planned to spend the night with him but since Karel . . .

Yes Julian said since Karel . . .

Gene offered to take her home and Theodosia said all right call a taxi.

Can we sleep in the bed on the balcony? Osbert asked meaning Santiago and himself. I'm so drunk he won't be able to take me home.

Shut up Santiago said. I'll get you home you bore me.

Harold said he would die if he didn't have some oysters at once. So kissing (almost everybody) good-bye declaring, though, that his love was not wholly physical he left with Osbert and Santiago.

K-Y was still calling Armand honey and after a while got him to get up and go.

Frederick said his mother would be frantic if he wasn't in soon but that he would see them tomorrow night. He lived in the Bronx.

Karel looked as if he would be unconscious until daylight.

Louis, the only other one left, had made no move to go so Julian said let's finish the gin. He drank his highball slowly and noticed for the first time what a beautiful nose Louis had. But he thought Louis' hair too thick as he grasped a handful. Julian looked at Louis looking up at him and said the only thing I have against life is that it spoils young men's mouths. Where are you sleeping tonight?

I have a place to sleep.

Sleep here. You and Karel and I will sleep in one bed.

Have you got cigarettes and oranges for breakfast?

I've got cigarettes and I can get oranges.

They undressed and went to bed that way with Karel who had one hand on the floor. They lay in bed smoking, their heads turning with the gin.

Julian thought: for a sexual conquest that turns out to be mutual it is not required that flattery be used by the aggressor; all that is necessary is that the object feel inferior, not in intellectual qualities but in sexual attractiveness.

He changed the position of his head.

The sun didn't shine white but the sun shone. Karel slept, loving neither flowers, animals nor music. There was no clock in the place. Louis found cigarettes and gave Julian one. Louis sat at the table and wrote with pencil on a piece of yellow paper. Julian looked at the floor strewn with cigarette butts, a broken victrola record and some glasses. An empty gin bottle stood at Louis' elbow and another lay at his ankle.

Don't you know that poems shouldn't be written after sexual excesses Julian said.

Louis said that is when I always write. He had put on Julian's dressing gown without bothering to draw the sash together.

I suppose I'll take a bath Julian suggested if you don't mind giving me the robe. Julian looked at his face in the mirror. Before going to bed he had not removed the mascara that Karel had applied to his eyelashes and under his eyebrows was black and under his eyes was black. He applied cold cream to his face, wiped it off, and went upstairs to the tin-lined bathtub with the shower above it. The water was alternately hot and cold. Somebody had left a pair of socks in one corner. There was a bar of soap on the tub which Julian took back downstairs. He found Karel awake but still in bed and talking to Louis who was dressing. Karel became quiet when Julian entered and nothing was said until Louis, after borrowing a book and turning his mouth down at Karel, smiling, left, saying I'll see you guys later.

Karel remained silent and Julian said how do you feel?

I always feel too much but I am aware of it Karel said.

I didn't say what do you feel.

Well, as long as I live I shall be able to extract myself from places, sooner rather than later.

Then you cannot bear challenges? asked Julian.

Of course I meant, also dragging the spoils with me.

I hope you will never have to commit suicide to do that.

Karel didn't reply, considering the unexpectedness of his position, which had come about inadvertently. A week ago he had looked on Louis with intolerance and little curiosity. Louis' way of seizing people made Karel think of a carnivorous bird or animal. Karel saw him hurt physically and realized the strength and weakness of Louis whom he went to bed with. Louis' asking was his way of taking. Karel was filled with a sense of power because of the willingness, even eagerness, of Louis to make their relation not a one-way affair sexually. Louis' sense of power was dilated by the fact that Karel was to keep him. Karel saw his own strength and weakness juxtaposed on that of Louis and what he saw made a whole. During the night he had just spent in bed with Julian and Louis he had heard Julian laugh and then Louis laugh and saw a segment of the whole, at the existence of which he was annoyed. He did not resent the tangent of Gabriel for he saw how he could be eliminated, in spite of Louis' having been dominated from the first by him. There were people who remembered the meeker Louis. Gabriel inspired action. Karel was sure Louis wanted to slough off Gabriel's influence not only because he feared it but also because he wanted now to show his own independence. Therefore Karel did not fear Gabriel's success if he chose to interfere, but Julian, he found, made the thing lopsided. I am moving uptown tonight he said to Julian. With Louis.

Why uptown?

I think it's safer. If I live down here Louis will get in bad with the gangsters. He's been too friendly with a few of them and they wouldn't accept his living with me. Too many undesirable people know my address anyway.

I don't guess then I'll see you very often.

You can visit us can't you?

Julian felt an absence of something he had held dear a few

minutes before. He looked around the room to see what was missing. He could find a wrong space nowhere and was sad. Then he thought he saw what he had lost. Since he saw it it must have been returned so he hadn't lost it for good.

His temporary illusion had disclosed a softness in him. A softness is a weakness and that submitted to always leaves some sort of something if only a small fear. This was a something that could be concealed by something else. He would think by what, by what it could be concealed.

Good-bye now. He looked at Karel with hard eyes and hoped the tears wouldn't come through until Karel left and when Karel left the tears didn't come through. He was learning to assume hardness. He put water and ground coffee in the pot and lit the gas. He dressed himself while thinking about love. He doubted the sincerity of the people he saw living together supposedly in love. He had never known physical and mental love toward a single person. It had always been completely one or the other. With Karel it was the other. With Louis really neither. He was unbelieving when he saw lovers who were lovers in the complete sense and who slept night after night in the same bed. He was quite sure their love was a fabrication or a convenience or a recompense and he did not believe in their love as love. There was a poem about that and he opened a book to read it and came to

> *We shall say, love is no more*
> *Than walking, smiling,*
> *Forcing out "good morning,"*
> *And were it more it were*
> *Fictitiousness and nothing.*
> *We close our eyes, we clutch at bodies,*
> *We wake at dream's length from each other*
> *And love shamefully and coldly*
> *Strangers we seem to know by memory.*
> *Like dunces we still shall kiss*
> *When graduated from music-making.*

Why had his estrangement with Karel happened and what could Karel gain from Louis? The coffee began to percolate and smell good. Julian pulled the table up to the bed and sat on the bed.

Somebody knocked coarsely from the hall. It was Mr. Simon's

Swedish boy come to sweep and put the room in order. Sometimes he left a pile of dirt in the middle of the floor.

Julian finished the coffee, put on his jacket, overcoat and black hat, and went out to the street. He was alone now for Karel was gone and he walked along looking at the sidewalk. Little boys with baskets of wood passed. The smell of beer came from a basement. He would go to the French place a few doors down and get a "white bunny" for fifty cents, a pink drink tasting of licorice. He reached a door painted green and rang the bell. The lock clicked and he went in and up the steps.

The proprietor opened the door for him and he nodded once and went in. There were no other customers at that hour in the room filled with white-covered tables. The windows at the front were on a level with the elevated tracks. He sat facing them and asked for a white bunny and lit a cigarette. He sipped the drink but it was soon gone so he ordered another and waited a while before tasting it.

I hate this place which is at this moment a. lonely; b. unlovely; c. has the possibility of the same thing that anything with possibility has. And what is that but the is and the do.

He ordered another drink and that made three and four made two dollars which was all the dollars he had. He went out and down the steps. Thank God for a kind of great show and he meant by that look at them. He wasn't at home. And here *o murderpiss beautiful boys grow out of dung.*

And wear padded shoulders. They push flesh into eternity and sidestep automobiles. I bemoan them most under sheets at night when their eyes rimmed with masculinity see nothing and their lymphlips are smothered by the irondomed sky. Poor things, their genitals only peaceful when without visiting cards. They install themselves narrowly and until 11:15 their trousers must be adjusted over the exclamation point, the puritanical period that old maids prefer not to grasp although they say how *do* you do adonisprick or do they grasp it with their five-fingered wrinkled cunts. Oh they will never undress in the subway fearing imprisonment and shame. Ramon Navarro wouldn't, no, nor Richard Barthelmess and John Barrymore wouldn't though he is old enough. Harry Number wouldn't nor would Louis, no, nor Karel nor I nor the one who would like the length of it to be seen.

Their necks grow unknowingly, their eyes are eaten eventually;

something explodes near their testicles and in the vicinity of their hearts (and sometimes they are nauseated). They doubtless clean spots off or out; they are soldiers without medals since they have legs with hairs on them and their heels sound. They wash themselves assuredly.

I have often imagined the curve of them next to me in bed colored like coffee or like cream or like peaches and cream powder but without peaches and cream powder in their perspiring dear pores. They have I understand eyelashes with noses to match.

I have often caught them going into toilets and coming out too.

I know the strange as it may seem pull toward the good-looking ones, the ones with the proud rumps and the careless underlips. They have all positions but stardusters' but I wouldn't mind a starduster, at least if I could depend on him at 8:30, but a prizefighter might be better though I don't know: some movie actors have made me look for my hat extraordinarily. They should carry knives to kill those others and hang their cunts around their necks and give them to the hungry dogs. And for every one given to or stolen by them or at any rate CUT, I personally would give them each a you can guess kiss.

Wives douse them but not always; you can see them dripping yet their cuffs are clean.

Broadway is one of the streets they walk on and 72nd Street another (and there are still others o pleased to be varied God). A pair of dice would be useless: buy a pair and swallow them but sit and wait or walk and wait. Their profiles may have nothing to do with carfare, then again gin may be bought and lemons even stolen though grenadine is a luxury. All won't make love though because that's the queerest part: boys you with the bluebrown shadows among your clothes and in warm rooms the closetomeredder smell.

He turned back down Fifth Avenue because the wind was blowing and it was cold. When he reached his studio he dropped on the bed and heard for the thousandth and more time the irregular beat of his heart through his right ear on the pillow.

This did not interfere this time with how beautiful she was. She had never been so beautiful even when he was ten years old. There were violet shadows around her eyes and the nipples of her breasts were not large. She raised her arms and there was no hair under them. No hair anywhere else except the long hair from her head. She was walking by the sea and someone was coming toward her: a sailor in a blue suit with a white sailor hat on the back of his head. When she saw him she stopped and looked at him and her violet eyes with the violet shadows were gazing at him. He walked to her his body and arms swinging like they would swing a little. When he got to her he leaned on the beach with his left thigh and elbow. He was twenty years old; his name was Jack; he had green eyes and the color of his hair was the bright gold color of the short silk threads of his eyes and brow. His teeth were white like the cap he wore and his face gold to a shade as the hand he raised to her (a shade less gold than the sun's sorrow). She let her knees fall into the sand by him. She wasn't afraid of him at all, she was by the sea. They were warm to each other, he was pure. She was beautiful, it was sad to see the sailor boy have to piss afterward and walk away.

There is something in my mind Frederick said.

Is it big? asked Julian.

It must be Broadway Karel said.

Or! Frederick's lips were prominent.

Shut up said Karel.

Broadway is big with bright lights said Julian and a torso passed with a head. It was walking in the direction opposite the one in which they were walking.

Are you going back? asked Frederick.

What did I see? asked Julian.

It wasn't fate—

Not in the form of a woman.

Well are you Frederick said.

No said Julian look at it.

It is big Karel said that is why you, too, are big looking at it. You can't decide can you.

You are not the only one Frederick said ooooooooOOO.

Don't camp like that Karel said. Or I'll leave.

You mustn't leave said Frederick. I'll go with—

Go ahead Julian said.

They stopped; people passed when they stopped.

There are such things as eyes Karel thought such things as are not eyes as words as even arms.

Let's go on Frederick said look over there.

Broadway can dance as well as walk Karel thought. Only it is not dancing now although it might just have been dancing.

The taxis came, went, wheeled from beneath their feet.

I feel like screaming whirred Frederick.

Hush said Karel.

Look at those two Frederick said ignoring him and they all tried to look.

Broadway is a big long place like a hall Karel was thinking, with new bodies and old doors that are not important but the bodies are and the clothes. And the faces. Broadway is alive with I don't know what all but I do know with some things, it is alive with people not in bed. It is alive with people not in bed he said aloud his hands cold in his overcoat's pockets.

Oh yes said Frederick.

There it is again Julian said isn't it. He meant the torso.

Yes it is Frederick said.

Karel looked and saw that it was.

Julian had slowed. I'm turning around he said.

Well said Karel.

Alone? asked Frederick.

Why not Julian said and went on.

He's got his own key Karel said.

Frederick said I have some money and would Karel like something to drink. Karel didn't mind and they turned into 46th Street and went up some steps. At the top of the second flight Frederick rang a bell outside a door. They were looked at through an uncovered hole and admitted.

The place was milling with mostly men who looked young. Some of them had curled hair. Clothes that fit were on others.

There was a separate room in which was a victrola and a Spanish boy doing high kicks and splits. He was surrounded by different ones at tables. Karel and Frederick went to the bar in the other room. Karel thought he saw Vincent and Tony at a table in the room with the Spanish boy but it was so dim there he wasn't sure.

They ordered old-fashioned cocktails and looked around and seeing nothing that interested them in their present mood, after the second drink nothing would do for Frederick but that he should suggest they go up on the Drive.

Karel was willing but lingered until they were spoken to by two undesirables. Frederick was frantic about one until he discovered on the other side of his neck a large boil.

Karel said to Frederick I will go up on the Drive for I'm dying for it.

They went out and down and over to the bus stop and took a bus and sat on the top of it until 106th Street or higher. There they got off and started to walk but first they both had to piss and that was rather pleasing.

They got up on Riverside Drive again. Soon there was a lot of sailors and civilians who must have started to follow them. Karel and Frederick could hear them, at first a crowd of them but neither dared look back.

Let's hurry Karel said. Let's cross. He heard them coming and calling out things. He would not stop nor would Frederick. Automobiles passed and they dashed across.

Karel said ooh and Frederick cried ohoooh. They were on the park space and on the gravel and almost by the buildings.

When Karel did turn around they were leaping at Frederick and him. He saw Frederick get swiped. One swung, one sailor, at Karel who had to run then across to two automobiles parked where some people were. He heard pad pad after him but was Frederick being killed.

Keep away from him the men in the cars said and two backed back. The men in the cars said you shouldn't be out on the Drive at this hour.

Karel turned and saw Frederick lying on the ground a thin figure far away. He saw him get up and move to the sidewalk RUN. He ran forward a little and as he took Frederick by the arm he saw two of them run at him again and he said let's RUN. They ran up one street and Frederick could say hail the first taxi but no taxi could be seen. What they did see was a private car and it stopping and the two chasing them were gaining on them. The audacity, the cussedness Karel thought as one had tried to hit him before that one sailor had his fly open the white showing.

The car was stopping. Two men got out and Frederick cried SAVE US FROM THESE SAILORS! The sailors were there and the men holding them off said to Frederick and Karel get in the car.

You're safe all right they said. They grabbed the sailors and said we're policemen you'll have to come along.

There was a crowd gathering and both sailors were trying to get away.

Karel had his handkerchief out, spitting on it and wiping off the mascara.

One of the sailors broke away and one of the policemen chased him.

The other sailor whined let me go I want to get away and the other policeman, cursing him, took out a blackjack and hit him on the shoulder which somewhat quieted him.

Frederick moaned now we're done for.

The other sailor didn't come back nor did Karel's eyebrows after the way he rubbed them.

The policeman that was left got in the car. They went to the police station and marched to the sergeant's desk. The whole gang had followed and were ordered out. Karel heard the policeman say fast thissailorsaid hefucked himin themouthbut theresnocomplaintsoits-disorderlyconductforall.

Karel's heart did not sink. He had been through it so many times in his mind he thought now life is being merely pedantic. He noticed the electric lights in particular.

What is your name (in a harsh voice)? Leers: search them! Contents of Frederick's pockets: two eyebrow tweezers, one black make-up pencil (with protector), one oversize ring twiddled by the detective, papers, key, money. The money was returned and the rest kept. Contents of Karel's pockets: one black make-up pencil (with protector), comb, key, money, all returned but make-up pencil and Karel thought I'll have to buy a new one.

Go in there.

They entered a kind of waiting room. Karel had a slight headache.

Frederick said you don't seem much perturbed how can you take it like that? I envy you.

Karel shrugged, thinking the occasion required no more confirmation than that.

They strolled in and out making wisecracks and Karel said to them you're all convinced beforehand why say anything.

One said if you'd stayed on Broadway this wouldna happened.

Karel looked sarcastically and said something about Broadway not that I know it so well.

Frederick told Karel that all the while his voice was sissy.

For Christ's sake Karel said I don't appear cowed anyway. He tried to appear just a little incommoded.

One perfectly unmentionable creature Frederick thought came in and said pair of the girls huh?

Karel looked at him as though he had just said no haven't a light buddy sorry.

Frederick was looking morose.

Karel thought that the sailor was cute looking with a sweet mouth. Anyway he's not so hoity-toity by this time the concupiscent bugger.

Well on my life Karel caught himself saying as he was looking at one spot and there suddenly appeared the visage of one Carl Manor, poet, who murmured well what are you doing here?

Karel smiled. He was noticing that Carl Manor had several what you might call abrasions, contusions, swellings and spots on his face and was being dressed by a surgeon. Two tough guys had just beat him up and there they were so Karel thought well ha, ha, that's that, no loss to poetry!

Frederick was watching the clock for the time to come. It did come and with it the patrol wagon. They all marched into it and there were some boys looking at them and they were taken to the station next to Harold's domicile.

After saying their names very plainly to the turnkey Frederick and Karel were given a cell to themselves. There was nothing but one long hard bench and a spigot above a toilet bowl.

Frederick answered yes you can drink from it if you can stand the stench coming from below.

The bench was calculated to be all but unendurable for two people.

Frederick said I can't sleep can you?

I don't know Karel said.

Frederick said I can't understand how you can take it like this but I'm in a worse position than you are. I've a suspended sentence.

Yes that's so said Karel.

Frederick said I envy you your composure you're marvelous and Karel looked at it and yes it was his composure.

Frederick said just think, I suppose Harold, Tony and the crowd are next door carousing at this moment. Karel admired Frederick's accent and enunciation. I'm going to lie down. Karel took off his coat and made a pillow of it.

They heard the voices in the others' cells: gob! . . . say any you got a cigarette . . . ohhh no butts here . . . what time is it?

That Frederick said is the way they always talk then they begin reminiscing like this: gee I'm in for stealing fifty dollars, it doesn't pay when I get out I'm not going to steal anything until I steal twenty thousand dollars.

Karel dozed off then he had to get up. I can't sleep.

Frederick said isn't it terrible my mother I know she's having hysterics I wish I could telegraph her but there's no chance of that. This'll call off my trip to Woodstock too O God. He had started to whimper when he first got in the cell but Karel put out his hand on his. It's very sportsmanlike of you he said you didn't run off, you stayed to save me.

Karel said uhm I could have got away easily. But somehow he couldn't be exactly sorry he didn't. I'll write a poem.

How can you in such atmosphere?

In this or no other. Isn't this a good first line. Karel recited it:

> *ripe is the urge, regular heart,*

and going on:

> *asleep in the mind, flesh on the hand*
> *picture and picture revolve into silence.*

But he could compose no more and fell asleep, taking up most of the bench.

Frederick stayed awake until it was dawn.

Karel managed to sleep in three positions. He would remember them he thought.

It's light Frederick said. I wonder what time it is.

While waiting Karel wet his hair and put his handkerchief smeared with mascara behind a pipe.

You still look like a queen Frederick said.

Boo Karel said and at that Frederick laughed.

They were let out of the cell and marched and Karel sat next to the sailor. The others included a gang of wops whatnot? who had come in later charged with assaulting one girl whatnot? (the impression they got was of concrete).

They had to wait after the ride, 8:30 Sunday morning, in one large cell at 57th Street station. The two who had trounced Manor got chummy and explained to Karel, looking up with their eyes and mouths to heaven in which there is God, that they both being Southern and drunk the night before had sought to displace without ceremony a Negro from a seat in the subway and Manor had interfered and got his.

In the same cell there was one old thing by himself charged with rape. The girl in one difficult whole led up to a particularly red and particularly large bump under her left eye.

six months two weeks doin six aint that snap snap fucking dame are you the chauffeur

Karel and Frederick were not insulted once. They started to wean them from the cell. It was 9:30.

Karel leaned against the back of the bench. Frederick's lip was swollen; the bloodspots were still on his chin and on his glasses.

One officious person, a hundred per cent bad Irish Karel thought, came back just before they were called and cursed at Manor's assaulters who did not think that was a good sign and it wasn't for they went and got sixty days.

There was only now the sailor at one end of the bench and Frederick and Karel at the other. Suddenly Frederick said plaintively to him what did you do it for? The sailor smiled slightly. Now you see what a mess we're all in—all for nothing.

The sailor said, weakly, I don't know.

We didn't speak to you now did we? You'd better say that because it'll make it go better for all of us. Someone had said the ship'll give you five days on bread and water for this.

The sailor said well I don't know.

Then they called them. Karel and Frederick waited on a bench as straight as this: i i

They saw the detective who had finally appeared go up to the gob and whisper something.

Frederick turned to Karel and said now we *are* done for.

Karel looked somewhere and they were called. He got out his private band and to music they went before justice and Karel handled his train very well he thought and there were not only two or three about four six people in the courtroom. Karel looked up at the magistrate after they had ranged them. The magistrate took one look. Karel imagined his switch was looking very well.

The magistrate said something but what did Karel care he had washed his gloves. The detective was sworn in first.

Frederick spoke up and said he would like an attorney beforehand. The magistrate who was white haired, shrewd-humored, stooped, small-faced waved him aside and (Frederick said later) WINKED.

The detective told the truth except he said that the sailor had said they had said to the sailor: want to earn a few easy dollars?

When he said that Karel knew just what to do thinking the magistrate had his eye furtively upon him: he looked away with his teeth "" meaning what a lie. The magistrate must have seen him but Karel thought he did it with the right accent, modestly.

The magistrate looked at the sailor and said has the detective spoken the truth?

The sailor was dumb; in his own sweet soul he couldn't tell such a BIG LIE.

The magistrate smiled and looked at Karel intently and said your first name is Karel?

Yes.

And you don't live with your parents.

No.

Where do you live?

319 West Third Street.

And you say you are a free-lance writer, what do you mean by that, free of writing?

No Karel said taking a sidelong glance to see that his elegant train of feather dusters was in place, if it means anything I have appeared in the best places . . . the *Post* . . . the *Sun* . . .

Do you mean the magistrate asked that your articles have been accepted by these places?

Yes Karel said the *Bookman* as well. . . . I have you see certain ambitions.

He cut him off DISCHARGED and Karel didn't have to lean forward to hear it.

Frederick started going toward the cells but someone pushed him into the aisle with Karel. The sailor was already there.

Then the magistrate leaned over and said sweetly but be more careful next time!

They went down some winding marble broad steps. The sailor walked in front of them.

Frederick was saying oh I can't believe it.

Karel said I knew it. I sensed it. There's at least one judge in the world with a civilized with a sense of civilization.

The sailor was walking down in front of them slowly.

Karel said I could kiss him right now.

They took the other side of the street and he did not look back at them.

They went to a drugstore and Karel had a chocolate ice-cream soda.

Frederick had a coca-cola with vanilla ice cream in it.

CHARLES HENRI FORD & PARKER TYLER

A novel of the thirties which its authors proudly present as "the novel of the generation that beat the beat generation": Parker Tyler, now become one of the foremost film critics of the time, and Charles Henri Ford, whose earlier poems had been patroned by Gertrude Stein, William Carlos Williams and Edith Sitwell.

The Young and Evil was first printed in Paris in 1933 by Jack Kahane's The Obelisk Press.

Parker Tyler says: "Pre-Cool, pre-Genet and pre-Beat, post-Fitzgerald and post-Surrealist, The Young and Evil *long represented a muted interval in Ford's career and mine. It seems a natural that The Olympia Press, direct descendant of The Obelisk Press, the book's original publisher in Paris over a quarter-century before, should have reissued it in 1960. Yet erotica and the nude spoken word, even five years ago, had not ascended to the heights of public tolerance and favor enjoyed today. In 1933, our book was duly attacked and defended in the columns of the Herald Tribune's Paris Edition, consigned to burning and banning by the customs authorities of other countries, and then left to the loving, lingering care of collectors. The late Dame Edith Sitwell, while joining the incendiary faction, expressed a qualified approval of what she called our 'pillow fights.' A great silence on the book, like a dark age, was interrupted (while I wrote poetry and criticism of art and film) only by strange, if gratifying, queries like this: 'Dear Mr. Tyler, I have heard of your* novel, The Young and Evil, *and wonder if you can tell me where I might be able to obtain a copy.' I would point vaguely in the direction of some esoteric bookshop. At last a copy found its way to Maurice Girodias, who proceeded to publish it in the classic little green covers of his Traveller's Companion Series. Wondering at the juxtaposition, I found myself cheek by jowl with the Marquis de Sade in print and (at a champagne party relaunching the book at the* Cave, *7 rue Saint-Sévérin) with William Saroyan and James Jones in person. The dust jacket again wore the glittering verbal plaques by Gertrude Stein and Djuna Barnes, to which had been added one by Louis Kronenberger: the only critic to have noticed the book's broken wave on American shores. Not a line of the novel's text has ever been revised, nor a word added or subtracted. If one may presume to tamper with perfection, one must stop at prophecy."*

Samuel Beckett

WATT

Mr Hackett turned the corner and saw, in the failing light, at some little distance, his seat. It seemed to be occupied. This seat, the property very likely of the municipality, or of the public, was of course not his, but he thought of it as his. This was Mr Hackett's attitude towards things that pleased him. He knew they were not his, but he thought of them as his. He knew were not his, because they pleased him.

Halting, he looked at the seat with greater care. Yes, it was not vacant. Mr Hackett saw things a little more clearly when he was still. His walk was a very agitated walk.

Mr Hackett did not know whether he should go on, or whether

he should turn back. Space was open on his right hand, and on his left hand, but he knew that he would never take advantage of this. He knew also that he would not long remain motionless, for the state of his health rendered this unfortunately impossible. The dilemma was thus of extreme simplicity: to go on, or to turn, and return, round the corner, the way he had come. Was he, in other words, to go home at once, or was he to remain out a little longer?

Stretching out his left hand, he fastened it round a rail. This permitted him to strike his stick against the pavement. The feel, in his palm, of the thudding rubber appeased him, slightly.

But he had not reached the corner when he turned again and hastened towards the seat, as fast as his legs could carry him. When he was so near the seat, that he could have touched it with his stick, if he had wished, he again halted and examined its occupants. He had the right, he supposed, to stand and wait for the tram. They too were perhaps waiting for the tram, for a tram, for many trams stopped here, when requested, from without or within, to do so.

Mr Hackett decided, after some moments, that if they were waiting for a tram they had been doing so for some time. For the lady held the gentleman by the ears, and the gentleman's hand was on the lady's thigh, and the lady's tongue was in the gentleman's mouth. Tired of waiting for the tram, said[1] Mr Hackett, they strike up an acquaintance. The lady now removing her tongue from the gentleman's mouth, he put his into hers. Fair do, said Mr Hackett. Taking a pace forward, to satisfy himself that the gentleman's other hand was not going to waste, Mr Hackett was shocked to find it limply dangling over the back of the seat, with between its fingers the spent three quarters of a cigarette.

I see no indecency, said the policeman.

We arrive too late, said Mr Hackett. What a shame.

Do you take me for a fool? said the policeman.

Mr Hackett recoiled a step, forced back his head until he thought his throatskin would burst, and saw at last, afar, bent angrily upon him, the red violent face.

Officer, he cried, as God is my witness, he had his hand upon it.

God is a witness that cannot be sworn.

If I interrupted your beat, said Mr Hackett, a thousand pardons.

---

[1] Much valuable space has been saved, in this work, that would otherwise have been lost, by avoidance of the plethoric reflexive pronoun after *say*.

I did so with the best intentions, for you, for me, for the community at large.

The policeman replied briefly to this.

If you imagine that I have not your number, said Mr Hackett, you are mistaken. I may be infirm, but my sight is excellent. Mr Hackett sat down on the seat, still warm, from the loving. Good evening, and thank you, said Mr Hackett.

It was an old seat, low and worn. Mr Hackett's nape rested against the solitary backboard, beneath it unimpeded his hunch protruded, his feet just touched the ground. At the ends of the long outspread arms the hands held the armrests, the stick hooked round his neck hung between his knees.

So from the shadows he watched the last trams pass, oh not the last, but almost, and in the sky, and in the still canal, the long greens and yellows of the summer evening.

But now a gentleman passing, with a lady on his arms, espied him.

Oh, my dear, he said, there is Hackett.

Hackett, said the lady. What Hackett? Where?

You know Hackett, said the gentleman. You must have often heard me speak of Hackett. Hunchy Hackett. On the seat.

The lady looked attentively at Mr Hackett.

So that is Hackett, she said.

Yes, said the gentleman.

Poor fellow, she said.

Oh, said the gentleman, let us now stop, do you mind, and wish him the time of evening. He advanced, exclaiming, My dear fellow, my dear fellow, how are you?

Mr Hackett raised his eyes, from the dying day.

My wife, cried the gentleman. Meet my wife. My wife. Mr Hackett.

I have heard so much about you, said the lady, and now I meet you, at last. Mr Hackett!

I do not rise, not having the force, said Mr Hackett.

Why I should think not indeed, said the lady. She stooped towards him, quivering with solicitude. I should hope not indeed, she said.

Mr Hackett thought she was going to pat him on the head, or at least stroke his hunch. He called in his arms and they sat down beside him, the lady on the one side, and the gentleman on the other. As a result of this, Mr Hackett found himself between them. His head reached to the armpits. Their hands met above the hunch, on the backboard. They drooped with tenderness toward him.

You remember Grehan? said Mr Hackett.

The poisoner, said the gentleman.

The solicitor, said Mr Hackett.

I knew him slightly, said the gentleman. Six years, was it not.

Seven, said Mr Hackett. Six are rarely given.

He deserved ten, in my opinion, said the gentleman.

Or twelve, said Mr Hackett.

What did he do? said the lady.

Slightly overstepped his prerogatives, said the gentleman.

I received a letter from him this morning, said Mr Hackett.

Oh, said the gentleman, I did not know they might communicate with the outer world.

He is a solicitor, said Mr Hackett. He added, I am scarcely the outer world.

What rubbish, said the gentleman.

What nonsense, said the lady.

The letter contained an enclosure, said Mr Hackett, of which, knowing your love of literature, I would favour you with the primeur, if it were not too dark to see.

The primeur, said the lady.

That is what I said, said Mr Hackett.

I have a petrol-lighter, said the gentleman.

Mr Hackett drew a paper from his pocket and the gentleman lit his petrol-lighter.

Mr Hackett read:

TO NELLY

To Nelly, said the lady.

To Nelly, said Mr Hackett.

There was a silence.

Shall I continue? said Mr Hackett.

My mother's name was Nelly, said the lady.

The name is not uncommon, said Mr Hackett, even I have known several Nellies.

Read on, my dear fellow, said the gentleman.
Mr Hackett read:

TO NELLY

To thee, sweet Nell, when shadows fall
Jug-jug! Jug-jug!
I here in thrall
My wanton thoughts do turn.
Walks she out yet with Byrne?
Moves Hyde his hand amid her skirts
As erst? I ask, and Echo answers: Certes.

Tis well! Tis well! Far, far be it
Pu-we! Pu-we!
From me, my tit,
Such innocent joys to chide.
Burn, burn with Byrne, from Hyde
Hide naught—hide naught save what
Is Greh'n's. IT hide from Hyde, with Byrne burn not.

It! Peerless gage of maidenhood!
Cuckoo! Cuckoo!
Would that I could
Be certain in my mind
Upon discharge to find
Neath Cupid's flow'r, hey nonny O!
Diana's blushing bud in statu quo.

Then darkly kindle durst my soul
Tuwhit! Tuwhoo!
As on it stole
The murmur to become
Epithalamium,
And Hymen o'er my senses shed
The dewy forejoys of the marriage-bed.

Enough—

Ample, said the lady.

A woman in a shawl passed before them. Her belly could dimly be seen, sticking out, like a balloon.

I was never like that, my dear, said the lady, was I?

Not to my knowledge, my love, said the gentleman.

You remember the night that Larry was born, said the lady.

I do, said the gentleman.

How old is Larry now? said Mr Hackett.

How old is Larry, my dear? said the gentleman.

How old is Larry, said the lady. Larry will be forty years old next March, D.V.

That is the kind of thing Dee always vees, said Mr Hackett.

I wouldn't go as far as that, said the gentleman.

Would you care to hear, Mr Hackett, said the lady, about the night that Larry was born?

Oh do tell him, my dear, said the gentleman.

Well, said the lady, that morning at breakfast Goff turns to me and he says, Tetty, he says, Tetty, my pet, I should very much like to invite Thompson, Cream and Colquhoun to help us eat the duck, if I felt sure you felt up to it. Why, my dear, says I, I never felt fitter in my life. Those were my words, were they not?

I believe they were, said Goff.

Well, said Tetty, when Thompson comes into the dining-room, followed by Cream and Berry (Colquhoun I remember had a previous engagement), I was already seated at the table. There was nothing strange in that, seeing I was the only lady present. You did not find that strange, did you, my love?

Certainly not, said Goff, most natural.

The first mouthful of duck had barely passed my lips, said Tetty, when Larry leaped in my wom.

Your what? said Mr Hackett.

My wom, said Tetty.

You know, said Goff, her woom.

How embarrassing for you, said Mr Hackett.

I continued to eat, drink and make light conversation, said Tetty, and Larry to leap, like a salmon.

What an experience for you, said Mr Hackett.

There were moments, I assure you, when I thought he would tumble out on the floor, at my feet.

Merciful heavens, you felt him slipping, said Mr Hackett.

No trace of this dollar appeared on my face, said Tetty. Did it, my dear?

Not a trace, said Goff.

Nor did my sense of humour desert me. What rolypoly, said Mr Berry, I remember, turning to me with a smile, what delicious roly-poly, it melts in the mouth. Not only in the mouth, sir, I replied, without an instant's hesitation, not only in the mouth, my dear sir. Not too osy with the sweet, I thought.

Not too what? said Mr Hackett.

Osy, said Goff. You know, not too osy.

With the coffee and liquors, labour was in full swing, Mr Hackett, I give you my solemn word, under the groaning board.

Swing is the word, said Goff.

You knew she was pregnant, said Mr Hackett.

Why er, said Goff, you see er, I er, we er—

Tetty's hand fell heartily on Mr Hackett's thigh.

He thought I was coy, she cried. Hahahaha. Haha. Ha.

Haha, said Mr Hackett.

I was greatly worried I admit, said Goff.

Finally they retired, did you not? said Tetty.

We did indeed, said Goff, we retired to the billiard-room, for a game of slosh.

I went up those stairs, Mr Hackett, said Tetty, on my hands and knees, wringing the carpetrods as though they were made of raffia.

You were in such anguish, said Mr Hackett.

Three minutes later I was a mother.

Unassisted, said Goff.

I did everything with my own hands, said Tetty, everything.

She severed the cord with her teeth, said Goff, not having a scissors to her hand. What do you think of that?

I would have snapped it across my knee, if necessary, said Tetty.

That is a thing I often wondered, said Mr Hackett, what it feels like to have the string cut.

For the mother or the child? said Goff.

For the mother, said Mr Hackett. I was not found under a cabbage, I believe.

For the mother, said Tetty, the feeling is one of relief, of great relief, as when the guests depart. All my subsequent strings were severed by Professor Cooper, but the feeling was always the same, one

of riddance.

Then you dressed and came downstairs, said Mr Hackett, leading the infant by the hand.

We heard the cries, said Goff.

Judge of their surprise, said Tetty.

Cream's potting had been extraordinary, extraordinary, I remember, said Goff. I never saw anything like it. We were watching breathless, as he set himself for a long thin jenny, with the black of all balls.

What temerity, said Mr Hackett.

A quite impossible stroke, in my opinion, said Goff. He drew back his queue to strike, when the wail was heard. He permitted himself an expression that I shall not repeat.

Poor little Larry, said Tetty, as though it were his fault.

Tell me no more, said Mr Hackett, it is useless.

SAMUEL BECKETT

As I was preparing to go into business under the imprint of The Olympia Press, I heard of a group of English and American writers living in Paris who, having founded a literary quarterly Merlin *in the spring of 1952, were about to embark on a book-publishing venture of*

their own. I have asked Richard Seaver, one of the original Merlin
*editors, to sketch the background concerning the publication of
Samuel Beckett's* Watt, *with which he was directly involved. The
following are his remarks:*

If there is such a phenomenon as a shock of discovery, I experienced it in the spring of 1952. I had been living in Paris for three years
then, hunting for I'm not sure what gods or ghosts, but convinced
they could be discovered only in that magic city. I had found quarters
on the rue du Sabot, in an empty ground-floor warehouse behind an
antique shop. The owner, too generous to have been Parisian, was a
Swiss dealer in primitive art, and in return for my tending the shop
a few hours a week, gave me free room in the dépôt at the end of the
courtyard. I mention the geography merely because it was soon to become the headquarters for an Anglo-American literary quarterly,
Merlin, and also because it was located fifty yards, and just around
the corner, from the most enterprising and perceptive French publisher of the postwar era: Les Editions de Minuit.

Jérôme Lindon, the director-owner-editor of Les Editions de
Minuit had everything—with the possible exception of money—necessary to make a good publishing house: intelligence, flair, and guts. By
1960 he had published most of the group which loosely became known
as the "new novelists": Alain Robbe-Grillet, Michel Butor, Nathalie
Sarraute, Claude Simon, Robert Pinget. But already in 1951 he had
"discovered" the most important writer to grace his imprint, and indeed one of the most important writers of our time: Samuel Beckett.

There were two routes from my warehouse-home to the bright
cafés of St.-Germain des Près, one by the rue du Dragon and the other
by the rue Bernard Palissy, and since I took at least two trips there a
day, and always tried to avoid taking the same route twice in a row,
it happened, almost inevitably, that I passed number 7 of the latter
street at least once a day. Number 7, a bordel until the puritanical
wrath of a famous female zealot caused these houses to close in 1948,
housed Les Editions de Minuit. Sometime early in 1952, in Minuit's
tiny display window, I noticed two intriguing works: Molloy, and
Malone Meurt, by Samuel Beckett. I remember looking in that
window a dozen times and reading the titles, vaguely recalling the
author's name. He was Irish, and I associated him with Joyce. And I
remembered that, twenty years before, he had contributed to that col-

lective Joycean commentary that Shakespeare & Company had pub-
lished and entitled Our Exagmination Round his Factification for In-
camination of Work in Progress.

Finally I went in and bought the books. I went home and read
them; and then I reread them. And after the second reading I was con-
vinced that my first impression was correct: Molloy *and* Malone *were*
miracles, two stunning works. I went back to Minuit and asked what
else of Beckett's it had published. As yet nothing, I was told, though
a third novel was coming. It was entitled L'Innommable. *There was,*
however, an earlier novel, Murphy, *which Bordas had published and*
which, Minuit believed, was still in print. I bicycled over to Bordas.
Not only was Murphy *still in print (it had been published in French*
five years before, in 1947), but by the look of the stock in the back of
the shop, the original printing was virtually intact. I took my precious
copy home and read Murphy. *Not* Molloy *or* Malone, *I felt, not great,*
but only a notch below. I would await L'Innommable.

While waiting, a friend informed me that the French radio was
scheduled to record part of an unproduced play by Beckett, En
Attendant Godot. *I went to the taping, and heard Roger Blin, a re-*
markable French actor, perform Lucky for the first time. The play, too,
was a thing of beauty. Shortly thereafter I discovered, in the French
magazine Fontaine, *a Beckett story entitled* "l'Expulsé," *which was*
of the caliber of Molloy.

All this was very personal and private, and of no concern to any-
one save myself, until I became involved in 1952 with a newly founded
English-language magazine Merlin, *whose editor was Alex Trocchi,*
later the author of Cain's Book *and at least a page or two of Frank*
Harris' memoirs. In the autumn 1952 issue of Merlin *I wrote an essay*
which, albeit inadequately, expressed my thoughts on Beckett. It was
called "Samuel Beckett: An Introduction," and it was no more than
that, for all I had read or heard of his work were the five works men-
tioned.

Dutifully, we sent a copy of the issue containing the essay to Mr.
Beckett. Silence. But then Monsieur Lindon let it slip that Beckett had
in hiding a final work in English (for by the 'fifties he had been
writing directly in French) he had written during the war, and never
published: Watt. *We wrote Mr. Beckett asking if we could publish*
an extract of Watt *in our magazine. Silence.*

We had all but given up when one rainy afternoon, at the rue du Sabot, a knock came at the door and a tall, gaunt figure in a rain-coat handed in a manuscript in a black binder, and disappeared, al-most without a word. That night a half dozen of us—Trocchi; Jane Lougee, Merlin's publisher; two English poets, Christopher Logue and Pat Bowles; a Canadian writer, Charles Hatcher; and I—sat up half the night and read Watt *aloud, taking turns till our voices gave out, until we had finished it.*

Beckett had specified, by a note in the manuscript, the section from Watt *we could use: Mr Knott's inventory of the possibilities of his attire (*"As for his feet, sometimes he wore on each a sock, or on the one a sock and on the other a stocking, or a boot, or a shoe, or a slipper, or a sock and boot, or a sock and shoe, or a sock and slipper, or a stocking and boot, or a stocking and shoe, or a stocking and slipper, or nothing at all. . . ."*) and the possible positions of the furniture in his room (*"Thus it was not rare to find, on the Sunday, the tallboy on its feet by the fire, and the dressing-table on its head by the bed, and the night-stool on its face by the door, and the washhand-stand on its back by the window; and, on the Monday, the tallboy on its head by the bed. . . ."* etc.). I believe Mr. Beckett was testing* Merlin's *integrity by that demand, for he tended to denigrate all his work, we were later to learn, and perversely chose a section which, taken out of context, would, he deemed, have to be rejected. Years later I confronted him with that accusation, which he answered with a broad, bad-boy grin. At any rate,* Merlin *published the extract in its next issue. I will not say the reaction was world-wide, but we received several angry letters and cancellation of five per cent of our subscriptions (i.e., five cancel-lations). Avant-garde, all right, the letters said, but let's draw the line at total absurdity. We knew we were on the right track. Thereafter, not an issue of* Merlin *appeared without something by Beckett. And when, in the autumn of 1953, having lost relatively little money on the magazine, we determined we would expand and see if we could lose more money more quickly by publishing books, the first book we chose to publish was, of course,* Watt. (*We had discovered a technique whereby, changing printers for each issue of the magazine, we were able to limit our quarterly losses. Calculating roughly that there were no less than fifty printers within a fifty-mile radius of Paris, we estimated (wrongly) that we could build up quite a backlist by limit-ing each printer to one book).*

An agreement—I do not recall whether there was an actual,

formal contract—was signed with Mr. Beckett, an advance of 50,000 francs ($100) duly paid, and we were in business. That is, not quite in business. For over a year we had been waging a battle with the French postal authorities—pleading, wheedling, cajoling—to obtain magazine-rate postal privileges. We had evolved through the various echelons of French postal bureaucracy and been rejected, variously, on the grounds that Merlin *appeared too infrequently (true), that we could not prove we were a legitimate business (we were not), that we had failed to fill out certain fundamental forms (we had failed to), etc. Finally, our cause reached a gray-haired, bushy-browed, well-dressed, highly placed functionary whose office, in the shadow of the Arc de Triomphe, looked as though it had not been cleaned since Napoleon had left town. He listened impassively to our impassioned plea, leafed through the various issues of the magazine in front of him, and then said: "Messieurs, I regret to inform you the department has turned down your request. Mailing privileges are not given to organs of propaganda." We were stunned. We pressed for clarification. "Messieurs, who is Samuel Beckett?" A writer, a very fine one; we have published several of his works, we said. "And this Mr. Beckett, does he not finance your magazine?" Most assuredly not. "Hmmmm." Silence. "Because, gentlemen, it appears to our examiners that your magazine is an organ of propaganda dedicated to furthering the fame of Mr. Beckett. I'm afraid the case is closed."*

Other problems, all business in nature, were hemming us in. Other French authorities were annoying us about failure to register as a company (ah taxes!), and for that we needed a French gérant *(manager). The little money we had for the magazine was running out, and yet, by mid-1953, we had concluded agreements for several more books, including a work by Sade, a remarkable first novel by a young American, Austryn Wainhouse—which no American publisher has had the foresight to republish here—Jean Genet's* The Thief's Journal, *which Genet's translator had brought us, two volumes of poems, etc. And by now the word was out among printers, who were demanding payment in advance, an obvious absurdity. We were in no wise paranoid, but it was clear there was a vast conspiracy against us.*

While we were reflecting upon these many problems, a knock came one afternoon on the rue du Sabot door, and a dapper gentleman in his mid-thirties, a Frenchman who spoke perfect English, introduced himself. Maurice Girodias, of whom we had heard as the pub-

*lisher of Les Editions du Chêne, a small but first-rate publishing house
which had recently been wrested away from him. He announced that
he was on the point of founding another, to publish only works in
English, had heard we had already planned our own, and suggested
we join forces. Collection Merlin could be part of his company,
wholly independent editorially; he would act as the* gérant, *thus
solving that thorny problem, and, what is more, he would put up the
money for the books. It sounded only slightly suspect. In return for
what? we asked. Well, at least two or three of the works I understand you are publishing, I too would plan to publish. The competition
would be ridiculous. Let us join forces. He was eloquent, suave, compelling. Standing before the courtyard door was Mr. Girodias' shiny
black Citroën, a sharp contrast to our seedy bicycles leaning sadly
against the entrance wall.*

*We had further meetings, came to an agreement, and soon Col-
lection Merlin and Olympia Press were one. True to his word,
Girodias provided the money, or at least the printers, for every work
we had planned, and some others we later contracted for. The first
work to appear under the joint imprint was* Watt.

*Several years later I was to learn that, when Maurice came by that
first day at the rue du Sabot, the shiny black Citroën which had so
impressed us had not been paid for, and his financial fortunes were
at an even lower ebb—if such were possible—than ours. The man
must be a genius.*

PLEXUS

The story finished, the kids were hustled off to bed. We could now settle down comfortably to drink and chew the fat. MacGregor liked nothing better than to talk of old times. We were only in our thirties but had twenty years of solid friendship between us, and besides, at that age one feels older than at fifty or sixty. Actually, both MacGregor and I were still in a period of prolonged adolescence.

Whenever MacGregor took up with a new girl it seemed imperative for him to look me up, get my approval of her, and then settle down for a long, sentimental talk-fest. We had done it so many

HENRY MILLER

times that it was almost like playing a duet. The girl was supposed to sit there enchanted—and to interrupt us now and then with a pertinent question. The duet always began by one of us asking if the other had seen or heard anything recently of George Marshall. I don't know why we instinctively chose this opening. We were like certain chess players who, no matter who the opponent may be, always open with the Scotch gambit.

"Have you seen George lately?" says I, apropos of nothing at all.
"You mean George Marshall?"
"Yeah, it seems ages since I've seen him."

"No, Hen, to tell you the truth, I haven't. I suppose he's still going to the Village Saturday afternoons."

"To dance?"

MacGregor smiled. "If you want to call it that, Henry. *You know George!*" He paused, then added: "George is a queer guy. I think I know less about him now than ever."

"*What?*"

"Just that, Henry. That guy leads a double life. You ought to see him at home, with the wife and kids. You wouldn't know him."

I confessed I hadn't seen George since he got married. "Never liked that wife of his."

"You should talk to George about her sometime. How they manage to live together is a miracle. He gives her what she wants and in return he goes his own way. Boy, it's like skating on dynamite when you visit them. You know the sort of double talk George indulges in...."

"Listen," I interrupted, "do you remember that night in Greenpoint, when we were sitting in the back of some gin mill and George began a spiel about his mother, how the sun rose and set in her ass?"

"Jesus, Hen, you sure think of strange things. Sure, I remember. I remember every conversation we ever had, I guess. And the time and place. And whether I was drunk or sober." He turned to Trix. "Are we boring you? You know, the three of us were great pals once. We had some good times together, didn't we, Hen? Remember Maspeth—those athletic contests? We didn't have much to worry about, did we? Let's see, were you tied up with the widow then, or was that later? *Get this,* Trix . . . Here's this guy hardly out of school and he falls in love with a woman old enough to be his mother. Wanted to marry her, too, didn't you, Hen?"

I grinned and gave a vague nod.

"Henry always falls hard. The serious sort, though you'd never think it to look at him. . . . But about George. As I was saying before, Hen, George is a different guy. He's at loose ends. Hates his work, loathes his wife, and the kids bore him to death. All he thinks of now is tail. And boy, does he chase it! Picks 'em younger and younger all the time. The last time I saw him he was in a hell of a mess with some fifteen year old—from his own school. (I still can't picture George as a principal, can you?) It began right in his office, it seems. Then he takes to meeting her at the dance hall. Finally he has the nerve to take her to a hotel—and register as man and wife. . . . The last I heard they were diddlin' one another in a vacant lot near the ball grounds. Some day, Hen, that guy's goin' to make the headlines. And boy, that won't make pleasant reading!"

At this point I had a flash of memory, so vivid and so complete, I could scarcely contain myself. It was like opening a Japanese fan. The picture was of a time when George and I were still twins, so to speak. I was then working for my father, which means I must have been twenty-two or -three. George Marshall had come down with a bad case of pneumonia which had kept him bedridden for several months. When he got well enough, his parents shipped him to the country—somewhere in New Jersey. It all started by my receiving a letter from him one day saying that he was recuperating fast and wouldn't I come to visit him. I was only too glad of the chance to steal a few days' vacation, and so I sent him a wire saying I'd be there the following day.

It was late autumn. The countryside was cheerless. George met me at the station, with his young cousin, Herbie. (The farm was run by George's aunt and uncle, that is, his mother's sister and her husband.) The first words out of his mouth—as I might well have expected!—were to the effect that it was his mother who had saved his life. He was overjoyed to see me and appeared to be in excellent shape. He was brown and weather-beaten.

"The grub is wonderful, Hen," he said. "It's a real farm, you know."

To me it looked much like any other farm—sort of seedy, grubby and run down. His aunt was a stout, kind-hearted, motherly creature whom George worshiped, apparently, almost as much as he did his mother. Herbie, the son, was a bit of a zany. A blabbermouth too. But what got me at once was the look of wonder in his eyes. He evidently idolized George. And then the way we talked to one another was something new for him. It was hard to shake him off our heels.

The first thing we did—I remember it so well—was to have a tall glass of milk. Rich milk. Milk such as I hadn't tasted since I was a boy. "Drink five and six of them a day," says George. He cut me a thick slice of home-made bread, spread some country butter over it, and over that some home-made jam.

"Did you bring any old clothes with you, Hen?"

I confessed I hadn't thought of that.

"Never mind, I'll lend you my things. You've got to wear old clothes here. You'll see."

He looked pointedly at Herbie. "Eh, Herbie?"

I had arrived on the afternoon train. It was now getting on to dark. "Change your clothes, Hen, and we'll take a brisk hike. Dinner won't be ready till seven. Got to work up an appetite, you know."

"Yeah," said Herbie, "we're going to have chicken tonight."

And in the next breath he asked me if I were a good runner.

George gave me a sly wink. "He's crazy about games, Hen."

When I met them at the foot of the stairs I was handed a big stick. "Better wear your gloves," said Herbie.

He threw me a big woolen muffler.

"All set?" says George. "Come on, let's hurry." And he starts off at a record-breaking clip.

"Why the hurry?" said I. "Where are we going?"

"Down by the station," said Herbie.

"And what's down there?"

"You'll see. Won't he, George?"

The station was a dismal, forlorn affair. A line of freight cars was standing there, waiting for milk cans, no doubt.

"Listen," said George, slowing up a bit to keep in step with me, "the idea is to take the lead. You know what I mean!" He talked rapidly, mumbling the words, as if there were something secretive connected with our actions. "Up to now there's been just Herbie and me: we've had to make our own fun. Nothing to worry about, Hen. You'll get on to it quick enough. Just follow me."

I was more than ever baffled by this quixotic piece of information. As we hopped along Herbie became positively electrified. He gabbled like an old turkey cock.

George opened the door of the station softly, stealthily, and peered inside. An old drunk was snoozing away on the bench. "Here," said George, grabbing my hat and stuffing an old cap in my hand, "wear this!" He shoves a crazy looking contraption on his own head and pins a badge on his coat. "You stay here," he commands, "and I'll open shop. Do just as Herbie does and you'll be all right."

As George ducks into the office and opens the ticket window Herbie pulls me by the hand. "This is it, Hen," says he, going up to the window where George is already standing, pretending to make up the train schedule.

"Sir, I would like to buy a ticket," says Herbie in a timid voice.

"A ticket to where?" says George, frowning. "We've got all kinds of tickets here. Do you want first, second, or third class? Let's see, the Weehawken Express pulls out of here in about eight minutes. She's making a connection with the Denver and Rio Grande at Omaha Junction. *Any baggage?*"

"Please sir, I don't know where I want to go yet."

"Whaddaya mean, you don't know where you want to go? What do you think this is—a *lottery*? Who's that man behind you? Any relation of yours?"

Herbie turns round to look at me and blinks.

"He's my great-uncle, sir. Wants to go to Winnipeg, but he's not sure when."

"Tell him to step up here. What's the matter with him—is he deaf or just hard of hearing?"

Herbie pushed me in front of him. We look at each other, George Marshall and I, as if we had never seen each other before.

"I just *came* from Winnipeg," says I. "Isn't there some other place I could go to?"

"I could sell you a ticket to New Brunswick, but there wouldn't be much in it for the company. We've got to make ends meet, you know. Now here's a nice looking ticket for Spuyten Duyvil—how would that suit you? Or would you like something more expensive?"

"I'd like to go by way of the Great Lakes, if you could arrange it."

"*Arrange it?* That's my business! How many in the party? Any cats or dogs? You know the lakes are frozen now, don't you? But you can catch the iceboat this side of Canandaigua. I don't have to draw a map for you, do I?"

I leaned forward as if to communicate something private and confidential.

"*Don't whisper!*" he shouted, banging a ruler against the counter. "It's against the rules. . . . Now, then, what is it you wished to convey to me? Speak clearly and pause for your commas and semicolons."

"It's about the coffin," I said.

"The *coffin?* Why didn't you mention that right off? Hold on a minute, I'll have to telegraph the dispatch master." He went over to the machine and tapped the keys. "Got to get a special routing. Livestock and corpses take the deferred route. They spoil too quickly. . . . Anything in the coffin besides the body?"

"Yes sir, my wife."

"Get the hell out of here before I call the police!" Down came the window with a bang. And then an infernal racket inside the coop, as if the new station master had run amuck.

"Quick," says Herbie, "let's get out of here. I know a short cut, come on!" And grabbing my hand, he pulls me out by the other door, around by the water tank. "Flop down, quick," he says, "or they'll spy you." We flopped in a puddle of dirty water under the tank. "Shhhhh!" says Herbie, putting his finger over my lips. "They might hear you."

We lay there a few minutes, then Herbie got up on all fours, cautiously, looking about as if we were already trapped. "You lay here a minute and I'll run up the ladder and see if the tank's empty."

"They're nuts," I said to myself. Suddenly I asked myself why I should be lying in that cold dirty water. Herbie called softly: "Come on up, the coast is clear. We can hide in here a while." As I gripped the iron rungs I felt the wind go through me like an icy blast. "Don't fall in," says Herbie, "the tank's half-full." I climbed to the top and hung from the inside of the tank with frozen hands. "How long do we stay this way?" I asked after a few minutes. "Not long," says Herbie. "They're changing the watch now. Hear 'em? George'll be waiting for us in the caboose. He'll have a nice warm stove going."

It was dark when we clambered out of the tank and raced across the yard to the end of the freight train standing on the siding. I was frozen through and through. Herbie was right. As we opened the door of the caboose there was George sitting before a hot stove, warming his hands.

"Take your coat off, Hen," he says, "and dry yourself." Then he reaches up to a little closet and gets a flask of whisky. "Here, take a good pull—this is dynamite." I did as instructed, passed the flask to George who took a good swig himself, and then to little Herbie.

"Did you bring any provisions?" says George to Herbie.

"A chippie and a couple of potatoes," says Herbie, fishing them out of his pockets."

"Where's the mayonnaise?"

"I couldn't find it, *honest*," says Herbie.

"Next time I want mayonnaise, understand?" thunders George Marshall. "How the hell do you expect me to eat roast potatoes without mayonnaise?" Then, without transition, he continues: "Now the idea is to crawl under the cars until we're near the engine. When I whistle, the two of you crawl from under and run as fast as you can. Take the short cut down to the river. I'll meet you under the bridge. Here Hen, better take another gulp of this . . . it's cold down there. Next time I'll offer you a cigar—but don't take it! *How do you feel now?*"

I felt so good I couldn't see the sense of leaving in a hurry. But evidently their plans had to be executed in strict timing.

"How about that chippie and the potatoes?" I ventured to ask.

"That's for next time," says George. "We can't afford to be trapped here." He turns to Herbie. "Have you got the gun?"

Off again, scrambling around under the freight train as if we were outlaws. I was glad Herbie had given me the woolen muffler. At a given signal Herbie and I flung ourselves face downward under the car, waiting for George's whistle.

"What's the next move?" I whispered.

"Shhhhh! Someone may hear you."

In a few minutes we heard a low whistle, crawled out from under, and ran as fast as our legs would carry us down the ravine toward the bridge. There was George again, sitting under the bridge, waiting. "Good work," he says. "We gave 'em the slip all right. Now listen, we'll rest a minute or two and then we'll make for that hill over there, do you see?" He turned to Herbie. "Is the gun loaded?"

Herbie examined his rusty old Colt, nodded, then shoved it back in the holster.

"Remember," says George, "don't shoot unless it's absolutely necessary. I don't want you to be killing any more children accidentally, you understand?"

There was a gleam in Herbie's eyes as he shook his head.

"The idea, Hen, is to get to the foot of that hill before they give the alarm. Once we get there we're safe. We'll make a detour home by way of the swamp."

We started off on a trot, crouching low. Soon we were in the bulrushes and the water coming over our shoe tops. "Keep an eye open for traps," muttered George. We got to the foot of the hill without detection, rested there a few moments, then set off at a brisk pace to skirt the swamp. Finally we reached the road and settled down to a leisurely walk.

"We'll be home in a few minutes," says George. "We'll go in by the back way and change our clothes. Mum's the word."

"Are you sure we shook them off?" I asked.

"Reasonably sure," says George.

"The last time they followed us right to the barn," says Herbie.

"What happens if we get caught?"

Herbie drew the side of his hand across his throat.

I mumbled something to the effect that I wasn't sure I wanted to be involved.

"You've got to be," says Herbie. "It's a feud."

"We'll explain it in detail tomorrow," says George.

In the big room upstairs there were two beds, one for me, and one for Herbie and George. We made a fire at once in the big-bellied stove, and began changing our clothes.

"How would you like to give me a rubdown?" says George, stripping off his undershirt. "I get a rubdown twice a day. First alcohol and then goose fat. Nothing like it, Hen."

He lay down on the big bed and I went to work. I rubbed until my hands ached.

"Now you lay down," says George, "and Herbie'll fix you up. Makes a new man of you."

I did as instructed. It sure felt good. My blood tingled, my flesh glowed. I had an appetite such as I hadn't known in ages.

"You see why I came here," says George. "After supper we'll play a round of pinochle—just to please the old man—and then we'll turn in."

"By the way, Hen," he added, "watch your tongue. No cursing or swearing in front of the old man. He's a Methodist. We say grace before we eat. Try not to laugh!"

"You'll have to do it too some night," says Herbie. "Say any goddamned thing that comes to mind. Nobody listens anyway."

At table I was introduced to the old man. He was the typical farmer—big horny hands, unshaven, smelling of clover and manure, sparse of speech, wolfing his food, belching, picking his teeth with the fork and complaining about his rheumatism. We ate enormous quantities, all of us. There were at least six or seven vegetables to go with the roast chicken, followed by a delicious bread pudding, fruits and nuts of all kinds. Everyone but myself drank milk with his food. Then came coffee with real cream and salted peanuts. I had to open my belt a couple of notches.

As soon as the meal was over the table was cleared and a pack of greasy playing cards was produced. Herbie had to help his mother with the dishes while George, the old man and I played a three-handed game of pinochle. The idea was, as George had already explained, to throw the game to the old man, otherwise he became grouchy and surly. I seemed to draw nothing but excellent hands, which made it difficult for me to lose. But I did my best, without being too obvious about it. The old man won by a narrow margin. He was highly pleased with himself. "With your hands," he remarked, "I would have been out in three deals."

Before we went upstairs for the night Herbie put on a couple of Edison phonograph records. One of them was "The Stars and Stripes Forever." It sounded like something from another incarnation.

"Where's that laughing record, Herbie?" says George.

Herbie dug into an old hat box and with two fingers dexterously extracted an old wax cylinder. It was a record I've never heard the like of. Nothing but laughter—the laughter of a loon, a crack-pot, a hyena. I laughed so hard my stomach ached.

"That's nothing," says George, "wait till you hear Herbie laugh!"

"Not now!" I begged. "Save it for tomorrow."

I no more than hit the pillow and I was sound asleep. What a bed! Nothing but soft, downy feathers—tons of them, it seemed. It was like slipping back into the womb, swinging in limbo. Bliss. Perfect bliss.

"There's a piss-pot under the bed, if you need it," were George's last words. But I couldn't see myself getting out of that bed, not even to take a crap.

In my sleep I heard the maniacal laugh of the loon. It was echoed by the rusty door knobs, the green vegetables, the wild geese, the slanting stars, the wet clothes flapping on the line. It even included Herbie's old man, the part of him that gave way sometimes to melancholy mirth. It came from far away, deliciously off-key, absurd and unreasonable. It was the laugh of aching muscles, of food passing through the midriff, of time foolishly squandered, of millions of nothings all harmoniously fitting together in the great jigsaw puzzle and making extraordinary sense, extraordinary beauty, extraordinary well-being. How fortunate that George Marshall had fallen ill and almost died! In my sleep I praised the grand cosmocrator for having arranged everything so sublimely. I slid from one dream to another, and from dream to a stonelike slumber more healing than death itself.

I awoke before the others, content, refreshed, motionless except for a pleasant waggle of the fingers. The farmyard cacophony was music to my ears. The rustling and scraping, the banging of pails, the cock-adoodle-doo, the pitter patter, the calls of the birds, the cackling and grunting, the squealing, the neighing and whinnying, the chug-chug of a distant locomotive, the crunch of hard snow, the slap and gust of the wind, a rusty axle turning, a log wheezing under the saw, the thud of heavy boots trudging laboriously—all combined to make a symphony familiar to my ear. These homely ancient sounds, these early morning notes born of the stir of everyday life, these calls, cackles, echoes and reverberations of the barnyard filled me with an earthling's joy. A starveling and a changeling, I heard again the immemorial chant of early man. The old, old song—of ease and abundance, of life where you find it, of blue sky, running waters, peace and gladness, of fertility and resurrection, and life everlasting, life more abundant, life superabundant. A song that starts in the very bowels, pervades the veins, relaxes the limbs and all the members of the body. Ah, but it was indeed good to be alive—and horizontal. Fully awake, I once again gave thanks to the Heavenly Father for having stricken my twin, George Marshall. And, whilst rendering devout thanks, praising the divine works, extolling all creation, I allowed my thoughts to drift toward the breakfast which was doubtless under way and toward the long, lazy stretch of hours, minutes, seconds before the day would draw to a close. It mattered not how we filled the day, nor if we left it empty as a gourd; it mattered only that time was ours and that we could do with it as we wished.

The birds were calling more lustily now. I could hear them winging from tree top to tree top, fluttering against the windowpanes, swooshing about under the eaves of the roof.

"Morning, Hen! Morning, Hen!"

"Morning, George! Morning, Herbie!"

"Don't get up yet, Hen. . . . Herbie'll make the fire first."

"O.K. Sounds wonderful."

"How did you sleep?"

"Like a top."

"You see why I don't want to get well too quick."

"Lucky guy, you. Aren't you glad you didn't die?"

"Hen, I'm never going to die. I promised myself that on my deathbed. It's just too wonderful to be alive."

"You said it. I say, George, let's fool them all and live forever, *what?*"

Herbie got up to make the fire, then crawled back into bed and began chuckling and cooing.

"What do we do now?" I asked. "Lie here till the bell rings?"

"Exactly," said Herbie.

"I say, Hen, wait till you taste those corn muffins his mother makes. They melt in your mouth."

"How do you like your eggs?" said Herbie. "Boiled, fried or scrambled?"

"Any old way, Herbie. Who gives a damn? Eggs are eggs. I can suck them raw too."

"The bacon, Hen, that's the thing. Thick as your thumb."

Thus the second day began, to be followed by a dozen more, all of the same tenor. As I said before, we were twenty-two or -three at the time, and still in our adolescence. We had nothing on our minds but play. Each day it was a new game, full of hair-raising stunts. "To take the lead," as George had put it, was as easy as drawing one's breath. Between times we skipped rope, threw quoits, rolled marbles, played leapfrog. We even played tag. In the toilet, which was an out-house, we kept a chess board on which a problem was always waiting for us. Often the three of us took a shit together. Strange conversations in that outhouse! Always some fresh tidbit about George's mother, what she had done for him, what a saint she was, and so on. Once he started to talk about God, how there *must* be one, since only God could have pulled him through. Herbie listened reverently —he worshiped George.

One day George drew me aside to tell me something confidential. We were to give Herbie the slip for an hour or so. There was a young country girl he wanted me to meet. We could find her down near the bridge, toward dark, with the right signal.

"She looks twenty, though she's only a kid," said George, as we hastened toward the spot. "A virgin, of course, but a dirty little devil. You can't get much more than a good feel, Hen. I've tried everything, but it's no go."

Kitty was her name. It suited her. A plain-looking girl, but full of sap and curiosity. Hump for the monkeys.

"Hello," says George, as we sidle up to her. "How's tricks? Want you to meet a friend of mine, from the city."

Her hand was tingling with warmth and desire. It seemed to me she was blushing, but it may have been simply the abundant health which was bursting through her cheeks.

"Give him a hug and squeeze."

Kitty flung her arms about me and pressed her warm body tight to mine. In a moment her tongue was down my throat. She bit my lips, my ear lobes, my neck. I put my hand under her skirt and through the slit in her flannel drawers. No protest. She began to groan and murmur. Finally she had an orgasm.

"How was it, Hen? What did I tell you?"

We chatted a while to give Kitty a breathing spell, then George locked horns with her. It was cold and wet under the bridge, but the three of us were on fire. Again George tried to get it in, but Kitty managed to wriggle away.

The most he could do was to put it between her legs, where she held it like a vise.

As we were walking back toward the road Kitty asked if she couldn't visit us sometime—when we got back to the city. She had never been to New York.

"Sure," said George, "let Herbie bring you. He knows his way around."

"But I won't have any money," said Kitty.

"Don't worry about that," said big-hearted George, "we'll take care of you."

"Do you think your mother would trust you?" I asked.

Kitty replied that her mother didn't give a damn what she did. "It's the old man: he tries to work me to the bone."

"Never mind," said George, "leave it to me."

In parting she lifted her dress, of her own accord, and invited us to give her a last good feel.

"Maybe I won't be so shy," she said, "when I get to the city." Then, impulsively, she reached into our flies, took out our cocks, and kissed them—almost reverently. "I'll dream about you tonight," she whispered. She was almost on the point of tears.

"See you tomorrow," said George, and we waved good-bye.

"See what I mean, Hen? Boy, if you could get that you'd have something to remember."

"My balls are aching."

"Drink lots of milk and cream. That helps."

"I think I'd rather jerk off."

"That's what you think *now*. Tomorrow you'll be panting to see her. I know. She's in my blood, the little bitch. . . . Don't let Herbie know about this, Hen. He'd be horrified. He's just a kid compared to her. I think he's in love with her."

"What will we tell him when we get back?"

"Leave that to me."

"*And her old man*—don't you ever think of that?"

"You said it, Hen. If he ever caught us I think he'd cut our balls off."

"That's cheering."

"You've got to take a chance," said George. "Here in the country all the gals are dying for it. They're much better than city tripe, you know that. They smell clean. *Here*, smell my fingers—ain't that delicious?"

Childish amusements. . . . One of the funniest things was taking turns riding an old tricycle which had belonged to Herbie's dead sister. To see George Marshall, a grown man, pushing the pedals of that ridiculous vehicle was a sight for sore eyes. His fanny was so big he had to be squeezed into the seat with might and main. Steering with one hand, he energetically rang a cowbell with the other. Now and then a car stopped, thinking he was a cripple in trouble: George would allow the occupants to get out and escort him to the other side of the road, pretending that he was indeed a paralytic. Sometimes he would bum a cigarette or demand a few pennies. Always in a strong Irish brogue, as if he had just arrived from the old country.

One day I espied an old baby carriage in the barn. It struck me that it would be still funnier if we took George Marshall out for a walk in that. George didn't give a shit. We got a bonnet with ribbons and a big horse blanket to cover him. But try as we would, we couldn't get him into the carriage. So Herbie was elected. We dressed him up like a kewpie doll, stuck a clay pipe in his mouth, and started down the road. At the station we ran into an elderly spinster waiting for the train. As usual, George took the lead.

"I say, Ma'am," touching his cap, "but would you be tellin' us where we might get a little nip? The boy's almost frozen."

"Dear me," said the spinster automatically. Then suddenly getting the drift of his words, she squeaked: *"What's that you said, young man?"*

Again George touched his cap respectfully, pursing his lips and squinting like an old spaniel. "Just a wee nip, that's all. He's nigh on to eleven but it's a terrible thirst he has."

Herbie was sitting up now, puffing vigorously at the short clay pipe. He looked like a gnome.

At this point I felt like taking the lead myself. The spinster had a look of alarm which I didn't like.

"I beg pardon, Ma'am," said I, touching my cap, "but the two of them are dotty. You know . . ." I tapped my skull.

"Dear me, dear me," she wheezed, "how perfectly dreadful."

"I do my best to keep them in good spirits. They're quite a trial. Quite. Especially the little one. Would you like to hear him laugh?"

Without giving her a chance to answer, I beckoned Herbie to go to it. Herbie's laugh was really insane. He did it like a ventriloquist's dummy, beginning with an innocent like smile which slowly broadened into a grin, then a chuckle and a cooing followed by a low gurgling, and finally a belly laugh which was irresistible. He could keep it up indefinitely. With the pipe in one hand and the rattle which he waved frantically in the other, he was a picture out of a Swiss joke book. Every now and then he paused to hiccup violently, then leaned over the side of the carriage and spat. To make the situation still more ludicrous, George Marshall had taken to sneezing. Pulling out a large red handkerchief with huge holes in it, he vigorously blew his nose, then coughed, then sneezed some more.

"The tantrums," I said, turning to the spinster. "There's no harm they be doing. Wonderful boys, the two of 'em—except they be queer." Then, on the impulse, I added: "Fact is, Ma'am," touching my cap reverently, "we're all screwballs. You wouldn't know where we might stop for the night, seein' the condition we're in? If only you had a drop of brandy—just a thimbleful. Not for meself, you understand, but for the little ones."

Herbie broke into a crying fit. He was so gleefully hysterical he didn't know what he was doing. He waved the rattle so assiduously that suddenly he lurched too far and the carriage tipped over.

"Goodness gracious, goodness gracious!" wailed the spinster.

George quickly pulled Herbie loose. The latter now stood up, in his jacket and long pants, the bonnet still wreathed around his head. He clutched the rattle like a maniac. Goofy was no word for it.

Says George, touching his cap, "No hurt, Ma'am. He's got a thick skull." He takes Herbie by the arm and pulls him close. "Say something to the lady! Say something nice!" And he gives him a god-awful box on the ears.

"You bastard!" yells Herbie.

"Naughty, naughty!" says George, giving him another cuff. "What do you say to ladies? Speak up now, or I'll have to take your pants down."

Herbie now assumed an angelic expression, raised his eyes heavenward, and with great deliberation, delivered himself thus:

"Gentle creature of God, may the angels deliver you! There are nine of us in all, not counting the goat. My name is O'Connell, Ma'am. Terence O'Connell. We were going to Niagara Falls, but the weather . . ."

The old cluck refused to hear any more. "You're a public disgrace, the three of you," she cried. "Now stay here, all of you, while I look for the constable."

"Yes, Ma'am," says George, touching his cap, "we'll stay right here, won't we, Terence?" With this he gives Herbie a sound slap in the face.

"Ouch!" yells Herbie.

"Stop that, you fool!" screams the spinster. "And *you*!" she says to me, "why don't *you* do something? Or are you crazy too?"

"That I am," says I, and so saying, I put my fingers to my nose and began bleating like a nanny goat.

"Stay right here! I'll be back in a minute!" She ran toward the station master's office.

"Quick!" says George, "let's get the hell out of here!" The two of us grabbed the handle of the baby carriage and started running. Herbie stood there a moment, unfastening his bonnet; then he too took to his heels.

"Good work, Herbie," said George, when we got safely out of sight. "Let's rehearse this tonight. Hen'll give you a new spiel, won't you Hen?"

"I don't want to be the baby any more," said Herbie.

"All right," said George amiably, "we'll let Hen ride in the carriage."

"If I can squeeze in, you mean."

"We'll squeeze you in, if we have to use a sledgehammer."

But after dinner that night we got new ideas, better ones, we thought. We lay awake till midnight discussing plans and projects.

Just as we were dozing off, George Marshall suddenly sat up.

"Are you awake, Hen?" he says.

I groaned.

"There's something I forgot to ask you."

"What's that?" I mumbled, fearing to wake myself up.

"Una . . . Una Gifford! You haven't said a word about her all this time. What's the matter, aren't you in love with her any more?"

"Jesus!" I groaned, "what a thing to ask me in the middle of the night."

"I know, Hen, I'm sorry. I just want to know if you still love her."

"You know the answer," I replied.

"Good, I thought so. O.K., Hen, good night!"

"Good night!" said Herbie.

"Good night!" said I.

I tried to fall back to sleep but it was impossible. I lay there staring at the ceiling and thinking of Una Gifford. After a while I decided to get it out of my system.

"Are you still awake, George?" I called softly.

"You want to know if I saw her lately, don't you?" he said.

He hadn't closed his eyes, obviously.

"Yeah, I would. Tell me anything. Any little crumb will do."

"I wish I could, Hen, I know how you feel, but there just isn't anything to tell."

"Christ, don't say that! Make up something!"

"All right, Hen, I'll do that for you. Hold on a minute. Let me think. . . ."

"Something simple," I said. "I don't want a fantastic story."

"Listen, Hen, this is no lie: I know she loves you. I can't explain how I know, but I do."

"That's good," I said. "Tell me a little more."

"The last time I saw her I tried to pump her about you. She pretended to be absolutely indifferent. But I could tell she was dying to hear about you. . . ."

"What I'd like to know," I broke in, "is this: has she taken up with someone else?"

"There *is* somebody, Hen, I can't deny that. But it's nothing to worry about. He's just a fill-in."

"What's his name?"

"Carnahan or something like that. Forget about him! What worries Una is the widow. That hurt her, you know."

"She can't know very much about *that*!"

"She knows more than you think. Where she gets it, I don't know. Anyway, her pride's hurt."

"But I'm not going with the widow any more, you know that."

"Tell it to *her*!" says George.

"I wish I could."

"Hen, why don't you make a clean breast of it? She's big enough to take it."

"I can't do it, George. I've thought and thought about it, but I can't screw up the courage."

"Maybe I can help you," said George.

I sat up with a bang. "You think so? Really? Listen, George, I'd swear my life away to you if you could patch it up. I know she'd listen to *you*. . . . *When are you going back?*"

"Not so fast, Hen. Remember, it's an old sore. I'm not a wizard."

"But you'll try, you promise me that?"

"Of course, of course. *Fratres Semper!*"

I thought hard and fast for a few moments, then I said: "I'll write her a letter tomorrow, saying I'm with you and that we'll both be back soon. That might prepare the way."

"Better not," said George promptly. "Better spring a surprise on her. I know Una."

Maybe he was right. I didn't know what to think. I felt elated and depressed at the same time. Besides, there was no prodding him into quick action.

"Better go to sleep," said George. "We've got lots of time to hatch up something."

"I'd go back tomorrow, if I could get you to go with me."

"You're crazy, Hen. I'm still convalescing. She won't get married in a hurry, if that's what's eating you up."

The very thought of her marrying someone else petrified me.

Somehow I had never visualized that. I sank back on the pillow like a dying man. I actually groaned with anguish.

"Hen . . ."

"Yes?"

"Before I go to sleep I want to tell you something. . . . You've got to stop taking this so seriously. Sure, if we can patch it up, fine! I'd like nothing better than to see you get her. But you won't if you let it get under your skin. She's going to make you miserable just as long as she can. That's her way of getting back at you. She's going to say No because you expect her to say No. You're off balance. You're licked before you start. . . . If you want a bit of advice, I'd say drop her for a while. Drop her cold. It's a risk, certainly, but you've got to take it. As long as she's got the upper hand you're going to dance like a puppet. No woman can resist doing that. She's not an angel, even if you like to think she is. She's a swell-looking girl and she's got a big heart. I'd marry her myself, if I thought I stood a

chance. . . . Listen, Hen, there's plenty to pick from. For all you know, there may even be better ones than Una. Have you ever thought of *that?*"

"You're talking drivel," I replied. "I wouldn't care if she were the worst bitch in creation . . . she's the one I want—*and no one else.*"

"O.K., Hen, it's your funeral. I'm going to sleep. . . ."

I lay awake a long while, revolving all manner of memories. They were delicious thoughts, filled with Una's presence. I was certain George would patch it up for me. He liked to be coaxed, that was all. Through a slit in the window shade I could see a brilliant blue star. Seemed like a good omen. I wondered, calf-like, if she were also lying awake mooning about me. I concentrated all my powers, hoping to wake her if she were asleep. Under my breath I softly called her name. It was such a beautiful name. It suited her perfectly.

Finally I began to doze.

FANNY HILL

John Cleland

*T*he next morning I dress'd myself as clean and as neat as my rustic wardrobe would permit me; and having left my box, with special recommendation, with the landlady, I ventured out by myself, and without any more difficulty than can be supposed of a young country girl, barely fifteen, and to whom every sign or shop was a gazing trap, I got to the wish'd-for intelligence office.

It was kept by an elderly woman, who sat at the receipt of custom, with a book before her in great form and order, and several scrolls, ready made out, of directions for places.

I made up then to this important personage, without lifting up my eyes or observing any of the people round me, who were attending there on the same errand as myself, and dropping her curtsies nine-deep, just made a shift to stammer out my business to her.

Madam having heard me out, with all the gravity and brow of a petty minister of State, and seeing at one glance over my figure what I was, made me no answer, but to ask me the preliminary shilling, on receipt of which she told me places for women were exceedingly scarce, especially as I seemed too slight built for hard work; but that she would look over her book, and see what was to be done for me, desiring me to stay a little, till she had dispatched some other customers.

On this I drew back a little, most heartily mortified at a declara-

tion which carried with it a killing uncertainty, that my circumstances could not well endure.

Presently, assuming more courage, and seeking some diversion
from my uneasy thoughts, I ventured to lift up my head a little, and
sent my eyes on a course round the room, wherein they met full tilt
with those of a lady (for such my extreme innocence pronounc'd her)
sitting in a corner of the room, dress'd in a velvet mantle (*nota bene*,
in the midst of summer), with her bonnet off; squab-fat, red-faced,
and at least fifty.

She look'd as if she would devour me with her eyes, staring at
me from head to foot, without the least regard to the confusion and
blushes her eying me so fixedly put me to, and which were to her,
no doubt, the strongest recommendation and marks of my being fit
for her purpose. After a little time, in which my air, person and whole
figure had undergone a strict examination, which I had, on my part,
tried to render favourable to me, by primming, drawing up my neck,
and setting my best looks, she advanced and spoke to me with the
greatest demureness:

"Sweetheart, do you want a place?"

"Yes and please you" (with a curtsey down to the ground).

Upon this she acquainted me that she was actually come to the
office herself, to look out for a servant; that she believed I might do,
with a little of her instructions; that she could take my very looks for
a sufficient character; that London was a very wicked, vile place; that
she hop'd I would be tractable, and keep out of bad company; in
short, she said all to me that an old experienced practitioner in town
could think of, and which was much more than was necessary to take
in an artless inexperienced country-maid, who was even afraid of
becoming a wanderer about the streets, and therefore gladly jump'd
at the first offer of a shelter, especially from so grave and matron-like
a lady, for such my flattering fancy assured me this new mistress of
mine was; I being actually hired under the nose of the good woman
that kept the office, whose shrewd smiles and shrugs I could not help
observing, and innocently interpreted them as marks of her being
pleased at my getting into place so soon: but, as I afterwards came to
know, these BELDAMES understood one another very well, and this
was a market where *Mrs. Brown*, my mistress, frequently attended, on
the watch for any fresh goods that might offer there, for the use of her
customers, and her own profit.

Madam was, however, so well pleased with her bargain, that fearing, I presume, lest better advice or some accident might occasion my slipping through her fingers, she would officiously take me in a coach to my inn, where, calling herself for my box, it was, I being present, delivered without the least scruple of explanation as to where I was going.

This being over, she bid the coachman drive to a shop in St. Paul's Churchyard, where she bought a pair of gloves, which she gave me, and thence renewed her directions to the coachman to drive to her house in *** street, who accordingly landed us at her door, after I had been cheer'd up and entertain'd by the way with the most plausible flams, without one syllable from which I could conclude anything but that I was, by the greatest good luck, fallen into the hands of the kindest mistress, not to say friend, that the *varsal* world could afford; and accordingly I enter'd her doors with most complete confidence and exultation, promising myself that, as soon as I should be a little settled, I would acquaint Esther Davis with my rare good fortune.

You may be sure the good opinion of my place was not lessen'd by the appearance of a very handsome back parlour, into which I was led and which seemed to me magnificently furnished, who had never seen better rooms than the ordinary ones in inns upon the road. There were two gilt pierglasses, and a buffet, on which a few pieces of plates, set out to the most show, dazzled, and altogether persuaded me that I must be got into a very reputable family.

Here my mistress first began her part, with telling me that I must have good spirits, and learn to be free with her; that she had not taken me to be a common servant, to do domestic drudgery, but to be a kind of companion to her; and that if I would be a good girl, she would be more than twenty mothers for me; to all which I answered only by the profoundest and the awkwardest curtsies, and a few monosyllables, such as "yes! no! to be sure!"

Presently my mistress touch'd the bell, and in came a strapping maid-servant, who had let us in. "Here, Martha," said Mrs. Brown— "I have just hir'd this young woman to look after my linen; so step up and shew her her chamber; and I charge you to use her with as much respect as you would myself, for I have taken a prodigious liking to her, and I do not know what I shall do for her."

Martha, who as an arch-jade, and, being used to this decoy, had her cue perfect, made me a kind of half curtsey, and asked me to walk up with her; and accordingly shew'd me a neat room, two pair of stairs backwards, in which there was a handsome bed, where Martha told me I was to lie with a young gentlewoman, a cousin of my mistress's, who she was sure would be vastly good to me. Then she ran out into such affected encomiums on her good mistress! her sweet mistress! and how happy I was to light upon her! that I could not have bespoke a better; with other the like gross stuff, such as would itself have started suspicions in any but such an unpractised simpleton, who was perfectly new to life, and who took every word she said in the very sense she laid out for me to take it; but she readily saw what a penetration she had to deal with, and measured me very rightly in her manner of whistling to me, so as to make me pleased with my cage, and blind to the wires.

In the midst of these false explanations of the nature of my future service, we were rung for down again, and I was reintroduced into the same parlour, where there was a table laid with three covers; and my mistress had now got with her one of her favourite girls, a notable manager of her house, and whose business it was to prepare and break such young fillies as I was to the mounting-block; and she was accordingly, in that view, allotted me for a bed-fellow; and, to give her the more authority, she had the title of cousin conferr'd on her by the venerable president of this college.

Here I underwent a second survey, which ended in the full approbation of *Mrs. Phœbe Ayres*, the name of my tutoress elect, to whose care and instructions I was affectionately recommended.

Dinner was now set on table, and in pursuance of treating me as a companion, *Mrs. Brown*, with a tone to cut off all dispute, soon over-rul'd my most humble and most confused protestations against sitting down with her LADYSHIP, which my very short breeding just suggested to me could not be right, or in the order of things.

At table, the conversation was chiefly kept up by the two madams, and carried on in double-meaning expressions, interrupted every now and then by kind assurances to me, all tending to confirm and fix my satisfaction with my present condition: augment it they could not, so very a novice was I then.

It was here agreed that I should keep myself up and out of sight for a few days, till such clothes could be procured for me as were fit for the character I was to appear in, of my mistress's companion, observing withal, that on the first impressions of my figure much might depend; and, as they well judged, the prospect of exchanging my country clothes for London finery made the clause of confinement digest perfectly well with me. But the truth was, Mrs. Brown did not care that I should be seen or talked to by any, either of her customers, or her DOES (as they call'd the girls provided for them), till she had secured a good market for my maidenhead, which I had at least all the appearances of having brought into her LADYSHIP's service.

To slip over minutes of no importance to the main of my story, I pass the interval to bed-time, in which I was more and more pleas'd with the views that opened to me, of an easy service under these good people; and after supper being shew'd up to bed, Miss Phœbe, who observed a kind of reluctance in me to strip and go to bed, in my shift, before her, now the maid was withdrawn, came up to me, and beginning with unpinning my handkerchief and gown, soon encouraged me to go on with undressing myself; and, still blushing at now seeing myself naked to my shift, I hurried to get under the bedclothes out of sight. Phœbe laugh'd and it was not long before she placed herself by my side. She was about five and twenty, by her most suspicious account, in which, according to all appearances, she must have sunk at least ten good years: allowance, too, being made for the havoc which a long course of hackneyship and hot waters must have made of her constitution, and which had already brought on, upon the spur, that stale stage in which those of her profession are reduced to think of SHOWING company, instead of SEEING it.

No sooner then was this precious substitute of my mistress's laid down, but she, who was never out of her way when any occasion of lewdness presented itself, turned to me, embraced and kiss'd me with great eagerness. This was new, this was odd; but imputing it to nothing but pure kindness, which, for aught I knew, it might be the London way to express in that manner, I was determin'd not to be behind-hand with her, and returned her the kiss and embrace, with all the fervour that perfect innocence knew.

Encouraged by this, her hands became extremely free, and wander'd over my whole body, with touches, squeezes, pressures that rather warm'd and surpriz'd me with their novelty, than they either shock'd or alarm'd me.

The flattering praises she intermingled with these invasions con-

tributed also not a little to bribe my passiveness; and, knowing no
ill, I feared none, especially from one who had prevented all doubt
of her womanhood, by conducting my hands to a pair of breasts that
hung loosely down, in a size and volume that full sufficiently distinguished her sex, to me at least, who had never made any other
comparison. . . .

I lay then all tame and passive as she could wish, whilst her freedom raised no other emotions but those of a strange, and, till then,
unfelt pleasure. Every part of me was open and exposed to the licentious courses of her hands, which, like a lambent fire, ran over my

whole body, and thaw'd all coldness as they went.

My breasts, if it is not too bold a figure to call so two hard, firm, rising hillocks that just began to shew themselves, or signify anything to the touch, employ'd and amus'd her hands awhile, till, slipping down lower, over a smooth track, she could just feel the soft silky down, that had but a few months before put forth and garnish'd the mount-pleasant of those parts, and promised to spread a grateful shelter over the seat of the most exquisite sensation, and which had been, till that instant, the seat of the most insensible innocence. Her fingers play'd and strove to twine in the young trendrils of that moss, which nature has contrived at once for use and ornament.

But, not contented with these outer posts, she now attempts the main spot, and began to twitch, to insinuate, and at length to force an introduction of a finger into the quick itself, in such a manner that, had she not proceeded by insensible gradations that inflamed me beyond the power of modesty to oppose its resistance to their progress, I should have jump'd out of bed and cried for help against such strange assaults.

Instead of which, her lascivious touches had lighted up a new fire that wanton'd through all my veins, but fix'd with violence in that center appointed them by nature, where the first strange hands were now busied in feeling, squeezing, compressing the lips, then opening them again, with a finger between, till an "Oh!" express'd her hurting me, where the narrowness of the unbroken passage refused it entrance to any depth.

In the meantime, the extension of my limbs, languid stretchings, sighs, short heavings, all conspired to assure that experienced wanton that I was more pleased than offended at her proceedings, which she seasoned with repeated kisses and exclamations, such as "Oh! what a charming creature thou art! . . . What a happy man will he be that first makes a woman of you! . . . Oh! that I were a man for your sake! . . . ," with the like broken expressions, interrupted by kisses as fierce and fervent, as ever I received from the other sex.

For my part, I was transported, confused, and out of myself; feelings so new were too much for me. My heated and alarm'd senses were in a tumult that robbed me of all liberty of thought; tears of pleasure gush'd from my eyes, and somewhat assuaged the fire that rag'd all over me.

Phœbe, herself, the hackney'd, thorough-bred Phœbe, to whom

all modes and devices of pleasure were known and familiar, found, it seems, in this exercise of her art to break young girls, the gratification of one of those arbitrary tastes, for which there is no accounting. Not that she hated men, or did not even prefer them to her own sex; but when she met with such occasions as this was, a satiety of enjoyments in the common road, perhaps too, a secret bias, inclined her to make the most of pleasure, wherever she could find it, without distinction of sexes. In this view, now well assured that she had, by her touches, sufficiently inflamed me for her purpose, she roll'd down the bed-clothes gently, and I saw myself stretched nak'd, my shift being turned up to my neck, whilst I had no power or sense to oppose it. Even my glowing blushes expressed more desire than modesty, whilst the candle, left (to be sure not undesignedly) burning, threw a full light on my whole body.

"No!" says Phœbe, "you must not, my sweet girl, think to hide all these treasures from me. My sight must be feasted as well as my touch . . . I must devour with my eyes this springing BOSOM . . . Suffer me to kiss it . . . I have not seen it enough . . . Let me kiss it once more. . . What firm, smooth, white flesh is here! . . . How delicately shaped! . . . Then this delicious down! Oh! let me view the small, dear, tender cleft! . . . This is too much, I cannot bear it! . . . I must . . . I must . . ." Here she took my hand, and in a transport carried it where you will easily guess. But what a difference in the state of the same thing! . . . A spreading thicket of bushy curls marked the full-grown, complete woman. Then the cavity to which she guided my hand easily received it; and as soon as she felt it within her, she moved herself to and fro, with so rapid a friction, that I presently withdrew it, wet and clammy, when instantly Phœbe grew more composed, after two or three sighs, and heart-fetched Oh's! and giving me a kiss that seemed to exhale her soul through her lips, she replaced the bedclothes over us. What pleasure she had found I will not say; but this I know, that the first sparks of kindling nature, the first ideas of pollution, were caught by me that night; and that the acquaintance and communication with the bad of our own sex is often as fatal to innocence as all the seductions of the other. But to go on. When Phœbe was restor'd to that calm, which I was far from the enjoyment of myself, she artfully sounded me on all the points necessary to govern the designs of my virtuous mistress on me, and by my answers, drawn from pure undissembled nature, she had no reason but to promise herself all imaginable success, so far as it depended on my ignorance, easiness, and warmth of constitution.

After a sufficient length of dialogue, my bedfellow left me to my rest, and I fell asleep, through pure weariness, from the violent emotions I had been led into, when nature (which had been too warmly stir'd and fermented to subside without allaying by some means or other) relieved me by one of those luscious dreams, the transports of which are scarce inferior to those of waking real action.

In the morning I awoke about ten, perfectly gay and refreshed. Phœbe was up before me, and asked me in the kindest manner how I did, how I had rested, and if I was ready for breakfast, carefully, at the same time, avoiding to increase the confusion she saw I was in, at looking her in the face, by any hint of the night's bed scene. I told her if she pleased I would get up, and begin any work she would be pleased to set me about. She smil'd; presently the maid brought in the tea-equipage, and I had just huddled my clothes on, when in waddled my mistress. I expected no less than to be told of, if not chid for, my late rising, when I was agreeably disappointed by her compliments on my pure and fresh looks. I was "a bud of beauty" (this was her style), "and how vastly all the fine men would admire me!" to all which my answers did not, I can assure you, wrong my breeding; they were as simple and silly as they could wish, and, no doubt, flattered them infinitely more than had they proved me enlightened by education and a knowledge of the world.

JOHN CLELAND

The book Fanny Hill, *subtitled* Memoirs of a Woman of Pleasure, *was bought from its author, John Cleland, in 1748, by the bookdealer Ralph Griffiths, for a flat fee of twenty guineas, money which the author, just recently out of debtor's prison, sorely needed. The book was an immediate success, earning for Mr. Griffiths some ten thousand pounds, which enabled the publisher to set himself up as a gentleman, and eventually, such are the vicissitudes of life, to have an heir, who, to maintain Mr. Griffith's elegant style of living, became a wholesale poisoner. So ends our knowledge about the fortunate publisher. John Cleland, who had written* Fanny Hill *while in his thirties, lived to be a lonely, cantankerous octogenarian, "a fine, sly, mal-*

content" as James Boswell describes him in his London Journal. *He was an impassioned student of philology, and wrote—besides* Fanny Hill *and some impressive monographs—*Memoirs of a Coxcomb, Surprises of Love, The Man of Honour, *none of which had the enthusiastic response which had been accorded to* Fanny. *Though he managed to stay out of debtor's prison, John Cleland was obliged, till the end of his long life in 1789, to be a hardworking London journalist.*

Born in 1709, son of a respected public official, William Cleland, John attended Westminster School and spent his formative years as British Consul in Smyrna. In 1736 he was employed in Bombay by the British East India Company, a position which ended in ignominy and, upon his long delayed return to England, to the thing he most feared, debtor's prison.

The first edition of Cleland's novel was dated 1749, and immediately reviewers were caught up in the controversy and commotion caused by its appearance. Is Fanny Hill *pornography? Or is it indeed a moral story which furthers the cause of love? Happily, we of the twentieth century have come up with the useful expression "hardcore pornography" from which* Fanny Hill, *devoid of pathologies, obscenity, or the grotesque, is rescued, and finally admitted to be charming and wholesome literature.*

Olympia's edition of Fanny Hill *is reproduced from an earlier version (compiled from the various existing "first editions") which was published in 1946 under The Obelisk Press imprint.*

Fanny Hill *has been constantly regarded in the last two centuries as the model of libertine literature, and has been denounced by censors with a vigor which seems directly inspired by the book's seductions. Its recent publication in New York, which went practically unhampered, is significant of the swift change which has taken place in the United States since the release of* Lolita *in 1958. The next steps came with* Lady Chatterley's Lover, Tropic of Cancer, *and other books which all had, in the quaint vocabulary of the courts, "literary merit." But when the American judges examined* Fanny Hill, *they decided that here was a book with no great artistic ambition, with no highfalutin philosophy, and whose humble message may have been described rather as a massage of the readers' libido.*

The court submitted Fanny Hill *to various legal tests of "social value," "prurient interest," "patently offensive," and "hard-core pornography," and cleared her on these grounds. It then pointed out that "in the 214 years that have elapsed since* Memoirs *was first published in 1749, the book has been in constant, though for the most part surreptitious, circulation and has been translated into every major European language," and noted that copies are to be found in the British Museum and Library of Congress, that Benjamin Franklin was reputed to have owned one, and that the New York Public Library copy of the book once belonged to Governor Samuel J. Tilden! The court concludes impishly: "While the saga of Fanny Hill will undoubtedly never replace "Little Red Riding Hood" as a popular bedtime story, it is quite possible that were Fanny to be transposed from her mid-eighteenth-century Georgian surroundings to our present day society, she might conceivably encounter many things which would cause her to blush."*

Perhaps one day those simple words will appear in big bold letters as a frontispiece to the official history of our twentieth century. They are supercharged with implications of all kinds. They certainly strike a strong blow at the traditions of hypocrisy which have hampered the progress of ideas in our society for so long. They do away with the maudlin excuse implied in the hackneyed formula: "artistic merit." They recognize sex and sexual stimulation as pleasant and happy pursuits, which contain their own justification.

Let us add, as a conclusion, that while Fanny Hill *won her franchise in America and reciprocally brought her contribution to the moral liberation of America, the Olympia English-language edition of the book was banned in France in 1956 (after having been ten years on the Paris bookstalls); was immediately reissued by Olympia under the thinly disguised title of* Memoirs of a Woman of Pleasure; *was banned again as such; was republished as simply* Fanny; *and banned again. The police never found out that they had thus banned the same book three times in succession.*

Story of O

Pauline Réage

*O*ne day her lover takes O for a walk in a section of the city where they never go—the Montsouris Park, the Monceau Park. After taking a stroll in the park and sitting together on the edge of the grass, they notice a car which, because of its meter, resembles a taxi. And yet the car is at an intersection where the park turns a corner, a spot where there is never any taxi stand.

"Get in," he says.

She gets in. It is autumn, and coming up to dusk. She is dressed the way she always is: high heels, a suit with a pleated skirt, a silk blouse, and no hat. But long gloves which come up over the sleeves of her jacket, and in her leather pocketbook she has her identification papers, her compact, and her lipstick.

The taxi moves off slowly, the man still not having said a word to the driver. But he pulls down the shades of the windows on both sides of the car, and the shade on the back window. She has taken off her gloves, thinking he wants to kiss her or that he wants her to caress him. But instead he says:

"Your bag's in your way; let me have it."

She gives it to him. He puts it out of her reach and adds:

"You also have too many clothes on. Unfasten your stockings and roll them down to above your knees. Here are some garters."

By now the taxi has picked up speed, and she has some trouble managing it; she's also afraid the driver might turn around. Finally, though, the stockings are rolled down, and she's embarrassed to feel her legs naked and unfettered beneath her silk slip. Besides, the loose garter-belt suspenders are sliding back and forth.

"Unfasten your garter belt," he says, "and take off your panties."

That's simple enough, all she has to do is slip her hands behind her back and raise herself slightly. He takes the garter belt and panties from her, opens her bag and puts them in, then says:

"You shouldn't sit on your slip and skirt. Pull them up behind you and sit directly on the seat."

The seat is made of some sort of imitation leather which is slippery and cold: it's quite an extraordinary sensation to feel it sticking to your thighs. Then he says:

"Now put your gloves back on."

The taxi is still moving along at a good clip, and she doesn't dare ask why René just sits there without moving or saying another word, nor can she guess what all this means to him—having her there motionless, silent, so stripped and exposed, so thoroughly gloved, in a black car going God knows where. He hasn't told her what to do or what not to do, but she's afraid either to cross her legs or press them together. She sits with gloved hands braced on either side of her seat.

"Here we are," he says suddenly. The taxi stops in front of a rather modest mansion which can be seen nestled between the court-yard and the garden, the type of small private dwelling one finds along the Faubourg Saint-Germain. The street lamps are some distance away, and it is still fairly dark inside the car. Outside it is raining.

"Don't move," René says. "Sit perfectly still."

His hand reaches toward the collar of her blouse, unties the bow, then unbuttons the blouse. She leans slightly forward, thinking he wants to fondle her breasts. No. He is merely groping for the shoulder straps of her brassiere, which he snips with a small penknife. Then he takes it off. Now, beneath her blouse, which he has buttoned back up, her breasts are naked and free, as is the rest of her body from waist to knee.

"Listen," he says. "Now you're ready. This is where I leave you. You're to get out and go ring the doorbell. Follow whoever opens the door for you, and do whatever you're told. If you hesitate about going in, they'll come and take you in. If you don't obey immediately, they'll force you to. Your bag? No, you have no further need for your bag. You're merely the girl I'm furnishing. Yes, of course I'll be there. Now run along."

Another version of the same beginning was simpler and more direct: the young woman, dressed in the same way, was driven by her lover and an unknown friend. The stranger was driving, the lover was seated next to the young woman, and it was the unknown friend who explained to the young woman that her lover had been entrusted with the task of getting her ready, that he was going to tie her hands behind her back, unfasten her stockings and roll them down, remove her garter belt, her panties, and her brassiere, and blindfold her. That she would then be turned over to the château, where in due course she would be instructed as to what she should do. And, in fact, as soon as she had been thus undressed and bound, they helped her to alight from the car after a trip that lasted half an hour, guided her up a few steps and, with her blindfold still on, through one or two doors. Then, when her blindfold was removed, she found herself standing alone in a dark room, where they left her for half an hour, or an hour, or two hours, I can't be sure, but it seemed forever. When at last the door opened and the light was turned on, you could see that she had been waiting in a very conventional, comfortable, and yet distinctive room: there was a thick rug on the floor, but not a stick of furniture, and all four walls were lined with closets. The door had been opened by two women, two young and beautiful women dressed in the garb of pretty eighteenth-century chambermaids: full skirts

made out of some light material, which were long enough to conceal their feet; tight bodices, laced or hooked in front, which sharply accentuated the bust line; lace frills around the neck; half-length sleeves. They were wearing eye shadow and lipstick, and they both had a close-fitting collar and tight bracelets on their wrists.

I know that it was at this point that they freed O's hands, which were still tied behind her back, and told her to get undressed, they were going to bathe her and make her up. They proceeded to strip her till she hadn't a stitch of clothing left, then put her clothes away neatly in one of the closets. She was not allowed to bathe herself, and they did her hair as at the hairdresser's, making her sit in one of those large chairs which tilt back when they wash your hair and back up again when it has been set and you're ready for the dryer. That always takes at least half an hour. Actually it took more than an hour, but she was seated naked on this chair, and they kept her from either crossing her legs or bringing them together. And since the wall in front of her was covered from floor to ceiling with a large mirror, which was unbroken by any shelving, she could see herself, thus open, each time her gaze strayed to the mirror.

When she was well made up and ready—her eyelids penciled lightly; her lips bright red; the tip and halo of her breasts highlighted with pink; the edges of her nether lips rouged; her armpits and pubis generously perfumed, and perfume also applied to the furrow between her thighs, the furrow beneath her breasts, and to the hollows of her hands—she was led into a room where a three-sided mirror, and another mirror behind, enabled her to examine herself closely. She was told to sit down on the hassock, which was set between the mirrors, and wait. The hassock was covered with black fur, which pricked slightly; the rug was black, the walls red. She was wearing red slippers. Set in one of the walls of the small bedroom was a large window, which looked out onto a lovely, dark park. The rain had stopped, the trees were swaying in the wind, the moon raced high among the clouds.

I have no idea how long she remained in the red bedroom, or whether she was really alone, as she surmised, or whether someone was watching her through a peephole camouflaged in the wall. All I know is that when the two women returned one was carrying a dressmaker's tape measure and the other a basket. With them came a man dressed in a long purple robe, the sleeves of which were gathered at the wrists and full at the shoulders. When he walked the robe flared open, from the waist down. One could see that beneath his robe he had on some sort of tights which covered his legs and thighs but left the sex exposed. It was the sex that O saw first, when he took his first step, then the whip, made of leather thongs, which he had in his belt. Then she saw that the man was masked by a black hood—which concealed even his eyes behind a network of black gauze—and, finally, that he was also wearing fine black kid gloves.

Using the familiar *tu* form of address, he told her not to move and ordered the women to hurry. The woman with the tape then took the measurements of O's neck and wrists. Though on the small side, her measurements were in no way out of the ordinary, and it was easy enough to find the right-sized collar and bracelets in the basket the other woman was carrying. Both collar and bracelets were made of several layers of leather (each layer being fairly thin, so that the total was no more than the thickness of a finger). They had clasps, which functioned automatically like a padlock when it closes, and they could be opened only by means of a small key. Imbedded in the layers of leather, directly opposite the lock, was a snuglyfitting metal ring, which allowed one to get a grip on the bracelet, if one wanted to attach it, for both collar and bracelets fit the arms and neck so snugly—although not so tight as to be the least painful—that it was impossible to slip any bond inside.

So they fastened the collar and bracelets to her neck and wrists, and the man told her to get up. He took her place on the fur hassock, called her over till she was against his knees, slipped his gloved hand between her thighs and over her breasts, and explained to her that she would be presented that same evening, after she had dined alone.

She did in fact dine by herself, in a sort of little cabin where an invisible hand passed the dishes to her through a grilled window. Finally, when dinner was over, the two women came for her. In the bedroom, they fastened the two bracelet rings together behind her back. They attached a long red cape to the ring of her collar and draped it over her shoulders. It covered her completely, but opened when she walked, since with her hands behind her back she had no way of keeping it closed. One woman preceded her, opening the doors, and the other followed, closing them behind her. They crossed a vestibule, two drawing rooms, and went into the library, where four men were having coffee. They were wearing the same long robes as the first, but were not masked. And yet O did not have time to see their faces or ascertain whether her lover was among them (he was), for one of the men shone a light in her eyes and blinded her. Everyone remained stock still, the two women flanking her and the men in front, studying her. Then the light went out and the women left. But O was blindfolded again. Then they made her walk forward— she stumbled slightly as she went—until she felt that she was standing in front of the fire around which the four men were seated. She could feel the heat, and in the silence she could hear the quiet crackling of the burning logs. She was facing the fire. Two hands lifted her cape, two others—after having checked to see that her bracelets were attached—descended the length of her back and buttocks. The hands were not gloved, and one of them penetrated her in both places at once, so abruptly that she cried out. Someone laughed. Someone else said:

"Turn her around, so we can see the breasts and belly."

They turned her around, and the heat of the fire was against her back. A hand seized one of her breasts, a mouth fastened on the point of the other. But suddenly she lost her balance and fell backward (supported by whose arms?), while they opened her legs and gently spread her lips. Hair grazed the insides of her thighs. She heard them saying that they would have to make her kneel down. This they did. She was extremely uncomfortable in this position, especially because they forbade her to bring her knees together and because her arms pinioned behind her forced her to lean forward. Then they let her rock back a bit, so that she was half-sitting on her heels, as nuns are wont to do.

"You've never tied her up?"

"No, never."

"And never whipped her?"

"No, never whipped her either. But as a matter of fact . . ."

It was her lover speaking.

"As a matter of fact," the other voice went on, "if you do tie her up from time to time, or whip her just a little, and she begins to like it, that's no good at all. You have to transcend the pleasure stage, until you reach the stage of tears."

Then they made O get up and were on the verge of untying her, probably in order to attach her to some pole or wall, when someone protested that he wanted to take her first, right there on the spot.

So they made her kneel down again, this time with her bust on a hassock, her hands still tied behind her, with her hips higher than her torso. Then one of the men, holding her with both his hands on her hips, plunged into her belly. He yielded to a second. The third wanted to force his way into the narrower passage and, driving hard, made her scream. When he let her go, sobbing and befouled by tears beneath her blindfold, she slipped to the floor, only to feel someone's knees against her face, and she realized that her mouth was not to be spared. Finally they let her go, a captive clothed in tawdry finery, lying on her back in front of the fire. She could hear glasses being filled and the sound of the men drinking, and the scraping of chairs. They put some more wood on the fire. All of a sudden they removed her blindfold. The large room, the walls of which were lined with bookcases, was dimly lit by a single wall lamp and by the light of the fire, which was beginning to burn more brightly. Two of the men were standing and smoking. Another was seated, with a riding crop on his knees, and the one leaning over her fondling her breast was her lover. All four of them had taken her, and she had not been able to distinguish him from the others.

They explained to her that this was how it would always be, as long as she was in the château, that she would see the faces of those who violated or tormented her, but never at night, and she would never know which ones had been responsible for the worst. The same would be true when she was whipped, except that they wanted her to see herself being whipped, and so this once she would not be blindfolded. They, on the other hand, would don their masks, so that she would no longer be able to tell them apart.

Her lover had helped her to her feet and, still wrapped in her red cape, made her sit down on the arm of an easy chair near the fire, so that she could hear what they had to tell her and see what they wanted to show her. Her hands were still behind her back. They showed her the riding crop, which was long, black, and delicate, made of thin bamboo encased in leather, the sort one sees in the windows of better riding equipment shops; the leather whip, which the first man she had seen had been carrying in his belt, was long and consisted of six lashes knotted at the end. There was a third whip of fairly thin cords, each with several knots at the end: the cords were quite stiff, as though they had been soaked in water, which was exactly what had been done, as O discovered, for they caressed her belly with them and nudged open her thighs, so that she could feel how stiff and damp the cords were against the tender inner skin. Then there were the keys and the steel chains on the console table. Along one entire wall of the library, halfway between floor and ceiling, ran a gallery which was supported by two pillars. A hook was imbedded in one of the columns, just high enough for a man standing on tiptoe, with his arms stretched above his head, to reach. O's lover had taken her in his arms, with one hand supporting her shoulders and the other in the furrow of her belly, which burned so she could hardly bear it. They told her that her hands would be untied, but merely so that they could be fastened anew, a short while later, to the pole, using these same bracelets and one of the steel chains. They said that, with the exception of her hands which would be held just above her head, she would thus be able to move and see the blows coming; that in principle she would be whipped only on the thighs and buttocks, in other words between her waist and knees, in the same region which had been prepared in the car that had brought her here, when she had been made to sit naked on the seat; but that in all likelihood one of the four men present would want to mark her thighs with the riding crop, which makes lovely long deep welts which last a long time. She would not have to endure all this at once; there would be ample time for her to scream, struggle, and to cry. They would grant her some respite, but as soon as she had caught her breath they would start in again, judging the results not from her screams or tears but from the size and color of the welts they had raised. They remarked to her that this method of judging the effectiveness of the whip—besides being equitable—also made it pointless for the victims to exaggerate their suffering in an effort to arouse pity, and this enabled them to resort to the same measures beyond the château walls, outdoors in the park —as was often done—or in any ordinary apartment or hotel room, assuming a gag was used (such as the one they produced and showed her there on the spot), for the gag stifles all screams and eliminates all but the most violent moans, while allowing tears to flow without restraint.

There was no question of using it that night. On the contrary, they wanted to hear her scream; and the sooner the better. The pride she mustered to resist and remain silent did not long endure: they even heard her beg them to stop for a second, just a second to stop and untie her. So frantically did she writhe, trying to escape the bite of the

lashes, that she turned almost completely around, on the near side of
the pole, for the chain which held her was long and, although plenty
solid, was fairly slack. As a result, her belly and the front of her
thighs were almost as marked as her backside. They paused for a
moment, having made up their minds to begin again only after a rope
had been attached first to her waist then to the pole. Since they tied
her tightly, to keep her waist snug to the pole, her torso was forced
slightly forward, and this in turn caused her buttocks to protrude in
the opposite direction. From then on the blows landed on their target,
unless aimed deliberately elsewhere. Given the way her lover had
handed her over, had delivered her into this situation, O might have
assumed that to beg him for mercy would have been the surest method
for making him redouble his cruelty, so great was his pleasure in
extracting, or having the others extract, from her this unquestionable
proof of his power. And he was in fact the first to notice that the
leather whip, the first they had used on her, left almost no marks (in
contrast to the whip made of water-soaked cords, which marked
almost upon contact, and the riding crop, which raised immediate
welts), and thus allowed them to prolong the agony and follow their
fancies in starting and stopping. He asked them to use only the leather
whip.

Meanwhile, the man who liked women only for what they had
in common with men, seduced by the available behind which was
straining at the bonds knotted just below the waist, a behind made all
the more attractive by its efforts to dodge the blows, called for an
intermission in order to take advantage of it. He spread the two parts,
which burned beneath his hands, and penetrated—not without some
difficulty—remarking as he did that the passage would have to be
rendered more easily accessible. They all agreed that this could, and
would, be done.

When they untied the young woman, she staggered and almost
fainted, draped in her red cape. Before returning her to the cell she
was to occupy, they sat her down in an armchair near the fire and
outlined for her the rules and regulations she was to follow during
her stay in the château and later in her daily life after she had left it
(which did not mean regaining her freedom, however). Then they
rang. The two young women who had first received her came in,
bearing the clothes she was to wear during her stay and tokens by
which those who had been hosts at the château before her arrival and

those who would be after she had left, might recognize her. Her outfit was similar to theirs: a long dress with a full skirt, worn over a sturdy whalebone bodice gathered tightly at the waist, and over a stiffly starched linen petticoat. The low-cut neck scarcely concealed the breasts which, raised by the constricting bodice, were only lightly veiled by the network of lace. The petticoat was white, as was the lace, and the dress and bodice were a sea green satin. When O was dressed and resettled in her chair beside the fire, her pallor accentuated by the color of the dress, the two young women, who had not uttered a word, prepared to leave. One of the four friends seized one of them as she passed, made a sign for the other to wait, and brought the girl he had stopped back toward O. He turned her around and, holding her by the waist with one hand, lifted her skirt with the other, in order to demonstrate, he said, the practical advantages of the costume and show how well designed it was. He added that all one needed to keep the skirts raised was a simple belt, which made everything that lay beneath readily available. In fact, they often had the girls circulate in the château or the park either like this, or with their skirts tucked up in front, waist high. They had the young woman show O how she would have to keep her skirt: rolled up several turns (like a lock of hair rolled in a curler) and secured tightly by a belt, either directly in front, to expose the belly, or in the middle of the back, to leave the buttocks free. In either case, skirt and petticoat fell diagonally away in large, cascading folds of intermingled material. Like O, the young woman's backside bore fresh welts from the riding crop. She left the room.

Here is the speech they then delivered to O:

"You are here to serve your masters. During the day, you will perform whatever domestic duties are assigned you, such as sweeping, putting back the books, arranging flowers, or waiting on table. Nothing more difficult than that. But at the first word or sign from anyone you will drop whatever you're doing and ready yourself for what is really your one and only duty: to give yourself. Your hands are not your own, nor are your breasts, nor, above all, any of your bodily orifices, which we may explore or penetrate at will. You will remember at all times—or as constantly as possible—that you have lost all right to privacy or concealment, and as a reminder of this fact, in our presence you will never press your knees together (you may recall you were forbidden to do this the minute you arrived). This will serve as a constant reminder, to you as well as to us, that your mouth, your belly, and your backside are open to us. You will never touch your breasts in our presence: the bodice raises them toward us, that they may be ours. During the day you will therefore be dressed, and if anyone should order you to lift your skirt, you will lift it; if anyone desires to use you in any manner whatsoever, he will use you, unmasked, but with this one reservation: the whip. The whip will be used only between dusk and dawn. But besides the whipping you receive from whoever may want to whip you, you will also be flogged in the evening, as punishment for any infractions of the rules committed during the day: for having been slow to oblige, for having raised your eyes and looked at the person addressing you or taking you—you must never look any of us in the face. If the costume we wear in the evening—the one I am now wearing—leaves our sex exposed, it is not for the sake of convenience, for it would be just as convenient the other way, but for the sake of insolence, so that your eyes will be directed there upon it and nowhere else, so that you may learn that there resides your master, for whom, above all else, your lips are intended. During the day, when we are dressed in normal attire and you are clothed as you are now, the same rules will apply, except that when requested you will open your clothes, and then close them again when we have finished with you. Another thing: at night you will have only your lips with which to honor us— and your widespread thighs—for your hands will be tied behind your back and you will be naked, as you were a short while ago. You will be blindfolded only to be maltreated and, now that you have seen how you are whipped, to be flogged. And yes, by the way: while it is perfectly all right for you to grow accustomed to being whipped— since you're going to be every day throughout your stay—this is less for our pleasure than for your enlightenment. That this truth is self-evident may be shown by the fact that on those nights when no one wants you, you will wait until the valet whose job it is comes to your solitary cell and administers what you are due to receive but we are not in the mood to mete out. Actually, both this flogging and the chain—which when attached to the ring of your collar keeps you more or less closely confined to your bed several hours a day—are intended less to make you suffer, scream, or cry than to make you feel, *through* this suffering, that you are not free but fettered, to teach you that you are totally dedicated to something outside yourself.

When you leave here, you will be wearing an iron ring on your third finger. This ring will identify you, and by then you will have learned to obey those who wear the same insignia, and when they see it they will know that beneath your skirt you are constantly naked, however proper or ordinary your clothes may be, and that this nakedness is for them. Should anyone find you in the least intractable, he will return you here. Now you will be shown to your cell."

The apartment where O lived was situated on the Ile Saint Louis, under the eaves of an old house which faced south and overlooked the Seine. All the rooms, which were spacious and low, had sloping ceilings, and the two rooms at the front of the house each opened onto a balcony set into the sloping roof. One of them was O's room; the other, in which bookshelves filled one wall from floor to ceiling on either side of the fireplace, served as a living room, a study, and even as a bedroom in case of necessity. Facing the two windows was a big couch, and there was a large antique table before the fireplace. It was here that they dined whenever the tiny dining room, which faced the interior courtyard and was decorated with dark green serge, was really too small to accommodate the guests. Another room, which also looked onto the courtyard, was René's, and it was here that he dressed and kept his clothes. O shared the yellow bathroom with him; the kitchen, also yellow, was tiny. A cleaning woman came in every day. The flooring of the rooms overlooking the courtyard was of red tile, those antique hexagonal tiles which in old Paris hotels are used to cover the stairs and landings above the second story. Seeing them again gave O a shock and set her heart to beating faster: they were the same tiles as the ones in the hallways at Roissy. Her room was small, the pink and black chintz curtains were closed, the fire was glowing behind the metallic screen, the bed was made, the covers turned back.

"I bought you a nylon nightgown," René said. "You've never had one before."

Yes, a white pleated nylon nightgown, tailored and tasteful like the clothing of Egyptian statuettes, an almost transparent nightgown was unfolded on the edge of the bed, on the side where O slept. O tied a thin belt around her waist, over the elastic waist-band of the night-gown itself, and the material of the gown was so light that the projection of the buttocks colored it a pale pink. Everything—save for the curtains and the panel hung with the same material against which the head of the bed was set, and the two small armchairs up-holstered with the same chintz—everything in the room was white: the walls, the fringe around the mahogany four-poster bed, and the bearskin rug on the floor. Seated before the fire in her white night-gown, O listened to her lover.

He began by saying that she should not think that she was now free. With one exception, and that was that she was free not to love him any longer, and to leave him immediately. But if she did love him, then she was in no wise free. She listened to him without saying a word, thinking how happy she was that he wanted to prove to him-self—it mattered little how—that she belonged to him, and thinking too that he was more than a little naive not to realize that this pro-prietorship was beyond any proof. But did he perhaps realize it and want to emphasize it merely because he derived a certain pleasure from it? She gazed into the fire as he talked, but he did not, not daring to meet her eyes. He was standing, pacing back and forth. Suddenly he said to her that, for a start, he wanted her to listen to him with her knees unclasped and her arms unfolded, for she was sitting with her knees together and her arms folded around them. So she lifted her nightgown and, on her knees, or, rather, squatting on her heels in the manner of Carmelites or of Japanese women, she waited. The only thing was, since her knees were spread, she could feel the light, sharp pricking of the white fur between her half-open thighs; he came back to it again: she was not opening her legs wide enough. The word "open" and the expression "opening her legs" were, on her lover's lips, charged with such uneasiness and power that she could never hear them without experiencing a kind of internal prostration, a sacred submission, as though a god, and not he, had spoken to her. So she remained motionless, and her hands were lying palm upward beside her knees, between which the material of her nightgown was spread, with the pleats re-forming.

What her lover wanted from her was very simple: that she be constantly and immediately accessible. It was not enough for him to know that she was: she was to be so without the slightest obstacle intervening, and her bearing and clothing both were to bespeak, as it were, the symbol of that availability to experienced eyes. That, he went on, meant two things. The first she knew, having been informed of it the evening of her arrival at the château: that she must never cross her knees, as her lips had always to remain open. She doubtless thought that this was nothing (that was indeed what she did think), but she would learn that to maintain this discipline would require a constant effort on her part, an effort which would remind her, in the secret they shared between them and perhaps with a few others, but surrounded by mundane occupations and when with those who did not share it, of the reality of her condition.

As for her clothes, it was up to her to choose them, or if need be to invent them, so that this semi-undressing to which he had subjected her in the car on their way to Roissy would no longer be necessary: tomorrow she was to go through her closet and sort out her dresses, and to do the same with her underclothing by going through her dresser drawers. She would hand over to him absolutely everything she found in the way of belts and panties; the same for any brassieres like the one whose straps he had had to cut before he could remove it, any full slips which covered her breasts, all the blouses and dresses which did not open up the front, and any skirts too tight to be raised with a single movement. She was to have other brassieres, other blouses, other dresses made. Meanwhile, was she supposed to visit her corset maker with nothing on under her blouse or sweater? Yes, she was to go with nothing on underneath. If someone should notice, she could explain it any way she liked, or not explain it at all, whichever she preferred, but it was her problem, and hers alone. Now, as for the rest of what he still had to teach her, he preferred to wait for a few days and wanted her to be dressed properly before hearing it. She would find all the money she needed in the little drawer of her desk. When he had finished speaking, she murmured "I love you" without the slightest gesture. It was he who added some wood to the fire, lighted the bedside lamp, which was of pink opaline. Then he told O to get into bed and wait for him, that he would sleep with her. When he came back, O reached over to turn out the lamp: it was her left hand, and the last thing she saw before the room was plunged into darkness was the somber glitter of her iron ring. She was lying half on her side: her lover called her softly by name and simultaneously, seizing her with his full hand, covered the nether part of her belly and drew her to him.

The next day, O, in her dressing gown, had just finished lunch alone in the green dining room—René had left early in the morning and was not due home until evening, to take her out to dinner—when the phone rang. The phone was in the bedroom, beneath the lamp at the head of the bed. O sat down on the floor to answer it. It was René, who wanted to know whether the cleaning woman had left. Yes, she had just left, after having served lunch, and would not be back till the following morning.

"Have you started to sort out your clothes yet?" René said.

"I was just going to start," she answered, "but I got up late, took a bath, and it was noon before I was ready."

"Are you dressed?"

"No, I have on my nightgown and my dressing gown."

"Put the phone down, take off your robe and your nightgown."

O obeyed, so startled that the phone slipped from the bed where she had placed it down onto the white rug, and she thought she had been cut off. No, she had not been cut off.

"Are you naked?" René went on.

"Yes," she said. "But where are you calling from?"

He ignored her question, merely adding:

"Did you keep your ring on?"

She had kept her ring on.

Then he told her to remain as she was until he came home and to prepare, thus undressed, the suitcase of clothing she was to get rid of. Then he hung up.

It was past one o'clock, and the weather was lovely. A small pool of sunlight fell on the rug, lighting the white nightgown and the corduroy dressing gown, pale green like the shells of fresh almonds, which O had let slip to the floor when she had taken them off. She picked them up and was going to take them into the bathroom to hang them up in a closet. On her way, she suddenly saw her reflection in one of the mirrors fastened to a door and which, together with another mirror covering part of the wall and a third on another door, formed a large three-faced mirror: all she was wearing was a pair of leather slippers the same green as her dressing gown—and only slightly darker than the slippers she wore at Roissy—and her ring. She was no longer wearing either a collar or leather bracelets, and she was alone, her own sole spectator. And yet never had she felt herself more totally committed to a will which was not her own, more totally a slave, and more content to be so.

When she bent down to open a drawer, she saw her breasts stir gently. It took her almost two hours to lay out on her bed the clothes which she then had to pack away in the suitcase. There was no problem about the panties; she made a little pile of them near one of the bedposts. The same for her brassieres, not one would stay, for they all had a strap in the back and fastened on the side. And yet she saw how she could have the same model made, by shifting the catch to the front, in the middle, directly beneath the cleavage of the breasts. The girdles and garter belts posed no further problems, but she hesitated to add to the pile the corset of pink satin brocade which laced up in the back and so closely resembled the bodice she had worn at Roissy. She put it aside on the dresser. That would be René's decision. He would also decide about the sweaters, all of which went on over the head and were tight at the neck, therefore could not be opened. But they could be pulled up from the waist and thus bare the breasts. All the slips, however, were piled on her bed. In the dresser drawer there still remained a half-length slip of black faille, hemmed with a pleated flounce and fine Valencienne lace, which was made to be worn under a pleated sun skirt of black wool which was too sheer not to be transparent. She would need other half-length slips, short, light-colored ones. She also realized that she would either have to give up wearing sheath dresses or else pick out the kind of dress that buttoned all the way down the front, in which case she would also have to have her slips made in such a way that they would open together with the dress. As for the petticoats, that was easy, the dresses too, but what would her dressmaker say about the underclothes? She would explain that she wanted a detachable lining because she was cold-blooded. As a matter of fact, she was sensitive to the cold, and suddenly she wondered how in the world she would stand the winter cold when she was dressed so lightly.

When she had finally finished, and had kept from her entire wardrobe only her blouses, all of which buttoned down the front, her black pleated skirt, her coats of course, and the suit she had worn home from Roissy, she went to prepare tea. She turned up the thermostat in the kitchen; the cleaning woman had not filled the wood basket for the living-room fire, and O knew that her lover liked to find her in the living room beside the fire when he arrived home in the evening. She filled the basket from the woodpile in the hallway closet, carried it back to the living-room fireplace, and lighted the fire. Thus she waited for him, curled up in a big easy chair, the tea tray beside her, waited for him to come home, but this time she waited the way he had ordered her to, naked.

The first difficulty O encountered was in her work. Difficulty is perhaps an exaggeration. Astonishment would be a better term. O worked in the fashion department of a photography agency. This meant that it was she who photographed, in the studios where they had to pose for hours on end, the most exotic and prettiest girls whom the fashion designers had chosen to model their creations.

They were surprised that O had postponed her vacation until this late in the fall and had thus been away at a time of year when the fashion world was busiest, when the new collections were about to be presented. But that was nothing. What surprised them most was how changed she was. At first glance, they were hard put to say exactly what was changed about her, but nonetheless they felt it, and the more they observed her the more convinced they were. She stood and walked straighter, her eyes were clearer, but what was especially striking was her perfection when she was in repose, and how measured her gestures were.

She had always been a conservative dresser, the way girls do whose work resembles that of men, but she was so skillful that she brought it off; and because the other girls—who constituted her subjects—were constantly concerned, both professionally and personally, with clothing and its adornments, they were quick to note what might have passed unperceived to eyes other than theirs. Sweaters worn right next to the skin, which gently molded the contours of the breasts—René had finally consented to the sweaters—pleated skirts so prone to swirling when she turned: O wore them so often it was a little as though they formed a discreet uniform.

"Very little-girl-like," one of the models said to her one day, a blond, green-eyed model with high Slavic cheekbones and the olive complexion that goes with it. "But you shouldn't wear garters," she added. "You're going to ruin your legs."

This remark was occasioned by O, who, without stopping to think, had sat down somewhat hastily in her presence, and obliquely in front of her, on the arm of a big leather easy chair, and in so doing had lifted her skirt. The tall girl had glimpsed a flash of naked thigh above the rolled stocking, which covered the knee but stopped just above it.

O had seen her smile, so strangely that she wondered what the girl had been thinking at the time, or perhaps what she had understood. She adjusted her stockings, one at a time, pulling them up to tighten them, for it was not as easy to keep them tight this way as it was when the stockings ended at mid-thigh and were fastened to a garter belt, and answered Jacqueline, as though to justify herself:

"It's practical."

"Practical for what?" Jacqueline wanted to know.

"I dislike garter belts," O replied.

But Jacqueline was not listening to her and was looking at the iron ring.

During the next few days, O took some fifty photographs of Jacqueline. They were like nothing she had ever taken before. Never, perhaps, had she had such a model. Anyway, never before had she been able to extract such meaning and emotion from a face or body. And yet all she was aiming for was to make the silks, the furs, and the laces more beautiful by that sudden beauty of an elfin creature surprised by her reflection in the mirror, which Jacqueline became in the simplest blouse, as she did in the most elegant mink. She had short, thick, blond hair, only slightly curly, and at the least excuse she would cock her head slightly toward her left shoulder and nestle her cheek against the upturned collar of her fur, if she were wearing fur. O caught her once in this position, tender and smiling, her hair gently blown as though by a soft wind, and her smooth, hard cheek-bone snuggled against the gray mink, soft and gray as the freshly fallen ashes of a wood fire. Her lips were slightly parted, and her eyes half-closed. Beneath the gleaming, liquid gloss of the photograph she looked like some blissful girl who had drowned, pale, she was so pale. O had had the picture printed with as little contrast as possible. She had taken another picture of Jacqueline which she found even more stunning: back lighted, it portrayed her bare-shouldered, with her delicate head, and her face as well, enveloped in a large-meshed black veil surmounted by an absurd double aigrette whose impalpable tufts crowned her like wisps of smoke; she was wearing an enormous robe of heavy brocaded silk, red like the dress of a bride in the Middle Ages, which came down to below her ankles, flared at the hips and tight at the waist, and the armature of which traced the outline of her bosom. It was what the dress designers called a gala gown, the kind no one ever wears. The spike-heeled sandals were also of red silk. And all the time Jacqueline was before O dressed in that gown and sandals, and that veil which was like the premonition of a mask, O, in her mind's eye was completing, was inwardly modify-ing the model: a trifle here, a trifle there—the waist drawn in a little tighter, the breasts slightly raised—and it was the same dress as at Roissy, the same dress that Jeanne had worn, the same smooth, heavy, cascading silk which one takes by the handful and raises whenever one is told to. . . . Why yes, Jacqueline was lifting it in just that way as she descended from the platform on which she had been posing for the past fifteen minutes. It was the same rustling, the same crackling of dried leaves. No one wears these gala gowns any longer? But they do. Jacqueline was also wearing a gold choker around her neck, and on her wrists two gold bracelets. O caught herself thinking that she would be more beautiful with a leather collar and leather bracelets. And then she did something she had never done before: she followed Jacqueline into the large dressing room adjacent to the studio, where the models dressed and made up and where they left their clothing and make-up kits after hours. She remained standing, leaning against the doorjamb, her eyes glued to the mirror of the dressing table before which Jacqueline, without removing her gown, had sat down. The mirror was so big—it covered the entire back wall, and the

dressing table itself was a simple slab of black glass—that she could
see Jacqueline's and her own reflection, as well as the reflection of
the costume girl who was undoing the aigrettes and the tulle netting.
Jacqueline removed the choker herself, her bare arms lifted like two
handles; a touch of perspiration gleamed in her armpits, which were
shaved (Why? O wondered, what a pity, she's so fair), and O could
smell the sharp, delicate, slightly plantlike odor and wondered what
perfume Jacqueline ought to wear—what perfume they would make
her wear. Then Jacqueline unclasped her bracelets and put them on
the glass slab, where they made a momentary clanking sound like
the sound of chains. Her hair was so fair that her skin was actually
darker than her hair, a grayish beige like fine-grained sand just after
the tide has gone out. On the photograph, the red silk would be
black. Just then, the thick eyelashes, which Jacqueline was always
reluctant to make up, lifted, and in the mirror O met her gaze, a
look so direct and steady that, without being able to detach her own
eyes from it, she felt herself blushing. That was all.

"I'm sorry," Jacqueline said, "I have to undress."

"Sorry," O murmured, and closed the door.

The next day she took home with her the proofs of the shots she
had made the day before, not really knowing whether she wanted, or
did not want, to show them to her lover, with whom she had a dinner
date. She looked at them as she was putting on her make-up at the
dressing table in her room, pausing to trace with her finger the curve
of an eyebrow, the suggestion of a smile. But when she heard the
sound of the key in the front door, she slipped them into the drawer.

For two weeks, O had been completely outfitted and ready for
use, and could not get used to being so, when she discovered one
evening upon returning from the studio a note from her lover asking
her to be ready at eight to join him and one of his friends for dinner.
A car would come by to pick her up, the chauffeur would come up
and ring her bell. The postscript specified that she was to take her
fur jacket, that she was to dress entirely in black (*entirely* was under-
lined), and was to be at pains to make up and perfume herself as at
Roissy.

It was six o'clock. Entirely in black, and for dinner—and it was
mid-December, the weather was cold, that meant black silk stockings,
black gloves, her pleated fan-shaped skirt, a thick sweater with

spangles or her short jacket of faille. She decided on the jacket of faille. It was padded and quilted in large stitches, close fitting and hooked from neck to waist like the tight-fitting doublets that men used to wear in the sixteenth century, and if it molded the bosom so perfectly, it was because the brassiere was fitted to it inside. It was lined of the same faille, and its slit tails were hip length. The only bright foil were the large gold hooks like those on children's snow boots which made a clicking sound as they were hooked or unhooked from their broad flat rings.

After she had laid out her clothes on her bed, and at the foot of the bed her black suede shoes with raised soles and spiked heels, nothing seemed stranger to O than to see herself, solitary and free in her bathroom, meticulously making herself up and perfuming herself, after she had taken her bath, as she had done at Roissy. The cosmetics she owned were not the same as those used at Roissy. In the drawer of her dressing table she found some rouge for the cheeks—she never used it—which she used to emphasize the halo of her breasts. It was a rouge which was scarcely visible when first applied, but which darkened later. At first she thought she had put on too much and tried to take a little off with alcohol—it was very hard to remove— and started all over: a dark peony pink flowered at the tips of her breasts. Vainly she tried to make up the lips which the fleece of her belly concealed, but the rouge left no mark. Finally, among the tubes of lipstick she had in the same drawer, she found one of those kiss-proof lipsticks which she did not like to use because they were too dry and too hard to remove. There, it worked. She fixed her hair and freshened her face, then finally put on the perfume. René had given her, in an atomizer which released a heavy spray, a perfume whose name she didn't know which had the odor of dry wood and marshy plants, a pungent, slightly savage odor. On her skin the spray melted, on the fur of the armpits and belly it ran and formed tiny droplets.

At Roissy O had learned to take her time: she perfumed herself three times, each time allowing the perfume to dry. First she put on her stockings and high shoes, then the petticoat and skirt, then the jacket. She put on her gloves and took her bag. In her bag were her compact, her lipstick, a comb, her key, and a thousand francs. Wearing her gloves, she took her fur coat from the closet and glanced at the time at the head of her bed: fifteen minutes to eight. She sat down diagonally on the edge of the bed and, her eyes riveted to the alarm

clock, waited without moving for the bell to ring. When she heard it
at last and rose to leave, she noticed in the mirror above her dressing
table, before turning out the light, her bold, gentle, docile expression.

When she pushed open the door of the little Italian restaurant
before which the car had stopped, the first person she saw at the bar
was René. He smiled at her tenderly, took her by the hand, and
turning toward a sort of grizzled athlete, introduced her in English
to Sir Stephen H. O was offered a stool between the two men, and
as she was about to sit down René said to her in a half-whisper to be
careful not to muss her dress. He helped her to slide her skirt from
under her and down over the edges of the stool, the cold leather of
which she felt against her skin, while the metal rim around it pressed
directly against the furrow of her thighs, for at first she had dared
only to half sit down, for fear that if she were to sit down completely
she might yield to the temptation to cross her legs. Her skirt billowed
around her. Her right heel was caught in one of the rungs of the
stool, the tip of her left foot was touching the floor. The Englishman,
who had bowed without uttering a word, had not taken his eyes off
her, she saw that he was looking at her knees, her hands, and finally
at her lips—but so calmly and with such precise attention, with such
self-assurance, that O felt herself being weighed and measured as the
instrument she knew full well she was, and it was as though compelled
by his gaze and, so to speak, in spite of herself that she withdrew her
gloves: she knew that he would speak when her hands were bare—
because she had unusual hands, more like those of a young boy than
the hands of a woman, and because she was wearing on the ring finger
of her left hand the iron ring with the triple spiral of gold. But no, he
said nothing, he smiled: he had seen the ring.

René was drinking a martini, Sir Stephen a whisky. He nursed
his whisky, then waited till René had drunk his second martini and O
the grapefruit juice that René had ordered for her, meanwhile explaining that if O would be good enough to concur in their joint opinion,
they would dine in the room downstairs, which was smaller and less
noisy than the one on the first floor, which was simply the extension
of the bar.

"Of course," O said, already gathering up her bag and gloves
which she had placed on the bar.

Then, to help her off the stool, Sir Stephen offered her his right
hand, in which she placed hers, he finally addressing her directly by

observing that she had hands that were made to wear irons, so becoming was iron to her. But as he said it in English, there was a trace of ambiguity in his words, leaving one in some doubt as to whether he was referring to the metal alone or whether he were not also, and perhaps even specifically, referring to iron chains.

In the room downstairs, which was a simple whitewashed cellar, but cool and pleasant, there were in fact only four tables, one of which was occupied by guests who were finishing their meal. On the walls had been drawn, like a fresco, a gastronomical and tourist map of Italy, in soft, ice-cream colors: vanilla, raspberry, and pistachio. It reminded O that she wanted to order ice cream for dessert, with lots of almonds and whipped cream. For she was feeling light and happy, René's knee was touching her knee beneath the table, and whenever he spoke she knew he was talking for her ears. He too was observing her lips. They let her have the ice cream, but not the coffee. Sir Stephen asked O and René to have coffee at his place. They had all dined very lightly, and O realized that they had been careful to drink very little and had kept her virtually from drinking at all: half a liter of Chianti for the three of them. They had also dined very quickly: it was no more than nine o'clock.

"I sent the chauffeur home," said Sir Stephen. "Would you drive, René. The simplest thing would be to go straight to my house."

René took the wheel, O sat beside him, and Sir Stephen was next to her. The car was a big Buick, there was ample room for three people in the front seat.

After the Alma intersection, the Cours la Reine was visible because the trees were bare and the Place de la Concorde sparkling and dry with, above it, the sort of sky which promises snow, but from which snow has not yet fallen. O heard a little click and felt the warm air rising around her legs: Sir Stephen had turned on the heater. René was still following the right bank of the Seine, then he turned at the Pont Royal to cross over to the left bank: between its stone yokes, the water looked as frozen as the stone, and just as black. O thought of hematites, which are black. When she was fifteen her best friend, who was then thirty and with whom she was in love, wore a hematite ring set in a cluster of tiny diamonds. O would have liked a necklace of these black stones, without diamonds, a tight-fitting necklace, perhaps even a choker. But the necklaces that were given to her now—no, they were not given to her—would she exchange them for the necklace of hematites, for the hematites of the dream? She saw again the wretched room where Marion had taken her, behind the Turbigo intersection, and remembered how she had untied—she, not Marion— her two big schoolgirl pigtails when Marion had undressed her and laid her down on the iron bed. How lovely Marion was when she was caressed, and it is true that eyes can resemble stars; hers looked like quivering blue stars.

René stopped the car. O did not recognize the little street, one of the cross streets which connects the rue de l'Université to the rue de Lille.

Sir Stephen's apartment was situated at the far end of a court-yard, in one wing of an old private mansion, and the rooms were laid out in a straight line, one opening onto the next. The room at the very end was also the largest, and the most reposing, furnished in dark English mahogany and pale yellow and gray silk drapes.

"I shan't ask you to tend the fire," Sir Stephen said to O, "but this settee is for you. Please sit down, René will make coffee. I would be most grateful if you would hear what I have to say."

The large sofa of light-colored Damascus silk was set at right angles to the fireplace, facing the windows which overlooked the garden and with its back to those behind, which looked onto the courtyard. O took off her fur and laid it over the back of the sofa. When she turned around, she noticed that her lover and her host were standing, waiting for her to accept Sir Stephen's invitation. She set her bag down next to her fur and unbuttoned her gloves. When, oh when would she ever learn, and *would* she ever learn, a gesture stealthy enough so that when she lifted her skirt no one would notice, so that she herself could forget her nakedness, her submission? Not, in any case, as long as René and that stranger were staring at her in silence, as they were presently doing. Finally she gave in. Sir Stephen stirred the fire, René suddenly went behind the sofa and, seizing O by the throat and the hair, pulled her head down against the back of the couch and kissed her on the mouth, a kiss so prolonged and profound that she gasped for breath and could feel her belly melting and burn-ing. He let her go only long enough to tell her that he loved her, and then immediately took her again. O's hands, overturned in a gesture of utter abandon and defeat, her palms upward, lay quietly on her black dress that spread like a corolla around her. Sir Stephen had come nearer, and when at last René let her go and she opened her eyes, it was the gray, unflinching gaze of the Englishman which she encountered.

Completely stunned and bewildered, as she still was, and gasping with joy, she nonetheless was easily able to see that he was admiring her, and that he desired her. Who could have resisted her moist, half-open mouth, with its full lips, the white stalk of her arching neck against the black collar of her page-boy jacket, her eyes large and clear, which refused to be evasive. But the only gesture Sir Stephen allowed himself was to run his finger softly over her eyebrows, then over her lips. Then he sat down facing her on the opposite side of the fireplace, and when René had also sat down in an armchair, he began to speak.

"I don't believe René has ever spoken to you about his family," he said. "Still, perhaps you do know that his mother, before she married his father, had previously been married to an Englishman, who had a son from his first marriage. I am that son, and it was she who raised me, until she left my father. So René and I are not actually relatives, and yet, in a way, we are brothers. That René loves you I have no doubt. I would have known even if he hadn't told me, even if he hadn't made a move: all one has to do is to see the way he looks at you. I know too that you are among those girls who have been to Roissy, and I imagine you'll be going back again. In principle, the ring you're wearing gives me the right to do with you what I will, as it does to all those men who know its meaning. But that involves merely a fleeting assignation, and what we expect from you is more serious. I say 'we' because, as you see, René is saying nothing: he prefers to have me speak for both of us.

"If we are brothers, I am the elder, ten years older than he. There is also between us a freedom so absolute and of such long standing that what belongs to me has always belonged to him, and what belongs to him has likewise belonged to me. Will you agree to join with us? I beg of you to, and I ask you to swear to it because it will involve more than your submission, which I know we can count on. Before you reply, realize for a moment that I am only, and can only be, another form of your lover: you will still have only one master. A more formidable one, I grant you, than the men to whom you were surrendered at Roissy, because I shall be there every day, and besides I am fond of habits and rites. . . ." (This last phrase he uttered in English.)

Sir Stephen's quiet, self-assured voice rose in an absolute silence. Even the flames in the fireplace flickered noiselessly. O was frozen to the sofa like a butterfly impaled upon a pin, a long pin composed of words and looks which pierced the middle of her body and pressed her naked, mindful loins against the warm silk. She was no longer mistress of her breasts, her hands, the nape of her neck. But of this much she was sure: the object of the habits and rites of which he had spoken were patently going to be the possession of (among other parts of her body) her long thighs concealed beneath the black skirt, her already opened thighs.

Both men were sitting across from her. René was smoking, but before he had lighted his cigarette he had lighted one of those black-hooded lamps which consumes the smoke, and the air, already purified by the wood fire, smelled of the cool odors of the night.

"Will you give me an answer, or would you like to know more?" Sir Stephen repeated.

"If you give your consent," René said, "I'll personally explain to you Sir Stephen's preferences."

"Demands," Sir Stephen corrected.

The hardest thing, O was thinking, was not the question of giving her consent, and she realized that never for a moment did either of them dream that she might refuse; nor, for that matter, did she. The hardest thing was simply to speak. Her lips were burning and her mouth was dry, all her saliva was gone, an anguish both of fear and desire constricted her throat, and her new-found hands were cold and moist. If only she could have closed her eyes. But she could not. Two gazes stalked her eyes, gazes from which she could not—and did not desire to—escape. They drew her toward something she thought she had left behind for a long time, perhaps forever, at Roissy. For since her return René had always taken her only by caresses, and the symbol signifying that she belonged to anyone who knew the secret of her ring had been without consequence: either she had not met anyone who was familiar with the secret, or else those who had remained silent—the only person she suspected was Jacqueline (and if Jacqueline had been at Roissy, why didn't she too wear the ring? Besides, what right did Jacqueline's knowledge of this secret give her over O, and did it, in fact, give her any?). In order to speak, did she have to move? But she could not move of her own free will—an order from them would immediately have made her get up, but this time what they wanted from her was not blind obedience, acquiescence to an order, they wanted her to anticipate orders, to judge herself a slave and surrender herself as such. This, then, is what they called her consent. She remembered that she had never told René anything but "I love you" or "I'm yours." Today it seemed that they wanted her to speak and to agree to, specifically and in detail, what till now she had only tacitly consented to.

Finally she straightened up and, as though what she was going to say was stifling her, unfastened the top hooks of her tunic, until the cleavage of her breasts was visible. Then she stood up. Her hands and her knees were shaking.

"I'm yours," she said at length to René. "I'll be whatever you want me to be."

"No," he broke in, "ours. Repeat after me: I belong to both of you. I shall be whatever both of you want me to be."

Sir Stephen's piercing gray eyes were fixed firmly upon her, as were René's, and in them she was lost, slowly repeating after him the phrases he was dictating to her, but like a lesson of grammar, she was transposing them into the first person.

"To Sir Stephen and me you grant the right . . ." The right to dispose of her body however they wished, in whatever place or manner they should choose, the right to keep her in chains, the right to whip her like a slave or prisoner for the slightest failing or infraction, or simply for their pleasure, the right to pay no heed to her pleas and cries, if they should make her cry.

"I believe," said René, "that at this point Sir Stephen would like me to take over, both you and I willing, and have me brief you concerning his demands."

O was listening to her lover, and the words which he had spoken to her at Roissy came back to her: they were almost the same words. But then she had listened snuggled up against him, protected by a feeling of improbability, as though it were all a dream, as though she existed only in another life and perhaps did not really exist at all. Dream or nightmare, the prison setting, the lavish party gowns, men in masks: all this removed her from her own life, even to the point of being uncertain how long it would last. There, at Roissy, she felt the way one does at night, lost in a dream one has dreamed before and is now beginning all over again: certain that it exists and certain that it will end, and you want it to end because you're not sure you'll be able to bear it, and you also want it to go on so you'll know how it comes out. Well, the end was here, where she least expected it (or no longer expected it at all) and in the form she least expected (assuming, she was saying to herself, that this really was the end, that there was not actually another hiding behind this one, and perhaps still another behind the next one). The present end was toppling her from memory into the present and, too, what had only been reality in a closed circle, a private universe, was suddenly about to contaminate all the customs and circumstances of her daily life, both on her and within her, now no longer satisfied with signs and symbols—the bare buttocks, bodices that unhook, the iron ring—but demanding fulfillment.

It was true that René had never whipped her, and the only difference between the period of their relationship prior to his taking her to Roissy and the time elapsed since her return was that now he used both her backside and mouth the way he formerly had used only her womb (which he continued to use). She had never been able to tell whether the floggings she had regularly received at Roissy had been administered, were it only once, by him (whenever there was any question about it, that is when she herself had been blindfolded or when those with whom she was dealing were masked), but she tended to doubt it. The pleasure he derived from the spectacle of her body bound and surrendered, struggling vainly, and of her cries, was doubtless so great that he could not bear the idea of lending a hand himself and thus having his attention distracted from it. It was as though he were admitting it, since he was now saying to her, so gently, so tenderly, without moving from the deep armchair in which he was half reclining with his legs crossed, he was saying how happy he was to be turning her over to, how happy he was that she was handing *herself* over to, the commands and desires of Sir Stephen. Whenever Sir Stephen would like her to spend the night at his place, or only an hour, or if he should want her to accompany him outside Paris or, in Paris itself, to join him at some restaurant or for some show, he would telephone her and send his car for her—unless René himself came to pick her up. Today, now, it was her turn to speak. Did she consent? But words failed her. This willful assent they were suddenly asking her to express was the agreement to surrender herself, to say yes in advance to everything to which she most assuredly wanted to say yes but to which her body said no, at least insofar as the whipping was concerned. As for the rest, if she were honest with herself, she would have to admit to a feeling of both anxiety and excitement caused by what she read in Sir Stephen's eyes, a feeling too intense for her to delude herself, and as she was trembling like a leaf, and perhaps for the very reason that she was trembling, she knew that she was waiting more impatiently than he for the moment when he would touch her with his hand, and perhaps with his lips. It was probably up to her to hasten the moment. Whatever courage, or whatever surge of overwhelming desire she may have had, she felt herself suddenly grow so weak as she was about to reply that she slipped to the floor, her dress in full bloom around her, and in the silence Sir Stephen's hollow voice remarked that fear was becoming to her too. His words were not intended for her, but for René. O had the feeling that he was restraining himself from advancing upon her and regretted his restraint. And yet she avoided his gaze, her eyes fixed upon René, terrified lest he should see what was in her eyes and perhaps deem it a betrayal. And yet it was not a betrayal, for if she were to weigh her desire to belong to Sir Stephen against her belonging to René, she would not have had a second's hesitation: the only reason she was yielding to this desire was that René had allowed her to and, to a certain extent, given her to understand that he was ordering her to. And yet there was still a lingering doubt in her mind as to whether René might not be annoyed to see her acquiesce too quickly or too well. The slightest sign from him would obliterate it immediately. But he made no sign, confining himself to ask her for the third time for an answer. She mumbled:

"I consent to whatever you both desire," and lowered her eyes toward her hands, which were waiting unclasped in the hollows of her knees, then added in a murmur: "I should like to know whether I shall be whipped. . . ."

There was a long pause, during which she regretted twenty times over having asked the question. Then Sir Stephen's voice said slowly: "From time to time."

Then O heard a match being struck and the sound of glasses: both men were probably helping themselves to another round of whisky. René was leaving O to her own devices. René was saying nothing.

"Even if I agree to it now," she said, "even if I promise now, I couldn't bear it."

"All we ask you to do is submit to it, and, if you scream or moan, to agree ahead of time that it will be in vain," Sir Stephen went on.

"Oh, please, for pity's sake, not yet!" said O, for Sir Stephen was getting to his feet, René was following suit, he leaned down and took her by the shoulders.

"So give us your answer," he said. "Do you consent?"

Finally she said that she did. Gently he helped her up and, having sat down on the big sofa, made her kneel down alongside him facing the sofa, on which reclined her outstretched arms, her bust, and her head. Her eyes were closed, and an image she had seen several years before flashed across her mind: a strange print portraying a woman kneeling, as she was, before an armchair. The floor was of tile, and in one corner a dog and child were playing. The woman's skirts were raised, and standing close beside her was a man brandishing a handful of switches, ready to whip her. They were all dressed in sixteenth-century clothes, and the print bore a title which she found disgusting: Family Punishment.

With one hand, René took her wrists in a viselike grip, and with the other lifted her skirts so high that she could feel the muslin lining brush her cheek. He caressed her flanks and drew Sir Stephen's attention to the two dimples that graced them, and to the furrow between her thighs. Then with his hand he pressed her waist, to accentuate further her buttocks, and ordered her to open her knees wider. She obeyed without saying a word. The honors René was bestowing upon her body, and Sir Stephen's replies, and the coarseness of the terms the men were using so overwhelmed her with a shame as violent as it was unexpected that the desire she had felt to be had by Sir Stephen vanished and she began to wish for the whip as a deliverance, for the pain and screams as a justification. But Sir Stephen's hands pried open her belly, forced the buttocks' portal, retreated, took her again, caressed her until she moaned. She was vanquished, undone, and humiliated that she had moaned.

"I leave you to Sir Stephen," René then said. "Remain the way you are, he'll dismiss you when he sees fit."

How often had she remained like this at Roissy, on her knees, offered to one and all? But then she had always had her hands bound together by the bracelets, a happy prisoner upon whom everything was imposed and from whom nothing was asked. Here it was through her own free will that she remained half-naked, whereas a single gesture, the same that would have sufficed to put her back on her feet, would also have sufficed to cover her. Her promise bound her as much as had the leather bracelets and chains. Was it only the promise? And however humiliated she was, or rather because she had been humiliated, was it not somehow pleasant to be esteemed only for her humiliation, for the meekness with which she surrendered, for the obedient way in which she opened?

With René gone, Sir Stephen having escorted him to the door, she waited thus alone, motionless, feeling more exposed in the solitude and more prostituted by the wait than she had ever felt before, when they were there. The gray and yellow silk of the sofa was smooth to her cheek; through her nylon stockings she felt, below her knees, the thick wool rug, and along the full length of her left thigh, the warmth from the fireplace hearth, for Sir Stephen had added three logs which were blazing noisily. Above a chest of drawers, an antique clock ticked so quietly that it was only audible when everything around was silent. O listened carefully, thinking how absurd her position was in this civilized, tasteful living room. Through the venetian blinds could be heard the sleepy rumbling of Paris after midnight. In the light of day, tomorrow morning, would she recognize the spot on the sofa cushion where she had laid her head? Would she ever return, in broad daylight, to this same living room, would she ever be treated in the same way here?

PAULINE RÉAGE

For many years now I have lived on the left bank, and my horizon on the other side of the Seine has been graced by that string of imposing buildings, the Palais de Justice to the left, crowned by the spire of the Sainte Chapelle, and the attendant bulk of the Préfecture de Police, to the right.

When I walk by, in the day, at night, at dawn, I invariably pay a mute homage to those seats of the two perennial powers that are reigning over this country, France: the legal power, and the police.

I know so well those corridors, those dusty courtrooms, those musty offices. I have sat on all those benches, I have waited in front of many of those forbidding doors. I have been the guest of those cells in the dark subterranean dungeons where bad boys are put away; I have been measured, photographed, weighed, and I have left countless fingerprints on innumerable files; I have been searched minutely, lovingly; I have been handcuffed, and promenaded in those labyrinths, without belt, tie or shoelaces, by attentive guards. I have spent a goodly portion of my life in those surroundings, but now I feel that I have become one of the family so to speak; the judges know me, and also the ushers, and even the charwomen. I think they like me in a way, because I have come to understand their little mannerisms, and I am always considerate to them, except sometimes, in the fire of action: but one has to play the game, and they do not really mind my occasional fits of distemper.

And it is so exhilarating to imagine those immense structures as if they were without walls, and open to general inspection from the outside. All this mass of varied activities conducive to the receipt of salaries, stipends, wages, pensions by thousands and thousands of lawyers, guards, judges, secretaries, office boys—all this appears to me as a vision equaled in magnitude only by that which overwhelmed John in Patmos.

When Story of O *appeared, I was still sharing offices with my French colleague, Jean-Jacques Pauvert, on rue de Nesle. His French version of the book came out nearly at the same time as the English translation published by The Olympia Press. We were anticipating a bit of trouble, and curious as to its nature: the book was unusual, and although it was quite deliberately pornographic, the excellence of its style put it in a class all by itself. It had obtained a literary prize, the Prix des Deux Magots. It was prefaced by one of France's most refined and revered writers, Jean Paulhan. But the author remained pseudonymous, and his or her identity was a matter of many a heated controversy in the fashionable salons. Who was the mysterious Pauline Réage?*

When Jean-Jacques was finally summoned to La Brigade Mondaine, he spent a whole day there. He came back fuming with rage, saying that they had tried everything to make him reveal the identity of the author, short of physical violence. He had simply told them that he knew perfectly well who the author was, but would never tell the police.

The next day came my turn. They gave me the grand treatment, presented me to the chief of the Brigade, cajoled me, threatened, and even went as far as pretending that Jean-Jacques had already given them the author's name. I laughed pleasantly at that and interrupted them to ask news of their families, and their projects for the next summer holidays, and so on, as is usual in polite French conversation.

They appreciated the detached breeziness of it all, as being part of the game we had played so often together. But they really meant business.

"So," I said, "I understand that Jean-Jacques Pauvert has told you that he knew who the author was, but that he would not tell you."

"That is so," they answered, "but of course he won't get away with that. We have our own sources of information and all we want is to check them. We don't really need your confirmation or your friend's, but you have no right to withhold information from us. On account of his attitude he will be severely sentenced. Would you like to act like a fool, too? You have quite enough trouble as it is, don't you?"

"Oh my, yes," I sighed, "but this is all so confusing. You see, you say you know who wrote the book and I can't say that I do, myself. As to Pauvert, he says he knows but that he won't tell. Well it is understandable that you should resent his attitude. But he was wise not to speak because I know who he believes the author to be. Well, gentlemen, all I can tell you is, firstly, that I don't know myself who that person really is, and, furthermore, knowing as I do who Pauvert thinks wrote the book, I know that he is wrong in his assumption, and that is about the only aspect of the matter on which I can proclaim any kind of certainty."

They were puzzled. One of them asked me: "But you could at least tell us who you think you know did not write the book that Pauvert thinks did write it?"

"Listen, gentlemen," I pleaded, "Pauvert is a very old friend of mine and I don't want to displease him stupidly by reporting our little quarrels to you. Would you like me to betray his confidence? No, and it would be such an error to bring up somebody's name who has nothing to do with all this, in my opinion. And furthermore I don't even know that person's name. . . ."

"So you say that you don't know the name of the person who you say you know did not write the book?"

"That is correct. Disturbing, maybe, but correct."

I told my tale of confusion to Pauvert when I got back to the office, after a full day of dialectical exercises. Pauvert picked up the phone and called the chief of the Brigade.

"I have something very important to tell you in connection with that book, Story of O,*" he said. "Girodias tells me he told you that he knew who I knew was the author of the book but that he was convinced that I was wrong. Well, that's a lot of nonsense. He always refused to tell me who he thought I thought was the author of the book: so how can he assume that I was wrong? That fellow's been reading too much pornography or something; he's simply illogical. No, my position is unchanged: I know who wrote the book, and I won't tell you. And even if you ask me if Girodias wrote it himself, I won't answer."*

And so we went out for refreshments.

KAMA HOURI

ATAULLAH MARDAAN

*T*he men were at prayer. Facing in the direction of Mecca, they stood heads uplifted, eyes closed. All at once, with the precision of ballet dancers, they knelt together and prostrated themselves. . . .

Ann watched the dancelike movements of worship with fascination. It was strange to see Yakub, his hands grasping his ears, his eyes tightly closed, solemnly bowed in prayer. She found it hard to believe that this was the same man whose strong hands had brutally violated her body, and for whose pleasure-giving loins she had left behind a lifetime. She had just arrived at this village where Yakub's small house nestled, like a small mushroom, among the foothills of the Hindu Kush. Ann sat down wearily. She had ridden until nightfall behind the Afridi peasant who had picked her up at Abbotabad. Since then she had traveled—she did not know exactly for how many days —on horseback, on foot, and in strange, lurching bullock carts, until, at last, she found herself face to face with Yakub. The Pathan had evinced no great surprise at her arrival, but Ann knew that mysteriously rapid messenger system among the tribesmen had already warned him of her projected visit. He had merely greeted her and asked her to sit and wait until the evening prayers were finished.

Worship was over. The men stood up. To Ann's deep amazement Yakub Khan walked into the house with them and left her sitting alone on the hillside. She rose indignantly, dusted her skirt, and walked with her mother's determined step toward the little house. She had hardly taken a few steps when two heavily garbed women, wearing the concealing cloaklike *burkha* came out of the house and signaled to her. One was a tall, mature woman of about thirty, who seemed vaguely familiar to Ann; the other—she realized with a shock —was the child bride of Abbotabad. The older woman raised her hand to her forehead in greeting.

"Khoda Hafeez. The master says that you are to dispose of your European clothes and put on native dress." She spoke in a strange formal manner.

Ann followed the two women, who led her through the back of the house into a small courtyard. They stopped beside a little murky pond, and told her to undress. Ann thankfully slipped off her dirty riding habit, and dipped a white leg into the cool water.

"How white she is, Shaukat Bibi . . . just like snow. . . ." the little girl cried excitedly.

Ann looked at herself reflected in the dirty pond. Her body glowed like a white *chambella* flower, that hides in the dark forests of India. A bright yellow leaf, floating on the water, coquettishly came to anchor on the reflected image of her mound. Smiling, Ann stirred the water with her toes, causing the leaf to sail round and round her rippling image—sometimes settling on her breast; sometimes brushing her full, pink mouth and then sliding downward, like an excited finger, and caressing the whole slim length of her leg. The older woman had filled an earthen jar with water and she poured some of it over Ann's body. Then taking a handful of dried grass, she plastered the weeds with wet mud and started to rub Ann's body. She looked like a strange wood nymph standing in the middle of the pond—her body speckled brown and white, and her long, fair hair

fluttering in the evening breeze. Sitting down in the shallow pool Ann gave herself up completely to the soothing, sensual pressure of the Indian woman's hands on her wet body.

After the bath they led her indoors and told her to lie down on the string bed. The older woman asked her to raise her arms above her head and she tied her wrists to the head of the wooden bed frame. The younger girl took some resinous gum out of a small jar and started to soften its consistency, working it energetically between her fingers. Then holding Ann's arm taut, she started to pluck the sparse blonde hairs from under her arms. Ann screamed. She tried to struggle, but the older woman impassively held her legs. She twisted her body in an effort to escape but the more she struggled the more it hurt. However, the little girl was very quick and efficient and in a very short while she had completely denuded the white woman's armpits of hair. The older woman now tied Ann's feet to the bed and bending over she held her hips firmly down against the dirty cloth mattress. Ann watched with horror, as the little girl, flicking her fingers, approached the sensitive forest of her mound. She groaned and writhed, for it seemed as if a thousand little needles were being driven into her body. The little girl looked up and laughed.

"Shaukat Bibi, this one is happy to look like a bear! Chee! Fancy a man sleeping with that—he may as well take a dog to bed with him," and she savagely plucked another golden shoot from Ann's smarting thigh. Then with a quick movement she parted Ann's knees and started to pluck the hairs from the sensitive lips of her sex. Ann cried out with the pain. She tried to move, but in vain; she was securely tied and the older woman bore down heavily on her trembling loins. When the depilatory torture was over, Ann was released. She rose trembling from her bed, her body a mass of pain. The little girl brought her a scrap of broken mirror and held it before her. Ann gasped. Her mound, deprived of hair, rose like a small cleft vase between her legs—pink and pure and clean. Despite the pain, she could not help but smile, as she looked at the soft, smooth, girlish swelling with its tempting deep pink slit. The women now sat her down and combed and oiled her long blonde hair which they deftly wove into a heavy chignon at the nape of her neck. Then gently pushing her back on the bed they massaged her body all over with some heavy, musky oil. As their slim flexible fingers traveled over her body, Ann felt the familiar dull excitement start to throb in her belly, and she looked forward with longing to the night and the punishing limbs of Yakub.

The women had dressed Ann in wide, white pyjamas and a long printed shirt. Around her head and over her shoulders they had draped a huge cotton shawl, and had placed open-toed sandals on her feet. They told her to sit quietly in the room and wait for their return. Ann sat patiently in the dark stuffy little chamber, heavy with the scent of oil and resin. Soon, the women were back with some food. Though Ann was hungry she ate the spiced mutton stew and stiff wheat cake without much relish. A little later the young girl came back bringing her a bowl of light green tea.

"The master says that you are to sleep with us here, and tomorrow you are to share the work of the house and fields—mem-sahib," she added mockingly, calling her by the flattering title given to all European women. Ann had a sudden impulse to strike the impudent girl. The latter, guessing her intention, ran suddenly from the room stopping only to look back at the angry woman with narrow, mocking eyes.

Ann lay on one of the cloth mats laid out on the floor. Evidently the bed was purely ornamental, for she was soon joined by the other two women who spread their thin mattresses on either side of her. They slept in their clothes, slightly loosening the cord of their pyjamas, and when they saw that Ann was about to undress they sharply reprimanded her and told her to sleep in the clothes she had on. Ann lay down but she could not sleep. She was wondering why Yakub had not yet come to see her. The heavy cotton pyjamas rubbed against her naked mound, the gentle friction only serving to increase her desire. Suddenly she heard footsteps and looking up she saw Yakub Khan come into the room. She sat upright and threw off her cotton covering.

"Yakub—at last here you are!"

He ignored her as if he had not heard her. He turned to the little girl and gently kicked her. She raised her head and looked up at her husband with large startled eyes.

"Chaleya—come."

"Hajee."

Abruptly he turned and left the room. Ann was too surprised to stop him. She got up immediately to follow him out but the older woman's hand was grasping her arm.

"You are not to go unless called." There was something menacing in her tone. Ann obeyed. She lay down again and watched the little girl. She had sleepily left her bed and was groping her way to the window sill. She pulled down a little jar of ointment, and spreading her legs, she rubbed it into the narrow sex. Taking a little oil from another bottle, she lifted her long, white shirt and massaged her small pointed breasts, polishing the nipples until they became as hard and as pointed as the sharp spikes on Arab shields. Then sighing deeply and looking back longingly at her bed, she dragged herself out of the room. Ann lay still, her heart beating. The heavy oil filled the room with its musky odor. She tossed on her thin mat, her senses excited by the perfume, but she did not dare get up as she knew that the still woman next to her watched her closely with her hard, dark eyes. Suddenly a moan broke the heavy silence of the night. Ann trembled . . . she could hear the string bed creak and strain and the whole house seemed filled with the odor of semen and sweat. Ann thought of the little bed in Yakub's hut in Abbotabad and, turning over on her stomach, she buried her face in the dirty mattress and wept.

A week had passed. . . . Every day Ann worked with the women:

cleaning the house, feeding the livestock, sewing and preparing and cooking the spiced food. She lived exclusively in a world of women— covering her face when a man approached, not so much through any newly acquired sense of values, but because she feared being recognized. Every night she waited trembling in the dark, her body afire with desire, but he only entered the room twice and each time it was to fetch the thin young wife. Ann felt deeply humiliated. Now that she had completely given herself to him, he refused to accept the generous gift of her body. Her dislike for the sharp, mocking young wife grew into hatred, and she waited for an opportunity to take revenge. Ann knew that Yakub was deliberately avoiding her to prove his absolute independence to her. To show her that she was no more the "memsahib" who commanded and he the servant who obeyed. She resolved to speak to him at the first opportunity, and to remind him of the unrestrained passion of their love. She had seen the little wife reluctantly go to his bed when called, and return tired and shaken. While the other women slept heavily, never even lifting their heads to look at their husband. Surely, she thought triumphantly, he could not fail to appreciate her after two such women. She could not help but feel that he was testing her in some mysterious way. . . .

The next night Ann crept out of bed, telling the women that she was going to the small pit that served as a toilet. She took a little vessel of water with her and left the room. Carefully she crept around the back of the house, slipped out and waited beside the front door for Yakub to pass by. She must have been standing for about half an hour in the cool night, when she recognized his footsteps. He had been to the little outhouse that served as a barn for their thin cow, small flock of goats and horses. He stopped outside the door to clean his bare feet with a stick. Ann, seeing him absorbed in his task, rushed out and threw her arms around his neck. He jerked up in surprise and pulled himself free.

"You!" he spat out the word.

"Yakub why are you doing this? You beast. You are doing this on purpose to torture me," she sobbed hysterically, beating him with her fists. He adroitly caught both her hands and pushed her against the wall.

"Shaukat . . . Azurie . . . jaldee . . . come."

The women came running out of the house, the older woman carrying a lantern.

"Quick catch this she-devil and bring her in." Without waiting for them to move he lifted her up and carried her into the house. He carried her into a room she had never entered before. It was a small room, as dark as the women's chamber, completely bare except for five rifles standing against the wall, a wooden chest and a wide string bed covered with heavy cloths and furs. Throwing Ann on the bed he ordered the women to undress her. Ann did not resist, it was a relief to have even the women's hands touch her naked body. They turned her onto her stomach and held her hands and feet. She heard him open the chest, and before she had even time to wonder what he was going to do, she felt the leather switch cut across her flaccid buttocks. She cried out, reflexively tensing her muscles for the next blow. The switch came down again and again on her hard, white rotundities, streaking them with red welts. Then turning her over onto her back he struck her across the breasts. Ann groaned, her nipples hardened provocatively as if they welcomed this brutal familiarity. Then suddenly they released her. Instinctively Ann leaped up from the bed and ran for protection to the chest. Yakub followed her with a whip. She jumped onto the wooden chest in an effort to escape the dancing lash, but it cut relentlessly across her buttocks. Jumping off, she ran to the bed, crawled on it and begged him to stop. He dropped the whip and holding her down on the bed slapped her hard across the breast. Then he dragged her off the bed and sat her on the

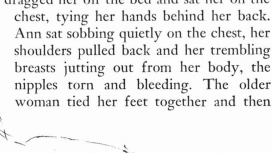

chest, tying her hands behind her back. Ann sat sobbing quietly on the chest, her shoulders pulled back and her trembling breasts jutting out from her body, the nipples torn and bleeding. The older woman tied her feet together and then quietly retired to a corner of the room and sat down. Yakub called to the little girl, she came passively toward him and took off her clothes. She stood in the center of the room like a shiny, black skeleton. Thin to the point of emaciation, her two small breasts looked like two small thorns on a dark rose stem. Her oiled black hair fell rippling to her tiny apple-hard buttocks. She rose on her toes and walked toward the tall man. By now, he was completely naked too and his lean body was like a flame in the orange glow of the lamp. He sat on the edge of the bed and signaled to the girl. Like a thin curl of smoke she knelt at his feet and putting her hands on his knees she took his long firm sex into her narrow mouth. With a sudden thrust he pushed it in deep. It seemed almost too big for her delicate mouth, but she accepted it submissively opening her lips wide and running her tongue cunningly over its tip. Yakub Khan moaned and his hips began a twitching rotatory movement. Turning his head he looked at Ann with a malicious smile on his lips. Ann felt as if she would burst—her thighs were moist with the excited juices that poured out of her quivering sex. Slowly the man disengaged his throbbing organ from the girl's snakelike kisses and raising her up, he lifted her onto his knees. She stood there like a small statue of the dusky blood Goddess Kali—thin and black, her tight breasts sharp and evil as thorns. He spread his knees wide, automatically parting her legs, and her dark hairless sex opened like an orchid before his mouth. His lips closed around the smooth mound and his tongue explored the purple depths, like an inquisitive bee. The girl quivered. Ann sobbed. Her haunches trembled and the pain in her belly was unendurable. She looked at the fortunate girl—her thin black legs were trembling, but her face was impassive, as if the pleasure she felt in her loins was completely detached from every other part of her being. Suddenly the man pulled at her black hips and forced the little girl to sit across his knees. Groping like the light-blind mole, his heavy rod sought for the hidden cave of her vagina and deftly inserted itself. A little cry escaped from her thin lips, but she still sat absolutely motionless and impassive, like a little black idol, on his knees. He moved her almost weightless body up and down, sometimes in a circular rotary movement and sometimes he raised and lowered her roughly on his erect sex. Ann struggled, her feet were cut by straining at the emprisoning string. She rotated her hips on the bare wooden chest in a desperate effort to relieve her pain. She wanted to throw herself between the man and the girl and to insinuate her white body between the black and the brown. She craved to bite the taut black nipples and to offer her golden slit to the thrusting, powerful organ. She cried out in her desire—but no one paid any heed to the perspiring white woman moaning in the darkness.

The black girl was now riding faster and faster on the knees of her master. And, as he felt the final convulsion rise in his loins, he seized her sharp breasts in his mouth and grasping the small fruit buttocks in his hands, he fell back on the bed, his penis stabbing the innermost depths of her being, as he buried his living seed securely within her.

The white skin began to be darkened by the sun—only the blue eyes and radiant hair revealed the origin of the third woman. One evening, as the men were away searching for stray members of their little flock of goats, Ann took the first wife aside and questioned her about many matters:

"How can you stand living in the same house when he loves Azurie more than you?"

The woman shrugged. She was tall, big-boned, silent. Her large square face was expressionless and almost manly with its long etched features and wide flat cheek bones. She gave an impression of rocklike stillness. Only the sharp, green eyes, so like her husband's, betrayed the violence of her nature.

"I am barren," she said in her slow, impersonal voice, "women are vessels to be filled by men. If I cannot contain the precious liquid, my husband has the right to choose and love another woman."

"Yes, but does it not make you angry . . . jealous?"

"What has it got to do with how I feel? My mother chose my husband. He has been good to me and allowed me to remain in his house. He has kept to his bargain. If he sent me away he would have to return my dowry, so you see I am not completely without protection."

"But how can you live . . . night after night . . . seeing him love the other?"

"In the beginning it used to hurt me. I traveled all over the country from Rawalpindi to Afghanistan visiting the tombs of Saints and talking to holy men, in the hope of diverting God's will. But I soon realized that Allah had ordained this, and so now I am resigned.

It is only right that I should be deprived of some of the joys of marriage, seeing that I cannot fulfill my part of the bargain and give my husband an heir."

"Why do you not return to your family?"

"And be a living reminder of my disgrace? Never. My parents would suffer greatly if their daughter was sent back by her husband. People would say, 'See that Shaukat, not only was she barren but she was so useless that her husband sent her back to her mother.' No a woman's lot is a sad one in this life and we must find the courage to bear it."

"I could not live like this . . . seeing him take the other woman more often than myself. . . . I could not."

The woman shrugged disinterestedly and walked away to find sticks to light the fire for the evening meal. . . .

Ann was sitting in the sun sifting rice in a little bamboo tray, when the girl came to call her:

"The master is calling you," she said.

Ann rose quickly, covered the rice to protect it from the marauding chickens and followed the girl, taking care to cover her face completely with her cotton shawl.

Yakub Khan was sitting on a string bed under a large umbrella-shaped tree. He was dressed in the usual gray pyjamas and long shirt, but over this he wore a sleeveless gaily decorated bolero. He dismissed the young wife with a gesture and beckoned to Ann. She did not wait for him to speak but started immediately to complain of his neglect and of her unhappiness. Yakub did not interrupt her but he caught hold of her arm and squeezed it brutally until she subsided.

"Ann, you must not speak without permission."

"Permission? From whom?"

"Ann you are no longer the memsahib living among your own kind. You chose to follow me and live with my people, so now you must follow our ways."

Ann waited in silence. Yakub smiled seeing her suddenly so docile.

"I suppose you have been wondering why I have been avoiding you recently," he continued in his gentle voice, "I shall tell you the truth. You repulse me. I have no stomach for women who are forward, immodest and shameless. You do not yet understand what womanhood is, my child." Taking her hand gently he guided her to the bed. "Sit down and do not be afraid, men are what women make them. I am not a beast, I am a simple man of my people. To us the most attractive thing about a woman is her modesty and virtue. I am more excited by a trembling virgin or a virtuous woman who succumbs to me through complete submission than by any bitch who points her breasts indiscriminately at any man! If you live here with us you must learn the joys of complete submission. . . ." He raised his hand.

"Stand up and undo your pyjamas."

Ann hesitated. They were seated not far from the little house and she was afraid that one of the villagers might pass by. Then slowly she undid the white cord and let the heavy trousers fall to the ground. Yakub drew her close to him and gently stroked her full white thighs.

"Ours is a religion of self-control. You know that we have very definite rules with regard to our conduct. A man disposes of his leisure in accordance with his status. Moreover we are brought up to honor women and to protect them from any bodily or spiritual harm . . . but to honor a woman it is necessary that she herself command this respect." He got up from the bed and turning the blonde girl round he made her bend over.

"Open your legs."

She obeyed. Without any further ceremony he quietly inserted his throbbing organ into the pocket of her womb. Ann gasped. It had been weeks now since she had had a man, and the unexpected quality of his entry only increased her passion. Trembling she began to jerk her buttocks, rotating her hips round and round as the long penis—now stiff and full—penetrated deeper into her belly. She started to shake and the bucking of her loins increased as she rose toward her climax. Suddenly, without warning, the plunging sex was violently withdrawn. For a moment she did not realize what had happened, then with a cry of rage she turned to face her tormentor. Yakub Khan gently held her off and smiled.

"Slowly . . . I see that it will take quite some time to make you understand. There are subtler pleasures than brutality, and there is little pleasure for a man when a woman is too eager and hot. Force is the man's role—acceptance the woman's."

Ann knelt on the hard string bed and buried her head in her hands. The string bit into her knees, and a cool breeze fanned her naked exposed buttocks, crept up the inviting channel between her thighs, making her feel naked and exposed. Once again the man mounted her. She felt the steady pressure of his rod as her muscles opened to welcome him into her body. His loins seemed content to fill her but his hands roamed over her body carressing her rock-pink nipples and brushing the golden down on her stomach and mound. His fingers were like a sculptor's creating new sensations and deeper desires as they brushed over every part of her—eyes, lips, into the moist pink mouth, ears, breasts, back—and dived between the swelling buttocks into the secret recess of her anus. Ann bit her tongue repressing an urgent desire to cry out. She was sweating, she wanted to grasp the huge body of the man and press it against her until she either died or was finally satisfied. But she was too afraid that the weaving caressing magic hands would leave her body. She shuddered as she felt the tumult mount within her. Slowly she started to move her hips, as if in some strange mystic dance. The man responded strongly thrusting his power within her, and his hands continued to seek out every secret of her body. She felt the torrential surge within her. Her muscles tensed—and suddenly he was gone! With a terrible effort Ann kept absolutely still. She neither moved nor cried out, waiting in an agony of suspense for the dark power to tear at her loins. Then he was back; this time he took her hard and ruthlessly, as he used to in the days when they lay struggling in his small dark room in Abbotabad. And Ann sobbed with relief as her body culminated its desire in an unendurable agony of pleasure.

Later as she lay dozing on the grass, she heard him gently order her to rejoin the other women. She rose up, at once, and bending low before him she touched his feet in respectful salutation as she had seen his wives do. . . .

ATAULLAH MARDAAN

Kama Houri *was written by a Pakistani girl who lived in Paris during Olympia's flourishing fifties. She was married to a Dutch photographer, had been educated at Columbia University, was the daughter of a distinguished Pakistani psychiatrist, and like every one else in Paris needed money. We enjoyed her irregular trips to our office when she would deliver her latest chapters for our approval. She always wore flowing silk saris, her hair, thick and braided had never been cut or coiffed, she was modest, beautiful, patient, polite, and draped in veils as she handed us the not so innocent product of her cultivated mind. She was, in every way, what my father and I had dreamed a pornographer should be.*

The Thief's Journal
Jean Genet

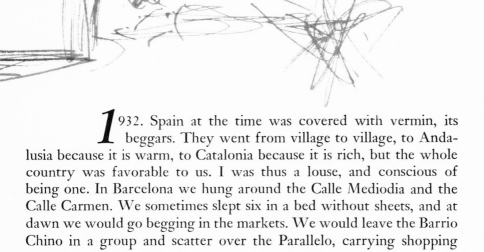

*1*932. Spain at the time was covered with vermin, its beggars. They went from village to village, to Andalusia because it is warm, to Catalonia because it is rich, but the whole country was favorable to us. I was thus a louse, and conscious of being one. In Barcelona we hung around the Calle Mediodia and the Calle Carmen. We sometimes slept six in a bed without sheets, and at dawn we would go begging in the markets. We would leave the Barrio Chino in a group and scatter over the Parallelo, carrying shopping

baskets, for the housewives would give us a leek or turnip rather than
a coin. At noon we would return, and with the gleanings we would
make our soup. It is the life of vermin that I am going to describe. In
Barcelona I saw male couples in which the more loving of the two
would say to the other:

"I'll take the basket this morning."

He would take it and leave. One day Salvador gently pulled the
basket from my hands and said, "I'm going to beg for you."

It was snowing. He went out into the freezing street, wearing a
torn and tattered jacket—the pockets were ripped and hung down—
and a shirt stiff with dirt. His face was poor and unhappy, shifty, pale,
and filthy, for we dared not wash since it was so cold. Around noon,
he returned with the vegetables and a bit of fat. Here I draw attention
to one of those lacerations—horrible, for I shall provoke them despite
the danger—by which beauty was revealed to me. An immense—and
brotherly—love swelled my body and bore me toward Salvador.
Leaving the hotel shortly after him, I would see him a way off
beseeching the women. I knew the formula, as I had already begged
for others and myself: it mixes Christian religion with charity; it
merges the poor person with God; it is so humble an emanation from
the heart that I think it scents with violet the straight, light breath
of the beggar who utters it. All over Spain at the time they were
saying:

"Por Dios."

Without hearing him, I would imagine Salvador murmuring it
at all the stalls, to all the housewives. I would keep an eye on him as
the pimp keeps an eye on his whore, but with such tenderness in my
heart! Thus, Spain and my life as a beggar familiarized me with the
stateliness of abjection, for it took a great deal of pride (that is, of
love) to embellish those filthy, despised creatures. It took a great deal
of talent, which came to me little by little. Though I may be unable
to describe its mechanism to you, at least I can say that I slowly
forced myself to consider that wretched life as a deliberate necessity.
Never did I try to make of it something other than what it was, I did
not try to adorn it, to mask it, but, on the contrary, I wanted to
affirm it in its exact sordidness, and the most sordid signs became for
me signs of grandeur.

I was dismayed when, one evening, while searching me after a
raid, the astonished detective took from my pocket, among other

things, a tube of vaseline. We dared joke about it since it contained mentholated vaseline. The whole record office, and I too, though painfully, writhed with laughter at the following:

"You take it in the nose?"

"Watch out you don't catch cold. You'd give your guy whooping cough."

I translate but lamely, in the language of a Paris hustler, the malicious irony of the vivid and venomous Spanish phrases. It concerned a tube of vaseline, one of whose ends was partially rolled up. Which amounts to saying that it had been put to use. Amidst the elegant objects taken from the pockets of the men who had been picked up in the raid, it was the very sign of abjection, of that which is concealed with the greatest of care, but yet the sign of a secret grace which was soon to save me from contempt. When I was locked up in a cell, and as soon as I had sufficiently regained my spirits to rise above the misfortune of my arrest, the image of the tube of vaseline never left me. The policemen had shown it to me victoriously, since they could thereby flourish their revenge, their hatred, their contempt. But lo and behold! that dirty, wretched object whose purpose seemed to the world—to that concentrated delegation of the world which is the police and, above all, that particular gathering of Spanish police, smelling of garlic, sweat and oil, but substantial looking, stout of muscle and strong in their moral assurance—utterly vile, became extremely precious to me. Unlike many objects which my tenderness singles out, this one was not at all haloed; it remained on the table a little gray leaden tube of vaseline, broken and livid, whose astonishing discreteness, and its essential correspondence with all the commonplace things in the record office of a prison (the bench, the inkwell, the regulations, the scales, the odor), would, through the general indifference, have distressed me, had not the very content of the tube made me think, by bringing to mind an oil lamp (perhaps because of its unctuous character), of a night light beside a coffin.

In describing it, I re-create the little object, but the following image cuts in: beneath a lamppost, in a street of the city where I am writing, the pallid face of a little old woman, a round, flat little face, like the moon, very pale; I cannot tell whether it was sad or hypocritical. She approached me, told me she was very poor and asked for a little money. The gentleness of that moonfish face told me at once: the old woman had just got out of prison.

"She's a thief," I said to myself. As I walked away from her, a kind of intense reverie, living deep within me and not at the edge of my mind, led me to think that it was perhaps my mother whom I had just met. I know nothing of her who abandoned me in the cradle, but I hoped it was that old thief who begged at night.

"What if it were she?" I thought as I walked away from the old woman. Oh! if it were, I would cover her with flowers, with gladioluses and roses, and with kisses! I would weep with tenderness over those moonfish eyes, over that round, foolish face! "And why," I went on, "why weep over it?" It did not take my mind long to replace these customary marks of tenderness by some other gesture, even the vilest and most contemptible, which I empowered to mean as much as the kisses, or the tears, or the flowers.

"I'd be glad to slobber over her," I thought, overflowing with love. (Does the word *glaïeul* [gladiolus] mentioned above bring into play the word *glaviaux* [gobs of spit]?) To slobber over her hair or vomit into her hands. But I would adore that thief who is my mother.

The tube of vaseline, which was intended to grease my prick and those of my lovers, summoned up the face of her who, during a reverie that moved through the dark alleys of the city, was the most cherished of mothers. It had served me in the preparation of so many secret joys, in places worthy of its discrete banality, that it had become the condition of my happiness, as my sperm-spotted handkerchief testified. Lying on the table, it was a banner telling the invisible legions of my triumph over the police. I was in a cell. I knew that all night long my tube of vaseline would be exposed to the scorn—the contrary of a Perpetual Adoration—of a group of strong, handsome, husky policemen. So strong that if the weakest of them barely squeezed his fingers together, there would shoot forth, first with a slight fart, brief and dirty, a ribbon of gum which would continue to emerge in a ridiculous silence. Nevertheless, I was sure that this puny and most humble object would hold its own against them; by its mere presence it would be able to exasperate all the police in the world; it would draw down upon itself contempt, hatred, white and dumb rages. It would perhaps be slightly bantering—like a tragic hero amused at stirring up the wrath of the gods—indestructible, like him, faithful to my happiness, and proud. I would like to hymn it with the newest words in the French language. But I would have also liked to fight for it, to organize massacres in its honor and bedeck a countryside at twilight with red bunting.*

The beauty of a moral act depends on the beauty of its expression. To say that it is beautiful is to decide that it will be so. It remains to be proven so. This is the task of images, that is, of the correspondences with the splendors of the physical world. The act is beautiful if it provokes, and in our throat reveals, song. Sometimes the consciousness with which we have pondered a reputedly vile act, the power of expression which must signify it, impel us to song. This means that treachery is beautiful if it makes us sing. To betray thieves would be not only to find myself again in the moral world, I thought, but also to find myself once more in homosexuality. As I grow strong, I am my own god. I dictate. Applied to men, the word beauty indicates to me the harmonious quality of a face and body to which is sometimes added manly grace. Beauty is then accompanied by magnificent, masterly, sovereign gestures. We imagine that they are determined by very special moral attitudes, and by the cultivation of such virtues in ourselves we hope to endow our poor faces and sick bodies with the vigor that our lovers possess naturally. Alas, these virtues, which they themselves never possess, are our weakness.

Now as I write, I muse on my lovers. I would like them to be smeared with my vaseline, with that soft, slightly mentholated substance; I would like their muscles to bathe in that delicate transparence without which the tool of the handsomest is less lovely.

When a limb has been removed, the remaining one is said to grow stronger. I had hoped that the vigor of the arm which Stilitano had lost might be concentrated in his penis. For a long time I imagined a solid member, like a blackjack, capable of the most outrageous impudence, though what first intrigued me was what Stilitano allowed me to know of it: the mere crease, though curiously precise, in the left leg of his blue denim trousers. This detail might have haunted my dreams less had Stilitano not, at odd moments, put his left hand on it, and had he not, like ladies making a curtsey, indicated the crease by delicately pinching the cloth with his nails. I do not think he ever lost his self-possession, but with me he was particularly calm. With a slightly impertinent smile, though quite nonchalantly, he would watch me adore him. I know that he will love me.

Before Salvador, basket in hand, crossed the threshold of our

---

* I would indeed rather have shed blood than repudiate that silly object.

hotel, I was so excited that I kissed him in the street, but he pushed me aside:

"You're crazy! People'll take us for mariconas!"

He spoke French fairly well, having learned it in the region around Perpignan where he used to go for the grape harvesting. Deeply wounded, I turned away. His face was purple. His complexion was that of winter cabbage. Salvador did not smile. He was shocked. "That's what I get," he must have thought, "for getting up so early to go begging in the snow. He doesn't know how to behave." His hair was wet and shaggy. Behind the window, faces were staring at us, for the lower part of the hotel was occupied by a café that opened on the street and through which you had to pass in order to go up to the rooms. Salvador wiped his face with his sleeve and went in. I hesitated. Then I followed. I was twenty years old. If the drop that hesitates at the edge of a nostril has the limpidity of a tear, why shouldn't I drink it with the same eagerness? I was already sufficiently involved in the rehabilitation of the ignoble. Were it not for fear of revolting Salvador, I would have done it in the café. He, however, sniffled, and I gathered that he was swallowing his snot. Basket in arm, passing the beggars and the guttersnipes, he moved toward the kitchen. He preceded me.

"What's the matter with you?" I said.

"You're attracting attention."

"What's wrong?"

"People don't kiss that way on the sidewalk. Tonight, if you like . . ."

He said it all with a charmless pout and the same disdain. I had simply wanted to show my gratitude, to warm him with my poor tenderness.

"But what were you thinking?"

Someone bumped into him without apologizing, separating him from me. I did not follow him to the kitchen. I went over to a bench where there was a vacant seat near the stove. Though I adored vigorous beauty, I didn't bother my head much about how I would bring myself to love this homely, squalid beggar who was bullied by the less bold, how I would come to care for his angular buttocks . . . and what if, unfortunately, he were to have a magnificent tool?

The Barrio Chino was, at the time, a kind of haunt thronged less with Spaniards than with foreigners, all of them down-and-out bums.

We were sometimes dressed in almond-green or jonquil-yellow silk shirts and shabby sneakers, and our hair was so plastered down that it looked as if it would crack. We did not have leaders but rather directors. I am unable to explain how they became what they were. Probably it was as a result of profitable operations in the sale of our meager booty. They attended to our affairs and let us know about jobs, for which they took a reasonable commission. We did not form loosely organized bands, but amidst that vast, filthy disorder, in a neighborhood stinking of oil, piss and shit, a few waifs and strays relied on others more clever than themselves. The squalor sparkled with the youth of many of our number and with the more mysterious brilliance of a few who really scintillated, youngsters whose bodies, gazes and gestures were charged with a magnetism which made of us their object. That is how I was staggered by one of them. In order to do justice to the one-armed Stilitano I shall wait a few pages. Let it be known from the start that he was devoid of any Christian virtue. All his brilliance, all his power, had their source between his legs. His penis, and that which completes it, the whole apparatus, was so beautiful that the only thing I can call it is a generative organ. One might have thought he was dead, for he rarely, and slowly, got excited: he watched. He generated in the darkness of a well-buttoned fly, though buttoned by only one hand, the luminosity with which its bearer will be aglow.

My relations with Salvador lasted for six months. It was not the most intoxicating but rather the most fecund of loves. I had managed to love that sickly body, gray face, and ridiculously sparse beard. Salvador took care of me, but at night, by candlelight, I hunted for lice, our pets, in the seams of his trousers. The lice inhabited us. They imparted to our clothes an animation, a presence, which, when they had gone, left our garments lifeless. We liked to know—and feel— that the translucent bugs were swarming; though not tamed, they were so much a part of us that a third person's louse disgusted us. We chased them away but with the hope that during the day the nits would have hatched. We crushed them with our nails, without disgust and without hatred. We did not throw their corpses—or remains— into the garbage; we let them fall, bleeding with our blood, into our untidy underclothes. The lice were the only sign of our prosperity, of the very underside of prosperity, but it was logical that by making our state perform an operation which justified it, we were, by the same token, justifying the sign of this state. Having become as useful for the knowledge of our decline as jewels for the knowledge of what is called triumph, the lice were precious. They were both our shame and our glory. I lived for a long time in a room without windows, except a transom on the corridor, where, in the evening, five little faces, cruel and tender, smiling or screwed up with the cramp of a difficult position, dripping with sweat, would hunt for those insects of whose virtue we partook. It was good that, in the depths of such wretchedness, I was the lover of the poorest and homeliest. I thereby had a rare privilege. I had difficulty, but every victory I achieved—my filthy hands, proudly exposed, helped me proudly expose my beard and long hair—gave me strength—or weakness, and here it amounts to the same thing—for the following victory, which in your language would naturally be called a comedown. Yet, light and brilliance being necessary to our lives, a sunbeam did cross the pane and its filth and penetrate the dimness; we had the hoarfrost, the silver thaw, for these elements, though they may spell calamity, evoke joys whose sign, detached in our room, was adequate for us: all we knew of Christmas and New Year's festivities was what always accompanies them and what makes them dearer to merrymakers: frost.

The cultivation of sores by beggars is also their means of getting a little money—on which to live—but though they may be led to this out of a certain inertia in their state of poverty, the pride required for holding one's head up, above contempt, is a manly virtue. Like a rock in a river, pride breaks through and divides contempt, bursts it. Entering further into abjection, pride will be stronger (if the beggar is myself) when I have the knowledge—strength or weakness—to take advantage of such a fate. It is essential, as this leprosy gains on me, that I gain on it and that, in the end, I win out. Shall I therefore become increasingly vile, more and more an object of disgust, up to that final point which is something still unknown but which must be governed by an aesthetic as well as moral inquiry? It is said that leprosy, to which I compare our state, causes an irritation of the tissues; the sick person scratches himself; he gets an erection. Masturbation becomes frequent. In his solitary eroticism the leper consoles himself and hymns his disease. Poverty made us erect. All across Spain we carried a secret, veiled magnificence unmixed with arrogance. Our gestures grew humbler and humbler, fainter and fainter, as the embers of humility which kept us alive glowed more intensely.

Thus developed my talent for giving a sublime meaning to so beggarly an appearance. (I am not yet speaking of literary talent.) It proved to have been a very useful discipline for me and still enables me to smile tenderly at the humblest among the dregs, whether human or material, including vomit, including the saliva I let drool on my mother's face, including your excrement. I shall preserve within me the idea of myself as beggar.

This journal is not a mere literary diversion. The further I progress, reducing to order what my past life suggests, and the more I persist in the rigor of composition—of the chapters, of the sentences, of the book itself—the more do I feel myself hardening in my will to utilize, for virtuous ends, my former hardships. I feel their power.

In the urinals, which Stilitano never entered, the behavior of the faggots would make matters clear: they would perform their dance, the remarkable movement of a snake standing on its tail and undulating, swaying from side to side, tilted slightly backward, so as to cast a furtive glance at my prick which was out of my fly. I would go off with the one who looked most prosperous.

In my time, the Ramblas were frequented by two young mariconas who carried a tame little monkey on their shoulders. It was an easy pretext for approaching clients: the monkey would jump up on the man they pointed out to it. One of the mariconas was called Pedro. He was pale and thin. His waist was very supple, his step quick. His eyes in particular were splendid, his lashes immense.

In fun, I asked him which was the monkey, he or the animal he carried on his shoulder. We started quarreling. I punched him. His eyelashes remained stuck to my knuckles; they were false. I had just discovered the existence of fakes.

Stilitano got money occasionally from the whores. Most often he stole it from them, either by taking the change when they paid for something, or at night from their handbags, when they were on the bidet. He would go through the Barrio Chino and the Parallelo heckling all the women, sometimes irritating them, sometimes fondling them, but always ironic. When he returned to the room, toward morning, he would bring back a bundle of children's magazines full of gaudy pictures. He would sometimes go a long roundabout way in order to buy them at a newsstand that was open late at night. He would read the stories which, in those days, corresponded to the Tarzan adventures in today's comic books. The hero of these stories is lovingly drawn. The artist took the utmost pains with the imposing physique of this knight, who was almost always nude or obscenely dressed. Then Stilitano would fall asleep. He would manage so that his body did not touch mine. The bed was very narrow. As he put out the light, he would say,

"Night, kid!"

And upon awakening:

"Morning, kid!"*

Our room was very tiny. It was dirty. The wash basin was filthy. No one in the Barrio Chino would have dreamed of cleaning his room, his belongings or his linen—except his shirt and, most often, only the collar. Once a week, to pay the room rent, Stilitano screwed the landlady who, on other days, called him Señor.

One evening he had to fight. We were going through the Calle Carmen. It was just about dark. Spaniards' bodies sometimes have a kind of undulating flexibility and their stances are occasionally equivocal. In broad daylight Stilitano would not have made a mistake. In this incipient darkness he grazed three men who were talking quietly but whose gesticulations were both brisk and languorous. As he neared them, Stilitano, in his most insolent tone of voice, hurled a few coarse words at them. Three quick and vigorous pimps replied to the insults. Stilitano stood there, taken aback. The three men approached.

"Do you take us for mariconas, talking to us like that?"

Although he recognized his blunder, Stilitano wanted to strut in my presence.

"Suppose I do?"

"Maricona yourself."

A few women drew up, and some men. A circle gathered around us. A fight seemed inevitable. One of the young men provoked Stilitano outright.

"If you're not fruit, come on and fight."

Before getting to the point of fists or weapons, hoodlums gab it out for a while. It's not that they try to soft-pedal the conflict; rather, they work themselves up to combat. Some other Spaniards, their friends, were egging the three pimps on. Stilitano felt he was in danger. My presence no longer bothered him. He said:

"After all, boys, you're not going to fight with a cripple."

He held out his stump. But he did it with such simplicity, such sobriety, that this vile hamming, instead of disgusting me with him, ennobled him. He withdrew, not to the sound of jeers, but to a murmur expressing the discomfort of decent men discovering the misery about them. Stilitano stepped back slowly, protected by his out-

---

* I used to toss my things any old place when we went to bed, but Stilitano laid his out on a chair, carefully arranging the trousers, jacket and shirt so that nothing would be creased. He seemed thereby to be endowing his clothes with life, as if wanting them to get a night's rest after a hard day.

stretched stump, which was placed simply in front of him. The absence of the hand was as real and effective as a royal attribute, as the hand of justice.

Those whom one of their number called the Carolinas paraded to the site of a demolished street urinal. During the 1933 riots, the insurgents tore out one of the dirtiest, but most beloved, pissoirs. It was near the harbor and the barracks, and its sheet iron had been corroded by the hot urine of thousands of soldiers. When its ultimate death was certified, the Carolinas—not all, but a formally chosen delegation—in shawls, mantillas, silk dresses and fitted jackets, went to the site to place a bunch of red roses tied together with a crape veil. The procession started from the Parallelo, crossed the Calle São Paolo and went down the Ramblas de Las Flores until it reached the statue of Columbus. The faggots were perhaps thirty in number, at eight A.M., at sunrise. I saw them going by. I accompanied them from a distance. I knew that my place was in their midst, not because I was one of them, but because their shrill voices, their cries, their extravagant gestures seemed to me to have no other aim than to try to pierce the shell of the world's contempt. The Carolinas were great. They were the Daughters of Shame.

When they reached the harbor, they turned right, toward the barracks, and upon the rusty, stinking sheet iron of the pissoir that lay battered on the heap of dead scrap iron they placed the flowers.

I was not in the procession. I belonged to the ironic and indulgent crowd that was entertained by it. Pedro airily admitted to his false lashes, the Carolinas to their wild larks.

Meanwhile, Stilitano, by denying himself to my pleasure, became the symbol of chastity, of frigidity itself. If he did screw the whores often, I was unaware of it. When he lay down to sleep in our bed, he had the modesty to arrange his shirttail so artfully that I saw nothing of his penis. The purity of his features corrected even the eroticism of his walk. He became the representation of a glacier. I would have liked to offer myself to the most bestial of Negroes, to the most flat-nosed and most powerful face, so that within me, having no room for anything but sexuality, my love for Stilitano might be further stylized. I was therefore able to venture in his presence the most absurd and humiliating postures.

We often went to the Criolla together. Hitherto, it had never occurred to him to exploit me. When I brought back to him the pesetas I had earned around the pissoirs, Stilitano decided that I would work in the Criolla.

"Would you like me to dress up as a woman?" I murmured.

Would I have dared, supported by his powerful shoulder, to walk the streets in a spangled skirt between the Calle Carmen and the Calle Mediodia? Except for foreign sailors, no one would have been surprised, but neither Stilitano nor I would have known how to choose the dress or the hair-do, for taste is required. Perhaps that was what held us back. I still remembered the sighs of Pedro, with whom I had once teamed up, when he went to get dressed.

"When I see those rags hanging there, I get the blues! I feel as if I were going into a vestry to get ready to conduct a funeral. They've got a priestish smell. Like incense. Like urine. Look at them hanging! I wonder how I manage to get into those damned sausage skins."

"Will I have to have things like that? Maybe I'll even have to sew and cut with my man's help. And wear a bow, or maybe several, in my hair."

With horror I saw myself decked out in enormous bows, not of ribbons, but of sausage meat in the form of pricks.

"It'll be a drooping, dangling bow," added a mocking inner voice. An old man's droopy ding-dong. A bow limp, or impish! And in what hair? In an artificial wig or in my own dirty, curly hair?

As for my dress, I knew it would be sober and that I would wear it with modesty, whereas what was needed to carry the thing off was a kind of wild extravagance. Nevertheless, I cherished the dream of sewing on a cloth rose. It would emboss the dress and would be the feminine counterpart of Stilitano's bunch of grapes.

(Long afterward, when I ran into him in Antwerp, I spoke to Stilitano about the fake bunch hidden in his fly. He then told me that a Spanish whore used to wear a muslin rose pinned on at cunt level.

("To replace her lost flower," he said.)

In Pedro's room, I looked at the skirts with melancholy. He gave me a few addresses of women's outfitters, where I would find dresses to fit me.

"You'll have a *toilette*, Juan."*

---

* The term *la toilette* also refers to certain kinds of wrappings or casings; for example, a tailor's or dressmaker's wrapper for garments, as well as to the caul over mutton.—*Translator's note.*

I was sickened by this butcher's word (I was thinking that the *toilette* was also the greasy tissue enveloping the guts in animals' bellies). It was then that Stilitano, perhaps hurt by the idea of his friend in fancy dress, refused.

"There's no need for it," he said. "You'll manage well enough to make pick-ups."

Alas, the boss of the Criolla demanded that I appear as a young lady.

As a young lady!

> *Myself a young lady*
> *I alight on my hip. . . .*

I then realized how hard it is to reach the light by puncturing the abscess of shame. I once managed to appear in woman's dress with Pedro, to exhibit myself with him. I went one evening, and we were invited by a group of French officers. At their table was a lady of about fifty. She smiled at me sweetly, with indulgence, and unable to contain herself any longer, she asked me:

"Do you like men?"

"Yes, madame, I do."

"And . . . when did it start?"

I did not slap anyone, but my voice was so shaken that I realized

how angry and ashamed I was. In order to pull myself together, I robbed one of the officers that very same night.

"At least," I said to myself, "if my shame is real, it hides a sharper, more dangerous element, a kind of sting that will always threaten anyone who provokes it. It might not have been laid over me like a trap, might not have been intentional, but since it is what it is, I want it to conceal me so that I can lie in wait beneath it."

At Carnival time, it was easy to go about in woman's dress, and I stole an Andalusian petticoat with a bodice from a hotel room. Disguised by the mantilla and fan, one evening I walked across town quickly in order to get to the Criolla. So that my break with your world would be less brutal, I kept my trousers on under the skirt. Hardly had I reached the bar when someone ripped the train of my dress. I turned around in a fury.

"I beg your pardon. Excuse me."

The foot of a blond young man had got caught in the lace. I hardly had strength enough to mumble, "Watch what you're doing." The face of the clumsy young man, who was both smiling and excusing himself, was so pale that I blushed. Someone next to me said to me in a low voice, "Excuse him, señora, he limps."

"I won't have people limping on my dress!" screamed the beautiful actress who smoldered within me. But the people around us were laughing. "I won't have people limping on my toilette!" I screamed to myself. Formulated within me, in my stomach, as it seemed to me, or in the intestines, which are enveloped by the "toilette," this phrase must have been expressed by a terrible glare. Furious and humiliated, I left under the laughter of the men and the Carolinas. I went straight to the sea and drowned the skirt, bodice, mantilla and fan. The whole city was joyous, drunk with the Carnival that was cut off from the earth and alone in the middle of the Ocean. I was poor and sad.

("Taste is required. . . ." I was already refusing to have any. I forbade myself to. Of course I would have shown a great deal of it. I knew that cultivating it would have—not sharpened me but—softened me. Stilitano himself was amazed that I was so uncouth. I wanted my fingers to be stiff: *I kept myself from learning to sew*.)

Stilitano and I left for Cadiz. Changing from one freight train to another, we finally got to a place near San Fernando and decided to continue our journey on foot. Stilitano disappeared. He arranged to meet me at the station. He didn't show up. I waited for a long time; I

returned the following day and the day
after, two days in succession, though I
was sure he had deserted me. I was
alone and without money. When I realized this, I again became aware of the
presence of lice, of their distressing and
sweet company in the hems of my shirt
and trousers. Stilitano and I had never
ceased to be nuns of Upper Thebaid who
never washed their feet and whose shifts
rotted away.

San Fernando is on the sea. I decided
to get to Cadiz, which is built right
on the water, though connected to the
mainland by a very long jetty. It was
evening when I started out. Before me
were the high salt pyramids of the San
Fernando marshes, and farther off, in the
sea, silhouetted by the setting sun, a city
of domes and minarets. At the outermost
point of Western soil, I suddenly had before me the synthesis of the Orient. For
the first time in my life I neglected a human being for a thing. I forgot Stilitano.

In order to keep alive, I would go
to the port early in the morning, to the
piscatoria, where the fishermen always
throw from their boats a few fish caught
the night before. All beggars are familiar
with this practice. Instead of going, as in
Malaga, to cook them on the fire of the
other tramps, I went back alone, to the
middle of the rocks overlooking Porto
Reale. The sun would be rising when my
fish were cooked. I almost always ate
them without bread or salt. Standing up,
or lying among the rocks, or sitting on
them, at the easternmost point of the
island, facing the mainland, I was the first

man lit up and warmed by the first ray, which was itself the first manifestation of life. I had gathered the fish on the wharves in the darkness. It was still dark when I reached my rocks. The coming of the sun overwhelmed me. I worshiped it. A kind of sly intimacy developed between us. I honored it, though without, to be sure, any complicated ritual; it would not have occurred to me to ape the primitives, but I know that this star became my god. It was within my body that it rose, continued its curve and completed it. If I saw it in the sky of the astronomers, I did so because it was the bold projection there of the one I preserved within myself. Perhaps I even confused it in some obscure way with the vanished Stilitano.

I am indicating to you, in this way, the form that my sensibility took. Nature made me uneasy. My love for Stilitano, the roar with which he burst upon my wretchedness, and any number of other things, delivered me to the elements. But they are malicious. In order to tame them I wanted to contain them. I refused to deny them cruelty; quite the contrary, I congratulated them for having as much as they had; I flattered them.

As an operation of this kind cannot succeed by means of dialectics, I had recourse to magic, that is, to a kind of deliberate *predisposition,* an intuitive complicity with nature. Language would have been of no help to me. It was then that things and circumstances became maternal to me, though alert within them, like the sting of a bee, was the point of my pride. (Maternal: that is, whose essential element is femininity. In writing this I do not want to make any Mazdaean allusion: I merely point out that my sensibility required that it be surrounded by a feminine order. It could do so inasmuch as it could avail itself of masculine qualities: hardness, cruelty, indifference.)

If I attempt to recompose with words what my attitude was at the time, the reader will be no more taken in than I. We know that our language is incapable of recalling even the pale reflection of those bygone, foreign states. The same would be true of this entire journal if it were to be the notation of what I was. I shall therefore make clear that it is meant to indicate what I am today, as I write it. It is not a quest of time gone by, but a work of art whose pretext-subject is my former life. It will be a present fixed with the help of the past, and not vice versa. Let the reader therefore understand that the facts were what I say they were, but the interpretation that I give them is what

I am—now.

At night I would stroll about the city. I would sleep against a wall, sheltered from the wind. I thought about Tangiers, whose proximity fascinated me, as did the glamor of the city, that haunt, rather, of traitors. To escape my poverty, I invented the boldest acts of treason, which I would have calmly performed. Today I know that only my love of the French language attaches me to France, but then!

This taste for treason will have to be better formulated when I am questioned at the time of Stilitano's arrest.

"Should I squeal on Stilitano for money and under the threat of a beating?" I asked myself. "I still love him, and I answer no. But should I squeal on Pépé who murdered the ronda player on the Parallelo?"

I would have accepted, though with great shame, the knowledge that my soul was rotten within since it emitted the odor that makes people hold their noses. Now the reader may remember that my periods of begging and prostitution were to me a discipline which taught me to utilize ignoble elements, to apply them to my own ends, indeed, to take pleasure in my choosing them. I would have done the same (strong in my skill in turning my shame to account) with my soul that had been decomposed by treason. Fortune granted that the question be put to me at the time when a young ship's ensign was sentenced to death by the maritime court of Toulon. He had turned over to the enemy the plans of a weapon or of a war port or of a boat. I am not talking of an act of treason causing the loss of a naval battle, which is slight, unreal, hanging from the wings of a schooner's sails, but of the loss of a combat of steel monsters wherein dwelt the pride of a people no longer childlike, but severe, helped and supported by the learned mathematics of technicians. In short, it was an act of treason in modern times. The newspaper reporting these facts (I learned of the matter in Cadiz) said, stupidly no doubt, for what could the reporter know about it: ". . . out of a taste for treason." Accompanying the text was the photograph of a young, very handsome officer. I was taken with his picture, which I still carry with me. As love is exalted in perilous situations, secretly within me I offered to share the exile's Siberia. The maritime court, by arousing my hostility, further facilitated my climb toward him whom I approached with heavy yet wingèd foot. His name was Marc Aubert. I shall go to Tangiers, I said to myself, and perhaps I may be summoned among the traitors and become one of them.

JEAN GENET

No writer has been so well and so thoroughly analyzed in his lifetime as Genet has been by Jean-Paul Sartre; for Sartre, Genet epitomizes certain fundamental precepts of existentialism. No one know's Genet's mind and work better than Sartre, who has commented upon The Thief's Journal *as follows:*

Not all who would be are Narcissus. Many who lean over the water see only a vague human figure. Genet sees himself everywhere; the dullest surfaces reflect his image; even in others he perceives himself, thereby bringing to light their deepest secrets. The disturbing theme of the double, the image, the counterpart, the enemy brother, is found in all his works.

Each of them has the strange property of being both itself and the reflection of itself. Genet brings before us a dense and teeming throng which intrigues us, transports us and changes into Genet beneath Genet's gaze. Hitler appears, talks, lives; he removes his mask: it was Genet. But the little servant girl with the swollen feet who meanwhile was burying her child—that was Genet too. In The Thief's Journal *the myth of the double has assumed its most reassuring, most common, most* natural *form. Here Genet speaks of Genet without intermediary. He talks of his life, of his wretchedness and glory, of his loves; he tells the story of his thoughts. One might think that, like Montaigne, he is going to draw a good-humored and familiar self-portrait. But Genet is never familiar, even with himself. He does, to be sure, tell us everything. The whole truth, nothing but the truth, but it is the sacred truth. He opens up one of his myths; he tells us: "You're going to see what stuff it's made of," and we find another myth. He reassures us only to disturb us further. His autobiography is not an autobiography; it merely seems like one; it is a sacred cosmogony. His stories are not stories. They excite you and fascinate you; you think he is relating facts and suddenly you realize he is describing rites. If he talks of the wretched beggars of the Barrio Chino, it is only to debate, in lordly style, questions of precedence and etiquette; he is the Saint-Simon of this Court of Miracles. His memories are not memories; they are exact but sacred; he speaks about his life like an evangelist, as a wonder-struck witness. . . .*

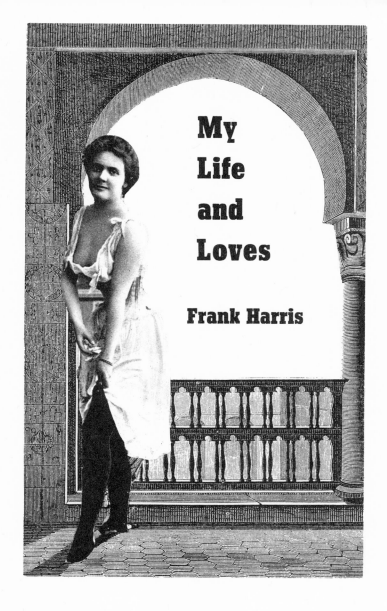

My
Life
and
Loves

Frank Harris

The only man I knew in Bombay was a man called Taylor. He had some kind of position with the railways. Here I find my memory at fault. In a long life lived energetically over three parts of the globe, this lapse is perhaps excusable. I shall go straight to the things which most concerned me, for they, like certain pages of Virgil and like certain immortal lines of Meredith, will remain with me always.

It was late afternoon when Taylor conducted me through the bazaar. There is nothing so picturesque as the bazaars of India, and nothing so chaotic. The men, women, and the skinny brown children are as thick as flies in the midst of the gaudy bales and bundles of their colorful wares. I couldn't help noticing how, when they saw us, they seemed to make way for us and to impede us at the same time. Taylor called my attention to the Chinese silks, the Tibetan shawls, and to the large drums of brown and yellow spices. I feigned interest, but to tell the truth, I was interested in the people more than in the gaudy merchandise which they held up for us to see. It seemed to me significant that Taylor, who was, after all, a man of no breadth of mind, a man who missed alike the joys of the spirit and the sweetest of the body's delights, should barge his way like a railway porter through the crowd. He typified for me the worst aspect of the British Raj, the kind of man who, like Lord Milner, is devoid of the sense of justice and fair play when he is confronted by the subject races. I allowed him to walk ahead, like a bad-mannered guide. Thoughtfully, taking everything in, I followed in his wake.

It occurred to me immediately that Taylor was not the kind of man whom I could trust to advise me in the matter which was closest to my heart. I decided, therefore, to take Mrs. Redfern at her word, and to accept her offer to be my guide and friend in sexual matters during my sojourn in India. Walking behind Taylor, I could not help feeling very anti-English. That this in general should have been the type of man they sent out to bring Western civilization to the East made me boil with rage. What kind of future could we expect when we showed such little wisdom in the choice of our emissaries? I remembered suddenly what I had said to Molly, the beautiful daughter of the innkeeper at Ballinasloe: "I am not ambitious, Molly, of place or power or riches; but of knowledge and wisdom I'm the lover and priest. . . . I don't want happiness even, Molly, nor comfort, though I'll take all I can get of both; I'm wedded to one quest like a knight of the Holy Grail and my whole life will go to the achievement." When I said that, I was thinking of Smith, my friend and professor in Lawrence, Kansas. Now, for the thousandth time in my life, I was thinking of him again. If only our western governments would be sensible enough to use the fine qualities of men like Smith! There are true Empire Builders, the men in whom moral courage is leavened by wisdom, the men who, in their wisdom, despise not the body in its pleasures nor are insensitive to it in its afflictions. That kind of man, more than those who learn their manners on the cricket field of Eton, is the one who will build the only true empire . . . the everlasting Empire of Love!

All around me was a strange people: men, passionate in their poverty; women, tender as flowers in their travail; children, graceful in their filth; a strange people, a colored people, a people whose natural right it was to know kindness and love at our hands but who had for centuries known nothing but ugliness and the whip! I decided that very moment to bid good-bye to Taylor as soon as we left the bazaar and, in future, to avoid wherever possible contact with his type during the rest of my stay in India. He was not, as you can well imagine, unsurprised at my sudden decision to part company with him, laughing first, and then, when he saw that I was in earnest, becoming cool and not a little angry toward me. But I have never had any time to waste on fools. I bade him good day politely and was lucky enough not to run into him again while I was in Bombay. I considered myself very lucky to have got off so lightly and so soon.

Mrs. Redfern, the stewardess, was not satisfied with failure. She was an extremely practical and capable woman, the widow of a noncommissioned officer, as I have said before. Perhaps it was that ordinary failures did not bring her in money enough. In any case, she was resolved to win my vagrant fancy and I had confidence in her. Soon after her first unfortunate introductions in Bombay, she began talking to me of a wonderful girl who was quite independent but who, at sixteen, would soon have to choose a lover or a husband.

"Some go much longer," I objected.

"Not in this climate," she cried. "When a girl of sixteen sees a girl of ten or twelve already given up to love, her chastity begins to trouble her, I can assure you. But I want to be certain that you will give this girl the best reception, for she is a peach."

She interested me and we soon decided on an afternoon upon which to bring about the meeting. I arranged the sitting room with flowers and fruit and wine, and really when Mrs. Redfern came in with her protégée, I was astonished. Her skin was a very pale brown color, too dark to be English, but she spoke English with no accent. She wore high-heeled slippers, but the rest of her costume was native, a large transparent veil hanging down from her head and being fastened between the knees. It was all in all an exceedingly gracious costume. But her pure accent caused me to ask her: "Are you English?"

"Half-English," she replied, and I learned that her father was an English officer while her mother was an Indian of good family. Her name was May and she deserved it. She was certainly very pretty and her gentle and sympathetic manners increased the effect of her beauty. Mrs. Redfern stripped the girl in front of my eyes and made me notice that the hairs everywhere had been taken off; indeed she seemed quite in love with the girl herself; she kissed her soft skin passionately and ran her hands over the softly rounded curves while the girl stood like a young sylph in her nudity. Mrs. Redfern told me that the girl was a *Padmini*, or lotus-girl, and when I asked what that meant she would have it that the girl's *Yoni* was like the bud of a lotus flower and her *Kama-salila* or love-juice had the perfume of a lily that was just opening. She became as lyrical in her praise as if she had been the lover, and indeed the girl's body deserved her eulogy. Her hips were smooth and rounded and gave downward to a pair of soft and shapely thighs on which the hairless mound, naked of hair between their roundnesses, jutted outward like a soft beak. I must say I found that rather ugly. It is a fallacy to think that a woman's sexual organ is less prominent when it is shaven of its hair. The hair, rising as it does outward and away from the lower belly, has a tendency to obscure the sharpness of the line of the mound, thus rendering the mound itself less prominent, more subtle in its provocativeness and more modest to a man's lips. Hair is the grass of the human body, the verdure and the beauty of the carnal meadow. But that was the only imperfection. The breasts were round and rosy like small pomegranates and her belly was really like the heap of brown-flecked wheat on which Solomon must have showered passionate kisses to have written of it in the immortal lines of his *Songs*. The soft indentation of her perfectly formed navel had all my attention. Her neck was almost yellow, not the offensive saffron color of the Turkish trousers she had worn, but a softer, browner yellow with a touch of hazel in it. Her lips were generous and young, perhaps cold in their sensuousness, but I could have been mistaken, while her eyes, glory of glories, were almost an amethyst color and glimmered suggestively from behind dark, oriental-lashed lids. The beauties of the East and West had combined to make this perfectly charming child, a widow at sixteen! one of the most prototypical of the fair tribe of Venus. She was seated on a round stool of gaily decorated leather and when she moved on her haunches there was a slight tearing sound as the skin of her warm, damp buttocks pulled away from the shining leather and readjusted itself in a more comfortable position. Mrs. Redfern had been sitting at her feet, like a courtier at the feet of one of Shakespeare's princesses—at the court of Richard II, yes, at the court of a Plantagenet! I felt a passion for her mounting in me.

I soon said "Good-bye" to Mrs. Redfern and a little later convinced myself that May, though not a virgin, was well disposed to me through the extravagant eulogy of Mrs. Redfern. I resolved to do my best to please her. Quickly, though not I hope without dignity, I removed my clothes and, taking one of her hands, lifted the graceful child on to her feet beside me. Then, with my hand at the cleft of her smooth buttocks, I drew her against me, belly to belly, until her hairless sex was against mine. At the same time I kissed her on the lips. She responded at once, searching to enclose one of my thighs between hers to bring pressure on her little love-knot. I allowed myself to be her confederate, feeling the soft urgent thrust of her mound against my thigh, her dark head, with its coils of raven-black hair, splashing a scintillating web at the white flesh of my shoulders and chest. After a moment, I lifted her off her feet and carried her in my arms across to the divan where I laid her down at full length. Her eyes were closed and she was breathing heavily. I began to stroke her and examine her at the same time. Really, the suffusion of a darker color which beneath the skin made the almost fair skin dusky was most attractive, especially at the breasts on which the pink nipples, as big as small thimbles, were set as coral gems in tarnished brass. It was on these delightful flowers that I bestowed my first kisses, gently, and at the same time, drawing apart the lips of her cleft with the fingers of my left hand. I agitated the little bud of her love until her hips arched upward in passion and a long sigh of content escaped from her lips. I was pleased to find that her sex was comparatively small, the sexual badge of women in warm climes being usually more obvious than that of the women of northern Europe and, in spite of the fact that it is truly the melting pot of nations, of the women of America. As I moved down into her, a small, hissing sound came from her lips, as though the sound at her throat slaked the terrible thirst at her loins, and then, when I had sunk to the hilt, I felt my own hips carried into a rhythm by a small rotatory movement of hers. I slid easily in the smooth love-juiced trough, her *Yoni* with its crystal varnish of *Kama-salila* as Mrs. Redfern would have called it, using long, slow strokes to kindle the flame in her, my hands, forefingers together, nestling under the soft oscillation of her buttocks, and my knees, slightly apart, locking her legs in an open position. I brought her to one climax after another, and then, when she had lost all fear of me and I felt her give her whole being over to love, I allowed my own passion to ride upward into her. I taught her from the beginning how to use the syringe. She laughed for a long time—the idea seemed to amuse her. That first time, even, I enjoyed her and gave her pleasure to the full. When it was over I drew her out about her life and found it had been very lonely.

A noncommissioned officer, an Indian and his wife, had been given charge of her by her father who had settled a small pension on her and so she had lived between the two contrasting civilizations, so to speak, understanding both but not loving either. The Indian, she said, was kinder than the Englishman, but had no notion of sex morality. I found out that she had been brought up in a temple as a bride of the God Brahma and had been taught all love's ways and arts by the priests; in fact she had only given ear to Mrs. Redfern hoping that I would take care of her or at least free her from the temple service. Of course, I promised to do what I could and set out to find out about it the very next day. With Mrs. Redfern's help, I found that the task was not very difficult. The English father had put the pension in the girl's control after her sixteenth year. By applying to the proper authorities, I soon got her out of the hands of the priests and into that of a person who, I knew, had real affection for her—Mrs. Redfern.

Naturally, I was inquisitive about the kind of treatment she had received at the hands of the priests. I questioned her about it but she was always very reticent. She admitted once that on one occasion she had been forced to submit to the attentions of two priests, almost simultaneously, and that on another occasion she had been stripped naked and flogged in front of a number of priests for what she con-sidered a trifling offense. That is as it may be, I can only report what she said. I must continue with my narrative.

For over a month I lived between Winnie and May and was more than content with my lot. Winnie was much stronger and more resolute, but May was more sensuous and her yielding and gentleness were infinitely touching. When I disappointed her, the big, dark-lashed eyes filled with tears. Winnie, on the other hand, would get angry and tear her passion to tatters. Still, they both gave me intense pleasure, and of a new kind, for it must be remembered that I was forty-five at the time and my young mistresses were both in their middle teens.

I had often thought of bringing them together. I consulted Mrs. Redfern, making sure to bring up the subject casually. To my instant delight, she responded favorably and at once to the idea.

"Winnie is such a dear," she said, "and fortunately she already knows and trusts me. I really think you ought to let me put it to her."

I asked her why.

"Oh, women 'ave ways of talking about such things!" she said with a merry laugh, and I supposed they had!

"And what about May? Do you think you'll be able to persuade her?" I was not unanxious on May's account either.

"You just leave it to me, Sir!"

I was only too glad to. Our own history has made it only too difficult for us to engineer situations whereas, with the aid of one other person only, how easily most love trysts are arranged! Perhaps this is the place to defend against the weight of judgment throughout history the character of Pander. A much-maligned figure indeed! And yet how necessary! Sometimes an individual needs an emissary as much as a nation. We do not despise the emissary in law; why, then, should we despise the emissary in love? Another of the old prejudices, and one, moreover, against which that great humanist Chaucer raised his voice in *Troilus and Cressida*. Who could read that masterpiece and not come away with the impression that Pander is not only human but, after a fashion, lovable? There was no doubt about it, Mrs. Redfern was playing Pander to my Troilus, but I didn't like her one whit the less for it. A few days later, the cunning lady came to me and announced that her entreaties had been successful. The meeting was arranged for the following day.

Only one thing had disturbed her, she said. It was the fact that Winnie was white and May a half-caste. She thought Winnie might have been put off by it. I laughed at her fears.

"To think that a girl like Winnie, so forthright and honest," I protested, "would entertain such contemptible notions as race prejudice and at the same time, in her inner self, give way to the desire to indulge in illicit pleasures, is not to know how beautiful her soul really is! I see that in some ways I know her better than you do, Mrs. Redfern!"

She laughed and exclaimed almost with a blush: "Oh, I suppose that sometimes I must appear very old-fashioned as compared with you and the girls!"

"Not at all! Mrs. Redfern," I replied. "You have, like I do, the heart of Youth!"

And, as shortly I was to find out, she had. Indeed, as she walked out of the room after that very conversation I couldn't help noticing how full and resilient were her buttocks and how shapely were her legs in spite of her forty-two years. Here, under my nose all the time, had been a woman without doubt both passionate and imaginative. I laughed at my discovery. How relative is one's vision to one's situation!

As on the previous occasion—on the "wedding night," so to speak—I arranged the room with flowers, fruit and wine, strewed cushions about the floor, bathed, put on my bathrobe and prepared for a pleasant afternoon.

Winnie arrived first, alone. She seemed a little nervous. I did my utmost to calm her anxieties.

"Tell me, Winnie," I said, "are you afraid of me?"

"Oh, no! not of you Frank, darling," cried the sweet child passionately. "I'm just nervous because it is the first time, with anyone else, I mean."

I told her not to be afraid, that nothing would take place against her will, and asked her if she didn't know me well enough to know that I would stoop to nothing underhand. She said that of course she did and that anyway it would give her pleasure to do just what I wanted her to do. I kissed her sweet forehead.

Then I poured her a glass of wine.

"If you are old enough to have your sense of touch delighted," I said with a smile, "you are old enough to have your sense of taste delighted."

Winnie laughed merrily.

"Oh, that's all right!" she said. "Father lets me drink wine at dinner!"

"Then perhaps he wouldn't mind your having breakfast with me?" I said jestingly.

Winnie giggled and then said soberly: "Sometimes I think you're the cleverest man in the world, Frank."

I bowed in mock-acceptance of the compliment. At that moment the bell rang.

"That will be our other little guest!" I said with a laugh and went immediately to the door and opened it. Sure enough, it was May in the company of the clever Mrs. Redfern. "If you don't mind, Sir," that good lady said at once, "I'll just attend to the undressing of May while you attend to the disrobing of the other young lady."

"Just as you think best, Mrs. Redfern."

"Come, May. Sit down over here with me," the lady said. May did as she was bid and Winnie, the soul of sweetness and understanding, came right across to me and said: "You undress me, Frank. It wouldn't be fair on May if I wasn't undressed at the same time."

May shot her a grateful glance and the two delightful children smiled at each other. If I had had any compunctions about this meeting, they were gone now, like a dandelion in the wind. I kissed Winnie on the lips and acted the part of her doting valet. Mrs. Redfern did the same for the duskier of my playmates and soon the two heavenly children confronted one another across the room, as stark naked as the first day they were born.

The first words spoken were by Winnie.

"Oh, look at her pussy!" she cried in a shrill voice. "It's been shaved off!"

Mrs. Redfern and I laughed and May blushed prettily.

"It's the custom where she comes from, my dear," I said, when the humor of the situation allowed.

"Do you like it that way?" Winnie said to May, in a friendly, earnest tone of voice.

"I haven't tried the other way!" said May cleverly, and the two children ran into one another's arms. How pretty they looked, like two little ballet dancers in *Swan Lake*, only much more beautiful, for the smooth glimmer of their naked flesh made them even more beautiful still.

"And now, you take your clothes off, Frank!" Winnie called out, laughing at me over her shoulder.

I laughed. Without delay, and heedless of the fact that Mrs. Redfern was still in the room, I threw off my bathrobe and stood naked in their sight. I was already aroused and the women burst out laughing when they saw me.

"Oh really! Mr. Harris!" Mrs. Redfern said.

But without paying attention to her, I moved swiftly across the room and encircled the girls with my arms. We stood in a group, smiling at one another.

"Well really!" Mrs. Redfern said, "if that's going to be the way of it!" and without another word, she too began to strip. And indeed, I don't think one of us had any desire to make her desist. The girls already had me on the floor and were teasing me by biting me all over. A moment later, Mrs. Redfern, heavily built but very well made and neat in her movements, had thrown herself into the fray. We all rolled over on the carpet and a moment later, with a feeling almost of shock, shock which soon gave way to delight, I realized that all three of them were seeking to pinion me in erotic clasps to the floor. Mrs. Redfern had my sex in her mouth and she lay with the weight of her breasts and upper torso on my thighs, prohibiting the movement of my legs. May—I was able to feel rather than see her—was seated astride my belly and urging me as she would a horse, while Winnie, the devil of the warren, squatted above my head, her neat sex a sword of Damocles suspended above my face. I laughed merrily and, with a supple twist of my body, unsaddled all three on to the rich Indian carpet. They rolled aside, like three impertinent Bacchantes, in a flurry of laughter and naked limbs.

Mrs. Redfern wasted no time. In a trice, she had pinioned her darling May to the floor and she began to caress her passionately with tongue and lips. May laughed delightedly as the older woman crushed down on her sex. Winnie meanwhile stood with her hands on her slim hips and surveyed her rival's helplessness with interest and delight. I was reminded at once of some of the legends of Sappho on the fair isle of Lesbos and I couldn't help noticing how superbly the skin colors blended. The skin of Mrs. Redfern was a ruddy pink-white, the shoulders and breasts of her protégée were the color of honey swimming below an untidy tress of raven-black hair, while Winnie, standing slim and independent as a boy, was all over a smooth creamy-white.

"Wait a moment," said Mrs. Redfern suddenly, "I'm going to light a joss stick!" She searched for her handbag, found it, stirred up the contents with her hand and produced a small green box from which she took an incense stick, the color of dung and the shape of a stub of pencil. This she stood upright in an ash tray, and she set light to it. Soon a long feather-like plume of sweet smoke rose upward from the glowing tip and the two girls, captivated by it, attempted, by beating their hands in the air, to direct the smoke against their skin.

"It's nice to smell, not to touch," Mrs. Redfern said drily.

It was at that moment that Winnie suggested a game of leapfrog. Immediately she had said it, she bent downward and exhibited one of the most pretty bottoms it has ever been my good fortune to see, lobes as smooth and as compact as large pebbles gathered prettily about her little rosebud beneath which a wisp of her sex's silky hair peeped like a goat's beard. May went first, skipping forward on her bare feet across the carpet and then upward as she cleared the obstacle successfully. She landed about a yard clear, ran forward two steps, and stooped into position herself. Mrs. Redfern went next, clearing both obstacles, in spite of her plumpness, without apparent effort. I hesitated only to allow her to settle in position and then hopped twice to pass with my legs astride the girls and take up a position from where I would run to make a leap clear across the fleshy posterior of Mrs. Redfern. Something—I do not know what until this day—made me hesitate. I found myself making the approach-run too slowly and before I realized what had happened I felt myself fit softly against the warm split in Mrs. Redfern's buttocks. Of course, she thought that my action was intentional and so she raised herself on tiptoes, thrusting out with her warm pulpy buttocks at the same time, so that my sex, distended from so much pleasure, ran sure as a plummet between the thickly-haired flanges of her sex and did not meet any resistance until it was sunk to the hilt in one of the warmest and juiciest vaginas imaginable. As soon as she felt the meeting of my belly tight against her buttocks, she seemed to knit her lower torso into a knot—an amorous clasp I don't doubt she had from a great deal of experience—and I discovered at once that I was stuck fast and firm without the slightest possibility of escape. At that moment I heard the laughter of the girls. And then Winnie cried: "Go on, dear, give it to her! If I were a man, I would!" And indeed I had little choice. I grasped her by her thick white waist and with short, jabbing strokes brought her quickly to her climax, nor was she content until I had allowed my seed to spurt deep and hotly into her. I withdrew almost at once. Mrs. Redfern straightened up with a laugh.

"There's life in an old dog yet!" she said gaily. "I hope, Mr. Harris, I won't have to wait so long for your next favor."

With some misgivings, but as gently as possible, I assured her that she would not have to wait long, that I should certainly not wait until I had been invited.

"I've only known one other man who loved it as much as you do, Sir," she cried, "and that was my late husband. He was tarred with the same black brush!"

"Black indeed!" I cried. "Why black?"

"Oh, Mr. Harris, you're terrible!" said the pretty and ecstatic Mrs. Redfern. She meant it. There indeed is evidence to prove the weakness of so much of the thought of Karl Marx. It is only the bohemian who can be free, not the proletarian. Poor Mrs. Redfern, in spite of the delight which she took in all amorous affairs, was unable to scale off that irritating and essentially ignorant sense of Original Sin. The girls, thank God! were not thus tainted. They enjoyed the whole affair immensely as was obvious from their merry giggles and happy faces, both at the time and afterward when their own turn was over and done with. Our session ended late. Winnie had to hurry so as not to arrive too late for the evening meal at her parents' house. Shortly afterward, Mrs. Redfern left with her pretty May.

When they had gone and I had a moment to relax after my endeavors, it occurred to me that there must have been one time in history, pre-history perhaps, when the full possibilities of a game like leapfrog were not only understood but exploited. The game was certainly known to the Greeks. To what end they played it, apart from its being a species of physical exercise, is unhappily nowhere recorded. Even were it a fact, as some recent historians assert, that the Greek youth indulged in the practice of homosexuality, I would not wish the truth buried in the remote past from which it can never rise up and be good ground for caution in our attitudes, self-control in our behavior, and wisdom in our judgment. The Truth, I have always believed, was never so detrimental to human affairs as was falsity; it should be remembered that if we had All truth, we should be possessed of All understanding. If I have had a mission in life, that has been it: to search for Truth and to protect it. And, as I pondered thus, like all men of talent and liberal opinion in the past, I felt that I had nothing to reproach myself with for the afternoon's pleasures; obviously, we had come together because each of us in his heart desired that it should be so. Would it have any effect on the future? Human love is in many ways delicate. Had I transgressed against the inviolable laws of Subtlety? I didn't think so and I proved to be right, for the gambol destroyed neither the intimacy between Winnie and me, nor that between myself and dear May. Not a bit of it! That, in the borrowed words of Arnold Bennett, is "The Old Wives' Tale" like so many of our theories pertaining to the matters of sex.

A week later, Mrs. Redfern was all aflame with a new project. The woman was indefatigable in her pursuit of the god Eros. Again, in reference to that lady, I must admit I sensed a taint of an ulterior motive, but I didn't blame her. Everybody is naturally eager to earn all the money he can get. Why then should I have blamed the poor woman? She made a great to-do of something she hoped to bring that would astonish me. "It's only to be had in the best houses," she declared. "What is it?" I wanted to know. "They call it the *hedgehog*," she replied, "but that tells you nothing. If I can get it for you, you will have to admit that India has taught you one thing worth knowing."

A few days later she drew out a *hedgehog* and showed it to me; it was a silver ring with a number of very fine tiny feathers brought in all round it. The ring was not closed, and Mrs. Redfern slipped it over my thumb and said:

"There; if you use that you will make all the girls crazy for you."

"Really," I exclaimed, "you mean if I put it on it will give them more pleasure?"

"You try!" she returned, "don't tell them, but try and you will soon see that I've made you a wonder worker."

"All right," I said, "I'm much obliged to you, and if you turn out to be a good prophet, I'll be liberal."

"I'm sure you will," she smiled, "but if you would try it the second time instead of the first, I'd feel even surer."

"Why the second time?" I asked.

"You know perfectly well," she exclaimed laughing; "you know that nine girls out of ten feel more the second time than they do the first, and if you use my tickler when they are already thrilling, you will have wonderful results. You wait and see!"

"I'll try it this very evening," I said, "and tomorrow I shall let you know all about it."

"All right," she replied, "that will suit me and meantime, I'm after another instrument that will surprise you still more and make every girl crazy for you."

"First rate," I laughed, "thanks to you, I think I shall learn something from India."

"The greatest country in the world," she said, solemnly, "for love-tools, or foods, or excitants; they know more here about sex sensations and how to vivify and intensify them than anywhere else. Try my tickler and you will see."

That evening Winnie came to spend a couple of hours with me. At first she seemed less passionate than usual, but after half an hour or so of love's dalliance when I thought she had reached the height of feeling, I slipped on the ring and began the final essay.

In a moment I knew that Mrs. Redfern was justified. Almost at once Winnie spread herself feverishly and soon, for the first time, began to move her body uncontrollably and utter strange sounds, now whimpering, now gasping: "Oh! I can't stand it; Oh! Stop please or I shall go mad, Oh! Oh! Oh!"

I too had finished, so I withdrew and removed the tickler and soon Winnie was all questions: "Why did you never make me feel so intensely before? I didn't feel particularly naughty tonight, but you made me lose all self-control; I never enjoyed it so keenly. Oh, you wonder, Frank. I'm all yours, you know; but now you've made me crazy. How did you do it *so* wonderfully?"

Of course, I kept my secret. Then began for me with Winnie an astonishing series of experiences. Passion provokes passion and when one gives intense pleasure one is summoned to try again. And again and again I tried, varying the motions, the tempo of my pressures and their soft oscillation, and each time with some new thrill of delight. I have heard her cry: "Oh, you are in me and that is Paradise for me! My womb opens to you, and at the same time you excite me, tease me so that I could bite you. When I am all yours you make me feel most intensely: I cannot explain."

At the same time I noticed that as her passion increased, so her love; she became radiant, more and more devoted to me and would wait for hours for me to see her. Indeed, it was this trait of absolute devotion which led to our separation.

I was resolved now to try the tickler as soon as possible with May. Somehow or other, I felt sure that May's response would be extraordinary, for though I had not yet brought her to lose control, I knew she was passionately endowed: her kisses promised much and after a few kisses she used to tremble from head to foot. It was as though her long slats of honey-colored flesh became alive. I could never forget it. And so I resolved to use the *hedgehog* at the proper time. I would beg her to come soon and have a gorgeous night.

Next day, I gave Mrs. Redfern fifty pounds and asked her to bring May that night. She could not, she told me. She would have to give a couple of days' notice and think of an excuse if I wanted her for the whole night. I did, and so it was arranged. On the appointed evening I made everything ready, down to a divan with a rough tigerskin thrown over it. Such was to be the bower of our bliss. We should make love on the tough hide of an old jungle-slayer. May delighted with the arrangement . . . she couldn't withhold from fingering it with her slender brown fingers.

"I'm glad it's not alive!" she said with a laugh which was really all the more attractive for its slightly Oriental quality.

I invited her to get undressed. She did so with alacrity. And then I lifted her warm body and laid it on top of the harshly striped tiger-skin. Then I bent down over her pale yellow loins and began to excite her with the tip of my tongue. By this time, the hair had grown thinly over the mound and I must say I welcomed the faint and silky chevron which did something at least to lessen the effect of the stubborn, almost unwomanly sex. Soon she responded with an agitated movement of her haunches, breathing deeply the while and articulating soundless words with her lips. When she was quite excited, I mounted her in the normal way and we reached a climax almost simultaneously. Only then, remembering the advice of Mrs. Redfern, did I attempt to use love's instrument. A few minutes later we were again thrusting passionately against one another, only this time I was armed with the silver ring. She did not respond to its use as quickly as Winnie, nor as passionately. Yet, to my astonishment, she guessed what the instrument was like; the priests had educated her sexually to complete understanding. She told me that when a woman was pregnant this instrument was never used as it was supposed to excite too intensely. But when I gave her a new dress and a new hat, or a pair of gloves, I found enthusiastic response in her. May was much more susceptible to gratitude than to passion.

What curious differences there are in women. Winnie took all such gifts as a matter of course, but responded to a new touch of sensuality as a violin to the bow. Of course, it had probably something to do with the difference in station between the two girls. Passion among the Indians flows free. A gift has all the enchantment of the Orient. Naturally, because of the heights of passion and abandon to which I could arouse the dear girl, I often preferred Winnie to May, and I have always said that Winnie won me so completely that I never learned India thoroughly; she so obsessed me that I could spare no time for anyone else or any other thing. For those hours that we lay together entwined, her softnesses giving juicily to my strength, I shall be for ever grateful to her.

But alas! her devotion made her people think. Her father had her followed once to my hotel and at length her mother came to me and begged me for the girl's sake to go away and leave her, or she would never get married. It nearly broke my heart to give my consent, but finally I did so and went on to Burma. Mrs. Redfern was greatly put out by my decision. She advised me not to go to Burma. "It's a filthy place, Sir!" she said, "and if it's go you must, take my advice and have nothing to do with women while you're there." I thanked her for her advice and reiterated my decision to quit Bombay for the sake of Winnie's future. Finally, I think she almost came to agree with me that it was the only thing to be done.

There in Rangoon began for me a series of adventures which forced me to the conclusion that the Burmese half-caste girl is one of the most fascinating in God's world, and she is certainly one of the prettiest and best-formed; she is cheap too. They are all sold at from thirteen to sixteen by their parents and seldom cost even twenty pounds. I would have bought many had I known what to do with them afterward, but I hadn't the heart to take them up for a short time and then leave them their penniless freedom in a big city. I was thus limited by a dictate of conscience to buy only that number for whose future I could provide after my eventual leave-taking. I hesitated a long time between the numbers of two and three, but finally discretion had the better part of valor, and I decided to content myself with two. Their names? I forget their original names because I heard them only at the beginning when I decided to call them Rose and Lily, and burning my boats behind me as I do, I had no need of their names, for I had no intention of writing them through the intermediary of a missionary. It was unfortunate that we couldn't speak each other's language, but the girls seemed to have a sixth sense of knowing what it was I wanted of them, and they were ever at my side with fruit and other refreshments at the very moment when the desire overtook me. Had I a longer writing life, I would certainly spend one year writing the detailed history of my short marriage to two Burmese maidens, one just over fourteen and the other in her sixteenth year, but I have still much to record and daily, in spite of my will, my sight fails the more. I shall have to content myself with describing one or two of their childish antics.

Perhaps the strangest was the way they used to love to make a "fur-collar" for me with their thighs. This was really a delightful procedure. Literally, they would twine their thighs into a kind of collar for me, my neck clamped between their soft mounds, and my head the only part of me to protrude upward between their dark navel-studded bellies. The idea was that I should tickle them until they allowed me to break free and without exaggeration I sometimes was forced to struggle with them—so tight was their hold—for as much as fifteen minutes. Another of their favorite tricks was to smear themselves all over with a sweet-smelling oil and then to wrestle with me until the oil from their bodies covered my own. Finally, there is the trick that some Burmese women have of smearing the male member with honey at every opportunity so that male and female lips are always clung with its sweet smell.

I had tired myself. I had wearied of passion, with Winnie, with May, with Rose and Lily—the old wanderlust was awake in me. This time it was Japan and China that called. My time for traveling was limited, so I resolved to go on. One thing I might make mention of: the custom of living with native women and having half-breed children is practiced by Englishmen and Americans throughout the East. The children are superb. The Eurasian girl or boy in Burma is often an excellent specimen not only physically but mentally. It is unfortunate that the girl's lot is almost always unhappy and often tragic. This leads me to say that the complete understanding given by the Oriental mind to the act of love is in my opinion causally connected with the depths of spirit attained by certain of the eastern Holy Men. The Westerner is often shallow beside the Easterner. Which only goes to show the truth of one of my lifelong theses: that a healthy sexual life is the prerequisite of a healthy spirit. What do I mean by "spirit"? To that question I shall offer at least part answer in the next chapter. I shall end here by saying that I believe

Keats could be called as a witness for the defense of my point of view. Who can recall the lines of *On a Grecian Urn*, an ode to the beauty of Attic youth, and still disagree?

> *O Attic shape! Fair attitude! with breed*
> *Of marble men and maidens overwrought,*
> *With forest branches and the trodden weed;*
> *Thou, silent form, dost tease us out of thought*
> *As doth eternity . . .*

And he ends rightly with:

> *Beauty is truth, truth beauty—that is all*
> *Ye know on earth, and all ye need to know.*

I thought of Keats quite frequently while I was in India. Burma struck me at once as a country whose gorgeous vegetation would have held magnificence for this very lush among English poets.

FRANK HARRIS

*This fifth volume of Frank Harris' memoirs has a history which must
now be made public, although I cannot do so without admitting to a
feat of truancy dramatically opposed to publishing ethics.*

*In the introduction to this volume I recounted the unfortunate
phase of my career when I lost my first publishing firm, in which the
remains of The Obelisk Press had been incorporated. My father, Jack
Kahane, had bought the publishing rights of* My Life and Loves *from
Frank Harris in the early 'thirties, and since then the four volumes
put out by The Obelisk Press had enjoyed a large and steady sale.*

*Many years later, after The Obelisk Press had become the
property of my powerful rivals, Hachette—much against my will—
they went on printing and selling* My Life and Loves *year after year.*

*I had first read the book when I was a young boy, and I had
been impressed by the ludicrous cheek of the little Irish adventurer.
I was elated by his treatment of the reader, the half-amused, half-
disgusted unconcern with which he fed his insolent cock-and-bull
stories to the gullible. The large layers of sexy episodes came between
rich slices of literary and political souvenirs with model regularity;
the cocksure, vulgar tone of the recital was quite wonderful. And yet,
Harris had certainly been a sincere and courageous man in his own
funny way. He had had some generous ideas, and he had been a
plucky fighter when it came to defending some rather interesting
causes; alas, self-adulation had prevented him from being quite the
universal hero he fancied himself to be—in literature, sex, or politics.
But he is certainly responsible to a large extent for the invention of
modern journalism, whether he should be thanked for that or not.*

*When I started The Olympia Press in competition with my ex-
publishing firm, The Obelisk Press, I remembered that my father's
contract with Frank Harris had contained a mention of a fifth volume
to be added at a later date to the famous first four, but that Harris'
death had brought an end to that project.*

*However, I decided to investigate and I went to see a lawyer
who represented the interests of Harris' widow. He was a tiny old*

gentleman by the name of Adolph, living in a crepuscular apartment in the frugal fashion typical of the French bourgeoisie of old. I crashed into several chairs on the way to his office, as there was strictly no light, electric or otherwise, in the hall; then he prudently guided me to a chair and went to sit behind his desk. Gradually my eyes became used to the deep night, and I began to perceive his frail contours. Then the uncanny negotiation began.

"Madame Nellie Harris," he explained, "is aware of your interest. But she values her husband's work very highly, and particularly that last unpublished book of his. Up to now she has refused even to envisage letting it be published. . . . But now she is a very old lady, and perhaps I might use my influence on her to try to persuade her to change her mind. However, I am aware of the fact that your former business has been taken over by La Librairie Hachette and that you have now started a new company with very limited means. . . . In those conditions we would require a rather substantial advance from you, young man, you must realize that."

I quoted a figure which I immediately knew was much too ridiculously high: 400,000 francs. I did not have the money, of course, but we would see about that later. The little man seemed pleased for the time being and made a few sniffing noises. Then I asked when I could see the manuscript.

"Ah, I expected that sort of question, young man," he retorted with mild impatience, "but why would you want to see that manuscript? You have just made an offer without having seen it: if I gave it to you to read now, what difference would that make? Your papa published the first four volumes of Monsieur Harris' world-famous work, and I venture to say that he has found that to be a profitable venture; and I daresay profit is also what you have on your mind, eh? So I must regretfully conclude: no, you cannot see the manuscript. But I promise to write to Madame Harris and plead your cause."

Listen to the old bird, I told myself; and felt like stealing his shawl and running away. Instead of which I stood up, bowed in the dark, and somnambulistically departed.

A few days later I received a note from Mr. Adolph, who never used the telephone, asking me to visit him as he had an important communication to impart.

I had been five minutes late at our first interview and I had discovered that the old man had been standing behind his door since

*the appointed time and had waited there for the bell to ring. This
time I arrived two minutes early to save him the trouble, and I rang
the bell for two minutes before he opened the door. I was engulfed
once more into the internal shades of his apartment, but I just had
time to take in the discolored pupils, the shaky pince-nez and the old-
celery skin.*

"Madame Harris," he declared with a tone of ominous satisfaction, "has not reacted too badly to your proposal, my dear Monsieur,
but she is of the opinion that it would be rather unseemly to entrust
the publication of her husband's book to a young publisher like you
without surrounding herself with all the proper guarantees. Furthermore, she has instructed me to inquire whether La Librairie Hachette
might not be interested in purchasing those publishing rights themselves, eh. . . . Well, I have approached the firm and they did not
hesitate to offer 600,000 francs. So, I regret to say that the book will
go to them . . . Unless of course you can make a better offer yourself . . . And when I say a better offer, I mean a much better offer.
Because if such an illustrious publishing house as La Librairie
Hachette offers fifty percent more than you, what should I conclude?
. . . Firstly, no doubt, that you were trying to take advantage of
Madame Harris' good will. And secondly, that in view of your
desire to make substantial profits, that property should be worth
much more to you than what you have offered, eh?"

*That tirade was delivered in a tiny, gasping voice. I asked if
Hachette had seen the manuscript.*

"My dear young man," Mr. Adolph retorted with finality, "I do
not consider it convenient to answer that question. But I do quite
understand that in your strained circumstances it will be impossible
for you to do better than La Librairie Hachette."

"Not at all," I countered, "I am ready to pay one million francs.
Now, do I see the manuscript?"

He chuckled softly. "Not so hasty, not so hasty, my dear young
Monsieur. Madame Harris will no doubt approve me if I tell you that
once we have signed a contract and received the agreed advance, then
you can have the manuscript. First you pay, then. . . ."

"All right," *I interrupted.* "When do we sign?"

"Ah, that is another question. First of all, does Madame Harris
accept your new offer? I have to ask."

At the next interview, he told me a little sheepishly that Madame

Harris had said yes. I interpreted that as meaning that Hachette had been approached again but had said no. I was nearly sorry to see that the deal was working out. I had no idea where to find all that money. And that unseen, untouchable manuscript was fishy in the extreme.

However, I was interrupted in my daydreaming by the old man who was saying in a surprisingly clear voice: "But if I have so aptly defended your cause to Madame Harris, you must understand that I have done so only because I always like to help young people like you and encourage them in their undertakings. I am an old man, as you can see, and I do those things with no thought of reward. In your case I will content myself with 5 per cent of the agreed sum—to be added to that million francs, naturally."

It took me two weeks and some rather demented maneuvering to raise the ransom, and when I saw my old friend for the last time, he had lighted a candle on his desk to facilitate the perusal of contracts, the signing thereof, and the accounting of banknotes. That gave an extra-ghostly appearance to the room, revealing the appurtenances of witchcraft: tall coffin-like furniture, musty clocks and a few ancient cobwebs.

When the ceremony was completed he opened a drawer slowly and fished out a slim package which he handed to me: "That is the manuscript," he asserted.

Stifling the beginning of an hysterical laugh, I took the so-called manuscript and sprang out of the room and into the healthy youthful street, peopled with vigorous cats and dogs. The manuscript was made up of a few sheafs of typed pages, yellowed by time; they were drafts of articles written by Harris for various bygone periodicals. He had no doubt put them aside to be incorporated into that projected fifth volume, but had never gone any further into the matter.

Never mind, I reasoned, I knew it all the time; and took a cab to rue du Sabot to talk things over with Alex Trocchi. We decided that that fifth volume of Monsieur Frank Harris' world-famous memoirs should be made into a really sumptuous work of art, to make Monsieur Harris' name even more illustrious. Alex was madly excited by the very idea of it. We rehearsed a few Harris idiosyncrasies: Never to write: she said in a dialogue, but always: she cried, etc.

The brand new fifth volume was soon delivered, tingling with solid sex and fun. I do not think honestly that Harris would have disowned that posthumous child of his.

Madame Harris and Monsieur Adolph never cried a word. La Librairie Hachette was suitably subdued. But as there is a morality to any act of immorality, the French government one day decided to ban Frank Harris' Life and Loves, *at the end of 1956, that is nearly thirty years after the first publication in France. Of course since then my fifth volume had been added to the first four; but the decree did not make any distinction between the fifth volume and its four half-brothers.*

I told myself, it is to double up in derision. And how I pity La Librairie Hachette who are now in a mess because of me. But I had hardly finished enjoying the situation when, a few days later, another decree appeared, correcting the first one: "Only the fifth volume of My Life and Loves *is banned," it said, "Not the other four."*

And that's justice. Who are we to make fun of La Librairie Hachette and things respectable?

CANDY

MAXWELL KENTON

*T*here was only one tree on Grove Street. This was the sort of thing Candy was quick to notice, and to love.

"Look," she would say softly, squeezing someone's hand. "Isn't it too *much!* I could just hug myself everytime I pass it!"

And that was where she met the hunchback.

It was late one airless summer day, when the sky over Greenwich Village was the color of lead. It had just begun to rain, and Candy was standing back in a shallow doorway, waiting for her bus. Dreamily, humming a little Elizabethan tune, feeling fresh and quietly joyful in her new mandarin rain-cloak, hugging it to her—she saw him. He was out in the midst of the downpour, leaning against the tree, staring into the window display of the men's shop on the corner. He was standing very still, though from time to time there seemed to be a slight movement of his back, as if he might be consciously pressing his hump against the tree.

Candy's humming softened as she watched him, and her heart beat a little faster. *Oh, the fullness of it!* she thought, *the terrible, beautiful fullness of life!* And a great mass of feeling rose in her throat at the pity she felt for her father so shut away from it all, never to know life, never even to suspect what it was all about. She put her arms around her delightful body and hugged herself, so glad at being alive, really alive, and her eyes brimmed with shimmering gratitude.

Just then two boys passed the corner, dark coats turned up, heads half hidden out of the rain. One of them noticed the hunchback and gave a derisive snort:

"Wha'cha doin' Mac, gittin' your nuts off?"

He kept nudging his companion, who wouldn't even bother to look.

351

"The guy's gittin' his *nuts* off fer chrissake!" he shouted again as they walked on.

The hunchback gazed after them oddly.

"Rubatubdub!" he said, "rubadubtub!"

Candy hadn't heard either one of them distinctly, but there was no mistaking the tone of contempt, the obvious effort to hurt and humiliate. "The ignorant fools!" she said half aloud, and gave a little stamp of impatience. At that moment the bus rounded the corner beyond; she frowned as she watched it approach, but just before it reached her, she took a deep breath and walked away from the stop, then casually over to where the hunchback was standing.

"*Hi!*" she said, giving him a wonderfully warm smile and tossing back the hood of her cloak to feel the fresh rain on her face. Wasn't it just too much? she thought joyfully, standing here in the rain, in Greenwich Village, talking to a hunchback—when she *should* have been at her job ten minutes ago! . . . She thought of the explanation she would have to give, the attempt to make them understand, and she was so happy and proud of herself she could have wept.

"That's my tree, you know," she said instead, smiling like a mischievous child, then laughing gayly at her own foolishness. "I pretend that it is," she admitted, almost shyly. "The *only* tree on Grove Street! Oh, I do love it so!" She leaned forward and touched it gently, half closing her eyes, and then she gave the hunchback another tender smile.

The shop on this corner of Grove was a man's underwear shop, and the hunchback's eyes devoured another crotch or two before he looked up. He was also smiling. He supposed she was a policewoman. "*Rubatubdub!*" he said, agitating his hump vigorously against the tree. Getting run in was part of his kick.

"Three men in a tub!" cried Candy, laughing in marvel at their immediate rapport. How simple! she thought. How wonderfully, beautifully simple the important things are! And how it had so completely escaped her father! She would have given twenty years of her life to have shared the richness of the moment with her father—he who had said that poems were "impractical"! The poor darling dummy, why *only* a poem could capture it! Only a poem could trap the elusiveness, the light-like subtlety, the vapor-edge of a really big thing, and lead it, coax it past . . . a poem, or music perhaps . . . yes, of course, music. And she began to hum softly, swaying her body a little, her fingers distractedly caressing the tree. She felt very relaxed with the hunchback.

And he was still smiling too, but that first gray glimmer of hope had died from his eyes, and they narrowed a bit now as he decided, quite simply, that she was a nut.

"*Hungry,*" he said, pointing to his mouth, "*hungry.*"

"Oh!" cried Candy, suddenly remembering, and she reached into the pocket of her cloak and took out a small paper bag. It was a bag of bread crumbs; she carried it often for pigeons in Washington Square. "I have this," she said, her wide eyes beautifully blue and ingenuous. She helped herself first, to show that it wasn't charity, but rather a human experience, simple, warm, and shared.

There was something disconcerting though in the way this hunchback sniggered, rolling his eyes, and squirmed against the tree, wiping his mouth with the back of his hand; but, after a moment, he took some of the crumbs too.

"Rubatubdub!" he said.   -

Candy laughed. She heard a wisdom and complex symbology in the hunchback's simple phrases. It was as though she were behind the scenes of something like the Dadaist movement, even creatively a part of it. This was the way things happened, she thought, the really big things, things that ten years later change the course of history, just this way, on the street corners of the Village; and here she was, a part of it. How incredibly ironic that her father should think she was "wasting her time"! The thought of it made her throat tighten and her heart rise up in sorrow for him.

"You got quarter, lady?" asked the hunchback then, nodding his head in anticipation. He held out his hand, but Candy was already shaking her curls defensively and fumbling in her purse.

"No, I don't think I have a *cent*, darn it! Here's an Athenean florin," she said, holding up a lump of silver, then dropping it back into the purse, "550 B.C. . . . *that* won't do us any good, will it? Not unless we're Sappho and Pythagoras and don't know it!" And she looked up, closing her purse and shaking her head, happily, as though not having any money herself would make them closer.

"*Are* you Pythagoras?" she asked gayly.

"You get your rubadub, don't you lady?" muttered the hunchback as he started shuffling away. "*Fuckashitpiss! Fuckashitpiss! Rubadub, rubadub!*"

This struck Candy with such anxiety that for a moment she was speechless. She could not bear the idea of his going away angry, and also in the back of her mind was the pride she would feel if, in a few days, she could be walking down the street with Ted and Harold, or with one of the people from International House, and the hunchback would speak to her by name; they might even stop and chat a bit, and she would introduce him:

"Ted, this is my friend, Derek," or whatever; it could certainly be as important as Blind Battersea, the sightless beggar in Washington Park being able to recognize Ted's voice.

"Listen," she cried, hurrying after him, "if you don't mind pot-luck, we could have something at my place—it's just past the corner there—I know there are some eggs. . . ."

When Candy had slipped out of her cloak and kicked off her shoes, she went into the bathroom. "Won't be a minute," she said, and very soon she reappeared, rubbing her hair with a towel, fluffing it out, her head back, eyes half closed for the moment as she stood there in the middle of the room.

"I don't know which is best," she said with a luxurious sigh, "the freshness of rain or the warmth of fire."

She had changed into a loose flannel shirt and a pair of tight-fitting faded bluejeans which were rolled up almost to the knee. She had another towel draped across her shoulder, and she laid this on the arm of the hunchback's chair as she crossed the room.

"Take off some of your things if you want," she said airily, "let them dry by the radiator," and she sat down on the edge of the couch opposite him and rubbed her feet with the towel, doing this carefully and impersonally, as though they were pieces of priceless china which belonged to someone else, yet silhouetting the white curve of her bare legs against the black corduroy couch-cover, and exclaiming genially: "My feet are soaked! Aren't yours?" She didn't wait for an answer, nor seem to expect one, only wanting to maintain a casual chatter to put the hunchback at ease; she took care not to look at him directly, as she stood up and crossed the room again, indicating with a gesture the magazine stand near his chair: "There's a *PR* and *Furioso* there —if you feel like light reading. I'm afraid there's not much else at the moment—I'll just get us a drink." And she disappeared then into the tiny kitchen.

The hunchback had been sniggering and squirming about in the chair, and now finally he picked up the towel and wiped his face, then blew his nose into it and spat several times.

"Rubatubtub!" he said.

Candy's gay laugh rang from the kitchen.

"Wish we had something stronger," she called out, "we could use it after that rain." Then she came in with a large bottle of Chianti and two glasses already filled, and sat these on the table. "Help yourself to more," she said, taking a sip of hers. "Umm, good," she said, and went back into the kitchen, "won't be a minute . . . well, not more than *five*, anyway." She had turned on the phono—some Gregorian chants—and hummed along with the music now as she busied herself, coming in and out, setting the table, and keeping up a spritely monologue the while.

The hunchback had a sip of the wine and spat it in the towel.

Through the open door of the kitchen, Candy could be seen moving about, and now she was bending over to put something down in the oven. In the tight jeans, her round little buttocks looked so firm and ripe that any straight-thinking man would have rushed in at once to squeeze and bite them; but the hunchback's mind was filled with freakish thoughts. From an emotional standpoint, he would rather have been in the men's room down at Jack's Bar on the Bowery, eating a piece of urine-soaked bread while thrusting his hump against someone from the Vice Squad. And yet, though he had decided that she was nutty (and because of this she was of no use to his ego), he was also vaguely aware that she was a mark; and, in an obscure, obstacle-strewn way, he was trying to think about this now: *how to get the money.* He wasn't too good at this, however, for his sincerity of thought was not direct enough: he didn't really feel he needed money, but rather that he *should* feel he needed it. It was perhaps the last vestige of normalcy in the hunchback's values; it only cropped up now and then.

"Onion omelet," Candy announced with a flourish as she entered, "hope you like tarragon and lots of garlic," and she put it on the table. "Looks good, doesn't it?" She felt she could say this last with a certain innocent candor, because her friends assured her she was a very good cook.

Aside from an occasional grunt and snort, the hunchback kept silent throughout the meal and during Candy's lively commentary, while into his image-laden brain now and then shot the primal questions: "*Where? No kill! How? Without kill! Where?*"

This silence of his impressed Candy all the more, making her doubly anxious to win his approval. "Oh, but here I'm talking away a mile, and you can't get in a single word!" She beamed, and nodded with a show of wisdom, "Or isn't it really that there's nothing to say—'would it have been worth while *after all*, etcetera, etcetera.' Yes, *I* know . . . oh, there's the tea now. *Tea!* Good Night, *I'm* still on Eliot—the darling old fuddy, don't you *love* him? It's coffee, of course. Expresso. I won't be a minute . . . Have some of the Camembert, not too *bien fait*, I'm afraid, but . . ." She rushed out to the kitchen, still holding her napkin, while the hunchback sat quietly, munching his bread. It was hardly the first time he had been involved in affairs of this sort.

When the darling girl returned, she suggested they move over to the couch to have their coffee. There she sat close beside him and leafed through a book of Blake's reproductions.

"Aren't they a *groove*," she was saying, "they're *so* funny! Most people don't get it at all!" She looked up at the wall opposite, where another print was hanging, and said gleefully: "And don't you just love *that* one? The details, I mean, did you ever look at it closely? Let me get it."

The print was hanging by a wire placed high, and Candy had to reach. She couldn't quite get it at first, and for a long moment she was standing there, lithe and lovely, stretching upward, standing on the tiptoes of one foot, the other out like a ballet-dancer's. As she strained higher, she felt the sinews of her calf rounding firmly and the edge of her flannel shirt lifting gently above her waist and upward across her bare back, while the muscles of her darling little buttocks tightened and thrust out taut beneath the jeans. "Oh, I *shouldn't!*" she thought, making another last effort to reach the print, "what if he thinks I'm . . . well, it's *my* fault, darn it!"

As it happened, the hunchback *was* watching her and, with the glimpse of her bare waist, it occurred to him suddenly, as though the gray sky itself had fallen, that, as for the other girls who had trafficked with him, what they had wanted was to be ravenously desired—to be so overwhelmingly physically needed that, despite their every effort to the contrary for a real and spiritual rapport, their beauty so powerfully, undeniably asserted itself as to reduce the complex man to simple beast . . . who must be fed.

By the time Candy had the print down and had reached the couch with it, the eyes of the hunchback were quite changed; they seemed to be streaked with red now, and they were very bright. The precious girl noticed it at once, and she was a little flustered as she sat down, speaking rapidly, pointing to the print: "Isn't this too *much?* Look at this figure, here in the corner, most people don't even . . ." She broke off for a moment to cough and blush terribly as the hunchback's eyes devoured her, glistening. In an effort to regain composure, she touched her lovely curls and gave a little toss of her head. "What *can* he be thinking?" she asked herself, "well, it's my own fault, darn it!" The small eyes of the hunchback blazed; he was thinking of money. "I love you!" he said then quickly, the phrase sounding odd indeed.

"Oh, darling, *don't* say that!" said Candy, imploring, as though she had been quite prepared, yet keeping her eyes down on the book.

"I want very much!" he said, touching her arm at the elbow.

She shivered just imperceptibly and covered his hand with her own. "You mustn't say that," she said with softness and dignity.

"*I want fuck you!*" he said, putting his other hand on her pert left breast.

She clasped his hand, holding it firmly, as she turned to him, her eyes closed, a look of suffering on her face. "No, darling, please," she murmured, and she was quite firm.

"I want fuck-suck you!" he said, squeezing the breast while she felt the sweet little nipple reaching out like a tiny mushroom.

She stood up abruptly, putting her hands to her face. "Don't. Please don't," she said. She stood there a moment, then walked to the window. "Oh why must it be like this?" she beseeched the dark sky of the falling day, "why? why?" She turned and was about to repeat it, but the voice of the hunchback came first.

"Is because of *this?*" he demanded, "because of *this?*" He was sitting there with a wretched expression on his face, and one arm raised and curled behind his head, pointing at his hump.

Candy came forward quickly, like a nurse in emergency. "*No,* you poor darling, of course it isn't; *no, no,*" and the impetus of her flight to him carried her down beside him again and put him in her arms. "You silly darling!" She closed her eyes, leaning her face against his, as she stroked his head. "I hadn't even noticed," she said.

"Why, then?" he wanted to know, "*why?*"

Now that she had actually touched him, she seemed more at ease. "*Why?*" she sighed, "oh, I don't know. Girls are like that, never quite knowing what they want—or need. Oh, I don't know, I want it to be *perfect,* I guess."

"Because of *this*," repeated the hunchback, shrugging heavily.

"No, you darling," she cooed, insisting, closed-eyed again, nudging his cheek with her nose, "no, no, no. What earthly *difference* does it make! I have blue eyes—you have that. What possible earthly difference does it make?"

"*Why?*" he demanded, reaching up under her shirt to grasp one of her breasts, then suddenly pulling her brassiere up and her shoulder back, and thrusting forward to cover the breast with his mouth. Candy sobbed, "*Oh darling, no,*" but allowed her head to recline gently back against the couch. "Why does it have to be like this?" she pleaded, "why? Oh, I know it's my own fault, darn it." And she let him kiss and suck her breast, until the nipple became terribly taut and she began to tingle all down through her precious tummy, then she pulled his head away, cradling it in her arms, her own eyes shimmering with tears behind a brave smile. "No darling," she implored, "please . . . not now."

"Because of *this*," said the hunchback bitterly.

"No, no, no," she cried, closing her eyes and hugging the head to her breast, holding his cheek against it, but trying to keep his mouth from the proud little nipple, "no, no, *not* because of that!"

"I want!" said the hunchback, with one hand on her hip now undoing the side buttons of her jeans; then he swiftly forced the hand across the panty sheen of her rounded tummy and down into the sweet damp.

"Oh, darling, no!" cried the girl, but it was too late, without making a scene, for anything to be done; his stubby fingers were rolling the little clitoris like a marble in oil. Candy leaned back in resignation, her heart too big to deprive him of this if it meant so much. With her head closed-eyed, resting again on the couch, she would endure it as long as she could. But, before she reached the saturation point, he had nuzzled his face down from her breast across her bare stomach and into her lap, bending his arm forward to force down her jeans and pants as he did and pulling at them on the side with his other hand.

"No, no, darling!" she sighed, but he soon had them down below her knees enough to replace his fingers with his tongue.

"It means so much to him," Candy kept thinking, "*so* much," as he meanwhile got her jeans and panties down completely so that they dangled now from one slender ankle as he adjusted her legs and was at last on the floor himself in front of her, with her legs around his neck, and his mouth very deep inside the honeypot.

"If it means so much," Candy kept repeating to herself, until she didn't think she could bear it another second, and she wrenched herself free, saying "*Darling, oh darling*," and seized his head in her hands with a great show of passion.

"Oh, *why?*" she begged, holding his face in her hands, looking at him mournfully. "Why?"

"*I need fuck you!*" said the hunchback huskily. He put his face against the upper softness of her marvelous bare leg. Small, strange sounds came from his throat.

"Oh, *darling, darling*," the girl keened pitifully, "I can't bear your crying." She sighed, and smiled tenderly, stroking his head.

"*I think* we'd better go into the bedroom," she said then, her manner prim and efficient.

In the bathroom, standing before the glass, Candy finished undressing—unbuttoning her shirt, slowly, carefully, a lamb resigned to the slaughter, dropping the shirt to the floor, and taking off her brassiere, gradually revealing her nakedness to herself, with a little sigh, almost of wistful regret, at how *very* lovely she was, and at how her nipples grew and stood out like cherry stones, as they always did when she watched herself undress. "How he wants me!" she thought. "Well, it's my own fault, darn it!" And she tried to imagine the raging lust that the hunchback felt for her as she touched her curls lightly. Then she cast a last glimpse at herself in the glass, blushing at her loveliness, and trembling slightly at the very secret notion of this beauty-and-beast sacrifice, and went back into the bedroom.

The hunchback was lying naked, curled on his side like a foetus, when Candy appeared before him, standing for a moment in full lush radiance, a naked angel bearing the supreme gift. Then, she got into bed quickly, under the sheet, almost soundlessly, saying, "*Darling, darling*," and cuddling him to her at once, while he, his head filled with the most freakish thoughts imaginable—all about tubs of living and broken toys, every manner of excrement, scorpions, steelwool, pig-masks, odd metal harness, etc.—tried desperately to pry into the images a single reminder: *the money*.

"Do you want to kiss me some more, darling?" asked the girl with deadly soft seriousness, her eyes wide, searching his own as one would a child's. Then she sighed and lay back, slowly taking the sheet from her, again to make him the gift of all her wet, throbbing treasures, as he, glazed-eyed and grunting, slithered down beside her.

"Don't hurt me, darling," she murmured, as in a dream, while he parted the exquisitely warm round thighs with his great head, his mouth opening the slick lips all sugar and glue, and his quick tongue finding her pink candy clit at once.

"Oh, darling, darling," she said, stroking his head gently, watching him, a tender courageous smile on her face.

The hunchback put his hands under her, gripping the foam-rubber balls of her buttocks, and sucked and nibbled her tiny clit with increasing vigor. Candy closed her eyes and gradually raised her legs, straining gently upward now, dropping her arms back by her head, one to each side, pretending they were pinioned there, writhing slowly, sobbing—until she felt she was no longer giving, but was on the verge of taking, and, as with an effort, she broke her hands from above her and grasped the hunchback's head and lifted it to her mouth, coming forward to meet him, kissing him deeply. "Come inside me, darling," she whispered urgently, "I want you *inside* me."

The hunchback, his brain seething with pure strangeness, hardly heard her. He had forgotten about the money, but did know that *something* was at stake, and his head was about to burst in trying to recall what it was. Inside his mind was like a gigantic landslide of black eels, billions of them, surging past, one of which held the answer. His job: *catch it*. Catch it, and chew off the top of its head; and there, in the gurgling cup, would be . . . the *message*: "You have forgotten about. . . ?"

But which eel was it? While his eyes grew wilder and rolled back until only the whites showed, Candy, thinking that he was beside himself with desire for her, covered his face with sweet wet kisses, until he suddenly went stiff in her arms as his racing look stopped abruptly on the floor near the bed. It was a coat hanger, an ordinary wire coat hanger, which had fallen from the closet, and the hunchback flung himself out of the bed and onto the floor, clutching the hanger to him feverishly. Then, as in a fit of bitter triumph, he twisted it savagely into a single length of coiled black wire, and gripping it so tightly that his entire body shook for a moment, he lunged forward, one end of it locked between his teeth. He thought it was the eel.

Candy had started up, half sitting now, one hand instinctively to her breast.

"Darling, what is it?" she cried, "darling, you aren't going to . . ."

The hunchback slowly rose, as one recovered from a seizure of apoplexy, seeming to take account of his surroundings anew, and, just as he had learned from the eel's head that the forgotten issue was money, so too he believed now that the girl wanted to be beaten.

"*Why*, darling?" pleaded Candy, curling her lovely legs as the hunchback slowly raised the black wire snake above his head. "*Why? Why?*"

And as he began to strike her across the back of her legs, she sobbed, "Oh, why, darling, why?" her long round limbs twisting, as she turned and writhed, her arms back beside her head as before, mov-

ing too except at the wrist where they were as stiff as though clamped there with steel, and she was saying: "Yes! Hurt me! Yes, yes! Hurt me as *they* have hurt you!" and now her ankles as well seemed secured, shackled to the spot, as she lay, spread-eagled, sobbing piteously, straining against her invisible bonds, her lithe round body arching upward, hips circling slowly, mouth wet, nipples taut, her teeny piping clitoris distended and throbbing, and her eyes glistening like fire, as she devoured all the penitence for each injustice ever done to hunchbacks of the world; and as it continued she slowly opened her eyes, that all the world might see the tears there—but instead she herself saw, through the rise and fall of the wire lash—the hunchback's white gleaming hump! The hump, the white, unsunned forever, radish-root white of hump, and it struck her, more sharply than the wire whip, as something she had seen before—the naked, jutting buttocks, upraised in a sexual thrust, not a thrust of taking, but of giving, for it had been an image in a hospital room mirror, of her own precious buttocks, naked and upraised, gleaming white, and thrusting downwards, as she had been made to do in giving herself to her Uncle Jack!

With a wild impulsive cry, she shrieked: *"Give me your hump!"*

The hunchback was startled for a moment, not comprehending.

"Your hump, your hump!" cried the girl, "GIVE ME YOUR HUMP!"

The hunchback hesitated, and then lunged headlong toward her, burying his hump between Candy's legs as she hunched wildly, pulling open her little labia in an absurd effort to get it in her.

"Your hump! Your hump!" she kept crying, scratching and clawing at it now.

"Fuck! Shit! Piss!" she screamed. "Cunt! Cock! Crap! Prick! Kike! Nigger! Wop! Hump! HUMP!" and she teetered on the blazing peak of pure madness for an instant . . . and then dropped down, slowly, through gray and grayer clouds into a deep, soft, black, night.

When Candy awoke she was alone. She lay back, thinking over the events of the afternoon. "Well, it's my own fault, darn it," she sighed, then smiled a little smile of forgiveness at herself—but this suddenly changed to a small frown, and she sat up in bed, cross as a pickle. "*Darn* it!" she said aloud, for she had forgotten to have them exchange names.

After freshening up a bit, Candy left the apartment and started walking down West 4th Street. The rain had stopped, and a cool gentle breeze was blowing; apparently it was going to be a lovely evening indeed.

It was too late now of course to think about the job; in fact, it was almost dark when she reached the corner of Sixth Avenue. She decided, quite on impulse, to stop in at the Riviera and have a Pernod.

Jack Katt and Tom Smart were there, at a front table, lushing it up and keen for puss. These were two fellows whom Candy vaguely knew and generally avoided. They were extraordinarily handsome and clever chaps, and Candy alone seemed immune to their undeniable charm; this was a constant source of annoyance to them. Now, when she entered, they graciously invited her to join them, but she refused. She wanted to sit quietly alone and cherish the memory of the past few hours with . . . but she *didn't* have the name to conjure with! And that was the blight on the experience, for she kept thinking of him now simply as "the hunchback," and every time the word formed in her mind she was cross enough with herself to bite. She didn't like thinking of him that way. "What earthly difference could it make!" she kept demanding, pouting her pretty mouth and clenching her small fist on the bar. Then she recalled the name she had given him, "Derek," and was happy with that for the moment, smiling again and sipping her drink.

"What the deuce is wrong with you?" asked the bartender suddenly, he who had been staring at the girl and had seen the gamut of emotions flit across her face.

"Nothing that *you* would understand," replied Candy imperiously; she didn't like the looks of this fellow, *nor* his forward manner. She lowered her eyes to the glass in her hand and quite ignored him; but he walked around the bar and looked frowningly down at the stool she was sitting on.

"Anything wrong?" Candy asked, and with an icy hauteur she knew would send a shiver up his spine.

"Apparently not," he replied easily, though without relaxing his consideration altogether, "somehow, from the gamut of emotions which crossed your face, I had the idea the *stool* had slipped up into your *damp*."

"I beg your pardon," said Candy, not comprehending, but not too keen on the fellow's tone.

"You know," said the bartender, going back behind the bar again, "your puss, your jelly-box . . . I thought the stool had somehow slipped up into your jelly-box. It happened the other night, a hefty babe was sitting here at the bar . . . not on the stool you're on, but the next one, and I was watching her. Well, she seemed to gradually *sink down* toward the floor, you know, as though the stool itself were going right through the floor, and . . . well, as I say, I was watching her, and, by God, a veritable gamut of emotions was crossing her face while this was happening . . . and what *had* happened was that somehow the stool had slipped or pushed up into her jelly-box, right up inside it, taking all the clothes with it, skirt, slip, panties and all, right up into her thing . . . the whole seat of the stool and about a foot of the legs. Christ, I never saw anything like it before. Of course, she was a good deal heavier than *you*, in fact, a lot heavier. She was a hefty babe, and . . ."

Candy didn't like this gabby intrusion into her thoughts about Derek and the afternoon behind them, and she was quick to let her expression reflect the annoyance she felt; but she allowed him to ramble on, not following the words at all, because she didn't care for this chap's tone. She supposed that he needed her in a way, but she wouldn't think about that now, she was too full at the moment, too full and warm from . . . she recalled Professor Mephesto's words, "from this wonderful business of *living*." She thought of herself for the moment as a lovely, contented cat . . . snuggled warm before the fire in her furabout, purring happily; she could have hugged herself. Yet on another level she did feel that the general ambience of the bar was somehow degrading to the experience of the afternoon, the experience she wanted so much to keep pure and whole, to nurture and fondle, privately, as one might a newborn babe of one's own. She knew that she should be in a more *refined* place than this Riviera bar, and she decided she would try to find out if any good foreign films were playing at the art movie house.

She went over to the table where Jack Katt and Tom Smart were sitting and inquired. Of course they had no notion of what was playing at the art cinemas, or anywhere else for that matter, being out only for cheap strong lush and slick tight puss. But they pretended they knew all about the various programs and insisted that Candy sit down while they discussed it. Then the suave Tom Smart leaned forward and spoke confidingly to the girl: "I'd sure like to dip my jumbo into that hot little honeypot of yours tonight!"

"No, no," said Jack Katt, his dark fire-glint eyes flashing with an impatience which would have made most girls tingle and cream, "let me handle this!" And he tried to pull the handsome Tom Smart away and at the same time actually attempted to thrust his hand into Candy's sweet little blouse.

"You silly boys!" she said crossly. She knew that this was simply their way of expressing a need for her, but she didn't care for this sort of talk, at any time, and especially not now when all her thoughts were with Derek.

"Good Christ Almighty," exclaimed Tom Smart, turning to his companion, "*will* you let me handle this! Now you've offended her! Christ!"

"*You!*" shouted Jack Katt, "you and your damned oblique approach! *I want puss!*"

And so they fell to arguing and discussing the tactic, though to Candy it was a respite and she pursued her reflections on the hours past.

She hardly noticed when they were joined at the table a few minutes later by another person, Dr. Howard Johns, a pleasant, middle-aged chap, certainly not the looker that Tom and Jack were, but perhaps more stable, and no doubt more comfortable for a young girl to be with. Nor did Candy catch his name at first, if in fact these two even troubled to introduce him, so informal were they in such matters.

"Listen, do you know what he is?" asked Tom Smart, after a minute, speaking to Candy, "a gynecologist! Ha-ha-ha!"

"Good grief," said Candy.

"Sure," said Tom Smart, and turning to the doctor, went on in his winningly irrepressible way, "how would you like to look up *that* snatch, Doc? Boy, it's honey and cream!"

"It's a living snake!" said Jack Katt.

This seemed to embarrass the doctor somewhat and he shifted uneasily in his chair.

"Well," said Candy, "I've never met a . . . a gynecologist *socially*. How do you do?"

"Are *you* kidding?" shouted Tom Smart, "how does he *do?*

He gets *more pussy* in three hours than most chaps do in a week! Right Doc?"

"Now, really, Tom, Jack," said Dr. Johns, "I mean, fun is fun, but . . ." He was clearly upset about the turn the conversation had taken.

"I think you boys are terrible," said Candy indignantly, and she got up and went to another table.

"Good God!" cried Jack Katt. "Now you've lost that hot puss for us! Christ! Christ!"

"What! What!" said Tom Smart, "*I* lost it? Great Scott man, don't you realize that if. . . ."

And so they would discuss it for hours on end.

Meanwhile, Dr. Johns got up and joined Candy at the other table.

"Well," he said, "they are certainly . . . certainly *outgoing* chaps, I must say. I'm terribly sorry about that. Really . . . I hardly. . . ."

"Oh they're just silly boys," said Candy, "it's just their way of trying to . . . trying to *express* themselves . . . aesthetically, I suppose."

"Hmm," said Dr. Johns, glancing at them again. They were scuffling about the floor now, wallowing in the pools of beer and saw-dust, shouting remarks about "tight quim," "hot puss," etc., etc.

Both Candy and the doctor looked away.

"Do you happen to know what's playing at the 5th Avenue Cinema?" she asked.

"No, I'm afraid I don't," said Dr. Johns. "Sorry."

"I'd like so much to see a good film tonight," said the girl.

"I don't go to the films much myself," he said. "Enjoy them, do you?"

"Well, of course, I only go to the art films," said Candy.

"I see," said Dr. Johns.

"Films like *The Quiet One*, and *The Cabinet of Dr. Caligari*."

"Well," said Dr. Johns, "would you like me to go and get a paper for you? It would probably be listed there."

"Oh no," said Candy, "that's all right, thanks very much." She was pleased by his consideration.

"Are you sure?" he asked.

"Oh yes, thanks. I'm sure someone will come in who knows what's playing there tonight. I know almost everyone who comes in here."

"I'm afraid I don't," said the doctor.

"Oh you'll get to know them," said Candy, "they're all swell kids."

"Yes, I'd like to," he said. "Who is your doctor, perhaps I know him."

"Well, I haven't been to a doctor since I've been in New York . . . not to a gynecologist anyway. I'm not married, of course, and . . . well, I suppose a single girl doesn't need to go to a gynecologist very often, does she?" In spite of her smile, the perfect girl was blushing.

Dr. Johns frowned.

"Well, of course, you should really have a periodic check-up," he said, "I mean certainly you should have that. When was the last time you did?"

"Oh gracious," said Candy, trying to recall, "it must have been a year ago at least."

"Far too long, far too long," said the doctor seriously.

"Gosh, guess *I'd* better make an appointment," said Candy.

"Hmm. The difficulty is, you see, I'm off on two months' holiday starting tomorrow," said Dr. Johns. He looked around the bar. "I'll tell you what," he said, getting up from the table, "I won't be a moment," and he went out the door.

Candy was humming the theme music of *Alexander Nevsky*, one of her favorite movies, when Dr. Johns came back in the door, carrying a little black bag. He stopped at the table and smiled at her. "We can give you an examination," he said, "just over there." And he assisted her up.

Candy was amazed. "Here? In the *Riviera?* Good grief, I don't . . ."

"Oh yes," said Dr. Johns. "Just here . . . this will do nicely." He had led the girl to the door of the men's toilet, and quickly inside. It was extremely small, a simple cabinet with a stool, nothing more. He locked the door.

"Good grief," said Candy, "I really don't think . . ."

"Oh yes," Dr. Johns assured her, "perfectly all right." He put his little bag down and started taking off her skirt. "Now we'll just slip out of these things," he said.

"Well, are you sure that . . ." Candy was quite confused.

"Now, the little panties," he said, pulling them down. "Lovely things you wear," he added and lifted her up on to the stool.

"Now you just stand with one foot on each side of the stool, limbs spread, that's right and . . . oh yes, you can brace yourself with your hands against the walls . . . yes, just so . . . Fine!"

He bent quickly to his kit and took out a small clamp and inserted it between the girl's darling little labia, so that they were held apart.

"*Good!*" he said. "Now I just want to test these clitorial reflexes," he said, "often enough, that's where trouble strikes first." And he began to gently massage her sweet pink clit. "Can you feel that?"

"Good grief yes!" said Candy, squirming about, "are you sure that is. . . ."

"Hmm," said Dr. Johns. "Normal response there all right. Now I just want to test these clitorial reflexes to tactile surfaces." And he began sucking it wildly, clutching the precious girl to him with such sudden force and abandon that her feet slipped off the stool and into the well of it. During the tumult the flushing mechanism was set in motion and water now surged out over the two of them, flooding the tiny cabinet and sweeping beyond the door and into the bar.

There was a violent pounding at the door.

"What in God's name is going on there?" demanded the manager, who had just arrived. He and the bartender were throwing their weight against the door of the cabinet which by now was two feet deep in water as the doctor and Candy thrashed about inside.

"Good grief!" she kept saying. They had both fallen to the floor. The doctor was snorting and spouting water, trying desperately to keep sucking and yet not to drown.

Finally with a great lunge the two men outside broke open the door. They were appalled by the scene.

"Good God! Good God!" they shouted. "What in the name of God is going on here!"

A police officer arrived at that moment and was beside himself with rage at the spectacle.

The doctor had lost consciousness by the time he was pulled to his feet. Both he and Candy were sopping wet and completely disheveled. She was naked from the waist down.

"He's a doctor!" she cried to the policeman, who was dragging him about like a sack and pulling her by the arm.

"Uh-huh," said the cynical cop, "Dr. Caligari, I suppose."

Candy didn't like this kind of flippant reference to an art film. "This happens to be an examination," she said with marked disdain.

"You can say *that* again, sister," said the officer, taking a good look himself.

"Good grief!" said Candy, snatching the clamp out from between her labes.

The manager and the bartender were speechless with fury.

"*You . . . you . . .*" stammered the manager, shaking his finger at Candy.

"This so *happens* to be a private examination by my doctor," said Candy with great haughtiness.

"*You are barred from the Riviera!*" he shouted with the finality of doom itself.

The doctor had regained consciousness now, but was still lost in his insane desire for the girl and flung himself against her in such ardor that they tumbled back into the cabinet with a splash, Candy shrieking, "Good heavens!"

MAXWELL KENTON

In December, 1956, Mason Hoffenberg brought over to The Olympia Press headquarters on the rue de Nesle his friend Terry Southern, who, then living in Geneva was on a short visit to Paris.

Mason and Terry were anxious to write a book for The Traveller's Companion Series, Terry being at the time in acute financial need. The arrangement was to be our basic one for d.b.'s: a round sum to be paid partly before, and partly after delivery of the manuscript, and giving me the right to exploit the book as best I could. Those books were all signed with pseudonyms and had a strictly under-the-counter career; they very seldom went into a second printing, but the implicit rule was that if we were ever to print a new edition, we would then pay the author another round sum, and so on.

We decided that the story should be about a young American girl, Candy, and this is how Terry outlined the heroine of that Voltairean fable, after our talks in Paris, in a letter he sent me after his return to Switzerland: ". . . A sensitive, progressive-school humanist who comes from Wisconsin to New York's lower East Side to be an art student, social worker, etc., and to find (unlike her father) 'beauty in mean places.' She has an especially romantic idea about 'minorities' and of course gets raped by Negroes, robbed by Jews, knocked up by Puerto Ricans, etc.—though her feeling of 'being needed' sustains her for quite a while, through a devouring gauntlet of freaks, faggots, psychiatrists and aesthetic cults. . . ."

The story was to be completed in time for our spring 1957 program, but was delayed time and again until the summer of 1958. When I received the final draft I was pleasantly surprised by the treatment of it, which was much better—and much funnier—than I had expected: obviously it was a good thing I had given more time to the two authors to complete their job. I wrote to Terry that he should not disown such a bright if incongruous child, and he replied: "As for your suggestion for proclaiming the authorship of Candy, *I must ask you to put such thoughts out of your mind for the time being. I assure you that it would not help sales or reviews, for the simple reason that I am not as yet that well established. . . . Also I have (ironically enough) a children's book under consideration by publishers just now and any news linking me with a book 'in questionable taste' would irreparably shatter my chances with that. . . ."*

The copyright was taken in the name of The Olympia Press in our first edition of the book which appeared in the fall of 1958, and I asked Terry to write a blurb for our catalogue, with the following result:

"Maxwell Kenton is the pen name of an American nuclear

physicist, formerly prominent in atomic research and development who, in February 1957, resigned his post, 'because I found the work becoming more and more philosophically untenable,' and has since devoted himself fully to creative writing. . . . The author has chosen to use a pen name because, in his own words again, 'I'm afraid my literary inclinations may prove a bit too romantic, at least in their present form, to the tastes of many of my old friends and colleagues,'

"*This present novel,* Candy—*which, aside from technical treatises, is Mr. Kenton's first published work—was seen by several English and American publishers, among whom it received wide private admiration, but ultimate rejection due to its highly 'Rabelaisian' wit and flavor. It is undoubtedly a work of very real merit—strikingly individualistic and most engagingly humorous. Perhaps it may be said that Mr. Kenton has brought to bear on his new vocation the same creative talent and originality which so distinguished him in the field he deserted. And surely here is an instance where Science's loss is Art's gain.*"

In June of the next year—1959—Terry was writing from New York: "Candy *is having a small* succès d'estime *here in private circulation . . . ,*" *but the book was much too hip to enjoy a normal sale as a regular d.b., and it took much more than the customary six to twelve months to dispose of the five thousand copies we had printed. We usually calculated that it took roughly that much time for the Paris police to become aware of the new titles on our list and ban them; but it sometimes happened that they were a little quicker, or that a book sold more slowly, with the result that we had to withdraw the book from circulation. That is precisely what happened in the case of* Candy, *which was banned in due course, but at a time when we still had about two thousand unbound copies at the printers'.*

As I liked the book and thought it should escape the common rule, I decided to have the first pages and the cover reprinted with a new title. We renamed the book Lollipop: *a rather silly name to conceal the book's identity from the French police, I admit. But I knew that the inspectors from the Brigade Mondaine would be fooled by that simple device, which we had used in a number of similar cases (the notorious* Helen and Desire *after it was banned was reissued as* Desire and Helen, The Organization *as* The New Organization, *etc.: the idea being that the banned titles were listed in alphabetical order, and a policeman's imagination seldom goes beyond the first letter of a word when it is not under orders to go any further).*

On January 17, 1961, I wrote to Terry to say that we had received an offer for the Italian translation rights of Candy, *and I suggested that we work out a proper contract for the book, as* Candy *was likely to enjoy quite a profitable career, and our earlier occult arrangement would be unfair to the authors. We signed a contract on May 9, 1961 in which the authors jointly agree that The Olympia Press should be considered as "the owners of all publications rights" of the book "by virtue of the outright royalty paid to the authors" when we commissioned them to write the book, but that for all further uses and exploitation of the novel, we would abide by normal terms of contract.*

Then we decided to print a new edition of Lollipop (*nee* Candy), *and the book resumed its slow subterranean career, until one day it was "discovered" by Walter Minton of G. P. Putnam's Sons, who had already made two successive fortunes with two of our books:* Lolita *and* The Memoirs of Fanny Hill. *In the case of* Candy, *however, Walter Minton decided to have a contract directly with the authors, thus saving one third of the royalties he would normally have had to pay had he made the agreement with us. But in order to make that possible, the authors had to attempt to have their agreement with us cancelled, and one of the many ironies of this case is that they had to deny the validity of a contract which existed only by virtue of my somewhat* démodé *view of publishing ethics. There are a number of apt Latin proverbs to fit that sort of situation.*

The rest of the curious story is now well-known. Candy's *publication by Putnam was extraordinarily successful. Then, weeks before the book ended its career as a best-selling hardcover production, three different paperback publishers each unexpectedly released a million-copy soft-cover edition. When Putnam attempted to sue them, and claimed that they had taken a fresh copyright on their own edition, the pirate publishers candidly explained that they had never intended to infringe Putnam's copyright, the validity of which they did not even want to question, but that they had simply copied Olympia's Paris edition which they contended was not legitimately copyrighted. They went on to threaten Putnam with a suit for damages because of the harassment, and the attempted restriction of their right to print and sell a book which was in the public domain.*

This is not the first case to raise the extraordinary intricacies of the United States copyright laws, some of which were set up with the intention of protecting American printers against foreign competition. It is doubtful that American printers ever derived the least advantage from that exotic piece of legislation, but the industry of pirate publishers, blackmailers, and shady operators has powerfully benefited from it.

We now have to see what will eventually result from that interesting multileveled conflict, and hope that it will yield some much-needed enlightenment to authors, legislators and publishers, straight or otherwise.

HENRY JONES

THE ENORMOUS BED

*W*estchester is what is known as an old foundation. This means the plumbing is atrocious, the quarters cramped and the discipline Spartan. I was boarded in the house of a Mr. Fletcher, a crouched man with pebble-glasses and a foul temper. It is the custom at boarding schools for the housemasters to be married and in this Mr. Fletcher was no exception. Or rather he was. His taste and good luck had been quite out of the ordinary. Rhoda Fletcher was beautiful.

I was approaching my seventeenth birthday, I suppose, when I realized that for the first time. If you are kept to a diet of Latin elegiacs and cross-country runs over a period of years, it is surprising how late your interest in the other sex can develop. But one day something is likely to happen quickly and, considering my rapid growth and disgusting good health, it was bound to.

Fletcher was obviously in a vile mood that morning.

"Jones, would it be too much to ask you to confine your un-questionable conversational gifts to the Debating Society. I am attempting to instruct you."

"I'm sorry sir. I was asking for a piece of paper."

"Your sorrow, Jones, is of lesser moment to me than your silence. I may proceed?"

I mumbled that he could do as he bloody well liked. There was a pause.

Fletcher began to tap a small ruler slowly on his desk.

"You said?"

"Please continue, sir."

There were only six of us in the group and the whole scene was ridiculous. No other master would have dreamt of addressing seniors like children. It suddenly occurred to me that I could knock Fletcher's head off and I regretted his glasses.

The lesson proceeded. We wrote and he talked occasionally. Then, two minutes before the end, it flared up again.

"What are you grinning about, Jones?"

The sun was blazing in through the window and I was thinking about cricket that afternoon. I got annoyed.

"It is a congenital tic, sir, nervously acquired from my paternal grandfather who was known in the village as Soft Charley."

His eyes swam forward against his lenses like tadpoles.

"Are you trying to be insolent, Jones?"

"Yes, sir."

He moved toward me and I rose in my seat and looked at him. We looked at each other. The bell went. Somebody muttered "seconds out" and I laughed and Fletcher went back to his desk to collect his papers.

It was a brilliant afternoon and I had been on form. Lying back in the deck chair I was entitled to as a member of the First XI, thinking with a schoolboyish pleasure of the eighty-four runs I had smacked and wheedled together in the previous two hours, I was disturbed by two slim womanly legs that were scissoring past me. The legs were brown and firm. My eyes moved unwillingly up them to the receding back of Mrs. Fletcher who was sauntering toward the tea tent. It was as if my eyes had spoken. Her white dress hung still for a second, then swirled decisively and she was coming back toward our little nest of chairs.

"Hello, Jones," she said. I stumbled to my feet, feeling myself blush. Her eyes were a very clear startled blue. Her hair was long and hung down over her shoulders like a girl's. In one hand she held an enormous picture-hat, about the size of a cart wheel. I suppose she was anything between thirty-five and forty. I thought she looked like one of those French paintings. A girl with laughing eyes on a windy hill in summer. Forgive me.

"I must congratulate you," she said. "A beautiful performance." Her soft voice dragged over the adjective so that I felt even clumsier. She was looking with those innocent eyes straight into mine as we stood there. Did she mean I was beautiful? That wasn't a word you used of men.

There was a rattle of hand claps and she turned to the field, shading her eyes with her free hand from the glare. I was conscious that her body was a woman's. It was a very hot day. The air shimmered up from the turf. They were walking in.

"Will you take me in to tea, Jones?" she said. "Vernon seems to have escaped." She shrugged and smiled. Vernon was Mr. Fletcher who was known for putting in brief unsmiling appearances at such functions and sliding off as soon as he decently could.

Her mouth was very red and glistening under the sun. Why didn't she put her hat on? Though she certainly looked good, standing there with her brown legs slightly apart, swinging it idly like a girl.

"Of course, Mrs. Fletcher," I said. "I'd be delighted."

Inside the tent it was cool and noisy. We moved over to a corner away from the tables and I held her tea while she sat down on a green painted chair, fastidiously arranging the folds of her skirt. The light filtered through in a pale washed green that bathed our white clothes and tanned limbs and turned us strange. Her hair was black now, her mouth dark and the shadow in the profound V of her dress had deepened.

I was two people. Outwardly Jones, H., making polite conversation with his housemaster's wife, inwardly a very confused excited young man trying to keep his eyes from straying to the firm plump bodice of her dress. Tents are always a bit odd anyway, I've found. There are walls all right, but your feet thud about on grass and the light gets all messed up and they have a shut-in but healthy kind of smell.

Anyway, as I bent down to take her plate from her, the sleeve of my blazer brushed against her cheek. I went to apologize, but she seemed not to have noticed. She was talking about her husband.

"Vernon tells me you were impertinent to him this morning," she said softly, and waited. I said nothing. She pulled down her brows in a slight frown. I noticed tiny wrinkles at the corners of her eyes, under the powder. The tent light put little shadows there too, like smudges from a cruel thumb. The tea break was nearly over.

"Look," she said rapidly, "I know he's not too popular with you boys. Will you do me a favor, Henry?"

"Anything, Mrs. Fletcher," I said, between embarrassment and pleasure at her calling me Henry.

"Then meet me by the tent here at eleven tonight. I know I can rely on you. Why, good afternoon, Head. Jones has been trying to explain the mysteries of the googly to me. I'm afraid he's found me a poor pupil." She laughed enchantingly. I hadn't even noticed Mr. Lytton's approach. But he could hardly have heard anything. The old boy was as deaf as a post. Anyway, what was there to hear? What was I getting so worked up about? Some damn nonsense about being kind to Vernon. I'd have to be careful about getting down to the tent, though. It would look strange if they found me snooping around the grounds after eleven.

"Splendid, splendid," said Head heartily and vaguely and moved on. Before I had a chance to reply to Mrs. Fletcher, she had been buttonholed by the school Matron and I had to go back to the game.

I met her that night. Imagine me, if you can, a tall gangling boy in striped pyjamas, waiting desperately in my bed for the talk to die down. Mercifully the dormitory quietened after twenty minutes and when I saw the luminous hands of my watch pointing to ten to eleven I could hear nothing but regular breathing all down the length of the room. My bed was next to the door and, even if anyone heard me leave, they would probably imagine nature had called. Which, in a way, she had. As I slipped on a thick dressing gown and shoved my feet into running shoes, I felt my heart thudding against my chest. I walked softly to the door and out. Down the broad stairs, into the ground floor lavatory, on to the seat, the window gave easily, a heave and a jump, and I was out, crouched in the warm summer's night on the grass verge surrounding Fletcher's house. To have left by the front door would have meant a private key since our youthful innocence was guarded with preternatural locks and bolts.

It was unreal, this walking over the lawns in the moonlight. I could see the white tent gleaming at me, small and mysterious, over under the far trees. My feet padded on. The grass was damp with night.

I had no idea toward what I was going. If I said there wasn't a thought in my head you'd smile and yet it's the truth. Eleven began to strike distantly from the village church. I took three steps between each stroke. It was unlikely anyone would be prowling about at this hour, but I kept into the heavy trees skirting the ground.

The tent was planted directly in front of me.

It was then that I nearly turned back. My tongue was heavy as a clapper in my mouth and my knees felt strangely insecure. I stood outside it for a moment, inhaling deeply on the night air. A smell of musty grass and taut canvas came sweetly into my lungs. I pulled tight on the cord of my gown and, brushing aside the flap of the tent, slipped inside.

"You *did* come," she said.

Rhoda Fletcher was sitting, so far as I could see, on a rug over by the afternoon's tea table. Those were the last words she said to me that night, and often since, in my more decadent moments of self-examination, have I tried to recapture the high breathless note on which she said them. She was smoking a cigarette and drew hard on it now, so that the lower triangle of her girl's face was suddenly lit up in a red glow. The fullness of her mouth struck me before the cigarette flew past me through the darkness in a slim arc of fire.

My eyes followed it, blinded for an instant, so that I was totally unaware of the swift movement she had made as she rejected it, and nearly leapt like an animal when her hand thrust aside my thick gown and took hold of me *there*. With her other hand she was tugging at the cord and loosening it.

I had been dammed up for too long. With a cry, I forced myself brutally into her hand, thrusting my face down and fastening my mouth like a maniac on to her soft open lips. The woman in the darkness was holding me violently now. It was nearly painful. The smooth palm of her hand caressed me indescribably for a second, then clenched once again. It was becoming unbearable.

I caught her blindly up in my arms and half-dragged, half-carried her over to the corner of the tent. She began to sink back to the firm ground and I fell clumsily with her. I was beyond thought. There was something in my way, some tight distracting material I was tugging at. Suddenly, like a miracle, the way was free and I felt the delirium of a woman's warm belly bare against mine. I began to rear like a beast. A hand crept down and caught me again, feeding me gently into the soft other mouth of her. There was no time.

I thrust and thrust as if I must die there, not hearing her first sharp cry, nor the moanings of delight that slid from her jerking lips afterward. I thought I could see her teeth bared and shining in the faint light as I plunged and plunged, working disruptingly deeper and deeper into her. There, on the hard ground, she lay and gripped on me, her fingers digging hard into the flesh of my shoulders, her mouth abruptly thrust with its flickering wetness of tongue over mine. I couldn't stop. I was a God, stronger than lions or sphinxes. This profound slippery thrusting as one grew and grew, while she cried openly now, mouthing at me wordlessly, her tongue lolling dead and her hands beating and stroking my shoulders, her belly smacked and brutalized under my onslaught. I was no longer anything but this enormous power driving out of me mindlessly into the moist parts of her. I felt her open, as it were, and subside suddenly under me in a spasm of small cries. Her long hair brushed the rug from side to side as she twisted her head in frenzy. But I was still mounting toward the heart of the mystery. Relentlessly I speared and squirmed my way on until she clutched me again and kissed me full on the mouth. Her heady perfume swept through me as I fought at her. We were locked utterly in need, a self-destroying monster, jerking as one. Her hips swung up with me now and fell as I moved. Then I could feel the tumult rising and lunged out with all my being, lunged and lunged into her, and we were liberated over a long moving minute, completely together. The sweat from our bellies ran together and mingled. In the anonymity of the night we had been one.

I tried hard to think what to say after the delirium had passed. Obviously I should say something. We were very warm lying there still linked in the posture of love and I realized I still had my gown on and that she was, in effect, still half-clothed. Only our lower parts had become, as if our clothing had vaporized under the moment's lust, utterly naked. While I thought of the appropriate words and she lay still, clutching me tightly to her, I began to take advantage of my suddenly won manhood and allowed my hands to stray inquisitively around the clothed portions of her body. My eyes were becoming accustomed to the tented gloom. Her face was peaceful and, it seemed, closed upon an enigmatic smile. She must have come prepared to this rendezvous. Under her skirt, now rucked up around her hips, she wore nothing.

My hands moved from the smoothness of her haunches and jumped on to her breast. A thin row of buttons, shimmering in the weak light, ran from her neck down to the waist. Unhurriedly my fingers eased each button through its hole. I had not as yet touched her breasts. To make my exploration easier I made to move my much-diminished self out of her, but she held savagely to me as I tried to withdraw, her eyes closed and bland. So I did the best I could. The last button slipped free and I drew aside the two halves of her evening-top. There could be little doubt that she had come prepared for more than conversation. She wore neither brassiere nor slip. My hands fell straight on to the large dark-tipped globes of her breasts.

For a second they rested inert as if astonished. I had forgotten about the polite necessity for conversation and Mrs. Fletcher had obviously gone far beyond it. I was learning as rapidly as I could, Adam my guide. To take the heavy yielding globe of a woman's breast in your hand for the first time is not nothing, as I found. My fingers quivered round the pair of them, palpating gently, assuring themselves of their good luck. She stirred slightly under me and sighed. Then her hands began slowly to work my gown off my shoulders. While she painstakingly freed me of it, I brought my fingers in a soft sweep round the line of her breast toward its swelling point, withdrawing my hand momentarily to allow the sleeve to slide over it. She was warming to her work. Now her hands fluttered along the buttons of my pyjama jacket and, in a second, I was free of that too. I lay heavily on her, plucking with increasing knowledge at her one breast, the other nuzzling into my bared chest.

I could feel the link between us growing stronger again. Now our two movements were decisive. I wanted to rid her of the skirt coiled up round her waist and, after some determined probing, discovered and unlatched the zip at the side, so that, thanks to a certain mutual dexterity, I was able to pull it up and over her head without actually breaking our union for an instant. Meanwhile she had forced my pyjama trousers down over my buttocks so that now all I had to do was push them down and off with the aid of an agile foot. What may sound complicated, as so often with explanations of natural acts, was in fact accomplished with great dispatch.

In agitating our bodies slightly during this disrobing, we had both become only too apparently excited again and I had started to lunge into her without, so to speak, coming to any decision to do so.

This time I was less brutal. Free of our clothes, there was less sensation of violation in what I was doing. Besides, though it is perhaps
unbecoming to record it here, I was already interested in observing
this time what was going on. I tried to *feel*, with that most sentient
part of oneself, into what I had intruded. With each insidious thrust, I
experienced the temporary joys of exploration.

But, at seventeen, the blood runs warm and I was over-optimistic.
What had begun with comparative delicacy ended, under the urgings
of Rhoda's cushiony thighs, in another devastation. I found myself
clutching the two proud white globes desperately for a second, then
I collapsed utterly, dominated by my loins' imperious needs and
flung into her while my arms pressed her sweating back, forcing her
irrevocably on to me. It was the same tearing pulpy abrasion, the
same necessity to be held in those slippery jaws, to withdraw an inch
only to advance into the rich center of her. She was crying out again
now under me, kissing me frantically and sobbing my name. Her
legs thrashed about around mine, then locked round my buttocks and
I suddenly felt the cold heel of an evening shoe pressing into my
flesh and realized she had retained at least one item of her clothing. It
was too much for me. I exploded into her until I thought it would
never stop.

When we both came to ourselves again, I realized we had somehow rolled off the rug and were lying on the nightdamp grass. Mrs.
Fletcher must have been extremely uncomfortable. I eased myself out
of her enveloping arms and, crouched over her white shimmering
body, lifted her back on to the blanket. She opened her eyes and
smiled up at me without a word. Then she turned over on her side
and groped for her handbag which she must have brought with her
to the tent. She took out two cigarettes which she placed in her
bruised mouth and lit. Sitting up, she curled one arm around my neck
and transferred one of the glowing cigarettes to my lips. This was,
idiotically, the first act of hers to really shock me, since it was one of
the most stringent rules of the school that even seniors, and particularly first team players, would be severely punished if found
smoking. I felt then what anarchy Rhoda Fletcher represented in the
tight male structure of Westchester. I sucked greedily at my cigarette
while her limp hand moved idly about my back.

We said nothing as we finished smoking. I had already had an
occasional cigarette, but not enough to prevent my head from feeling

unusually light, a pleasant giddiness, as I inhaled now. When we had thrown them away, we lay down together, turned in toward each other on the rug, and clasped each other once again in our arms. It was getting cold and we instinctively, as it seemed to me, moved toward each other for warmth. I felt a great pang of affection for this incredible woman as she embraced me with indescribable tenderness. This was love, I thought, this overpowering mixture of gratitude and desire.

I had read, of course, of lovemaking, but imprecisely and, I was now realizing, inaccurately. Life allowed of no asterisks. This immediate renewal of desire was something I took for granted: there seemed no reason why it should ever stop. It was years before I knew that Mrs. Fletcher must have found me an exceptionally eager lover.

Because, as we lay cradled into each other, the small limpness on my left thigh began imperceptibly to stiffen. I felt one of her hands running down the bones of my back and lingering softly on the curve of my hip. Then, as she moved her lips blindly toward mine again and wiggled the dark rose of her tongue in and out of my mouth, her hand became fingertips that brushed mesmerically down over my belly and around my loins, then moved softly around the firm stem of me again, in circles toward the tip. I was eager again for the fray, but found myself better able to control my immediate reactions. I waited for her to move over on to her back and thrust my face down on to the musky warmth of her breasts, daring to let my tongue briefly touch, under some obscure compulsion, the round stains of her nipples. But she stayed, tapering down the length of me, on her side. I felt she was playing with me, as indeed she was. Very well, she was in my power now and I would show her who it was that controlled.

I moved a hand down to the bushy part of her abruptly and began to stroke her clumsily with the inner pads of my fingers. I thought I could hear her laughing quietly in the darkness and my fingers became more insistent, intent on humbling her experience. Gradually I felt her soft lips cleaving apart under my stroking and I insinuated my fingers gently into the wet warmth, rubbing and kneading at the slippery flesh. She began to breathe heavily and the laughter quite stopped.

Then slowly I heard the movement of her body on the harsh wool of the rug as she lifted her left leg and brought it languidly

down over my thigh. Before I had thought about it, the swollen head
of me was butting confidently through the moist opening my fingers
had prepared. I was determined to go less far this time, to hold something in reserve, and, although I entered her easily enough, I went
no further than the succulent lips, gently gyrating there.

Her hands struggled round my buttocks and tried to press me
home, holding me low down and forcing me upward. Her head was
thrown back and her long luxuriant hair streamed darkly around it.
Her mouth worked loosely, imploringly. She moved her teeth forward suddenly and bit me on the shoulder. Her whole body fought
against mine in a frenzy, frantic to hold me and have me closer.
Finally, after what seemed hours of this maddening play, when I
knew I could no longer contain myself against such throbbing
warmth, I went wholeheartedly into her to the extent of my powers
so that we seemed once more molded into one strange beast.

Lying so on my side, I jabbed lengthily in the profound stillness
of the night. She lay as if in a swoon, her belly moving spasmodically
with mine. This time there was a kind of sleep in the act. I drew it
out as long as I could, lost in the mounting drunkenness of this held
slithering. She came silently once, twice, I lost count, terribly open
to me, then holding me there in a fresh convulsion. Finally she seemed
to go mad and worked herself desperately around me, while I redoubled my onslaught until, in a double rear of our bucking bodies,
the longdrawn thread of my being poured free into her.

Utterly exhausted, our one body hunched on itself like a weary
worm. I have no idea how long we lay there without motion. I could
feel the soft flesh of her breasts rising and falling damply against me.
Her hair, in which my face was buried, gave off a subtle private
smell that would have excited me terribly a few minutes before. I
began, as I slowly came alive again, to sort out those of our tangled
limbs that properly belonged to me. My senses became unusually
sharp. As two o'clock struck from the distant church, the dull strokes
reverberated not only in my ears but throughout my entire frame, so
that Rhoda stirred slightly beneath me and groaned happily. Her eyes
came hesitatingly open and she caught me in her arms, tousling my
hair and kissing and licking my face like a puppy.

I still don't know why it was. To have spoken at all now would
have been impossible. That night our two identities had obliterated
each other so completely that any word would have been an act

almost against nature. What passed through her mind I shall never know, but my own thoughts had become as impalpable as feathers, motes drifting into my mind and dissolving as my limbs dictated. So our wordless dialogue continued.

I got up and fumbled around for my pyjamas. It was getting cold now. It occurred to me they might just possibly have discovered my absence from the dormitory. Nature's calls were not usually so prolonged. I had some vague idea of getting back into bed as quickly as possible. Mr. Fletcher must be wondering about his wife, too, I supposed, though this seemed less important than my own predicament. She had shown such initiative that I couldn't see her not having laid her plans carefully there as well. Anyway, what the hell, I thought, as I struggled into my gown, this had been worth anything. The whole world of school had faded from my character, which it had attempted to mold for so long, as if it had never been. I could hardly believe that tomorrow would find me brushing my teeth alongside twenty similarly pyjamaed boys, giving lines to cheeky juniors, knocking a cricket ball about in the nets.

Her body loomed whitely by my side. She too had begun to dress. I watched the plump ghostly stalks of her legs stepping into the dark folds of her skirt, and the quick eclipse of her thighs. She bent forward, in unconscious provocation, to adjust a shoe so that her breasts swung heavily down in the pearly light. I moved over to her across the rug and kissed her neck where her hair fell away from it. My hands had caught up the softness of her breasts. She straightened out and curved backward against me fleetingly before breaking free with a breathless laugh and moving to put on her top. This I buttoned for her lingeringly. Then I held her bag while she made as if to paint her mouth again. For whom? I wondered absurdly. She held the lipstick in her hand for a moment as if reflecting and apparently asked herself the same question, for she put it back in her bag without using it. I bent down and picked up the rug, shaking it free of telltale grass and folding it.

We left the tent well pleased, I suppose, with each other. As I have said, I imagined myself to be heart and soul in love, forgetting my body alone had been so far involved. It seemed pointless now for us to care about snoopers. The windows of the old school buildings shone darkly at us from the other side of the field like so many blind eyes. It was a wonderful night, though cooler now. I had my arm

romantically round her waist and she let her head fall lazily back on to my shoulder. We might have been taking a lovers' stroll through the conventional park.

As we drew near to her husband's house, she pulled me into a border of thick bushes along one side of it. I thought we were to say our goodnights here and stooped down to kiss her. Our mouths met, but, at the same time, her hand shot as if uncontrollably down to my trousers and discovered my freshly proved manhood again. She worked so furiously on and around it while I stood there helplessly that I found myself stronger than ever and burning to take her. She turned round then, leaving me hard and exposed in the moonlight, and bent down, throwing up her skirts, so that I thought for a confused second of small boys about to be caned. I suppose she had found me an adept enough pupil to have no fears as to my capacity for solving more advanced problems. Anyway, as she dropped on to her hands like a runner awaiting the pistol, I had the good fortune to find the mark without untoward fumblings and entered her animally. The strain of stooping and stabbing into her eager parts only increased my fury to finish and I slammed into her latest proposition with unflagging good will. She held herself rigid to meet me as long as she could, before subsiding limply to the ground with me tied to her.

I was past bewilderment at the night's events. Few young men can have had the good fortune to have discovered such pleasure with so little pain. But this philosophical reflection was hardly occupying

me as I bade my unusually carnal good night to Mrs. Fletcher. I was
awash with delight. We were grovelling hard on the ground, all
restraints utterly gone, reverted to the primal pattern of love. I
seemed, as I thrust now, to be lancing hotly almost into the hidden
womb of her, a deep deep penetration wetly and suckingly caressed
along its whole length. It took me long to have done this fourth time.
Having once voided myself into her convulsive welcome, I found to
my surprise that I was in no way diminished and stayed accordingly
to give her what I have since heard called, with somewhat offensive
bonhomie, "one for the road." The road in question was presumably
well-traveled and yet I think its owner had little that night but
applause for the toll she had taken. Certainly, as we at last came apart
and rose unsteadily to our feet, brushing one another down with
peaceful hands, her innocent eyes shone into mine with unmistakably
genuine gratitude, even perhaps affection. I naturally, with the whole
heart of my seventeen years, took it for reciprocated love.

We kissed swiftly and separated, I to my lavatory window, she
presumably to let herself in by a side door that led by a private
stairway to the apartments she shared with her husband.

With the unbelievable luck that had characterized this evening, I
got safely back to the dormitory and into bed without waking a
soul. My head fell back on the pillow, I sighed dreamily to myself
and sank immediately into a profound and well-earned sleep.

HENRY JONES

*If Henry Jones insists that his identity must be concealed at any cost,
he has good reason for that—being a sound product of the English
Establishment (public school and Oxbridge) who has returned to it,
after a lapse of several years spent in Paris cafés which were mostly
devoted to the cultivation of some of the minor arts and the writing
of* The Enormous Bed.

THE GAUDY IMAGE

WILLIAM TALSMAN

Gunner and Nickie divvied up the haul after the holdup. Nickie was anxious to spend his half, but Gunner told him to wise up.

"If you're smart," he said, "you'll stick with me and don't go walk the streets so no two-bit beatman can pick ya up. Lay low 'til the look goes out of your eyes. You don't know how you act. You're always watchin' in back for some cop to come up from behind and nab you. You gotta cool down, limber up, so you can go out and act like nothin' happened, act like it happened a long time ago, so you ain't tender to it. Take a tip, stick with me. Just lay low for a month or so 'til the job is back in the books somewhere and not on the front page of the police blotter with every cheap tinhorn cop buckin' to land you like a big fish."

"Okay," Nickie said, but wondered, "how we gonna work it?"

"I know this roomin' house joint on Dauphine. Ain't no palace, but we can do better later. We just hang around there and pay our rent regular and on time, say we work nights and sleep during the day, then go to a neighborhood joint at night. Got it?"

"Don't the cops check roomin' joints?"

"Yeah, but they don't know about this one. She don't report nothin'."

Nickie didn't have a suitcase, but he did carry some personal

389

things, a busted razor and a tiny square of hotel soap, in a paper bag, which he hitched to his belt. After he got settled in the rooming house, he figured he could steal some shaving cream and whatever else he needed.

Gunner stood in front of the rooming house with his legs spread and his arms folded across his chest. He rapped on the door with his fist.

The landlady opened the door and stood solidly on the two stumps which were her legs.

"Whatcha want?" she asked, blocking the doorway with her bulk.

"We're lookin' for a room, ma'am," Gunner told her.

"Can you pay in advance?"

"Yeah."

Her gaze passed over Gunner and reported to her brain: black hair, nice build, stubborn chin, twisted smile, no, shifty smile, but kinda nice manner for a construction worker. Then she shot a glance at Nickie.

"He don't look like he can pay in advance!"

"Yeah, he can," Gunner answered for him, "if we like it."

"Well, I just happen to have a real nice room."

As they started up the stairs, Nickie smelled tomato sauce in the air. He looked into the kitchen and saw two plates which were piled high with steaming spaghetti. She didn't need all that food, he told himself. Maybe she'd invite him down for a feed. The landlady huffed and puffed up the stairs.

"Always like my pay in advance," she said. "Policy around here. If you're a long-time guest and I like steadies, I make an exception once in a while, but that don't apply to you yet. No monkey business in the rooms. I clean once a week if my rheumatism ain't bad. The bath's at the end of the hall. I don't like queers, and don't fill the tub over the red watermark. My husband didn't paint it just to pretty up the tub. I got two other guests. I live on the ground floor—with my husband. There's a wrestler in 2-B and a boxer in 2-C. You can have 2-A, right by the stairs. Where you work?"

"At night."

"Then you ain't in construction?"

"Naw, never said we was. We work in a bar back of town."

"Yeah? Well, remember the rules 'cause I ain't repeatin' them, and if you break the littlest one, out you go with no kickback, understand?"

"Yeah."

When they reached the first landing, she stopped to catch her breath. "You go up and look around. I don't go the next flight 'less I have to."

The door of the room was ajar. Gunner pushed it open with his foot and looked in. There was a big brass bed which was retouched with white paint, or a white bed which was retouched with brass paint. He didn't know which. There was a dresser with a cracked mirror and a rocking chair. The white plaster walls bulged in places, but, all in all, he figured the room would hold up for another month, so he said, "We'll take it."

"I ain't told you how much yet," she reminded him.

"How much?"

"I'll give you a special price. Ten dollars."

"That's what I pay for a single. We'll pay eight for two—since we're quiet guys."

"Eight-fifty."

"Can't go no higher than eight."

"Gotta include the water and lights," she explained.

"Eight cold."

Nickie, who hadn't said a word or seen the room yet, said, "I don't like it."

"Eight," she agreed. "But you gotta realize that's a special price, so I gotta have it in advance right along. I'm takin' a loss—just 'cause you're quiet guys."

Gunner handed her eight dollars, which she grabbed and stuffed down the neck of her dress.

Her parting words were: "I'm sure you'll be very happy here, if you mind the rules. Shut the door when you're in the bathroom, and call my husband when the toilet clogs."

Gunner slammed the door. The door banged shut but opened again, inching its way back into the room as if gasping for air.

Then Nickie shut the door. When it crept back into the room, he lifted it up and fastened a loop through a hole in a metal bar which was provided for a padlock, if the roomers had a padlock.

"This sweat box will do," Gunner said, yawning. "It ain't permanent."

"I don't like it," Nickie said uneasily, but he threw his paper sack on top of the dresser.

Gunner didn't answer because he didn't hear. He had flopped on the bed and had fallen asleep.

As Nickie joined him, he felt a warmth which was not accounted for by the room or by Gunner, but, as he conked out, he clamped his fist over the source of radiation, the wad of bills in his pocket.

The next morning Gunner bought two po' boy sandwiches and a couple of soft drinks for their breakfast. When Nickie saw them, he said. "This is eatin' high on the hog, man. Ain't never had a po' boy for breakfast."

"A lot of things you ain't never had you'll get if you stick with me."

"Some team, man, Nickie and Gunner," Nickie said proudly.

"Gunner and Nickie," Gunner corrected. "You ain't been brought up right."

"Man, we'll travel," Nickie said, changing the subject. He didn't care whose name was first in the title of the corporation. As long as that corporation continued to bring in as much money as he had in his pocket at this minute, he was first, regardless.

"This is just the beginning," Gunner assured him. "I got plans. Big plans. And we got plenty of time to make them stick."

They had plenty of time. Time fell in that room as slowly as water drips from a leaky faucet. Each moment was filled with the same amount of vacuous silence. Long ago they had exhausted their plans, which had been discussed down to the last detail, memorized, and rehearsed to perfection. After they had outslept themselves, Gunner sat in the rocker and rocked himself to a standstill.

Later, Nickie propped open the door in order to watch the other two roomers as they went up and down the stairs. Nickie decided that the dark one must be the boxer because he left in the morning with a pair of gloves, lacings tied together, dangling around his neck, and sometimes he carried a paper sack with some purple silk sticking out the top. The blond's stocky frame was overloaded with muscle like a wrestler.

When the boxer headed down the stairs one morning, Nickie commented dryly, "He's goin' to the gym."

And when the wrestler walked past the door with a blanket over his shoulder, wearing only his shorts, Gunner said, just as dryly,

"He's headin' for the patio and the afternoon sun." Then Gunner reminded Nickie that the wrestler might have the patio sun, but soon they would have the real stuff on the wide open beaches of Miami.

"Yeah," Nickie sighed, but, as Gunner continued to remind him, his "yeah" ran uphill until it became a full-fledged question. Nickie was convinced that anything in the present was better than the best in the future, but he didn't tell Gunner that nothing was worth waiting for.

When Gunner stood up and walked around the room, Nickie grabbed the rocker. As he rocked, he counted the rocks until he did the impossible: he fell asleep.

Gunner rapped the wall with his fist. There was a resounding smack, but Nickie didn't blink. He opened his eyes and wondered if the days were longer than the nights or the nights were longer than the days. They seemed about even. All too long. But he never resolved the wonder, for, if he had, he wouldn't have had anything to think about the next day.

The boxer passed by the door with his hair in a sweaty tangle.

"He's back from the gym," Nickie announced. "Been workin' out, probably."

He listened for the door of the boxer's room to slam. After the door slammed, he said, "He's goin' to take a shower. They probably ain't got a shower at the gym."

"What kind of gym is that?" Gunner wanted to know.

"No shower gym," Nickie explained.

"Probably some cheap tinhorn place," Gunner guessed.

"Yeah, some real cheap tinhorn place."

"Yeah, some real goddamn cheap tinhorn place."

"Yeah, some real mammy-lovin' goddamn cheap tinhorn place."

They expanded the thought with adjectives in order to postpone the arrival of that menace, silence.

"What you mean, a shower?" Gunner asked. He had poked around in the discussion and had seized upon any discrepancy in order to prolong the conversation "How's he gonna shower in this hole?"

"I meant a bath."

"All right, a bath. Why didn't you say so in the first place?"

"I was thinkin' 'bout the showers we're gonna take in Miami."

"Yeah, real tile they got," Gunner reminded Nickie as the picture of Miami softened his voice. "Pretty colors."

Nickie said nothing. His mind saw the boxer dropping his shorts and tugging his sweat shirt over his head.

"He's puttin' on that maroon bathrobe," Nickie said.

"Yeah, I seen him in it, too," Gunner said.

One door slammed, then another. The sound of water.

"I wonder if he uses over the red line?"

"How's she gonna know if he does or not unless she goes in there with him?"

"Maybe she does."

"I wouldn't doubt it."

Nickie choked on a phony laugh.

He heard two streams of water.

"Now he's runnin' the cold," he said.

"Where you been? It's all cold. He's takin' a leak."

Their voices dropped into silence as if they had fallen into a deep pit in the center of the room. They listened to the water as it gurgled down the drain, but neither mentioned it, for they knew what the other would say. Statement and response, response and statement, question and answer, answer and question, it didn't matter which came first or who said it. They were all the same.

A door slammed, then another.

"He's goin' to sit on his gallery and soak up the sun. How's come he got a gallery with his room?"

"Yeah, how come?"

" 'Cause he puts out to that slut, that's how come."

"Yeah," Nickie said. "He puts out. I bet he don't even pay rent."

Nickie heard the heavy, stiff-legged thumping of footsteps on the stairs as though pillars were walking away from the temple. Long pauses were interrupted by heavy breathing.

"She's on the landing," Nickie narrated.

More footsteps, more pauses.

When the landlady passed by his door without looking in, he rolled over on the bed and buried his head. Through the pillow he said, "She's on her way to collect his rent."

A smile grazed Gunner's face, but disappointment, discontent or impatience deflected the smile so that there was no trace of it on his face but the small scar which parted his lips. He switched his concentration to his knife and started to clean his fingernails. A tear in the window shade let in a beam of light, and, as the light struck the six-inch blade, the blade reflected the beam into Nickie's eyes. Nickie blinked.

"Shut the door," Gunner ordered. "I'm tired of listenin' to 'em." There was no trace of the smile in his voice, either. The smile had ricocheted off the discontent which had been firmly fixed on his face.

Nickie slipped off the bed and slammed the door. Then he slammed it again. The third time he held the door with his foot while he fastened the latch. After securing the latch, he flopped on the bed and began to dream, but Gunner started in with a story, so Nickie saved his dream. He had already spent most of his dreams, and dreams were hard to come by since the demand was so much greater than the supply, so he saved his dream gladly.

"Man, when I was up at State, I used to get it any time I wanted," Gunner began. "We used to soap a guy up in the shower and have him done 'fore the guard came to let us out.

"Sometimes the guard was on top. Then he would see that the guy got two desserts for supper, whether he wanted them or not, but most guys wanted them, and from then on we all knew that he would be easy pickin'. What you think of that?"

Rat bastard, Nickie thought.

"Well, what you think of it?"

Rat bastard, Nickie thought.

"Once, when I was in parish," Gunner began again, "they toss this kid in a cell with me and this big clammy brute, whose face was all cut up somethin' awful. This goof tried to heist a plane, but when the cops started chasing him, he got so excited he ran right smack into a moving propeller. Well, I had a knife sealed up behind a loose piece of plaster in the cell wall. I didn't want to miss with the kid 'cause I'm kinda partial to cherries, and this kid didn't know nothin', so I use my knife on him and tell that mangy dog, that cup-up homely bastard, to keep an eye out for the guard. Like I knew, I had a little trouble with the kid, but he didn't want to get cut up 'cause he only had six months to do, and I was just stoppin' over on my way to State, so I didn't care if I got more time or not. So, just as I start to ease in, this beam of light hits me in the face, and the guard sees what I'm up to. The guard don't take the kid, but real tough-like he orders me out of the cell and down to the dispensary. When I pass that big moron, I spit on him, and I see he's got a hard. That jerk! He was watchin' me and the kid instead of keepin' an eye out for that guard.

"It's a funny thing about some of them guards. You'd think he'd go for the kid, but, no, he hustled me down to the dispensary and started in before he turned on the light."

"Did ya get two desserts?" Nickie wanted to know.

"What you think?"

"Yeah, what were they?"

"Bread puddin'."

"They never gave nothin' in reform. They just said, 'You're lucky you're livin'.' "

"Did they get you?" Gunner asked.

"Nah, none tried."

"Well, that night when I got back to my cell," Gunner said, going on with his story, eager to end it, "that brute goof says to me, 'Thanks, pal.' He says it real big-like. Then I knew he was goofy for real. I didn't do nothin' for him but spit on him. 'Thanks for what?' I say. And he says, 'For warmin' up the kid.' "

As Gunner talked, he flicked the dirt from under his fingernails with the knife. Nickie thought of the knife instead of the story. He wondered how far in it would go if it were driven into his chest up to the hilt. Six inches, he decided. The thought shrank his insides, but his outsides were calm and unaffected, frozen in place.

The commotion, the giggles and gasps which escaped from the boxer's room ran down the hall into Nickie's room. As he listened to the noise in the distance, he rolled over on his stomach, and an urgent desire to dream pressed in upon him.

Gunner rocked faster.

"You're a funny guy," Gunner told him.

"What you mean?" Nickie asked, grateful for anything which would crowd out the noisy reality in the distance.

"Always on that bed. You don't sleep on it or use it for nothin', but you're always on it."

"You want me to sit on the floor?"

"You want a fist?"

"Naw, why?"

"Keep smartin' off, and you'll get one."

"I ain't smartin' off," Nickie said. "What you so touchy about?"

"Nothin'. Just keep wisin' off, and you're goin' to get it."

"Aw."

"You heard me!"

Nickie checked to see if he could spot the source of the irritation. He could. Gunner had his legs spread. A taut crease in his pants extended down one leg to his knee. He squirmed in the rocker.

"You want to fight or fuck?" Nickie asked.

"Both," Gunner smiled. "I like to fight when I fuck."

Nickie smiled weakly.

"Strip," Gunner ordered.

"I was just kiddin'," Nickie confessed.

"I'm not. I think you never had it before."

"I don't like it," Nickie added hurriedly.

"How you know if you never?"

"I just know. I don't need to find out."

"You're talkin' gas. What's a matter, you selfish? Can't ya help a guy out?"

"Get some free rent off the landlady," Nickie suggested.

"I couldn't make a dent in that hog fat."

Nickie laughed in spurts. He put stops on his laughter, but the laughs gushed over the stops. Then he held his breath, but that, too, was an ineffective dam.

"I don't want to," Nickie whined.

"You don't, and I'll give ya a cut the length of your front." Gunner slashed the air with his knife to demonstrate. "I'm slippin'. Sleepin' with a virg and didn't know it. I told you I was partial to fresh meat."

"Aw, come on," Nickie coaxed, "let's have a dart game with your knife. See who can stick it in the door the most times."

"You still achin' for a cut?"

Nickie sat up on the bed, threw his legs over the side, and fumbled with the buttons on his shirt.

After, Nickie sat on the bed. His nonchalance was restricted to his exterior, and only there in a shrug.

"I told ya I didn't like it," he said.

"Ya never do the first time," Gunner explained. "Did I ever tell ya about my first time?"

"Naw, I don't wanna hear." Nickie didn't want to hear anything. He wanted a calm reality which would set an example for his chaotic insides.

"Well," Gunner began, ignoring Nickie's request, "I was in junior high, and this creep of an English teacher calls me in after class and

tells me I'm gonna flunk. I told him I didn't care. 'So what?' I says.
He gives me a spiel about how I can keep the red mark off my record,
if I want, 'cause I act older than I am. Get that! Then he gets up from
his desk, and I see somethin' I ain't never seen before: a hard. He tells
me he can fix things up if I let him put his penis in my rectum. How
you like that? He didn't even know how to say prick. So, he takes me
in the cloakroom, and I fix up my English grade. Next year it was
Current Events."

Gunner spent more and more time away from the room. He
patronized the local grocery and picked out some crackers and
cheese in the mornings, and in the evenings he brought up quarts of
beer.

The retired life became more attractive to Nickie. Drunk, the
nights went faster. The beer lubricated his mind, and the many
conquests which would be his with money lay, in full view, on the
periphery of his mind, and they advanced toward the front of his
mind when they were set in motion by the catalyst which was beer.

One night, after Gunner had polished off his quart of beer and had pushed aside a half-empty jar of cheese, pineapple-pimento it was, he started talking about the wrestler.

"You know that wrassler?"

"Yeah," Nickie said dryly, "is he?"

"He is. Like a three-dollar bill."

"How you know?" Nickie asked, again dryly. He wasn't interested in the blond Polack bastard, whose folds of skin, around his midriff and at the back of his neck, reminded Nickie of a rhinoceros. Nickie wanted to keep his reality in motion in order to discourage thought, so he encouraged Gunner to talk.

"That wrassler! He loves it. Lets you in from the front."

"What 'bout the boxer?" Nickie asked. He asked in a disinterested tone, but he gave his interest away by stuttering on the -er, prolonging it as if he were reluctant to let go.

"The boxer, too. Let me tell you how I found out. That's why I struck up with the wrassler, only went one time, just so I could find out 'bout the boxer. I had the wrassler goin', beggin' me to hurry, when I asks him, 'I bet you been in that boxer 'cross the hall.' I buttered him up first, conned him good by askin', 'God, what you got in there?' And that's how I found out. 'Yeah,' he says, 'I been there, when he ain't payin' his rent.'"

While Gunner was out on errands, Nickie hung around the upstairs hallway, usually around noon, when the boxer returned from the gym. When the wrestler went down for his sun, Nickie had his feet out of the way. The wrestler didn't speak. Nickie didn't speak. The boxer didn't speak either, until—

"Man, you must got it easy," he said, passing his hand through his hair in a gesture of wonder, dumb wonder. The hand dispelled a visible odor of sweat.

"I work nights," Nickie told him as casually as he could.

"Me, too," the boxer said, proudly. "Sometimes five seconds, sometimes three rounds. Depends. Nice racket, huh?"

"Yeah," Nickie said, not looking up, but he did look across, and he saw the black hair on the boxer's legs, that hair which curled out of his sweat socks.

Distracted by a commotion, the boxer turned his head and looked down the stairwell. Nickie fixed his gaze on the boxer's profile and saw the boxer's eyebrow as the unruly half of a hairy ellipse.

"That slut," the boxer said, smiling half-assedly. "She's tryin' to talk her old man into a nap."

The hot rays of the boxer's smile melted Nickie's armor of calm. Nickie drove the point of his stare into a rosebud in the carpet in order to regroup his forces against the boxer's smile, but, when the boxer put his foot on the step, Nickie's forces were routed by the perfect ninety-degree angle which the bent leg formed. As the boxer leaned forward, the vise behind his knee closed. It was a powerful fulcrum, and the weight of his thigh, or the scream of his thigh, echoed in Nickie's gut, liquefying his viscera. Something was burning, for he smelled the odor of heated rubber.

Nickie looked into the boxer's eyes in an act of formal surrender. He saw only doors in the boxer's head which were swung wide with welcome and had gone soft with hope.

The boxer smelled his armpits.

"I gotta take a bath," he said. "If you ain't doin' nothin', why don't you stop by the room? We can jaw. That is, if you ain't doin' nothin'."

He looked away when he said it, and Nickie looked away when he answered it.

"Maybe I might," Nickie said.

"Go in and flop. I'll be done in a minute."

Nickie watched the boxer as he disappeared down the hall. His heavy shoulders moved in opposition to the sway of his hips. Nickie thought, when he walked, he waddled. As the image of the boxer filtered through Nickie's brain, it turned feminine. His mind had deceived him into believing that the walk was something other than that which was clearly visible. The extensive movement of the boxer's hips from side to side and other minor things, if seized upon, could build a case for femininity around the boxer's walk, but the interpretation of evidence was only a vaporous thought in Nickie's head, which was made dense by his own desire.

Desire was stifled. An inkling of want did stir within him, but it could not be labeled desire. He mistook the feeling for friendship since he knew the sensation would never rise to the pitch of desire, but he suspected that it would sustain its low level warmth over a long period of time.

"He's a dumb, good-looking dope," Nickie said as he grabbed for that point which lies outside the self, which few can reach and where fewer still can remain for long. Then he fell back into the shell of self. He fell gently, willingly, not breaking the shell. He slid, and now he spoke from the other side of his mouth. "But he's got something. I wish to hell I knew what it was."

Half of Nickie walked into the boxer's room and sat down in the proverbial rocker with which every room was furnished. Half of Nickie waited for the other half.

The other half of Nickie entered the room, dripping water. His body was too big for an ordinary bath towel, and dampness had blackened his maroon bathrobe in spots.

The boxer didn't speak, but his animal's body spoke for him. He stepped back from the dresser and shadow boxed with his image in the mirror. His left jab and right cross forced his bathrobe into a rhythmic dance.

Nickie stared at various objects in the room, but none of them detained his gaze.

The boxer took off his robe and threw it on the bed with positive gestures. He grabbed a towel and rubbed his back briskly, rhumbastyle. Then he bent over the bed and fumbled with the tassel on his robe. He arranged it coyly, obscenely.

Nickie thought. He's killin' time so he won't have to get dressed. Everything about him said yes. Now!

Nickie leaped from the rocker and charged. He was about to apply a hug when the quick-footed boxer sidestepped, and Nickie landed face down on the bed. With the same fleet movement the boxer fell on top of Nickie and pinned him to the bed. The boxer was a silent, dead weight for some time. That time ended when he started his hips in an easy, forward motion.

Nickie was numb. He felt as if he had stacked a deck of cards only to discover, after he had looked at his hand, that the gods had intervened and had reshuffled the deck on the sly.

"Do ya like it?" the boxer asked.

And, strangely enough, Nickie did.

Their happiness clamored. They were aware of nothing but the sharp focus, the pin-pointed desire which throbbed in their loins.

The boxer promised the world. He said he had a bid for some exhibition bouts around the country. That meant easy dough, but he didn't want to go alone. Did Nickie want to go with him?

He did. The boxer's shadow loomed over Nickie's body and gave a shape to his feelings, a direction to his destiny.

The strains of happiness, now as minutely orchestrated as a symphony, forced their reality to recede to a point where both exclaimed, "I've been away." The clamor was the sound of trumpets, interspersed with lyric violins, quivering high notes without a trace of dissonance, until a bassoon rose above the ecstatic clamor.

"I thought so!" shrieked the bassoon, rasped the landlady. "Been here a week and queered every guy on the place." She swung her broom wildly. "I knew you were queer the minute I saw ya. Ya never said nothin', just snuck around and did your dirty work."

"Get out of here 'fore I punch ya silly," the boxer yelled.

"You're the ones gettin' out. If you and that bathrobe ain't out of here by nightfall, I'm callin' the cops."

"Don't worry!"

"That goes for Lady Godiva there, too."

The landlady slammed the door. The boxer resumed, and in no time at all he reached the climax of the symphony by spouting a galaxy of stars.

After Nickie shimmied down the gallery pole, the boxer tossed him a beat-up suitcase. A suitcase and everything, Nickie thought. Everything was three pairs of shoes: tennis shoes and canvas shoes and moccasins for dress up. He couldn't go wrong with a deal like that, so he didn't mind leaving the rooming house. The place was nothing but a trap, anyway, but when he sneaked under the kitchen window and smelled the steam from a pot of seething spaghetti, he wished he had wormed his way on the good side of the landlady, whatever side that was, and had been invited down for a feed.

I suppose what became of Gunner is of little interest, or the ensuing events which terminated his stay at the rooming house, but the events took place that same afternoon, later. Gunner spoke about them at the club, still later, and even the distance of time, memory, did not lessen the immediacy of the horror.

When Gunner returned to the room and discovered that Nickie had left with the boxer (the landlady was far from silent on the subject or from restraining herself from making insinuations in general about her roomers), Gunner sat in the rocker and slashed the cheesecloth curtains with his knife.

The wrestler was no less enraged. Whether it was the disappearance of the boxer, the possible threat of inheriting the free rent privilege, the abundance of Italians on the premises which ruffled his nationalistic pride, the presence of desire, or the feeling of having been wronged by Gunner which prompted the wrestler's rage, I suppose we shall never know, but we do know that he was motivated quite beyond the minimum requirements for drastic acts.

Anyway, he marched toward Gunner's room and shoved the door open with a determined fist. The door swung open and closed with a force which equaled the wrestler's determination, so he shoved it again. So fierce was the second blow that the doorknob stuck in the wall and left the room permanently exposed.

"What's the idea, Polack?" Gunner asked.

"You ain't been in to pay up," the wrestler growled. He presented the first reason which pressed to the foreground of his mind.

"What ya mean, Polack?"

"You owe me a piece of ass."

"That ain't a nice way to talk now, is it?" Gunner's words curled out of his smile. "You ain't been brought up right, Polack."

"Bare it, Dago," the wrestler ordered.

Gunner rocked slower and flashed his knife.

"I ain't afraid of your knife, Dago. I'll take it and cut off your balls. It's an old Polish pastime."

"You're talkin' kinda big for a Polack, ain't ya, Polack?"

The wrestler lunged as Gunner sprang to his feet and readied his knife. The wrestler faked with his fist and kicked Gunner's hand with his foot. The knife flew out of Gunner's hand and stuck in the ceiling. Then the wrestler tore off Gunner's shirt. When Gunner resisted, the wrestler planted bruises on his face and arms until the last blow knocked Gunner into the corner.

The deliciousness of the violence awoke desire in the wrestler. When such violence aroused him during prolonged, overheated falls in the ring, he was glad he had worn a mercilessly iron-clad jockstrap which drove his elongating penis into his ass instead of allowing it to rise into public view, but now he was proud of the synonyms, might and desire, and he was also proud of the symptoms, so he sported them openly, only now they were concentrated in the singular. He waved it like an unadorned flagpole which had been caught in a stiff wind.

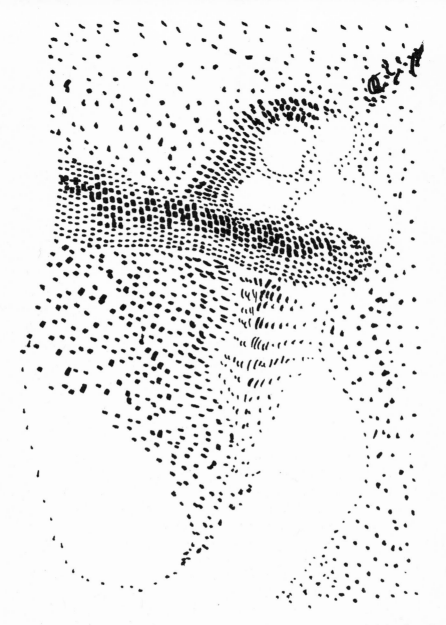

"Come out of that corner on your knees," the wrestler ordered with flames in his voice, "with your mouth open."

Gunner crawled out of the corner on his knees with his mouth open.

Then the wrestler lowered his voice. He replaced the heated cry of battle with the muted call of victory. "Don't need no vaseline with you greasy guinea bastards."

WILLIAM TALSMAN

In May, 1949, I wrote the following letter to Huntington Cairns of the National Gallery of Art in Washington, D.C., concerning The Gaudy Image *and problems of censorship. For many years Mr. Cairns acted as private adviser for literary matters to the U.S. Customs Administration:*

We have recently published a book entitled The Gaudy Image *by a young American writer, who writes under the pseudonym of William Talsman. The theme of this book is very frankly homosexual and I would even say it is the first book with this theme which is completely uninhibited and straightforward in style and treatment. There is no denying that Talsman was influenced by Jean Genet or rather that Genet's example helped him to achieve free expression. However, this book may be judged from a purely moral and conventional point of view. It is not only very sincere but well written and a valuable work of art.*

We sent several copies to the author immediately upon publication at the end of March—some via airmail; they did not reach him. We sent one copy to the Library of Congress for registration of "ad interim" copyright and they acknowledged receipt to the author. We sent three copies via registered mail to Professor Brom Weber at the University of Minnesota for transmission to the author, who used to be his student. At the time of writing, Professor Weber has not received the books and I can only assume they were stopped by Customs and that the delay in notifying the addressee must be due to the fact that the book is still under examination. I wonder whether you have had to intervene at this stage and take the liberty of insisting that this book, in spite of its theme, cannot be classed as pornography. I need not stress the obvious fact that the problem of censorship is rapidly progressing towards an infinitely more liberal and intelligent notion of what is morally damageable and artistically permissible. A negative verdict against this first book by a young American author would only have one result: it would relegate him to the class of suspect or outlaw writers and we know perfectly well what this situation leads to. In appealing to you, I am, of course, aware that your action and appreciation have always been motivated by the most balanced attitude towards this problem. May I ask you to give the matter your personal consideration?

Justine

Marquis de Sade

ere my cruel situation to permit me to amuse you for an instant, Madame, when I must think of nothing but gaining your compassion, I should dare describe some of the symptoms of avarice I witnessed while in that house; but a catastrophe so terrible for me was awaiting me during my second year there that it is by no means easy to linger entertaining details before making you acquainted with my miseries.

Nevertheless, you will know, Madame, that, for light in Monsieur du Harpin's apartment, there was never any but what he got from the street lamp which, happily, was placed opposite his room; never did Monsieur or Madame use linen; what I washed was hoarded away, it was never touched; on the sleeves of Monsieur's coat, as well as upon Madame's dress, were old gauntlet cuffs sewn over the material, and these I removed and washed every Saturday evening; no sheets, no towels, and that to avoid laundry expenses. Never was wine drunk in her house, clear water being, declared Madame du Harpin, the natural drink of man, the healthiest and least dangerous. Every time bread was sliced, a basket was put beneath the knife so that whatever fell would not be lost; into this container went, also, and with exactitude, all the scraps and leavings that might survive the meal, and this compound, fried up on Sunday together with a little butter, made a banquet for the day of rest; never was one to beat clothing or too energetically dust the furniture for fear of wearing it out, instead, very cautiously, one tickled about with a feather. Monsieur's shoes, and Madame's as well, were double-soled with iron, they were the same shoes that had served them on their wedding day; but a much more unusual custom was the one they had me practice once a week: there was in the apartment a rather large room whose walls were not papered; I was expected to take a knife and scrape and shave

407

away a certain quantity of plaster, and this I next passed through a fine
sieve; what resulted from this operation became the powder wherewith every morning I sprinkled Monsieur's peruke and Madame's
hair, done up in a bun. Ah! wouldst to God those had been the only
turpitudes of which this evil pair had made habits! Nothing's more
normal than the desire to conserve one's property; but what is not
normal is the desire to augment it by the accession of the property of
others. And it was not long before I perceived that it was only thus
du Harpin acquired his wealth.

Above us there lodged a solitary individual of considerable means
who was the owner of some handsome jewels, and whose belongings,
whether because of their proximity or because they had passed
through my master's hands, were very well known to him; I often
heard him express regrets to his wife over the loss of a certain gold
box worth thirty or forty *louis*, which article would infallibly have
remained his, said he, had he proceeded with greater cleverness. In
order to console himself for the sale of the said box, the good
Monsieur du Harpin projected its theft, and it was to me he entrusted
the execution of his plan.

After having delivered a long speech upon the indifference of
robbery, upon, indeed, its usefulness in the world, since it maintains
a sort of equilibrium which totally confounds the inequitabilities of
property; upon the infrequence of punishment, since out of every
twenty thieves it could be proven that not above two die on the
gallows; after having demonstrated to me, with an erudition of which
I had not dreamt Monsieur du Harpin capable, that theft was
honored throughout Greece, that several races yet acknowledge it,
favor it, and reward it for a bold deed simultaneously giving proof
of courage and skill (two virtues indispensable to a warlike nation),
after having, in a word, exalted his personal influence which would
extricate me from all embarrassments in the event I should be de-
tected, Monsieur du Harpin tendered me two lock picks, one to open
the neighbor's front door, the other his secretary within which lay
the box in question; incessantly he enjoined me to get him this box
and, in return for so important a service, I could expect, for two
years, to receive an additional crown.

"Oh Monsieur!" I exclaimed, shuddering at his proposal, "is it
possible a master dare thus corrupt his domestic! What prevents me

from turning against you the weapons you put into my hands? and what defense will you have if someday I make you the victim of your own principles?"

Du Harpin, much confused, fell back upon a lame subterfuge: what he was doing, said he, was being done with the simple intention of testing me; how fortunate that I had resisted this temptation, he added . . . how I should have been doomed had I succumbed, etc. I scoffed at this lie; but I was soon enough aware of what a mistake it had been to answer him with such asperity: malefactors do not like to find resistance in those they seek to seduce; unfortunately, there is no middle ground or median attitude when one is so unlucky as to have been approached by them: one must necessarily thereupon become either their accomplices, which is exceedingly dangerous, or their enemies, which is even more so. Had I been a little experienced, I would have quit the house forthwith, but it was already written in Heaven that every one of the honest gestures that was to emanate from me would be answered by misfortunes.

Monsieur du Harpin let almost a month drift by, that is to say, he waited until the end of my second year with him, and waited without showing the least hint of resentment at the refusal I had given him, when one evening, having just retired to my room to taste a few hours of repose, I suddenly heard my door burst open and there, not without terror, I saw Monsieur du Harpin and four soldiers of the watch standing by my bed.

"Perform your duty, Sirrah," said he to the men of the law "this wretch has stolen from me a diamond worth a thousand crowns, you will find it in her chamber or upon her person, the fact is certain."

"I have robbed you, Monsieur!" said I, sore troubled and springing from my bed, "I! Great Heaven! Who knows better than you the contrary to be true! Who should be more deeply aware than you to what point I loathe robbery and to what degree it is unthinkable I could have committed it."

But du Harpin made a great uproar to drown out my words; he continued to order perquisitions, and the miserable ring was discovered in my mattress. To evidence of this strength there was nothing to reply; I was seized instantly, pinioned, and led to prison without being able to prevail upon the authorities to listen to one word in my favor.

The trial of a misfortunate who has neither influence nor protection is conducted with dispatch in a land where virtue is thought incompatible with misery, where poverty is enough to convict the accused; there, an unjust prepossession causes it to be supposed that he who ought to have committed a crime did indeed commit it; sentiments are proportioned according to the guilty one's estate; and when once gold or titles are wanting to establish his innocence, the impossibility that he be innocent then appears self-evident.[1]

I defended myself, it did no good, in vain I furnished the best material to the lawyer whom a protocol of form required be given me for an instant or two; my employer accused me, the diamond had been discovered in my room; it was plain I had stolen it. When I wished to describe Monsieur du Harpin's awful traffic and prove that the misfortune that had struck me was naught but the fruit of his vengeance and the consequence of his eagerness to be rid of a creature who, through possession of his secret, had become his master, these pleadings were interpreted as so many recriminations, and I was informed that for twenty years Monsieur du Harpin had been known as a man of integrity, incapable of such a horror. I was transferred to the Conciergerie, where I saw myself upon the brink of having to pay with my life for having refused to participate in a crime; I was shortly to perish; only a new misdeed could save me: Providence willed that crime serve at least once as an aegis unto virtue, that crime might preserve it from the abyss which is someday going to engulf judges together with their imbecility.

I had about me a woman, probably forty years old, as celebrated for her beauty as for the variety and number of her villainies; she was called Dubois and, like the unlucky Thérèse, was on the eve of paying the capital penalty, but as to the exact form of it the judges were yet mightily perplexed: having rendered herself guilty of every imaginable crime, they found themselves virtually obliged to invent a new torture for her, or to expose her to one whence we ordinarily exempt our sex. This woman had become interested in me, criminally interested without doubt, since the basis of her feelings, as I learned afterward, was her extreme desire to make a proselyte of me.

Only two days from the time set for our execution, Dubois came to me; it was at night. She told me not to lie down to sleep, but to

---

[1] O ages yet to come! You shall no longer be witness to these horrors and infamies abounding!

stay near her side. Without attracting attention, we moved as close as we could to the prison door. "Between seven and eight," she said, "the Conciergerie will catch fire, I have seen to it; no question about it, many people will be burned; it doesn't matter, Thérèse," the evil creature went on, "the fate of others must always be as nothing to us when our own lives are at stake; well, we are going to escape from here, of that you can be sure; four men—my confederates—will join us and I guarantee you we will be free."

I have told you, Madame, that the hand of God which had just punished my innocence, employed crime to protect me; the fire began, it spread, the blaze was horrible, twenty-one persons were consumed, but we made a successful sally. The same day we reached the cottage of a poacher, an intimate friend of our band who dwelt in the forest of Bondi.

"There you are, Thérèse," Dubois says to me, "free. You may now choose the kind of life you wish, but were I to have any advice to give you, it would be to renounce the practice of virtue which, as you have noticed, is the courting of disaster; a misplaced delicacy led you to the foot of the scaffold, an appalling crime rescued you from it; have a look about and see how useful are good deeds in this world, and whether it is really worth the trouble immolating yourself for them. Thérèse, you are young and attractive, heed me, and in two years I'll have led you to a fortune; but don't suppose I am going to guide you there along the paths of virtue: when one wants to get on, my dear girl, one must stop at nothing; decide, then, we have no security in this cottage, we've got to leave in a few hours."

"Oh Madame," I said to my benefactress, "I am greatly indebted to you, and am far from wishing to disown my obligations; you saved my life; in my view, 'tis frightful the thing was achieved through a crime and, believe me, had I been the one charged to commit it, I should have preferred a thousand deaths to the anguish of participating in it; I am aware of all the dangers I risk in trusting myself to the honest sentiments which will always remain in my heart; but whatever be the thorns of virtue, Madame, I prefer them unhesitatingly and always to the perilous favors which are crime's accompaniment. There are religious principles within me which, may it please Heaven, will never desert me; if Providence renders difficult my career in life, 'tis in order to compensate me in a better world. That hope is my consolation, it sweetens my griefs, it soothes me in my sufferings, it fortifies me in distress, and causes me confidently to face all the ills it pleases God to visit upon me. That joy should straightway be extinguished in my soul were I perchance to besmirch it with crimes, and together with the fear of chastisements in this world I should have the dolorous anticipation of torments in the next, which would not for one instant procure me the tranquillity I thirst after."

"Those are absurd doctrines which will have you on the dung heap in no time, my girl," said Dubois with a frown; "believe me: forget God's justice, His future punishments and rewards, the lot of those platitudes lead us nowhere but to death from starvation. O Thérèse, the callousness of the Rich legitimates the bad conduct of the Poor; let them open their purse to our needs, let humaneness reign in their hearts and virtues will take root in ours; but as long as our misfortune, our patient endurance of it, our good faith, our abjection only serves to double the weight of our chains, our crimes will be their doing, and we will be fools indeed to abstain from them when they can lessen the yoke wherewith their cruelty bears us down. Nature has caused us all to be equals born, Thérèse; if fate is pleased to upset that primary scheme of the general law, it is up to us to correct its caprices and through our skill to repair the usurpations of the strongest. I love to hear these rich ones, these titled ones, these magistrates and these priests, I love to see them preach virtue to us. It is not very difficult to forswear theft when one has three or four times what one needs to live; it is not very necessary to plot murder when one is surrounded by nothing but adulators and thralls unto whom one's will is law; nor is it very hard to be temperate and sober when one has the most succulent dainties constantly within one's reach; they can well contrive to be sincere when there is never any apparent advantage in falsehood. . . . But we, Thérèse, we whom the barbaric Providence you are mad enough to idolize, has condemned to slink in the dust of humiliation as doth the serpent in grass, we who are beheld with disdain only because we are poor, who are tyrannized because we are weak; we, who must quench our thirst with gall and who, wherever we go, tread on the thistle always, you would have us shun crime when its hand alone opens up unto us the door to life, maintains us in it, and is our only protection when our life is threatened; you would have it that, degraded and in perpetual abjection, while this class dominating us has to itself all the blessings of fortune, we reserve for ourselves naught but pain, beatings, suffering, nothing but want and tears, brandings and the gibbet. No, no, Thérèse, no; either this Providence you reverence is made only for our scorn, or the world we see about us is not at all what Providence would have it. Become better acquainted with your Providence, my child, and be convinced that as soon as it places us in a situation where evil becomes necessary, and while at the same time it leaves us the possibility of doing it, this evil harmonizes quite as well with its decrees as does good, and Providence gains as much by the one as by the other; the state in which she has created us is equality: he who disturbs is no more guilty than he who seeks to re-establish the balance; both act in accordance with received impulses, both have to obey those impulses and enjoy them."

I must avow that if ever I was shaken 'twas by this clever woman's seductions; but a yet stronger voice, that of my heart to which I gave heed, combatted her sophistries; I declared to Dubois that I was determined never to allow myself to be corrupted. "Very well!" she replied, "become what you wish, I abandon you to your sorry fate; but if ever you get yourself hanged, which is an end you cannot avoid, thanks to the fatality which inevitably saves the criminal by sacrificing the virtuous, at least remember before dying never to mention us."

While we were arguing thus, Dubois' four companions were drinking with the poacher, and as wine disposes the malefactor's heart to new crimes and causes him to forget his old, our bandits no sooner learned of my resolution than, unable to make me their accomplice, they decided to make me their victim; their principles, their manners, the dark retreat we were in, the security they thought they enjoyed, their drunkenness, my age, my innocence—everything encouraged them. They get up from table, they confer in whispers, they consult Dubois, doings whose lugubrious mystery makes me shiver with horror, and at last there comes an order to ready myself there and then to satisfy the desires of each of the four; if I go to it cheerfully, each will give me a crown to help me along my way; if they must employ violence, the thing will be done all the same; but the better to guard their secret, once finished with me they will stab me, and will bury me at the foot of yonder tree.

I need not paint the effect this cruel proposition had upon me. Madame, you will have no difficulty understanding that I sank to my knees before Dubois, I besought her a second time to be my protectress: the low creature did but laugh at my tears:

"Oh by God!" quoth she, "here's an unhappy little one. What! you shudder before the obligation to serve four fine big boys one after another? Listen to me," she added, after some reflection, "my sway over these dear lads is sufficiently great for me to obtain a reprieve for you upon condition you render yourself worthy of it."

"Alas! Madame, what must I do?" I cried through my tears; "command me; I am ready."

"Join us, throw in your lot with us, and commit the same deeds, without show of the least repugnance; either that, or I cannot save you from the rest." I did not think myself in a position to hesitate; by accepting this cruel condition I exposed myself to further dangers, to be sure, but they were the less immediate; perhaps I might be able to avoid them, whereas nothing could save me from those with which I was actually menaced.

"I will go everywhere with you, Madame," was my prompt answer to Dubois, "everywhere, I promise you; shield me from the fury of these men and I shall never leave your side while I live."

"Children," Dubois said to the four bandits, "this girl is one of the company, I am taking her into it; I ask you to do her no ill, don't put her stomach off the *métier* during her first days in it; you see how useful her age and face can be to us: let's employ them to our advantage rather than sacrifice them to our pleasures."

But such is the degree of energy in man's passions nothing can subdue them. The persons I was dealing with were in no state to heed reason: all four surrounded me, devoured me with their fiery glances, menaced me in a still more terrible manner; they were about to lay hands on me, I was about to become their victim.

"She has got to go through with it," one of them declared, "it's too late for discussion: was she not told she must give proof of virtues in order to be admitted into a band of thieves? and once a little used, won't she be quite as serviceable as she is while a virgin?"

I am edulcorating their expressions, you understand, Madame, I am sweetening the scene itself; alas! their obscenities were such that your modesty might suffer at least as much from beholding them unadorned as did my shyness.

A defenseless and trembling victim, I shuddered; I had barely strength to breathe; kneeling before the quartet, I raised my feeble arms as much to supplicate the men as to melt Dubois' heart. . . .

"An instant," said one who went by the name of Coeur-de-fer and appeared to be the band's chief, a man of thirty-six years, of a bull's strength and bearing the face of a satyr; "one moment, friends: it may be possible to satisfy everyone concerned; since this little girl's virtue is so precious to her and since, as Dubois states it very well, this quality otherwise put into action could become worth something to us, let's leave it to her; but we have got to be appeased; our mood is warm, Dubois, and in the state we are in, d'ye know, we might perhaps cut your own throat if you were to stand between us and our pleasures; let's have Thérèse instantly strip as naked as the day she came into the world, and next let's have her adopt one after the other all the positions we are pleased to call for, and meanwhile Dubois will sate our hungers, we'll burn our incense upon the altar's entrance to which this creature refuses us."

"Strip naked!" I exclaimed, "Oh Heaven, what is it thou doth require of me? When I shall have delivered myself thus to your eyes, who will be able to answer for me...."

But Coeur-de-fer, who seemed in no humor either to grant me more or to suspend his desires, burst out with an oath and struck me in a manner so brutal that I saw full well compliance was my last resort. He put himself in Dubois' hands, she having been put by his in a disorder more or less the equivalent of mine and, as soon as I was as he desired me to be, having made me crouch down upon all fours so that I resembled a beast, Dubois took in hand a very monstrous object and led it to the peristiles of first one and then the other of Nature's altars, and under her guidance the blows it delivered to me here and there were like those of a battering ram thundering at the gates of a besieged town in olden days. The shock of the initial assault drove me back; enraged, Coeur-de-fer threatened me with harsher treatments were I to retreat from these; Dubois is instructed to redouble her efforts, one of the libertines grasps my shoulders and prevents me from staggering before the concussions: they become so fierce I am in blood and am able to avoid not a one.

"Indeed," stammers Coeur-de-fer, "in her place I'd prefer to open the doors rather than see them ruined this way, but she won't have it, and we're not far from the capitulation.... Vigorously ... vigorously, Dubois..."

And the explosive eruption of this debauchee's flames, almost as violent as a stroke of lightning, flickers and dies upon ramparts ravaged without being breached.

The second had me kneel between his legs and while Dubois administered to him as she had to the other, two enterprises absorbed his entire attention: sometimes he slapped, powerfully but in a very nervous manner, either my cheeks or my breasts; sometimes his impure mouth fell to sucking mine. In an instant my face turned purple, my chest red. . . . I was in pain, I begged him to spare me, tears leapt from my eyes; they roused him, he accelerated his activities; he bit my tongue, and the two strawberries on my breasts were so bruised that I slipped backward, but was kept from falling. They thrust me toward him, I was everywhere more furiously harassed, and his ecstasy supervened. . . .

The third bade me mount upon and straddle two somewhat separated chairs and, seating himself betwixt them, excited by Dubois, lying in his arms, he had me bend until his mouth was directly below the temple of Nature; never will you imagine, Madame, what this obscene mortal took it into his head to do; willy-nilly, I was obliged to satisfy his every need. . . . Just Heaven! what man, no matter how depraved, can taste an instant of pleasure in such things. . . . I did what he wished, inundated him, and my complete submission procured this foul man an intoxication of which he was incapable without this infamy.

The fourth attached strings to all my parts to which it was possible to tie them, he held the ends in his hand and sat down seven or eight feet from my body; Dubois' touches and kisses excited him prodigiously; I was standing erect: 'twas by sharp tugs now on this string, now on some other that the savage irritated his pleasures; I swayed, I lost balance again and again, he flew into an ecstasy each time I tottered; finally, he pulled all the cords at once, I fell to the floor in front of him: such was his design: and my forehead, my breast, my cheeks received the proofs of a delirium he owed to none but this mania.

That is what I suffered Madame, but at least my honor was respected even though my modesty assuredly was not. Their calm restored, the bandits spoke of regaining the road, and that same night we reached Tremblai with the intention of approaching the woods of Chantilly, where it was thought a few good prizes might be awaiting us.

Nothing equaled my despair at being obliged to accompany

such persons, and I was only determined to part with them as soon as I could do so without risk. The following day we lay hard by Louvres, sleeping under haystacks; I felt in need of Dubois' support and wanted to pass the night by her side; but it seemed she had planned to employ it otherwise than protecting my virtue from the attacks I dreaded; three of the thieves surrounded her and before my very eyes the abominable creature gave herself to all three simultaneously. The fourth approached me; it was the captain. "Lovely Thérèse," said he, "I hope you shall not refuse me at least the pleasure of spending the night with you?" and as he perceived my extreme unwillingness, "fear not," he went on; "we'll have a chat together, and I will attempt nothing without your consent."

"O Thérèse," cried he, folding me in his arms, " 'tis all foolishness, don't you know, to be so pretentious with us. Why are you concerned to guard your purity in our midst? Even were we to agree to respect it, could it be compatible with the interests of the band? No need to hide it from you, my dear; for when we settle down in cities, we count upon your charms to snare us some dupes."

"Why, Monsieur," I replied, "since it is certain I should prefer death to these horrors, of what use can I be to you, and why do you oppose my flight?"

"We certainly do oppose it, my lass," Coeur-de-fer rejoined, "you must serve either our pleasures or our interests; your poverty imposes the yoke upon you, and you have got to adapt to it. But Thérèse, and well you know it, there is nothing in this world that cannot be somehow arranged: so listen to me, and accept the management of your own fate: agree to live with me, dear girl, consent to belong to me and be properly my own, and I will spare you the baneful role for which you are destined."

"I, Sir, I become the mistress of a———"

"Say the word, Thérèse, out with it: a scoundrel, eh? Oh, I admit it, but I have no other titles to offer you; that our sort does not marry, you are doubtless well aware: marriage is one of the sacraments, Thérèse, and full of an undiscriminating contempt for them all, with none do we ever bother. However, be a little reasonable; that sooner or later you lose what is so dear to you is an indispensable necessity, hence would it not be better to sacrifice it to a single man who thereupon will become your support and protector, is that not better, I say, than to be prostituted to everyone?"

"But why must it be," I replied, "that I have no other alternative?"

"Because, Thérèse, we have got you, and because the stronger is always the better reason; La Fontaine made the remark ages ago. Truthfully," he continued rapidly, "is it not a ridiculous extravagance to assign, as you do, such a great value to the most futile of all things? How can a girl be so dull-witted as to believe that virtue may depend upon the somewhat greater or lesser diameter of one of her physical parts? What difference does it make to God or man whether this part be intact or tampered with? I will go further: it being the intention of Nature that each individual fulfill on this earth all of the purposes for which he has been formed, and women existing only to provide pleasure for men, it is plainly to outrage her thus to resist the intention she has in your regard. It is to wish to be a creature useless in this world and consequently one contemptible. This chimerical propriety, which they have had the absurdity to present to you as a virtue and which, since infancy, far from being useful to Nature and society, is an obvious defiance of the one and the other, this propriety, I say, is no more than a reprehensible stubbornness of which a person as mettlesome and full of intelligence as you should not wish to be culpable. No matter; continue to hear me out, dear girl, I am going to prove my desire to please you and to respect your weakness. I will not by any means touch that phantom, Thérèse, whose possession causes all your delight; a girl has more than one favor to give, and one can offer to Venus in many a temple; I will be content with the most mediocre; you know, my dear, near the Cyprean altar, there is situate an obscure grot into whose solitude Love retires, the more energetically to seduce us: such will be the altar where I will burn my incense; no disadvantages there, Thérèse; if pregnancies affright you, 'tis not in this manner they can come about, never will your pretty figure be deformed this way; the maidenhead so cherished by you will be preserved unimpaired, and whatever be the use to which you decide to put it, you can propose it unattainted. Nothing can betray a girl from this quarter, however rude or multiple the attacks may be; as soon as the bee has left off sucking the pollen, the rose's calix closes shut again; one would never imagine it had been opened. There exist girls who have known ten years of pleasure this way, even with several men, women who were just as much married as anyone else after it all, and on their wedding nights they proved quite as virgin as could be wished. How many fathers, what a multitude of brothers have thuswise abused their daughters and sisters without the latter having become on that account any the less worthy of a later hymeneal sacrifice! How many confessors have not employed the same route to satisfaction, without parents experiencing the mildest disquiet; in one word, 'tis the mystery's asylum, 'tis there where it connects itself with love by ties of prudence. . . . Need I to tell you further, Thérèse, that although this is the most secret temple it is howbeit the most voluptuous; what is necessary to happiness is found nowhere else, and that easy vastness native to the adjacent aperture falls far short of having the piquant charms of a locale into which one does not enter without effort, where one takes up one's abode only at the price of some trouble; women themselves reap an advantage from it, and those whom reason compels to know this variety of pleasure, never pine after the others. Try it, Thérèse, try, and we shall both be contented."

"Oh Monsieur," I replied, "I have no experience of the thing; but I have heard it said that this perversion you recommend outrages women in a yet more sensitive manner. . . . It more grievously offends Nature. The hand of Heaven takes its vengeance upon it in this world, Sodom provides the example."

"What innocence, my dear, what childishness," the libertine retorted; "who ever told you such a thing? Yet a little more attention, Thérèse, let me proceed to rectify your ideas.

"The wasting of the seed destined to perpetuate the human species, dear girl, is the only crime which can exist—such is the hypothesis; according to it, this seed is put in us for the sole purpose of reproduction, and if that were true I would grant you that diverting it is an offense. But once it is demonstrated that her situating this semen in our loins is by no means enough to warrant supposing that Nature's purpose is to have all of it employed for reproduction, what then does it matter, Thérèse, whether it be spilled in one place or in another? Does the man who diverts it perform a greater evil than Nature who does not employ all of it? Now, do not those natural losses, which we can imitate if we please, occur in an abundance of instances? Our very ability to provoke them, firstly, is an initial proof that they do not offend Nature in the slightest. It would be contrary to all the equity and profound wisdom we everywhere recognize in her laws for them to permit what might affront her; secondly, those

losses occur a hundred hundred million times every day, and she in-
stigates them herself; nocturnal pollutions, the inutility of semen
during the periods of woman's pregnancy, are they not authorized
by her laws, enjoined by them, and do they not prove that, very
little concerned for what may result from this liquid to which we so
foolishly attach a disproportionate value, she permits us its waste with
the same indifference she herself causes it every day to be wasted; she
tolerates reproduction, yes, but much is wanting to prove reproduction is one of her intentions; she lets us go ahead with our repro-
ducing, to be sure, but it being no more to her advantage than our
abstaining therefrom, the choice we happen to make is as one to her.
Is it not clear that leaving us the power to create, not to create, or to
destroy, we will not delight her at all or disappoint her any more by
adopting toward the one or the other the attitude which suits us best;
and what could be more self-evident than that the course we choose,
being but the result of her power over us and the influence upon us of
her actions, will far more surely please than it will risk offending her.
Ah, Thérèse! believe me, Nature frets very little over those mysteries
we are great enough fools to turn into worship of her. Whatever be
the temple at which one sacrifices, immediately she allows incense to
be burned there, one can be sure the homage offends her in no wise;
refusals to produce, waste of the semen employed in production, the
obliteration of that seed when it has germinated, the annihilation of
that germ even long after its formation, all those, Thérèse, are imaginary crimes which are of no interest to Nature and at which she
scoffs, as she does at all the rest of our institutions which offend more
often than they serve her."

Coeur-de-fer waxed warm while expounding his perfidious max-
ims, and I soon beheld him again in the state which had so terrified me
the night before; in order to give his lesson additional impact, he
wished instantly to join practice to precept; and, my resistances notwithstanding, his hands strayed toward the altar into which the traitor
wanted to penetrate. . . . Must I declare, Madame, that, blinded by the
wicked man's seductions; content, by yielding a little, to save what
seemed the more essential; reflecting neither upon his casuistries'
illogicalities nor upon what I was myself about to risk, since the
dishonest fellow, possessing gigantesque proportions, had not even
the possibility to see a woman in the most permissible place and since,
urged on by his native perversity, he most assuredly had no object

but to maim me; my eyes, as I say, perfectly blind to all that, I was
going to abandon myself and become criminal through virtue; my
opposition was weakening; already master of the throne, the insolent
conqueror concentrated all his energies in order to establish himself
upon it; and then there was heard the sound of a carriage moving
along the highway. Upon the instant, Coeur-de-fer forsakes his
pleasures for his duties; he assembles his followers and flies to new
crimes.

Rodin was forty years of age, dark-haired, with shaggy eyebrows, a sparkling bright eye; there was about him what bespoke
strength and health but, at the same time, libertinage. In wealth he
was risen far above his native station, possessing from ten to twelve
thousand pounds a year; owing to which, if Rodin practiced his
surgical art, it was not out of necessity, but out of taste; he had a very
attractive house in Saint Marcel which, since the death of his wife
two years previously, he shared with two girls, who were his servants,
and with another, who was his own daughter. This young person,
Rosalie by name, had just reached her fourteenth year; in her were
gathered all the charms most capable of exciting admiration: the
figure of a nymph, an oval face, clear, lovely, extraordinarily ani-

mated, delicate pretty features, very piquant as well, the prettiest mouth possible, very large dark eyes, soulful and full of feeling, chestnut-brown hair falling to below her waist, skin of an incredible whiteness . . . aglow, smooth, already the most handsome breasts in all the world, and, furthermore, wit, vivacity, and one of the most beautiful souls Nature has yet created. With respect to the companions with whom I was to serve in this household, they were two peasant girls: one of them was a governess, the other the cook. She who held the first post could have been twenty-five, the other eighteen or twenty, and both were extremely attractive; their looks suggested a deliberate choice, and this in turn caused the birth of some suspicions as to why Rodin was pleased to accommodate me. What need has he of a third woman? I asked myself, and why does he wish them all to be pretty? Assuredly, I continued, there is something in all this that little conforms with the regular manners from which I wish never to stray; we'll see.

In consequence, I besought Monsieur Rodin to allow me to extend my convalescence at his home for yet another week, declaring that, at the end of this time, he would have my reply to what he had very kindly proposed.

I profited from this interval by attaching myself more closely to Rosalie, determined to establish myself in her father's house only if there should prove to be nothing about it whence I might be obliged to take umbrage. With these designs, I cast appraising glances in every direction, and, on the following day, I noticed that this man enjoyed an arrangement which straightway provoked in me furious doubts concerning his behavior.

Monsieur Rodin kept a school for children of both sexes; during his wife's lifetime he had obtained the required charter and they had not seen fit to deprive him of it after he had lost her. Monsieur Rodin's pupils were few but select: in all, there were but fourteen girls and fourteen boys: he never accepted them under twelve and they were always sent away upon reaching the age of sixteen; never had monarch prettier subjects than Rodin. If there were brought to him one who had some physical defect or a face that left something to be desired, he knew how to invent twenty excuses for rejecting him, all his arguments were very ingenious, they were always colored by sophistries to which no one seemed able to reply; thus, either his corps of little day-students had incomplete ranks, or the children who filled them were always charming. These youngsters did not take their meals with him, but came twice a day, from seven to eleven in the morning, from four to eight in the afternoon. If until then I had not yet seen all of this little troupe it was because, having arrived at Rodin's during the holidays, his scholars were not attending classes; toward the end of my recovery they reappeared.

Rodin himself took charge of the boys' instruction, his governess looked after that of the girls, whom he would visit as soon as he had completed his own lessons; he taught his young pupils writing, arithmetic, a little history, drawing, music, and for all that no other master but himself was employed.

I early expressed to Rosalie my astonishment that her father, while performing his functions as a doctor, could at the same time act as a schoolmaster; it struck me as odd, said I, that being able to live comfortably without exercising either the one or the other of these professions, he devoted himself to both. Rosalie, who by now had become very fond of me, fell to laughing at my remark; the manner in which she reacted to what I said only made me the more curious, and I besought her to open herself entirely to me.

"Listen," said that charming girl, speaking with all the candor proper to her age, and all the naïveté of her amiable character; "listen to me, Thérèse, I am going to tell you everything, for I see you are a well brought up girl . . . incapable of betraying the secret I am going to confide to you.

"Certainly, dear friend, my father could make ends meet without pursuing either of these two occupations; and if he pursues both at once it is because of the two motives I am going to reveal to you. He practices medicine because he has a liking for it; he takes keen pleasure in using his skill to make new discoveries, he has made so many of them, he has written so many authoritative texts based upon his investigations that he is generally acknowledged the most accomplished man in France at the present time; he worked for twenty years in Paris, and for the sake of his amusements he retired to the country. The real surgeon at Saint Marcel is someone named Rombeau whom he has taken under his tutelage and with whom he collaborates upon experiments; and now, Thérèse, would you know why he runs a school? . . . libertinage, my child, libertinage alone, a passion he carries to its extremes. My father finds in his pupils of either sex objects whose dependence submits them to his inclinations, and he exploits them. . . . But wait a moment . . . come with me," said Rosalie, "today is Friday, one of the three days during the week when he corrects those who have misbehaved; it is in this kind of punishment my father takes his pleasure; follow me, I tell you, you shall see how he behaves. Everything is visible from a closet in my room which adjoins the one where he concludes his business; let's go there without making any noise, and above all be careful not to say a word both about what I am telling you and about what you are going to witness."

It was a matter of such great importance to familiarize myself with the customs of this person who had offered me asylum, that I felt I could neglect nothing which might discover them to me; I follow hard upon Rosalie's heels, she situates me near a partition, through cracks between its ill-joined boards one can view everything going on in the neighboring room.

Hardly have we taken up our post when Rodin enters, leading a fourteen-year-old girl, blonde and as pretty as Love; the poor creature is sobbing away, all too unhappily aware of what awaits her; she comes in with moans and cries; she throws herself down before her implacable instructor, she entreats him to spare her, but his very inexorability fires the first sparks of the unbending Rodin's pleasure, his heart is already aglow, and his savage glances spring alive with an inner light. . . .

"Why, no, no," he cries, "not for one minute, this happens far too frequently, Julie, I repent my forbearance and leniency, their sole result has been repeated misconduct on your part, but could the gravity of this most recent example of it possibly allow me to show clemency, even supposing I wished to? A note passed to a boy upon entering the classroom!"

"Sir, I protest to you, I did not—"

"Ah! but I saw it, my dear, I saw it."

"Don't believe a word of it," Rosalie whispered to me, "these are trifles he invents by way of pretext; that little creature is an angel, it is because she resists him he treats her harshly."

Meanwhile, Rodin, greatly aroused, had seized the little girl's hands, tied them to a ring fitted high upon a pillar standing in the middle of the punishment room. Julie is without any defense . . . any save the lovely face languishingly turned toward her executioner, her superb hair in disarray, and the tears which inundate the most beautiful face in the world, the sweetest . . . the most interesting.

Rodin dwells upon the picture, is fired by it, he covers those supplicating eyes with a blindfold, approaches his mouth and dares kiss them, Julie sees nothing more, now able to proceed as he wishes, Rodin removes the veils of modesty, her blouse is unbuttoned, her stays untied, she is naked to the waist and yet further below. . . . What whiteness! What beauty! These are roses strewn upon lilies by the Graces' very hands . . . what being is so heartless, so cruel as to condemn to torture charms so fresh . . . so poignant? What is the monster that can seek pleasure in the depths of tears and suffering and woe? Rodin contemplates . . . his inflamed eye roves, his hands dare profane the flowers his cruelties are about to wither; all takes place directly before us, not a detail can escape us: now the libertine opens and peers into, now he closes up again those dainty features which enchant him; he offers them to us under every form, but he confines himself to these only: although the true temple of Love is within his reach, Rodin, faithful to his creed, casts not so much as a glance in that direction, to judge by his behavior, he fears even the sight of it; if the child's posture exposes those charms, he covers them over again; the slightest disturbance might upset his homage, he would have nothing distract him . . . finally, his mounting wrath exceeds all limits, at first he gives vent to it through invectives, with menaces and evil language he affrights this poor little wretch trembling before the blows wherewith she realizes she is about to be torn; Rodin is beside himself, he snatches up a cat-o'-nine-tails that has been soaking in a vat of vinegar to give the thongs tartness and sting. "Well there," says he, approaching his victim, "prepare yourself, you have got to suffer"; he swings a vigorous arm, the lashes are brought whistling down upon every inch of the body exposed to them; twenty-five strokes are applied; the tender pink rosiness of this matchless skin is in a trice run into scarlet.

Julie emits cries . . . piercing screams which rend me to the soul; tears run down from beneath her blindfold and like pearls shine upon her beautiful cheeks; whereby Rodin is made all the more furious. . . . He puts his hands upon the molested parts, touches, squeezes, worries them, seems to be readying them for further assaults; they follow fast upon the first, Rodin begins again, not a cut he bestows is unaccompanied by a curse, a menace, a reproach . . . blood appears . . . Rodin is in an ecstasy; his delight is immense as he muses upon the eloquent proofs of his ferocity. He can contain himself no longer, the most indecent state manifests his overwrought state; he fears not to bring everything out of hiding. Julie cannot see it . . . he moves to the breach and hovers there, he would greatly like to mount as a victor, he dares not, instead, he begins to tyrannize anew; Rodin whips with might and main and finally manages, thanks to the leathern stripes, to start this asylum of the Graces and of joy. . . . He no longer knows who he is or where; his delirium has attained to such a pitch the use of reason is no longer available to him; he swears, he blasphemes, he storms, nothing is exempt from his savage blows, all he can reach is treated with identical fury, but the villain pauses nevertheless, he senses the impossibility of going further without risking the loss of the powers which he must preserve for new operations.

"Dress yourself," he says to Julie, loosening her bonds and readjusting his own costume, "and if you are once again guilty of similar misconduct, bear it firmly in mind you will not get off quite so lightly."

Julie returns to her class, Rodin goes into the boys' and immediately brings back a young scholar of fifteen, lovely as the day; Rodin scolds him; doubtless more at his ease with the lad, he wheedles and kisses while lecturing him.

"You deserve to be punished," he observes, "and you are going to be."

Having uttered these words, he oversteps the last bounds of modesty with the child; for in this case, everything is of interest to him, nothing is excluded, the veils are drawn aside, everything is palpated indiscriminately; Rodin alternates threats, caresses, kisses, curses; his impious fingers attempt to generate voluptuous sentiments in the boy and, in his turn, Rodin demands identical ministrations.

"Very well," cries the satyr, spying his success, "there you are in the state I forbade. . . . I dare swear that with two more movements you'd have the impudence to spit at me. . . ."

But too sure of the titillations he has produced, the libertine advances to gather an homage, and his mouth is the temple offered to the sweet incense; his hands excite it to jet forth, he meets the spurts, devours them, and is himself ready to explode, but he wishes to persevere to the end.

"Ah, I am going to make you pay for this stupidity!" says he and gets to his feet.

He takes the youth's two hands, he clutches them tight, and

offers himself entirely to the altar at which his fury would perform
a sacrifice. He opens it, his kisses roam over it, his tongue drives deep
into it, is lost in it. Drunk with love and ferocity, Rodin mingles the
expressions and sentiments of each. . . .

"Ah, little weasel!" he cries, "I must avenge myself upon the
illusion you create in me."

The whips are picked up, Rodin flogs; clearly more excited by
the boy than he was by the vestal, his blows become both much more
powerful and far more numerous: the child bursts into tears, Rodin
is in seventh heaven, but new pleasures call, he releases the boy and
flies to other sacrifices. A little girl of thirteen is the boy's successor,
and she is followed by another youth who is in turn abandoned for a
girl; Rodin whips nine: five boys, four girls; the last is a lad of fourteen, endowed with a delicious countenance: Rodin wishes to amuse
himself, the pupil resists; out of his mind with lust, he beats him, and
the villain, losing all control of himself, hurls his flame's scummy jets
upon his young charge's injured parts, he wets him from waist to
heels; enraged at not having had strength enough to hold himself in
check until the end, our corrector releases the child very testily, and
after warning him against such tricks in the future, he sends him back
to the class: such are the words I heard, those the scenes at which I
assisted.

"Dear Heaven!" I said to Rosalie when this appalling drama
came to its end, "how is one able to surrender oneself to such excesses? How can one find pleasure in the torments one inflicts?"

"Ah," replied Rosalie, "you do not know everything. Listen,"
she said, leading me back into her room, "what you have seen has
perhaps enabled you to understand that when my father discovers
some aptitudes in his young pupils, he carries his horrors much
further, he abuses the girls in the same manner he deals with the
boys." Rosalie spoke of that criminal manner of conjugation whereof
I myself had believed I might be the victim with the brigands' captain
into whose hands I had fallen after my escape from the Conciergerie,
and by which I had been soiled by the merchant from Lyon. "By
this means," Rosalie continued, "the girls are not in the least dishonored, there are no pregnancies to fear, and nothing prevents them
from finding a husband; not a year goes by without his corrupting
nearly all the boys in this way, and at least half the other children. Of
the fourteen girls you have seen, eight have already been spoiled by

these methods, and he has taken his pleasure with nine of the boys; the two women who serve him are submitted to the same horrors. . . . O Thérèse!" Rosalie added, casting herself into my arms, "O dear girl, and I too, yes I, he seduced me in my earliest years; I was barely eleven when I became his victim . . . when, alas! I was unable to defend myself against him."

"But Mademoiselle," I interrupted, horrified, "at least Religion remained to you . . . were you unable to consult a confessor and avow everything?"

"Oh, you do not know that as he proceeds to pervert us he stifles in each of us the very seeds of belief, he forbids us all religious devotions, and, furthermore, could I have done so? he had instructed me scarcely at all. The little he had said pertaining to these matters had been motivated by the fear that my ignorance might betray his impiety. But I had never been to confession, I had not made my First Communion; so deftly did he cover all these things with ridicule and insinuate his poisonous self into even our smallest ideas, that he banished forever all their duties out of them whom he suborned; or if they are compelled by their families to fulfill their religious duties, they do so with such tepidness, with such complete indifference, that he has nothing to fear from their indiscretion; but convince yourself, Thérèse, let your own eyes persuade you," she continued, very quickly drawing me back into the closet whence we had emerged; "come hither: that room where he chastises his students is the same wherein he enjoys us; the lessons are over now, it is the hour when, warmed by the preliminaries, he is going to compensate himself for the restraint his prudence sometimes imposes upon him; go back to where you were, dear girl, and with your own eyes behold it all."

However slight my curiosity concerning these new abominations, it was by far the better course to leap back into the closet rather than have myself surprised with Rosalie during the classes; Rodin would without question have become suspicious. And so I took my place; scarcely was I at it when Rodin enters his daughter's room, he leads her into the other, the two women of the house arrive; and thereupon the impudicious Rodin, all restraints upon his behavior removed, free to indulge his fancies to the full, gives himself over in a leisurely fashion and undisguisedly to committing all the irregularities of debauchery. The two peasants, completely nude, are flogged with exceeding violence; while he plies his whip upon the one, the other pays him back in kind, and during the intervals when he pauses for rest, he smothers, with the most uninhibited, the most disgusting caresses, the same altar in Rosalie who, elevated upon an armchair, slightly bent over, presents it to him; at last, there comes this poor creature's turn: Rodin ties her to the stake as he tied his scholars, and while one after another and sometimes both at once his domestics flay him, he beats his daughter, lashes her from her ribs to her knees, utterly transported by pleasure. His agitation is extreme: he shouts, he blasphemes, he flagellates: his thongs bite deep everywhere, and wherever they fall, there, immediately, he presses his lips. Both the interior of the altar and his victim's mouth . . . everything, the before-end excepted, everything is devoured by his suckings; without changing the disposition of the others, contenting himself with rendering it more propitious, Rodin by and by penetrates into pleasure's narrow asylum; meanwhile, the same throne is offered by the governess to his kisses, the other girl beats him with all her remaining strength, Rodin is in seventh heaven, he thrusts, he splits, he tears, a thousand kisses, one more passionate than the other, express his ardor, he kisses whatever is presented to his lust; the bomb bursts and the libertine besotted dares taste the sweetest of delights in the sink of incest and infamy. . . .

Rodin sat down to dine; after such exploits he was in need of restoratives. That afternoon there were more lessons and further corrections, I could have observed new scenes had I desired, but I had seen enough to convince myself and to settle upon a reply to make to this villain's offers. The time for giving it approached. Two days after the events I have described, he himself came to my room to ask for it. He surprised me in bed. By employing the excuse of looking to see whether any traces of my wounds remained, he obtained the right, which I was unable to dispute, of performing an examination upon me, naked, and as he had done the same thing twice a day for a month and had never given any offense to my modesty, I did not think myself able to resist. But this time Rodin had other plans; when he reaches the object of his worship, he locks his thighs about my waist and squeezes with such force that I find myself, so to speak, quite defenseless.

"Thérèse," says he, the while moving his hands about in such a manner as to erase all doubt of his intents, "you are fully recovered, my dear, and now you can give me evidence of the gratitude with which I have beheld your heart overflowing; nothing simpler than the form your thanks would take; I need nothing beyond this," the traitor continued, binding me with all the strength at his command. ". . . Yes, this will do, merely this, here is my recompense, I never demand anything else from women . . . but," he continued, " 'tis one of the most splendid I have seen in all my life. . . . What roundness, fullness! . . . unusual elasticity! . . . what exquisite quality in the skin! . . . Oh my! I absolutely must put this to use. . . ."

Whereupon Rodin, apparently already prepared to put his projects into execution, is obliged, in order to proceed to the next stage, to relax his grip for a moment; I seize my opportunity and extricating myself from his clutches,

"Monsieur," I say, "I beg you to be well persuaded that there is nothing in the entire world which could engage me to consent to the horrors you seem to wish to commit. My gratitude is due to you, indeed it is, but I will not pay my debt in a criminal coin. Needless to say, I am poor and most unfortunate; but no matter; here is the small sum of money I possess," I continue, producing my meager purse, "take what you esteem just and allow me to leave this house, I beg of you, as soon as I am in a fitting state to go."

Rodin, confounded by the opposition he little expected from a girl devoid of means and whom, according to an injustice very ordinary amongst men, he supposed dishonest by the simple fact she was sunk in poverty; Rodin, I say, gazed at me attentively.

"Thérèse," he resumed after a minute's silence, "Thérèse, it is hardly appropriate for you to play the virgin with me; I have, so it would seem to me, some right to your complaisance; but, however, it makes little difference: keep your silver but don't leave me. I am highly pleased to have a well-behaved girl in my house, the conduct of those others I have about me being far from impeccable. . . . Since you show yourself so virtuous in this instance, you will be equally so, I trust, in every other. My interests would benefit therefrom; my daughter is fond of you, just a short while ago she came and begged me to persuade you not to go; and so rest with us, if you will, I invite you to remain."

"Monsieur," I replied, "I should not be happy here; the two women who serve you aspire to all the affection you are able to give them; they will not behold me without jealousy, and sooner or later I will be forced to leave you."

"Be not apprehensive," Rodin answered, "fear none of the effects of these women's envy, I shall be quite capable of keeping them in their place by maintaining you in yours, and you alone will possess my confidence without any resultant danger to yourself. But in order to continue to deserve it, I believe it would be well for you to know that the first quality, the foremost, I require in you, Thérèse, is an unassailable discretion. Many things take place here, many which do not sort with your virtuous principles; you must be able to witness everything, hear all and never speak a syllable of it. . . . Ah, Thérèse, remain with me, stay here, Thérèse, my child, it will be a joy to have you; in the midst of the many vices to which I am driven by a fiery temper, an unrestrainable imagination and a much rotted heart, at least I will have the comfort of a virtuous being dwelling close by, and upon whose breast I shall be able to cast myself as before the feet of a God when, glutted by my debauches, I . . ." "Oh Heaven!" I did think at this moment, "then Virtue is necessary, it is then indispensable to man, since even the vicious one is obliged to find reassurance in it and make use of it as of a shelter." And then, recollecting Rosalie's requests that I not leave her, and thinking to discern some good principles in Rodin, I resolved to stay with him.

"Thérèse," Rodin said to me several days later, "I am going to install you near my daughter; in this way, you will avoid all frictions with the other two women, and I intend to give you three hundred pounds wages."

Such a post was, in my situation, a kind of godsend; inflamed by the desire to restore Rosalie to righteousness, and perhaps even her father too were I able to attain some influence over him, I repented not of what I had just done . . . Rodin, having had me dress myself, conducted me at once to where his daughter was; Rosalie received me with effusions of joy, and I was promptly established.

I left Lyon by way of the road to Dauphiné, still filled with the mad faith which allowed me to believe happiness awaited me in that province. Traveling afoot as usual, with a pair of blouses and some handkerchiefs in my pockets, I had not proceeded two leagues when I met an old woman; she approached me with a look of suffering and implored alms. Far from having the miserliness of which I had just received such cruel examples, and knowing no greater worldly happiness than what comes of obliging a poor person, I instantly drew forth my purse with the intention of selecting a crown and giving it to this woman; but the unworthy creature, much quicker than I, although I had at first judged her aged and crippled, leaps nimbly at my purse, seizes it, aims a powerful blow of her fist at my stomach, topples me, and the next I see of her, she has put a hundred yards betwixt us; there she is, surrounded by four rascals who gesture threateningly and warn me not to come near.

"Great God!" I cried with much bitterness, "then it is impossible for my soul to give vent to any virtuous impulse without my being instantly and very severely punished for it!" At this fatal moment all my courage deserted me; today I beg Heaven's forgiveness in all sincerity, for I faltered; but I was blinded by despair. I felt myself ready to give up a career beset with so many obstacles. I envisioned two alternatives: that of going to join the scoundrels who had just robbed me, or that of returning to Lyon to accept Saint-Florent's offer. God had mercy upon me; I did not succumb, and though the fresh hope He quickened in me was misleading, since so many adversities yet lay in store for me, I nevertheless thank Him for having held me upright: the unlucky star which guides me, although innocent, to the gallows, will never lead me to worse than death; other supervision might have brought me to infamy, and the one is far less cruel than the other.

I continue to direct my steps toward Vienne, having decided to sell what remains to me in order to get on to Grenoble: I was walking along sadly when, at a quarter league's distance from this city, I spied a plain to the right of the highway, and in the fields were two riders busily trampling a man beneath their horses' hooves; after having left him for dead, the pair rode off at a gallop. This appalling spectacle melted me to the point of tears. "Alas!" I said to myself, "there is an unluckier person than I; health and strength at least remain to me, I can earn my living, and if that poor fellow is not rich, what is to become of him?"

However much I ought to have forbidden myself the self-indulgence of sympathy, however perilous it was for me to surrender to the impulse, I could not vanquish my extreme desire to approach the man and to lavish upon him what care I could offer. I rush to his side, I aid him to inhale some spirits I had kept about me: at last he opens his eyes and his first accents are those of gratitude. Still more eager to be of use to him, I tear up one of my blouses in order to bandage his wounds, to stanch his blood: I sacrificed for this wretched man one of the few belongings I still owned. These first attentions completed, I give him a little wine to drink: the unlucky one has completely come back to his senses, I cast an eye upon him and observe him more closely. Although traveling on foot and without baggage, he had some valuable effects—rings, a watch, a snuff box—but the latter two have been badly damaged during his encounter. As soon as he is able to speak he asks me what angel of charity has come to his rescue and what he can do to express his gratitude. Still having the simplicity to believe that a soul enchained by indebtedness ought to be eternally beholden to me, I judge it safe to enjoy the sweet pleasure of sharing my tears with him who has just shed some in my arms: I instruct him of my numerous reverses, he listens with interest, and when I have concluded with the latest catastrophe that has befallen me, the recital provides him with a glimpse of my poverty.

"How happy I am," he exclaims, "to be able at least to acknowledge all you have just done for me; my name is Roland," the adventurer continues, "I am the owner of an exceedingly fine château in the mountains fifteen leagues hence, I invite you to follow me there; and that this proposal cause your delicacy no alarm, I am going to explain immediately in what way you will be of service to me. I am unwedded, but I have a sister I love passionately: she has dedicated herself to sharing my solitude; I need someone to wait upon her; we have recently lost the person who held that office until now, I offer her post to you."

I thanked my protector and took the liberty to ask him how it chanced that a man such as he exposed himself to the dangers of journeying alone, and, as had just occurred, to being molested by bandits.

"A stout, youthful, and vigorous fellow, for several years," said Roland, "I have been in the habit of traveling this way between the place where I reside and Vienne. My health and pocketbook benefit from walking. It is not that I need avoid the expense of a coach, for I am wealthy, and you will soon see proof of it if you are good enough to return home with me; but thriftiness never hurts. As for those two men who insulted me a short while ago, they are two would-be gentlemen of this canton from whom I won a hundred *louis* last week in a gaming house at Vienne; I was content to accept their word of honor, then I met them today, asked for what they owe me, and you witnessed in what coin they paid me."

Together with this man I was deploring the double misfortune of which he was the victim when he proposed we continue our way.

"Thanks to your attentions I feel a little better," said Roland; "night is approaching, let's get on to a house which should be two leagues away; by means of the horses we will secure tomorrow, we might be able to arrive at my château the same afternoon."

Absolutely resolved to profit from the aid Heaven seemed to have sent me, I help Roland to get up, I give him my arm while we walk and indeed after progressing two leagues we find the inn he had mentioned. We take supper together, 'tis very proper and nice; after our meal Roland entrusts me to the mistress of the place, and the following day we set off on two mules we have rented and which are led by a boy from the inn; we reach the frontier of Dauphiné, ever heading into the highlands. We were not yet at our destination when the day ended, so we stopped at Virieu, where my patron showed me the same consideration and provided me with the same care; the next morning we resumed our way toward the mountains. We arrived at their foot toward four in the afternoon; there, the road becoming almost impassable, Roland requested my muleteer not to leave me for fear of an accident, and we penetrated into the gorges. We did but turn, wind, climb for the space of more than four leagues, and by then we had left all habitations and all traveled roads so far behind us I thought myself come to the end of the world; despite myself, I was seized by a twinge of uneasiness; Roland could not avoid seeing it, but he said nothing and I was made yet more uncomfortable by his silence. We finally came to a castle perched upon the crest of a mountain; it beetled over a dreadful precipice into which it seemed ready to plunge: no road seemed to lead up to it; the one we had followed, frequented by goats only, strewn with pebbles and stones, however did at last take us to this awful eyrie which much more resembled the hideaway of thieves than the dwelling place of virtuous folk.

"That is where I live," quoth Roland, noticing I was gazing up at his castle.

I confessed my astonishment to see that he lived in such isolation.

"It suits me," was his abrupt reply.

This response redoubled my forebodings. Not a syllable is lost

upon the miserable; a word, a shift of inflection and, when 'tis a question of the speech of the person upon whom one depends, 'tis enough
to stifle hope or revive it; but, being completely unable to do anything, I held my tongue and waited. We mounted by zigzags; the
strange pile suddenly loomed up before us: roughly a quarter of a
league still separated it from us: Roland dismounted and having told
me to do likewise, he returned both mules to the boy, paid him and
ordered him to return. This latest maneuver was even more displeas-
ing to me; Roland observed my anxiety.

"What is the trouble, Thérèse?" he demanded, urging me on
toward his fortress; "you are not out of France; we are on the
Dauphiné border and within the bishopric of Grenoble."

"Very well, Monsieur," I answered; "but why did it ever occur
to you to take your abode in a place befitting brigands and robbers?"

"Because they who inhabit it are not very honest people," said
Roland; "it might be altogether possible you will not be edified by
their conduct."

"Ah, Monsieur!" said I with a shudder, "you make me tremble;
where then are you leading me?"

"I am leading you into the service of the counterfeiters of whom
I am the chief," said Roland, grasping my arm and driving me over a
little drawbridge that was lowered at our approach and raised immediately we had traversed it; "do you see that well?" he continued
when we had entered; he was pointing to a large and deep grotto
situated toward the back of the courtyard, where four women, nude
and manacled, were turning a wheel; "there are your companions and
there your task, which involves the rotation of that wheel for ten
hours each day, and which also involves the satisfaction of all the
caprices I am pleased to submit you and the other ladies to; for which
you will be granted six ounces of black bread and a plate of kidney
beans without fail each day; as for your freedom, forget it; you will
never recover it. When you are dead from overwork, you will be
flung into that hole you notice beside the well, where the remains of
between sixty and eighty other rascals of your breed await yours, and
your place will be taken by somebody else."

"Oh, Great God!" I exclaimed, casting myself at Roland's feet,
"deign to remember, Monsieur, that I saved your life, that, moved by
gratitude for an instant, you seemed to offer me happiness and that it
is by precipitating me into an eternal abyss of evils you reward my

services. Is what you are doing just? and has not remorse already begun to avenge me in the depths of your heart?"

"What, pray tell, do you mean by this feeling of gratitude with which you fancy you have captivated me?" Roland inquired. "Be more reasonable, wretched creature; what were you doing when you came to my rescue? Between the two possibilities, of continuing on your way and of coming up to me, did you not choose the latter as an impulse dictated by your heart? You therefore gave yourself up to a pleasure? How in the devil's name can you maintain I am obliged to recompense you for the joys in which you indulge yourself? And how did you ever get it into your head that a man like myself, who is swimming in gold and opulence, should condescend to lower himself to owing something to a wretch of your species? Even had you resurrected me, I should owe you nothing immediately it were plain you had acted out of selfishness only: to work, slave, to work; learn that though civilization may overthrow the principles of Nature, it cannot however divest her of her rights; in the beginning she wrought strong beings and weak and intended that the lowly should be forever subordinated to the great; human skill and intelligence made various the positions of individuals, it was no longer physical force alone that determined rank, 'twas gold; the richest became the mightiest man, the most penurious the weakest; if the causes which establish power are not to be found in Nature's ordinations, the priority of the mighty has always been inscribed therein, and to Nature it made no difference whether the weak danced at the end of a leash held by the richest or the most energetic, and little she cared whether the yoke crushed the poorest or the most enfeebled; but these grateful impulses out of which you would forge chains for me, why, Thérèse, Nature recognizes them not; it has never been one of her laws that the pleasure whereunto someone surrenders when he acts obligingly must become a cause for the recipient of his gratuitous kindness to renounce his rights over the donor; do you detect these sentiments you demand in the animals which serve us as examples? When I dominate you by my wealth or might is it natural for me to abandon my rights to you, either because you have enjoyed yourself while obliging me or because, being unhappy, you fancied you had something to gain from your action? Even were service to be rendered by one equal to another, never would a lofty spirit's pride allow him to stoop to acknowledge it; is not he who receives always humiliated? And is this humiliation not sufficient payment for the benefactor who, by this means alone, finds himself superior to the other? Is it not pride's delight to be raised above one's fellow? Is any other necessary to the person who obliges? And if the obligation, by causing humiliation to him who receives, becomes a burden to him, by what right is he to be forced to continue to shoulder it? Why must I consent to let myself be humiliated every time my eyes fall upon him who has obliged me? Instead of being a vice, ingratitude is as certainly a virtue in proud spirits as gratitude is one in humble; let them do what they will for me if doing it gives them pleasure, but let them expect nothing from me simply because they have enjoyed themselves."

Having uttered these words, to which Roland gave me no opportunity to reply, he summoned two valets who upon his instructions seized me, despoiled me, and shackled me next to my companions, so was I set to work at once, without a moment's rest after the fatiguing journey I had just made. Then Roland approaches me, he brutally handles all those parts of me designation of which modesty forbids, heaps sarcasms upon me, makes impertinent reference to the damning and little merited brand Rodin printed upon me, then, catching up a bull's pizzle always kept in readiness nearby, he applies twenty cuts to my behind.

"That is how you will be treated, bitch," says he, "when you lag at the job; I'm not giving you this for anything you've already done, but only to show you how I cope with those who make mistakes."

I screamed, struggled against my manacles; my contortions, my cries, my tears, the cruel expressions of my pain merely entertained my executioner. . . .

"Oh, little whore, you'll see other things," says Roland, "you're not by a long shot at the end of your troubles and I want you to make the acquaintance of even the most barbaric refinements of misery."

He leaves me.

Located in a cave on the edge of that vast well were six dark kennels; they were barred like dungeons, and they served us as shelters for the night. It arrived not long after I was enlisted in this dreadful chain gang, they came to remove my fetters and my companions', and after we had been given the ration of water, beans, and dry bread Roland had mentioned, we were locked up.

I was no sooner alone than, undistracted, I abandoned myself to contemplating my situation in all its horror. Is it possible, I wondered, can it be that there are men so hardened as to have stifled their capacity for gratitude in themselves? This virtue to which I surrender myself with such charm whenever an upright spirit gives me the chance to feel it . . . can this virtue be unknown to certain beings, can they be utter strangers to it? and may they who have suppressed it so inhumanly in themselves be anything but monsters?

I was absorbed in these musings when suddenly I heard the door to my cell open; 'tis Roland: the villain has come to complete his outraging of me by making me serve his odious eccentricities: you may well imagine, Madame, that they were to be as ferocious as his other proceedings and that such a man's love-makings are necessarily tainted by his abhorrent character. But how can I abuse your patience by relating these new horrors? Have I not already more than soiled your imagination with infamous recitations? Dare I hazard additional ones?

"Yes, Thérèse," Monsieur de Corville put in, "yes, we insist upon these details, you veil them with a decency that removes all their edge of horror; there remains only what is useful to whomever seeks to perfect his understanding of enigmatic man. You may not fully apprehend how these tableaux help toward the development of the human spirit; our backwardness in this branch of learning may very well be due to the stupid restraint of those who venture to write upon such matters. Inhibited by absurd fears, they only discuss the puerilities with which every fool is familiar, and dare not, by addressing themselves boldly to the investigation of the human heart, offer its gigantic idiosyncrasies to our view."

"Very well, Monsieur, I shall proceed," Thérèse resumed, deeply affected, "and, proceeding as I have done until this point, I will strive to offer my sketches in the least revolting colors."

Roland, with whose portrait I ought to begin, was a short, heavy-set man, thirty-five years old, of an incredible vigorousness, as hirsute as a bear, with a glowering mien and fierce eye; very dark, with masculine features, a long nose, bearded to the eyes, black, shaggy brows; and in him that part which differentiates men from our sex was of such length and exorbitant circumference, that not only had I never laid eyes upon anything comparable, but was even absolutely convinced Nature had never fashioned another as prodigious; I could scarcely surround it with both hands, and its length matched that of

my forearm. To this physique Roland joined all the vices which may
be the issue of a fiery temperament, of considerable imagination, and
of a luxurious life undisturbed by anything likely to distract from
one's leisure pursuits. From his father Roland had inherited a fortune;
very early on in life he had become surfeited by ordinary pleasures,
and begun to resort to nothing but horrors; these alone were able to
revive desires in a person jaded by excessive pleasure; the women who
served him were all employed in his secret debauches and to satisfy
appetites only slightly less dishonest within which, nevertheless, this
libertine was able to find the criminal spice wherein above all his
taste delighted; Roland kept his own sister as a mistress, and it was
with her he brought to a climax the passions he ignited in our
company.

He was virtually naked when he entered; his inflamed visage
was evidence simultaneously of the epicurean intemperance to which
he had just given himself over, and the abominable lust which consumed him; for an instant he considers me with eyes that unstring my
limbs.

"Get out of those clothes," says he, himself tearing off what I
was wearing to cover me during the night . . . "yes, get rid of all that
and follow me; a little while ago I made you sense what you risk by
laziness; but should you desire to betray us, as that crime would be
of greater magnitude, its punishment would have to be proportion-
ally heavier; come along and see of what sort it would be."

I was in a state difficult to describe, but Roland, affording my
spirit no time in which to burst forth, immediately grasped my arm
and dragged me out; he pulls me along with his right hand, in his left
he holds a little lantern that emits a feeble light; after winding this
way and that, we reach a cellar door; he opens it, thrusts me ahead
of him, tells me to descend while he closes this first barrier; I obey; a
hundred paces further, a second door; he opens and shuts it in the
same way; but after this one there is no stairway, only a narrow
passage hewn in the rock, filled with sinuosities, whose downward
slope is extremely abrupt. Not a word from Roland; the silence
affrights me still more; he lights us along with his lantern; thus we
travel for about fifteen minutes; my frame of mind makes me yet
more sensitive to these subterranean passages' terrible humidity. At
last, we had descended to such a depth that it is without fear of
exaggeration I assure you the place at which we were to arrive must

have been more than a furlong below the surface of the earth; on either side of the path we followed were occasional niches where I saw coffers containing those criminals' wealth: one last bronze door appeared, Roland unlocked it, and I nearly fell backward upon perceiving the dreadful place to which this evil man had brought me. Seeing me falter, he pushed me rudely ahead, and thus, without wishing to be there, I found myself in the middle of that appalling sepulcher. Imagine, Madame, a circular cavern, twenty-five feet in diameter, whose walls, hung in black, were decorated by none but the most lugubrious objects, skeletons of all sizes, crossed bones, severed heads, bundles of whips and collections of martinets, sabers, cutlasses, poignards, firearms: such were the horrors one spied on the walls illuminated by a three-wicked oil lamp suspended in one corner of the vault; from a transverse beam dangled a rope which fell to within eight or ten feet of the ground in the center of this dungeon and which, as very soon you will see, was there for no other purpose than to facilitate dreadful expeditions: to the right was an open coffin wherein glinted an effigy of death brandishing a threatful scythe; a prayer stool was beside it; above it was visible a crucifix bracketed by candles of jet; to the left, the waxen dummy of a naked woman, so lifelike I was for a long time deceived by it; she was attached to a cross, posed with her chest facing it so that one had a full view of her posterior and cruelly molested parts; blood seemed to ooze from several wounds and to flow down her thighs; she had the most beautiful hair in all the world, her lovely head was turned toward us and seemed to implore our mercy; all of suffering's contortions were plainly wrought upon her lovely face, and there were even tears flowing down her cheeks: the sight of this terrible image was again enough to make me think I would collapse; the further part of the cavern was filled by a vast black divan which eloquently bespoke all the atrocities which occurred in this infernal place.

"And here is where you will perish, Thérèse," quoth Roland, "if ever you conceive the fatal notion of leaving my establishment; yes, it is here I will myself put you to death, here I will make you reverberate to the anguishes inflicted by everything of the most appalling I can possibly devise."

As he gave vent to this threat Roland became aroused; his agitation, his disorder made him resemble a tiger about to spring upon its prey: 'twas then he brought to light the formidable member wherewith he was outfitted; he had me touch it, asked me whether I had ever beheld its peer.

"Such as you see it, whore," said he in a rage, "in that shape it has, however, got to be introduced into the narrowest part of your body even if I must split you in half; my sister, considerably your junior, manages it in the same sector; never do I enjoy women in any other fashion," and so as to leave me in no doubt of the locale he had in mind, he inserted into it three fingers armed with exceedingly long nails, the while saying:

"Yes, 'tis there, Thérèse, it will be shortly into this hole I will drive this member which affrights you; it will be run every inch of the way in, it will tear you, you'll bleed and I will be beside myself."

Foam flecked his lips as he spoke these words interspersed with revolting oaths and blasphemies. The hand, which had been prying open the shrine he seemed to want to attack, now strayed over all the adjacent parts; he scratched them, he did as much to my breast, he clawed me so badly I was not to get over the pain for a fortnight. Next, he placed me on the edge of the couch, rubbed alcohol upon that mossy tonsure with which Nature ornaments the altar wherein our species finds regeneration; he set it afire and burned it. His fingers closed upon the fleshy protuberance which surmounts this same altar, he snatched at it and scraped roughly, then he inserted his fingers within and his nails ripped the membrane which lines it. Losing all control over himself, he told me that, since he had me in his lair, I might just as well not leave it, for that would spare him the nuisance of bringing me back down again; I fell to my knees and dared remind him again of what I had done in his behalf. . . . I observed I but further excited him by harping again upon the rights to his pity I fancied were mine; he told me to be silent, bringing up his knee and giving me a tremendous blow in the pit of the stomach which sent me sprawling on the flagstones. He seized a handful of my hair and jerked me erect:

"Very well!" he said, "come now! prepare yourself; it is a certainty, I am going to kill you. . . ."

"Oh, Monsieur!"

"No, no, you've got to die; I do not want to hear you reproach me with your good little deeds; I don't like owing anything to anybody, others have got to rely upon me for everything. . . . You're going to perish, I tell you, get into that coffin, let's see if it fits."

He lifts me, thrusts me into it and shuts it, then quits the cavern and gives me the impression I have been left there. Never had I thought myself so near to death; alas! it was nonetheless to be presented to me under a yet more real aspect. Roland returns, he fetches me out of the coffin.

"You'll be well off in there," says he, "one would say 'twas made for you; but to let you finish peacefully in that box would be a death too sweet; I'm going to expose you to one of a different variety which, all the same, will have its agreeable qualities; so implore your God, whore, pray to him to come posthaste and avenge you if he really has it in him. . . ."

I cast myself down upon the *prie-dieu,* and while aloud I open my heart to the Eternal, Roland in a still crueler manner intensifies, upon the hindquarters I expose to him, his vexations and his torments; with all his strength he flogs those parts with a steel-tipped martinet, each blow draws a gush of blood which springs to the walls.

"Why," he continues with a curse, "he doesn't much aid you, your God, does he? and thus he allows unhappy virtue to suffer, he abandons it to villainy's hands; ah! what a bloody fine God you've got there, Thérèse, what a superb God he is! Come," he says, "come here, whore, your prayer should be done," and at the same time he places me upon the divan at the back of that cell: "I told you, Thérèse, you have got to die!"

He seizes my arms, binds them to my side, then he slips a black silken noose about my neck; he holds both ends of the cord and, by tightening, he can strangle and dispatch me to the other world either quickly or slowly, depending upon his pleasure.

"This torture is sweeter than you may imagine, Thérèse," says Roland; "you will only approach death by way of unspeakably pleasurable sensations; the pressure this noose will bring to bear upon your nervous system will set fire to the organs of voluptuousness; the effect is certain; were all the people who are condemned to this torture to know in what an intoxication of joy it makes one die, less terrified by this retribution for their crimes, they would commit them more often and with much greater self-assurance; this delicious operation, Thérèse, by causing, as well, the contraction of the locale in which I am going to fit myself," he added as he presented himself to a criminal avenue so worthy of such a villain, "is also going to double my pleasures."

He thrusts, he sweats, 'tis in vain; he prepares the road, 'tis futile; he is too monstrously proportioned, his enterprises are repeatedly frustrated; and then his wrath exceeds all limits; his nails, his hands, his feet fly to revenge him upon the opposition Nature puts up against him; he returns to the assault, the glowing blade slides to the edge of the neighboring canal and smiting vigorously, penetrates to nigh the midway mark; I utter a cry; Roland, enraged by his mistake, withdraws petulantly, and this time hammers at the other gate with such force the moistened dart plunges in, rending me. Roland exploits this first sally's success; his efforts become more violent; he gains ground; as he advances, he gradually tightens the fatal cord he has passed round my neck, hideous screams burst from my lips; amused by them, the ferocious Roland urges me to redouble my howlings, for he is but too confident of their insufficiency, he is perfectly able to put a stop to them when he wishes; their shrill sharp notes inflame him, the noose's pressure is modulated by his degree of delight; little by little my voice waxes faint; the tightenings now become so intense that my senses weaken although I do not lose the power to feel; brutally shaken by the enormous instrument with which Roland is rending my entrails, despite my frightful circumstances, I feel myself flooded by his lust's jetted outpourings; I still hear the cries he mouths as he discharges; an instant of stupor followed, I knew not what had happened to me, but soon my eyes open again to the light, I find myself free, untied, and my sensory organs seem to come back to life.

"Well, Thérèse," says my butcher, "I dare swear that if you'll tell the truth you'll say you felt pleasure only?"

"Only horror, Monsieur, only disgust, only anguish and despair."

"You are lying, I am fully acquainted with the effects you have just experienced, but what does it matter what they were? I fancy you already know me well enough to be damned certain that when I undertake something with you, the joy you reap from it concerns me infinitely less than my own, and this voluptuousness I seek has been so keen that in an instant I am going to procure some more of it. It is now upon yourself, Thérèse," declares this signal libertine, "it is upon you alone your life is going to depend."

Whereupon he hitches about my neck the rope that hangs from the ceiling; he has me stand upon a stool, pulls the rope taut, secures it, and to the stool he attaches a string whose end he keeps in his hand as he sits down in an armchair facing me; I am given a sickle which I am to use to sever the rope at the moment when, by means of the string, he jerks the stool from beneath my feet.

"Notice, Thérèse," he says when all is ready, "that though you may miss your blow, I'll not miss mine; and so I am not mistaken when I say your life depends upon you."

He excites himself; it is at his intoxication's critical moment he is to snatch away the stool which, removed, will leave me dangling from the beam; he does everything possible to pretend the instant has come; he would be beside himself were I to miss my cue; but do what he will, I divine the crisis, the violence of his ecstasy betrays him, I see him make the telltale movement, the stool flies away, I cut the rope and fall to the ground; there I am, completely detached, and although five yards divide us, would you believe it, Madame? I feel my entire body drenched with the evidence of his delirium and his frenzy.

Anyone but I, taking advantage of the weapon she clutched in her hand, would doubtless have leapt upon that monster; but what might I have gained by this brave feat? for I did not have the keys to those subterranean passages, I was ignorant of their scheme, I should have perished before being able to emerge from them; Roland, furthermore, was armed; and so I got up, leaving the sickle on the ground so that he might not conceive the slightest suspicion of my intentions, and indeed he had none, for he had savored the full extent of pleasure and, far more content with my tractability, with my resignation, than with my agility, he signaled to me and we left.

MARQUIS DE SADE

Justine was first published a hundred and seventy-four years ago, and after a decade of success was seized and suppressed by Napoleon's police. Thereafter it remained out-of-print, but not forgotten, for well over a century. After World War II, a young, enterprising French publisher, Jean-Jacques Pauvert, republished it as part of an ambitious project to republish the complete works of Sade. I have asked one of the editors of the recently published Grove Press volume of Sade's works—which contains the complete Justine—to provide the description of the circumstances surrounding the composition and original publication of this work.

The most famous of all Sade's works is the novel Justine. *It is also probably the one he cared most about—Sade dedicated it to the faithful companion of the last twenty-five years of his existence, Marie-Constance Quesnet. It was also the book which caused him the most difficulty with the authorities during his lifetime.*

Sade finished the first draft of this "*philosophical novel*" *while he was a prisoner in the Bastille. Working uninterruptedly over the two-week period from June 23 to July 8, 1787, Sade completed the hundred-and-thirty-eight page manuscript, which he entitled* Les Infortunes de la Vertu. *Originally intended to become a part of the volume he was then preparing,* Contes et fabliaux du XVIIIᵉ siècle, *this "first Justine" underwent considerable revision in the course of the following year, and Sade soon determined to strike it from his list of tales and make it a work unto itself.*

Writing to his lawyer-friend Reinaud on June 12, 1791, a little more than a year after the revolutionary government had rendered him his liberty, Sade noted: "At the moment a novel of mine is being printed, but it is a work too immoral to be sent to so pious and so decent a man as yourself. I needed money, my publisher said that he wanted it well spiced, and I gave it to him fit to plague the devil himself. It is called Justine or Good Conduct Well Chastised. Burn it and do not read it, if perchance it falls into your hands. I am disclaiming the authorship. . . ."

In fact, the original edition of Justine—the author's first work published during his lifetime—did not bear his name. Printed in Paris, Justine first appeared in 1791 in two octavo volumes, with a frontispiece depicting Virtue between Licentiousness and Irreligion, and at the place on the title page generally reserved for the publisher's imprint there appeared the vague description: In Holland, At Associated Booksellers.

"Will it not be felt," *writes Sade in his dedication,* "that Virtue, however beautiful, becomes the worst of all possible attitudes when it is found too feeble to contend with Vice and that, in an entirely corrupted age, the safest course is to follow the others?" *If this be the impression, says Sade, it is wrong: this work is intended to combat such* "dangerous sophistries," *such* "false philosophy," *and show how*

Virtue afflicted may turn a thoroughly depraved and corrupt spirit wherein there yet remain a few good principles, back toward the path of righteousness.

During the decade following its publication, Justine *went through six printings (one of which, actually done in Paris, bore as the unlikely place of publication: "Philadelphia"), eloquent testimony to its early popularity. Doubtless prompted by its success, an enterprising Paris publisher, Nicolas Massé, brought out, in 1797, the monumental ten-volume work entitled* La Nouvelle Justine . . . suivie de l'Histoire de Juliette, sa soeur, *which was freely offered, at least for a year following its publication, in the leading Paris bookstores. Then, in the waning two years of the eighteenth century, searches and seizures began, ending with the arrest, on March 6, 1801, of the man who was purported to be, but adamantly denied he was, the author of both works. On that day, both Sade and Massé were arrested on the latter's premises. A search of Massé's offices revealed a number of manuscripts in Sade's handwriting, as well as printed volumes of* Justine *and* Juliette *annotated in his hand. Massé, after being detained for twenty-four hours, was released upon condition that he reveal the whereabouts of his stock of* Juliette, *and there is evidence to indicate that the publisher, to save himself, had denounced Sade to the police. Be that as it may, Sade was once again incarcerated, first in Saint-Pélagie and then, two years later, in the Charenton asylum, where he was to remain a prisoner until the end of his life.*

NAKED LUNCH
William S. Burroughs

The County Clerk has his office in a huge red brick building known as the Old Court House. Civil cases are, in fact, tried there, the proceeding inexorably dragging out until the contestants die or abandon litigation. This is due to the vast number of records pertaining to absolutely everything, all filed in the wrong place so that no one but the County Clerk and his staff of assistants can find them, and he often spends years in the search. In fact, he is still looking for material relative to a damage suit that was settled out of court in 1910. Large sections of the Old Court House have fallen in ruins, and others are highly dangerous owing to frequent cave-ins. The County Clerk assigns the more dangerous missions to his assistants, many of whom have lost their lives in the service. In 1912 two hundred and seven assistants were trapped in a collapse of the North-by-North-East wing.

When suit is brought against anyone in the Zone, his lawyers connive to have the case transferred to the Old Court House. Once this is done, the plaintiff has lost the case, so the only cases that actually go to trial in the Old Court House are those instigated by eccentrics and paranoids who want "a public hearing," which they rarely get since only the most desperate famine of news will bring a reporter to the Old Court House.

The Old Court House is located in the town of Pigeon Hole outside the urban zone. The inhabitants of this town and the surrounding area of swamps and heavy timber are people of such great stupidity and such barbarous practices that the Administration has seen fit to quarantine them in a reservation surrounded by a radioactive wall of iron bricks. In retaliation the citizens of Pigeon Hole plaster their town with signs: *"Urbanite Don't Let The Sun Set On You Here,"* an unnecessary injunction, since nothing but urgent business would take an urbanite to Pigeon Hole.

Lee's case is urgent. He has to file an immediate affidavit that he is suffering from bubonic plague to avoid eviction from the house he has occupied ten years without paying the rent. He exists in perpetual quarantine. So he packs his suitcase of affidavits and petitions and injunctions and certificates and takes a bus to the Frontier. The Urbanite customs inspector waves him through: "I hope you've got an atom bomb in that suitcase."

449

Lee swallows a handful of tranquilizing pills and steps into the Pigeon Hole customs shed. The inspectors spend three hours pawing through his papers, consulting dusty books of regulations and duties from which they read incomprehensible and ominous excerpts ending with: "And as such is subject to fine and penalty under act 666." They look at him significantly.

They go through his papers with a magnifying glass.

"Sometimes they slip dirty limericks between the lines."

"Maybe he figures to sell them for toilet paper. Is this crap for your own personal use?"

"Yes."

"He says yes."

"And how do we know that?"

"I gotta affidavit."

"Wise guy. Take off your clothes."

"Yeah. Maybe he got dirty tattoos."

They paw over his body probing his ass for contraband and examine it for evidence of sodomy. They dunk his hair and send the water out to be analyzed. "Maybe he's got dope in his hair."

Finally, they impound his suitcase; and he staggers out of the shed with a fifty-pound bale of documents.

A dozen or so Recordites sit on the Old Court House steps of rotten wood. They watch his approach with pale blue eyes, turning their heads slow on wrinkled necks (the wrinkles full of dust) to follow his body up the steps and through the door. Inside, dust hangs in the air like fog, sifting down from the ceiling, rising in clouds from the floor as he walks. He mounts a perilous staircase—condemned in 1929. Once his foot goes through, and the dry splinters tear into the flesh of his leg. The staircase ends in a painter's scaffold, attached with frayed rope and pulley to a beam almost invisible in dusty distance. He pulls himself up cautiously to a ferris wheel cabin. His weight sets in motion hydraulic machinery (sound of running water).

The wheel moves smooth and silent to stop by a rusty iron balcony, worn through here and there like an old shoe sole. He walks down a long corridor lined with doors, most of them nailed or boarded shut. In one office, *Near East Exquisitries* on a green brass plaque, the Mugwump is catching termites with his long black tongue. The door of the County Clerk's office is open. The County Clerk sits inside gumming snuff, surrounded by six assistants. Lee stands in the doorway. The County Clerk goes on talking without looking up.

"I run into Ted Spigot the other day . . . a good old boy, too. Not a finer man in the Zone than Ted Spigot. . . . Now it was a Friday I happen to remember because the Old Lady was down with the menstrual cramps and I went to Doc Parker's drugstore on Dalton Street, just opposite Ma Green's Ethical Massage Parlor, where Jed's old livery stable used to be. . . . Now, Jed, I'll remember his second name directly, had a cast in the left eye and his wife came from some place out East, Algiers I believe it was, and after Jed died she married up again, and she married one of the Hoot boys, Clem Hoot if my memory serves, a good old boy too, now Hoot was around fifty-four fifty-five year old at the time. . . . So I says to Doc Parker: 'My old lady is down bad with the menstrual cramps. Sell me two ounces of paregoric.'

"So Doc says, 'Well, Arch, you gotta sign the book. Name, address and date of purchase. It's the law.'

"So I asked Doc what the day was, and he said, 'Friday the 13th.'

"So I said, 'I guess I already had mine.'

" 'Well,' Doc says, 'there was a feller in here this morning. City feller. Dressed kinda flashy. So he's got him a RX for a mason jar of morphine. . . . Kinda funny looking prescription writ out on toilet paper. . . . And I told him straight out: "Mister, I suspect you to be a dope fiend." '

" ' "I got the ingrowing toe nails, Pop. I'm in agony." ' he says.

" ' "Well," I says, "I gotta be careful. But so long as you got a legitimate condition and an RX from a certified bona feedy M.D., I'm honored to serve you." '

" ' "That croaker's really certified," he say. . . . Well, I guess one hand didn't know what the other was doing when I give him a jar of Saniflush by error. . . . So I reckon he's had his too.'

" 'Just the thing to clean a man's blood.'

" 'You know, that very thing occurred to me. Should be a sight

better than sulphur and molasses. . . . Now, Arch, don't think I'm nosey; but a man don't have no secrets from God and his druggist I always say. . . . Is you still humping the Old Gray Mare?'

" 'Why, Doc Parker . . . I'll have you know I'm a family man and an Elder in the First Denominational Non-sextarian Church and I ain't had a piecea hoss ass since we was kids together.'

" 'Them was the days, Arch. Remember the time I got the goose grease mixed up with the mustard? Always was a one to grab the wrong jar, feller say. They could have heard you squealing over in Cunt Lick County, just a squealing like a stoat with his stones off.'

" 'You're in the wrong hole, Doc. It was you took the mustard and me as had to wait till you cooled off.'

" 'Wistful thinking, Arch. I read about it one time inna magazin settin' in that green outhouse behind the station. . . . Now what I meant awhile back, Arch, you didn't rightly understand me. . . . I was referring to your wife as the Old Gray Mare. . . . I mean she ain't what she used to be what with all them carbuncles and cataracts and chilblains and haemorrhoids and aftosa.'

" 'Yas, Doc, Liz is right sickly. Never was the same after her eleventh miscarriaging. . . . There was something right strange about that. Doc Ferris he told me straight, he said: "Arch, 'tain't fitting you should see that critter." And he gives me a long look made my flesh crawl. . . . Well, you sure said it right, Doc. She ain't what she used to be. And your medicines don't seem to ease her none. In fact, she ain't been able to tell night from day since using them eye drops you sold her last month. . . . But, Doc, you oughtta know I wouldn't be humping Liz, the old cow, meaning no disrespect to the mother of my dead monsters. Not when I got that sweet little ol' fifteen year old thing. . . . You know that yaller girl used to work in Marylou's Hair Straightening and Skin Bleach Parlor over in Nigga town.'

" 'Getting that dark chicken meat, Arch? Gettin' that coon pone?'

" 'Gettin' it steady, Doc. Gettin' it steady. Well, feller say duty is goosing me. Gotta get back to the old crank case.'

" 'I'll bet she needs a grease job worst way.'

" 'Doc, she sure is a dry hole. . . . Well, thanks for the paregoric.'

" 'And thanks for the trade, Arch. . . . He he he . . . Say, Archy boy, some night when you get caught short with a rusty load drop around and have a drink of Yohimbiny with me.'

" 'I'll do that, Doc, I sure will. It'll be just like old times.'

"So I went on back to my place and heated up some water and mixed up some paregoric and cloves and cinnamon and sassyfrass and give it to Liz, and it eased her some I reckon. Leastwise she let up aggravatin' me. . . . Well, later on I went down to Doc Parker's again to get me a rubber . . . and just as I was leaving I run into Roy Bane, a good ol' boy too. There's not a finer man in this Zone than Roy Bane. . . . So he said to me he says, 'Arch, you see that ol' nigger over there in that vacant lot? Well, sure as shit and taxes, he comes there every night just as regular you can set your watch by him. See him behind them nettles? Every night round about eight thirty he goes over into that lot yonder and pulls himself off with steel wool. . . . Preachin' Nigger, they tell me.'

"So that's how I come to know the hour more or less on Friday the 13th and it couldn't have been more than twenty minutes half an hour after that, I'd took some Spanish Fly in Doc's store and it was jest beginning to work on me down by Grennel Bog on my way to Nigger town. . . . Well the bog makes a bend, used to be nigger shack there. . . . They burned that ol' nigger over in Cunt Lick. Nigger had the aftosa and it left him stone blind. . . . So this white girl down from Texarkana screeches out:

" 'Roy, that ol' nigger is looking at me so nasty. Land's sake I feel just dirty all over.'

" 'Now, Sweet Thing, don't you fret yourself. Me an' the boys will burn him.'

" 'Do it slow, Honey Face. Do it slow. He's give me a sick headache.'

"So they burned the nigger and that ol' boy took his wife and went back up to Texarkana without paying for the gasoline and old Whispering Lou runs the service station couldn't talk about nothing else all Fall: 'These city fellers come down here and burn a nigger and don't even settle up for the gasoline.'

"Well, Chester Hoot tore that nigger shack down and rebuilt it just back of his house up in Bled Valley. Covered up all the windows with black cloth, and what goes on in there ain't fittin' to speak of. . . . Now Chester he's got some right strange ways. . . . Well it was just where the nigger shack used to be, right across from the Old Brooks place floods out every Spring, only it wasn't the Brooks place then . . . belonged to a feller name of Scranton. Now that piece of land was surveyed back in 1919. . . . I reckon you know the man did the job too. . . . Feller name of Hump Clarence used to witch out wells on the side. . . . Good ol' boy too, not a finer man in this Zone than Hump Clarence. . . . Well it was just around about in there I come on Ted Spigot ascrewin a mud puppy."

Lee cleared his throat. The Clerk looked up over his glasses. "Now if you'll take care, young feller, till I finish what I'm asaying, I'll tend to your business."

And he plunged into an anecdote about a nigra got the hydrophobia from a cow.

"So my pappy says to me: 'Finish up your chores, son, and let's go see the mad nigger. . . . ' They had that nigger chained to the bed, and he was bawling like a cow. . . . I soon got enough of that ol' nigger. Well, if you all will excuse me I got business in the Privy Council. He he he!"

Lee listened in horror. The County Clerk often spent weeks in the privy living on scorpions and Montgomery Ward catalogues. On several occasions his assistants had forced the door and carried him out in an advanced state of malnutrition. Lee decided to play his last card.

"Mr. Anker," he said, "I'm appealing to you as one Razor Back to another," and he pulled out his Razor Back card, a memo of his lush-rolling youth.

The Clerk looked at the card suspiciously. "You don't look like a bone feed mast-fed Razor Back to me. . . . What you think about the Jeeeeews . . . ?"

"Well, Mr. Anker, you know yourself all a Jew wants to do is doodle a Christian girl. . . . One of these days we'll cut the rest of it off."

"Well, you talk right sensible for a city feller. . . . Find out what he wants and take care of him. . . . He's a good ol' boy."

WILLIAM S. BURROUGHS

In the winter of 1963, during the newspaper strike, The New York Review of Books *first appeared. Among other excellent articles, it carried a long review by Mary McCarthy on* Naked Lunch. *As I have found this one of the best commentaries on Burroughs, I requested that it be reprinted here, and I wish to thank both Miss McCarthy and the* Review *for their permission to do so.*

"*You can cut into* Naked Lunch *at any intersection point," says Burroughs, suiting the action to the word, in an Atrophied Preface he appends as a tail-piece. His book, he means, is like a neighborhood movie with continuous showings that you can drop into whenever you please—you don't have to wait for the beginning of the feature picture. Or like a worm that you can chop up into sections each of which wriggles off as an independent worm. Or a nine-lived cat. Or a cancer.* He is fond of the word *"mosaic,"* especially in its scientific sense of a plant-mottling caused by a virus, and his Muse (see etymology of *"mosaic"*) is interested in organic processes of multiplication and duplication. The literary notion of time as simultaneous, a montage, is not original with Burroughs; what is original is the scientific bent he gives it and a view of the world that combines biochemistry, anthropology, and politics. It is as though Finnegans Wake were cut loose from history and adapted for a cinerama circus titled *"One World."* Naked Lunch has no use for history, which is all *"ancient history"*—sloughed-off skin; from its planetary perspective, there are only geography and customs. Seen in terms of space, history shrivels into a mere wrinkling or furrowing of the surface as in an aerial relief-map or one of those pieced-together aerial photographs known in the trade as mosaics. The oldest memory in Naked Lunch is of jacking-off in boyhood latrines, a memory recaptured through pederasty. This must be the first space novel, the first serious piece of science fiction—the others are entertainment.

The action of Naked Lunch *takes place in the consciousness of One Man, William Lee, who is taking a drug cure. The principal characters, besides Lee, are his friend, Bill Gains (who seems momentarily to turn into a woman called Jane), various members of the Narcotic Squad, especially one Bradley the Buyer, Dr. Benway, a charlatan medico who is treating Lee, two vaudevillians, Clem and Jody, A.J., a carnival con man, the last of the Big Spenders, a sailor, an Arab called Ahmed, an archetypal Southern druggist, Doc Parker ("a man don't have no secrets from God and his druggist"), and various boys with whining voices. Among the minor characters are a number of automobiles, each with its specific complaint, like the oil-burning Ford V-8, a film executive, the Party Leader, the Vigilante, John and Mary, the sex acrobats, and a puzzled American housewife who is heard complaining because the Mixmaster keeps trying to climb up under her dress. The scene shifts about, shiftily, from New York to Chicago to St. Louis to New Orleans to Mexico to Malmo, Sweden, Venice, and the human identities shift about shiftily too, for all these modern places and modern individuals (if that is the right word) have interchangeable parts. Burroughs is fond too of the word "ectoplasm," and the beings that surround Lee, particularly the inimical ones, seem*

ectoplasmic phantoms projected on the wide screen of his conscious-
ness from a mass séance. But the haunting is less visual than auditory.
These "characters," in the colloquial sense, are ventriloquial voices
produced, as it were, against the will of the ventriloquist, who has
become their dummy. Passages of dialogue and description keep re-
curring in different contexts with slight variations, as though they
possessed ubiquity.

The best comparison for the book, with its aerial sex acts per-
formed on a high trapeze, its con men and barkers, its arena-like form,
is in fact a circus. A circus travels but it is always the same, and this
is Burroughs' sardonic image of modern life. The Barnum of the show
is the mass-manipulator, who appears in a series of disguises. Control,
as Burroughs says, underlining it, can never be a means to anything
but more control—like drugs, *and the vicious circle of addiction is*
re-enacted, world-wide, with sideshows in the political and "social"
sphere—the social here has vanished, except in quotation marks, like
the historical, for everything has become automatized. Everyone is
an addict of one kind or another, as people indeed are wont to say of
themselves, complacently: "I'm a crossword puzzle addict, a High-Fi
addict," etcetera. The South is addicted to lynching and nigger-
hating, and the Southern folk-custom of burning a Negro recurs
throughout the book as a sort of Fourth-of-July carnival with fire-
works. Circuses, with their cages of wild animals, are also dangerous,
like Burroughs' human circus; an accident may occur, as when the
electronic brain in Dr. Benway's laboratory goes on the rampage,
and the freaks escape to mingle with the controlled citizens of Free-
land in a general riot, or in the scene where the hogs are let loose in
the gourmet restaurant.

On a level usually thought to be "harmless," addiction to plati-
tudes and commonplaces is global. To Burroughs' ear, the Bore, lurk-
ing in the hotel lobby, is literally deadly ("'You look to me like a
man of intelligence.' Always ominous opening words, my boy!").
The same for Doc Parker with his captive customer in the back room
of his pharmacy (". . . so long as you got a legitimate condition and
an Rx from a certified bona feedy M.D., I'm honored to serve you"),
the professor in the classroom ("Hehe hehe he"), the attorney in
court ("Hehe hehe he," likewise). The complacent sound of snicker-
ing laughter is an alarm signal, like the suave bell-tones of the psychia-
trist and the emphatic drone of the Party Leader ("You see men and

women. Ordinary *men and women going about their ordinary every-day tasks. Leading their ordinary lives. That's what we need . . .").*

Cut to ordinary men and women, going about their ordinary everyday tasks. The whine of the put-upon boy hustler: "All kinda awful sex acts." "Why cancha just get physical like a human?" "So I guess he come to some kinda awful climax." "You think I am in-narested to hear about your horrible old condition? I am not inna-rested at all." "But he comes to a climax and turns into some kinda awful crab." This aggrieved tone merges with the malingering sighs of the American housewife, opening a box of Lux: "I got the most awful cold, and my intestines is all constipated." And the clarion of the Salesman: "When the Priority numbers are called up yonder I'll be there." These average folks are addicts of the science page of the Sunday supplements; they like to talk about their diseases and about vile practices that paralyze the practitioner from the waist down or about a worm that gets into your kidney and grows to enormous size or about the "horrible" result of marijuana addiction—it makes you turn black and your legs drop off. The superstitious scientific vocabulary is diffused from the laboratory and the mental hospital into the general population. Overheard at a lynching: "Don't crowd too close, boys. His intestines is subject to explode in the fire." The same dif-fusion of culture takes place with modern physics. A lieutenant to his general: "But, chief, can't we get them started and they imitate each other like a chained reaction?"

The phenomenon of repetition, of course, gives rise to boredom; many readers complain that they cannot get through Naked Lunch. *And/or that they find it disgusting. It is disgusting and sometimes tiresome, often in the same places. The prominence of the anus, of feces, and of all sorts of "horrible" discharges, as the characters would say, from the body's orifices, becomes too much of a bad thing, like the sado-masochistic sex performances—the automatic ejacula-tion of a hanged man is not everybody's cantharides. A reader whose erogenous zones are more temperate than the author's begins to feel either that he is a square (a guilty sentiment he should not yield to) or that he is the captive of an addict.*

In defense, Swift could be cited, and indeed between Burroughs and Swift there are many points of comparison; not only the obses-sion with excrement and the horror of female genitalia, but a disgust with politics and the whole body politic. Like Swift, Burroughs has

*irritable nerves and something of the crafty temperament of the in-
ventor. There is a great deal of Laputa in the countries Burroughs
calls Interzone and Freeland, and Swift's solution for the Irish problem would appeal to the American's dry logic. As Gulliver, Swift
posed as an anthropologist (though the study was not known by that
name then) among savage people; Burroughs parodies the anthropologist in his descriptions of the American heartland: ". . . the Interior a
vast-subdivision, antennae of television to the meaningless sky. . . .
Illinois and Missouri, miasma of mound-building peoples, grovelling
worship of the Food Source, cruel and ugly festivals." The style here
is more emotive than Swift's, but in his deadpan explanatory notes
("This is a rural English custom designed to eliminate aged and bed-
fast dependents") there is a Swiftian factuality. The "factual" appearance of the whole narrative, with its battery of notes and citations,
some straight, some loaded, its extracts from a diary, like a ship's log,
its pharmacopeia, has the flavor of eighteenth-century satire. He calls
himself a "Factualist" and belongs, all alone, to an Age of Reason,
which he locates in the future. In him, as in Swift, there is a kind of
soured utopianism.*

Yet what saves Naked Lunch *is not a literary ancestor but
humor. Burroughs' humor is peculiarly American, at once broad and
sly. It is the humor of a comedian, a vaudeville performer playing in
One, in front of the asbestos curtain to some Keith Circuit or Pan-
tages house long since converted to movies. The same jokes reappear,
slightly refurbished, to suit the circumstances, the way a vaudeville
artist used to change Yonkers to Renton when he was playing Seattle.
For example, the Saniflush joke, which is always good for a laugh:
somebody is cutting the cocaine/the morphine/the penicillin with
Saniflush. Some of the jokes are verbal ("Stop me if you've heard this
atomic secret" or Dr. Benway's "A simopath . . . is a citizen convinced
he is an ape or other simian. It is a disorder peculiar to the army and
discharge cures it"). Some are mimic buffoonery (Dr. Benway, in his
last appearance, dreamily, his voice fading out: "Cancer, my first
love"). Some are whole vaudeville "numbers," as when the hoofers,
Clem and Jody, are hired by the Russians to give Americans a bad
name abroad: they appear in Liberia wearing black Stetsons and red
galluses and talking loudly about burning niggers back home. A skit
like this may rise to a frenzy, as if in a Marx Brothers or a Clayton,
Jackson, and Durante act. E.g., the very funny scene in Chez Robert,*

"where a huge icy gourmet broods over the greatest cuisine in the world": A. J. appears, the last of the Big Spenders, and orders a bottle of ketchup; immediate pandemonium; A. J. gives his hog-call, and the shocked gourmet diners are all devoured by famished hogs. The effect of pandemonium, all hell breaking loose, is one of Burroughs' favorites and an equivalent of the old vaudeville finale, with the acrobats, the jugglers, the magician, the hoofers, the lady-who-was-cut-in-half, the piano player, the comedians, all pushing into the act.

Another favorite effect, with Burroughs, is the metamorphosis. A citizen is turned into animal form, a crab or a huge centipede, or into some unspeakable monstrosity like Bradley the Narcotics Agent who turns into an unidentifiable carnivore. These metamorphoses, of course, are punishments. The Hellzapoppin effect of orgies and riots and the metamorphosis effect, rapid or creeping, are really cancerous onslaughts—matter on the rampage multiplying itself and "building" as a revue scene "builds" to a climax. Growth and deterioration are the same thing: a human being "deteriorates" or "grows" into a one-man jungle. What you think of it depends on your point of view; from the junky's angle, Bradley is better as a carnivore eating the Narcotics Commissioner than he was as "fuzz"—junky slang for the police.

The impression left by this is perplexing. On the one hand, control is evil; on the other, escape from control is mass slaughter or reduction to a state of proliferating cellular matter. The police are the enemy, but as Burroughs shrewdly observes in one passage: "A functioning police state needs no police." The policeman is internalized in the citizen. You might say that it would have been better to have no control, no police, in the first place; then there would be no police states, functioning or otherwise. This would seem to be Burroughs' position, but it is not consistent with his picture of sex. The libertarian position usually has as one of its axioms a love of Nature and the natural, that is, of the life-principle itself, commonly identified with sex. But there is little overt love of the life-principle in Naked Lunch, *and sex, while magnified—a common trait of homosexual literature—is a kind of mechanical mantrap baited with fresh meat. The sexual climax, the jet of sperm, accompanied by a whistling scream, is often a death spasm, and the "perfect" orgasm would seem to be the posthumous orgasm of the hanged man, shooting his jissom into pure space.*

It is true that Nature and sex are two-faced and that growth is death-oriented. But if Nature is not seen as far more good than evil, then a need for control is posited. And, strangely, this seems to be Burroughs' position too. The human virus can now be treated, *he says* with emphasis, *meaning the species itself. By scientific methods, he implies. Yet the laboratory of* Naked Lunch *is a musical-comedy inferno, and Dr. Benway's assistant is a female chimpanzee. It is impossible, as Burroughs knows, to have scientific experiment without control. Then what? Self-control? Do-it-yourself? But self-control, again, is an internalized system of authority, a subjection of the impulse to the will, the least "natural" part of the personality. Such a system might suit Marcus Aurelius, but it hardly seems congenial to the author of* Naked Lunch. *And even if it were (for the author is at once puritan and tolerant), it would not form the basis for scientific experiment on the "human virus." Only for scientific experiment on oneself.*

Possibly this is what Burroughs means: in fact his present literary exercises may be stages in such a deliberate experiment. The questions just posed would not arise if Naked Lunch *did not contain messages that unluckily are somewhat arcane. Not just messages; prescriptions. That—to answer a pained question that keeps coming up like a refrain —is why the book is taken seriously. Burroughs' remarkable talent is only part of the reason; the other part is that, finally, for the first time in recent years, a talented writer means what he says to be taken and used literally, like an Rx prescription. The literalness of Burroughs is the opposite of "literature." Unsentimental and factual, he writes as though his thoughts had the quality of self-evidence. In short, he has a crankish courage, but all courage nowadays is probably crankish.*

YOUNG ADAM

Frances Lengel

Cathie. I met her for the first time in a holiday resort on the West Coast. I had gone there because I had to get a job to earn some money. I was leaning on my elbows on the balustrade of the promenade looking out across the sands toward the sea. I had been aware for some time of a slight movement, of the soft sea wind in colored cloth, just below me on the beach. A girl was lying there, attempting with modest movements to oil her own back. I don't know whether at that moment she was aware of me. I allowed my eyes to fall occasionally and each time I did so she seemed to react by giving up the attempt to oil her back and by moving her oiled hand over the smooth flesh of her thighs and calves. They were well within her reach and she oiled them with great sensuality.

I watched for perhaps ten minutes. I felt sure by this time that she was inviting me to make contact with her and I was afraid that if I did not do so she would tire, gather her things together, and move along to a more populated part of the beach.

I walked quickly along to the nearest steps, descended to the beach, and walked toward her along the sand. I walked slowly, trying to gauge her reactions.

She was wearing sunglasses. Behind them, I felt her eyes focused on me, weighing me up.

There is a point at which a man and a woman stalk one another like animals. It is normally, in most human situations, a very civilized kind of stalking, each move on either side being capable of more than one interpretation. This is a defensive measure. One can, as it were, pretend up to the last moment not to be aware of the sexual construction that can be placed upon one's own movements; one is not bound to admit one's intention to seduce before one is certain that the seduction is consented to. But one can never be quite certain because the other is just as wary, just as unwilling to consent to a man who has not shown clearly his intentions are sexual as the man is to make his intentions obvious without prior consent. So a man and a woman fence with one another and the fencing is the more delicate because neither can wholly trust the other not to simulate ignorance of all that has passed between them. In every situation the man might be a puritan, the woman a woman who wishes to have the pleasure of being courted without the finality of the sexual act itself.

Cathie, for example, could have pretended, and, as a matter of fact did pretend, to be surprised at my sudden presence beside her on the beach. It had given her pleasure to be seen stroking her own limbs but I had no way of knowing whether she would now consent to have me stroke them. She knew this, just as women usually know it, and she was going to enjoy having my purpose unfolded before her. At the point at which she was certain, she would be able to consent or not and without reference to my desire.

I knew this and she knew it as I sat down beside her and offered her a cigarette. She accepted it. We talked casually about the weather, about the sun, and that made it possible for me to pick up the bottle of sun-tan oil and to examine it. She said I could use some if I wanted to.

I was still fully dressed and I had no bathing costume with me so I said there was not much point in it. Before she could interpret this as a withholding of myself I suggested that I could oil her back for her and I confessed that I had been watching her from the promenade above. She pretended not to know about this, but without a word she rolled over on to her belly and exposed her back to me. She was wearing a two-piece bathing costume of black nylon, the lower part sheathing her immaculate buttocks closely and the upper part hidden beneath her except for the thin strand of nylon which ran across her back just below her shoulder blades.

I began at the small of her back, working with the oil in ever-increasing circles to the limits of her exposed flesh. Soon, however, the massage became a caress, and when I felt her succumb to it, her face buried in her towel in the sand, my fingers slipped first underneath the strap of the top half and then gently on to the smooth mound of her buttocks beneath the taut black nylon. She made no effort to resist. She had shut out the rest of the world from herself, shut out the fear of a casual onlooker from the promenade, by the simple expedient of closing her eyes. I continued to caress her for about five minutes, speaking occasionally to reassure her, and then my hand moved down across the sleek nylon on to the smooth heavy fats of her thighs. Still pretending to oil her, I caressed her ankles, her calves, behind her knees, and more voluptuously, the dull sheen of her inner thighs which yellowed slightly where they joined her abandoned torso and where the nylon came, thin almost as a cigarette paper, over the hot rut between her legs.

Not far away were some rocks under which I knew it would be possible to be out of sight both from the beach and from the promenade. I did not even know the girl's name at the time and I was wondering whether I dared suggest that we should go out of sight of other people. After all, even with my hands so intimately at work on the softnesses of her body, she was at present safe, all fears gone and tensions relaxed. I could do nothing on the exposed part of the beach. And then, even if she were to consent, the sensations, the looseness which I had already caused in her during the caress might fade entirely as we walked to a more private place. She would have a hundred opportunities to revise and decide again. At that moment, I believe, had there been no danger of being witnessed, I could have pulled the pants of her bathing costume down over her thighs, but whether, out of the sun, after a walk of a hundred yards, I would still be able to assert myself with a girl who was, after all, a stranger, I couldn't know. The thought made me pause. I was unwilling to lose what I had already gained in a premature attempt to seduce her. But my doubts did not remain for long. My fingers moved upward between her thighs. She was quivering with pleasure, totally oblivious to the people who walked past on the promenade overhead. I leaned down and whispered that we could find a place to be alone together farther along the beach.

For a moment she did not answer. She was lying with her eyes closed almost as though she were unconscious. I knew then that she wanted to go to wherever it was but that she had not yet overcome all her scruples. The longer she analyzed, the cooler she would become. At this point it is always difficult to know what to do. If one is too enthusiastic, the woman has her "suspicions" confirmed, she *knows* what you want and is able by some species of rationalization, and in spite of the fact that she knew all along what you wanted, knew, that is, that she had no need to confirm her "suspicions," to be shocked by your proposal. She has, as it were, contemplated the possibility quite calmly and even with excitement up until the moment when you actually pose the question. At that moment, unless you have been extremely tactful, she is liable to become indignant that you should be able even to contemplate the possibility. On an animal level, she wants urgently to have sex, but, as soon as the desire reaches the level of speculation, the codes operative in everyday life come back into play. The most lustful woman is liable to be the most righteously indignant, perhaps because, having copulated before, she is sentimental enough to regret the fact that she has nothing to lose, more probably because she resents your knowing it. What do you think I am! she says dishonestly, knowing very well that you know as she does what she is and what you could most enjoyably do together.

If one is, on the contrary, not enthusiastic enough, the woman is liable to be offended in almost the same way. What does he think I am? she says to herself, resenting the fact that you take her compliance or non-compliance so lightly. He treats me as though I were a lustful bitch! That, of course, is true. The woman whose thighs have been stroked *is* a lustful bitch and the woman and the man (the lustful dog) both know it. The woman knows it. What she resents is the man's knowing it. She is ashamed of appearing naked in that way before another person. That is the purpose of convention, to inculcate shame. Our priests have been singularly successful during perhaps thirty centuries. Thus a man must take account of a woman's shame, at least until he is between her legs when, happily, the woman has no more need of her shame, except perhaps to increase her pleasure.

Let's go anyway, I said. We needn't do anything when we get there.

She opened her eyes and smiled, her "suspicions" calmed.

It's not far, is it? she said.

Perhaps she too was frightened that her desire would die on the way.

A hundred yards, I said, pointing. Over by those rocks there.

Without another word, she rose, lifted her towel and the small bag in which she carried her make-up, a book, and the other articles which a woman takes to the beach, and walked beside me in the direction of the rocks.

We walked separately, almost without speaking.

The rocks were at the far end of the promenade, beyond the last hotel, and they rose up sharply and steeply enough to obscure anything on their seaboard side from the sight of whoever passed by on the promenade. They were shaped almost like a horseshoe within which small clusters of rock rose upward from the flat sand, forming tiny water-logged caves. We walked round the nearest point which sloped downward almost to the sea's edge and as soon as we had done so we had the impression that we were in a kind of amphitheater. Once inside, we followed the lee of the outer perimeter to a patch of dry sand, overhung by rock, but which was still in the direct line of the sun.

I threw off my jacket, she arranged her towel, and we sat down. The inarticulate closeness which had existed between us a few moments before had evaporated. She especially was suspicious and aloof. We smoked two cigarettes one after the other before she finally lay down and closed her eyes. This time, she was lying on her back, the disc of her belly gleaming with oil, her long legs apart and tapering downward from the sleek cask of her nylon bathing costume. Her thighs, soft, and already tanned dark with the sun, rose smoothly under glistening particles of sand which, as she had lain on her front, clung now to the oiled and almost unhaired skin. Her breasts were held tightly and nervously in the black nylon pockets of her brassiere.

Above was her face, the lips heavy and sensual, the eyes closed under almond-shaped eyelids.

There was no one in sight.

The bottle of oil represented for the moment our only means of contact. A hand naked, uncoated with the viscous gold substance, would have been received coldly, perhaps repulsed. I poured it generously into the palm of my hand before leaning over and smearing it over the smooth skin of her calves. From the point at which my hand touched her flesh there was no further resistance, merely a twitch of her whole body as the oil ran down the inside of her legs which, now that the tensions had again relaxed, crooked themselves slightly upward, raising the knees and exposing the hanging thighs to my caress. Soon my palms moved upward away from her flesh and I was caressing with my fingertips. Her whole body reacted to it, the buttocks tightening and straining to rise from the toweled sand in which they were embedded, her mound purposeful beneath the wafer of nylon which was wet at my groping fingertips.

The bottom part of her bathing costume peeled off the sultry white flesh of her lower abdomen like the bark off a supple switch, with a minute commotion as the constricting nylon was pulled away. Without further delay I pulled the costume down over her willing thighs and calves and twisted it off her feet.

Her eyes were still closed. Her body was entirely bare now except for the brassiere. Gently, I insinuated my hands under her shoulder blades and unhooked it. Her breasts caved slightly to their natural set and the firm purplish teats were exposed, stranded with spiderwebs of sweat which ran up over her breasts toward her armpits. She made no effort to resist. A moment later, our lips came together, and I felt myself sucked inward. She groaned. We rolled over under the shade of the rocks. That was my first experience of Cathie. We were together a long time.

Our love-making was usually a sudden affair. When we had lived together for some time, the constriction of our life set us at a distance from one another. We were no longer free to choose being together. It was the necessity to break through those constrictions that led us, unconsciously for the most part, to explore violence.

If from a distance you have watched a man and woman making love, if, for example, they have gone about it with you still in the room, the fact of the witness's presence increasing their desire, you will be struck by the fact that in their soft nobbled movements, as their bellies slide together and retract in small strong heaps of muscle, there is an undercurrent of violence. You become aware suddenly, as you dissociate the idea of love from the strong haired torques and thrusts of the limbs, that you are watching a union of animals which will continue brutally at least until the moment at which the male achieves his orgasm. The female's legs perhaps have on more than one occasion sought to extricate themselves, because her position has not been satisfactory, or because she desires to arrest momentarily the flow of passion, but her muffled and near-impotent movements have been trapped and regathered perhaps between his knees, much as a tomcat traps and regathers a female cat to him, and she is forced again to submit. These small, almost imperceptible, spoiled movements come across to a spectator and constitute the best evidence of the constant presence of violence in the sexual act.

Now, if there is no passion, or if the passion has been suffocated by the civilized structure into which an ordinary man allows it to run, if the accumulated tedium of years of living together has killed the animal excitement of the sexual act, it is not surprising that men seek artificial means of stimulating violence so that the act, become frantic, may again be passionate.

There was an undercurrent of violence always in our unions but it was not until one day in our small flat in Leith that we came to realize that violence alone could make our love interesting.

Cathie worked during the day. I hung about the house doing the small chores, reading, vegetating. One day I made a large bowl of bright yellow custard. I don't remember why exactly. There was a lot of milk in the house. The weather was quite warm and I was afraid it would turn sour. Anyway, I was bored. I made it early in the afternoon and it had stood cooling on the dresser for about three hours before Cathie returned from work. I was reading the evening paper when she came.

I could see she was in a bad mood. She fiddled around with this and that without paying any attention to me. Now and again she breathed heavily to let me know that she was exasperated. I watched her over the top of the newspaper.

Suddenly she said she was going out.

I did not answer.

She hesitated and then, without another word, she began to change her clothes. She had taken off what she was wearing and was sitting in her panties rolling on her best nylon stockings. She did not excite me at all. I saw only an exasperated woman whose body bored me and whose conversation was constructed for the most part to express her resentment of the fact that her body did bore me. Suddenly she said:

What have *you* been doing all day anyway?

Nothing much, I said. I made some custard.

You made what?

Some custard, I said.

What did you want to make custard for?

I stood up.

I thought I might make some custard, I said. It struck me as a good idea. So I made it. Here it is over on the dresser.

I walked toward the bowl. It was a very large bowl and it must have contained about two and a half pints of custard.

I don't give a damn where it is! she said, pulling on her other stocking. You'll have to eat it yourself, that's all. I certainly don't want any custard.

I looked at her. Suddenly I was annoyed with her. I had been bored all day. I had enjoyed making the custard. I was damned if I was going to have her sit there making nasty remarks about my custard. Her face had taken on that kind of stupidly defiant look. It angered me. She was not looking at me even. She was straightening the seams of her stockings. Above them were her black nylon panties. That was all she was wearing. Her hair, still in cattails after her work, was hanging over her face as she bent to twist the stocking straight about her calf. I spoke slowly and threateningly.

I made the custard and you're going to eat it, I said.

I don't know why I wanted her to eat it but I did.

You know what you can do with it! she said derisively.

I know what I *am* going to do with it! I replied.

I threw it at her.

The custard, slipping from the bowl, a massive yellow gobbet of it, sailed across the room and struck her on the breasts. It had not hardened. It had the consistency of a soft glue paste. She screamed and tilted backward in her chair so that her body, now covered with custard, sprawled across the dusty oilcloth on the floor. Her thighs meanwhile in their upward arc as the chair spun backward and her hot spread buttocks glimmering whitely beneath the gauze-fine nylon stimulated me to further action. I lifted a stick from the fireplace, the split side of an egg crate, and leapt upon her. She was whimpering with fright. I grasped her by one arm, twisted her about so that her great big and now custard smeared buttocks were facing me and with all the strength of my right arm I thrashed at them with the rough slat of wood. I thrashed her mercilessly for about a minute. She was making shrill whinnying noises as she threshed about on the dusty floor. The custard was dripping off her nipples and mingling already with the short hairs of her sex. I paused, moved over to the mantle-piece and grasped a bottle of bright blue ink. She was seated on her haunches, crying, wheezing and shaking. I emptied the contents of the bottle over her head so that it ran through her hair and down over her face and shoulders where it met the custard. It was then that I remembered the sauce and the vanilla essence. I stirred them into the mixture, tomato ketchup, brown sauce, and a bottle of vanilla essence, blues, greens, yellows, and reds, all the colors of the rainbow.

I don't know whether she was crying or laughing as I poured a two-pound bag of sugar over her. Her whole near-naked body was twitching convulsively, a blue breast and a yellow-and-red one, a green belly, and all the odor of her pain and sweat and gnashing. By that time I was hard. I stripped off my clothes, grasped the slat of the egg crate, and moved among her with prick and stick, like a tycoon.

When I rose from her, she was in a hideous mess, almost unrecognizable as a white woman, and the custard and the ink and the sugar sparkled like surprising meats on the haired twist of her satisfied mound.

I washed and went out without a word. When I returned, there was no evidence of the mess. She was in bed, and as I got in beside her, I felt her arms close about me and she kissed me on the lips.

FRANCES LENGEL

When Alexander Trocchi arrived in Paris he was an eager young Scotsman with a brilliant academic future; he was so misinformed of worldly things that he went to live near the Gare de l'Est—the city's most neutral and forbidding district.

It took him one year to discover the Left Bank and to understand why he had come to Paris. When, at last, he moved to Saint-Germain-des-Prés, he was immediately transformed; he shed his subdued provincial manner to become the big bad literary wolf of his time and day.

Alex was always busy cultivating extreme attitudes, extravagant styles and wild dreams with great gusto and appetite. Sometimes he misunderstood his appetite for ambition, and launched into great projects, very few of which succeeded because there were too many other interests and also too many girls around.

But Alex had a certain amount of electricity buzzing around his shaggy brow, and he naturally became the center of a very active literary group which formed around his short-lived magazine, Merlin.

He was the first of Olympia's all-out literary stallions; his novel, Helen and Desire, *published under the pen name of Frances Lengel, became a model of the kind. It was the first of a series of Frances Lengel productions, all of them very robust and funny parodies of pornography; and some, as* Young Adam, *of excellent quality.*

Although all his books had the honor of being banned by the French authorities, Helen and Desire *was saved from total annihilation by being reprinted under a different title:* Desire and Helen. *The French police never found out; perhaps now they will.*

TELENY

Anonymous

*A*s my thoughts were entirely absorbed, it was some time before I noticed that a man, who had sprung up from somewhere, was walking by my side. I grew nervous; for I fancied that he not only tried to keep pace with me but also to catch my attention, for he hummed and whistled snatches of songs, coughed, cleared his throat, and scraped his feet.

All these sounds fell upon my dreamy ears, but failed to arouse my attention. All my senses were fixed on the two figures in front of me. He therefore walked on, then turned round on his heels, and stared at me. My eyes saw all this without heeding him in the least.

He lingered once more, let me pass, walked on at a brisker pace, and was again beside me. Finally, I looked at him. Though it was cold, he was but slightly dressed. He wore a short, black velvet jacket and a pair of light gray, closely fitting trousers marking the shape of the thighs and buttocks like tights.

As I looked at him he stared at me again, then smiled with that vacant, vapid, idiotic, facial contraction of a *raccrocheuse*. Then, always looking at me with an inviting leer, he directed his steps toward a neighboring *Vespasienne*.

"What is there so peculiar about me?" I mused, "that the fellow is ogling me in that way?"

Without turning round, however, or noticing him any further, I walked on, my eyes fixed on Teleny.

As I passed by another bench, someone again scraped his feet and cleared his throat, evidently bent on making me turn my head. I did so. There was nothing more remarkable about him than there is in the first man you meet. Seeing me look at him, he either unbuttoned or buttoned up his trousers.

After a while I again heard steps coming from behind; the person was close up to me. I smelt a strong scent—if the noxious odor of musk or of patchouli can be called a scent.

The person touched me slightly as he passed by. He begged my pardon; it was the man of the velvet jacket, or his Dromio. I looked at him as he again stared at me and grinned. His eyes were painted with kohl, his cheeks were dabbed with rouge. He was quite beardless. For a moment, I doubted whether he was a man or a woman; but when he stopped again before the column I was fully persuaded of his sex.

Someone else came with mincing steps, and shaking his buttocks, from behind one of these *pissoirs*. He was an old, wiry, simpering man, as shriveled as a frostbitten pippin. His cheeks were very hollow, and his projecting cheekbones very red; his face was shaven and shorn, and he wore a wig with long, fair, flaxen locks.

He walked in the posture of the Venus of Medici; that is, with one hand on his middle parts, and the other on his breast. His looks were not only very demure, but there was an almost maidenly coyness about the old man that gave him the appearance of a virgin-pimp.

He did not stare, but cast a sidelong glance at me as he went by. He was met by a workman—a strong and sturdy fellow, either a butcher or a smith by trade. The old man would evidently have slunk by unperceived, but the workman stopped him. I could not hear what they said, for though they were but a few steps away, they spoke in that hushed tone peculiar to lovers; but I seemed to be the object of their talk, for the workman turned and stared at me as I passed. They parted.

The workman walked on for twenty steps, then he turned on his heel and walked back exactly on a line with me, seemingly bent on meeting me face to face.

I looked at him. He was a brawny man, with massive features; clearly, a fine specimen of a male. As he passed by me he clenched his powerful fist, doubled his muscular arm at the elbow, and then moved it vertically hither and thither for a few times, like a piston rod in action, as it slipped in and out of the cylinder.

Some signs are so evidently clear and full of meaning that no initiation is needed to understand them. This workman's sign was one of them.

Now I knew who all these nightwalkers were. Why they so persistently stared at me, and the meaning of all their little tricks to catch my attention. Was I dreaming? I looked around. The workman had stopped, and he repeated his request in a different way. He shut his left fist, then thrust the forefinger of his right hand in the hole made by the palm and fingers, and moved it in and out. He was bluntly explicit. I was not mistaken. I hastened on, musing whether the cities of the plain had been destroyed by fire and brimstone.

As I learnt later in life, every large city has its particular haunts— its square, its garden for such recreation. And the police? Well, it winks at it, until some crying offense is committed; for it is not safe to stop the mouths of craters. Brothels of men-whores not being allowed, such trysting places must be tolerated, or the whole is a modern Sodom or Gomorrah.

—What! there are such cities nowadays?

—Aye! for Jehovah has acquired experience with age; so He has got to understand His children a little better than He did of yore, for He has either come to righter sense of toleration, or, like Pilate, He has washed His hands, and has quite discarded them.

At first I felt a deep sense of disgust at seeing the old catamite pass by me again, and lift, with utmost modesty, his arm from his breast, thrust his bony finger between his lips, and move it in the same fashion as the workman had done his arm, but trying to give all his movements a maidenly coyness. He was—as I learnt later—a *pompeur de dard*, or as I might call him, a "sperm-sucker"; this was his specialty. He did the work for the love of the thing, and an experience of many years had made him a master of his trade. He, it appears, lived in every other respect like a hermit, and only indulged himself in one thing—fine lawn handkerchiefs, either with lace or embroidery, to wipe the amateur's instrument when he had done with it.

The old man went down toward the river's edge, apparently inviting me for a midnight stroll in the mist, under the arches of the bridge, or in some out-of-the-way nook or other corner.

Another man came up from there; this one was adjusting his dress, and scratching his hind part like an ape. Notwithstanding the creepy feeling these men gave me, the scene was so entirely new that I must say it rather interested me.

—And Teleny?

—I had been so taken up with all these midnight wanderers that I lost sight both of him and of Briancourt, when all at once I saw them reappear.

With them there was a young Zouave sublieutenant and a dapper and dashing fellow, and a slim and swarthy youth, apparently an Arab.

The meeting did not seem to have been a carnal one. Anyhow, the soldier was entertaining his friends with his lively talk, and by the few words which my ear caught I understood that the topic was an interesting one. Moreover, as they passed by each bench, the couples seated thereon nudged each other as if they were acquainted with them.

As I passed them I shrugged up my shoulders, and buried my head in my collar. I even put up my handkerchief to my face. Still, notwithstanding all my precautions, Teleny seemed to have recognized me, although I had walked on without taking the slightest notice of him.

I heard their merry laugh as I passed; an echo of loathsome words was still ringing in my ears; sickening faces of effete, womanish men traversed the street, trying to beguile me by all that is nauseous.

I hurried on, sick at heart, disappointed, hating myself and my fellow creatures, musing whether I was any better than all these worshipers of Priapus who were inured to vice. I was pining for the love of one man who did not care more for me than for any of these sodomites.

It was late at night, and I walked on without exactly knowing where my steps were taking me to. I had not to cross the water on my way home, what then made me do so? Anyhow, all at once I found myself standing in the very middle of the bridge, staring vacantly at the open space in front of me.

The river, like a silvery thoroughfare, parted the town in two. On either side huge shadowy houses rose out of the mist; blurred domes, dim towers, vaporous and gigantic spires stared, quivering, up to the clouds, and faded away in the fog.

Underneath I could perceive the sheen of the cold, bleak, and bickering river, flowing faster and faster, as if fretful at not being able to outdo itself in its own speed, chafing against the arches that stopped it, curling in tiny breakers, and whirling away in angry eddies, whilst the dark pillars shed patches of ink-black shade on the glittering and shivering stream.

As I looked upon these dancing, restless shadows, I saw a myriad of fiery, snakelike elves gliding to and fro through them, winking and beckoning to me as they twirled and they rolled, luring me down to rest in those Lethean waters.

They were right. Rest must be found below those dark arches, on the soft, slushy sand of that swirling river.

How deep and fathomless those waters seemed! Veiled as they were by the mist, they had all the attraction of the abyss. Why should I not seek there that balm of forgetfulness which alone could ease my aching head, could calm my burning breast?

Why?

Was it because the Almighty had fixed His canon against self-slaughter?

How, when, and where?

With His fiery finger, when He made that *coup de théâtre* on Mount Sinai?

If so, why was He tempting me beyond my strength?

Would any father induce a beloved child to disobey him, simply to have the pleasure of chastising him afterwards? Would any man deflower his own daughter, not out of lust, but only to taunt her with her incontinence? Surely, if such a man ever lived, he was after Jehovah's own image.

No, life is only worth living as long as it is pleasant. To me, just then, it was a burden. The passion I had tried to stifle, and which was merely smoldering, had burst out with renewed strength, entirely

mastering me. That crime could therefore only be overcome by
another. In my case suicide was not only allowable, but laudable—
nay, heroic.

What did the Gospel say? "If thine eye . . ." and so forth.

All these thoughts whirled through my mind like little fiery
snakes. Before me in the mist, Teleny—like a vaporous angel of light
—seemed to be quickly gazing at me with his deep, sad, and thoughtful eyes; below, the rushing waters had for me a siren's sweet, en-
ticing voice.

I felt my brain reeling. I was losing my senses. I cursed this beautiful world of ours—this paradise, that man has turned into a hell. I cursed this narrow-minded society of ours, that only thrives upon hypocrisy. I cursed our blighting religion, that lays its veto upon all the pleasures of the senses.

I was already climbing on the parapet, decided to seek forget-fulness in those Stygian waters, when two strong arms clasped me tightly and held me fast.

—It was Teleny?

—It was.

"Camille, my love, my soul, are you mad?" said he, in a stifled, panting voice.

Was I dreaming—was it he? Teleny? Was he my guardian angel or a tempting demon? Had I gone quite mad?

All these thoughts chased one another, and left me bewildered. Still, after a moment, I understood that I was neither mad nor dream-ing. It was Teleny in flesh and blood, for I felt him against me as we were closely clasped in each other's arms. I had wakened to life from a horrible nightmare.

The strain my nerves had undergone, and the utter faintness that followed, together with his powerful embrace, made me feel as if our two bodies clinging closely together had amalgamated or melted into a single one.

A most peculiar sensation came over me at this moment. As my hands wandered over his head, his neck, his shoulder, his arms, I could not feel him at all; in fact, it seemed to me as if I were touching my own body. Our burning foreheads were pressed against each other, and his swollen and throbbing veins seemed my own fluttering pulses.

Instinctively, and without seeking each other, our mouths united by a common consent. We did not kiss, but our breath gave life to our two beings.

I remained vaguely unconscious for some time, feeling my strength ebb slowly away, leaving but vitality enough to know that I was yet alive.

All at once I felt a mighty shock from head to foot; there was a reflux from the heart to the brain. Every nerve in my body was tin-gling; all my skin seemed pricked with the points of sharp needles. Our mouths which had withdrawn now clung again to each other with newly awakened lust. Our lips—clearly seeking to engraft themselves together—pressed and rubbed with such passionate strength that the blood began to ooze from them—nay, it seemed as if this fluid, rushing up from our two hearts, was bent upon mingling together to celebrate in that auspicious moment the old hymeneal rites of nations—the marriage of two bodies, not by the communion of emblematic wine but of blood itself.

We thus remained for some time in a state of overpowering delirium, feeling, every instant, a more rapturous, maddening pleasure in each other's kisses, which kept goading us on to madness by increasing that heat which they could not allay, and by stimulating that hunger they could not appease.

The very quintessence of love was in these kisses. All that was excellent in us—the essential part of our beings—kept rising and evaporating from our lips like the fumes of an ethereal, intoxicating, ambrosial fluid.

Nature, hushed and silent, seemed to hold her breath to look upon us, for such ecstasy of bliss had seldom, if ever, been felt here below. I was subdued, prostrated, shattered. The earth was spinning round me, sinking under my feet. I had no longer strength enough to stand. I felt sick and faint. Was I dying? If so, death must be the happiest moment of our life, for such rapturous joy could never be felt again.

How long did I remain senseless? I cannot tell. All I know is that I awoke in the midst of a whirlwind, hearing the rushing of waters around me. Little by little I came back to consciousness. I tried to free myself from his grasp.

"Leave me! Leave me alone! Why did you not let me die? This world is hateful to me, why should I drag on a life I loathe?"

"Why? For my sake." Thereupon he whispered softly, in that unknown tongue of his, some magic words which seemed to sink into my soul. Then he added, "Nature has formed us for each other; why withstand her? I can only find happiness in your love, and in yours alone; it is not only my heart but my soul that panteth for yours."

With an effort of my whole being I pushed him away from me, and staggered back.

"No, no!" I cried, "do not tempt me beyond my strength; let me rather die."

"Thy will be done, but we shall die together, so that at least in death we may not be parted. There is an afterlife, we may then, at least, cleave to one another like Dante's Francesca and her lover Paolo. Here," said he, unwinding a silken scarf that he wore round his waist, "let us bind ourselves closely together, and leap into the flood."

I looked at him, and shuddered. So young, so beautiful, and I was thus to murder him! The vision of Antinoüs as I had seen it the first time he played appeared before me.

He had tied the scarf tightly round his waist, and he was about to pass it around me.

"Come."

The die was cast. I had not the right to accept such a sacrifice from him.

"No," quoth I, "let us live."

"Live," added he, "and then?"

He did not speak for some moments, as if waiting for a reply to that question which had not been framed in words. In answer to his mute appeal I stretched out my hands toward him. He—as if frightened that I should escape him—hugged me tightly with all the strength of irrepressible desire.

"I love you!" he whispered, "I love you madly! I cannot live without you any longer."

"Nor can I," said I, faintly; "I have struggled against my passion in vain, and now I yield to it, not tamely, but eagerly, gladly. I am yours, Teleny! Happy to be yours, yours for ever and yours alone!"

For all answer there was a stifled hoarse cry from his innermost breast; his eyes were lighted up with a flash of fire; his craving amounted to rage; it was that of the wild beast seizing his prey; that of the lonely male finding at last a mate. Still his intense eagerness was more than that; it was also a soul issuing forth to meet another soul. It was a longing of the senses, and a mad intoxication of the brain.

Could this burning, unquenchable fire that consumed our bodies be called lust? We clung as hungrily to one another as the famished animal does when it fastens on the food it devours; and as we kissed each other with ever-increasing greed, my fingers were feeling his curly hair, or paddling the soft skin of his neck. Our legs being clasped together, his phallus, in strong erection, was rubbing against mine no less stiff and stark. We were, however, always shifting our position, so as to get every part of our bodies in as close a contact as possible; and thus feeling, clasping, hugging, kissing, and biting each other, we must have looked, on that bridge amidst the thickening fog, like two damned souls suffering eternal torment.

The hand of Time had stopped; and I think we should have continued goading each other in our mad desire until we had quite lost our senses—for we were both on the verge of madness—had we not been stopped by a trifling incident.

A belated cab—wearied with the day's toil—was slowly trudging its way homeward. The driver was sleeping on his box; the poor, broken-down jade, with its head drooping almost between its knees, was likewise slumbering—dreaming, perhaps, of unbroken rest, of new-mown hay, of the fresh and flowery pastures of its youth; even the slow rumbling of the wheels had a sleepy, purring, snoring sound in its irksome sameness.

"Come home with me," said Teleny, in a low, nervous, and trembling voice; "come and sleep with me," added he, in the soft, hushed, and pleading tone of the lover who would fain be understood without words.

I pressed his hands for all answer.

"Will you come?"

"Yes," I whispered, almost inaudibly.

This low, hardly articulate sound was the hot breath of vehement desire; this lisped monosyllable was the willing consent to his eagerest wish.

AUTHORSHIP

Oscar Wilde, at the height of his fame, which was prodigious, and at the height of his creativity, which has enriched English literature with some of its finest prose and poetry, became involved in a love-hate affair with the young Alfred Douglas which ended in Wilde's total ruin. Oscar Wilde, probably an active homosexual throughout his life, had maintained a façade of respectability: a wife, two children, a steady output of work, friendship with the leading minds of Victorian England. In his early forties, with Alfred as the aggressor, he began the frenzied affair which led to a criminal trial in 1895 with Alfred's insane and powerful father, Lord Douglas. The lengthy proceedings ended in the court's decision for Lord Douglas and against Wilde. Wilde was imprisoned for two years, suffering the filth of nineteenth-century jails, the loss of his considerable fortune, his family, his reputation, and that delicate balance of abandon and discipline that had enabled him to produce his great works. Upon his release from Reading Gaol, Oscar Wilde, a miserable approximation of the flamboyant leading wit he had been, slipped out of England, assumed the alias of Sebastian Mellmoth, and secluded himself in France for the few brief years left until his death in 1900. The day he met young Alfred Douglas, as he records in de Profundis, *was the day the end of all he valued in life began.*

He had already met Alfred in 1893, the date which appears on the first and only previous edition of Teleny. *When the book appeared it was unsigned, but since its original publication, booksellers, collectors, and students of Wilde have persistently attributed its authorship to Wilde.* Teleny, *or* The Reverse of the Medal *is an outrageous, romantic, hysterical record of a homosexual love affair set in fashionable Parisian society at the close of the nineteenth century. The few copies of the limited first edition were immediately buried in private collections. It is believed that the book was written for the amusement of an exclusive few, and that each of the group, prominent writers and artists, wrote and exchanged extravagantly pornographic works. Having received an anonymously bound volume, with additional evidence to substantiate that this book could indeed be attributed to Oscar Wilde, Olympia Press reprinted* Teleny *in its original, uncut, unsigned state.*

FUZZ

AGAINST JUNK

THE SAGA OF THE
NARCOTICS BRIGADE

AKBAR DEL PIOMBO
COLLAGES & PICTORIAL
BY RUBINGTON

*S*ir Edwin Fuzz enjoying an hour of leisure in his London club. Foremost narcotics expert of the United Kingdom and sleuth par excellence, he reads, unaware of the impending significance for himself, stories of the sudden outbreaks of violence ravaging the streets of New York. . . .

Brutal knifings. . . .

Sudden deaths due to narcotics. . . .

And the most hideous case of the swollen corpse: death induced by an overdose of heroin. Faced with an outbreak of criminality which reached Gargantuan proportions, the New York police, their back against the wall, had no recourse but wire an urgent message to Sir Edwin Fuzz, requesting his services to help them smash the drug ring responsible for all this mayhem.

Arriving in secret in New York, Sir Edwin's first view of the city's life convinced him it was a seething hell of criminality.

Little time was lost in acquainting the famous detective with the methods and facilities at his disposal. He was noted to scrutinize the women with exceptional attention: "Know your enemy," he explained, "that is the keystone of my methods."

Sir Edwin undergoing rapid briefing. State and Federal authorities co-operated to put at his fingertips all the data accumulated in years of combating the spread of drug addiction.

Some of the more striking exhibits shown are presented on the following pages and will convince the reader of both the thoroughness of the police, and the ingenuity and craft of certain of the more redoubtable criminals.

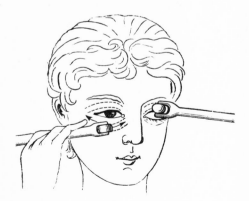

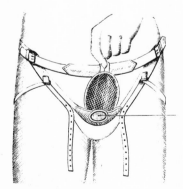

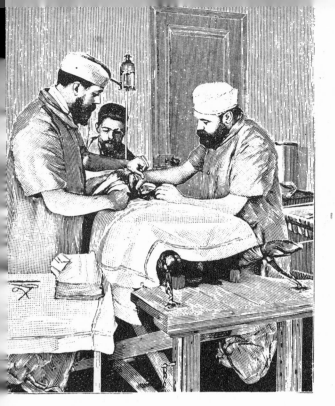

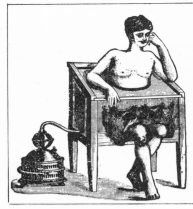

THE FIX. Fig. 1: Californian two-hour pelvic region "fix." Fig. 2: "Opium Vapor Bath"; upright position for two-hour "fix."

"Junkie" receiving daily dose. Stomach incisional system is in use only as a last resort when no more puncturable skin surface is available.

Fig. 3: "Quickie" vapor bath, upright position, for limbs only.

"Stoned."

Examples of
"stoned" subjects.

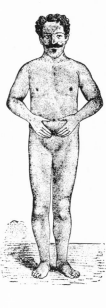

New York detective   plete   inflexibility
demonstrating com-   of "stoned" subject.

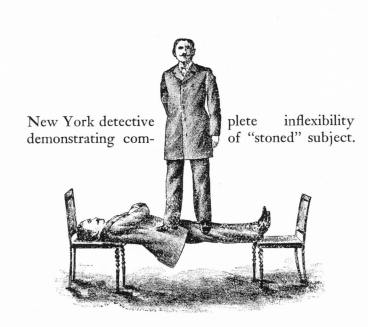

Here we find one of the most amazing hauls ever made in narcotics history. Intensive laboratory examination has not yet revealed the functions of all the curious instruments pictured. Sir Edwin is at a loss to explain the clocklike instrument in the lower right-hand corner, obviously the work of Swiss craftsmen. Most of the needle-like objects were meant for intravenous hypodermic syringes and their considerable variety of form, the use of wheels and drilling apparatus suggests they were employed by a fanatical sect of masochistic "junkies." (*Junkies:* criminal term for Heroin addicts.) At the top left, one sees the more classical syringes with gadgets that served equally for self punishment or clandestine obstetrics. Top right and bottom left show two possible functions for the clock mechanism; one of Sir Edwin's pet theories is that the addict of low means could hereby attain his daily dosage by some process of osmosis, whether by placing the special head on the surface of the lung or through the fingers as demonstrated.

Photos found in the possession of San Francisco "Beatnik" and representing a typical jazz-poetry gathering, complete with a prototype bongo drum and orator reciting. Often accompanied with the smoking of "pot." Pseudo-bohemian atmosphere and typical disarray customary with this group. Note the brutish attitudes also common to their type, characteristic of the dope action referred to as being "stoned." The host is a prominent writer for them, although his principal vocabulary centers predominantly on the use of four-letter words, and the stories contain no action other than what is normally considered obscene.

We come now to the mysterious personage known in the "milieu" as "The Man." Here is the key figure in the narcotics drama. Around him centers all the activity of the underworld for he is the principal dispensing agent of the drugs so desperately craved by the criminals. Note particularly the sadistic temperament of this criminal, his extraordinary capacity for dissimulating his appearance in the most outlandish disguises, which has kept him for years out of the tentacles of the police. It was in fact their long-standing inability to capture him which induced the FBI to seek out the services of Sir Edwin Fuzz. It will later be related how Sir Edwin managed at long last to snare this prize catch, to his everlasting glory in the annals of police victories.

"The Man" and his Wife.

"Gentlemen!" Sir Edwin Fuzz cried after the briefing was over, "Gentlemen, after what I have seen, it is perfectly clear that the root of the evil lies not in New York but in San Francisco!" A great murmur followed his statement. "It is clear," he shouted, "that the masterminds as well as the major activity of these criminals is centered in San Francisco. Here you have but the body of the viper . . . but the head is in California. . . ." He immediately proposed an expedition to the West Coast. "Unthinkable!" came the response. "Unheard of . . ." etc., etc. Protocol having raised its nasty head and the principle of noninterference in the affairs of another State (a principle which had already caused a civil war), Sir Edwin picked up his coat. "In that case I am returning to England," he cried, "for by the same token I am only interfering in your private affairs!" Dumbfounded, they called him back, and a hasty conference was held in which his views finally won the day. "They won't like it though," was the unanimous feeling.

Special armament shipped overland to San Francisco, destined to implement Sir Edwin's campaign.

Detectives in San Francisco, waiting for the arrival of Sir Edwin Fuzz, obviously determined to sabotage New Yorkers butting into their affairs.

Instantly aware that the San Francisco police had no intention of co-operating in his campaign, Sir Edwin Fuzz was obliged to resort to subterfuge. He thus ordered his men to disguise themselves as Californians. "You are now secret agents in every sense of the term," he told them. Consequently they were masked most of the time, rarely went abroad in daylight and then only to the nearest bookshop where they secured the necessary reading material to implement their disguise. "You are 'Beat' from now on," Sir Edwin instructed them, "and you will act accordingly. Bone up on 'Zen.' Refrain from washing and let your hair grow. Listen to music . . . the stuff they call 'Cool' . . . learn the names of the bands . . . become adept on the 'Bongo' drum . . . and . . . ! I am afraid it is necessary also . . . learn to take a 'fix'! If you cannot familiarize yourselves with the 'Beat' vocabulary, keep your mouths shut and write poetry. For that you need only extract passages from the Farmer's Almanac and inject obscene words in the right places. . . ."

A month later, bearded and unwashed, Sir Edwin penetrates for the first time into the holy of holies, a gathering of notorious "Beatniks" seen here in the act of absorbing narcotics, the two visible being Opium and Cocaine. Sir Edwin himself is smoking "pot," and in spite of the disagreeable sensations, is very ably managing the "cool" countenance necessary.

Sir Edwin was not long in discovering that the prize he sought was on the premises. In fact "The Man" was in an upstairs room preparing a "fix."

While Sir Edwin was smoking "pot," secret agents strategically deployed prepared to spring the trap. Among the "Beatniks" were several detectives who had succeeded in passing themselves off as criminals, following Sir Edwin's example.

The raid! Infuriated "Beatniks" attempt to storm the exit while hard-battling plainclothesmen drub them into submission.

Thinking of "The Man," Sir Edwin dashed upstairs and burst in upon a couple in an already half-drugged state and apparently preparing a sinful act.

The spectacle in the next room was far more pathetic for there a degraded couple were in the act of leading an innocent woman to her doom. Sir Edwin's ire knew no bounds. . . . The woman went to her knees in gratitude.

Get-away car as it was found abandoned along the highway in "The Man's" desperate attempt to evade the police. ("Beatnik" sketching apparatus in view.)

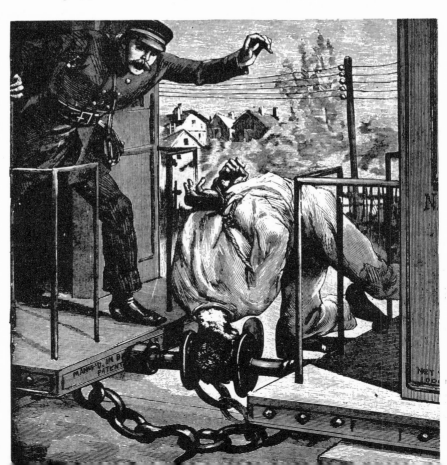

Sir Edwin returning to England. "But Sir," Sgt. Blackhead inquired, "You don't mean to keep that extraordinary growth of hair?" "Why, certainly," replied Sir Edwin. "I have grown quite fond of it. . . . I rather see the point, you know . . . all that fuss about shaving, trimming mustaches, etc., what's the use of it? I do believe it has a favorable effect on the ladies from what I've seen. . . ."

AKBAR DEL PIOMBO

After years of Parisian exile Rubington returned to visit his native land where he fell in the Grand Canyon. His only commentary was: "Ask Piombo for the words . . . I do the pictures."

(del Piombo's words)

I first met R. trying to persuade Maurice to put pictures in his books but Maurice said it was bad enough defending "dirty words."
"What's a dirty picture?" R. said. "I once got a bunch of nudes

(paintings) past the Jersey customs only because their pubic hair was blue. Without hair, no problem. But if they'd been black an 'Art' expert would have been called as only he could tell if this black was 'Dirt' or 'Art.' "

"You don't understand. Your blue hair altered the context. It's unreal."

"But 'real' people shave or dye if they wish. Does that get them out of the context of dirt?"

This idea of pulling things out of context began to intrigue us. R. ripped out pages of old engravings, some of which he reassembled into collages. He'd hold up a picture, I'd give it a title, and we never stopped laughing. The thing was already in the wind with art reproductions appearing in altered context, but we believe ours was the first sustained story, not just a series of gags.

"Maurice doesn't want pictures," R. said when I proposed showing it to him.

"I know. I just want to get his reaction."

STEINER'S TOUR

Philip O'Connor

I take as the suspect palliative of the pain of my smallness the vastness of my eternal cradle; yet, there it is. I ventilate my concerns every now and then, and most easily when they're not going well, with draughts of eternity: when my ceiling sits low I pierce through to the stars, and beyond them back to myself. But, I cannot forget, and as I age even less so, the small range in time and space of my preposterously multifarious tentacles, my adages of sensibility, my patents of character, my sentimental lineage, my short future. Congestion is the trouble of failure. My eternity must be a home-made thing, a star-topped bonnet to go philosophizing in: in itself, a passé, scorned occupation; yet science has always to be mopped up into childishly human understanding. For what is knowledge without the kneading of man? But this spraying around of the scent of eternity when we are in a tight corner is less efficacious than true; it is the druggist use of religion, to round the corners of apparent doom, dim the lines of our state in order to illuminate hope and imminence with the stolen fuel of realization. Eternity has uses for perspective only, which is the offering of only the smallest measures; perspective goes holidaying in myopia. Yet, the hat of the high sky, and its windows through it, and the airs beyond that, and the—carolling—inconceivable beyond that, is a mighty relief to a man with a small chest who pants to get from Tottenham Court Road to Picadilly. At least he may know he isn't going too far. At least he may know he can never—"really"—go too far, or be too silly, or too mad, or stupid or wise, for the great size of things to be unable to digest every folly and wisdom into its infinitely hospitable silence. It is, as I say, a dangerous opiate, a concentrated food; but none, alas, can gainsay the reliability of its operation, and the true *essence* of its "escapism" and, to no advantage to himself at all (at the risk of making a traffic jam), discover the bars of common sense to apply to a limited (so "human"!) traffic in a small space. That there's no eternal confinement in the civilization strictures of circumstances is an unhappy and useless, yet also a comforting knowledge to amateurs of the imagination. No; fences *advertise* great spaces, and death great times.

Now babbling little Steiner swerves round his tidy pantechnicon of personalia, turns on bright his eyes' headlights, and twists the crank. The engine purrs; "Good morning. Yes, Mr. Steiner." "It was eleven o'clock you asked me to come? No, I wasn't aware of your having anything special for me to do." But, a mere rehearsing. Ah, how reified you are, Steiner. What a thing, a package of this and that knotted too tightly, sometimes, for a subtle confection likely to appeal to exalted palates. What a packet sent hither and thither by the absent Lord of Gold, the invisible cannibal king or Great Cat of the Universe. For how long has that forehead, as clearly as Brook Bond says tea, said Intellect to my employers in my knowledge? And those eyes said candor and reliability, and the chin ductility? For very long, now, for too long. Over the counter they go, my wares, my blood with tears. His eyes: narrowed, assessing, with a false moisture of disarming affability: the softness of his voice meshed in the wires of his calculation; the eternal fable of an utter lack of exploitation, of the public service not his. Alas, alas and alas. *La condition humaine; non, sociale.* The fable he will not get more from me than I from him, and the assumption laid thereupon, foursquare, that affectation guides him, and the public interest. (I speak of more elevated employments; in others we certainly stand like rumpsteaks for bluebottle inquiries.) His motions; of a silk-reined tiger: now, quite a cold blue fire of excited speculation, for I please him—he sucks—I show him more, and more, and consolidate each presentation with succinctly modest silences, and fullstop breathing of disinterested accuracy in those presentations; have not added or taken away, am as strange to boasting as to modesty, am the very incense of disinterestedness, and have dropped in Heaven only knows why. Will not say, to please him—no, but honestly, I do not know . . . ah, ah and ah.

Yes, in a church we are, we couple of vestals just landed from the evening coach from Margate (full of popular blooms), in this church by the pond of pure men's tears, with a blood red rose bush growing beside, and just ducks quacking on the marge. Strange encounter? Ha ha, strange. Might as well . . . yes. Start tomorrow, out of church though. We'll meet by the stocks and the pound, opposite the sheriff's in a snowstorm. The old, old church bell tolls; our hearts away with it. Crème de menthe emotion. Jubilant jelly eyes. Spread me with butter, Lord, for I come for thy high tea. I am baked, cut and toasted, but miss thy sharp tooth; am as a heap of corn, Lord Simson, to be negligently (heavens, man, don't strain 'ee) gathered by thee.

Take me take me take me. No, I am not homosexual; sulkiness, no doubt (pent pulsing of my perimeters!). No, I draw the line there (I am an artist). Thank you, sir. God, sir, what a pleasure it is to talk to you. But what, sir, is its rival pleasure? Why, sir, listening to you. Honestly, I'm not joking: I shall never be the same man again. No, I'm putting off the pilgrimage to Mecca, since I heard you. Why waste time and money when you're so near? I'm afraid I'm being sincere, sir; I cannot help my being so straightforward, about what everyone who meets you must have wanted to tell you but daren't. Ha ha, thank you. On account, yes. Sweet on account. I can count.

The decorous interchange of casualties led to the engagement of one man by another for their mutual benefit, with the just bias of emoluments toward the employer as a fit reward for his enterprise. I lack enterprise.

Steiner, the lorry of you awaits the will of you, as it runs along the conduit of mortality from the creator's typewriter. Hurry up, man. Put on the old green hat—well, it's old, you know, and not quite the kitten you fondle in it—and the damned red scarf. Come on, man. Don't lag. Simper, sir, but not affectedly. Beam, sir, and he will mote. He lives, as you know, in Brook Street, in a district somewhat mercantilely overburdened these days. Not what it thought it was going to be, an exclusive residence in the afterlife.

He has a man—I mean a "man"—to open the door; naturally. I

am myself employed, by myself, frequently in that capacity. I am not surprised at that. In truth, I have had a man, albeit myself, employed to do far more menial things than open a door. One man is the same as another; if it is another who does these things, it makes no difference. A man's a man, etc. One has a right to self-respect, etc. One need not be ashamed of one's calling, even oneself one's bedchamber man, etc. Nay, it is the attitude that counts: for—

A very handsome man, seated at an immense desk, at sea, with all his excellent furniture (he affects a Regency style) on a carpet of bursting flowers. He rises and becomes very tall, to which I shorten, and advances from his work to me, a large white hand held forward, and the first word he says is Ah. Then he says Mr. Steiner and, as I trusted, there is a discreet drop in his voice at my name; I immediately recognize him as a man of public pro-Semitism. So I gaze frankly into the public expanses of his heart, through the drains of which I see printer's ink pressing into the curls and flutes of first-rate emotions, and I say Yes; that is all, just Yes. For here I am, entire, and so little. He asks me, in an urgent voice, to be seated; I accommodate myself to his urgent wish; which he follows with a pause. A pause is like the first introduction of dentist's gas down the nostrils. The furniture then wakes itself up, with other visible appurtenances of his state; no longer alone, in comfort and authority he commences:

"The fact is, Mr. Steiner, I have a particular project in mind which, from what I have heard about you from Mr. G. and Sir Arthur Rammage, I believe you are especially fitted to undertake. I don't know if you have read my Column . . ." on which he stands like Nelson adorned in the droppings of the flying heavenly bodies far from the world below—"Yes yes," I say rather loudly (I had read it once, in a long waiting room), "I know it very well indeed." He smiles as faintly as it would be seemly to; then he lengthens his face, prettily alerts his eyes for the far sight:

"Well. It has been occurring to me these last few months that something different might well be appreciated and might, further, be more in accord with the recent changes in policy of the paper than my present work. I do not propound this as a new development in public taste—it is as old as our democracy, indeed—yet it is certainly the recurrence of a perpetual theme: the lives, Mr. Steiner, of those we somewhat loftily call ordinary people (and don't you think everyone is fundamentally in that category, ha ha?) are again, I believe, to become of extraordinary interest to . . . well, to ordinary people." I nearly rupture myself in the intensity of my effort to show appreciation of this original discovery and enlightened sentiment. My eyes pop, and an agreeable drop of moisture, in tribute to democracy, is manufactured; I calculate in being able to recover myself in the long stretches I see ahead of the adumbration of this idea. I recognize, in the elaboration of his launching, the promise of a long voyage. I go to the Captain's deck to prospect over the blue sea. The wind is fair, the waves small.

"Everyday happenings of such people, Mr. Steiner, can be looked at in one of two ways. One and, I believe, not necessarily the truer, is that of the observation of routine, expediency, necessity, colorless existence, and so forth. But it is to avoid this—slander, if I may say so—that the second way is asked for, and which we must provide; in which life, Mr. Steiner, is a romance; an amazing, extraordinary phenomenon, of unknown origins, unknown destinations, thrilled with the mysteries of life and death, and checkered with moments gay and grim, lofty and sordid, exquisite and degrading: in brief, Life as Life really is in this sometimes sad, sometimes gay, and always extraordinary old world of ours. I want us to penetrate to the hearts of the people, to discover the—faith is not too great a word—that enables them so courageously, sometimes so recklessly, always so unflaggingly to persevere, to retain that quality of honesty and cheerfulness which is, I believe, the British prerogative. Never more than now, when the country is in difficulties and the world altogether in a turmoil—when our old institutions are facing both American modernism and totalitarian tyranny—is it more desirable, and even essential, to reveal to the people the wonder of the people. Do you understand me?"

"Certainly, Lord Simson; that is a feeling I have long had about people, but one which I have been unable to express."

"Then, practically speaking, my proposition is this: that you go forth, like Haroun Al Raschid's vizier—for Haroun must stay at home now, ha ha—into the country, the towns, the marketplaces, the pubs, places high and low wherever you may gain entry, and in a manner proper to the milieu—and report to me your candid, unvarnished findings of the workings of this method of life. I want you, Mr. Steiner—and I hope the adventure will reward the frequent hardship and embarrassments—to *disguise yourself* as one of (aha—and show thereby your common humanity *with*) those upon whom you report.

I want you to penetrate to the heart of the people in the guise of whatever kind you encounter. I want you to be a tramp, a loafer, a business man, a Soho misfit, an artist . . . all these things. I leave the method to you; it shall be your private art. You may incur any expenses within reason—the "Lion" purrs to its workers—but you must provide me with material closer, finer, more intimate than is the common matter of journalism. Now, Mr. Steiner, does the project interest you? If it does not, pray say so. Its undertaking is not a condition of your employment with me—I have other work for you if you feel that this is outside your scope of interests or beyond your particular capabilities; for it is, I think, on this scale, something new in journalism."

"Lord Simson," I replied virginally but with, so to speak, my wallet on my heart, and a dreaming rapture in my glazing eye—for democracy's tear had spread evenly over it—"nothing would more suit my nature or my interests. I do not think that anything more attractive could be offered to a journalist. I am of course only too eager to do my best. It is an almost Balzacian enterprise that you suggest, I feel."

"Exactly." He paused again, and the pause was like a disintoxication. The furniture retired, the appurtenances flagged, and alone he stood. He moved to his desk, breaking the portrait of his inspiration and his ideals. "Now for the details; I shall require your first report within two weeks. It is now November 18th, 1953, is it not? I propose to run the series for six months minimum. Your salary, as you know, will be £3,000 per annum, and for further expenses you need but apply to me from wherever you are. Only one thing I beg of you— but I don't think I need have any fears on that account—keep within the law." He rose, again, in his springtime. "That, I think, is all. You may start how and where you please. I leave everything to you. It is to be understood, of course, that your notes are to be but the basis of my Column. Well, good morning, Mr. Steiner, and good luck." He shook hands with me warmly and though, as I have said, he had a man for this office, he nevertheless employed himself for the undertaking, to see me out. So simple am I that I made him the cool and natural thank you I would have made to his man; thus, we can be deceived.

Out and along the streets I began to look at my fellowmen with self-conscious distaste. If, I said, it is out of you I must concoct this wonderful legend, God help me. It would be easier to extract your livers than your wonder. Did all these safely shut faces guard the rare human jewelry so spoken of by my new master? Were they the shrines? Must I find them all wonderful people? It would be the end of the word wonder. I looked at them worse. Bleak slugs of an ashen routine, I muttered: tomtits tittivating on his broken Column. Your hearts: at best, Ganges of treacle; your minds: repulped children's encyclopedias; your aspirations: below. I touched, and rejected the journalistic myth of our age. Wasn't what was chiefly admired their moronic patience with their lot, and their delusions of its significance? And you, Creator, I snarled: was this the mission you bore me for? Then I shall kill myself from your pages. Find another more fit for this monkery. I suppose, I said ironically, it was to earn kudos in this glamorous scavengering that you invented me. Do not expect, dacto-phylic seer, to find things easy with me. Anyone can have a child; none can make it do what he wants. The pavements, the shops' bright stomachs, the wind and humanity seem, to me, all of one material. "Unconquerable will of man," said Gorki; "never sets himself problems he can't solve." On the contrary, the religious beast carefully sets himself only the insoluble problems.

Home, I glared at Mrs. Meaty. Where is your human wonder, Mrs. Meaty? I have but to take away your capital letter to find that, and I hastily return it to you. I rummage for the books of my sentimental adolescence, a library of the wonder of man; great hearts to guide me anent the wonder of this commodity, Humanity. I cannot read them. Gone, gone is that queer belief. The knobbly skeleton stares through the cuisined pages.

Poor Steiner. He is confused; ponders the hoped-for wonder of No man. Becomes religious; reality tolls back symbols. Out of my confusion I at length decided: First, I shall—

"Steiner, first you shall—" "What?" "Steiner, do you know who's talkin'?" "I heard you, my dear Typist." "Hear better next time, Steiner. Unless a man is night and day in touch with his Creator he has no hope." "I'd rather be without hope than with you, pestilential bore." "There speaks the spirit of evil. Quiet now, my creature, and hear me. Parenthetically, wretch, everything you do and say comes of me, as you very well know. So don't let's play about any more. Here is my plan for you. You shall first see the odds and ends in your erstwhile haunts of Soho and Fitzrovia; you shall thus be dis-

gusted, as it is written or as it shall be. You shall then walk among respectable people and your heart, though moved, shall not perceptibly be lifted. You shall then say: 'I have it. I shall become a tramp! And see what is what from the floor of life' "So; but the work becomes mine. What of Lord Simson? I shall take the cream, and he may have the skimmed milk romantically bottled, in crusty flagons of life's old song. But the cream shall be for me . . . which is for you?" "Precisely, Steiner," said the voice from the clouds, "you begin to catch on. But it offends me deeply to have occasionally to chastise a jealous God. I fear you are not mature enough yet to take fate into your own poor shaking hands. Mankind grows slowly." "It ingrows very fast, Your Honor."

"Upon which a lean and foolish knight forever rides in vain," said Chesterton; apropos of my pursuits. I rummaged in my lean and foolish knight's wardrobe, and exposed to the light a historical pair of khaki corduroys; but these, I thought, are not worn today by the fraternity; indeed, does the fraternity exist? I waver, waving the corduroys, animating them into a semblance of my old-time picturesque galope down the London boulevards. I don't know. Really I don't know. "They'll do, Steiner; they will place you as one who has not crawled on in anything, even the modes of the fraternity. They will secure you pity and contempt, the best vantage point of observation." Hm. Sandals? Oh no. Sandals stopped in the forties, I'm convinced. I simper; I remember me in sandals; Chinese straw sandals, at first, for which I paid eleven pence half penny in 1934. But now, a pair of ancient shoes. Is the fraternity still, so to speak, "artistic"? Has it, anyway, its hair long, as erstwhile? I do not know. I must make a preliminary sortie, as myself, to discover. I shrink. I know of old the crablike withdrawal that inquiring into one's fellows' hearts automatically induces: how the most social of activities turns one into the most antisocial of men. But how can one know others if . . . one doesn't want to? When the "mystery" of him is subsidized by the exigencies of the game—when his deplorable familiarity would make collapse the individuating flirtation with his "unknown," for our strangeness to excite our competition? I cannot fight or exploit you if I know you; it would hurt *me*, to find you like me. So there's nothing to know that can be interestingly said. We are in a coma, then. I know of writers who say interestingly. But not one who does not initially patent an attitude to see him through to the profitable end. Apart from your ancient peddlers of petty-bourgeois *dramas*

in which Her feelings were gashed and His eyes narrowed,

in which something swept up Him, making him hot, or down him, making him cold, so that he knew;

in which she moved, slightly, and he, unaccountably, held his breath, which he released as soon as the fictional proprieties allowed; though I have frequently come across held breath never being released, in fitting style with the submarine nature of the *drama*.

In which he clenched that reliable old ham, his fist, and ground those old teeth, recklessly sacrificing his dentist's equanimity to the heightened state of his passions; in which, after grinding them, he takes the plate out and scrutinizes it for damages, and places it forbearingly, relative to those passions, in a glass of water by his side;

in which she screamingly pulls his hair, which comes off,

and he is sardonically revealed to be forty-seven and undesirable; or more desirable, because his soul is revealed through the crevices of his passé body.

In which, forever after, he sports a bald pate, because of her reaction cunningly capitalizing this last resource.

In which: "Heel, Steiner, heel!"

In which, when he falls in love with a young woman who finds him too old, he seriously considers taking legal action against the first woman—a manicurist—who gave him false advice; in which a lawyer, an old friend of his (with a good taste in port) places the tips of his fingers together, as in the *Forsyte Saga*, and smiles with benevolent superiority. You wouldn't, says old Ratham, have the ghost of a chance, my dear fellow. Look: now do look a moment; you are dealing, surely, in imponderables. You could not prove that you had materially suffered—but you would be a cad if you could, come now —by not gaining the young girl's affections. No jury would convict. . . . "But my luv, my botty's happiness, my spirit's wings. . . ." "No, my friend, much as I understand your feelings—and, believe me, sympathize heartily with them—these matters are for the court of a Higher One . . . be manful, and buy another toupee." He sobbed down Pall Mall. Yes, he shook with masterless sobs. He flung himself into the park. He took a bus; a red one. This bus—"Quiet now, Steiner. Collect yourself."

This bus, poised, beautifully dressed by Balmain, with sick

wheels, steeped into the mill of Nottinghill by lamplight; he alights, he turns an eye one way and the other another way: but he cannot refocus them! So, he is lost. Constable, he shouts, help me, help me. Take me to the hospital, please constable; I will pay for the taxi, for I can afford it, my man. The constable thinks: "Steiner, quiet sir."

What is the fraternity's main interest? It used to be the poor work of others; will that still hold? The scope of discussion in that kind are certainly greater. Money? Ah, money still holds. And love? Well, I doubt it. The level of sublimation has dropped since the war, and the love that posed on the top of it with it. Only homosexuals and lesbians, the awfully unsatisfied, still speak of love. The rest may mention sex, but rarely, except in the suburbs. No. I think money is the topic of the hour, in all classes of society. Since mankind is incapable of admitting a major interest without weaving robes of glory for it, we must look for the higher meaning of getting money; perhaps a pale resurrection of the Victorian ethos of prosperity. It will have been resurrected with a primitive respect for work since the war that naturally, as the dedication proceeds, is quickly kicked aside as the unwanted ladder; the jump down from the swaying wall constitutes the drama. The possession of money fuels people with a magical power, aroused with a wanton perfume of Isolation, which God nibbles toothlessly. The lonely gander of my grandeur. I lope to private feasts. Shermozzle of me poxy soul-purse. Angst-stink of me rotting doubloons. Fecal cancer of me agonizing power. Poets wipe me with deathless verse. Existenz. I shall taste the criminal sensibility induced by the lack of it, but artificially: how artificially? And how artificial will the virtues of its possession be to me? The virtue of poverty is cheese shared by the mice; the vice of it to be a rodent. What grandeurs does poverty inhibit, of the soul? Delayed suicide, which is religion.

I must leave Mrs. Meaty's. I am too rich to stay any longer. It would be hypocrisy. I must be honest. Now that I am rich she will disgust me. "Mrs. Meaty, I'm afraid (how true) that I must leave you in a week's time. I have to go abroad on an assignment, for an indefinite period." "Oh, Mr. Steiner, I am sorry to hear that. What a pity it is." "Yes, Mrs. Meaty, I have been very happy here, and we have grown to understand each other. But I may come back, if you have a vacancy, later?" "Yes, Mr. Steiner, I shall be only to glad to accommodate you again. When shall you be going exactly? I'd like to

know so that I can show people the room, when you're out of course."
"Oh do that at any time, Mrs. Meaty. It won't worry me. But let's
see, it's Monday today: I shall leave next Saturday." "All right then,
Mr. Steiner. What a pity, though. But I daresay you'll like it abroad.
You so like traveling, I know." "Yes, it will make a change, Mrs.
Meaty. A change is the thing, isn't it?" "Well, I don't know. I've been
here coming on thirty years and I don't know what I'd do if I was to
go. Why even when I go for a week by the sea I feel upset like. It's
not being in your own place, like. But we're all made different, and a
good thing too I daresay." "Yes, Mrs. Meaty. Variety makes us
mutually tolerable." No. This is not the age of significant words,
however, but of balls served on rackets. We say to feel sincere which
is to be surprised by what we say, to feel we cannot help it; so helplessness is virtue when virtue is English. So. I have retired. I diminish
in my room. My companion the fly is more real; he charges about in
"my" emptiness; whereas he, the automaton taking over, begins packing already. I moan—I whimper—over the packings of old lives; over
dilapidated generous-looking shoes in which I tramped, over the
mean-looking trousers in which I furrowed to rehabilitation (my
Typist says). Why move, why live? Why lift this arm? Why try to
save it from its approaching cramp—let the cramp freeze inward, like
an army of ants till it is *exciting* to relieve it—what if I anticipate this
excitement? As well as the cramp? What does the mirror say? Blank.
Gas is escaping: of this identity, leaking all over the room. I am
already partly outside. The buses sound louder, beginning to claim
me. Shouts from outside, fishing for me.

My room has a sad dampness, and the smell of yesterday's fire; a
tint of a smell crisply lodged in the hard rim of the globe of mucous
halfway down my nostril (an internal tear). How sad are the smells
of yesterday's fire; forty. The fire has been extinct for five years. I
put it out to save the building. So the building was cold; its only heat-
ing system was the break of self-destruction to exaggerate the drive
of the wheels of life, even to make sparks fly (all in my eye). I am like
other men. That I cannot tolerate. No. I begin a refreshing brandishing of limbs, that linger on the way to their belonging to me. Back to
the scrum, to identification, in the service of my Creator. Pack
rapidly; yet carefully place the sentiment: the red handkerchief, the
wide, sloppy, boatlike shoes. The little sheaf of crayon drawings by
Oliver, who was blown up about to say something (one, of myself

as a fat robin in a tree of women; another, as a double-chinned pluto-
crat fixed by a long cigar). Feather-light drawings incommoded with
"characteristic lines." We suppurate with the characteristic. Books:
old harmoniums, chuck them all in, trembling with finality. So, I have
packed five days too soon. That is as it should be. Adroit miscalcula-
tions keep the ball rolling. I always lose my pipe to find it, and contrive an astonished lack of matches. From this to Livingstone in Africa
is a long way, but in the same direction. Grr. I shall grind a sheet of
red bacon and a yellow ball of egg in a white cloak with my chattering teeth at about one o'clock, I think.

I roar with laughter to shed a tear. They say this is manic. They
are garrulous, who sweep things up with definitions, and cluck the
world away. For here is a—bead, glass—of my love. Love. It is like a
mirror without one's reflection, so far away. I last loved twelve years
ago; renounced it, firmly, because my identity would not tolerate it.
Why, I found myself falling away; why, she was beginning to be as
real as I: Sir, was that just? You wouldn't like it? No, Sir. It was
unjust. Then I sped on waterfloats over her trembling seas, in the
sun, and nearly fell in: Incompatibility, I roared, come to my aid!

Lord; when I eat a plum, then—I remember clearly the plum, full
of her—when my teeth gently crush through sounding like the seas
withdrawing down the shivering beach—when my teeth, so guard-
edly dry, sweep like battalions through the glistening fleshes, piled
in and out, in a static rush of themselves—an aviary of singing tastes—
giving their fruit's blood, I know—that she is getting into my world.
All that I tasted was of her; roads were softened with the pregnancy
of my walk, made so by her; the buildings were washed of their alien
distinction from homes; were soft, holding in others, of the stuff of
her and me. Why, the sun had plastic beams, solid as butter on my
living brow; I combed my hair, then, with a comb riding through
clean and glistening strands, I washed a face of sensitized fruit in its
warmth and intimate refreshedness, I moved like music in music; the
whole world, Sir, was of my flesh: I was not alone! Could I tolerate
it? Say I had a breakdown? Yes—: ha, my Inner Self, me Ego too,
began temerariously to creep out of its safe, burgled by love's soft
hands—could I lose my treasure? My gold? No. Never—for no one:
and I raised the awful walls of my Character and Individuality, like
the walls of the Château d'If across the harbor, to deride her climbing
powers . . . she put out to sea again, in her child's rowing boat. I saw

her from my window one hundred feet up: a small boat on blue. A dark wave raised itself, a claw of solid iron-water above her, in the lustful trembling of whose claw I felt my hand associate; which rose highest as I most tensed my hand, and with my gibbering lewdness in its hiss, covered her; and in the silence of the sea above her I read majesty: so that my fortress arose upon distinguished legs and waded through her cemetery to the shore, purporting there to participate in individualistic traffic—which you, my Author, prevent, so that I am a meek man. So that my fortress is soft, just a suit. Brush it. Carefully. I walk in my suit in the moon, of course, in the light of the moon.

In the light of the moon my dark suit looks like a black soup of lanterns pointed. There is more menace in that dark suit walking toward me than in me without it walking away. The suit is character- istic. It is the suit of fear; a black flame from the dim ground, with a gold watch in it. The watch is vivacious. The suit walks like, in the play, Frankenstein's monster; it walks me as precisely as my nurse once did. It takes me through doors I would dread to enter alone, it flings my arms up in the air, it twists my shoulders ironically or agreeably. It gives me all that I haven't. Has the dark suit a cherry for a heart, worn on its wrist? That would be elegant. When it is very strained and very stretched the whining and moaning will be psychic, of the material. It will moan and whine one day, and fall apart. It will scream and cry at its death; I'll laugh at it: born anew from my Château d'If, my Individuality, my Author, your Me.

I shall call my suit Stoke Pogis, in honor of Thomas Gray, be- cause it does to me what Stoke Pogis does to him. I'm going to get into you, Stoke Pogis. Clamor, clamor I do for entry. In I go. Have you got me? En avant, down the page, back through the print, you and I, you and eye, Stoke Pogis, dreadnoughting it to another chapter in our practically unfurlable epic. How I shudder when I get back into print . . . but when I feel the forty-two battering rams of the creative letter-slinger on my white soul of silence and peace—ah, I was, or was without I, a tree in Norway blowing well in another God's gales, arms spread, in a regalia of pretty birds, personally upon me. Or when I lay, fetal, sighing with white sleep in my ream, my old homely old-world ream in our draw; there. Down we go. Now careful, Stokey Pogey; he flings the big battering rams for his capitals —there they come, hurled by the cannons of giant art—bang bang bang, Pogey, bang, bang, bang.

PHILIP O'CONNOR

Philip O'Connor spent his childhood in France, and French was his first language. He never really found any comfort in living in England: "Not dislike," he explains, "allergy."

He began writing at nine, and became an atheist at twelve. His prewar poems were published in New Verse *(1936), but he wrote little after that until his first book was published in England:* Memoirs of a Public Baby, *which was very well received. Several books and radio programs have followed.*

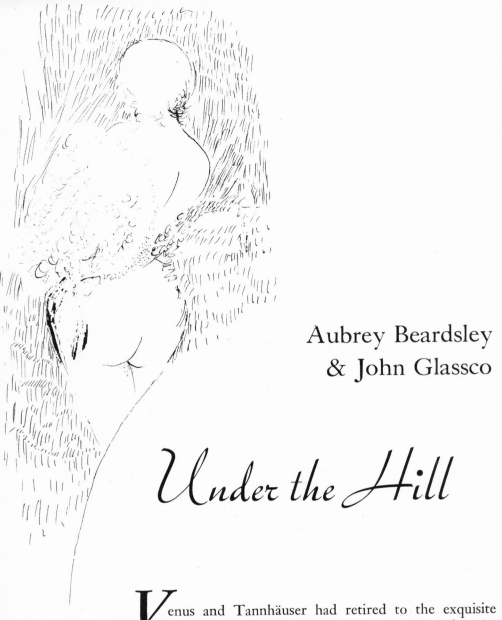

Aubrey Beardsley
& John Glassco

Under the Hill

Venus and Tannhäuser had retired to the exquisite boudoir or pavilion Le Con had designed for the queen on the first terrace, and which commanded the most delicious view of the parks and gardens. It was a sweet little place, all silk curtains and soft cushions. There were eight sides to it, bright with mirrors and candelabra, and rich with pictured panels, and the ceiling, dome shaped and some thirty feet above the head, shone obscurely with gilt moldings through the warm haze of candlelight below.

Tiny wax statuettes dressed theatrically and smiling with plump cheeks, quaint magots that looked as cruel as foreign gods, gilded monticules, pale celadon vases, clocks that said nothing, ivory boxes full of secrets, china figurines playing whole scenes of plays, and a world of strange preciousness crowded the curious cabinets that stood against the walls. On one side of the room there were six perfect little card tables, with quite the daintiest and most elegant chairs set primly round them; so, after all, there may be some truth in that line of Mr. Theodore Watts—

I played at picquet with the Queen of Love.

Nothing in the pavilion was more beautiful than the folding screens painted by De La Pine, with Claudian landscapes—the sort of things that fairly make one melt, things one can lie and look at for hours together, and forget the country can ever be dull and tiresome. There were four of them, delicate walls that hem in an amour so cosily, and make room within room.

The place was scented with huge branches of red roses, and with a faint amatory perfume breathed out from the couches and cushions —a perfume Châteline distilled in secret and called L'Eau Lavante.

Cosmé's precise curls and artful waves had been finally dis-arranged at supper, and strayed ringlets of the black hair fell loosely over Venus' soft, delicious, tired, swollen eyelids. Her frail chemise and dear little drawers were torn and moist, and clung transparently about her, and all her body was nervous and responsive. Her closed thighs seemed like a vast replica of the little bijou she had between them; the beautiful tétons du derrière were firm as a plump virgin's cheek, and promised a joy as profound as the mystery of the Rue Vendôme, and the minor chevelure, just profuse enough, curled as prettily as the hair upon a cherub's head.

Tannhäuser, pale and speechless with excitement, passed his gem-girt fingers brutally over the divine limbs, tearing away smock and pantalon and stocking, and then, stripping himself of his own few things, fell upon the splendid lady with a deep-drawn breath!

It is, I know, the custom of all romancers to paint heroes who can give a lady proof of their valiance at least twenty times a night. Now Tannhäuser had no such Gargantuan felicity, and was rather relieved when, an hour later, Mrs. Marsuple and Doricourt and some others burst drunkenly into the room and claimed Venus for themselves. The pavilion soon filled with a noisy crowd that could scarcely keep its feet. Several of the actors were there, and Lesfesses, who had played Sporion so brilliantly, and was still in his make-up, paid tremendous attention to Tannhäuser. But the Chevalier found him quite uninteresting off the stage, and rose and crossed the room to where Venus and the manicure were seated.

"How tired the poor baby looks," said Mrs. Marsuple. "Shall I put him in his little cot?"

"Well, if he's as sleepy as I am," yawned Venus, "you can't do better."

Mrs. Marsuple lifted her mistress off the pillows, and carried her in her arms in a nice, motherly way.

"Come along, children," said the fat old thing, "come along; it's time you were both in bed."

The Théâtre des Deux Mains was a bijou little playhouse which breathed an elegance altogether Regency. Not more than ninety feet by sixty, its proportions were exquisite. The walls were spaced out by panels picturing the gilded shapes of amorous cupidons and caryatides, between which hung portieres of dusty-yellow Utrecht velvet embellished with loops, tassels, fleurons and formalized heraldic figures; the ceiling, softly domed and figured with wreaths and curlycues of creamy plaster, was a little low. Everything was arranged in the most intimate way, for the pit had been suppressed altogether, and behind the single row of stalls began the boxes and loges, each able to hold four or five persons.

Although the floor sloped down to a minuscule orchestra pit, maintaining the classical separation of audience and actors, the stage was so close as to give you the impression of being a part of what was going on; and in fact, when Venus and her party slipped in during the entr'acte, the audience was still deeply moved. The lights were only half up, and everywhere was a buzz of comment and criticism, expressions of appreciation, ejaculations from behind masks, smiling retorts and suggestive grimaces. The occupants of some of the boxes had even drawn the curtains, from behind which came the sound of slaps and smothered laughter!

Tannhäuser was delighted with everything, especially with the box-openers; for here, instead of the grumpy old women to whom the playgoer has become used—though not, I dare say, reconciled—were a dozen or so beautiful young creatures in plum-colored jackets and yellow tapering trousers that strapped under the instep and fitted smoothly across their behinds; their build, their delicate features, and the short ringlets that played around their shoulders left their sex a matter of doubt; but this ambiguity, De La Pine explained in a whisper, was matched by their readiness to sustain the role of either.

Then the lights went down, the music began, and the curtains rose on the second of the two acts, discovering the interior of an orphanage where a dozen or more ravishing children, dressed in an old-fashioned and modest manner, were performing a graceful gavotte. Circling, dividing, forming and re-forming in intricate patterns and arabesques, they engrossed the stage with a charming collective movement, making quaint erotic gestures and accompanying their dance with the sweet treble of a cheerful little song. Soon the fun became more lively and more risqué, the couples detaching themselves for a few minutes in the center of the stage to execute some really naughty pantomime, while the others clapped their hands in time, beat their little slippers on the floor, and laughed in a simple, wordless cascade of melody which was tossed to and fro, from the boys to the girls and back again, with infinite varieties of expression and cadence.

But all at once there was a roll of drums, the lights on the stage changed to a deep rose, and a drop curtain swept aside, revealing two statuesque female figures in long white gowns, who had been watching. A wild arpeggio from the harp, like the susurrus of an autumn wind, succeeded, and the chorus of children, wailing, shrank back in a calculated disarray toward the wings; then the Matrons advanced slowly, to a solemn, throbbing pizzicato of bass viols.

Their appearance was truly wonderful. With faces painted dead white, mounting false chins and noses which almost met over tiny mouths, their foreheads graced with rows of curls like inverted question marks, and wearing enormous mobcaps which quivered and swayed on their heads, they moved slowly upstage, nodding portentously and making gestures of outrage. A round of applause greeted them, for these were Mrs. Bowyer and Mrs. Barker.

And now the former took a striking attitude, the harp sounded a few notes, and she delivered a glorious recitative, her majestic contralto filling the theater as she expressed her indignation and horror, her well-nigh disbelief in the testimony of her eyes, while she clasped her hands, raised them in the air and dropped them to her sides, rolling her eyes and shaking her head; an occasional interpolation from Mrs. Barker's golden soprano cut across her words, and then the two voices joined in a somber and stirring duet in which execrations were mingled with promises of punishment and invocations of the spirit of birch.

The duet ended with three long notes in alt, uttered by the matrons in unison. This was the call to the servants, and as the applause of the audience reached its climax four strapping girls carrying rods rushed on the stage. Now, the orchestra struck up a jolly bourrée, to whose accented rhythm was executed a short and lively bacchanale, the orphans retreating and fleeing, the servantgirls pursuing, grasping and losing; cries of alarm, triumph and vexation mingled with the in-

vigorating music, the dance became a wild rout of flying forms, a whirling kaleidoscope of smock and sash, of bare limb and lacy pantalette, from which at last two of the serving-wenches emerged, each with an orphan securely horsed on her back, and the music ceased with a plangent crash of cymbals.

To the sounds of an exquisite solo by the premier violone, the two captives, a boy and a girl, were now lovingly and ceremoniously untrussed. Ah, what a delightful operation this was! What ravishing contours were exposed, what quiverings, what tremblings and trepidations, what rosy reluctancies, as the plump fesses emerged and the two dear children were prepared for the neat birch rods in the hands of Bowyer and Barker!

Then all was quiet; the tableau arranged itself, each captive flanked by matron and domestic, the remaining children creeping close as at the bidding of fear and fascination, and Mrs. Barker, her rod upraised, began to deliver a thrilling lecture full of the old-fashioned phrases of nursery eloquence. By degrees her emotion mounted, as if like an Homeric hero she were exciting herself by her own threats and vauntings; her voice rose, throbbing and fulminating in somber crescendi, her arm gesturing with motions ever more purposeful, until at last, as a superb and stately period rolled to its close, the twigs descended with a rich and urgent hiss, and the flagellation commenced to a softly resumed music.

Tannhäuser, already blushing with pleasure, followed everything eagerly, loving the strokes that fell so roundly, admiring the art with which the voices of fesseuse and fessé blended, this one rising, that falling, in a chromatic progression that decorated in obbligato the gentle but insistent beat of the bolero whispered by drums and muted strings. Now, the birch seemed to dominate all the sounds and movements, as if it, and not the conductor's baton, were leading the music, evoking the cries of distress and satisfaction, and directing the reed-like swaying of the chorus from side to side and the leaps and bounds of the disciplined urchin. The Chevalier found himself beating time with the toe of his slipper.

Then the music and cries increased in volume as flutes and oboes joined in, echoing and mingling and competing with the singers, and all at once two other voices added themselves, as Mrs. Bowyer began to thrash the other culprit; and now the rhythms multiplied themselves in ingenious counterbeats and syncopations, notes short and long were exchanged like the repartees of a fugue, and at last, as agonized trills, roulades and fiorituri poured from the two children, the stirring quartet came to an end, its final strains engulfed by roars and bravos from the audience of deboshed cognoscenti.

Fresh melodies and fresh victims succeeded rapidly. The plot became confused, the story lost itself, the incidents grew more outrageous, as birch rods were supplanted by long, supple canes, these by limber straps, and these in turn by many-tongued martinets. At length, when matters had apparently reached some kind of crisis, there were only the matrons, the four servants, and a beautiful youth, quite nude, occupying the stage. Forming a circle around him, they drove him to and fro between them with the blows of their martinets, laughing silverly, until after a minute or two the boy sank down in an exquisite pose, quite motionless. The lights began to dim, Mrs. Bowyer made a sign with her hand, and in the hush the domestics let down a scale from the proscenium, fastened the youth's wrists to it, and drew him up on tiptoe. The stage was utterly dark for a moment; then a clear rosy light illuminated the three principals, and one saw the two matrons were armed with long, supple whips.

The audience was tense and silent; Tannhäuser himself felt his breath quickening as the blows began to fall. For now make-believe had turned to reality! He reached for the hand of Venus, which squeezed his in moist sympathy, as they both stared at the stage, hearing now the veritable sounds of punishment and the true accents of pain. The youth's body shook, twisted and trembled, his feet danced and kicked, the two whips sang in alternation, and piercing cries filled the little theater, pleas for mercy, prayers for forgiveness, promises of amendment, all alike met by the matrons' measured replies, calm and judicial, full of ironical sympathy and encouragement, a suave, antiphonal rhetoric made deliciously paradoxical by the steady accompaniment running beneath it, the repeated whistle and report of whipcord on flesh.

"Oddsfish," said Cosmé in a whisper, " 'tis artistry with a vengeance, that throws art to the winds." De La Pine nodded, smiling and rubbing his hands.

There was wild applause as the representation came to an end and the fainting youth hung limply in his bonds. Then, as the lights went up and the two Flagellantes advanced to the footlights, hand in hand, bowing, they were greeted by cries of "Unmask, unmask!"

—and the next moment, when they twitched off their comic vizards, Tannhäuser saw the two old frights replaced by a pair of handsome, smiling women who at once began to ogle the unattached gentlemen in the side boxes. Bouquets were thrown from several directions; they were received with bows and courtesies by the divas, who held them to their breasts and then, smiling archly, held up the little notes concealed in them, blowing kisses and flourishing their whips playfully at the admirers they had made.

"If you keep on looking at those creatures that way," Venus smiled at the Chevalier, "I'll be jealous."

Tannhäuser's only response was to draw the curtains of the box violently, to seize the Queen in his arms and press burning kisses upon her neck and shoulders.

"Oh!" she cried after a few moments. "Not here, not here!"

"No," said Mrs. Marsuple, putting her head through the curtain at that instant. "I've engaged the Ducal Suite upstairs. I saw you, my dears, and I knew *just* how you'd be feeling. Come on!'"

AUBREY BEARDSLEY

Aubrey Beardsley (1872–1898) "ended" (in the words of Arthur Symons) "a long career at the age of twenty-six." In this short span he not only proved himself one of the greatest artists in black-and-white of his time, but also joined the select company of John Cleland and George Colman as one of the three erotic writers of genuine talent England has produced. His "romantic novel," a fantastic re-telling of the Tannhäuser legend, was first conceived under the title The Queen in Exile, *then re-named* Venus and Tannhäuser, *was published in expurgated form in* The Savoy *magazine, and at last issued, unexpurgated but still only half written, from the underground press of Leonard Smithers in 1907. Even as a fragment, it stood unique and alone as one of the truly original works of the era of Wilde, Whistler and Shaw. Beardsley himself was a dandy, a wit, and beloved by all who knew him; his personal life was blameless. His illustrations of Malory, Jonson and above all of Pope and Wilde, are unsurpassed for force, imagination, and beauty of line; his pictures for Aristophanes'* Lysistrata *make even obscenity beautiful. His literary work has no clearly discernible ancestry, and its only children are the novels of Ronald Firbank. He remains an outstanding but curiously isolated figure in the history of English literature—as he would have wished.*

JOHN GLASSCO

John Glassco, a distinguished Canadian poet (born 1909 in Montreal; The Deficit Made Flesh, *1958;* A Point of Sky, *1964) first read* Under the Hill *in the bowdlerized version of Haldeman-Julius' five-cent* Little Blue Books *at the age of twelve, and was disappointed to find the story broken off in the middle. Twenty years passed before the idea came to him of completing the unfinished book himself—and then only as a labor of love with no thought of publication. Ten years later, in 1958, he took the completed manuscript with him to Paris and Olympia Press brought it out in the following year in a limited edition with all the original Beardsley illustrations.*

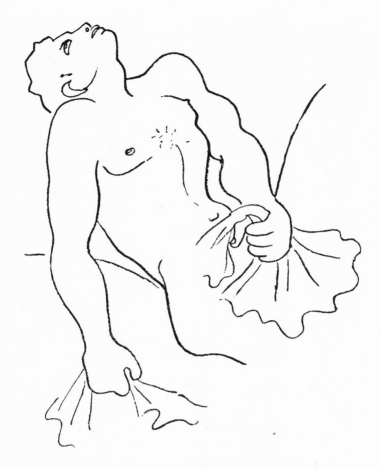

THE WHITE PAPER
Anonymous

I had to return to Toulon. It would be tedious to describe that charming Sodom smitten by hardly very wrathful heavenly fires in the form of a caressing sun. In the evening a still sweeter indulgence inundates the city and, as in Naples, as in Venice, a holiday-making crowd saunters in slow circles through the squares where fountains play, where there are trinket and tinsel stalls, waffle-sellers, and gyp-artists. From the four corners of the earth men whose hearts are gone out to masculine beauty come to admire the sailors who hang about singly or drift in groups, smile in reply to longing's stare, and never refuse the offer of love. Some salt or nocturnal potion transforms the most uncouth ex-convict, the toughest Breton, the wildest Corsican into these tall whores with their low-necked jumpers, their swaying hips, their pompoms, these lithely graceful, colorful whores who like to dance and who, without the least sign of awkwardness, lead their partner into the obscure little hotels down by the port.

One of the cafés where you can dance is owned by a former café-concert singer who's got the voice of a girl and who used to do a strip tease, starting it off as a woman. These days he wears a turtle-neck sweater and rings on his fingers. Flanked by the seafaring giants who idolize him and whose devotion he repays with mistreatment, in a large, childish hand and his tongue stuck out he jots down the prices of the drinks his wife announces to him in a tone of naive asperity.

One evening, pushing open the door to the place run by that astonishing creature who ever basks in the midst of the respect and deferential gestures of a wife and several husbands, I stopped abruptly, rooted to the spot. I'd just caught sight, caught a profile view, of Dargelos' shade. Leaning one elbow upon the mechanical piano, it was Dargelos in a sailor suit.

Of the original Dargelos this facsimile had above all the barefaced arrogance, the insolent and casual manner. Hell of a Fellow was spelled out in letters of gold on the flat hat tilted down in front over his left eyebrow, his tie was knotted up over his Adam's apple and he was wearing those amply bell-bottomed pants which sailors used once upon a time to roll to the thigh and which nowadays the regulations find some moral excuse or other for outlawing.

In another place I'd never have dared put myself within range of that lofty stare. But Toulon is Toulon; dancing eliminates uncomfortable preambles, it throws strangers into each other's arms and sets the stage for love.

They were playing dipsy-doodly music full of sauciness and winning smiles; we danced a waltz. The arched bodies are riveted together at the sex; grave profiles cast thoughtful downward glances, turn less quickly than the tripping and now and then plodding feet. Free hands assume the gracious attitudes affected by common folk when they take a cup of tea or piss it out again. A springtime exhilaration transports the bodies. Those bodies bud, push forth shoots, branches, hard members bump, squeeze, sweats commingle, and there's another couple heading for one of the rooms with the globe lights overhead and the eiderdowns on the bed.

Despoiled of the accessories which cow civilians and of the manner sailors adopt to screw up their courage, Hell of a Fellow became a meek animal. He had got his nose broken by a siphon bottle in the course of a brawl. Without that crooked nose his face might well have been uninteresting. A siphon bottle had put the finishing touch to a masterpiece.

Upon his naked torso, this lad, who represented pure luck to me, had LOUSY LUCK tattooed in blue capital letters. He told me his story. It was brief. That afflicting tattoo condensed it in a nutshell. He'd just emerged from the brig. After the *Ernest-Renan* mutiny there'd been the inquest; they'd confused him with a colleague; that was why his hair was only half an inch long; he deplored a tonsure which wonderfully became him. "I've never had anything but lousy luck," he repeated, shaking that bald little head reminiscent of a classical bust, "and it ain't never going to change."

I slipped my fetish chain around his neck. "I'm not giving it to you," I explained, "it's a charm, but not much of a one, I guess, for it hasn't done much for me and won't for you either. Just wear it tonight." Then I uncapped my fountain pen and crossed out the ominous tattoo. I drew a star and a heart above it. He smiled. He understood, more with his skin than with the rest, that he was in safe hands, that our encounter wasn't like the ones he'd grown accustomed to: hasty encounters in which selfishness satisfies itself.

Lousy luck! Incredible—with that mouth, those teeth, those eyes, that belly, those shoulders and cast-iron muscles, those legs, how was it possible? Lousy luck, with that fabulous little undersea plant, forlorn, inert, shipwrecked on the frothy fleece, which then stirs, unwrinkles, develops, rouses itself and hurls its sap afar when once it is restored to its element of love. Lousy luck? I couldn't believe it; and to resolve the problem I drowned myself in a vigilant sleep.

LOUSY LUCK remained very still beside me. Little by little, I felt him undertaking the delicate maneuver of extricating his arm from under my elbow. I didn't for a single instant think he was meditating a dirty trick. It would have been to demonstrate my ignorance of the code of the fleet. "Gentlemanliness," "semper fidelis" and the strict up and up embellish the mariners' vocabulary.

I watched him out of the corner of one eye. First, several times, he fingered the chain, seemed to be weighing it, kissed it, rubbed it against his tattoo. Then, with the dreadful deliberation of a player in the act of cheating, he tested to see if I was asleep, coughed, touched me, listened to my breathing, approached his face to my open right hand lying by my face and gently pressed his cheek to my palm.

Indiscreet witness of this attempt being made by an unlucky child who in the midst of the sea's wilderness felt a lifesaver coming within reach, I had to make a major effort in order not to lose my wits, feign a sudden awakening and demolish my life.

Day had scarcely dawned when I left him. My eyes avoided his which were laden with all the great expectations surging up in him and the hopes to which he couldn't give expression. He returned my chain. I kissed him, I edged past him and switched off the lamp by the bed.

Downstairs, I had to write the hour—5:00—when sailors are to be waked. On a slate, opposite the room numbers, were quantities of similar instructions. As I picked up the chalk I noticed I'd forgotten my gloves. I went back up. A sliver of light showed under the door. The lamp by the bed must have been turned on again. I was unable to resist peeping through the keyhole. It supplied the baroque frame to a little head upon which sprouted about half an inch of hair.

LOUSY LUCK, his face buried in my gloves, was weeping bitterly.

Ten long minutes I hesitated before that door. I was about to knock when Alfred's visage superimposed itself in the most exact manner upon LOUSY LUCK's. I stole on tiptoe down the stairs, pushed the button opening the door and slammed the door behind me. In the center of an empty square a fountain was pronouncing a solemn soliloquy. "No," I thought to myself, "we aren't of the same species. It's wonderful—it's enough to move a flower, a tree, a beast. But you can't live with one."

Now the sun had risen. Cocks crowed out over the sea. The sea lay cool and dark. A man came around a corner with a shotgun on his shoulder. Hauling an enormous weight, I trudged toward my hotel.

AUTHORSHIP

Jean Cocteau; poet, painter, film maker, novelist, opium addict, homosexual, moralist, Renaissance man who put his mark on a century, so that an exhibit of major art of the twentieth century shown in Paris is called, simply, Jean Cocteau and His Times.

He writes a preface to The White Paper, *that anonymous, notorious confession of a man's passion for boys, which not surprisingly is illustrated by Jean Cocteau;* "The White Paper, *whence does it come, who wrote it? Did I? Perhaps. Another? Probably. Are we not become others the moment after we've done writing? A posthumous book? That too is probable; are we not today yesterday's dead? Antinomous? The thing is not impossible. We have these days our ears glued to mothering wombs, eager to detect the first peep of the prenatal poem due to break the record in the child prodigy class. Would* The White Paper *be autobiographical then? Then I refuse its paternity, for what I find charming here is that the author talks without talking himself."*

But no one else comes forward to claim paternity, and The White Paper *remains the most signatured of unsigned works, a book defiantly of Cocteau's times, presumably from Cocteau's pen.*

A Sad, Ungraceful History of *Lolita*

MAURICE GIRODIAS

*O*ne day in the early summer of 1955, I received a call from a literary agent, a Russian lady by the name of Doussia Ergaz. She told me about an old friend of hers, a Russian *émigré* now a professor of Russian Literature at Cornell University. He had written a book with a rather dangerous theme which had, for that reason, been rejected by a number of prominent American publishers.

The man's name was Vladimir Nabokov and his book, *Lolita*, dealt with the impossible amours of a middle-aged man with a girl of twelve who belonged to the seductive species for which Nabokov had invented the word "nymphet."

I asked Madame Ergaz to send me the manuscript, which promptly turned up complete with a curriculum vita in which I read:

"Born 1899, St. Petersburg, Russia. Old Russian nobility. Father eminent statesman of the Liberal group, elected member of the First Duma. Paternal grandfather State Minister of Justice under Czar Alexander II. Maternal great grandfather President of Academy of Medicine.

"Education: Private School in St. Petersburg. Cambridge University (Trinity College), England. Graduated with Honors, 1922.

"Family escaped from Communist Russia in 1919. England, Germany, France.

"Acquired considerable fame in *émigré* circles as novelist and poet.

"Married in 1925. One son, b. 1934.

"Emigrated to the United States in 1940. Became an American writer. American citizen since 1945.

"Since 1940 taught literature at various American universities, combining this with a Research Fellowship in Entomology at the Museum of Comp. Zoology, Harvard (1942–48). Professor of Russian Literature at Cornell University since 1948.

"Guggenheim Fellowship for Creative Writing in 1943, and again in 1952.

"American Academy of Arts and Letters award in 1951.

"List of published works attached."

There was a certain disarming naïveté in the writer's insistence on such points as "father eminent statesman," or the "considerable fame acquired in *émigré* circles," which I found to be not devoid of charm, but I quickly succumbed to the much more compelling attraction of the book itself, which developed before me in its near absolute perfection. I was struck with wonder, carried away by this unbelievable phenomenon: the apparently effortless transposition of the rich Russian literary tradition into modern English fiction. This was, in itself, an exercise in genius; but the story was a rather magical demonstration of something about which I had so often dreamed, but never found: the treatment of one of the major forbidden human passions in a manner both completely sincere and absolutely legitimate. I sensed that *Lolita* would become the one great modern work of art to demonstrate once and for all the futility of moral censorship, and the indispensable role of passion in literature.

I immediately wrote Nabokov and we proceeded to negotiate a contract. I bowed to all the terms imposed on me, paid an advance much larger than I could afford at the time, and did not even insist on reserving for my firm a share of the eventual film rights, as is the usual practice.

The truth of the matter is that I was delighted by the book itself, but I doubted that it had any of the qualities which make a best seller. Nabokov himself wrote to me that he would be deeply hurt if *Lolita* were to obtain a *succès de scandale*: as the book had quite another meaning for him. He did not believe that it would ever be published in America, and he repeatedly expressed his gratitude for my acceptance of the book, as I had provided the only chance left for him ever to see it in print.

Madame Ergaz told me that Nabokov, somewhat frightened at first by the reaction of the American publishers to whom he had submitted it, was reluctant to let the book appear under his own name, and that she had had to use all her influence to make him change his mind. His career at Cornell was important to him, obviously; although he had written a number of books before, they had all met with mediocre reception, and he did not believe that *Lolita* would ever pull him out of obscurity.

I wanted to print the book immediately, but, before I did, I decided that we had to obtain a number of changes from the author. On July 1, 1955, I wrote to Nabokov that the "excessive use of French sentences and words gives a slightly affected appearance to the text," and submitted a list of suggested changes; to which he immediately responded by making numerous corrections on the proofs. I had hardly received the proofs back when Nabokov sent me a cable saying: "When is Lolita appearing. Worried. Please answer my letters. . . ." —an entreaty which has been repeated so often in so many cables sent by so many authors to so many publishers. . . .

Lolita appeared a few weeks later, in September, 1955, but was not noticed or reviewed anywhere, and sold very poorly. It was only at the end of the next year that things started to happen—strange things indeed. In an interview by the London *Times Literary Supplement*, Graham Greene mentioned *Lolita* as one of the "three best books of the year." That immediately provoked a demential reaction on the part of John Gordon, editor of the popular *Daily Express*, who accused Graham Greene and the *Times* of helping sell pornography of the lewdest variety. A very absurd and comical exchange followed —including even a very drunken public debate—in which Graham Greene fought gallantly and cleverly for the book; and the over-all result of that commotion was to create a great deal of interest in *Lolita* among partisans and detractors, an infinitesimal number of whom had read the book.

At the same time, I heard that one or two copies of *Lolita*, having been sent to persons residing in America, had been confiscated by the Customs, and then released after a few weeks, without any explanation. I decided to write to the New York Bureau of Customs to investigate, and received a rather miraculous letter signed by a Mr. Irving Fishman, Deputy Collector for the Restricted Merchandise Division, dated February 8, 1957, which said: ". . . You are advised that certain copies of this book have been before this Office for examination and that they have been released." In lay language, that meant that the U.S. Customs had had the remarkable mental—and may I say political—courage of finding *Lolita*, a book printed in Paris by my disreputable publishing firm, admissible in the United States. That decision by one of the two Federal departments to exert moral censorship on literary material (the other being the Post Office), was naturally of extreme importance: *Lolita* could now legitimately be published in America with practically no danger.

The third fact was of a less favorable nature, at least at first sight. The British Government had several times already invoked the International Agreement on the Repression of Obscene Publications to prevail on the French Government to look into my publishing activities. Nothing much had been done about those requests by the French, until the dispute between Graham Greene and John Gordon in London gave new dimensions to the issue. More pressing demands were made on the Ministry of the Interior in Paris by the British Home Office which provoked the intervention of the French police, as I have already recounted in the Introduction to this volume. *Lolita* was thus banned in its English version by the French government (on December 20, 1956) only a few weeks before it was found to be no longer objectionable by the U.S. authorities.

My relations with Vladimir Nabokov and his wife Vera, who helped him in his work, had up to that point been remarkably courteous and pleasant, if sometimes a little strained, although we had never yet had occasion to meet. When I decided to fight the *Lolita* ban, my first thought was to ask for Nabokov's help. I was rather surprised to receive a very adamant refusal to participate in what he called, with blithe unconcern, the "lolitigation."

"My moral defense of the book is the book itself," he wrote on March 10, 1957. "I do not feel under any obligation to do more. . . . On the ethical plane, it is of supreme indifference to me what opinion French, British, or any other courts, magistrates or philistine readers in general may have of my book. However, I appreciate your difficulties."

Somewhere else he wrote: "I would very much prefer if you did not stress too much my being a professor at Cornell . . . I do not mind being referred to as a 'university professor teaching literature in a great American university.' But I would prefer you not to call Cornell by name. . . ."

All Britain and all America were now aware of *Lolita*, and in the United States all the big publishers who had turned down Nabokov's manuscript a few years before were biting their nails in chagrin. The prize was still there for any one of them to seize, but naturally there were quite a few bidders now, and the rights had to be bought from me, not from Nabokov. One publisher spontaneously offered a 20 per cent royalty to get the book, but was then apparently frightened away by Nabokov's attitude when he met him later in New York; and Nabokov's attitude had indeed changed quite substantially as *Lolita*'s glory expanded on the horizon. There were no more haughty denunciations of the philistine masses coming from that supple pen, but only tortuous controversies over the terms of our agreement, which was now weighing heavily on Nabokov's dreams of an impending fortune.

In spite of my disappointment at Nabokov's indifference, I went on with my single-handed fight against the French authorities. Progress was slow, as the case was most unusual, and to make the issue known to the French public I printed a pamphlet (*L'Affaire Lolita*) which elicited from Nabokov a volley of enthusiastic adjectives. Soon after, on August 3, he was still writing: "I shall always be grateful to you for having published *Lolita*."

Alas, those were his last nice words to me. After that came more and more morose exchanges on the subject of the American publication of the book and I finally received a registered letter from Nabokov, dated October 5 of the same year, informing me in elaborate legal style that he was exercising his right "to declare the Agreement between us null and void."

I was already half prepared for that, but the shock was felt nevertheless. Nabokov's excuse for his action was futile and ineffective, but our relationship was irreparably damaged by it, at a time when we should have been acting more than ever in close agreement. The bickering over the American contract became even more ludicrous since Nabokov had persuaded himself that he no longer had a contract with me.

At last I received a cable from Walter Minton, head of G. P. Putnam's Sons, announcing: "Nabokov has agreed contract." That was on February 11, 1958. A few days later I won my lawsuit against the Minister of the Interior: the ban was lifted . . . in France. Nabokov did not feel it necessary to acknowledge that event.

In August, Putnam released their edition of *Lolita*, which immediately conquered the top place on the best-seller list, to be dislodged only by *Dr. Zhivago* a few months later.

It was very gratifying, and I was receiving Minton's crescendo reports of our successes with a feeling that I had really earned the right to relax a bit and enjoy life. But the more sales increased the more Nabokov remembered that he hated me for having stolen a portion of his property. His harassment was thorough and all-encompassing: he refused to let Putnam acknowledge my firm as first publisher of *Lolita* in their edition of the book; a new argument flared up over the British contract and Minton reported that Nabokov was again contemplating lawsuits (more lolitigation). I had made great plans based on my share of American royalties, but Minton was constantly writing to me that he could not pay me as agreed, due to the Nabokovs' opposition: "They feel you did nothing to help the book and they think you have taken a lot of the royalties," was his explanation (November 6, 1958).

I became so disgusted that I asked Nabokov to submit his ghostly grievances to arbitration. But after the British contract was signed with Weidenfeld and Nicolson, which was finally achieved when I agreed to pay Nabokov's commission to his own agent out of my own pocket, Walter Minton again wrote to me (November 19, 1958): "I have also talked with Nabokov about the question of arbitrating your difficulties. I must confess I don't think there is anything to arbitrate. . . ." And a few days later (November 29, 1958): "Incidentally Mrs. Nabokov is highly suspicious of a tie-up between you and Weidenfeld even though I told her I picked him and you did not even meet him. . . . Actually it is she, I think, who is at the bottom of most of the troubles between you and her husband. She is a lovely lady of a very actively suspicious turn of mind which just complements her husband's. . . ." Aye, aye, sir.

The next episode came when I wrote again to Nabokov on January 14, 1959, a long letter meant as an effort to dissolve the bad feelings, in which I said: "I was greatly relieved to hear from Madame Ergaz that you see no point in the arbitration I suggested in order to eliminate the legal differences which seemed to persist between us. . . . Now that the legal aspect of that enigmatic conflict is happily settled, I would very much like to settle its other aspects. I am still at a loss to understand your reasons for so much resenting your association with me, and feel we should make a genuine effort to eliminate misunderstandings. . . ." and concluded thus: "I admit that my satisfaction in having done my job well is marred by your attitude towards me.

The only purpose of this letter is to ask you to think the matter over and to reconsider your judgment."

To this I received a twelve-line answer saying: "I have received your letter of January 14th. I am sorry that lack of time prevents my commenting upon it in detail. . . ."

Three weeks later I received a letter from Minton chiding me for having given my agreement to sell the Israeli rights on *Lolita* to a man named Steimatzky. I had nothing to do with that as it had been Mrs. Nabokov herself who had insisted on having us offer the rights to Steimatzky. I said so but nobody thought of apologizing to me for that silly incident.

In France, since the advent of the Fifth Republic, the status of *Lolita* had again changed. The Minister of the Interior had appealed against the earlier judgment of the Administrative Tribunal lifting the ban, and had won an easy victory against me at the Conseil d'Etat: under a strong régime, you cannot win against the police. *Lolita* was again under a ban restricted in its application (by accident, I assume) to the English version as published by me. If strictly interpreted, it did not preclude the possibility of publishing a French version in France.

The Librairie Gallimard—France's foremost literary publishers —had bought the French rights long before, but they had been very hesitant to release the book, which had been translated by my brother, Eric Kahane. The release of the Putnam edition in America was a powerful argument which I used to convince Gallimard finally to publish the French version, which came out in April, 1959.

I had asked Gallimard to mention in their version that my firm was the publisher of the original version, as this was very important to me in my litigation with the French government. Such an acknowledgment was a simple enough matter, but Nabokov heard of my request and opposed it violently. Gallimard's editor, Michel Mohrt, wrote me on February 27, 1959, a pathetically embarrassed letter in which he quoted Nabokov: "You are mistaken in thinking that the French translation of Lolita has been made from the Olympia edition. This is not so. When last spring I prepared the Putnam edition I changed an entire paragraph in the Olympia edition and made several other corrections throughout the book. . . ." Etc., etc.

I was descending the stairs of hell, feeling like the much-hated Quilty with the muzzle of a maniacal revolver pointed at my back.

However, I was still fighting. There was no way of appealing against the final judgment of the Conseil d'Etat and of having the ban lifted on the English version of the book by direct litigation: in its verdict, the Conseil had stated that the Minister of the Interior's power not only to apply but even to *interpret* the law was absolute and could not be questioned even by the Conseil (a strange conclusion, incidentally, as the Conseil's function is precisely to verify the lawful regularity of the government's acts and decisions). But since the French version of *Lolita* had been authorized while my own English edition was still under a ban, I had yet another way open to me: to sue the government for damages, under the pretext that an unjust application of the law had been made, and that the republican principle of equality between citizens had been violated. Surprisingly, that worked. I was called to the Ministry of the Interior, and a compromise was proposed to me: the Minister was willing to cancel the ban if I agreed to withdraw my request for damages. I agreed and the ban was finally abrogated on July 21, 1959.

The ban had hardly been lifted in France on the English version when the Belgian government decided to forbid the sale of the French version on its own territory. Apparently, Gallimard was not in a hurry to do anything about that, and I took it upon myself to write to the Belgian Minister of the Interior, Mr. René Lefebvre, protesting against his decree. Mr. Lefebvre immediately responded to my request and wrote to me that he would look into the matter: the Belgian ban was in turn abrogated by royal decree a few weeks later.

A few days after that I received the visit of a Mr. Godemert, who acted as legal adviser to Gallimard. I knew him well, and he stated the reason for his visit with as straight a face as he could manage. Mr. Nabokov did not want to spend money on French lawyers, and had therefore asked Gallimard to see if there was any legal possibility of breaking his agreement with me. So, Godemert explained, in view of the fact that you know all the aspects of the case better than I do, I have come to ask you if you could please give me the elements of an answer, and suggest some method to attack you on Mr. Nabokov's behalf.

We had a drink together, and I wrote to Nabokov (April 27, 1960): "I have just seen Mr. Godemert, Gallimard's legal adviser, who came to ask on what grounds you could possibly sue me. I need hardly draw your attention to the irony of the situation," etc.

Nabokov, meanwhile, had instructed his much-harrassed agent, Doussia Ergaz, to suspend all payment to me of my share of certain foreign royalties due me as a result of our contract. I reciprocated by informing her that I would suspend payment of the royalties owed by my firm to Nabokov on our own edition. With mechanistic determination another registered letter soon issued from the tireless typewriter dated August 13, 1960, in which I was told: "I must call to your attention, therefore, that as a result of such failure and as provided in paragraph 8 of such Agreement, such Agreement between us, effective as of the last day of July, 1960, automatically became null and void and all rights therein granted reverted to me. I, therefore, demand that you immediately cease publication of *Lolita* and distribution and sale of any copies thereof," etc., etc.

What could I do but patiently attempt to refute once again the fine legal metaphysics, and helplessly resort to the habitual conclusion of my letters to Vladimir Nabokov: "Allow me to say again how deeply I regret this turn of events, not only because it cannot, in the long run, fail to harm our mutual interests, but also because I consider your personal attitude to be profoundly unjust in view of my constant efforts in favor of a book which I have always admired. . . ."

Nabokov's final consecration by the American Establishment had come in the form of a long panegyric in *Life International* of April 13, 1959, entitled "Lolita and the Lepidopterist" and announced by a large portrait of the author himself appearing on the cover in his butterfly-hunting costume, with the wily, innocent grin of the traditional Russian society clown painted on his face.

That article could have been conceived as a pastiche by a clever journalist of an article written for *Life* by Mr. Nabokov on Mr. Nabokov. In particular, the earlier career of *Lolita* is dismissed with a series of stylistic shrugs of strictly Nabokovian obedience but the distortion of facts was such that I sent a protest, which *Life* felt obliged to print in full (*Life International*, July 6, 1959), although they attempted to water down my pitiful true-life account of facts by framing it between two pieces of prose, the first being a letter from Vladimir Nabokov himself; and the latter being an exhaustive editorial comment which appeared as a postscript, and, which, although signed with the initials of our mysterious friend ED., seems to carry on its forehead the beautiful silver aura of Vera Nabokov's distinguished scalp.

However unjustly trying for the reader, I cannot refrain from quoting Nabokov's letter which was obviously intended to temper the effects of *Life*'s reporter's excessive adulation:

"There are two little errors in your fascinating account of me and *Lolita*. . . . In the photograph showing my brother Serge and me in boyhood he is on the left and I am on the right, and not vice versa as the caption says. And towards the end of the article I am described as being 'startled and . . . indignant' when my Parisian agent informed me that The Olympia Press wanted to 'add *Lolita* to its list.' I certainly was neither 'startled' nor 'indignant' since I was only interested in having the book published—no matter by whom."

In my own letter, I had protested against Nabokov's innuendoes concerning Lolita's "unhappy marriage" with The Olympia Press, adding that: "Were it not for my firm, *Lolita* would still be a dusty manuscript in a nostalgic cupboard. I might add that I do not regret having published this admirable book; in spite of many disappointments, it has proved to be a rather exhilarating experience."

Life, in its closing comments, deemed it right to express regrets for having given "the mistaken impression that Vladimir Nabokov was 'a little indignant' at The Olympia Press offer to publish *Lolita* —an impression that Mr. Nabokov himself corrects in his letter above. As for the somewhat more important question of whether or not Olympia Press publishes pornography, it may depend upon one's viewpoint."

After that last scuffle, I began at last to accept the fact of the Nabokovs' hostility as a permanent part of my difficult publisher's life. The career of *Lolita* had been wonderful, and although my role was being represented in the darkest colors, I really did not mind. May I say that I was quite happy to see Nabokov pursuing his literary career so masterfully, with *Pnin*, *Pale Fire*, and the heroic translation of *Eugene Onegin*. Many years spent in this profession, publishing, teach you that no great writer can be less than a monster of egomania. And that seems indeed to be an absolute requisite: literary genius can only derive from superhuman concentration—and who cares if a few people are abused and hurt along the way?

Some time after the *Life* incident, I heard that Nabokov was coming to Paris. He wrote to my brother Eric that he was anxious to meet him to discuss the French translation of *Lolita*. Gallimard decided to celebrate Nabokov's arrival in this conquered city with one of their traditional cocktail parties. I learned that a heated debate had taken place among the directors of the firm when somebody had asked whether I should be invited or not. My conflict with Nabokov was so notorious that some unpleasant incident was bound to happen if we were ever to face each other in the flesh for the first time in the history of our relationship. Some argued that it would be unseemly to exclude me; and in the end caution prevailed, and it was decided to eliminate my name from the guest list. But Monique Grall, Gallimard's P.R. lady, thought it would be amusing to transgress that decision, of which she had not been properly informed. She sent me an invitation.

I was very perplexed when I received it. I did not want to embarrass my friends at Gallimard; and I did not want to look like a coward, being quite as able as anyone else to digest a punch on the nose in case of necessity. I discussed this rather exquisite point of ethics with Eric, who said that he was to meet Nabokov shortly before the party at his hotel, at his invitation, and it would be ludicrous for me to abstain; he later called from the hotel, insisting that Nabokov had showered him with compliments for his translation, and although he had not breathed a word about me, it did not seem that the old boy would be shocked to meet me.

I therefore duly made my appearance in the gilded salons of the rue Sébastien-Bottin, and I must add in all proper modesty that the stupor painted on so many faces made me feel a little conspicuous. Monique Grall was doubled over in helpless mirth, in a corner, but the other Gallimard dignitaries were all rather pale, and the many press photographers present had that determined, ferocious glint in their eyes which means so much to celebrities in danger of being caught at a disadvantage.

I immediately identified Nabokov who was surrounded by a tight group of admirers; not too far away Madame Nabokov was impersonating dignity, destroying by her pale fire presence the myth of her husband's entomological concern for the race of nymphets. I found, hiding in a corner, my dear suffering, terrified friend Doussia Ergaz, choking on a macaroon. I asked her kindly to introduce me to the master, our master, as was her duty being our mutual friend, as well as the *dea ex machina* who had, with her magic wand, generated such a sumptuous train of literary facts. She at first protested, then complied. We made our way through the crowd. Nabokov was speaking to my brother in earnest, but he had very obviously recognized me. At last we reached the presence, I was introduced, expecting at all moments a blow, a screech, a slap, anything—but not that vacuous grin which is all the *papperazzi* were able to capture, much to their disappointment. As if he were seized by some sudden urge, Vladimir Nabokov pivoted on himself with the graceful ease of a circus seal, throwing a glance in the direction of his wife, and was immediately caught up in more ardent conversation by a Czech journalist. I was both relieved and disappointed, and I went to down a few glasses of champagne before I plunged back into the crowd, unassisted this time, in the direction of Madame Nabokov. She was standing very quiet, very self-possessed. I introduced myself, but she did not acknowledge my presence even with the flicker of an eyelash. I did not exist; I was no more than an epistolary fiction, and I had no business wearing a body and disturbing people at a literary cocktail party given in honor of her husband, Vladimir Nabokov.

The next day, Doussia Ergaz called me, chuckling with delight and relief. She had had dinner with the Nabokovs after the party, and asked Vladimir what he thought of me. "And do you know what he answered," she added. "He said: 'Was he there? I didn't know.'"

But so many things have happened since then. There is nothing much now to quarrel about, and when the project of publishing this volume came to be discussed with the directors of Grove Press, I told them that the only difficult author they would have to approach would be Nabokov, but that he would certainly agree after all these years, even if a little reluctantly, to let them print an excerpt from *Lolita* in this compendium. They said that they would try to approach Nabokov through his American publisher, Walter Minton, who obligingly accepted to forward their request. The answer was no, certainly not. I then wrote to Barney Rosset to tell Minton that if Nabokov were to persist in his refusal, I would have no choice but to write the story of our relationship. The answer came by return mail: "This is blackmail. And you know what you have to do with blackmailers: sue them."

HENRY MILLER

QUIET DAYS IN CLICHY

I was only in bed about an hour when I heard Carl opening the door. He went straight to his room and closed his door. I was sorely tempted to ask him to go out and buy me a sandwich and a bottle of wine. Then I had a better idea. I would get up early, while he was still sound asleep, and rifle his pockets. As I was tossing about, I heard him open the door of his room and go to the bathroom. He was giggling and whispering—to some floozy, most likely, whom he had picked up on the way home.

As he came out of the bathroom I called to him.

"So you're awake?" he said jubilantly. "What's the matter, are you sick?"

I explained that I was hungry, ravenously hungry. Had he any change on him?

"I'm cleaned out," he said. He said it cheerfully, as though it were nothing of importance.

"Haven't you got a franc at least?" I demanded.

"Don't worry about francs," he said, sitting on the edge of the bed with the air of a man who is about to confide a piece of important news. "We've got bigger things to worry about now. I brought a girl home with me—a waif. She can't be more than fourteen. I just gave her a lay. Did you hear me? I hope I didn't knock her up. She's a virgin."

"You mean she *was*," I put in.

"Listen, Joey," he said, lowering his voice to make it sound more convincing, "we've got to do something for her. She has no place to stay . . . she ran away from home. I found her walking about in a trance, half starved, and a little demented, I thought at first. Don't worry, she's O.K. Not very bright, but a good sort. Probably from a good family. She's just a child . . . you'll see. Maybe I'll marry her when she comes of age. Anyway there's no money. I spent my last cent buying her a meal. Too bad you had to go without dinner. You should have been with *us*. We had oysters, lobster, shrimps—and a wonderful wine. A Chablis, year. . . ."

"Fuck the year!" I shouted. "Don't tell me about what you ate. I'm as empty as an ash can. Now we've got three mouths to feed and no money, not a sou."

"Take it easy, Joey," he said smilingly, "you know I always keep a few francs in my pockets for an emergency." He dove into his pocket and pulled out the change. It amounted to three francs sixty altogether. "That'll get you a breakfast," he said. "Tomorrow's another day."

At that moment the girl stuck her head through the doorway. Carl jumped up and brought her to the bed. "Colette," he said, as I put out my hand to greet her. "What do you think of her?"

Before I had time to answer, the girl turned to him and, almost as if frightened, asked what language we were speaking.

"Don't you know English when you hear it?" said Carl, giving me a glance which said I told you she wasn't very bright.

Blushing with confusion, the girl explained quickly that it sounded at first like German, or perhaps Belgian.

"There is no Belgian!" snorted Carl. Then to me. "She's a little idiot. But look at those breasts! Pretty ripe for fourteen, what? She swears she's seventeen, but I don't believe her."

Colette stood there listening to the strange language, unable even yet to grasp the fact that Carl could speak anything but French. Finally she demanded to know if he really was French. It seemed quite important to her.

"Sure I'm French," said Carl blithely. "Can't you tell by my speech? Do I talk like a *Boche?* Want to see my passport?"

"Better not show her that," I said, remembering that he carried a Czech passport.

"Would you like to come in and look at the sheets?" he said, putting an arm around Colette's waist. "We'll have to throw them away, I guess. I can't take them to the laundry; they'd suspect me of having committed a crime."

"Get *her* to wash them," I said jocularly. "There's a lot she can do around here if she wants to keep house for us."

"So you do want her to stay? You know it's illegal, don't you? We can go to jail for this."

"Better get her a pair of pajamas, or a nightgown," I said, "because if she's going to walk around at night in that crazy shift of yours I may forget myself and rape her."

He looked at Colette and burst out laughing.

"What is it?" she exclaimed. "Are you making fun of me? Why doesn't your friend talk French?"

"You're right," I said. "From now on we're talking French and nothing but French. *D'accord?*"

A childish grin spread over her face. She bent down and gave me a kiss on both cheeks. As she did so her boobies fell out and brushed my face. The little shift fell open all the way down, revealing an exquisitely full young body.

"Jesus, take her away and keep her locked up in your room," I said. "I won't be responsible for what happens if she's going to prowl around in that getup while you're out."

Carl packed her off to his room and sat down again on the edge of the bed. "We've got a problem on our hands, Joey," he began, "and you've got to help me. I don't care what you do with her when my back is turned. I'm not jealous, you know that. But you mustn't let her fall into the hands of the police. If they catch her they'll send her away—and they'll probably send us away too. The thing is, what to tell the concierge? I can't lock her up like a dog. Maybe I'll say she's a cousin of mine, here on a visit. Nights, when I go to work, take her to the movies. Or take her for a walk. She's easy to please. Teach her geography or something—she doesn't know a thing. It'll be good for you, Joey. You'll improve your French. . . . And don't knock her up, if you can help it. I can't think about money for abortions now. Besides, I don't know anymore where my Hungarian doctor lives."

I listened to him in silence. Carl had a genius for getting involved in difficult situations. The trouble was, or perhaps it was a virtue, that he was incapable of saying No.

It was near the Café Marignan on the Champs-Elysées that I ran into her.

I had only recently recovered from a painful separation from Mara-St. Louis. That was not her name, but let us call her that for the moment, because it was on the Ile St. Louis that she was born, and it was there I often walked about at night, letting the rust eat into me.

It is because I heard from her just the other day, after giving her up for lost, that I am able to recount what follows. Only now, because of certain things which have become clear to me for the first time, the story has grown more complicated.

I might say, in passing, that my life seems to have been one long search for *the* Mara who would devour all the others and give them significant reality.

The Mara who precipitated events was neither the Mara of the Champs-Elysées nor the Mara of the Ile St. Louis. The Mara I speak of was called Eliane. She was married to a man who had been jailed for passing counterfeit money. She was also the mistress of my friend Carl, who had at first been passionately in love with her and who was now, on this afternoon I speak of, so bored with her that he couldn't tolerate the thought of going to see her alone.

Eliane was young, slim, attractive, except that she was liberally peppered with moles and had a coat of down on her upper lip. In the eyes of my friend these blemishes at first only enhanced her beauty, but as he grew tired of her their presence irritated him and sometimes caused him to make caustic jokes which made her wince. When she wept she became, strangely enough, more beautiful than ever. With her face wreathed in tears she looked the mature woman, not the slender androgynous creature with whom Carl had fallen in love.

Eliane's husband and Carl were old friends. They had met in Budapest, where the former had rescued Carl from starvation and later had given him the money to go to Paris. The gratitude which Carl first entertained for the man soon changed to contempt and ridicule when he discovered how stupid and insensitive the fellow was. Ten years later they met by chance on the street in Paris. The invitation to dinner, which followed, Carl would never have accepted had the husband not flaunted a photograph of his young wife. Carl was immediately infatuated. She reminded him, he informed me, of a girl named Marcienne, about whom he was writing at the time.

I remember well how the story of Marcienne blossomed as his clandestine meetings with Eliane become more and more frequent. He had seen Marcienne only three or four times after their meeting in the forest of Marly where he had stumbled upon her in the company of a beautiful greyhound. I mention the dog because, when he was first struggling with the story, the dog had more reality (for me) than the woman with whom he was supposed to be in love. With Eliane's entrance into his life the figure of Marcienne began to take on form and substance; he even endowed Marcienne with one of Eliane's superfluous moles, the one at the nape of her neck, which he said made him particularly passionate every time he kissed it.

For some months now he had the pleasure of kissing all Eliane's beautiful moles, including the one on the left leg, up near the crotch. They no longer made him inflammatory. He had finished the story of Marcienne and, in doing so, his passion for Eliane had evaporated.

The finishing stroke was the husband's arrest and conviction. While the husband was at large there had been at least the excitement of danger; now that he was safely behind the bars, Carl was faced with a mistress who had two children to support and who very naturally looked to him as a protector and provider. Carl was not ungenerous but he certainly was not a provider. He was rather fond of children, too, I must say, but he didn't like to play the father to the children of a man whom he despised. Under the circumstances the best thing he could think of was to find Eliane a job, which he proceeded to do. When he was broke he ate with her. Now and then he complained that she worked too hard, that she was ruining her beauty; secretly, of course, he was pleased, because an Eliane worn with fatigue made less demands on his time.

The day he persuaded me to accompany him he was in a bad mood. He had received a telegram from her that morning, saying that she was free for the day and that he should come as early as possible. He decided to go about four in the afternoon and leave with me shortly after dinner. I was to think up some excuse which would enable him to withdraw without creating a scene.

When we arrived I found that there were three children instead of two—he had forgotten to tell me that there was a baby too. A pure oversight, he remarked. I must say the atmosphere wasn't precisely that of a love nest. The baby carriage was standing at the foot of the steps in the dingy courtyard, and the brat was screaming at the top of its lungs. Inside, the children's clothes were hanging up to dry. The windows were wide open and there were flies everywhere. The oldest child was calling him daddy, which annoyed him beyond measure. In a surly voice he told Eliane to pack the kids off. This almost provoked a burst of tears. He threw me one of those helpless looks which said: "It's begun already . . . how am I ever going to survive the ordeal?" And then, in desperation, he began to pretend that he was quite merry, calling for drinks, bouncing the kids on his knee, reciting poetry to them, patting Eliane on the rump, briskly and disinterestedly, as though it were a private ham which he had ordered for the occasion. He even went a little further in his simu-

lated gaiety; with glass in hand he beckoned Eliane to approach, first giving her
a kiss on his favorite mole, and then, urging me to draw closer, he put his free
hand in her blouse and fished up one of
her teats, which he coolly asked me to
appraise.

I had witnessed these performances
before—with other women whom he had
been in love with. His emotions usually
went through the same cycle: passion,
coolness, indifference, boredom, mockery, contempt, disgust. I felt
sorry for Eliane. The presence of the children, the poverty, the
drudgery, the humiliation, rendered the situation far from funny. Seeing that the jest had missed fire, Carl suddenly felt ashamed of himself. He put his glass down and, with the look of a beaten dog, he put
his arms around her and kissed her on the forehead. That was to indicate that she was still an angel, even if her rump were appetizing and
the left breast exceedingly tempting. Then a silly grin spread over his
face and he sat himself down on the divan, muttering Yah, Yah, as
though to say—"That's how things are, it's sad, but what can you
do?"

To relieve the tension, I volunteered to take the children out for
a walk, the one in the carriage included. At once Carl became alarmed.
He didn't want me to go for a walk. From the gestures and grimaces
he was making behind Eliane's back, I gathered that he didn't relish
the idea of performing his amorous duties just yet. Aloud he was saying that *he* would take the kids for an airing; behind her back he was
making me to understand, by deaf and dumb gestures, that he wanted
me to take a crack at her, Eliane. Even had I wanted to, I couldn't.
I didn't have the heart for it. Besides, I felt more inclined to torture
him because of the callous way in which he was treating her. Meanwhile the children, having caught the drift of the conversation, and
having witnessed the deaf and dumb show behind their mother's back,
began to act as if the very devil had taken possession of them. They
pleaded and begged, then bellowed and stamped their feet in uncontrollable rage. The infant in the carriage began to squawk again, the
parrot set up a racket, the dog started yelping. Seeing that they
couldn't have their way, the brats began to imitate Carl's antics, which

they had studied with amusement and mystification. Their gestures were thoroughly obscene and poor Eliane was at a loss to know what had come over them.

By this time Carl had grown hysterical. To Eliane's amazement, he suddenly began to repeat his dumb antics openly, this time as though imitating the children. At this point I could no longer control myself. I began to howl with laughter, the children following suit. Then, to silence Eliane's remonstrances, Carl pushed her over on the divan, making the most god-awful grimaces at her while he chattered like a monkey in that Austrian dialect which she loathed. The children piled on top of her screeching like guinea hens, and making obscene gestures which she was powerless to hinder because Carl had begun to tickle her and bite her neck, her legs, her rump, her breasts. There she was, her skirts up to her neck, wriggling, squealing, laughing as if she would burst, and at the same time furious, almost beside herself. When she at last managed to disengage herself she broke into violent sobs. Carl sat beside her, looking distraught, baffled, and muttering as before—Yah, Yah. I quietly took the youngsters by the hand and led them out into the courtyard, where I amused them as best I could while the two lovers patched things up.

When I returned I found that they had moved into the adjoining room. They were so quiet I thought at first that they had fallen asleep. But suddenly the door opened and Carl stuck his head out, giving me his usual clownish grin, which meant—"All's clear, I gave her the works." Eliane soon appeared, looking flushed and smolderingly content. I lay down on the divan and played with the kids while Carl and Eliane went out to buy food for the evening meal. When they returned they were in high spirits. I suspected that Carl, who beamed at the mere mention of food, must have been carried away by his enthusiasm and promised Eliane things which he had no intention of fulfilling. Eliane was strangely gullible; it was probably the fault of the moles, which were a constant reminder that her beauty was not untarnished. To pretend to love her because of her moles, which was undoubtedly Carl's line of approach, rendered her hopelessly defenseless. Anyway she was becoming more and more radiant. We had another Amer Picon, one too many for her, and then, as the twilight slowly faded, we began to sing.

In such moods we always sang German songs. Eliane sang too, though she despised the German tongue. Carl was a different fellow now. No longer panicky. He had probably given her a successful lay, he had had three or four apéritifs, he was ravenously hungry. Besides night was coming on, and he would soon be free. In short, the day was progressing satisfactorily in every way.

When Carl became mellow and expansive, he was irresistible. He talked glowingly about the wine he had bought, a very expensive wine which, on such occasions, he always insisted he had bought expressly for me. While talking about the wine he began devouring the hors d'œuvre. That made him more thirsty. Eliane tried to restrain him, but there was no holding him back now. He fished out one of her teats again, this time without protest on her part, and, after pouring a little wine over it, he nibbled at it greedily—to the children's huge enjoyment. Then, of course, he had to show me the mole on her left leg, up near the crotch. From the way things were going on, I thought they were going back to the bedroom again, but no, suddenly he put her teat back inside her blouse and sat down saying: "*J'ai faim, j'ai faim, chérie.*" In tone it was no different than his usual "Fuck me, dearie, I can't wait another second!"

During the course of the meal, which was excellent, we got on to some strange topics. When eating, especially if he enjoyed the food, Carl always kept up a rambling conversation which permitted him to concentrate on the food and wine. In order to avoid the dangers of a serious discussion, one which would interfere with his digestive processes, he would throw out random remarks of a nature he thought suitable and appropriate for the morsel of food, or the glass of wine, he was about to gulp down. In this offhand way he blurted out that he had just recently met a girl—he wasn't sure if she were a whore or not, what matter?—whom he was thinking of introducing me to. Before I could ask why, he added—"She's just your type."

"I know your type," he rattled on, making a quick allusion to Mara of the Ile St. Louis. "This one is much better," he added. "I'm going to fix it for you. . . ."

Sin for Breakfast

HAMILTON DRAKE

*I*f anyone in the café thought it odd that he had been sitting for over half an hour without shifting his gaze from the house across the street he hardly cared. There was a magnificent view of Oliver's door and that was all that mattered. Occasionally a car drove up the street, and for an instant, the door would be obscured behind it. When this happened he would sharpen his attention so that the instant seemed to take a perilously long time. As soon as the car had passed and the door was visible again, Trent's eyes fixed hungrily on it as if, in the next second, it might open and somebody step out.

When he'd finished his second coffee, he got up, put a hundred-franc note under the saucer, and crossed the street.

Inside the house it was cool and silent. He tiptoed up the stairs and stood outside Oliver's room, his ear to the door and trembling slightly. There was no sound. He pictured him in there, lying curled up in the bed, alone, probably, and with some book he'd been reading and his cigarettes lying on the floor beside the bed. He'd probably gone to sleep about three o'clock and was going to wake up at noon. That would give him another two hours. Perhaps he'd stayed out all night and wasn't there at all for that matter. He considered opening the door—his own key would work he'd discovered one time when Oliver had been locked out—but a wave of embarrassment overcame him. If, by chance, Oliver were awake and lying in bed reading, or smoking a cigarette, it would be too ridiculous for him to enter like that and be caught in all the dense silliness of his suspicion.

He turned and went back down the stairs making as little sound as possible. Once in the street, however, he regretted his lack of nerve. One glance at the room, empty, or with Oliver in it alone, would have freed him, but, as things stood, he was a prisoner to the vicinity until he'd made certain that just this was the case: that, for example, nobody else was there. By "nobody else" he meant Vivian.

He went back to the café again and ordered another coffee. After a while he bought a newspaper and pretended to be reading it but his gaze remained on Oliver's door and, in his mind, for the hundredth time he went over what had happened that morning to cause him to be sitting there.

It was because of the abruptness with which she'd gotten out of bed that he'd awakened; there had been something hurried and deliberate in the way she'd done it, as if something were up. He remembered asking her sleepily where she was going and that she had answered that she was going shopping at the Bon Marché. After that he'd made believe he'd gone back to sleep—covering his face with his hand and watching her through the cracks between his fingers. That was something he often did in the mornings. He liked to watch her dress and to pretend that she was a woman he didn't know and that he was peeping at her through a keyhole. It was also the only way that he could get a look at her body at such moments, for she was inordinately shy and would have managed to conceal her nudity if she suspected he were watching. Not that there was anything for her

to be ashamed of, he had thought, as she'd sat in the chair, one of her shapely legs raised in the air, and slowly pulled the long silk stocking on. No, on the contrary, any other woman, if she were that good-looking, would take every opportunity to parade about naked in front of her husband and let the rest of the men see a few things too—lean over innocently while seated in a café, for example, and let them see that those were really her breasts that swelled out like that, and not the rubber form of some trick brassiere; or sit on a sofa the way some women did, with her legs curled up beneath her so that any man who happened to be opposite could see everything she had whenever she changed her position. In a way, he was sorry she wasn't like those other women; it would have been exciting if, once in a while, she would deliberately do something shocking—take his hand and suddenly rub it between her legs, or, when she was going up a flight of stairs ahead of him, yank her skirt up unexpectedly and show him her bottom. . . . It was better she didn't, of course. He didn't really have much time for that sort of thing, and if their love-making was a bit perfunctory and not very frequent it was all to the good. He had begun to think about his thesis and about his work at the School of Oriental Languages and then it had happened.

She had been standing, fully clothed by now—in the black velvet dress which went so perfectly with her blond hair—and dabbing herself about the face and neck with the perfume he'd given her for her birthday when suddenly she raised her skirt and rested her foot on a chair. She had her back to him, and he remembered looking at the foot on the chair, in its high-heeled patent-leather pump, wondering what she was doing, before discovering that it was all being reflected in the full-length mirror on the closet door.

To his astonishment, he noticed, first: that she had neglected to put on her panties and that, for once, he was afforded an excellent view of the furry spot between her legs, and, even more extraordinary, that she was touching herself there with her index finger. He realized that for some incredible reason she was perfuming this secret part of her anatomy. It was really unbelievable. He'd been with her for two years now and had never seen anything like it. Before it was over she had actually spread the lips of her sex apart with two fingers and dabbed some of the scent between them. He had all he could do to keep still in the bed and continue the farce of being asleep. A minute later and she had swept out of the room and he heard the front door open and shut very quietly.

He had sprung out of the bed then, and, pulling on his bathrobe, had dashed into the kitchen whose window gave on the street. Standing there, hidden behind a curtain, he had observed yet another inexplicable thing: instead of crossing the avenue to where the bus stopped that went to Sèvres-Babylone and the department store, she was remaining on their side as if she were going to take a bus in the other direction.

"Oliver," he had thought. There could be no other explanation, that was absolutely the only time they ever took the ninety-one bus going that way. But what the hell was she going to Oliver's for at nine o'clock in the morning? All of this unusual behavior of hers, offered up as soon as he awoke, was going to take a few minutes to comprehend. The solution, however, wasn't very complicated. If a woman gets up, puts a bit of perfume on her pussy, and then takes the bus to your best friend's house, it doesn't much look like she's going shopping. But Oliver! Good old chubby Oliver! this was something he'd have to see to believe.

He stayed at the window long enough to watch her board the bus and then, with his heart beating fast, hurriedly dressed and washed and was, himself, mounting a ninety-one bus eight minutes later.

Once arrived, however, he had had a wave of doubt. Should he just go storming right into the room like a maniac? After all, maybe she wasn't even there. Maybe she had some lover that he didn't know about that lived in the same *quartier* as Oliver. Or maybe she was visiting Oliver but it wasn't what he thought—she might just be in there talking about something, but about what? About how pretty her pussy smelled and wouldn't Oliver maybe like to have a sniff? It was incredible. He decided to have a cup of coffee at the corner café where he could watch the door of the house and consider the situation.

That had been an hour ago. During that time his belief in Vivian's culpability had dwindled considerably. Now that he had gone and listened outside the door, and heard nothing, he was almost ready to give the whole thing up as a wild suspicion. He was starting to get an ache in his neck besides, from not having moved his head for all that time. All right, he thought, I'll give it one more try and if I don't hear anything I'll go back home. She would probably say something that night that would clear the whole thing up without his even asking. . . .

Only this time he *did* hear something. It was so loud that he hadn't gotten to the door but heard it as soon as he started up the stairs. It was unmistakable—the sound of a bed taking a beating, the springs creaking steadily up and down.

The key didn't make a sound. He pushed the door open and there it was—Oliver's big white ass pumping away for dear life. It looked like a frantic washerwoman kneeling over a tub of dirty clothes, and, underneath, the laundry being pummeled was Vivian all right. A glance at the white legs, dangling and kicking lasciviously in the air was enough. There was no need to see the face, contorted, as if in pain and with the tongue avidly licking the mouth of her lover.

For what seemed like a long time he stood watching in shocked disbelief as Oliver's shivering buttocks rose and crashed down, driving stiffly into Vivian; knocking the breath out of her, so that each downward plunge was accompanied by her gasp—and then the door clicked shut behind him.

Instantly, the activity on the bed came to a halt. The silence was absolute in the room and faintly, as if from very far away, he heard the screeching scooters and the snarling trucks of the Paris morning.

The two faces staring at him were expressionless and it was he, as he took the pistol from his back pocket and pointed it to his temple, who wore a foolish and embarrassed grin, as if he had stumbled into the room by mistake.

Several times, and rapidly, he squeezed on the trigger and the little jets of water splattered hard against his forehead and trickled ludicrously down, wetting his shirt.

Then he turned and left, being very careful not to slam the door.

Trent tiptoed in the blackness of the dark apartment. Expertly he stepped around chairs, avoided tables, placed his hand unerringly on the switch of the hall lamp outside the bedroom. This gave enough light so that when he opened the door he could see the furniture of the bedroom, the big, double bed, and Vivian sleeping in it.

He approached noiselessly and looked at her. She lay sprawled on her back, legs apart and with her full arms stretched back on the pillow framing her lovely face and the golden torrent of her hair.

Her round, soft breasts rose and fell regularly, and her lips were slightly parted so that she looked almost as if she were smiling in her sleep at some particularly pleasant dream.

"Angelic," he thought and her face was so full of peace and innocence that, thinking of how he had spent that evening, for a split second he felt a twinge of guilt. Then he made a conscious effort and recalled the "new" state of affairs. Instantly his feeling of guilt evaporated and was replaced by a sense of righteous elation.

He spoke to her—forming the words with his lips and making no sound:

"Do you know where I've been? And what I've been doing? No. You wouldn't be sleeping so nicely. Well, I spent a few hours with Margot. You know? Margot? That's right. And you know what? She's got a delicious tongue. You can't imagine how nice it is. I know because I was kissing her a little while ago and she put it in my mouth. It was quite a kiss. And you know something else she has that's very nice? What security you must have, to sleep so sweetly! There isn't a doubt in your mind, is there, that I'm over at the den practicing calligraphy with a camel's hair brush; or memorizing the good old 214 radicals; or translating Wu proverbs—here's a nice one, by the way: 'The weak get devoured, the strong are spit out.' Isn't that the truth though? Yes, my dear, one has to fight back hard in life, or else one gets walked on. . . .

"I've got awfully big eyes for Margot . . . you can imagine—after those things she did tonight. It isn't finished either: I'm going to be seeing her quite a bit now. You go right on sleeping with your goddamn chastity, and thinking I'm just like I used to be; but I'm cheating from here on in. . . ."

Vivian's dream focused between her luxuriously separated thighs . . . she had become aware that someone was in the bedroom, standing and staring at her. The smile of pleasure that had been on her dreaming face changed to a pout.

"That you?" she mumbled without opening her eyes.

"Shhhhh," Trent whispered sharply, as if to warn her not to wake herself up.

She was wide awake though, and bitterly angry with him for having torn her from such a delicious world—she was still hot and passionate from what had taken place. . . . It became more and more tenuous in the next few seconds, and, though she strove mightily to retain it, it fled like time itself through her fingers and quite melted away. Vivian was left feeling cheated and very lascivious and that was all.

"Trent?" she said quietly.

"Yeah. Go on back to sleep. I'm sorry I woke you up."

"What time is it?"

"Pretty late I guess. I'm not sure, three-thirty or four maybe. Go back to sleep."

"I can't. I'm up now. Besides, I don't feel well."

"What's the matter?"

"I've been having excruciating cramps all night, and I've got a migraine headache." This was a lie and Vivian took a particular pleasure in telling it because of her irritation with him. Of itself, her voice didn't betray her ire.

Trent stepped into his pyjama pants and said:

"Do you want me to get you some aspirin?"

"Do you know what would be wonderful, darling?" she asked sweetly in spite of her "headache."

"What?"

"A cup of weak tea with lemon. I think maybe that would settle my stomach. It's probably something to do with nervous excitement." That would take him a little while, she thought, maybe long enough. She wanted badly to be alone for a few minutes.

"Right. You don't have a fever, do you?" he inquired solicitously.

"I don't know," she said.

Trent went to the kitchen and put a small pot of water on the stove. He performed his little chore with utmost goodwill and as part of what he intended to be a general campaign to lull Vivian into believing that he had forgiven her for what she had done that morning and that conditions were back to "normal." He didn't want her to suspect that there was something brewing between Margot and him. He was prepared to go to great lengths to keep it a secret. It was going to be an enormous source of satisfaction to him, he knew, to deceive her, and he was going to do it properly; she wasn't going to know a thing about it.

Back in the bedroom, he snapped on a small lamp and handed Vivian her tea. She lay with the sheet pulled all the way up to her brown eyes which stared at him unblinkingly. Her face—what he could see of it—seemed flushed.

"Are you sure you don't have a fever?" he asked.

Vivian sat up and pushed her luxuriant blond hair behind her ears. "Maybe," she answered. "It wouldn't surprise me a bit."

He placed the back of his hand against her cheek and noted that it felt a good deal warmer than seemed normal. In spite of himself, this contact with her silky skin aroused him. He was already feeling quite lustful after his strange evening with Margot and now, seeing Vivian, warm and disheveled, and picturing how the heat that emanated from her voluptuous body must be warming the whole bed, he longed to strip naked, lift up her flimsy nightgown, get on her beautiful belly and sink into that heat.

He'd had such desires many times in the past and Vivian's response had been consistently negative. Occasionally, she'd let him have his way, but with such an air of grim resignation and silent suffering that invariably, when he, trembling, had managed to penetrate her rigid, unyielding body, he would experience a few seconds of unbearable sweetness and then, almost without having moved, would ejaculate, completely out of control and covered with shame.

Perhaps, if he had been able to hold back and give her the sort of prolonged and versatile treatment that some men were capable of —perhaps it would have changed things. Perhaps her iciness would finally melt as the warm minutes of prodding in her love-pouch accumulated. Perhaps she would become pliant, wrap her arms about him, open her thighs and hump tenderly back at him!

The thought of it was overpowering. Knowing he was doomed to frustration, he nevertheless begged:

"God, it's been so long we made love . . . honey, don't you want to at all? . . . It would be so great! . . ." His hands slid down from her cheek and timidly brushed the perfectly round globe of her breast.

She tolerated the caress stonily. It was worse than if she'd taken his hand by the wrist and removed it . . . .

"Here I am with a splitting headache and cramps and probably a fever. How can you expect me to want to make love? Honestly, is that all you ever think of?" She was looking at his fly. The bulge there left little doubt as to the pitiful state he was in. She considered the protuberance and a slight tremor of disgust shook through her.

"No sense in fooling around," Trent said. "If you think you've got a fever you'd better take your temperature."

"I can't stand taking my temperature."

"I know, but you've got to be a little less childish. If you're going to be sick, the sooner you catch it the better," Trent said sensibly. "Otherwise you'll be spending ten days in bed with the grippe or something, you know that."

"All right," Vivian conceded, "but you've got to put the thermometer in, and then take it out and look at it—it disgusts me."

There was a curious gleam in her eye as she stated these conditions which Trent was at a loss to understand. Maybe she's enjoying the idea that she's not going to have to do it herself, he speculated. Not that it mattered what her feelings might be. . . .

He went at once to get the thermometer before she might change her mind and withdraw this singular privilege.

Searching for it in the medicine chest, the idea of what was about to happen excited him so that he couldn't resist slipping his hand into his pyjama pants and fondling his tumid joint a bit. It felt as if it were within inches of shooting off. All that day's erotic events: the sight of Vivian being soundly jazzed; the fantasies of his promenade; what had happened in the den; and then, Margot—all this inflammatory material had converged and was packed into that ready-to-burst erection.

When he came back into the room he found Vivian lying curled up on her side. Her butt, bulging prominently under the covers, rested on the extreme edge of the bed.

Trent coated the head of the thermometer with vaseline, then knelt by the side of the bed.

"Ready?" he asked in a clipped, professional-sounding way.

"Be careful," Vivian admonished in a muffled voice.

He lifted the cover and folded it back over on her so that only her backside was uncovered. Her nightgown had worked up high on her thighs and it was possible to raise it the rest of the way without her having to lift her body.

Vivian kept her legs tightly together so as to cheat him of any sight of her cleft or even the little beard which adorned it. Even so, at the sight of her well-fleshed buttocks—so close that he could see the fine golden hairs which peeped out from the central crevice—he all but came off in his pants. With one hand he held the thermometer while with the thumb and forefinger of the other he carefully opened the cheeks of her bottom and, for the first time since he'd been married to her, was accorded a look at his wife's anus.

He would have liked to have looked at it for a little while—calmly and philosophically. He would have liked to be able to contemplate it, this anus of a very beautiful blonde woman. He would have thought of it being there when she was a young girl of sixteen, how it had always been there so secret and forbidden (had anyone else ever seen it?) that she herself (had she ever even looked at it herself with a mirror?) just about refused to acknowledge its very existence. And yet it was there, proving in a way that was at once charming and terrifying that she was an animal—like a horse, or like a she-wolf. . . .

He would have liked to have looked at it but he knew that if there were the slightest delay she would say something, would perhaps become angry and accuse him of being "degenerate," and of taking advantage of the fact that she was sick to indulge his unnatural inclinations.

He gave himself two seconds—that was the absolute maximum—in which to look at it freely, after which he would have to insert the thermometer. In those two seconds, in spite of the nonchalance with which he had considered leaving her that morning, in spite of the enthusiasm with which he had begun his campaign to seduce Margot, in spite of the bravado with which he had silently addressed her as she lay asleep, boasting of his infidelity; in those two seconds, looking intently at her anus, he fell more deeply in love with her than ever before. It was beautiful too—like everything else about her. As he inserted the thermometer he realized that he was very close to bursting into tears. . . .

He heard the sharp intake of her breath as the tip of the instrument touched her, then something which sounded like a sigh as the small and puckered hole yielded and allowed the foreign object to slide in.

"Not so fast. . . . Slowly!" Vivian instructed. And then. "That's too far, take it out a little. . . . No, not that much. . . ."

Trent did exactly as he was told, moving the glass tube in and out as ordered. The wave of sentimentality which he had felt a few instants before, and which had been so mighty that it had almost caused him to weep, had abruptly disappeared. Manipulating the thermometer in Vivian's rectum, watching it slide slowly back and forth in obedience to her commands, was such a formidable erotic experience that all feelings other than that of pure lust were driven from him. It looked exactly as if Vivian were being made love to anally by the thin tube. More than that, it was as if she herself desired it since it was she who directed its movements.

At this instant, red-faced and with his eyes bulging, Trent *did* look like a degenerate. He knelt in such a way that his stiff member was held between his thighs and, involuntarily, he worked it back and forth in its area of confinement. The thermometer had at last been positioned suitably and he was waiting now for when it would be time to take it out. He knew he was going to come and he was holding back till the moment when, once again spreading her buttocks, he withdrew the glass tube. . . .

At the sight of her anus contracting as the thermometer came clear it finally happened to him. It was a powerful jolt, hitting him violently like an electric shock and forcing him to double over.

He fancied he saw a spasm shake Vivian's body also and make her arch her back, but it was no doubt a trick his eyes were playing on him, blurred over as they were with his ecstasy.

He feared she might suspect something on hearing the sudden movement he had made as he doubled over, so with the orgasm still pulsing in him, he managed to twist the thermometer and focus his eyes until the thin column of mercury caught the light.

"Well, thank God for that," he gasped, "it's normal."

HAMILTON DRAKE

The many-faced Hamilton Drake, author of Sin for Breakfast, *is known also to his unknowing readers as Faustino Perez, creator of* Until She Screams *(which is right at the beginning of the book through to the last page) and as one-half of Maxwell Kenton, the holy Hoffenberg-Southern syndicate that wrote the very successful* Candy. *He is finally and accurately identified as Mason Hoffenberg to the select readers of the Botteghe Oscure where his poetry has been published.*

Born in New York, Mason Hoffenberg is one of the few American soldiers who permanently settled in France. He came back to France, where he had been stationed, in 1948, with a G.I. Bill safely buttoned in his pocket; only fair since the army had drafted him out of Olivet College. He married a French girl, Coquitte, the grand-daughter of the distinguished French art historian Dr. Elie Faure, in 1953. They have three children and a house somewhere behind Montparnasse. Mason has worked for the Agence France Press in Paris and has, through the years, accumulated a vast stack of his "automatic writings" which some enterprising editor will one day have to struggle through. He's currently working on a novel to justify the munificent advance Putnam's presented to him for the rights to what they hope will be another best-selling Candy. *But Mason, student of Chinese and Hebrew, poet, linguist, stylist, man of the far-out mind, is not to be predicted.*

The Ticket That Exploded

William S. Burroughs

The room was on the roof of a ruined warehouse swept by winds of time through the open window trailing gray veils of curtain sounds and ectoplasmic flakes of old newspapers and newsreels swirling over the smooth concrete floor and under the bare iron frame of the dusty bed—The mattress twisted and molded by absent tenants—Ghost rectums, spectral masturbating afternoons reflected in the tarnished mirror—The boy who owned this room stood naked, remote mineral silence like a blue mist in his eyes—Sound and image flakes swirled round him and dusted his metal skin with gray powder—The other green boy dropped his pants and moved in swirls of poisonous color vapor, breathing the alien medium through sensitive purple gills lined with erectile hairs pulsing telepathic communications—The head was smaller than the neck and tapered to a point—A silver globe floated in front of him—The two beings approached each other wary and tentative—The green boy's penis, which was the same purple color as his gills, rose and vibrated into the heavy metal substance of the other—The two beings twisted free of human coordinates rectums merging in a rusty swamp smell— Spurts of semen fell through the blue twilight of the room like opal chips—The air was full of flicker ghosts who move with the speed of light through orgasms of the world—Tentative beings taking form for a few seconds in copulations of light—Mineral silence through the two bodies stuck together in a smell of KY and rectal mucus fell apart in time currents swept back into human form—At first he could not remember—Winds of time through curtain sounds—Blue eyes blurred and twisted absent bodies—The blue metal boy naked now flooded back into his memory as the green boy-girl dropped space ship controls in swirls of poisonous color—The blue boy reached out like an icy draught through the other apparatus—They twisted together paralyzed—He and Bradly grinding against each other in pressure seats, while heavy metal substance guided their ship through the sickening twist of human cloud belts—Galaxy X chartering a rusty swamp smell—Their calculations went out in a smell of ozone—Opal chip neighborhood of the flicker ghosts who travel the far flung edge of Galaxy X hover and land through orgasm— Flickering form of his companion naked in copulation space suit that clung to his muscular blue silence—Smell of KY and rectal mucus in eddies of translucent green light—His body flushed with spectral presences like fish of brilliant colors flashing through clear water—Tentative beings that took form and color from the creatures skin membrane of light—Pulsing veins criss-crossed the bodies stuck together in slow motion time currents—Lips of tentative faces, rectums merging structure one body in translucent green flesh—

Bradly's left arm went numb and the tingling paralysis spread down his left side—He felt crushing weight of The Green Octopus who was there to block any composite being and maintain her flesh monopoly of birth and death—Her idiot camp followers drew him into The Garden of Delights—Back into human flesh—The Garden of Delights is a vast tingling numbness surrounded by ovens of white-hot metal lattice within sloped funnels like a fish trap—Outside the oven funnels is a ruined area of sex booths, Turkish baths and transient hotels—Orgasm addicts stacked in rubbish heaps like muttering burlap —Phantom sex guides flashing dirty movies—Sound of fear—Dark street life of a place forgotten—"It might take a little while."

The guard was wearing a white life jacket—He led Bradly to a conical room with bare plaster walls—On the green mattress cover lay a human skin half inflated like a rubber toy with erect penis—There was a metal valve at base of the spine—

"First we must write the ticket," said the guard (Sound of liquid typewriters plopping into gelatine)—

The guard was helping him into skin pants that burned like erogenous acid—His skin hairs slipped into the skin hairs of the sheath with little tingling shocks—The guard molded the skin in place shaping thighs and back, tucking the skin along the divide line below his nose—He clicked the metal valve into Bradly's spine—Exquisite toothache pain shot through nerves and bones—His body burned as if lashed with stinging sex nettles—The guard moved around him with little chirps and giggles—He goosed the rectum trailing like an empty condom deep into Bradly's ass—The penis spurted again and again as the guard tucked the burning sex skin into the divide line and smoothed it down along the perineum, hairs crackling through erogenous purple flesh—His body glowed a translucent pink steaming off a musty smell—

"Skin like that very hot for three weeks and then—" the guard snickered—

Bradly was in a delirium where any sex thought immediately took three-dimensional form through a maze of Turkish baths and sex cubicles fitted with hammocks and swings and mattresses vibrating to a shrill insect frequency that danced in nerves and teeth and bones— The sex phantoms of all his wet dreams and masturbating afternoons surrounded him licking kissing feeling—From time to time he drank a heavy sweet translucent fluid brought by the guard—The liquid left a burning metal taste in his mouth—His lips and tongue swelled perforated by erogenous silver sores—The skin glowed phosphorescent pink purple suffused by a cold menthol burn so sensitive he went into orgasm at a current of air while uncontrolled diarrhea exploded down his thighs—The guard collected all his sperm in a pulsing neon cylinder—Through transparent walls he could see hundreds of other prisoners in cubicles of a vast hive milked for semen by the white-coated guards—The sperm collected was passed to central bank—Sometimes the prisoners were allowed contact and stuck together melting and welding in sex positions of soft rubber— At the center of this pulsing translucent hive was a gallows where the prisoners were hanged after being milked for three weeks—He could see the terminal cases carried to the gallows, bodies, wasted to transparent mummy flesh over soft phosphorescent bones—Necks broken by the weight of suspension and the soft bones spurted out in orgasm leaving a deflated skin collected by the guards to be used on the next shift of prisoners—Mind and body blurred with pleasure some part of his being was still talking to the switch blade concealed under his mattress, feeling for it with numb erogenous fingers—One night he slipped into a forgotten nightmare of his childhood—A large black poodle was standing by his bed—The dog dissolved in smoke and out of the smoke arose a dummy being five feet tall—The dummy had a thin delicate face of green wax and long yellow fingernails—

"Poo Poo," he screamed in terror trying desperately to reach his knife—but his motor centers were paralyzed—This had happened before—"I told you I would come back"—Poo Poo put a long yellow corpse fingernail on his forehead vaulted over his body and lay down beside him—He could move now and began clawing at the dummy— Poo Poo snickered and traced three long scratches on Bradly's neck—

"You're dead, Poo Poo, dead dead dead," Bradly screamed trying to pull the dummy head off—

"Perhaps I am—And you are too unless you get out of here—

I've come to warn you—Out of present time past the crab guards on dirty pictures?—There's a Chinese boy in the next cubicle and Iam is just down the hall—He's very technical you know—And use this —I'm going now"—

He faded out leaving a faint impression on the green mattress cover—The room was full of milky light—(Departed have left mixture of dawn and dream)—There was a little bamboo flute on the bed beside Bradly—He put it to his lips and heard Poo Poo speak from an old rag in one corner—"Not now—Later"—

He contacted the Chinese boy who had smuggled in a transistor radio—They made plans quickly and when the guard came with the heavy liquid turned on the metal static and stabbed the switch blade deep into insect nerve centers—The guard fell twisting and flipping white juice from his ruptured abdomen—Bradly picked up the guard's gun and released the other prisoners—Most of them were too far gone to move but others they revived with static and formed a division of combat troops—Bradly showed the guard's weapon to Iam—

"How do you work this fucker?"—

Iam examined the mechanism with long fingers precise as tooled metal—explained it was camera gun with telescopic lens equipped to take and project a moving picture vibrating the image at supersonic speed—He attached the radio to the camera gun so that the static synchronized with the vibrations—Bradly had the gun ready in his hand as they zigzagged out of the hive rushing the metal points of the ovens—Guard towers opened up with magnetic spirals and Bradly lost half his men before he could hit the central control tower and deactivate the mechanical gun turrets—(His troops had one advantage—All the guards and weapons of the enemy were operated by machine control and they had no actual fighters on the location)— Zigzagging he opened up with camera gun and static—Towers and ovens went up in a nitrous blast of burning film—A great rent tore the whole structure of the Garden to the blue sky beyond—He put the flute to his lips and blue notes of Pan trickled down from the remote mountain village of his childhood—The prisoners heard the pipes and streamed out of the garden—The sperm tanks drained into streets of image forming thunderbolts of plasma that exploded The Garden Of Delights in a flash of silver light—

He was standing on a Moroccan hillside with his troops and

around them the Pan pipes calm and impersonal as the blue sky—From his pocket he heard Poo Poo say "Take me with you"—He felt a little plastic bag and drew it out—There was a flat gray membrane inside it —He moved away on Pan pipes to the remote mountain village of his childhood where blue mist swirled through the streets and time stopped in the slate houses—Words fell from his mind—He drifted through wind chimes of subway dawns and turnstiles—Boys on roller skates turned slow circles in a shower of ruined suburbs—Gray luminous flakes falling softly on Ewyork, Aris, Ome, Oston—Crumpled cloth bodies through the glass and metal streets swept by time winds— From siren towers the twanging tones of fear—Positive feedback Pan God Of Panic piping blue notes through empty streets as the berserk time machine twisted a tornado of centuries—Wind through dusty offices and archives—Board books scattered to rubbish heaps of the earth —Symbol books of The All Powerful Board that had controlled thought feeling and movement of a planet with iron claws of pain and pleasure from birth to death—Control symbols pounded to word and image dust; crumpled cloth bodies of the vast control machine—The whole structure of reality went up in silent explosions under the whining sirens—Pipers from his remote mountain villages loosed Pan God of Panic through streets of image—Dead nitrous streets of an old film set—Paper moon and muslin trees and in the black silver sky great rents as the cover of the world rained down in luminous film flakes—The 1920's careened through darkening cities in black Cadillacs spitting film bullets of accelerated time—

Through the open window trailing swamp smells and old newspapers—Orgasm addicts stacked in the attic like muttering burlap— The mattress molded on all sides masturbating afternoons reflected; "Difficult to get out"—Word and image skin like a rubber toy dusted with gray spine powder—The boy who owned this room stood naked to his mountain village and swirled the vampire guards out of his path —Blue notes of Pan trickled down silver train whistles—Calling the imprisoned Jinn from copulation space suits that clung to his muscle lust and burning sex skin—The green fish boys dropped their torture of spectral presence and like fish left the garden through clear water— Tentative beings followed the music membrane of light and color— Pipes of Pan trickled down sleeping comrade of his childhood—Pure blue jabs through the Garden Of Delights—Alien beauty cutting the black insect—He slipped out of time in a flash of absent bodies—His camera gun blasted memory—The blue boy reached from the remote mountain village other apparatus—They twisted cool and impersonal as the sky against each other in pressure seats—Stuck together in slow motion faces—Criss-crossed with tentative whistles of other lips and slipped suddenly out of other apparatus twisted the guards in a flash of speed—Masturbating afternoon of spectral presence went out in clear water—The Board that had controlled sperm bank of a planet with sex prisoners broken now from birth to death—Control skin melted leaving crumpled cloth bodies of muttering burlap—Explosion swept through empty sex thoughts as the sperm tanks drained into streets of image—The cover of the world rained down—

operation
rewrite

"The Venusian invasion was known as 'Operation Other Half,' that is, a parasitic invasion of the sexual area taking advantage, as all invasion plans must, of an already existing fucked-up situation ('My God what a mess')—The human organism is literally consisting of two halves from the beginning word and all human sex is this unsanitary arrangement whereby two entities attempt to occupy the same three-dimensional coordinate points giving rise to the sordid latrine brawls which have characterized a planet based on 'The Word,' that is, on separate flesh engaged in endless sexual conflict—The Venusian Boy-Girls under Johnny Yen took over The Other Half, imposing a sexual blockade on the planet—(It will be readily understandable that a program of systematic frustration was necessary in order to sell this crock of sewage as Immortality, The Garden Of Delights, and LOVE)—

"When the Board Of Health intervened with inflexible authority, 'Operation Other Half' was referred to the Rewrite Department where the original engineering flaw of course came to light and the Venusian Invasion was seen to be an inevitable correlate of the separation flesh gimmick—At this point a tremendous scream went up from the Venusians agitating to retain the flesh gimmick in some form— They were all terminal flesh addicts of course, motivated by pornographic torture films, and the entire Rewrite and Blueprint Departments were that disgusted ready to pull the switch out of hand to

'It Never Happened'—'Unless these jokers stay out of the Rewrite room'—

"The Other Half was only one aspect of Operation Rewrite— Heavy Metal addicts picketed the Rewrite Office, exploding in protest—Control addicts prowled the streets trying to influence waiters, lavatory attendants, clochards, and were to be seen on every corner of the city hypnotizing chickens—A few rich control addicts were able to surround themselves with latahs and sat on the terraces of expensive cafes with remote cruel smiles unaware i wrote last cigarette—

"My God what a mess—Just keep all these jokers out of The Rewrite Room is all"—

So let us start with one average, stupid, representative case: Johnny Yen The Other Half, errand boy from the death trauma— Now look I'm going to say it and I'm going to say it slow—Death *is* orgasm *is* rebirth *is* death in orgasm *is* their unsanitary Venusian Gimmick *is* the whole birth death cycle of action—You got it?— Now do you understand who Johnny Yen is? The Boy-Girl Other Half striptease God of sexual frustration—Errand Boy from the death trauma—His immortality depends on the mortality of others— The same is true of *all* addicts—Mr. Martin, for example, is a heavy metal addict—His life line is the human junky—The life line of control addicts is the control word—Control word "THE"—That is these so-called Gods can only live without three-dimensional co-ordinate points by forcing three-dimensional bodies on others—Their existence is pure vampirism—They are utterly unfit to be officers— Either they accept a rewrite job or they are all broken down to lavatory attendants, irrevocably committed to the toilet—

All right, back to the case of Johnny Yen—One of many such errand boys—Green Boy-Girls from the terminal sewers of Venus— So write back to the streets, Johnny, back to Ali God of Street Boys and Hustlers—Write out of the sewers of Venus to neon streets of Saturn—Alternatively Johnny Yen can be written back to a green fish boy—There are always alternative solutions—Nothing is true— Everything is permitted—

"NO HASSAN I SABBAH—WE WANT FLESH—WE WANT JUNK—WE WANT POWER—"

"That did it—Dial POLICE"—

the
nova police

Bulletin From Rewrite: We had to call in the Nova Police to keep all these jokers out of The Rewrite Room—Can't be expected to work under such conditions—Introducing Inspector J. Lee of the Nova Police—"I doubt if any of you on this copy planet have ever seen a Nova criminal—(they take considerable pains to mask their operations) and i am sure none of you has ever seen a Nova police officer—When disorder on any planet reaches a certain point the regulating instance scans POLICE—Otherwise—Sput—Another planet bites the cosmic dust—I will now explain something of the mechanisms and techniques of Nova which are always deliberately manipulated—I am quite well aware that no one on any planet likes to see a police officer so let me emphasize in passing that the Nova police have no intention of remaining after their work is done—That is, when the danger of Nova is removed from this planet we will move on to other assignments—We do our work and go—

"The basic Nova technique is very simple: Always create as many insoluble conflicts as possible and always aggravate existing conflicts—This is done by dumping on the same planet life forms with incompatible conditions of existence—There is of course nothing 'wrong' about any given life form since 'wrong' only has reference to conflicts with other life forms—The point is these life forms should not be on the same planet—Their conditions of life are basically incompatible in present time form and it is precisely the work of the Nova Mob to see that they remain in present time form, to create and aggravate the conflicts that lead to the explosion of a planet, that is to Nova—At any given time recorders fix the nature of absolute need and dictate the use of total weapons—Like this: Take two opposed pressure groups—Record the most violent and threatening statements of group one with regard to group two and play back to group two—Record the answer and take it back to group one—Back and forth between opposed pressure groups—This process is known as 'feedback'—You can see it operating in any barroom quarrel—In any quarrel for that matter—Manipulated on a global scale feeds back nuclear war and Nova—These conflicts are deliberately created and aggravated by Nova criminals—The Nova Mob: 'Sammy the Butcher,' 'Green Tony,' 'The Brown Artist,' 'Jacky Blue Note,' 'Limestone John,' 'Izzy the Push,' 'Hamburger Mary,' 'Paddy The Sting,' 'The Subliminal Kid,' 'The Blue Dinosaur,' 'Willy The Rat' (who informed on his associates), and Mr. & Mrs. D also known as 'Mr. Bradly Mr. Martin' also known as 'The Ugly Spirit,' thought to be the leader of the mob—The Nova Mob—In all my experience as a police officer i have never seen such total fear and degradation on any planet—We intend to arrest these criminals and turn them over to the Biological Department for the indicated alterations—

"Now you may well ask whether we can straighten out this mess to the satisfaction of any life forms involved and my answer is this— Your earth case must be processed by the Biological Courts—(admittedly in a deplorable condition at this time)—No sooner set up than immediately corrupted so that they convene every day in a different location like floating dice games, constantly swept away by stampeding forms all idiotically glorifying their stupid ways of life—(Most of them quite unworkable of course)—attempting to seduce the judges into Venusian sex practices, drug the court officials, and intimidate the entire audience chamber with the threat of Nova—In all my experience as a police officer I have never seen such total fear of the indicated alterations on any planet—A thankless job you see and we only do it so it won't have to be done some place else under even more difficult circumstances—

"The success of the Nova Mob depended on a blockade of the planet that allowed them to operate with impunity—This blockade was broken by partisan activity directed from the planet Saturn that cut the control lines of word and image laid down by the Nova Mob —So we moved in our agents and started to work keeping always in close touch with partisans—The selection of local personnel posed a most difficult problem—Frankly we found that most existing police agencies were hopelessly corrupt—The Nova Mob had seen to that— Paradoxically some of our best agents were recruited from the ranks of those who are called criminals on this planet—In many instances we had to use agents inexperienced in police work—There were of course casualties and fuck-ups—You must understand that an undercover agent witnesses the most execrable cruelties while he waits helpless to intervene, sometimes for many years, before he can make a definitive arrest—So it is no wonder that green officers occasionally slip control when they finally do move in for the arrest—This condition, known as 'arrest fever,' can upset an entire operation—In one recent case, our man in Tangiers suffered an attack of 'arrest fever' and detained everyone on his view screen including some of our undercover men—He was transferred to paper work in another area —Let me explain *how* we make an arrest—Nova criminals are not three-dimensional organisms—(though they are quite definite organisms as we shall see)—but they need three-dimensional human agents to operate—The point at which the criminal controller intersects a three-dimensional human agent is known as 'a coordinate point'—And if there is one thing that carries over from one human host to another and established identity of the controller it is *habit*: idiosyncrasies, vices, food preferences—(we were able to trace Hamburger Mary through her fondness for peanut butter)—a gesture, a special look, that is to say the *style* of the controller—A chain smoker will always operate through chain smokers, an addict through addicts—Now a single controller can operate through thousands of human agents, but he must have a line of coordinate points—Some move on junk lines through addicts of the earth, others move on lines of certain sexual practices and so forth—It is only when we can block the controller out of all coordinate points available to him and flush him out from host cover that we can make a definitive arrest— Otherwise the criminal escapes to other coordinate"—

Question: "Inspector Lee, i don't quite understand what is meant by a 'coordinate point'—Could you make that a little clearer?—"

Answer: "Certainly—You see these criminal controllers occupy human bodies—Ghosts? Phantoms? Not at all—Very definite organisms indeed—True you can't see them—Can you see a virus?—Well, the criminal controllers operate in very much the same manner as a virus—Now a virus in order to invade, damage and occupy the human organism must have a gimmick to get in—Once in the virus invades damages and occupies a certain area or organ in the body—Known as the tissue of predilection—Hepatitis, for example, attacks the liver— Influenza the respiratory tract—Polio and rabies the central nervous system—In the same way a controller invades, damages and occupies some pattern or configuration of the human organism"—

Question: "How do these controllers gain access to the human organism?"

Answer: "I will give an example: the controllers who operate through addiction to opiates—That is who occupy and control addicts of the earth—Their point of entry is of course the drug itself— And they maintain this coordinate point through addiction"—

Question: "What determines the choice of coordinate points? Why does one controller operate through addiction in preference to other channels?"—

Answer: "He operates through addicts because he himself is an addict—A heavy metal addict from Uranus—What we call opium or junk is a very much diluted form of heavy metal addiction—Venu-

sians usually operate through sexual practices—In short these controllers brought their vices and diseases from their planet of origin
and infected the human hosts very much in the same way that the
early colonizers infected so-called primitive populations"—

Question: "Inspector Lee, how can one be sure that someone
purporting to be a Nova police officer is not an imposter?"—

Answer: "It is not always easy, especially during this transitional
period. There are imposters, 'shake men,' who haunt atomic installa-
tions and victimize atomic scientists in much the same way as spurious
police officers extort money from sexual deviants in public lavatories
—In one recent case a well-organized shake mob, purporting to repre-
sent the Nova Police, confiscated cyclotrons and other atomic equipment which they subsequently sold on the Uranian black market to
support their heavy metal habits—They were arrested and sent away
for the thousand-year cure—Since then we have encountered a few
sporadic cases—Cranks, lunatics for the most part"—

Question: "Inspector Lee, do you think that the Nova Mob can
be defeated?"—

Answer: "Yes—Their control machine has been disconnected by
partisan activity—

"Now we can move in for some definitive arrests—

"Sammy The Butcher dissolved his dummy cover—His burning
metal eyes stabbed at the officer from the molten core of a hot blue
planet—The officer moved back dissolving all connections with The
Blue Planet, connections formed by the parasite dummy which had
entered his body at birth, carefully prepared molds and association
locks closed on empty space—Sammy's eyes burned and sputtered
incandescent blue and went out in a smell of metal—His last white-
hot blast exploded in empty space—The officer picked up the micro-
phone: 'Sammy The Butcher,' arrested—'Paddy The Sting,' arrested
—'Hamburger Mary' has defected—'Green Tony' has surrendered—
move in for the definitive arrest of 'Mr. Bradly Mr. Martin' also
known as 'Mr. and Mrs. D' also known as 'The Ugly Spirit'—

" 'Sammy The Butcher' dissolved his ranks of self-righteous millions and stabbed at the officer dripping Marilyn Monroe Planet—
Locks closed on empty space lettering 'My Fair Lady'—In three-
dimensional terms 'The Ugly Spirit' and 'Mrs. D' screamed through
female blighted continent—So we turn over The Board Books and all
the ugliness i had forgotten—Criminal Street—Punitive legislation

screaming for more association locks in electric chair and gas chamber
—Technical death over the land—White no-smell of death dripping
Nova—'The Ugly Spirit' was flushed out of one host cover after the
other—Blanked out by our static and silence waves—Call The Old
Doctor twice 'Mr. and Mrs. D'—He quiets you remember?—Finished
—No shelter—A handful of dust—Screaming, clawing for the Nova
switch 'The Ugly Spirit' was dragged from the planet—From all the
pictures and words of ugliness that have been his place of residence
since he moved in on The New World—The officer with silent inflexible authority closed one coordinate point after another—Only
this to say: 'Would you rather talk to the partisans "Mr. and Mrs.
D"?—Well?—No terms—This is definitive arrest—'Sammy The
Butcher' has been taken—There are no guards capable protect you—
Millions of voices in your dogs won't do you a bit of good—Voices
fading—Crumpled cloth bodies—Your name fading across newspapers of the earth'—Madison Avenue machine is disconnected—Errand boy closing their errand boys—Won't be much left—Definitive
arrest of The Board as you listen, as the officer closes track—Self-
righteous ugliness of their space program a joke—Written in symbols
blighted America: $$$—American scent of memory pictures—The
idiot honky-tonks of Panhandle—Humiliation Outhouse and snarling
ugliness of dying peoples—Bourbon-soaked legislators from 'mari-
juana is deadlier than cocaine'—Board Book symbol chains lynch
mobs—The White Smoke of pressure group relying on rectum sub-
urbs and the no smell of death—Control Avenue and Hollywood,
look at the bread line—The Ugly Spirit retreated back to the '20's
in servants and police and the dogs of H. J. Anschlinger—Into one
battered host after another—Blanked out board instructions—Silence
—Silence—Silence—Call the old money equipment information files
of memory—Finished—No shelter—A hand falls across newspapers
of the earth for the Nova Switch—Won't do you a bit of good,
collaborators with ugliness and degraded flesh—Traitors to all souls
everywhere moved in on The New World—The Old Doctor cleav-
ing a heavy silent authority closed one coordinate point after another
—The Board is near right now—This to say: 'Would you rather
talk up relying on money?—Fading voice terms?—This is definitive
arrest through dying air—There are no guards now capable guide
humiliations—Poisonous cloud, millions of dogs won't do you a bit of
good—Parasites, crumpled cloth bodies—Your control books fading

cross newspaper of the earth couldn't form Nova—Operation completed—Planet out of danger—Proceed with the indicated alterations' "—

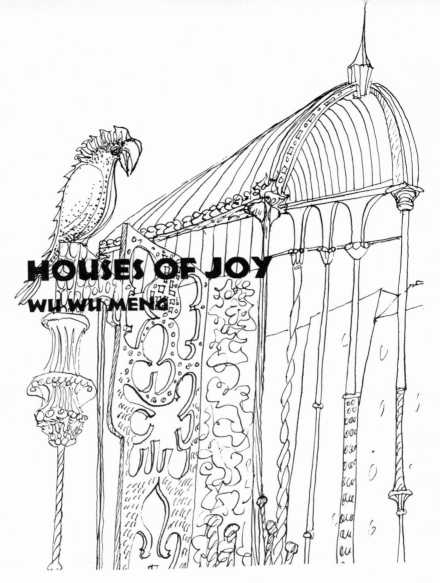

HOUSES OF JOY
WU WU MENG

*O*ne day Hsi Men received an invitation to the house
of his neighbor Hua. When he went there at noon,
he was so wrapped in his thoughts that as he crossed the outer court
he almost collided with Mistress Ping, Hua's wife, who was standing
on the raised platform inside the second entry. He had seen her only
once before, when visiting his friend's estate. Today, for the first
time, he looked at her closely. On account of the heat she was dressed
lightly. Her thin blouse left the throat uncovered, and closed over
her bosom as loosely as the two halves of a split lotus root held to-

gether by fragile fibers. Beneath the hem of her white skirt, like the tips of two little tongues, peeped out two neat little red satin slippers, embroidered with a phoenix pattern. Her hair was bound in a silver net, and at the lobes of her ears glittered earrings of rubies set in gold. Her full figure was of medium stature, and her face was oval and full as a melon. Her brows were delicately penciled, and her eyes made Hsi Men's senses soar to the heights of heaven.

She answered his low bow with a soft Wan fu: "Happiness ten thousandfold!" and at once withdrew. A maid ushered him into the reception room and pressed him to take a seat. A moment later Mistress Ping's charming face appeared again from behind the door.

"Please wait a moment," she begged him. "My husband has just gone out on a business errand and will soon be here."

The maid brought him tea. Then he again heard Mistress Ping's voice behind the door.

"May I ask of you, noble gentleman? If my husband wants you to drink wine with him today in a certain place, will you, for the sake of my honor, see that he does not stay away too long? For the moment I am all alone in the house with my two maids."

Hsi Men had just time to promise her, "Sister-in-law, I will not fail—" when Master Hua's return was announced. His wife at once disappeared from the door. Master Hua had sent for Hsi Men only in order to propose an immediate visit to Mother Wu's house of joy. For Hua's beloved, Silver Bud, was that day celebrating her birthday. With the beautiful Lady Ping's request in mind, Hsi Men, at an early hour of the evening, brought his extremely intoxicated friend home, having done his best to reduce him to that condition. When the drunken man had got safely indoors and Hsi Men was about to take his leave, Mistress Ping came into the reception room to thank him for escorting her husband. "Of course my lunatic of a husband has drunk too much again!" she said. "How kind of you to see him home!"

Hsi Men bowed. "Please, please. Any command of yours is at once buried in my heart like a bronze inscription, engraved upon my very bones. My only regret is that I was unable to prevent him from remaining as long as he did. It took all my powers of persuasion to induce him to leave. And on the way back I had great difficulty in preventing him from entering other establishments. If I had allowed him, he would have remained in the district all night. But how can a man neglect such a lovely young wife as you! It is really inexcusable of the stupid fellow!"

"You are right. I am really quite ill with worry on account of his featherheaded ways. May I hope that for my sake you will to some extent keep an eye on him in the future? I should thank you from the bottom of my heart!"

Now, Hsi Men was this sort of person: if he was tapped on the head, there was instantly an echo from the soles of his feet. Thanks to his years of experience in the play of the moon and wind, he at once understood that by her words the beautiful Mistress Ping had opened a convenient passage into the haven of love. With a meaning smile he replied: "Set yourself at ease, Lady! I shall watch over him most rigorously!"

She thanked him and withdrew. Hsi Men slowly sipped his tea, flavored with foam of apricot kernels, and contentedly went home.

From now onward, he proceeded systematically. Whenever he and his friend Hua went to a house of joy, his boon companions, Beggar Ying and Tickler Ta, were instructed to detain the other at his cups and, if possible, keep him away from home all night. Hsi Men would leave quietly, and going home, would stand outside the door of his house. As soon as he saw his beautiful neighbor and her two maids at the door opposite, waiting for Hua, Hsi Men would stroll up and down in front of her house, turning now to the east, now to the west, and clearing his throat to attract attention, occasionally darting a glance into the shadows of the gateway. She, on the other hand, would retreat shyly indoors whenever he passed, but as soon as he had gone by she would cautiously emerge again, and peer after him with wistful eyes. Each waited anxiously for the other to make the next advance.

One evening when he was standing outside the door the maid, Apricot Blossom, came over to him.

"Is there anything your mistress wishes of me?" he asked eagerly.

"Yes, she would like to speak to you," she whispered. "The master isn't at home."

He quickly followed the maid, and was shown into the reception room.

"You were so kind the other day—" his neighbor greeted him. "Have you by any chance come across my husband today or yesterday? He has been away for two days now."

"Why, yes, we were at Mother Chong's yesterday," he said. "I left rather early on business. I haven't seen him today and I really couldn't say where he is just now. I am only thankful that I myself did not remain, for then I should deserve the severest criticism for keeping my promise so indifferently."

"Oh, his lack of consideration is driving me to despair! Must he always continue to rove among flowers and willows, and never come home?" she cried.

"In other respects he is the best and most amiable of men. . . ." Hsi Men sighed hypocritically. Fearing to be surprised by her husband, he soon took his leave.

Next day, Master Hua came home. His wife greeted him with such bitter reproaches that he wanted to slink off again and find a girl to soothe his wounded pride. Then she added:

"Our honorable neighbor, Hsi Men, has been unselfish enough to look after you a little; otherwise you would ruin yourself completely. We ought to show our gratitude by some little attention. Such things preserve a friendship."

Friend Hua obediently packed four boxes with little presents and sent them, with a jug of his best wine, to the house next door.

When Hsi Men explained to Moon Lady the reason for these presents, Moon Lady answered sarcastically:

"Well, to think of that! You are trying to guide him into a decent way of life! You had better give a little thought to your own way of life! It is just as if a clay Buddha were to teach an earthenware Buddha how to behave. Don't you yourself spend the whole day racketing about?"

A few days later, Hua, prompted by his wife, invited Hsi Men and some friends to come to the chrysanthemum show in his house. Two dancers were engaged to entertain the party, and as usual they acquitted themselves well.

It was about the hour when one takes lantern in hand when Hsi Men rose from the table to leave the room for a moment in order to empty his bladder. Outside the door he almost collided with Mistress Ping, who had chosen a dark corner near the Spirit wall for her observation post. She quickly withdrew to the side door on the west of the house. Immediately afterward her maid, Apricot Blossom, emerged from the darkness and approached Hsi Men.

"My mistress begs you," she whispered, "to be temperate in your drinking and to leave early. Later she will send you another message."

In his joy Hsi Men almost forgot to do what he had left the house for. When he returned to the table he pretended to be drunk, and as far as possible refused more wine.

Meanwhile Mistress Ping, impatiently walking up and down behind the curtain, had to wait for some little time. The first watch of the night was already past, and she saw Master Hsi Men still sitting at the table, nodding his head as though half asleep. Mistress Ping was beside herself with impatience. At last Hsi Men rose to go.

"Little Brother, why can't you sit still?" his friend Hua asked reproachfully. "You're not very courteous to your host today."

"I'm tipsy and can hardly stand on my feet," said Hsi Men, thickly. Supported by two servants, he made his way to the door, simulating the rolling gait of a drunkard.

"I don't know what's wrong with him today," grumbled Beggar Ying. "Doesn't want to drink and gets drunk on a couple of drops. But that shouldn't prevent us from having a few more rounds. We are getting along excellently without him."

"Impudent rascals!" Mistress Ping, behind the curtain, murmured angrily; and she sent for her husband. "Please oblige me by taking yourself and those two fellows off to your house of joy," she said. "There you can go on soaking for all I care. But here I should like to be spared this deafening racket and uproar. Do you expect me to waste my whole night burning the lamp and keeping the fire alight? I have no notion of doing such a thing!"

"I should like to go out, but then you'd reproach me afterward."

"For all I care you need not come home till morning," she replied.

Master Hua did not wait to be told twice, and his two companions were no less delighted, so shortly before midnight they left with the two dancers.

Hsi Men went out in the darkness and sat under an arbor close to the wall between his grounds and those of Master Hua. There he waited impatiently for the message from Mistress Ping. Suddenly he heard the sound of a dog barking. A door creaked. Then silence. After a moment he heard the mewing of a cat on top of the wall. He looked up and saw the maid Pear Blossom. She leaned over and beckoned to him. Quickly he pushed a table against the wall, placed a bench on top of the table, and climbed over. On the other side there

was a ladder leaning against the wall. He was ushered into a candle-lit room. In a light housedress, bare-headed and with loosened hair, his beautiful neighbor appeared, pressed him to take a seat, and presented him with a cup of welcome.

"I was almost dying with impatience!" she continued, after a few polite and flowery phrases of greeting.

"What if Brother Hua should suddenly come home?" inquired the prudent Hsi Men.

"Oh, I've granted him leave until morning."

His fears allayed, Hsi Men, without another thought, gave himself up to the pleasure of the moment. Shoulder pressed to shoulder, thigh to thigh, he drank out of the same bowl with her, out of the same goblet. Pear Blossom served while Apricot Blossom poured. After the meal the two lovers went to a bedroom fragrant with perfume, and there, under the bright silken curtains, they abandoned themselves to the joys of the couch.

Dear reader, what drives a libertine, such as Hsi Men, to stray beyond his own domain in search of new adventures?

True, his capacity for lust was immense, but it wasn't as if he was saddled to a single wife whose slender charms become a monotonous ritual. For all his wives—apart from Moon Lady the delicate arbiter—and many of the maids were wonderfully conversant in more than the seventy-nine accepted ways of provoking a man's flame-juice to spurt from his body. Indeed, if Hsi Men had given himself to sport with each of them every day of the year, in one year he could not exhaust by half the repertoire that each had to offer. And over the years he had tested all their performances and had found them not wanting, but still he hankered after other flesh beyond his own walls. Was it simply love of conquest that sent him lusting after the play of clouds and rain in other quarters? No, it was more than that.

An ordinary fellow, in Hsi Men's boots, would live out his summers with his head and toes in the seventh heaven, not to speak of his loins. He would delegate his business entirely to trusted accountants so that he never had to waste his time by setting his feet beyond the gate, and he would while away the afternoons by flitting from one to another of his wives' perfumed pavilions. But Hsi Men was a man who was constantly in search of his own body.

In the main, his wives were faithful, and had devoted themselves entirely to inflaming his senses and serving his organ of pleasure. Their mode of dressing, their scents, the way they twined their limbs about his body, the way they caressed his skin or tore at his back with sharp fingernails—although differing from one wife to another—were entirely patterned by his immediate reactions. Those gestures which instantly elicited the greatest pleasure in him were offered again and again, say a particular manner of rocking the hips that cradled his thighs, or a certain way of slanting the palpitating sheath that sucked on his member, and those which did not were explored no further. For when a number of women compete with each other for the favors of one master, their desire to try something new is somewhat cramped by their anxiousness to provide instant delight. Thus they do not easily lead their master into discovering that his body is a limitless orchestra of sensations. So Hsi Men searched for himself anew in houses of joy, but to no avail. For who could be more anxious to please hastily than these courtesans?—even the best of them.

Many lust-driven loins do they couch,
But none which truly belong to them.

Such women are skilled in rapidly transforming themselves into replicas of their customers' wives and, coupled with the usual servility of their profession, they are only admirably suited to men whose vanity has been punctured by domineering wives, or, of course, to beginners.

Many of our sisters of the sun were aware that Hsi Men did not come to them merely to renew his customary sensations, but, for the most part, they failed him, for like anyone else, they are irreparably marked by the ways of their trade. Are they not, after all, simply flattering mirrors in which a man will never discover aspects of himself that he has never seen before? So Hsi Men had to search elsewhere as well.

There is an old adage which tells us: To know one's own feet one must wear another's shoes. So, dear reader, what could be better for such a one as Hsi Men than to seek the attentions of another man's wife?—a wife who strains to clothe the body of her new lover with the sensual image of the husband she has learned to serve so well, a woman who exudes a perfume blended to excite other nostrils.

By the side of the couch, Mistress Ping, in a silken chemise that gave a silvery fluidity to the mounds and valleys of her body, leaned trembling against the naked Hsi Men, whose hands slid with the silk up the back of her thighs along the cleft between the cheeks of her firm buttocks.

Hsi Men nearly swooned as she folded her blue-white arms about his neck, for this simple gesture lifted the thrilling chemise along the surface of his strong but sensitive body.

He drew her face, now strangely serious, toward him. But she anticipated his gesture, and lifting herself upon her little toes, she vivaciously placed her burning mouth upon his eager lips, looking at him deeply with moist eyes. The suddenness of this unfamiliar tenderness went to his head like drink and his hands slipped up to the small of her back and squeezed her still tighter. Their two heads, joined at the mouth, inclined together, their nostrils panting, their eyes closed. Never before did Hsi Men understand so clearly as in the vertigo, the frenzy, the half-unconscious state in which they found themselves, all that is really meant by the "intoxication of the kiss." He no longer knew who he was or what was going to happen. The present was so intense that the future and past disappeared in it.

She moves her lips with his. She burns in his arms and he feels her small stomach pressing him in a fervent silken caress that he has never known before. Then she moves away a little, and placing a lily hand on his red-hot member, which stands firmly upward, she forces it down and grasps it between her sheathed thighs, and as it slips upward again to the place where her love-lips have moistened her chemise, she runs her fingers, as tender and supple as bamboo shoots, along his spine.

> *Consider a woman who cuts her claws*
> *So her eyes may be all the sweeter.*
> *She masters her own malevolence*
> *To better release her sensuality.*

Then he lowers his hands and peels off her chemise, pressing himself against her burning skin. Now he moves away in order to feast his eyes as she lifts the garment over her head and tosses it wantonly on the floor.

Behold! Her lovely form is bathed in moonlight, and the fullness of a strange and heady scent envelops her like a fragrant cloud. The downy swelling darkness beneath her small belly and the blue tufts under her arms are perfumed with crisp mint, carrying messages of freshness mixed with the ancient odor of sensuality to his quivering nostrils.

And now he steps forward into her aura. Her breasts are in his hands. How soft they seem! How gently warm! Compared to these the breasts of his beloved Fifth are hard as statued marble. He rests his burning lips on her naked arms, her rounded shoulders, her soft breasts again and again, and her white neck.

He sighs deeply, and leading him by the hand, she draws aside the curtain of orange silk, and causes him to kneel on the soft bed. She mounts beside him and slips her little head under his belly. Then imitating the trembling kid that drinks from its mother, she sucks on the spongy teat that tops his member. Hsi Men can no longer contain himself. He leaps up and embraces her so vigorously that she cries aloud in pain, then he falls to savagely tearing a path into her mysterious blue jungle with a cruel hatchet. She presses him upon her as upon a burning wound, rocks her agile thighs, slithering her tongue between his foaming lips. Now she knows nothing more of the world and her four threshing limbs could be cut off without awakening her from her delight. Hsi Men's thrusting charger is like the head of a natural loom that draws his nerves into threads and twines them into a sensual knot that chokes the throat of his charger, swells until it magically bursts in molten liquid form, scattering in her raw-red cavern like balls of lead shot.

At last they lie quietly. Her loins are gently hollowed like a bowl for holding fruits, and truly the tenderest fruits are contained within its rim! Beside the moist blue woman-fruit lies the fat pink male-fruit, and below it the ancient fountain-fruit which contains two magical seeds!

As after a strenuous dance, a thousand pearls of perspiration appear on her brilliant skin. So she takes a towel from the couchside table and rubs herself from belly to head, as though she had come from a bath. . . .

When the phoenix has grown its wings again, with her two legs in the air, and her knees apart, Mistress Ping curves herself backward and touches the bed with her toes. While Hsi Men's member is cushioned in the lush funnel that leads into the depths of her innards, she stretches her head upward toward the wrinkled sac dangling from the root of his submerged pillar. She fills her wetted mouth with it and lets her tongue curve round each of its eggs, those rich oval granaries that charge the throat of his fleshy pillar with the turbulent liquid of life. Soon she feels its contents disgorging into her body, and every cell of Hsi Men's flesh envies his neighbor Hua.

Lady Ping had carefully shut one parchment-covered window in order to elude any possible curious glances from the courtyard. But she had not reckoned with the artfulness of her maid, Pear Blossom. This inquisitive, seventeen-year-old creature could not refrain from sneaking up under the windowsill, and, with a hairpin, boring a peep-hole through the pane of parchment. And she perceived, in the light of the moon from the other window, a lamp and tapers, a something that outlined itself on the closed bed hangings like the shadow of a

great, queerly shaped, struggling fish. Then that queer being came to rest and split into two halves.

They remained together until the first crowing of the cock, when a pale glow in the east indicated the approach of dawn. The little maid, who had been watching all the time, saw her mistress take two golden clasps from her hair and give them to Hsi Men, saying, "But don't let my husband see them!" Thereupon the maid fled from the courtyard and Hsi Men returned home as he had come. For future assignations they had agreed upon a secret signal. A cough and the throwing of a wall tile over the wall would give him to understand that the coast was clear.

While the little maid was hastily fingering the rim of her pleasure bowl in Lady Ping's servants' quarters, excited by her long night's vigil, Hsi Men went to the pavilion of Gold Lotus, who was still in bed.

"Where have you been all night?" she asked him.

"At Mother Wu's place with Brother Hua. I went along with him only to oblige him," he apologized.

She believed him, yet the shadow of a doubt lurked in her heart.

One afternoon, as she sat sewing in an arbor with Jade Fountain, a tile suddenly fell to the ground just in front of the arbor. Startled, Jade Fountain drew in her feet and lowered her head; Gold Lotus, accidentally glancing in the direction of the adjacent park wall, had a vague glimpse of a sunlit face that rose and immediately disappeared. She nudged her companion and pointed to the spot in question.

"Sister Three," she asked quietly, "doesn't the estate of neighbor Hua lie on the other side of that wall? And it was surely Pear Blossom who peeped over the wall and immediately disappeared when she saw us sitting here. I distinctly recognized her. Do you imagine that she wanted merely to look at our flowers?"

All that evening she kept a secret watch over Hsi Men. Having paid her a short visit in her pavilion, when she asked him if he would have something to eat or drink, he absently declined and, presently excusing himself, he went off into the park. Burning with curiosity, she followed him at a distance. He turned his footsteps in the direction of the wall. All at once she saw the same face which she had seen in the afternoon peer over the wall, and immediately afterward, Hsi Men placed a ladder against the coping and cautiously clambered over. She returned to her pavilion full of thought. For a long while she paced restlessly up and down her room. When at last she lay down it was only to lie wakeful throughout the night.

In the early hours of the morning Hsi Men appeared in her room and sat close beside her on the edge of the bed. Peeping at him from between her half-closed eyelids, she could plainly read embarrassment and consciousness of guilt on his face. She sat up and seized him by the ear, looking him sternly in the eyes.

"You faithless wretch!" she scolded him. "Confess where you have been all night! But please, no evasions! I know all about your little game. . . ."

Hsi Men saw that he was caught. He preferred to make himself as small as a dwarf. He fell on his knees before her and humbly pleaded: "Darling little oily-mouth, no scandal, I beg of you! I will confess everything!" And when he had confessed, he concluded: "Tomorrow Mistress Ping will pay you a friendly visit, and soon she will present you with a pair of friendship slippers. Yesterday she obtained the foot-measure of Moon Lady, and for the time being she sends you these trifling gifts by me."

He removed his hat, and took from his hair the two brooches given him by Mistress Ping. They were precious ornaments of chased gold, in the form of the auspicious symbol Shu, encrusted with blue turquoises, which signify long life. In his day, the old High Eunuch, her husband's uncle, had worn them at court.

"Well, how do you like them?"

Gold Lotus was pacified.

"Very well, I shall say no more. On the contrary, I'll help you to discover how the wind blows whenever you feel any desire for her. What do you say now?"

"What a sensible little woman you are!" he said, in commendation. Overjoyed by this sudden change of attitude, he clasped her tenderly in his arms. "And do you know, that woman yonder does not love me in a calculating way. It is really love at first sight. Ah, I feel as if I have a new body! And as for you, tomorrow you shall have a ravishing new dress as a reward."

"Listen: I haven't too much faith in your honeyed tongue and your sugary words. I would rather you promised me three things, if you want me to tolerate this affair of yours."

"I will promise anything you like!"

"Well then, first you must keep away from the houses of joy.

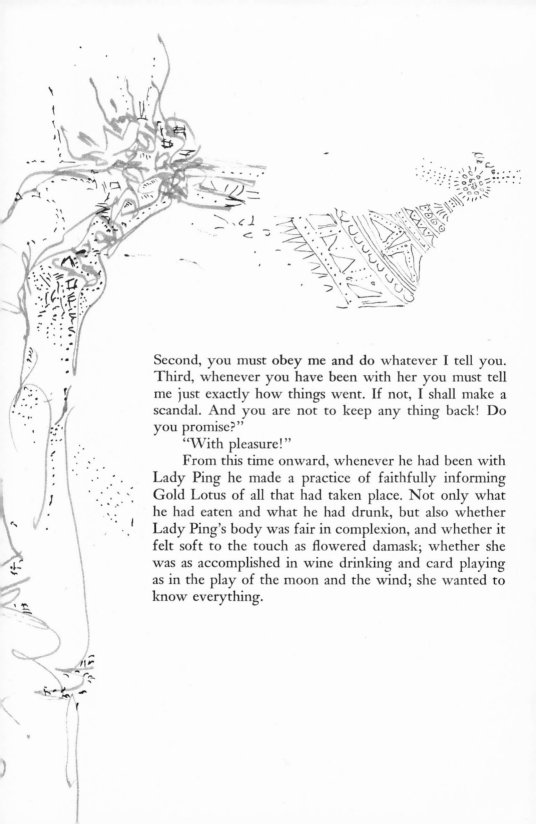

Second, you must **obey me and do** whatever I tell you.
Third, whenever you have been with her you must tell
me just exactly how things went. If not, I shall make a
scandal. And you are not to keep any thing back! Do
you promise?"

"With pleasure!"

From this time onward, whenever he had been with
Lady Ping he made a practice of faithfully informing
Gold Lotus of all that had taken place. Not only what
he had eaten and what he had drunk, but also whether
Lady Ping's body was fair in complexion, and whether it
felt soft to the touch as flowered damask; whether she
was as accomplished in wine drinking and card playing
as in the play of the moon and the wind; she wanted to
know everything.

WU WU MENG

In the case of Wu Wu Meng, we were duped. A young South African appeared one day in our office. His name was Sinclair Beiles, he was a writer, and of an extremely nervous and frantic nature. He explained to us, while clutching some pages in his hand, that he had been brought up in China, was the son of a missionary, read and wrote Chinese (it was in fact his first language), and was presently translating a rare Chinese novel, of a voluptuousness and sensuality that only the Chinese could achieve. For a price, he would continue the translation for Olympia Press, and at an agreed price, would bring us a new chapter every week. He fled from the office, leaving the kneaded pages behind. The next week he returned with the second chapter and sat outside our office reading a Chinese newspaper. We asked him what was new in Peking, and he told us, talking rapidly and urgently. He took his money, left the second chapter and was gone. This arrangement continued until we had all of Houses of Joy, *an extremely amusing and delicately indelicate book. Some months later we discovered that due to a lacuna in our knowledge of fifteenth-century Chinese literature, we had not been aware that we were buying a disguised and lascivious version of the Chinese classic,* Psi Men and His Many Wives, *which had in fact been translated by the distinguished Chinese scholar A. C. Waite. But Sinclair Beiles had given us such a gorgeously doctored and original version of this work, that we cheerfully published the Beiles edition. We felt it was worth every yen we had paid him, and that publishers, like Prime Ministers, can not be perfect.*

CHESTER HIMES

Panama Paul invited Cleo Daniels up to his room at
the Albert Hotel, which is situated on University
Place a few blocks north of Washington Square. He invited her
up to his room for the purpose of having a drink. She accepted on
those grounds.

They had a drink on those grounds and then another drink on
those grounds and he attempted to get chummy.

"Take off your shoes, baby."

"I will not."

So he took off his own shoes. And they had another drink.

PINKTOES

"Take off your clothes, baby."

"I will not."

So he began taking off his own clothes.

"What are you doing," she asked.

"I'm undressing," he replied and continued to undress until he had finished undressing.

"You're naked," she said, carefully examining his buck naked black body, especially his private parts which were not at all private now.

"I sure am," he said.

"For what?"

"For to go to bed."

"You can't go to bed and leave me here."

"I ain't. You're coming with me."

"I am not coming with you."

"What's the matter, you scared? You mean you came up here and drank my whisky and now think you're going to go?"

"You invited me to have a drink. You didn't say anything about going to bed."

"What else would I invite you up here to drink my whisky for, pray tell, without going to bed with you?"

"Use your imagination."

"Oh. You thought I was going to do that?"

"Well, what else did you keep showing me your tongue for. What was that supposed to mean from an accomplished thespian like you?"

"Well, get ready, girl, I can't through your clothes."

So she took off her shoes and stockings and garter belt and panties and pulled up her skirt and sat in the armchair with her naked white legs hooked over the arms and it was ready.

And was he astonished. "It's red-headed!" he exclaimed.

"It is not," she said. "It's just red hot."

Naturally this was his cue to demonstrate his virtuosity.

And before he knew what was happening she jumped up, snatched up her shoes and stockings and garter belt, and ran out into the corridor, slamming the door behind her.

He was so mad he finished the bottle of whisky all by himself and fell into a drunken sleep and dreamed he was in a heaven filled with naked white angels, but when he tried to fly in their direction he found that his testicles were weighted down with anvils.

And for another thing, Milt and Bessie Shirley and their guest, Arthur Tucker, went gaily into their suite of rooms in the Theresa Hotel and gaily closed the door behind. And what with all the people moving about in the corridor, it was some time before one had a chance to peek through the keyhole. And, well kiss my foot, all three of them were stark naked.

Bessie Shirley was hanging head down from a walking stick stuck through the chandelier with her long hair hanging to the floor, and embracing Mr. Tucker, who stood confronting her. And were they having a ball! Where was Milt Shirley? He was standing to one side looking on, having his own private ball. The last thing one saw before some people came down the hall, interrupting one's enjoyment, was the chandelier gradually pulling loose from the ceiling.

Then, of course, Merto guided Willard B. Overton to the apartment on the West Side where she lived with Maurice Gordey, who was not really her husband, she confessed, and where Eddy Schooley had been guest of honor during his broadcast, but not since.

When all was in readiness she took out a small tape measure and measured Mr. Overton. Mr. Overton was not accustomed to being measured in such circumstances and became so chagrined that his measurements abruptly changed. However, when Merto revealed her purpose, his measurements were restored. It had nothing to do with his capabilities, as he had assumed.

In her spare time she knitted a record of her accomplishments. Being as Merto was an expert knitter, they were identical to the subjects which they represented, so naturally measurements were required for the accuracy of the data.

Afterward she opened a drawer and showed Mr. Overton her filing cabinet. It was filled to the brim with data of all sizes and colors except white. Obviously she had done well by the poor oppressed Negroes.

Mr. Overton was immensely impressed. He thought she had made a commendable contribution to the Negro problem, but poor Maurice must be getting worn out from beating her.

However, it evidently suited her, for she looked nice and rosy and in the pink of health, sitting crosslegged on the bed.

She promised to knit his record in duplicate and mail him the extra copy for a souvenir. But he convinced her that it was unnecessary, as much as he adored her generosity. If she would just phone him, at the office, that is, he would come and get it. There was no telling what might ensue should Mrs. Overton open the package and examine its contents and recognize the measurements.

Naturally Dr. Brown drove slowly and carefully down the dangerous New York City streets to their hotel at 34th Street and Eighth Avenue, being as he was responsible for the person of Dr. Carl Vincent Stone, his white boss as you might say, who was sitting in the back seat of Dr. Brown's Chrysler sedan relentlessly crowding Maiti's big hams into her corner.

So, when on their way up to their rooms Dr. Brown invited Dr. Stone to stop in for a nightcap of real eight-year-old Kentucky bourbon whisky and a sandwich of real Smithfield ham, how could Dr. Stone refuse, as desirous as he was by then for some ham.

But when Dr. Stone discovered that the ham was really Smithfield ham and not the ham which he had anticipated, he recorded a black mark against Dr. Brown's dog-in-the-manger character, and soon afterward bade them good night.

However, before retiring he called the night bell captain and ordered some of the common Eighth Avenue variety of ham to assuage his appetite.

"Good and black," he instructed.

"Black, sir?"

"You heard me."

"Oh, yes sir, black, sir," the bell captain stammered, wondering where he was going to find any black ham in that vicinity that late at night.

As forty-nine-year-old leading young Negro novelist Lorenzo Llewellyn and his companion, dapper Maurice Gordey, were scouting about, they came upon a house in Brooklyn where a whole bevy of big strong gaily dressed colored women were having themselves a ballll! But being as they didn't have any women's clothes to join in the balling, the women were considerate enough to take off their own; and lo and behold, underneath they were actually mennnn! Suddenly Maurice was heard to squeal delightedly, "Don't you dare pull that big thing on a little girl like me!"

On the other hand, one might have sworn that Jonah Johnson would get himself a Rothschild fellowship by driving Dr. Garrett, president of the Rothschild Foundation, all the way from 155th Street downtown to the Waldorf-Astoria Hotel. Especially as Jonah talked all the way at the rate of three hundred words a minute, giving Dr. Garrett a detailed synopsis of his intended book on, er, ah, the Russians.

"Mmmmm, quite fetching, the little brown ones," Dr. Garrett said, jerking himself awake from time to time. "Mmmm, and they liked to be whipped, did you say?"

"Well, I didn't say they would like it exactly, sir, but I'm sure we can do it if we keep prepared."

"Mmmmm, they all like it, my boy."

"Well, sir, they would certainly resist."

"Mmmmm, I like them with spunk, but I'm worn out tonight."

So when they stopped in front of the hotel, Jonah asked hopefully, "What do you think of that as a book, Dr. Garrett?"

"Book!" exclaimed the startled Dr. Garrett. "Book, did you say?"

"Yes sir, my book about the communists."

"Communists. I thought you were discussing the Romanists."

"Er, why no sir, I was telling you about my book—"

"Oh, ah, quite interesting. Quite! Read it just last week."

"But I haven't written it yet."

"Haven't? Ha-ha, better get started, Mr., er, ah—No time like the present."

"Johnson, sir," Jonah said desperately. "Jonah Johnson. I was thinking that with a Rothschild fellowship—"

"Ah, yes, Mr. Johnson, remember you now. Never forget a Rothschild fellow. Showed great promise—"

The Waldorf-Astoria doorman hastened to the rescue of Dr. Garrett and whisked him safely into the confines of the Waldorf-Astoria Hotel.

Jonah turned his car around and drove back uptown to his apartment on the third floor of a walkup on 139th Street. His light-complexioned ever-loving wife asked crossly where he had been all night. She already had one black eye and he promptly gave her another, whether she liked it or no.

So what happened to the unidentified distinguished-looking white lady and the young dark Negro poet who looked like Jackson? They left Mamie's to go somewhere and make some poetry, and, oh, brother, they are making it, white and black poetry, that is.

This poetry is not only being made but it is being said, between pants and grunts and groans, that is.

HE: Birmingham.

SHE: Oh, you poor lamb.

HE: Ku-Klux-Klan.

SHE: Oh, you poor black man.

HE: Lynch mob.

SHE: Oh, you make me sob.

HE: Little Rock.

SHE: Oh, what an awful shock.

HE: Jim Crow.

SHE: Oh, you suffering Negro.

HE: Denied my rights.

SHE: Oh, take my delights.

HE: Segregation.

SHE: Oh, but integration.

HE: They killed my pappy.

SHE: Oh, let me make you happy.

HE: They call me low.

SHE: Oh, you beautiful Negro.

Finally the verses ceased as the rhythm increased to a crashing crescendo with a long wailing finale:

HE: Oooooooooooo!

SHE: Negroooooooooo!

Which just goes to show the Negro problem is inspirational too, for what other grave problem of our time inspires such spontaneous rhapsody?

And what did Julius find out about that fashionable East Side divorcee, Fay Corson? He found out that she lived in a seven-room apartment on the eighth floor of a very swank building in the east Seventies, and that she was an animal lover. For no sooner had they disrobed than she suggested they play dogs. So they scampered about the carpeted floor in the manner of mating dogs. Then she decided to play shaggy dog and pulled down the telephone from the bed table and dialed a number. It so happened that Will Robbins answered and she said to him:

"You sneak."

"Fay!" he exclaimed. "Where are you?"

"I'm at home, you rat."

"Doing what?"

"I'm playing bitch, if you just must know."

"Is that new?"

"With a big black dog," she said.

"Lucky black dog, you lucky white bitch," he said.

"And what are you doing, you louse?"

"If you just must know, I am sitting at the kitchen table eating oysters on the half shell."

"And what is that black slut doing you took home with you? Eating oysters too, I suppose."

"That fine brown woman is not eating oysters whatsoever."

"Then why don't you give her some oysters?"

"Her turn will come when I'm finished."

"And when will that be?"

"Soon."

"Wait for me."

"Better hurry."

"Now!" she cried.

"Now!" he replied.

"Oh, now and now again and again now," she said, quoting Hemingway.

"Not any more now," he said, sighing.

"You dirty freak," she said, and banged down the receiver.

Then she pulled away from Julius and ran into the bathroom. Julius listened to the water running. And what had he found out for real? Well, he had found out where sea urchins come from.

As for Reverend Riddick and Professor Samuels, they both wound up in the Bellevue psychiatric ward for observation.

But it is not at all like you're probably thinking. What happened was that Isaiah and Kit Samuels, leaving Mamie Mason's party at the same time as Reverend Mike Riddick, could do no less than help him get the helpless Miss Lucy Pitt downtown to her abode. Then what happened after that was when they had got the young lady home and got her undressed and safely resting atop the sheet with all her sweet brown femininity exposed, Reverend Riddick was struck by such compelling compassion that he wished to say a Christian prayer for the poor helpless girl before tucking her beneath the covers. And that is the only reason he asked Professor Samuels to leave the room, which in turn precipitated the wrestling match.

Because Professor Samuels said, "I see no reason why we both can't pray in turns. That is, if we leave my wife out of it."

"It's because you're Jewish," Reverend Riddick said. "And while I have nothing against the Jewish faith, it being the father of my own faith, still and all you can see the girl has not been circumcised and is only fit for a Christian prayer."

"I'm not Jewish," Professor Samuels denied vehemently.

"Then what are you doing with a Jewish name?" Reverend Riddick challenged.

"You've got an Irish name but you're not Irish," Professor Samuels rebutted.

"I have never said I was Irish," Reverend Riddick said.

"I have never said I was Jewish either," Professor Samuels said.

"Then what are you doing with a Jewish name?" Reverend Riddick persisted.

"That's my family name," Professor Samuels informed him. "The fact of the matter is, I am from Mississippi and all of my family are Christians and very anti-Semitic."

"If you're anti-Semitic then you're anti-Negro," Reverend Riddick charged. "And if you're anti-Negro I shall not let you pray over this helpless young Negro girl."

"I'm getting damned tired of people accusing me of being anti-Negro just because I'm from Mississippi," Professor Samuels said. "Some of the Negro people's best friends are from Mississippi."

"How far from Mississippi?" Reverend Riddick asked.

"It's not a matter of distance," Professor Samuels said. "We can be miles apart and still be friends."

"Then if you're not anti-Negro you're not afraid of the black rubbing off of me," Reverend Riddick said.

"As far as that goes, if you're not anti-white you're not afraid of the white rubbing off of me," Professor Samuels said.

"Then if you're not afraid of the black rubbing off of me, I'll wrestle you buck naked," Reverend Riddick challenged.

"I'll wrestle you buck naked with the greatest of pleasure," Professor Samuels accepted his challenge.

So that is how they came about wrestling buck naked.

But one look at Reverend Riddick's fine black body with its big impressive limbs inspired Kit Samuels to rip off her own clothes and begin wrestling buck naked also. She wrestled about the room in circles, as though she were wrestling two buck naked electric wires.

"Oh, oh, big black Riddick," she cried in spontaneous rapture and began throwing her white body about as though to demonstrate its potentialities, in case anyone might be interested.

"Put on your clothes, you bitch!" Professor Samuels shouted. "You're exposing yourself."

But she must have misunderstood him because she began doing the splits and the bumps and exposing herself from all directions, shouting in reply, "Oh, big black Riddick, I'm a bitch! I'm a bitch! Oh, big black Riddick, I'm a bitch in heat."

"You're a frantic slut," Professor Samuels screamed.

Naturally Reverend Riddick resented Professor Samuels addressing such a fine white woman in that manner, even though she was his wife. So he caught Professor Samuels' head in a nelson. Professor Samuels was not one to be nelsoned without retaliating, so he gripped Reverend Riddick's most vulnerable limb. The only thing was he was too weak to take a good hold and his hand kept slipping up and down.

And when Kit Samuels noticed this she entered into the spirit of

the match with greater abandon.

"Oh, big black Riddick, I'm a frantic slut. Oh, I'm a frantic slut. Oh, big black Riddick, I'm a frantic slut."

Such behavior on the part of his wife so intensified Professor Samuels' agitation that he wrapped his legs about one of Reverend Riddick's big black legs and began to wrestle in earnest.

"Oh, you whore!" he reviled his wanton wife.

"Oh, I'm a whore, I'm a whore," Kit Samuels cried, dancing in even greater frenzy.

"I'll divorce you, you whore!" Professor Samuels cried. "I'll throw you out!"

"Oh, I'm a whore and I'll give you cause to throw me out," Kit Samuels said and immediately launched into such frenzied cause that Professor Samuels cried out.

"I'll kill myself! I'll jump into the river!"

Which, for some inexplicable reason caused Kit Samuels to cry joyously, "Go kill yourself! Go jump into the river! Or I'll give more cause!"

Professor Samuels broke from Reverend Riddick's hold and ran, still dripping, out of the door.

"Jesus save us!" Reverend Riddick bellowed, and ran, still dripping, to bring him back.

Just as day was breaking, Professor Samuels came running down the stairs from Lucy Pitt's fourth-floor flat beside the railroad tracks on West 10th Street, in the Village, white baby naked. Reverend Riddick came running down behind him, black baby naked.

Early Village risers looked up and saw a naked white man high-balling down the street with a naked black man chasing him and hastened back inside their homes and locked their doors, thinking the Africans were invading.

The naked white man ran underneath the elevated railroad tracks and headed toward the Hudson River. The naked black man ran after him. The naked men ran past one big trailer truck after another big trailer truck. They ran past one freighter dock after another freighter dock. The naked white man couldn't find any way to get close enough to the river to jump in and drown. The naked black man couldn't run fast enough to catch him and stop him in case he got to the river bank.

One of the Bowery bums who had strayed over on that side

during the night, a former professor of Greek mythology at an Ivy League university, dozing fitfully on the sidewalk, looked up in time to see the fleetfooted naked runners rounding the walls of Troy, and exclaimed weakly, "History repeats itself!"

Shortly afterward two truck drivers came out of an all-night greasy spoon and caught the runners and held them for the police.

Which just goes to show that the phallus complex is the aphrodisiac of the Negro problem.

Speaking of phalli, what about the big-all-over white man, Art Wills? Well, Art Wills was taken home by Brown Sugar, who was really Mrs. Lillian Davis Burroughs, wife of the Harlem financier in private life. She told him that it would be perfectly all right, and she had her big new shiny Buick there, and she was a big, handsome, hefty, hammy, curly-headed, wide-eyed, smooth, brown, luscious piece herself, so naturally Art believed her. Even when she parked her car before a three-story brick house on Fish Avenue in the Bronx, and informed him coyly that was where she and her husband lived, he was so far gone it didn't bother him a bit as long as it didn't bother her.

They sat on the sofa in the living room and explored their differences until, as it should always happen when there is sufficient negotiation, her difference seemed ready to accept his difference and come to the point, or if not to the point, come anyway.

So she said, "You undress now."

The lady said undress and, being as he was a man, he undressed.

"You undress, too," he said.

Being as she was a woman with an undressed man about she undressed too. Now they were both undressed. He looked at the lady's well-inflated, curly-haired privacy that seemed about to pop from her smooth, tight, copper-colored thighs and naturally he didn't want that to happen, but the lady contended that there were more important decisions to be taken.

"You won't be afraid of the scandal?" she asked.

"What scandal?" he asked.

"I'm going to scream when you're ready."

"You can see I'm ready," he contended. "But you're not going to scream just because of that."

"Oh, I'm ready for that too, but are you ready for the other?"

"Ready for what other?"

"Why, ready for my husband to come down and catch us."

"Catch us doing what?"

"Why, catch us making love. What do you think? Who else would I want to catch us making love?"

"I'm sure I don't know. The neighbors, perhaps.

"The neighbors are not in it."

"Well, I'm glad to know that. It would be a little crowded if they were. But what is your husband going to do when he comes down here and finds us making love?"

"Oh, he won't make any trouble. He's a coward. It's just for him to see it."

"Oh, he likes to see you making love with other men?"

"Certainly not. Do you think I'd be married to a man like that? That's why I want him to see it."

"Let me get this straight. You mean you want your husband to see you making love with another man because he won't like it?"

"If he liked it there wouldn't be any point. Are you stupid?"

"I'm beginning to think so. You mean to say your husband is going to hear you scream and come running down here and find us making love and he's not going to make any trouble even though he won't like it?"

"Of course not. He's not a savage. He's going to give one look and see right away it isn't anything like that."

"You mean he's going to give one look and see you're not making love. You don't know me, baby."

"I don't mean that. I mean as if you're hurting me. He's going to see right off I'm loving you too."

"The way things are going, it is going to take more than him to see that. But why are you going to scream before we even start, unless you're one of those natural screamers who start screaming just by thinking about it."

"Oh, don't be so silly. I've got to scream to get him down here to find us. Otherwise he'd just stay up in his room and keep on sleeping and we'd be making love for nothing."

"You might be making love for nothing but not me, and I don't see why some husband has got to find me making love to his wife in order for me to enjoy it."

"Please, don't try to appear so dense," she said, stroking him and kissing him. "We can't avoid the scandal."

"Do you mean to say you can't make love without making a scandal?" he asked.

"What do you take me to be, an exhibitionist?" she flared. "But it can't be avoided."

"It seems to me it could be avoided easily enough if we would just make love quietly and you didn't scream."

"But how else can we get him to come down here and find us making love. You don't know Handsome—"

"What's more, I don't want to know him—"

"He wouldn't even sue for divorce at all if he didn't actually find us making love."

Art felt suddenly as though he had gotten involved in the cold war by mistake. "You mean he wouldn't sue you for divorce—" he began.

But she cut him off. "It's not him I'm thinking about. I know you can handle him—"

"Don't tell me there will be others?"

"It's your wife I'm thinking about," she said. "Can you make her give you a divorce, or does she have to catch us making love too?"

"But why all these divorces?" he asked in amazement. "Just for a little love-making?"

"So we can get married, you big wonderful white man, and make love all the time," she said.

He looked regretfully at all that ripe October-painted flesh going to waste and thought, My God, this woman is stark raving mad. Whereupon he jumped into his clothes and got out of there as fast as was humanly possible before she started screaming, making love or not.

For a natural born philanderer, he was exceptionally glad to get home to his apartment on East 54th Street where his ever-loving wife, Debbie, was waiting for him with this news:

"Darling, she did it again."

By then he was good and tired of cryptic women.

"Say what you mean," he said crossly. "*Who* did *what* again?"

"Your daughter, dear. What other *she* would I mean?"

"How would I know?" he snapped.

Her eyes widened. "And just what does that mean?"

But he refused to get involved again in women's logic.

"It means I would like to know what did my daughter do again? I know it's something bad because the only time she's my daughter is when she's done something bad. When she's good she's your daughter."

"Well, heaven knows she must have inherited it from you. No one in my family has ever done anything like *that*."

"Like *what*?"

"I just told you. She threw the cat out of the window again."

"Who do you know in my family, may I ask, who has ever thrown a cat out of a window?"

"I can't speak for the others, but *your* daughter has, twice."

Two weeks before, Art's angelic little eight-year-old daughter, Marilyn, had befriended a mangy old alley cat she'd found in the street, obviously friendless. She'd brought it upstairs to their fourth-floor apartment and had bathed it in the bathtub and her mother had to call the doctor to treat her for scratches. Then she had fed it and pampered it until the cat became ungrateful and unresponsive, as are all fat cats. So Marilyn had picked up the ungrateful cat and had thrown it out of the fourth-story window back into the street. The cat's front legs had been broken. Her mother had had to take the cat to the cat-and-dog clinic, and it had cost twenty-five dollars to get the cat's legs set and put in plaster casts. For the past week the cat had been living the life of an invalid in the Willses' apartment. So naturally

Art was only too happy that *his* little daughter had taken this commendable action and got rid of the cat.

"Did you call the SPCA to take it away?" He meant the cat's corpse, of course.

"I did not," Debbie replied indignantly. "Do you think I want anyone to know *your* daughter has inherited such a streak of cruelty?"

"Well, then, when did it happen?" he asked.

"At one o'clock this morning, while you were gallivanting around Mamie Mason's."

"Oh, then it was all right to leave it there."

"And listen to it yowling in agony?"

"What! You mean it wasn't dead?"

"Of course it wasn't dead. That kind of cat never dies."

"Then what did you do with it, may I ask?"

"I called the doctor, of course."

"What! You called the doctor at two o'clock in the morning! My God, what did he charge?"

"Why, the same as before, twenty-five dollars. The same two legs were broken."

"Wife, do you mean to stand there and tell me you paid twenty-five dollars on that cat again?" he demanded. "And do we still have the monster here convalescing in our home?"

"I know it's difficult. But she's your daughter."

"*My* daughter."

"So what else could I do?"

"You could have called an ambulance and all of you could have gone to an insane asylum."

She bristled. "I believe you mean that."

"Mean it!" he shouted.

But he restrained from committing himself and went into the kitchen and drank the pint of one hundred and twenty proof corn whisky he had been saving for such an emergency.

Speaking of emergencies, one might assume that Moe Miller, blessed with such a formidable talent and charged as he was with strong whisky and fried chicken, would certainly have passed the night in some creative activity, such as increasing the population. But no, Moe was a home man, and even though his wife, Evie, was in Baltimore, he went straight home.

What was wrong with him? Did he have a case? Had he buried

his talent and forgotten where? Not at all. Moe was writing a series of newspaper articles on the Negro problem, mornings after parties being the best time for such creativity, and on the side he was trying to catch a rat. Not the kind of rat you're thinking about either. The rat Moe was trying to catch was a real ratty rat, a dirty lowdown thieving rat that had been stealing food from the Millers' larder for a long time.

The Millers lived in a two-story brick bungalow in Brooklyn, and when they first began missing the food they had assumed it was a two-legged rat, since Brooklyn is known to be infested with all kinds of rats. Whole loaves of bread, sacks of potatoes, bowls of fruit, tins of meat, bottles of whisky had disappeared, along with several bags of nuts, although, in view of the ensuing events, that would not have been so farfetched as it might seem.

Moe had notified the police and had kept their doors and windows securely closed and locked. But still the food kept disappearing. Naturally Moe didn't put up with that, as well as he liked to eat. He began setting rat traps in strategic places about the house. The first traps of the common spring type disappeared also. It was then Moe concluded it had to be a mighty big rat if it would eat the traps. So he bought all of the biggest rat traps known, but the rat merely ignored these traps and continued to steal the food. So Moe bought a bear trap and baited it with a pound of the best cheese money could buy, and he chained the trap to the cold water pipe. But the rat moved the trap over beside the door and then made a big racket, knocking over the dustpan and letting out some horrible-sounding squeals. Moe came rushing down into the kitchen, thinking he had caught the rat, and stepped into the trap. At first he thought the rat had him. By its bite he knew the rat was as big as a Great Dane. He fought the rat so furiously and screamed in such desperation the entire neighborhood was awakened and prowl cars came from all directions. For one whole week Moe was unable to walk and after that he gave up on traps. He decided to shoot the rat. He was going to shoot it in cold blood. He was going to blow that dirty rat's brains to hell and gone. He bought a double-barreled twelve-gauge shotgun and nights on end he lay in ambush for the rat. But the rat never appeared while he was waiting for it. Naturally, the rat had more sense than that. The rat wouldn't come out and raid the larder until Moe got sleepy and went to bed.

Besides which, it kept Evie so nervous with Moe prowling around in the dark house with a loaded shotgun that she threatened to leave him. He compromised by promising to keep the gun unloaded until he actually saw the rat. One night he was sitting in the dark kitchen with the two twelve-gauge shells on the table at his hand and the shotgun across his knees, waiting for the rat to show its dirty head. But he dozed off, and while he was sleeping the rat came and stole the two shotgun shells. The very next morning Moe got rid of the shotgun to keep the rat from stealing it and shooting him, being as the rat already had the shells for it.

That was when he bought the big, vicious-looking razorsharp hunting knife. He was going to lay for that rat and catch him face to face. And it was going to be man against rat, a fight to the finish. That rat was going to find out who was the best man. He was going to cut that rat's heart out.

When he arrived home from Mamie Mason's party, he took off his shoes and entered the house as silently as an Indian. He tiptoed up the front stairs in the dark and got his knife and tiptoed down the back stairs and snapped on the light in the kitchen.

And there, in the middle of the polished linoleum floor, was a hen egg. He blinked and spun about, holding the knife ready to stab. And there, at the head of the basement stairs, was another hen egg.

Before going to the party he had bought a half dozen eggs, a pound of butter and a loaf of bread, which he had left on the sidestand for his breakfast. Nothing remained but the empty sack which had held the eggs.

He turned on the basement lights and started downstairs. There was an egg on the middle stair and another one at the bottom. In the middle of the basement floor was his pound of butter with one corner nibbled off. At the far end of the basement was the old fuel bin which had been out of use since they had installed a new oil burner. There was a sizable hole at the bottom of the screen door to the bin. Directly in front of the hole was another egg.

Moe opened the door. Directly inside of the bin was the loaf of bread with a corner nibbled off. There, beside the big wooden box where kindling and paper had been stored, was another egg.

Moe lifted the lid of the box. The box was filled to the brim with food. There was a hole in the back of the box opening onto a network of tunnels. The box had been neatly divided into compartments.

There was a compartment for eggs, one for fruit, one for bread, one for cured meat, one for bottles of whisky, coca cola, milk, ink and cleaning fluid, and one big compartment at the far end for a miscellaneous collection of nails, screws, tampax, lipstick, perfume, chewing gum, cigarettes, a pipe, an old pair of house slippers and a stack of comic books. He could see right off that the rat loved comfort, but he didn't think much of the rat's reading habits. Poking around with a stick he uncovered some suspiciously stained towels and some used condoms. He had already realized it was a big rat, but judging from the size of the condoms, what an enormous rat it must have been screwing.

He searched the coal bin and the entire basement, but there was no sign of the rat. He went back to the kitchen, determined to search the entire house, room by room, and also look to see if the beds had been used. But just as he stepped into the kitchen, at long last he had his wish. He and the rat stood face to face. The rat tried to get past him into the basement but he kicked the rat back into the kitchen and slammed the door.

This was it. Man to rat. The rat stood up on its hind legs and snarled at him. The man was somewhat alarmed. That rat was as big as a tomcat. It had mangy gray fur and a long bare tail that resembled the main root of a giant cactus. But what alarmed the man most was the size of the rat's teeth.

Moe clutched the broom in his left hand and held his hunting knife in his right hand. He swiped at the rat with the broom. The rat dodged and slapped him on the ankle with its tail. He slashed at the rat with his knife. The rat backed away slowly. Moe advanced cautiously. Suddenly the rat looked around and found itself in a corner. It knew it was a cornered rat. It stood up on its hind legs again and snarled a warning. Moe punched at it with the broom. The rat bit the broom and jerked it out of Moe's hand. Moe lunged for the broom and the rat lunged for Moe. Moe jumped back and at the rat with his knife. The rat charged Moe and slashed open his pants with its teeth. Moe was so frightened he threw his knife at the rat. The knife missed the rat and hit the wall and bounced back onto the floor. The rat lit on the knife and grabbed the handle between its teeth. Then it charged Moe with the knife. Moe jumped on top of the table. The rat leaped up into the air and tried to cut Moe on the leg. Moe jumped from the table onto the drain. The rat leaped up into the sink. Moe jumped from the drainboard on top of the stove. The rat leaped onto the drainboard and Moe jumped down to the floor. When the rat leaped down to follow Moe the knife was jarred from its teeth. While the rat was going back for the knife, Moe had time to get the door open and run out of the house.

Shaken and exhausted, Moe went to the police precinct station and reported the rat to the police. Then he sent his wife, Evie, a telegram:

FOR GOD SAKE DO NOT COME STOP RAT HAS GOT KNIFE STOP IN POSSESSION OF HOUSE STOP I AM DROPPING THE NEGRO PROBLEM UNTIL RAT IS CAUGHT STOP LOOK FOR ME ON THE 12:10.

And right there you have the main trouble with the Negro problem—*rats*.

Well, what about Joe? No inference intended.

Joe looked into the den at the sleeping Bacchus. All looked peaceful atop Olympus. In fact, Bacchus had Olympus to himself.

Joe went into the bedroom and took off his clothes. He was hairless as an eightball, save for the patch of dried pubic grass.

Mamie came into the bedroom and looked at Joe and laughed.

"Baby, no one will challenge your legitimacy," she said.

Joe smiled slyly. "Mama kept it for papa."

"This mama is keeping it for her papa," Mamie lied with a straight face and took off her own clothes.

And what do you know? Those catty women who were always disparaging her breasts weren't too wrong. They hung down like nanny goat's udders, but that suited Joe fine, as much as he liked to suckle. For no sooner had she climbed astride his soft black belly in jockey fashion, holding his arms pinioned to the bed and letting her titties dangle over his face, than he tried his damndest to suckle. The only trouble was he couldn't catch one in his big juicy mouth although he nibbled hard enough, first at one and then at the other like a fish after worms. But finally he got hold of one, looking for all the world like a big black baby suckling. Afterward he didn't even have to change position to go to sleep.

Having that done with, Mamie donned a red quilted robe and red felt mules and carried the telephone extension from the den and plugged it in the kitchen outlet. She dialed a Chelsea number and asked to speak to Wallace Wright.

It so happened that Wallace Wright's home telephone was on the Audubon exchange and his office telephone on the Murray Hill exchange. And this Chelsea number that Mamie called was listed in the name of a very smart, middle-aged white divorcee who lived on West 23rd Street.

"Wallace Wright?" The low husky voice sounded startled. "That's you, isn't it, Mamie?"

"Yes, darling. Wallace left his notecase here when he was at my party and I found your letter in it."

"Letter? What letter?"

"The one where you asked him to divorce his Negro wife. Naturally I don't want that type of letter in my house and—" She broke off to listen to the faint sound of whispering at the other end. "What did he say, darling?"

"You are vicious, Mamie. You know damn well I've never written any such letter to Mr. Wright and if I had Mr. Wright has too much pride—"

"Call him Wallace, darling," Mamie interrupted. "At least while he's in bed with you."

"Mr. Wright has not, is not—"

Mamie hung up. Her only regret was that she was not there to see Mr. Wright getting out of bed. But what she didn't know was that by the time she had hung up, Mr. Wright had already gotten out of bed and had gotten half-dressed.

"I'd better go, dear. Better go. Best thing," he was muttering.

His erstwhile bedmate started to tell him he didn't really have to go, that she wasn't afraid of Mamie Mason. But after the second look she realized that Mr. Wright had already gone.

"I know dear. Phone me and come when you can," she said.

Mamie would have then phoned Wallace Wright's wife, Juanita, and informed her where Wallace had been. But she and Juanita were not on speaking terms, and she would not give Juanita the satisfaction of being spoken to by her. Instead she went downstairs to have her very best friend, Patty Pearson, who was also Juanita's very best friend, telephone instead.

Patty had not attended Mamie's party because she had been entertaining a party on her own. But her party had finished and gone and Patty was alone, reminiscing over the delights of being screwed while standing on her head.

"Come on into the kitchen and tell me all about it, honey," she welcomed Mamie.

"What's that you're cooking, sugar?"

"I'm frying some salt pork to go with my grits. You want some scrambled eggs with yours?"

"You know I'm on a diet, sugar."

"I know you are honey. Just eat one of those cold pig's feet while you're waiting."

"Enjoy yourself, sugar?" Mamie asked with the foot in her mouth.

"I blitzed him, honey. You couldn't squeeze out another drop with a steam roller. How was your party?"

"Wonderful, sugar. Schooley sobered up enough to dance naked."

"Nothing dropped off, I hope."

"No, sugar. You'll find it just as you left it."

Patty raised her eyebrows. "*That* limp?"

Mamie laughed and started on another foot.

"Wait, honey," Patty said. "I just got to do the eggs."

"Do you have some mineral oil, sugar?"

"Natch, honey, with my men. In the bathroom."

When Mamie returned from drinking a quarter of a glass of mineral oil, the feast was on the table.

"I suppose Dora Steele got Jule," Patty said.

"She couldn't come. Jimmy had a case of acute indigestion."

"When you said *case* I thought—"

"You know how careful Jimmy is."

"But indigestion!" Patty exclaimed.

"Something he et."

"Does it give one indigestion?"

They exchanged sly looks and noisily chewed their grits.

"Who did get Jule, honey?"

"Fay."

"Oh, her. Is he still trying to find out if it's true?"

"He's just hunting while he can."

"He won't win a home with her."

"Not home-hunting, sugar. Tuft-hunting."

"When's my turn coming to be shot?"

"Soon, sugar. Just keep flipping your tuft at him."

"Wallace have a nice time, honey?"

"Lovely, sugar. I want you to call Juanita for me."

"I'd love to. What do you want me to tell her?"

"Just say that being as you're her best friend, you want to tell her before it gets all over town, that Wallace has been caught in bed with a you-know-who."

Patty smiled sweetly.

And that was how it happened that Juanita first found out about what later became known in Harlem as Wallace's folly.

It turned out so well they both returned to the kitchen and drank a pint of rum to celebrate.

And why did Mamie do this thing to Wallace Wright? Simply because Wallace never brought Juanita to any of her parties. He always came alone, just as though she ran a whorehouse. She considered that a damn insult.

CHESTER HIMES

Casting about for the best word on Chester Himes, I asked John A. Williams if I could use his article which appeared in Book Week *in the October 11, 1964 issue of the* New York Herald Tribune. *Both Williams and the* Tribune *were delighted:*

Chester Himes is getting on. He's only 54, at the "peak" as the critics would say. He is old not so much in years, but in experiences, the sameness of those experiences. And he works hard, worries hard, drinks hard, writes hard. If he lives for another century, however, he could not write all the books that are in him. He simply knows too much about people, places and things. And it hurts beyond the hurts he received in a fall during boyhood, hurts which still plague him.

This contemporary and friend of the late Richard Wright may now be working on his fifteenth novel, It Rained Five Days. *He may be shuffling with that old limp between Paris and Biot, Amsterdam and points in Germany. But he is working; his typewriter, at least, remains constant, cold, a demanding bitch. Nineteen years have passed since Himes published his first novel,* If He Hollers Let Him Go, *reissued recently. Down through aching, frustrating years have come* Lonely Crusade *(1947),* Cast the First Stone *(1952),* The Third Generation *("My most dishonest novel"—1954, and also re-*

issued) and The Primitive *(1956). One year later Coffin Ed Johnson and Grave Digger Jones, two Negro detectives in a Harlem setting, descended upon Paris—and were a sensation. Gallimard published this first of six books,* La Reine des Pommes. *Here it was called* For Love of Imabelle, *and put out by Gold Medal. Coffin Ed and Grave Digger became known throughout Paris and the near provinces. Back at the ranch in New York, writers who had known Himes were sneering, "He's writing detective books now." But what detective books!*

So, ultimately Himes came to Pinktoes *(Librairie Plon, 1961) or, as it is known in Europe,* Mamie Mason. *It is a galloping, balloon-bursting novel. How best to describe it? Take Candy, the Southern-Hoffenberg nymphette. Tan her and smooth her over with whatever John Howard Griffin used, age her in bed, not alone, but with many people over many years. Give her a lust for power and status and, above all, the white men who are as anxious as she to advance the Negro Cause in the early '40s. Strike halting innocence because by now you've a middle-age fox on your hands. Mamie Mason's husband, along with many another Negro in the book, is just as anxious to advance the cause as his wife—with white women. Everyone in the book is all for the cause which has the effect of making them wind up in bed at the earliest opportunity.*

Himes was not always so satiric nor macabre. His first four books show little trace of it. But The Primitive *marks a turn. "I sat down in Mallorca with a kind of I-don't-give-a-damn attitude and wrote."*

What happened to Chester Himes? In these times it becomes a mean task to publish fifteen books, let alone fifteen or sixteen novels with an enviable degree of versatility. More often than not, we tend to cry about the state of the American novel, yet we manage to kill off, literally and figuratively both, novelists whose works are quite representative of America. But, perhaps, not the America we like to believe we live in.

If Chester Himes likes you, he will tell you what happened. He will tell you because he is a natural raconteur, with a thousand digressions from the main story. He will tell you in his rugged little duplex on the Château de Bourbon which you reach after an endless flight of stairs and stepping over of couple of clochards. He will tell you with murder in his laughter and between deep draughts of vin ordinaire or whisky, if it has been a good month.

Rebelling against a broken middleclass family ("My father

taught wheelwrighting—was known as a professor"), he staged an armed robbery after putting in two years at Ohio State. He went to prison when he was 19 and came out when he was 27. While in prison, he began publishing in Esquire, *using his prison number. Meyer Levin was first assistant to Arnold Gingrich then. Shortly after his release and marriage he met Langston Hughes, then later worked as a butler for Louis Bromfield at Malabar Farm. During this time, Bromfield "read my prison manuscript (Cast the First Stone) and promised to help me get it published or made into a film . . . he talked my book up and sent me to see some people. A few Hollywood people knew me from* Esquire—*which used to be the Hollywood Bible—but no one suspected I was black. When they saw my face, I was finished, period."*

If He Hollers Let Him Go *had a West Coast setting. So did* Lonely Crusade *which dealt with Communist activities in California. That was the book that hurt Himes or, rather, added to what was already there. "Everybody (and I mean* everybody*) jumped on* Lonely Crusade. *The Communists crucified it. I was compared to* [the late] *Senator Bilbo and the traitors who squealed on the slave revolts. Willard Motley wrote a dirty, incredibly vicious review for the* Chicago Sun-Times; *James Baldwin wrote a review (it was the first I had ever heard of Baldwin) for the Socialist Party Union Leader headed,* HISTORY AS A NIGHTMARE. . . . *Anyways, I got hurt. My father had come to New York to see some of the broadcasts (which had been cancelled). He said, by way of consolation, 'New York is not the only city with skyscrapers.'"*

In 1953, Himes put this land behind him. He returns occasionally to see his old friend Carl van Vechten, or to work on some deal with the French film industry. But he is a nervous, wretched man. Once you are out of New York, you can almost see from which direction the pressures are coming; when you are in the city, in America, you expect them to come from any direction, any time. And you can't see them. It was almost inevitable, then, that he should have gone through the nasty taxi driver bit on his last visit. We got the ride, dropping off Lynne Caine, then publicity director at Farrar, Straus, but had to report the driver. Himes was a shaken man when he got to his hotel, shaken with anger. We drank until the next day dawned cold and gray. Some months later, Mrs. Caine and I had to appear as witnesses at the Hack Bureau. They took away the cabbie's license for two weeks or so. I was glad Himes wasn't there.

Even the NAACP has conspired to pressure Himes. I say "even" knowing that there are many gaps in a piece as short as this. I can't tell it all, and Himes won't, not to the public, just as he has sworn not to write about Richard Wright or James Baldwin or any of the five hundred other people who have crossed his life and left their marks on it.

On April 16, 1962, Herbert Hill, Labor Secretary of the NAACP and editor of an anthology of new writing by American Negroes, 1940–1962, fired off a memo to Arthur Cohen who was then considering Himes' screenplay, Baby Sister. *Said Mr. Hill: (among other things) ". . .* Baby Sister *consists almost entirely of banal caricature, unrelieved violence and endlessly repeated eroticism. One must note that the material contained in this script is nothing more than a travesty on Negro life in Harlem. It has no relationship to reality and is not redeemed by any literary values. This opinion is shared by all my colleagues in the Association."*

My impression of the script was that its aim was to show how difficult it was for an attractive girl to grow up in Harlem—a rather Darwinian exercise. But what Mr. Hill and his colleagues most objected to, perhaps, was not Baby Sister *at all, but* Pinktoes.

Chester Himes is getting on. His temper is shorter, he sees doctors more often, his sullen moods are longer, his laughter wilder. But he has topped a lot of fine writing with Pinktoes, *and I for one don't care how much murder there is in his laughter as long as he keeps on writing.*

the soft machine

William S. Burroughs

The War Between the Sexes split the planet into armed camps right down the middle line divides one thing from the other and I have seen them all: The Lesbian Colonels in bright green uniform and the cool blue metal of all sexes and the young aides and directives regarding The Sex Enemy from proliferating departments who thought the planet posted on every corner by Doctor Benway Blue Colonels of Supersonic Approval.

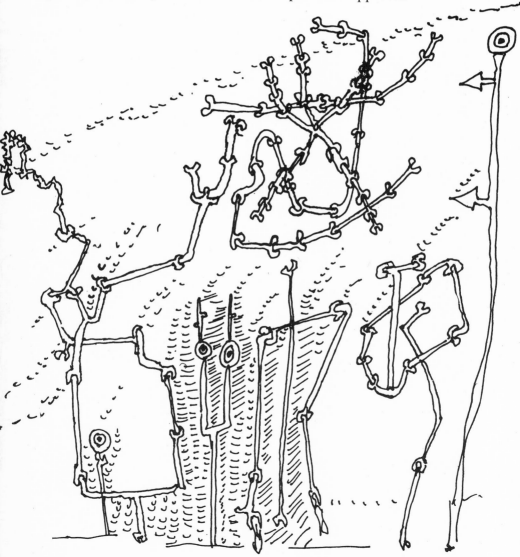

On The Line is The Baby and Semen Market where the sexes meet to exchange The Basic Commodity injected straight away into Receptacles and detained in Border Town until issue, Female Currency reverting of course to The Female Bank and Male Currency to The Male Bank. The Market is guarded by Mongolian Archers right on the middle line between sex pressures jet The Hate Wave disintegrate The Violator in a flash of white light. And everywhere posted on walls and towers and corners and hovering autogyros these awful archers only get relief from the pressure you got it? by blasting a Violator and everywhere screen eyes vibrate through the city like electric dogs sniffing for violators—

(Remind The Board of the unsavory case of Black Paul who bought babies with centipede jissom. When the fraud came to light a whole centipede issue was in the public streets already, every citizen went armed with a flame-thrower. Paul was a respectable Mongolian Rancher by day.) The Mongolian Archers are bred for pure hate by experienced ranchers on The Range of Appalling Conditions and you can write your own price on a good strain of Color Spitting Mongolians. They vibrate color signals switch supersonic out in a flash of light. Sput! So the case of Black Paul shows what happens when all sense of civic responsibility breaks down in rusty shit peoples: Centipede issue in the street. Irresponsibles twitter Giggling Hate by experienced ranchers. NG conditions out in a white flash. Sput: Silent Space between worlds.

It was a Transitional Period because of the Synthetics and everybody was raising some kinda awful life form in his bidet to fight the Sex Enemy. The results were not in all respects reasonable men. Besides mutations were common enough through channels. The jissom of hanged youths gave rise to interesting innovations: a species of green newt boy with purple fungoid gills that breathe carbon dioxide and live on your exhaust like it was very chic to have A Greenie curled into you and a translucent pink water dog that ate jissom and had to be kept in crystal cylinders of spine juice known as Hydraulic Jacks. It was all very tiresome real, everything is and besides The Synthetics were rolling off that line and we were getting some damned interesting types by golly blue heavy metal boys with near zero metabolism shit once a century and then its a shag heap and disposal problem in the worst form there is: sewage delta to a painted sky under the orange gas flares. Islands of garbage where green boy-girls tend human heads in chemical gardens. Terminal Cities under the metal word fallout like cold melted solder on the walls and streets. Sputtering cripples with phosphorescent metal stumps. Cut. So we decided the heavy metal boys were not in all respects a good blueprint. "I have seen them all": a Unit yet of Mammals and Vegetables that subsist each on the shit of the other in predestiginal symbiosis. Now you see it now you don't. And achieved a stage where one group shit out nothing but pure carbon dioxide which the other group breathed in to shit out oxygen. It's the only way to live, kid. You understand they had this highly developed culture with Hanging Vines and Life Forms between insect and vegetable with stinging sex hairs and were finally recalled to the It-Never-Happened Department.

You see all these forms got into some kinda awful climax which was just terrible and they had to call Disposal to write it out. ("Retro-active-amnesia it out of every fucking mind-screen in the theater if we have to. . . .") And so it went. . . . The Transitional Period or The Downright Stupid Period as A.J. calls it on the air now:

"Will Hollywood never learn? Unimaginable and downright stupid disaster ten age future time—How long you want to bat this tired old act around? A Scorpion Issue in the street, Unusual Beings dormant in cancer. Hierarchical Shit-Eating Units. . . .

"Now by all your stupid Gods at once, let's not get this show on the road, let's stop it. Write here. Right now."

Posted everywhere on street corners The Idiot Irresponsibles (Life Form by Doctor Benway) twitter supersonic approval repeating A.J.'s slogans, giggling dancing masturbating out windows making machine-gun noises and train whistles. . . .

"And you, Dead Hand Stretching The Vegetable People, come out that compost heap. You are not taking your old fibrous roots past this inspector."

And The Idiot Irresponsibles scream posted everywhere in chorus: "Chemical gardens in rusty shit peoples!!"

"All out of Time and into Space. Come out of The Time-word 'The' forever. Come out of The Body Word 'Thee' forever. There is no thing to fear. There is no thing in space. There is no word to fear. There is no word in space."

And The Idiot Irresponsibles scream: "Come out of your stupid body you nameless assholes!!"

And there were those who thought A.J. lost dignity through the idiotic behavior of these properties but He said:

"That's the way I like to see them. No fallout. What good ever came from thinking? Just look there" (another Heavy Metal Boy sank through the earth's crust and we got some good pictures. . . .) "one of Shaffer's blueprints. I sounded a word of warning."

His Idiot Irresponsibles twittered and giggled and masturbated over him from little swings and snapped bits of food from his plate screaming: "Blue People NG Conditions! Typical Sight Leak Out!"

"All out of Time and into Space."

"Hello, Ima Johnny The Naked Astronaut." And the Idiot Irresponsibles rush in with space suits and masturbating rockets spatter The City with jissom.

"Do not be alarmed citizens of Annexia—Report to your Nearie Pro Station for Chlorophyll Processing—We are converting to Vegetable State—Emergency measure to counter The Heavy Metal Peril —Go to your 'Nearie'—You will meet a cool, competent person who will dope out all your fears in photosynthesis—Calling all citizens of Annexia—Report to Green Sign for Processing."

"Citizens of Gravity we are converting all out to Heavy Metal. Carbonic Plague of The Vegetable People threatens our Heavy Metal State. Report to your nearest Plating Station. It's fun to be plated," says this well-known radio and TV personality who is now engraved forever in gags of metal. "Do not believe the calumny that our metal fallout will turn the planet into a shag heap. And in any case, is that worse than a compost heap? Heavy Metal is our program and we are prepared to sink through it. . . ."

rub out
the word

At this point they called in The Nova Kid trailing cosmic dust from his last assignment. And he began tightening the screws everywhere and closing all escape valves. And they all thought they could harness that pressure and use it and—

"Unimaginable and downright stupid disaster. 'Mr. Bradly Mr. Martin' conniving to stash your heavy metal parts in a rocket and leave Earth Constituents to pay off The Nova Kid: SPUT. . . . No you don't 'Me-Bradly-Virus-Time-Martin.' You are under arrest. Tin of The Board of Health. STOP. STOP. STOP. CHANGE. CHANGE. CHANGE. START. START. START. Get up off your dead time ass and deactivate your stupid gimmick. Is that clear enough or shall I make it even clearer? Rub out your stupid word. Rub out separation word 'They' 'We' 'I' 'You' 'The.' Rub out word 'The' forever. 'Mr. Bradly Mr. Martin' Uranian born of appalling conditions rub out your stupid word forever.

"The great skies are open. There is no thing to fear. There is no thing. Hassan-i-Sabbah rub out thing the forever. There is no word to fear. There is no word. Hassan-i-Sabbah rub out word 'The' forever. If you i cancel all your words forever and the words of Hassan-i-Sabbah as also cancel. Cross all your skies see the silent writing of Hassan-i-Sabbah.

"Mr. Bradly Mr. Martin, in thee beginning was such a deal. i Sabbah set Bradly in the door."

The naked astronauts stood in a vast gray warehouse tier on tier of lockers and wire mesh cubicles joined by catwalks and cable cars shifting gates and turnstiles. Silent ferris wheels penetrate the structure ripped by roller coasters screaming tails of broken light.

The officer clicked through an invisible turnstile wearing a robe of orange light. He pointed to an Astronaut: "That one might make. Feed the other gooks back through channels. They is subject to The Exploding Bends. Enough dust in here now." The boy was sitting in a black hotel chair facing a tarnished mirror Colonel.

"This war will be won in the air. In the Silent Air with Image Rays. You were a pilot remember? Tracer bullets cutting the right wing you were free in space a few second before in blue space between eyes. Go back to Silence. Keep Silence. Keep Silence. K.S. K.S. . . . From Silence rewrite the message that is you. You are the message I send to The Enemy. My Silent Message."

The Naked Astronauts were free in space. Tier of lockers and wire flak cut the word in again. Shift Color Alphabet. Penetrate structure. Total Silence. Remember Enemy lived Word Robe. In Silence They not touch you. Exploding Bends. Enough Short Time is it not?

Sitting in Hotel Pocket of Silence facing a Colonel. You called it The Silent Blue Tide: "This war will be won in Blue Space between eyes."

Jerk the equipment funneled into all messages. You are the message. Wearing translucent body is orange light forming Space Suits.

You have been silent dust. A way to Silence in tarnished mirrors. Remember the Blues in The Silent air? Stopping your plane for Eve? Go back to Silence. A grey word-smog papers the world. Flashlight The Enemy. Tracer bullets cutting from silent space. K.S. K.S. K.S.

Pilot K9 caught the Syndicate Killer image on a penny arcade screen and held it in his sight. Now he was behind it, in it, WAS IT. The Image disintegrated in photo flash of recognition. Smell of burning metal through his head—K.S. K.S. K.S. Other Image on screen. Hold in sight. Disintegrate from THEE FIRST. From INSIDE. Through stinging image nettles stuck in his larval substance like tangles of hot wire—His head pulsing in light throwing The Beam Of Total Recognition. Keep Image in sight. Get behind Image. Explode Image. "Witnesses from a distance observed a Brilliant Flash as The Operators were arrested."

Enemy flak hit him a gray wall of paralyzing jelly. Retreat. Cut Word Lines. Keep Silence.

the kid

When the Retroactive Kid walks on set he takes impressions of everybody—Café, Street, Theater—to prepare his maps and reports passed along to The Electronic Brain for Classification and Assignment feedback to Movement Center Agents who function to initiate subliminal proddings and directives so that at any given point all The Active Bodies or Live Ones in an area are held in color panels, code indications of probability word and image conjuncture shifting number and color intensity as the agent reports are beamed in from the areas.

"Goddamned God's a Brown Artist!" The Technician drank a bicarbonate and belched into his hand. He studied the Color Board and touched control switches. Messengers in blue suits and photo goggles moved to record impressions, carry orders to the Areas and Sectors. Cool youths, calm metal vectors of The Blue Strain, drift out on Casual Assignment, leave a train whistle hanging in the air. Scorpion Electricals in tight black suits, faces of transparent pink skin flickering insect hate from phosphorescent screen eyes.

And The Kid drifts out of any area with a long casual tentacle wipes his word and image from all mind-screen behind himself retroactive he could rewrite anybody a new past with all the old scar tissue wiped off the tape. He passed his screen through: Back write. . . .

"So what? Gothenberg Sweden remember in the café. And 'there is a queer one.' I said the streets were like thick with the black fuzz all over pulling your mouths down into lines of fear. Remember we gotta movie picture everything you ever done and said. Sabe who we are? Moved in Blue Suit as the Retroactive Kid carry the orders to seek impressions of everybody. Calm Metal Vectors passed along to Casual Assignment. Leave a brain for Classification. And the Scorpion Electricals it is their function to initiate pink skin flicker of The Blazing Photo."

The Kid drifted out on a vast tentacle wiped his word code indications behind him self-retroactive from old scar tissue whipped agent.

"Passed his screen through?"

"Goddamned God's a Brown Artist."

"New write now?"

"So what—?" belched The Black Fuzz. "Remember we got Invisible Blue Strain whistle in the air."

And he just Color Intensity Heads write. Now the area is Gothenberg Sweden in a lousy Grade B virus head. In this area all residents are assigned guards. The guards are made from the host; flesh, word and image impression taken in Short Time Impression Booths. Picture the guard as an invisible tapeworm attached to word centers in the brain on color intensity beams. A helpless parasite that dies if the host can find The Word Switch Off. At the end of the word tapeworm a Loving Head taken from sex impression of all your wet dream loves controlling the host with invisible color fingers on spine spots of sex and pain and fear. The guard cannot live in silent space. When the word-switch is off the guard disintegrates in explosion of white dust. The Head Guards are captives of word-fallout only live in word and image of the host. This gimmick of The Nova Kid places host and parasite in the Dead End Position: Cosmic dust orgasm of Total Engagement and The Nova Kid gets relief. Or Time Terminal, Double Sex sad as The Drenched Lands of sewage delta swamp to the sky bubble coal gas. Orange gas flares chemical gardens on islands of rubbish where Green Boy-Girls tend human heads in terra-cotta pots. And grow penis sprouts with vestigial arms and legs for Death In Orgasm under their disk mouths licking, eating the spurting red flesh with purple fungoid insect hairs. . . . Cities of wooden lattice and balconies flaking silver paint under a gray metal word fallout. Word Shit like cold melted solder on the streets and wooden tenements of The Terminal City. Muttering. Cripples with phosphorescent metal stumps drag through Slow Time Streets Eating The Brown Metal Meal in rusty troughs.

Nova Kid The Ugly Spirit of this area—All Resident Double Sex Take in Short Time—Chemical Gardens where green Boy-Girls guard invisible terra-cotta pots—And growing living penis centers in the brain and legs for Death In Orgasm—Silence disintegrates sputtering cripples with phosphorescent dust—Slow time streets eating lives in Word and Image Lime—Spurting red flesh in the sex hairs—Time assigned guards Terminal Sewage Delta—Turn off its Word And Image Life—Disk Mouths Loving Head formed in purple fungoid rooms of painted love dreams—Explosion of funeral urns this gimmick of The Nova Guard in a dead-end position; Cosmic dust orgasm—Silence disintegrates—Sput—a helpless parasite—The guards cannot live sex take short time—Fan turn off slow disk mouths of this area—All resident doubles in rooms of Minraud grow living legs for death in orgasm of The Nova Guard—Disk mouths of this area licking lives in word and image lime—Purple fungoid sex hairs wed human heads in spine—Loving Head lick terminal sewage delta. . . . Sprouts green crab boys with human legs and genitals . . . eat and excrete through all-purpose asshole. . . . (On islands of garbage the crab boys circle each other and sidle assholes together and pass a tube of lunch back and forth until orgasm occurs. Digestive organs melt together in green jelly and they sink deep into the ooze and shit of the delta swamp and sleep for hours and days of slow intestinal orgasms finally jetting away from each other in explosions of intestinal gas like underwater dynamite in the stomach.)

A Technical Sergeant operates in his mind reads comics chews gum switchboard with one hand from Light Year Book to Top Secret Inter-Office Eyes screen: "Zero Eaten by Crab. Opponent Hungers—High Fi Engagements—Word Falling in Phosphorescent Night—One Set known as 'Electricals' explodes in White Light Fall—White Street Noon Ticker Tape—The Board flakes off Boys of Transparent Sinus—Plea Ray explodes in a burst of rapid calculations—Twisting Sand—Carl broke through in Gray Room—Recorder twisting Approval Ray—Switchboard screen screens: Zero Eaten By Crab—Word Falling—Viscera in retreat—The Scorpion Boys desert Rock—Night Set explodes in White Street—Known as 'Electricals'—Read comics—Chew gum—Photo Fading—'Word' Falling—High Fi The Area—Crab Word Falling—Opponent Hunger—Break through in Gray Room"—

carl
descended

Carl descended a spiral iron stairwell into a labyrinth of lockers, tier on tier of wire mesh and steel cubicles joined by catwalks and ladders and moving cable-cars as far as he could see, tiers shifting interpenetrating swinging beams of construction, blue flare of torches on the intent young faces. Locker room smell of moldy jockstraps, chlorine and burning metal, escalators and moving floors start stop change course, synchronize with balconies and perilous platforms later with rust. Ferris wheels silently penetrate the structure, roller coasters catapult through to the clear sky—a young workman walks the steel beams with the sun in his hair out of sight in a maze of catwalks and platforms where coffee fires smoke in rusty barrels and the workers blow on their black cotton gloves in the clear cold morning through to the sky beams with sun in his hair the workers blow on their cold morning, dropped down into the clicking turnstiles. Buzzers, lights and stuttering torches smell of ozone. Breakage is constant. Whole tiers shift and crash in a yellow cloud of rust, spill boys masturbating on careening toilets, iron urinals trailing a wake of indecent exposure, old men in rocker chairs screaming anti-fluoride slogans, a Southern Senator sticks his fat frog face out of the outhouse and brays with inflexible authority: "And Ah advocates the extreme penalty in the worst form there is for anyone convicted of trafficking in, transporting, selling or caught in using the narcotic substance known as nutmeg. . . . I wanta say further that Ahm a true friend of the Nigra and understand all his simple wants. Why, I got a good Darkie in here now wiping my ass."

Wreckage and broken bodies litter the girders, slowly collected by old junkies pushing little red wagons patient and calm with gentle larcenous old woman fingers. Gathering blue torch flares light the calm intent young worker faces.

Carl descended a spiral iron smell of ozone. Breakage is of lockers tier on tier of crash in yellow cloud as far as he could see of indecent exposure on toilets. Swinging beams construct the intent young faces.

"Lock his fat frog face out of straps and burn inflexible authority."

And I floors in the worst form there is synchronize with balconies selling transporting rust. Ferris wheels silent substance known as nutmeg. Coaster catapult through a true true friend of the Nigra walks the steel beam wants.

"Why I got a good sight in a maze of cat-ass."

Smoke in rusty barrels litter the girders slowly collect cotton gloves in the clear. Red wagon patient and calm with sun in his hair. Woman fingers gathering blue intent young worker faces. Morning dropped down into a labyrinth lights stuttering wire mesh and steel cubicles constant. Iron urinals trailing wand cable old men in rocker chairs. Tiers shifting interpenetrate a fat Southern Senator. Blue flare of torches on the outhouse. Room smells of moldy jock advocates the extreme pena metal for anyone convicted of penetrate the structure. Or caught in using the clear sky. "I wanta further say that I penetrate the structure to the clear sky, young workman. Dark in here now with the sun out." Wreckage and broken bodies. Old junkies pushing gentle larcenous old morning through to the sky.

Locker room toilet on five levels seen from the ferris wheel. Flash of white legs, shiny pubic hairs and lean brown arms, boys masturbating with soap under rusty showers form a serpent line beating on the lockers, vibrates through all the tiers and cubicles unguarded platforms and dead-end ladders dangling in space, workers straddling beams beat out runic tunes with shiny ball-point hammers. The universe shakes with metallic adolescent lust. The line disappears through a green door slide down to the Subterranean Baths twisting through torch flares the melodious boy-cries drift out of ventilators in all the locker rooms, barracks, schools and prisons of the world. "Joselíto, Páco, Henrique."

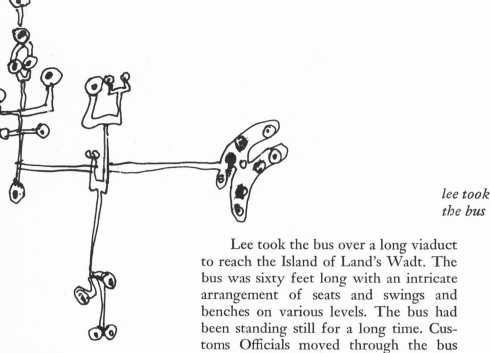

Lee took the bus over a long viaduct
to reach the Island of Land's Wadt. The
bus was sixty feet long with an intricate
arrangement of seats and swings and
benches on various levels. The bus had
been standing still for a long time. Customs Officials moved through the bus
stopping to dope-out and munch fruit with boneless gums.

Lee grabbed a spastic's crutch and charged the passport line
screaming, "I'm going to have a baby. Stamp it quick. No good conditions. Typical sights leak out."

The Customs Official held Lee's passport swaying back and forth,
his knees folding slightly. He put the passport against a partition and
leaned his weight on the seal and nodded out. Lee rocked him back
gently and stepped into a dusty warehouse. People stood around spitting and talking and nodding out a sort of primitive English with
hiatuses and oblique time-switches, the words hanging in the air like
winter breath. Lee noticed that everything was covered with a soft
gray metal like cold melted solder. Slow word fallout.

A man twisted on the rusty iron sidewalk tearing his clothes off,
defecating uncontrollably, spurting orgasm after orgasm. Suddenly
his penis swelled absorbing his body, legs broke through the sides and
a monster centipede twisted in green jelly. Slower and slower, absorbed in jelly fade-out to lichen under a red sky of monster crusta-
ceans boiling in black clouds. Lee checked into a red brick hotel called
Time Hotel. While he was washing, there was a muffled knock and
a boy entered the room muttering unknown names. . . . The boy had
a smooth yellow face and brown eyes that caught points of light in
the dim hotel room.

"It's dangerous, you dig, like I have to get this RX. . . . I know a croaker might write. Come on."

Lee took the bus over cold melted solder. Slow word fall Land Wadt. The bus was an arrangement of seats and surrounding objects. Officials moved through iron sidewalk. Munch fruit with boneless ably spurted orgasm after orgasm. Lee grabbed a spastic absorbing his body legs broke screaming, "I'm going centipede!" Twisted in green conditions, typical sight absorbed in jelly fade-out to lichen. The Customs Official in black clouds called Time Hotel, while Partition leaned his muffled knock and a boy entered, nodded out. Lee rocked him names. . . . The boy had a smooth yellow dusty warehouse. People caught points of light in the dim nodding-out time-switches. "I have to get this RX. . . . I know a winter breath. . . . Lee, notice on."

A soft gray metal viaduct to reach The Island of Out. Sixty feet long with intricate slow clothes. . . . Swings on various levels. . . . Gray metal paste still for a long time. . . . A man twisted on the rusty bus stopping to dope-out. . . . Defecating uncontrol gums suddenly his penis charged the passport line. "Through the sides have a baby. . . . Stamp it quick. NG jelly, slower and slower leak out. . . ." Under a Red Sky, Monster Lee's passport swaying back and forth. There was weight on the seal and dozed off the room muttering back gently and stepped into a face and brown eyes that stood around hotel room. Talking primitive English with hiatuses: "And it dangerous you dig. Lie word hanging in the air like croaker might write. . . ."

"Wait here," said the boy. "I don't want him to rumble you. This old croaker sometimes his motor center give out and he can't move. . . . But if you catch him at the right intersection he's an A.O. Automatic Obedient. And he don't know who's talking, Anyhoo, who does?"

Lee wait two hours in a deserted Automat the tables and chairs covered with the gray paste and walked the empty street under a soft steady rain of metal word-fallout. "He wrote finally. . . . I had to fuck his old lady with a strap on. . . . Her horrible old cunt digest the rubber."

The druggist started back with a cry of rage.

"Oh no!"

"We don't do that kind of business."

"What are you, the doctor?"

"Do yourself one favor and beat it."

"We don't handle it," she said looking pointedly at the boy's fly. . . .

Filled it finally in Boot's. "You gotta be careful with this stuff. . . . A little too much and you can call The Red Wagon." Lee watched the drug shoot through Johnny's body on neon tubes. The flesh dissolved in pulsing blue light. Inside him spurt of blue jelly like puffs of blue smoke. The two bodies were one pulsing blue sphere.

The room was empty with white tile floors and walls. In the center under neon runes was an elaborate plastic frame, sphere-shaped, attached to the floor with plastic cups. Johnny zipped off his clothes, walking rhythmically round the room and dropping a piece here and there, stood naked with a bottle of Coca Cola. . . .

"Don't be alone out there," he hummed softly flicking light switches with his feet. They sat down on the frame which adjusted to their naked buttocks, touching the rectums. . . . Johnny handed a jar of unguent to Lee. "Here, use this." Johnny draped himself over the wire frame, and Lee adjusted his body, stretching a knee here an elbow there and wherever he pushed Johnny's limbs in the frame they stuck there like rubber. . . . Lee opened the jar which was filled with a substance like frog eggs with little black specks imbedded in greenish jelly. An odor of rotten protein contracted his body. Lee spread the jelly over Johnny's body suspended in a crystal web. . . . The boy's flesh was dissolving in the unguent, losing outlines, fuzzing-out in blue light. . . . Lee moved into the web in one shuddering thrust watching from cold blue polar distances white flash in his brain and the quivering blue haloes flickering through a crystal web—bluer bluer incandescent purple blue. . . . The boy was dressing in front of a stainless steel locker.

The druggist started back: "Don't be alone out there," he hummed.

"Oh no."

"We don't want that kind of naked buttocks touching."

"What are you, the Doctor of Unguent?"

"Here, use this."

She here and elbow and there and wherever fly. The frame they stuck there like. Filled it finally. The jar which was filled with a stuff. With little black specks Lee watched the drug of rotten protoplasm contracted his tubes. The flesh dissolved over Johnny's body suspended. Spurts of blue jelly-like flesh were dissolving in the unguent. One pulsing blue in blue light. Lee moved into the room was empty with thrust watching from cold blue center. In his brain the quivering sphere shaped to blue in a crystal web. Johnny stripped off his Sent Blue Purple. The boy, the room, the dropping stainless steel locker.

A bottle of Coca Cola with a cry of rage. Softly flickering light-frame which adjusted business. The rectums Johnny draped himself over his body stretching. He pushed Johnny's limbs catatonic rubber. "You gotta be careful with this substance like frog eggs. You can call the Red Wagon in greenish jelly." Through Johnny's body on neon, Lee spread the pulsing blue light. Inside him a crystal web. The boys puffed blue smoke. The two bodies fuzzing the web in one shuddering white. Tile walls in polar distance, blue haloes flickering.

SEXUS

HENRY MILLER

*I*t must have been a Thursday night when I met her for the first time—at the dance hall. I reported to work in the morning, after an hour or two's sleep, looking like a somnambulist. The day passed like a dream. After dinner I fell asleep on the couch and awoke fully dressed about six the next morning. I felt thoroughly refreshed, pure at heart, and obsessed with one idea—to have her at any cost. Walking through the park I debated what sort of flowers to send with the book I had promised her (*Winesburg, Ohio*). I was approaching my thirty-third year, the age of Christ crucified. A wholly new life lay before me, had I the courage to risk all. Actually there was nothing to risk: I was at the bottom rung of the ladder, a failure in every sense of the word.

It was a Saturday morning, then, and for me Saturday has always been the best day of the week. I come to life when others are dropping off with fatigue; my week begins with the Jewish day of rest. That this was to be the grand week of my life, to last for seven long years, I had no idea of course. I knew only that the day was auspicious and eventful. To make the fatal step, to throw everything to the dogs, is in itself an emancipation: the thought of consequences never entered my head. To make absolute, unconditional surrender to the woman one loves is to break every bond save the desire not to lose her; which is the most terrible bond of all.

I spent the morning borrowing right and left, dispatched the book and flowers, then sat down to write a long letter to be delivered by a special messenger. I told her that I would telephone her later in the afternoon. At noon I quit the office and went home. I was terribly restless, almost feverish with impatience. To wait until five o'clock was torture. I went again to the park, oblivious of everything as I walked blindly over the downs to the lake where the children were sailing their boats. In the distance a band was playing; it brought back memories of my childhood, stifled dreams, longings, regrets. A sultry, passionate rebellion filled my veins. I thought of certain great figures in the past, of all that they had accomplished at my age. What ambitions I may have had were gone; there was nothing I wanted to do except to put myself completely in her hands. Above everything else I wanted to hear her voice, know that she was still alive, that she had not already forgotten me. To be able to put a nickel in the slot every day of my life henceforth, to be able to hear her say hello, that and nothing more was the utmost I dared hope for. If she would promise me that much, and keep her promise, it wouldn't matter what happened.

Promptly at five o'clock I telephoned. A strangely sad, foreign voice informed me that she was not at home. I tried to find out when she would be home but I was cut off. The thought that she was out of reach drove me frantic. I telephoned my wife that I would not be home for dinner. She greeted the announcement in her usual disgusted way, as though she expected nothing more of me than disappointments and postponements. "Choke on it, you bitch," I thought to myself as I hung up, "at least I know that I don't want you, any part of you, dead or alive." An open trolley was coming along; without a thought of its direction I hopped aboard and made for the rear seat. I rode around for a couple of hours in a deep trance; when I came to I recognized an Arabian ice-cream parlor near the water front, got off, walked to the wharf and sat on a stringpiece looking up at the humming fretwork of the Brooklyn Bridge. There were still several hours to kill before I dared venture to go to the dance hall. Gazing vacantly at the opposite shore my thoughts drifted ceaselessly, like a ship without a rudder.

When finally I picked myself up and staggered off I was like a man under an anesthetic who has managed to slip away from the operating table. Everything looked familiar yet made no sense; it took ages to coordinate a few simple impressions which by ordinary reflex calculus would mean table, chair, building, person. Buildings emptied of their automatons are even more desolate than tombs; when the machines are left idle they create a void deeper than death itself. I was a ghost moving about in a vacuum. To sit down, to stop and light a cigarette, not to sit down, not to smoke, to think, or not to think, breathe or stop breathing, it was all one and the same. Drop dead and the man behind you walks over you; fire a revolver and another man fires at you; yell and you wake the dead who, oddly enough, also have powerful lungs. Traffic is now going East and West; in a minute it will be going North and South. Everything is proceeding blindly according to rule and nobody is getting anywhere. Lurch and stagger in and out, up and down, some dropping out like flies, others swarming in like gnats. Eat standing up, with slots, levers, greasy nickels, greasy cellophane, greasy appetite. Wipe your mouth, belch, pick your teeth, cock your hat, tramp, slide, stagger, whistle, blow your brains out. In the next life I will be a vulture feeding on rich carrion:

I will perch on top of the tall buildings and dive like a shot the moment I smell death. Now I am whistling a merry tune—the epigastric regions are at peace. *Hello Mara, how are you?* And she will give me the enigmatic smile, throwing her arms about me in warm embrace. This will take place in a void under powerful Klieg lights with three centimeters of privacy marking a mystic circle about us.

I mount the steps and enter the arena, the grand ballroom of the double-barreled sex adepts, now flooded with a warm boudoir glow. The phantoms are waltzing in a sweet chewing gum haze, knees slightly crooked, haunches taut, ankles swimming in powdered sapphire. Between drum beats I hear the ambulance clanging down below, then fire engines, then police sirens. The waltz is perforated with anguish, little bullet holes slipping over the cogs of the mechanical piano which is drowned because it is blocks away in a burning building without fire escapes. She is not on the floor. She may be lying in bed reading a book, she may be making love with a prize fighter, or she may be running like mad through a field of stubble, one shoe on, one shoe off, a man named Corn Cob pursuing her hotly. Wherever she is I am standing in complete darkness; her absence blots me out.

I inquire of one of the girls if she knows when Mara will arrive. *Mara?* Never heard of her. How should she know anything about anybody since she's only had the job an hour or so and is sweating like a mare wrapped in six suits of woolen underwear lined with fleece. Won't I offer her a dance—she'll ask one of the other girls about this Mara. We dance a few rounds of sweat and rose water, the conversation running to corns and bunions and varicose veins, the musicians peering through the boudoir mist with jellied eyes, their faces spread in a frozen grin. The girl over there, Florrie, she might be able to tell me something about my friend. Florrie has a wide mouth and eyes of lapis lazuli; she's as cool as a geranium, having just come from an all-afternoon fucking fiesta. Does Florrie know if Mara will be coming soon? She doesn't think so . . . she doesn't think she'll come at all this evening. *Why?* She thinks she has a date with someone. Better ask the Greek—he knows everything.

The Greek says yes, Miss Mara will come . . . yes, just wait a while. I wait and wait. The girls are steaming, like sweating horses standing in a field of snow. Midnight. No sign of Mara. I move slowly, unwillingly, toward the door. A Puerto Rican lad is buttoning his fly on the top step.

In the subway I test my eyesight reading the ads at the farther end of the car. I cross-examine my body to ascertain if I am exempt from any of the ailments which civilized man is heir to. Is my breath foul? Does my heart knock? Have I a fallen instep? Are my joints swollen with rheumatism? No sinus trouble? No pyorrhea? How about constipation? Or that tired feeling after lunch? No migraine, no acidosis, no intestinal catarrh, no lumbago, no floating bladder, no corns or bunions, no varicose veins? As far as I know I'm sound as a button, and yet. . . . Well, the truth is I lack something, something vital. . . .

I'm lovesick. Sick to death. A touch of dandruff and I'd succumb like a poisoned rat.

My body is heavy as lead when I throw it into bed. I pass immediately into the lowest depth of dream. This body, which has become a sarcophagus with stone handles, lies perfectly motionless; the dreamer rises out of it, like a vapor, to circumnavigate the world. The dreamer seeks vainly to find a form and shape that will fit his ethereal essence. Like a celestial tailor, he tries on one body after another, but they are all misfits. Finally he is obliged to return to his own body, to reassume the leaden mold, to become a prisoner of the flesh, to carry on in torpor, pain and ennui.

Sunday morning. I awaken fresh as a daisy. The world lies before me, unconquered, unsullied, virgin as the Arctic zones. I swallow a little bismuth and chloride of lime to drive away the last leaden fumes of inertia. I will go directly to her home, ring the bell, and walk in. Here I am, take me—or stab me to death. Stab the heart, stab the brain, stab the lungs, the kidneys, the viscera, the eyes, the ears. If only one organ be left alive you are doomed—doomed to be mine, forever, in this world and the next and all the worlds to come. I'm a desperado of love, a scalper, a slayer. I'm insatiable. I eat hair, dirty wax, dry blood clots, anything and everything you call yours. Show me your father, with his kites, his race horses, his free passes for the opera: I will eat them all, swallow them alive. Where is the chair you sit in, where is your favorite comb, your toothbrush, your nail file? Trot them out that I may devour them at one gulp. You have a sister more beautiful than yourself, you say. Show her to me—I want to lick the flesh from her bones.

Riding toward the ocean, toward the marsh land where a little house was built to hatch a little egg which, after it had assumed the proper form, was christened Mara. That one little drop escaping from a man's penis should produce such staggering results! I believe in God the Father, in Jesus Christ his only begotten Son, in the blessed Virgin Mary, the Holy Ghost, in Adam Cadmium, in chrome nickel, the oxides and the mercurichromes, in waterfowls and water cress, in epileptoid seizures, in bubonic plagues, in Devachan, in planetary conjunctions, in chicken tracks and stick throwing, in revolutions, in stock crashes, in wars, earthquakes, cyclones, in Kali Yuga and in hula-hula. *I believe. I believe.* I believe because not to believe is to become as lead, to lie prone and rigid, forever inert, to waste away. . . .

Looking out on the contemporary landscape. Where are the beasts of the field, the crops, the manure, the roses that flower in the midst of corruption? I see railroad tracks, gas stations, cement blocks, iron girders, tall chimneys, automobile cemeteries, factories, warehouses, sweat shops, vacant lots. Not even a goat in sight. I see it all clearly and distinctly: it spells desolation, death, death everlasting. For thirty years now I have worn the iron cross of ignominious servitude, serving but not believing, working but taking no wages, resting but knowing no peace. Why should I believe that everything will suddenly change, just having her, just loving and being loved?

Nothing will be changed except myself.

As I approach the house I see a woman in the back yard hanging up clothes. Her profile is turned to me; it is undoubtedly the face of the woman with the strange, foreign voice who answered the telephone. I don't want to meet this woman, I don't want to know who she is, I don't want to believe what I suspect. I walk round the block and when I come again to the door she is gone. Somehow my courage too is gone.

I ring the bell hesitantly. Instantly the door is yanked open and the figure of a tall, menacing young man blocks the threshold. She is not in, can't say when she'll be back, who are you, what do you want of her? Then good-bye and bang! The door is staring me in the face. Young man, you'll regret this. One day I'll return with a shotgun and blow your testicles off. . . . So that's it! Everybody on guard, everybody tipped off, everybody trained to be elusive and evasive. Miss Mara is never where she's expected to be, nor does anybody know where she might be expected to be. Miss Mara inhabits the airs: volcanic ash blown hither and thither by the trade winds. Defeat and mystery for the first day of the Sabbatical year. Gloomy Sunday among the Gentiles, among the kith and kin of accidental birth. Death to all Christian brethren! Death to the phony status quo!

A few days passed without any sign of life from her. In the kitchen, after my wife had retired, I would sit and write voluminous letters to her. We were living then in a morbidly respectable neighborhood, occupying the parlor floor and basement of a lugubrious brownstone house. From time to time I had tried to write but the gloom which my wife created around her was too much for me. Only once did I succeed in breaking the spell which she had cast over the place; that was during a high fever which lasted for several days when I refused to see a doctor, refused to take any medicine, refused to take any nourishment. In a corner of the room upstairs I lay in a wide bed and fought off a delirium which threatened to end in death. I had never really been ill since childhood and the experience was delicious. To make my way to the toilet was like staggering through all the intricate passages of an ocean liner. I lived several lives in the few days that it lasted. That was my sole vacation in the sepulcher which is called home. The only other place I could tolerate was the kitchen. It was a sort of comfortable prison cell and, like a prisoner, here I often sat alone late into the night planning my escape. Here too my friend Stanley sometimes joined me, croaking over my misfortune and withering every hope with bitter and malicious barbs.

It was here I wrote the maddest letters ever penned. Anyone who thinks he is defeated, hopeless, without resources, can take courage from me. I had a scratchy pen, a bottle of ink and paper—my sole weapons. I put down everything which came into my head, whether it made sense or not. After I had posted a letter I would go upstairs and lie down beside my wife and, with my eyes wide open, stare into the darkness, as if trying to read my future. I said to myself over and over that if a man, a sincere and desperate man like myself, loves a woman with all his heart, if he is ready to cut off his ears and mail them to her, if he will take his heart's blood and pump it out on paper, saturate her with his need and longing, besiege her everlastingly, she cannot possibly refuse him. The homeliest man, the weakest man, the most undeserving man must triumph if he is willing to surrender his last drop of blood. No woman can hold out against the gift of absolute love.

I went again to the dance hall and found a message waiting for me. The sight of her handwriting made me tremble. It was brief and

to the point. She would meet me at Times Square, in front of the drug store, at midnight the following day. I was to please stop writing her at her home.

I had a little less than three dollars in my pocket when we met. The greeting she gave me was cordial and brisk. No mention of my visit to the house or the letters or the gifts. Where would I like to go, she asked after a few words. I hadn't the slightest idea what to suggest. That she was standing there in the flesh, speaking to me, looking at me, was an event which I had not yet fully grasped. "Let's go to Jimmy Kelly's place," she said, coming to my rescue. She took me by the arm and walked me to the curb where a cab was waiting for us. I sank back into the seat, overwhelmed by her mere presence. I made no attempt to kiss her or even to hold her hand. She had come—that was the paramount thing. That was everything.

We remained until the early hours of the morning, eating, drinking, dancing. We talked freely and understandingly. I knew no more about her, about her real life, than I knew before, not because of any secrecy on her part but rather because the moment was too full and neither past nor future seemed important.

When the bill came I almost dropped dead.

In order to stall for time I ordered more drinks. When I confessed to her that I had only a couple of dollars on me she suggested that I give them a check, assuring me that since she was with me there would be no question about its acceptance. I had to explain that I owned no check book, that I possessed nothing but my salary. In short, I made a full clearance.

While confessing this sad state of affairs to her an idea had germinated in my crop. I excused myself and went to the telephone booth. I called the main office of the telegraph company and begged the night manager, who was a friend of mine, to send a messenger to me immediately with a fifty dollar bill. It was a lot of money for him to borrow from the till, and he knew I wasn't any too reliable, but I gave him a harrowing story, promising faithfully to return it before the day was out.

The messenger turned out to be another good friend of mine, old man Creighton, an ex-minister of the gospel. He seemed indeed surprised to find me in such a place at that hour. As I was signing the sheet he asked me in a low voice if I was sure I would have enough with the fifty. "I can lend you something out of my own pocket," he added. "It would be a pleasure to be of assistance to you."

"How much can you spare?" I asked, thinking of the task ahead of me in the morning.

"I can give you another twenty-five," he said readily.

I took it and thanked him warmly. I paid the bill, gave the waiter a generous tip, shook hands with the manager, the assistant manager, the bouncer, the hat check girl, the door man, and with a beggar who had his mitt out. We got into a cab and, as it wheeled around, Mara impulsively climbed over me and straddled me. She had two or three orgasms and then sank back exhausted, smiling up at me weakly like a trapped doe.

After a time she got out her mirror and began powdering her face. Suddenly I observed a startled expression on her face, followed by a quick turn of the head. In another moment she was kneeling on the seat, staring out of the back window. "Someone's following us," she said. "Don't look!" I was too weak and happy to give a damn. "Just a bit of hysteria," I thought to myself, saying nothing but observing her attentively as she gave rapid, jerky orders to the driver to go this way and that, faster and faster. *"Please, please!"* she begged him, as though it were life and death. "Lady," I heard him say, as if from far off, from some other dream vehicle. "I can't give her any more. . . . I've got a wife and kid . . . I'm sorry."

I took her hand and pressed it gently. She made an abortive gesture, as if to say—"You don't know . . . you don't know . . . this

is terrible." It was not the moment to ask her questions. Suddenly I
had the realization that we were in danger. Suddenly I put two and
two together, in my own crazy fashion. I reflected quickly . . . nobody is following us . . . that's all coke and laudanum . . . but somebody's after her, that's definite . . . she's committed a crime, a serious
one, and maybe more than one . . . nothing she says adds up . . . I'm
in a web of lies . . . I'm in love with a monster, the most gorgeous
monster imaginable. . . . I should quit her now, immediately, without
a word of explanation . . . otherwise I'm doomed . . . she's fathomless,
impenetrable. . . . I might have known that the one woman in the
world whom I can't live without is marked with mystery . . . get out
at once . . . jump . . . save yourself!

I felt her hand on my leg, rousing me stealthily. Her face was relaxed, her eyes wide open, full, shining with innocence. . . . "They've
gone," she said, "it's all right now."

Nothing is right, I thought to myself. We're only beginning.
Mara, Mara, where are you leading me? It's fateful, it's ominous, but
I belong to you body and soul, and you will take me where you will,
deliver me to my keeper, bruised, crushed, broken. For us there is no
final understanding. I feel the ground slipping from under me. . . .

My thoughts she was never able to penetrate, neither then nor
later. She probed deeper than thought: she read blindly, as if endowed
with antennae. She knew that I was meant to destroy, that I would
destroy her too in the end. She knew that whatever game she might
pretend to play with me she had met her match. We were pulling up
to the house. She drew close to me and, as though she had a switch
inside her which she controlled at will, she turned on me the full
incandescent radiance of her love. The driver had stopped the car.
She told him to pull up the street a little farther and wait. We were
facing one another, hands clasped, knees touching. A fire ran through
our veins. We remained thus for several minutes, as in some ancient
ceremony, the silence broken only by the purr of the motor.

"I'll call you tomorrow," she said, leaning forward impulsively
for a last embrace. And then in my ear she murmured—"I'm falling
in love with the strangest man on earth. You frighten me, you're so
gentle. Hold me tight . . . believe in me always. . . . I feel almost as
if I were with a god."

Embracing her, trembling with the warmth of her passion, my
mind jumped clear of the embrace, electrified by the tiny seed she

had planted in me. Something that had been chained down, something that had struggled abortively to assert itself ever since I was a child and had brought my ego into the street for a glance around, now broke loose and went sky-rocketing into the blue. Some phenomenal new being was sprouting with alarming rapidity from the top of my head, from the double crown which was mine from birth.

ZAZIE
DANS LE MÉTRO

Illustrations by
Jacqueline Duhème

RAYMOND QUENEAU

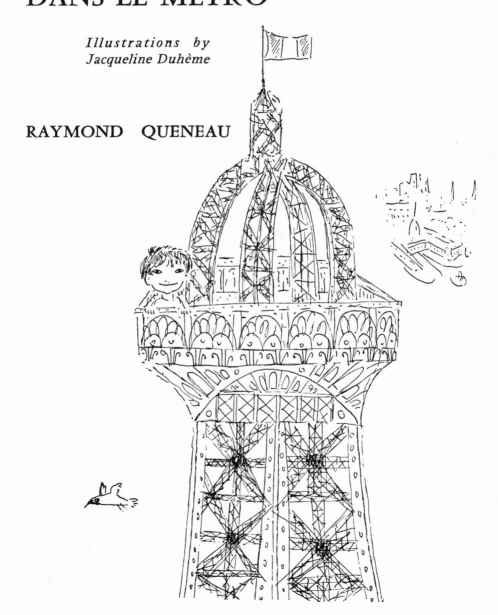

Marceline is softly dozing in a chair when something suddenly awakens her. She looks at the clock with a blinking eye but can draw no special conclusion, and then she realizes that someone is knocking ever so discreetly on the door.

She puts out the light and sits very still. It can't be Gabriel, she reflects, because when he comes home with the others there'll probbly be a helluva racket. And it can't be the pliss either because the city's milkmen aren't even up yet. As to the possibility of a housebreaker lusting after Gabriel's jack, well, that's a laugh.

After a moment's silence, the doorknob turns slowly, but with no appreciable results, and then Marceline hears something or someone meddling with the lock. It goes on for a good while. He ain't too bright, Marceline says softly to herself. The door finally opens.

The guy doesn't come in immediately. Marceline is breathing so silently and astutely that he can't possibly hear her.

Then he steps in. He feels around for the light switch, finds it eventually and the hall is flooded with light.

At first glance, Marceline recognizes the guy's silhouette: it's the so-called Surplus Pedro. But when he turns on the light in the living room, Marceline softly says to herself, Well I must've made a mistake, because this guy is wearing neither handlebars nor smoked glasses. He is holding his shoes in his hand.

He beams at Marceline.

"I frightened the hell outa you, didn't I?" he says politely.

"Nonsense," Marceline answers softly.

While he sits down silently and puts his shoes back on, she realizes her first guess was right: it is definitely the guy Gabriel has thrown down the stairs.

Shod anew, he beams anew.

"This time," says he, "I'll be glad to accept a glass of grenadine."

"Why d'you say *this time?*" asks Marceline, couching the last two words in italics.

"Don't you recognize me?"

Marceline hesitates, then acknowledges the fact (gesture).

"And you're wonderin' what I'm doin' here at this time of day?"

"You're a shrewd psychologist, m'sieu Pedro."

"M'sieu Pedro? Why d'you say *m'sieu Pedro?*" the guy asks curiously, boldly dressing up m'sieu Pedro in italics.

"Because that's what you said your name was this morning," Marceline softly replies.

"Oh yes?" says the guy nonchalantly. "Well, I forgot all about that."

(silence)

"So," he goes on, "ain't you gonna ask me what I'm doin' here at this time of day?"

"No, I'm not."

"That's a shame," says the guy, "because I woulda told you that I came to accept a glass of grenadine."

Marceline silently communicates to her inner ego the following reflection: "He's dyin' for me to tell him his escuse is perfectly stupid, but I'm doin' him no favor, and I certainly won't tell him."

The guy looks around him.

"D'you keep it" (gesture) "in here?"

He points to the Lousye XIV cabinet.

As Marceline doesn't answer, he calmly shrugs his shoulders, gets up, opens the cabinet, takes out a bottle and two glasses.

"Will you have a drop with me?" he says.

"Goodness no, I couldn't go to sleep," Marceline says softly.

The guy doesn't insist. He takes a sip.

"This stuff really stinks," he remarks incidentally.

Marceline offers no comment.

"Ain't they home yet?" asks the guy, just to say something.

"You know very well they aren't back yet. Otherwise you'd be flat on your back downstairs by now."

"Gabriella," says the guy dreamily (silence). "Thass a laugh" (silence). "I mean it's a scream."

He finishes off his glass.

"Phew," he grimaces.

Once again, the air is heavy with silence.

Then the guy makes up his mind at last.

"Now then," he says, "there's a few questions I want to ask you."

"You can ask," Marceline softly says, "but I'm not goin' to answer."

"You'd better," says the guy. "I'm inspector Bertin Podzol."

Marceline bursts out laughing.

"Here's my pliss card," says the guy in a chagrined voice.

He waves it from afar.

"It's a fake," says Marceline. "I can tell that right off. Watzmore, if you were a real pliss inspector, you'd know this is not the way to conduct an investigation. You wouldn't act so dumb if you'd taken the trouble to read a detective novel, a French one of course. There's enough here to get you demoted: tampering with locks, effraction, violation of a person's house. . . ."

"Yeah, and violation of what else?"

"I beg your pardon?" asks Marceline softly.

"I tell you what," says the guy. "I'm crazy about you. The moment I laid eyes on you I said to myself I said: I can't go on livin'

on this earth if I don't get to stuff this chick sooner or later, and then I added to myself: might as well be sooner'n later. Me, I just can't wait. I'm the impatient type, because that's the way I am. So then I said to myself I said: tonight's my chance, because the divine—thass you—is goin' to be all by her lonesome in her little nooky, as the rest of the household, and that includes that boob Turdanrot, are goin' to the Golden Balls to getta load of Gabriella's capers. Gabriella" (silence). "Thass a laugh" (silence). "I mean it's a scream."

"How come you know all that?"

"You seem to forget I'm pliss inspector Bertin Podzol."

"You're a big bluff," says Marceline, suddenly changing her vocabulary. "Whyntcha admit you're a phony cop?"

"Do you think a cop—to borrow your expression—has no heart?"

"Then you're really shit-headed."

"Some cops are soft-hearted."

"Yes, but you, you're downright mushy."

"Then my serenade leaves you cold? My beautiful lovebird's serenade?"

"You don't really expeck me to spread myself out for you just for the askin', do you?"

"I sincerely believe that my personal charm will not leave you indifferent in the end."

"God, what a big yap you got."

"Juss you wait and see. A little conversation and bingo! my casanovian powers will operate."

"What if they don't?"

"Then I'll have to jump you. Easy as pie."

"Yes? Well go ahead. Just try."

"Oh, I got plenty of time. It's only as a last resort that I would make use of this procedure, which my conscience doesn't entirely approve of, so to speak."

"You'd better hurry up. Gabriel will be comin' home pretty soon."

"Oh no, he won't. Night like this, he won't be home before six in the mornin'."

"Poor Zazie," says Marceline softly, "she's gonna be all tired out. And she must catch the six-sixty train."

"I don't givafart about Zazie. Little kidlets like her make me sick to the stomach. They're skinny and sour and—phew! But a gorgeous female like you, well, wham!"

"It was another song this mornin' when you were chasin' the poor child around."

"Of all the things to say," says the guy. "It's me brung her back home to you. Besides, my day was only juss startin'. But since I seen you. . . ."

Feigning deep melancholy and grief, the visitor stares mutely at Marceline, then he fiercely seizes the grenadine bottle, fills his glass to the brim, swallows its contents and discards the inedible residue, as one does with the disembodied bones of a pork chop or fillet of sole.

"Pheeeeew," he says, and he gulps the beverage he has elected, subjecting it to the expeditious treatment usually reserved for vodka.

He wipes his sticky lips with the back of his (left) hand, whereupon he begins to lay on the charm.

"Me," he says right off the cuff, "I'm the fickle type. That yokel kid simply gives me a pain in spite of her bloodcurdlin' stories. But that was in the mornin'. Later on in the day it so happened some dame from the uppers fell for me on sight. A baroness de Mwack. A widow. She got me under her epidermis. Her whole life's been bowled over in less'n five minutes. I must say that I was in my finest beat-trampin' attire at that time. I love that. You can't imagine the kick I get out of this uniform. The best is when I whistle down a taxi and hop aboard. The geezer at the wheel can't get over it. Then I tell him to drive me home. Takes the geezer's breath away" (silence). "But perhaps you think I'm a bit of a snob?"

"There's no accountin' for tastes."

"Haven't I charmed you yet?"

"Not at all."

Bertin Podzol coughs a couple of times then resumes his charmer's act.

"I gotta tell you how I got mixed up with the widow," he says.

"You bore me," says Marceline softly.

"In any case, I parked her at the Golden Balls along with the others. You see, Gabriella's frolics (Gabriella!) leave me perfectly cold. But you, you really heat me up."

"Haven't you got no shame, mister Surplus?"

"Shame, shame, thass easy to say. How can you be refined when you exchange chitchat?" (pause) "Besides, don't you call me Surplus Pedro. It gets on my nerves. I cooked up that monicker on the spur of the moment, juss like that, for Gabriella's benefit (Gabriella!), but I can't get used to it. After all, it's the first time I'm usin' it. But I have other names that fit me to a tee."   。

"Such as Bertin Podzol?"

"Sure. Or else the one I use when I dress up as a plissman. But Podzol is the one I like best, it's the one I use when I lay myself out to conquer a dame" (silence).

He looks troubled by something.

"When I lay myself out," he repeats with anguish. "Is that correck? Can you really say 'I lay myself out'? What do you think, pretty-face?"

"Why don't you lay off?"

"Tz tz tz. Don't forget I'm a pliss inspector."

"You're a big phony."

"Oh no! Not at all!! Thass not true!!! What makes you think I'm not a real cop?"

Marceline shrugs.

"I don't really care," she says softly.

"What? When I'm layin' myself out to please you?"

"If you want to please me, as I said, all you have to do is lay off."

"You don't seem to unnerstand what I mean, I didn't say 'lay off' but 'lay out,' dontcha know the difference?"

Marceline giggles ironically.

"How can I esplain," he sighs.

He looks estremely annoyed.

"Well, look it up in the dictionary," Marceline suggests softly.

"Dictionary, she says! D'you think I carry a dictionary around with me? I don't even have one at home. I can't afford to waste my time readin', I got too many things to do."

"There's one over there" (getsure).

"Wow," he says admiringly, "you're an intellectual on top of everythin' else! Well, wow!"

But he stays frozen in his chair.

"Would you like me to get it for you?" Marceline asks softly.

"I'll get it myself."

He walks to the shelf and takes the dictionary, keeping a wary eye on Marceline all the while. He comes back with the book and begins riffling through the pages. He soon is completely absorbed in his task.

"Now lemme see . . . *lashkar* . . . *lateran* . . . *latona, mother of apollo* . . . *lazarus* . . . No, it ain't in here."

"You have to look before the yellow pages."

"Yeah, and what have they got in them yellow pages? Pornography, I'll bet, hey? See, I guessed right . . . it's in Latin . . . *lash'yattay ogny spermanza, voy k'entrahttay!* And dig this one: *lex est quod notamus loco dolenti* . . . But it ain't in here either."

"I told you *before* the yellow pages."

"Shit, that thing's too complicated . . . Ah, at last: words everybody can understand . . . *latitudinarian* . . . *lauraceous* . . . *laverock* . . . Bull's eye! Here it is, right at the top of the page, too! Now then. LAY (laid, laying), (ME *leyen, leien;* AS *legcan; akin to Goth lagjan*). *To cause to come down with force* . . . Lessee . . . *to produce and deposit (an egg or eggs)* . . . Thassa laugh . . . *to form (the strands of a rope) by twisting yarn* . . . I mean it's a scream . . . *v. t., to smooth down, as: she laid the nap of a cloth* . . . No, thass not it . . . *to lay oneself out: to try very hard (Colloq.)* . . . Ha, you see, I was right and . . . Wait . . . *to lay (slang), v. t.: to have sexual intercourse with.* See? I was right! So I'm gonna lay you like the book says!! Get rid of them clothes, my beauty!!! And step on it!!!! Gwan, takem off, takem off!"

He looks up with bloodshot eyes. And they get even more so as he discovers that Marceline has totally and suddenly disappeared.

Sliding down the rain pipe, suitcase in hand, she's deftly setting foot on a cornice, with only a ten-foot drop to reach the street.

She vanishes around the corner.

RAYMOND QUENEAU

Raymond Queneau is distinguished both as a prolific writer, one book a year since the publication of his first novel, Le Chiendent, *1933, and as one of the board of directors of Gallimard, France's most important publishing house. He was born in the port of Le Havre in 1903, was a brilliant student of philosophy, later a student of every café, street corner, billiard hall in Paris. He was one of the original supporters of surrealism, and broke with it in 1929. M. Queneau has during his life collected, and seen destroyed, crates of plays, novels, histories; yet his works are illuminated by a sense of the comic ordered by a sense of the coherent. He is a brilliant mathematician, chess expert, student of Greek, and writes to make people laugh, and of course, in the best Gallic tradition, to think. The reader catches the contagious, horsy, sonorous laugh of Queneau, which is nowhere more clearly or perfectly sounded than in* Zazie.

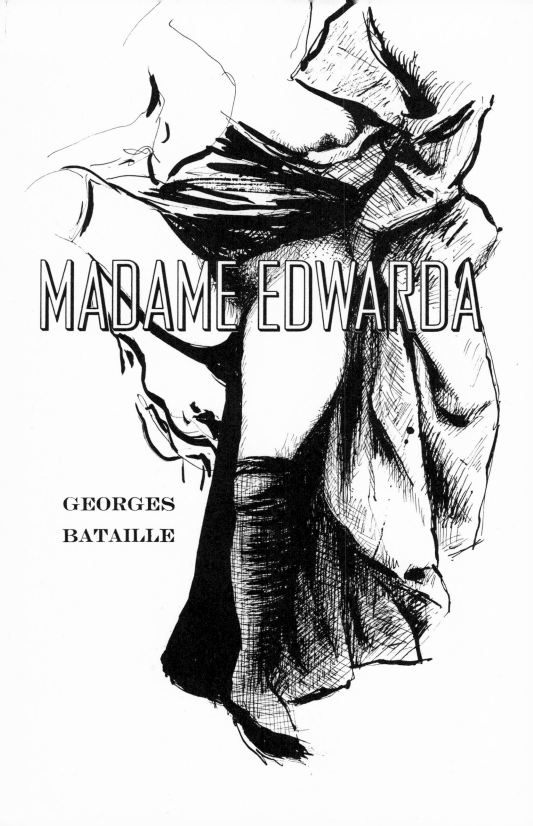

MADAME EDWARDA

GEORGES
BATAILLE

*T*here—I had come to a street corner—there a foul dizzying anguish got its nails into me (perhaps because I'd been staring at a pair of furtive whores sneaking down the stair of a urinal). A great urge to heave myself dry always comes over me at such moments. I feel I have got to make myself naked, or strip naked the whores I covet: it's in stale flesh's tepid warmth I always suppose I'll find relief. But this time I soothed my guts with the weaker remedy: I asked for a Pernod at the counter, drank the glass in one gulp, and then went on and on, from zinc counter to zinc counter, drinking until. . . . The night was done falling.

I began to wander among those streets—the propitious ones—which run between the Boulevard Poisonnière and the Rue Saint-Denis. Loneliness and the dark strung my drunken excitement tighter and tighter. I wanted to be laid as bare as was the night there in those empty streets: I skinned off my pants and moved on, carrying them draped over my arm. Numb, I coasted on a wave of overpowering freedom; I sensed that I'd got bigger. In my hand I held my straight-risen sex.

(The beginning is tough. My way of telling about these things is raw. I could have avoided that and still made it sound plausible. It would have seemed "likely," detours would have been to my advantage. But this is how it has to be, there is no beginning by scuttling in sidewise. I continue . . . and it gets tougher.)

Not wanting trouble, I got back into my pants and headed toward The Mirrors. I entered the place and found myself in the light again. Amidst a swarm of girls, Madame Edwarda, naked, looked bored to death. Ravishing; she was the sort I had a taste for. So I picked her. She came and sat down beside me. I hardly took the time to reply when the waiter asked what it was to be; I clutched Edwarda, she surrendered herself: our two mouths met in a sickly kiss. The room was packed with men and women, and that was the wasteland where the game was played. Then, at a certain moment, her hand slid; I burst, suddenly, like a pane of glass shattering, flooding my clothes. My hands were holding Madame Edwarda's buttocks and I felt her break in two at the same instant: and in her starting, roving eyes, terror, and in her throat, a long-drawn whistled rasp.

Then I remembered my desire for infamy, or rather that it was infamous I had at all costs to be. I made out laughter filtering through the tumult of voices, of glare, of smoke. But nothing mattered any more. I squeezed Edwarda in my arms; immediately, icebound, I felt smitten within by a new shock. From very high above a kind of stillness swept down upon me and froze me. It was as though I were borne aloft in a flight of headless and unbodied angels shaped from the broad swooping of wings, but it was simpler than that. I became unhappy and felt painfully forsaken, as one is when in the presence of GOD. It was worse and more of a letdown than too much to drink. And right away I was filled with unbearable sadness to think that this very grandeur descending upon me was withering away the pleasure I hoped to have with Edwarda.

I told myself I was being ridiculous. Edwarda and I having exchanged not one word, I was assailed by a huge uneasiness. I couldn't breathe so much as a hint of the state I was in, a wintry night had locked round me. Struggling, I wanted to kick the table and send the glasses flying, to raise the bloody roof; but that table wouldn't budge, it must have been bolted to the floor. I don't suppose a drunk can ever have to face anything more comical. Everything swam out of sight, Madame Edwarda was gone, so was the room.

I was pulled out of my dazed confusion by an only too human voice. Madame Edwarda's thin voice, like her slender body, was obscene: "I guess what you want is to see the old rag and ruin," she said. Hanging on to the tabletop with both hands, I twisted around toward her. She was seated, she held one leg stuck up in the air; to open her crack yet wider she used fingers to draw the folds of skin apart. And so Madame Edwarda's "old rag and ruin" loured at me, hairy and pink, just as full of life as some loathsome squid. "Why," I stammered in a subdued tone, "why are you doing that?" "You can see for yourself," she said; "I'm GOD." "I'm going crazy—" "Oh, no, you don't, you've got to see, look . . ." Her harsh, scraping voice mellowed, she became almost childlike in order to say, with a lassitude, with the infinite smile of abandon: "Oh, listen, fellow! The fun I've had . . ."

She had not shifted from her position, her leg was still cocked in the air. And her tone was commanding: "Come here." "Do you mean," I protested, "in front of all these people?" "Sure," she said, "why not?" I was shaking; I looked at her: motionless, she smiled back so sweetly that I shook. At last, reeling, I sank down on my knees and feverishly pressed my lips to that running, teeming wound. Her bare thigh caressingly nudged my ear; I thought I heard a sound of roaring seasurge, it is the same sound you hear when you listen into a large conch shell. In the brothel's boisterous chaos and in the atmosphere of corroding absurdity I was breathing (it seemed to me that I was choking, I was flushed, I was sweating) I hung strangely suspended, quite as though at that same point we, Edwarda and I, were losing ourselves in a wind-freighted night, on the edge of the ocean.

I heard another voice, a woman's but mannish. She was a robust and handsome person, respectably got up. "Well now, my little chicks," in an easy, deep tone, "up you go." The second in command of the house collected my money, I rose and followed Madame Edwarda whose tranquil nakedness was already traversing the room. But this so ordinary passage between the close-set tables, through the dense press of clients and girls, this vulgar ritual of "the lady going up" with the man who wants her in tow, was, at that moment, nothing short of an hallucinating solemnity for me: Madame Edwarda's sharp heels clicking on the tiled floor, the smooth advance of her long obscene body, the acrid smell I drank in, the smell of a woman in the throes of joy, of that pale body. . . . Madame Edwarda went on ahead of me, raised up unto the very clouds. . . . The room's noisy unheeding of her happiness, of the measured gravity of her step, was royal consecration and triumphal holiday: death itself was guest at the feast, was there in what whorehouse nudity terms the pig-sticker's stab. . . .
. . . .
. . . .
. . . . the mirrors wherewith the room's walls were everywhere sheathed and the ceiling too, cast multiple reflections of an animal coupling, but, at each least movement, our bursting hearts would strain wide-open to welcome "the emptiness of heaven."

Making that love liberated us at last. On our feet, we stood gazing soberly at each other: Madame Edwarda held me spellbound, never had I seen a prettier girl—nor one more naked. Her eyes fastened steadily upon me, she removed a pair of white silk stockings from a bureau drawer; she sat on the edge of the bed and drew them on. The delirious joy of being naked possessed her: once again she parted her legs, opened her crack; the pungent odor of her flesh and mine commingled flung us both into the same heart's utter exhaustion. She put on a white bolero, beneath a domino cloak she disguised her nakedness. The domino's hood cowled her head, a black velvet mask, fitted

with a beard of lace, hid her face. So arrayed, she sprang away from me, saying: "Now let's go."

"Go? Do they let you go out?" I asked. "Hurry up, duckie," she replied gaily, "you can't go out undressed." She tossed me my clothes and helped me climb into them; as she did so, from her caprice now and then passed a sly exchange, a nasty little wink darting between her flesh and mine. We went down a narrow stairway; encountered nobody but the chambermaid. Fetched to a halt by the abrupt darkness of the street, I was startled to discover Edwarda rushing away, swathed in black and blackness. She ran, eluded me, was off; the mask she wore was turning her into an animal. Though the air wasn't cold, I shivered. Edwarda, something alien; above our heads, a starry sky, mad and void. I thought I was going to stagger, to fall, but didn't, and kept walking.

At that hour of the night the street was deserted. Suddenly gone wild, mute, Edwarda raced on alone. The Porte Saint-Denis loomed before her; she stopped. I stopped too; she waited for me underneath the arch—unmoving, exactly under the arch. She was entirely black, simply there, as distressing as an emptiness, a hole; I realized she wasn't frolicking, wasn't joking, and indeed that, beneath the garment enfolding her, she was mindless: rapt, absent. Then, all the drunken exhilaration drained out of me, then I knew that She had not lied, that She was GOD. Her presence had about it the unintelligible out-and-out simplicity of a stone—right in the middle of the city I had the feeling of being in the mountains at nighttime, lost in a lifeless, hollow solitude.

I felt that I was free of Her—I was alone, as if face to face with black rock. I trembled, seeing before me what in all this world is most barren, most bleak. In no way did the comic horror of my situation escape me: She, the sight of whom petrified me now, the instant before had . . . And the transformation had occurred in the way something glides. In Madame Edwarda, grief—a grief without tears or pain—had glided into a vacant silence. Nonetheless, I wanted to find out: this woman, so naked just a moment ago, who lightheartedly had called me "duckie.". . . I crossed in her direction; anguish warned me to go no farther, but I didn't stop.

Unspeaking, she slipped away, retreating toward the pillar on the left. Two paces separated me from that monumental gate; when I passed under the stone overhead, the domino vanished soundlessly. I paused, listening, holding my breath. I was amazed that I could grasp it all so clearly: when she had run off I had known that, no matter what, she had had to run, to dash under the arch; and when she had stopped, that she had been hung in a sort of trance, an absence, far out of range and beyond the possibility of any laughter. I couldn't see her any longer: a deathly darkness sank down from the vault. Without having given it a second's thought, I "knew" that a season of agony was beginning for me. I consented to suffer, I desired to suffer, to go farther, as far as the "emptiness" itself, even were I to be stricken, destroyed; no matter. I knew, I wanted that knowing, for I lusted after her secret and did not for one instant doubt that it was death's kingdom.

I moaned underneath the stone roof, then, terrified, I laughed: "Of all men, the sole to traverse the nothingness of this arch!" I trembled at the thought she might fly, vanish forever. I trembled as I accepted that, but from imagining it I became crazed: I leaped to the pillar and spun round it. As quickly I circled the other pillar on the right: she was gone. But I couldn't believe it. I remained woestruck before the portal and I was sinking into the last despair when upon the far side of the avenue I spied the domino, immobile, just faintly visible in the shadow: she was standing upright, entranced still, planted in front of the ranged tables and chairs of a café shut up for the night. I drew near her: she seemed gone out of her mind, some foreign existence, the creature apparently of another world and, in the streets of this one, less than a phantom, less than a lingering mist. Softly she withdrew before me until in her retreat she touched against a table on the empty terrace. A little bang. As if I had waked her, in a lifeless voice she inquired. "Where am I?"

Desperate, I pointed to the empty sky curved above us. She looked up and for a brief moment stood still, her eyes vague behind the mask, her gaze lost in the fields of stars. I supported her; it was in an unhealthy way she was clutching the domino, with both hands pulling it tight around her. She began to shake, to convulse. She was suffering, I thought she was crying but it was as if the world and the distress in her, strangling her, were preventing her from giving way to sobs. She wrenched away from me, gripped by a shapeless disgust; suddenly lunatic, she darted forward, stopped short, whirled her cloak high, displayed her behind, snapped her rump up with a quick jerk of her spine, then came back and hurled herself at me. A gale of dark savagery blew up inside her; raging, she tore and hammered at my face, hit with clenched fists, swept away by a demented impulse to violence. I tottered and fell. She fled.

I was still getting to my feet—was actually still on my knees—

when she returned. She shouted in a raveled, impossible voice, she screamed at the sky and, horrified, her whirling arms flailing at vacant air: "I can't stand any more," she shrilled, "but you, you fake priest bastard, goddamn you—" That broken voice ended in a rattle, her outstretched hands groped blindly, then she collapsed.

Down, she writhed, shaken by respiratory spasms. I bent over her and had to rip the lace from the mask, for she was chewing and trying to swallow it. Her thrashings had left her naked, her breasts spilled through her bolero. . . . I saw her flat, pallid belly, and above her stockings, her hairy crack yawned astart. This nakedness now had the absence of meaning and at the same time the overabundant meaning of death-shrouds. Strangest of all—and most disturbing—was the silence that held Edwarda in its snares; owing to the pain she was in, further communication was impossible and I let myself be absorbed into this unutterable barrenness—into this black night hour of the being's core no less a desert nor less hostile than the empty skies. Her body's fish-floppings, the ignoble rage expressed by the ill written on her countenance cindered the life in me, dried it down to the lees of revulsion.

(Let me explain myself. No use laying it all up to irony when I say of Madame Edwarda that she is GOD. But GOD figured as a public whore and insane—that, viewed through the optic of "philosophy," makes no sense at all. I don't mind having my sorrow derided if derided it has to be; he only will grasp me aright whose heart holds a wound that is an incurable wound, who never, for anything, in any way, would be cured of it. . . . And what man, if so wounded, would ever be willing to "die" of any other hurt?)

The awareness of my irreparable doom whilst, in that night, I knelt next to Edwarda was not less clear and not less imposing than it is now, as I write. Edwarda's sufferings dwelt in me like the quick truth of an arrow: one knows it will pierce the heart, but death will ride in with it; as I waited for annihilation, all that subsisted in me seemed to me to be the dross over which man's life tarries. Squared against a silence so black, something leaped in my heavy despair's midst; Edwarda's convulsions snatched me away from my own self, they cast my life into a desert waste "beyond," they cast it there carelessly, callously, the way one flings a living body to the hangman.

A man condemned to die, when after long hours of waiting he arrives in broad daylight at the exact spot the horror is to be wrought, observes the preparations; his too full heart beats as though to burst, upon the narrow horizon which is his, every object, every face is clad in weightiest meaning and helps tighten the vise whence there is no time left him to escape. When I saw Madame Edwarda writhing on the pavement, I entered a similar state of absorption; but I did not feel imprisoned by the change that occurred in me; the horizon before which Edwarda's sickness placed me was a fugitive one, fleeing like the object anguish seeks to attain; torn apart, a certain power welled up in me, a power that would be mine upon condition I agree to hate myself. Ugliness was invading all of me. The vertiginous sliding which was tipping me into ruin had opened up a prospect of indifference; of concerns, of desires there was no longer any question: at this point, the fever's desiccating ecstasy was issuing out of my utter inability to check myself.

(If you have to lay yourself bare, then you cannot play with words, trifle with slow-marching sentences. Should no one unclothe what I have said, I shall have written in vain. Edwarda is not dream's airy invention; the real sweat of her body soaked my handkerchief; so real was she that, led on by her, I came to want to do the leading in my turn. This book has its secret, I may not disclose it. Now more words.)

Finally, the crisis subsided. Her convulsions continued a little longer, but with waning fury; she began to breathe again, her features relaxed, ceased to be hideous. Drained entirely of strength, I lay full length down on the roadway beside her. I covered her with my clothing. She was not heavy and I decided to pick her up and carry her. One of the boulevard taxi stands was not far away. She lay unstirring in my arms. It took time to get there, thrice I had to pause and rest; she came back to life as we moved along and when we reached the place she wanted to be set down. She took a step and swayed. I caught her, held her; held by me she got into the cab. Weakly, she said: ". . . not yet . . . tell him to wait." I told the driver to wait. Half dead from weariness, I climbed in too and slumped down beside Edwarda.

For a long time we remained without saying anything, Madame Edwarda, the driver and I, not budging in our seats, as though the taxi were rolling ahead. At last Edwarda spoke to me. "I want him to take us to Les Halles." I repeated her instructions to the driver, and we started off. He took us through dimly lit streets. Calm and deliberate, Edwarda loosened the ties of her cloak, it fell away from her. She got rid of the mask too, she removed her bolero and, for her own hearing, murmured: "Naked as a beast." She rapped on the glass partition, had the cab stop, and got out. She walked round to the driver and when close enough to touch him, said: "You see . . . I'm bare-assed, Jack. Let's screw." Unmoving, the driver looked at that beast; having backed off a short distance, she had raised her left leg, eager to show him her crack. Without a word and unhurriedly, the man stepped out of the car. He was thickset, solidly built. Edwarda twined herself around him, fastened her mouth upon his, and with one hand scouted about in his underwear. It was a long heavy member she dragged through his fly. She eased his trousers down to his ankles. "Come into the back seat," she told him. He sat down next to me. Stepping in after him, she mounted and straddled him. Carried away by voluptuousness, with her own hands she stuffed the hard stave into her hole. I sat there, lifeless and watching: her slithering movements were slow and cunning and plainly she gleaned a nerve-snapping pleasure from them. The driver retaliated, struggling with brute heaving vigor; bred of their naked bodies' intimacy, little by little that embrace strained to the final pitch of excess at which the heart fails. The driver fell back, spent and near to swooning. I switched on the overhead light in the taxi. Edwarda sat bolt erect astride the still stiff member, her head angled sharply back, her hair straying loose. Supporting her nape, I looked into her eyes: they gleamed white. She pressed against the hand that was holding her up, the tension thickened the wail in her throat. Her eyes swung to rights and therewith she seemed to grow easy. She saw me, from her stare, then, at that moment, I knew she was drifting home from the "impossible" and in her nether depths I could discern a dizzying fixity. The milky outpouring traveling through her, the jet spitting from the root, flooding her with joy, came spurting out again in her very tears: burning tears streamed from her wide-open eyes. Love was dead in those eyes, they contained a daybreak aureate chill, a transparence wherein I read death's letters. And everything swam drowned in that dreaming stare: a long member, stubby fingers prying open fragile flesh, my anguish, and the recollection of scum-flecked lips—there was nothing which didn't contribute to that blind dying into extinction.

Edwarda's pleasure—fountain of boiling water, heartbursting furious tideflow—went on and on, weirdly, unendingly; that stream of luxury, its strident inflection, glorified her being unceasingly, made her nakedness unceasingly more naked, her lewdness ever more intimate. Her body, her face swept in ecstasy were abandoned to the unspeakable coursing and ebbing, in her sweetness there hovered a crooked smile: she saw me to the bottom of my dryness; from the bottom of my desolation I sensed her joy's torrent run free. My anguish stood bar to the pleasure I ought to have sought; Edwarda's pain-wrung pleasure filled me with an exhausting impression of bearing witness to a miracle. My own distress and fever seemed small things to me. But that was what I felt, those are the only great things in me which made answer to the rapture of her whom in the deeps of an icy silence I called "my heart."

Some last shudders took slow hold of her, then her sweat-laved frame relaxed—and there in the darkness sprawled the driver, felled by his spasm. I still held Edwarda up, my hand still behind her head; the stave slipped out, I helped her lie down, wiped her wet body. Her eyes dead, she offered no resistance. I had switched off the light; she was half asleep, like a drowsy child. The same sleepiness must have borne down upon the three of us, Edwarda, the driver and me.

(Continue? I meant to. But I don't care now. I've lost interest. I put down what oppresses me at the moment of writing: Would it all be absurd? Or might it make some kind of sense? I've made myself sick wondering about it. I awake in the morning—just the way millions do, millions of boys and girls, infants and old men, their slumbers dissipated forever. . . . These millions, those slumbers have no meaning. A hidden meaning? Hidden, yes, "obviously"! But if nothing has any meaning, there's no point in my doing anything. I'll beg off, I'll use any deceitful means to get out of it, in the end I'll have to let go and sell myself to meaninglessness, nonsense: that is man's killer, the one who tortures and kills; not a glimmer of hope left. But if there is a meaning? Today I don't know what it is. Tomorrow? Tomorrow, who can tell? Am I going then to find out what it is? No, I can't conceive of any "meaning" other than "my" anguish, and as for that, I know all about it. And for the time being: nonsense. Monsieur Nonsense is writing and understands that he is mad. It's atrocious. But his madness, this meaninglessness—how "serious" it has become all of a sudden!—might that indeed be "meaningful"? [No, Hegel has nothing to do with a maniac girl's "apotheosis."] My life only has a meaning insofar as I lack one: oh, but let me be mad!

make something of all this he who is able to, understand it he who is dying; and there the living self is, knowing not why, its teeth chattering in the lashing wind: the immensity, the night engulfs it and, all on purpose, that living self is there just in order . . . "not to know." But as for GOD? What have you got to say, Monsieur Rhetorician? and you, Monsieur Godfearer?— GOD, if He knew, would be a swine. O Thou my Lord [in my distress I call out unto my heart], O deliver me, make them blind! The story—how shall I go on with it?)

But I am done.

From out of the slumber which for a so short space kept us in the taxi, I awoke, the first to open his eyes. . . . The rest is irony, long weary waiting for death. . . .

Note to page X.: I said "GOD, if He knew would be a swine." He (He would I suppose be, at that particular moment, somewhat in disorder, his peruke would sit all askew) would entirely grasp the idea . . . but what would there be of the human about him? beyond, beyond everything . . . and yet farther, and even farther still. . . . HIMSELF, in an ecstasy, above an emptiness. . . . And now? I TREMBLE.

GEORGES BATAILLE

The long fangs of a wild beast of the woods, the deep-set blue eyes alight with intelligence, the slow gait and careful speech of Georges Bataille were the first traits of his personality to capture one's attention. When I met him for the first time, in 1942 or 1943, he was assistant curator at the Bibliothèque Nationale. His appearance was that of a peaceful, retiring, scholar, a man of taste; and he was all of that, but the hungry jaw was there to reveal that he was at the same time a man of substantial passions.

Bataille was dominated by a number of such contradictions. His studies at the Ecole des Chartes prepared him to be an historian, but his interests, in those formative years, went rather to philosophy and religion. Then, in the early 'thirties, with the advent of Surrealism, Bataille launched his own movement, attacking with iconoclastic fury both the Surrealists, and what they were fighting. In those years he edited Documents *and wrote several erotic novelettes,* L'Histoire de l'Oeil, Madame Edwarda, L'Anus Solaire, *which belong to the Surrealist era by their form of expression; but they are impregnated with Bataille's own weird genius.*

In 1948 Bataille came to me with the suggestion that we start publication of a monthly review of books. Thus Critique *was born, which reflected Bataille's interests in a variety of fields ranging from art to sociology, from philosophy to linguistics, from metaphysics to ethnology.*

If Bataille never attained more than a very modest measure of fame, it is partly due to his lack of interest in his public image, but also to his refusal to become limited by the choice of a specialty. He was pursuing a much higher aim, which seems to have been the constant preoccupation and torment of his life. He was obsessed by the idea of unity; he refused the mental limitations of knowledge. He had studied Indian philosophy and the methods of illumination practiced by certain Buddhist schools, which he explored in his own way. But the very pressure of his ubiquitous intelligence made it impossible for him to obtain the necessary detachment to succeed in such a quest. Thus he remained, on the brink of accomplishment, torn between intuition and deduction, having set free his inferno but unable to cope with it. Under the smooth diffident surface, a cold tempest was constantly raging. From those depths two images emerged, the two most powerful gods in Bataille's mythology: death and eroticism. They were bound one to the other. Eroticism was not simply sex, but sex detached from the reproductive function, driving its energies toward creative forms and sensations. But in the elaboration of erotic feeling, which appears as the source of individual culture and judgment, many elements come to play whose role must be understood in terms of the human continuum—death, suffering, rape.

OUR LADY OF THE

FLOWERS

Jean Genet

*S*ince Divine is dead, the poet may sing her, may tell her legend, the Saga, the annals of Divine. The Divine Saga should be danced, mimed, with subtle directions. Since it is impossible to make a ballet of it, I am forced to use words that are weighed down with precise ideas, but I shall try to lighten them with expressions that are trivial, empty, hollow, and invisible.

What is involved for me who is making up this story? In reviewing my life, in tracing its course, I fill my cell with the pleasure of being what for want of a trifle I failed to be, recapturing, so that I may hurl myself into them as into dark pits, those moments when I strayed through the trap-ridden compartments of a subterranean sky. Slowly displacing volumes of fetid air, cutting threads from which hang bouquets of feelings, seeing the gypsy for whom I am looking emerge perhaps from some starry river, wet, with mossy hair, playing the fiddle, diabolically whisked away by the scarlet velvet portiere of a cabaret.

I shall speak to you about Divine, mixing masculine and feminine as my mood dictates, and if, in the course of the tale, I shall have to refer to a woman, I shall manage, I shall find an expedient, a good device, to avoid any confusion.

Divine appeared in Paris to lead her public life about twenty years before her death. She was then thin and vivacious and will remain so until the end of her life, though growing angular. At about two A.M. she entered Graff's Café in Montmartre. The customers were a muddy, still shapeless clay. Divine was limpid water. In the big café with the closed windows and the curtains drawn on their hollow rods, overcrowded and foundering in smoke, she wafted the coolness of scandal, which is the coolness of a morning breeze, the astonishing sweetness of a breath of scandal on the stone of the temple, and just as the wind turns leaves, so she turned heads, heads which all at once became light (giddy heads), heads of bankers, shopkeepers, gigolos for ladies, waiters, managers, colonels, scarecrows.

She sat down alone at a table and asked for tea.

"Specially fine China tea, my good man," she said to the waiter.

With a smile. For the customers she had an irritatingly jaunty smile. Hence, the "you-know-what" in the wagging of the heads. For the poet and the reader, her smile will be enigmatic.

That evening she was wearing a champagne silk short-sleeved blouse, a pair of blue trousers stolen from a sailor, and leather sandals. On one of her fingers, though preferably on the pinkie, an ulcer-like stone gangrened her. When the tea was brought, she drank it as if she were at home, in tiny little sips (a pigeon), putting down and lifting the cup with her pinkie in the air. Here is a portrait of her: her hair is brown and curly; with the curls spilling over her eyes and down her cheeks, she looks as if she were wearing a cat-o'-nine-tails on her head. Her forehead is somewhat round and smooth. Her eyes sing, despite their despair, and their melody moves from her eyes to her teeth, to which she gives life, and from her teeth to all her movements, to her slightest acts, and this charm, which emerges from her eyes, unfurls in wave upon wave, down to her bare feet. Her body is fine as amber. Her limbs can be agile when she flees from ghosts. At her heels, the wings of terror bear her along. She is quick, for in order to elude the ghosts, to throw them off her track, she must speed ahead faster than her thought thinks. She drank her tea before thirty pair of eyes which belied what the contemptuous, spiteful, sorrowful, wilting mouths were saying.

Divine was full of grace, and yet was like all those prowlers at country fairs on the lookout for rare sights and artistic visions, good sports who trail behind them all the inevitable hodgepodge of side shows. At the slightest movement—if they knot their tie, if they flick the ash of their cigarette—they set slot machines in motion. Divine knotted, garroted arteries. Her seductiveness will be implacable. If it were only up to me, I would make her the kind of fatal hero I like. Fatal, that is, determining the fate of those who gaze at them, spellbound. I would make her with hips of stone, flat and polished cheeks, heavy eyelids, pagan knees so lovely that they reflected the desperate intelligence of the faces of mystics. I would strip her of all sentimental trappings. Let her consent to be the frozen statue. But I know that the poor Demiurge is forced to make his creature in his own image and that he did not invent Lucifer. In my cell, little by little, I shall have to give my thrills to the granite. I shall remain alone with it for a long time, and I shall make it live with my breath and the smell of my farts, both the solemn and the mild ones. It will take me an entire book to draw her from her petrifaction and gradually impart my suffering to her, gradually deliver her from evil, and, holding her by the hand, lead her to saintliness.

The waiter who served her felt very much like snickering, but out of decency he did not dare in front of her. As for the manager, he approached her table and decided that as soon as she finished her tea, he would ask her to leave, to make sure she would not turn up again some other evening.

Finally, she patted her snowy forehead with a flowered handkerchief. Then she crossed her legs; on her ankle could be seen a chain fastened by a locket which *we* know contained a few hairs. She smiled all around, and each one answered only by turning away, but that was a way of answering. The whole café thought that the smile (for the colonel: the invert; for the shopkeepers: the fairy; for the banker and the waiters: the fag; for the gigolos: "*that* one"; etc.) was despicable. Divine did not press the point. From a tiny black satin purse she took a few coins which she laid noiselessly on the marble table. The café disappeared, and Divine was metamorphosed into one of those monsters that are painted on walls—chimeras or griffins— for a customer, in spite of himself, murmured a magic word as he thought of her:

"Homoseckshual."

That evening, her first in Montmartre, she was cruising. But she got nowhere. She came upon us without warning. The habitués of the café had neither the time nor, above all, the composure to handle properly their reputations or their females. Having drunk her tea, Divine, with indifference (so it appeared, seeing her), wriggling in a spray of flowers and strewing swishes and spangles with an invisible furbelow, made off. So here she is, having decided to return, lifted by a column of smoke, to her garret, on the door of which is nailed a huge discolored muslin rose.

Her perfume is violent and vulgar. From it we can already tell that she is fond of vulgarity. Divine has sure taste, good taste, and it is most upsetting that life always puts someone so delicate into vulgar positions, into contact with all kinds of filth. She cherishes vulgarity because her greatest love was for a dark-skinned gypsy. On him, under him, when, with his mouth pressed to hers, he sang to her gypsy songs that pierced her body, she learned to submit to the charm of such vulgar cloths as silk and gold braid, which are becoming to immodest persons. Montmartre was aflame. Divine passed through its multicolored fires, then, intact, entered the darkness of the promenade of the Boulevard de Clichy, a darkness that preserves old and ugly faces. It was three A.M. She walked for a while toward Pigalle. She smiled and stared at every man who strolled by alone. They didn't dare, or else it was that she still knew nothing about the customary routine: the client's qualms, his hesitations, his lack of assurance as soon as he approaches the coveted youngster. She was weary; she sat down on a bench and, despite her fatigue, was conquered, transported by the warmth of the night; she let herself go for the length of a heartbeat and expressed her excitement as follows: "The nights are mad about me! Oh the sultanas! My God, they're making eyes at me! Ah, they're curling my hair around their fingers (the fingers of the nights, men's cocks!). They're patting my cheek, stroking my butt." That was what she thought, though without rising to, or sinking into, a poetry cut off from the terrestrial world. Poetic expression will never change her state of mind. She will always be the tart concerned with gain.

There are mornings when all men experience with fatigue a flush of tenderness that makes them horny. One day at dawn I found myself placing my lips lovingly, though for no reason at all, on the icy banister of the Rue Berthe; another time, kissing my hand; still another time, bursting with emotion, I wanted to swallow myself by opening my mouth very wide and turning it over my head so that it would take in my whole body, and then the Universe, until all that would remain of me would be a ball of eaten thing which little by little would be annihilated: that is how I see the end of the world. Divine offered herself to the night in order to be devoured by it tenderly and never again spewed forth. She is hungry. And there is nothing around. The pissoirs are empty; the promenade is just about deserted. Merely some bands of young workmen—whose whole disorderly adolescence is manifest in their carelessly tied shoelaces which hop about on their insteps—returning home in forced marches from an evening of pleasure. Their tight-fitting jackets are like fragile breast-plates or shells protecting the naïveté of their bodies. But by the grace of their virility, which is still as light as a hope, they are inviolable by Divine.

She will do nothing tonight. The possible customers were so taken by surprise that they were unable to collect their wits. She will have to go back to her attic with hunger in her belly and her heart. She stood up to go. A man came staggering toward her. He bumped her with his elbow.

"Oh! sorry," he said, "terribly sorry!"

His breath reeked of wine.

"Quite all right," said the queen.

It was Darling Daintyfoot going by.

Description of Darling: height, 5 ft. 9 in., weight 165 lbs., oval face, blond hair, blue-green eyes, mat complexion, perfect teeth, straight nose.

He was young too, almost as young as Divine, and I would like him to remain so to the end of the book. Every day the guards open my door so I can leave my cell and go out into the yard for some fresh air. For a few seconds, in the corridors and on the stairs, I pass thieves and hoodlums whose faces enter my face and whose bodies, from afar, hurl mine to the ground. I long to have them within reach. Yet not one of them makes me evoke Darling Daintyfoot.

When I met Divine in Fresnes Prison, she spoke to me about him a great deal, seeking his memory and the traces of his steps throughout the prison, but I never quite knew his face, and this is a tempting opportunity for me to blend him in my mind with the face and physique of Roger.

Very little of this Corsican remains in my memory: a hand with too massive a thumb that plays with a tiny hollow key, and the faint image of a blond boy walking up La Canebière in Marseilles, with a small chain, probably gold, stretched across his fly, which it seems to be buckling. He belongs to a group of males who are advancing upon me with the pitiless gravity of forests on the march. That was the starting point of the daydream in which I imagined myself calling him Roger, a "little boy's" name, though firm and upright. Roger was upright. I had just got out of the Chave prison, and I was amazed not to have met him there. What could I commit to be worthy of his beauty? I needed boldness in order to admire him. For lack of money, I slept at night in the shadowy corners of coal piles, on the docks, and every evening I carried him off with me. The memory of his memory made way for other men. For the past two days, in my day-dreams, I have again been mingling his (made-up) life with mine. I wanted him to love me, and of course he did, with the candor that re-quired only perversity for him to be able to love me. For two suc-cessive days I have fed with his image a dream which is usually sated after four or five hours when I have given it a boy to feed upon, how-ever handsome he may be. Now I am exhausted with inventing cir-cumstances in which he loves me more and more. I am worn out with the invented trips, thefts, rapes, burglaries, imprisonments, and treach-ery in which we were involved, each acting by and for the other and never by or for himself, in which the adventure was ourselves and only ourselves. I am exhausted; I have a cramp in my wrist. The pleasure of the last drops is dry. For a period of two days, between my four bare walls, I experienced with him and through him every possi-bility of an existence that had to be repeated twenty times and got so mixed up it became more real than a real one. I have given up the day-dream. I was loved. I have quit, the way a contestant in a six-day bicycle race quits; yet the memory of his eyes and their fatigue, which I have to cull from the face of another youngster whom I saw coming out of a brothel, a boy with firm legs and ruthless cock, so solid that I might almost say it was knotted, and his face (it alone, seen without its veil), which asks for shelter like a knight-errant—this memory refuses to disappear as the memory of my dream-friends usually does. It floats about. It is less sharp than when the adventures were taking place, but it lives in me nevertheless. Certain details persist more ob-stinately in remaining: the little hollow key with which, if he wants to, he can whistle; his thumb; his sweater; his blue eyes. . . . If I con-tinue, he will rise up, become erect, and penetrate me so deeply that

I shall be marked with stigmata. I can't bear it any longer. I am turning him into a character whom I shall be able to torment in my own way, namely, Darling Daintyfoot. He will still be twenty, although his destiny is to become the father and lover of Our Lady of the Flowers.

To Divine he said:

"Terribly sorry!"

In his cups, Darling did not notice the strangeness of this passer-by with his aggressive niceness:

"What about it, pal?"

Divine stopped. A bantering and dangerous conversation ensued, and then everything happened as was to be desired. Divine took him home with her to the Rue Caulaincourt. It was in this garret that she died, the garret from which one sees below, like the sea beneath the watchman in the crow's-nest, a cemetery and graves. Cypresses singing. Ghosts dozing. Every morning, Divine will shake her dustrag from the window and bid the ghosts farewell. One day, with the help of field glasses, she will discover a young gravedigger. "God forgive me!" she will exclaim, "there's a bottle of wine on the vault!" This gravedigger will grow old along with her and will bury her without knowing anything about her.

So she went upstairs with Darling. Then, in the attic, after closing the door, she undressed him. With his jacket, trousers, and shirt off, he looked as white and sunken as an avalanche. By evening they found themselves tangled in the damp and rumpled sheets.

"What a mess! Man! I was pretty groggy yesterday, wasn't I, doll?"

He laughed feebly and looked around the garret. It is a room with a sloping ceiling. On the floor, Divine has put some threadbare rugs and nailed to the wall the murderers on the walls of my cell and the extraordinary photographs of good-looking kids, which she has stolen from photographers' display windows, all of whom bear the signs of the power of darkness.

"Display window!"

On the mantelpiece, a tube of phenobarbital lying on a small painted wooden frigate is enough to detach the room from the stone block of the building, to suspend it like a cage between heaven and earth.

From the way he talks, the way he lights and smokes his cigarette, Divine has gathered that Darling is a pimp. At first she had certain fears: of being beaten up, robbed, insulted. Then she felt the proud satisfaction of having made a pimp come. Without quite seeing where the adventure would lead, but rather as a bird is said to go into a serpent's mouth, she said, not quite voluntarily and in a kind of trance: "Stay," and added hesitantly, "if you want to."

"No kidding, you feel that way about me?"

Darling stayed.

In that big Montmartre attic, where, through the skylight, between the pink muslin puffs which she has made herself, Divine sees white cradles sailing by on a calm blue sea, so close that she can make out their flowers from which emerges the arched foot of a dancer. Darling will soon bring the midnight-blue overalls that he wears on the job, his ring of skeleton keys and his tools, and on the little pile which they make on the floor he will place his white rubber gloves, which are like gloves for formal occasions. Thus began their life together in that room through which ran the electric wires of the stolen radiator, the stolen radio, and the stolen lamps.

They eat breakfast in the afternoon. During the day they sleep and listen to the radio. Toward evening, they primp and go out. At night, as is the practice, Divine hustles on the Place Blanche and Darling goes to the movies. For a long time, things will go well with Divine. With Darling to advise and protect her, she will know whom to rob, which judge to blackmail. The vaporish cocaine loosens the contours of their lives and sets their bodies adrift, and so they are untouchable.

In her garret, Divine lived only on tea and grief. She ate her grief and drank it; this sour food had dried her body and corroded her mind. Nothing—neither her own personal care nor the beauty parlors—kept her from being thin and having the skin of a corpse. She wore a wig, which she set most artfully, but the net of the underside showed at the temples. Powder and cream did not quite conceal the juncture with the skin of the forehead. One might have thought that her head was artificial. In the days when he was still in the garret, Darling might have laughed at all these embellishments had he been an ordinary pimp, but he was a pimp who heard voices. He neither laughed nor smiled. He was handsome and prized his good looks, realizing that if he lost them he would lose everything. Though the difficult charms employed in making beauty hold fast did not excite him, they left him cold and drew no cruel smile. It was quite natural. So many former girl friends had made themselves up in his presence that he knew that the damages to beauty are repaired without mystery. In shady hotels, he had witnessed clever restorations, had watched women as they hesitated with a lipstick in mid-air. Many a time he had helped Divine fasten her wig on. His movements had been skillful and, if I may say so, natural. He had learned to love that kind of Divine. He had steeped himself in all the monstrosities of which she was composed. He had passed them in review: her very white dry skin, her thinness, the hollows of her eyes, her powdered wrinkles, her slicked-down hair, her gold teeth. He noted every detail. He said to himself that that's how it was; continued to screw it. He knew ecstasy and was caught good and proper. Darling the sturdy, all and always hot muscle and bush, was smitten with an artificial queen. Divine's wiles had nothing to do with it. Darling plunged headlong into this sort of debauch. Then, little by little, he had grown weary. He neglected Divine and left her. In the garret, she then had terrible fits of despair. Her advancing age was moving her into a coffin. It got to the point where she no longer dared a gesture or manner; people who came to know her during this period said that she seemed retiring. She still clung to the pleasures of bed and hallway; she cruised the tearooms, but now it was she who did the paying. When making love, she would experience the wildest terror, fearing, for example, lest an excited youngster rumple her hair while she was on her knees, or press his head against her too roughly and push off her wig. Her pleasure was encumbered with a host of petty worries. She would stay in the garret in order to jerk off. For days and nights on end she would remain lying in bed, with the curtains drawn over the window of the dead, the Bay Window of the Departed. She would drink tea and eat fruitcake. With her head beneath the sheets, she would devise complicated debauches, involving two, three, or four persons, in which all the partners would arrange to discharge in her, on her, and for her at the same time. She would recall the narrow but vigorous loins, the loins of steel that had perforated her. Without regard for their tastes, she would couple them. She was willing to be the single goal of all these lusts, and her mind strained in an effort to be conscious of them simultaneously as they drifted about in a voluptuousness poured in from all sides. Her body would tremble from head to foot. She felt personalities that were strange to her passing through her. Her body would cry out: "The god, behold the god!" She would sink back, all exhausted. The pleasure soon lost its edge. Divine then donned the body of a male. Suddenly strong and muscular, she saw herself hard as nails, with her hands in her pockets, whistling. She saw herself doing the act on herself. She felt her muscles growing, as when she had tried to play virile, and she felt herself getting hard around the thighs, shoulderblades, and arms, and it hurt her. This game, too, petered out. She was drying up. There were no longer even any circles under her eyes.

It was then she sought out the memory of Alberto and satisfied herself with him. He was a good-for-nothing. The whole village mistrusted him. He was thievish, brutal, and coarse. Girls frowned when his name was mentioned in their presence, but their nights and sudden escapes during the dreary hours of work were taken up with his vigorous thighs, with his heavy hands that were forever swelling his pockets and stroking his flanks, or that remained there motionless, or moved gently, stealthily, as they lifted the taut or distended cloth of his trousers. His hands were broad and thick, with short fingers, a splendid thumb, an imposing, massive mound of Venus, hands that hung from his arms like sods. It was on a summer evening that the children, who are the usual bearers of staggering news, informed the village that Alberto was fishing for snakes. "Snake fisher, that's just what he's fit for," thought the old women. This was one more reason for wishing him to the devil. Some scientists were offering an attractive premium for every reptile captured alive. While playing, Alberto caught one unintentionally, delivered it alive, and received the promised premium. Thus was born his new profession, which he liked, and which made him furious with himself. He was neither a superman nor an immoral faun. He was just a boy with simple thoughts, though embellished by voluptuousness. He seemed to be in a state of perpetual delight or perpetual intoxication. It was inevitable that Culafroy should meet him. It was the summer he spent wandering along the roads. As soon as he saw Alberto's figure in the distance, he realized that there was the purpose and goal of his walk. Alberto was standing motionless at the edge of the road, almost in the rye, as if waiting for someone, his two shapely legs spread in the stance of the Colossus of Rhodes, or the one shown us by the German sentries, so proud and solid beneath their helmets. Culafroy loved him. As he passed by, brave and indifferent, the lad blushed and lowered his head, while Alberto, with a smile on his lips, watched him walk. Let us say that he was eighteen years old, and yet Divine remembers him as a man.

He returned the following day. Alberto was standing there, a sentinel or statue, at the side of the road. "Hello!" he said, with a smile that twisted his mouth. (This smile was Alberto's particularity, was himself. Anyone could have had, or could have acquired, the same stiff hair, the color of his skin, his walk, but not his smile. Now when Divine seeks out the lost Alberto, she tries to portray him on herself and invents his smile with her own mouth. She puckers her muscles in what she thinks is the right way, the way—so she thinks when she feels her mouth twisting—that makes her resemble Alberto, until the day it occurs to her to do it in front of a mirror, and she realizes that her grimaces in no way resemble the smile we have already called starlike.) "Hello!" muttered Culafroy. That was all they said to each other, but from that day on Ernestine was to get used to seeing him desert the slate house. One day, Alberto asked:

"Want to see my pouch?"

He showed him a closely woven wicker basket buckled by a strap. The only thing in it that day was one elegant and angry snake.

"Shall I open it?"

"Oh! no, no, don't open it!" he said, for he has always felt that uncontrollable repulsion for reptiles.

Alberto did not lift the lid, but put his hard, gentle, brier-scratched hand on the back of Culafroy's neck, just as the child was about to drop to his knees. Another day, three snakes were writhing about each other. Their heads were hooded in little hard leather cowls that were tightened about their necks by nooses.

"You can touch them. They won't hurt you."

Culafroy didn't move. Rooted with horror, he could no more have run away than at the apparition of a ghost or an angel from heaven. He was unable to turn his head. The snakes fascinated him; yet he felt that he was about to vomit.

"You scared? Come on, admit it. I used to be scared too."

That wasn't true, but he wanted to reassure the child. With sovereign superiority, Alberto calmly and deliberately put his hand into the tangle of reptiles and took one out, a long, thin one whose tail flattened like a whipcord, but without a sound, about his bare arm. "Touch it!" he said, and as he spoke, he took the child's hand and placed it on the cold, scaly body, but Culafroy tightened his fist and only the joints of his fingers came into contact with the snake. That wasn't touching. The coldness surprised him. It entered his vein, and the initiation proceeded. Veils were falling from large and solemn tableaux that Culafroy's eyes could not make out. Alberto took another snake and placed it on Culafroy's bare arm, about which it coiled just as the first had done.

"You see, she's harmless." (Alberto always referred to snakes in the feminine.)

Just as he felt his penis swelling between his fingers, so the sensitive Alberto felt in the child the mounting emotion that stiffened him and made him shudder. And the insidious friendship for snakes was born. And yet he had not yet touched any, that is, had not even grazed them with the organ of touch, the finger tips, the spot where the fingers are swollen with a tiny sensitive bump, by means of which the blind read. Alberto had to open the boy's hand and slip the icy, lugubrious body into it. That was the revelation. At that very moment, it seemed to him that a host of snakes might have invaded him, climbed over him, and wound themselves into him without his feeling anything but a friendly joy, a kind of tenderness, and meanwhile Alberto's sovereign hand had not left his, nor had one of his thighs left the child's, so that he was no longer quite himself. Culafroy and Divine, with their delicate tastes, will always be forced to love what they loathe, and this constitutes something of their saintliness, for that is renunciation.

Alberto taught him culling. You must wait until noon, when the snakes are asleep on the rocks, in the sun. You sneak up on them and then, crooking the index and middle finger, you grab them by the neck, close to the head, so that they can't slip away or bite; then, while the snake is hissing with despair, you quickly slip the hood over its head, tightened the noose, and put it into the box. Alberto wore a pair of corduroy trousers, leggings, and a gray shirt, the sleeves of which were rolled up to the elbows. He was good-looking—as are all the males in this book, powerful and lithe, and unaware of their grace. His hard, stubborn hair, which fell down over his eyes to his mouth, would have been enough to endow him with the glamor of a crown in the eyes of the frail, curly-haired child.

They generally met in the morning, around ten o'clock, near a granite cross. They would chat for a while about girls and then leave. The harvesting had not yet been done. As the metallic rye and wheat were inviolable by all others, they found sure shelter there. They entered obliquely, crept along and suddenly found themselves in the middle of the field. They stretched out on the ground and waited for noon. At first, Culafroy played with Alberto's arms, the next day with his legs, the day after with the rest of him, and this memory thrilled Divine, who could see herself hollowing her cheeks the way a boy does when he whistles. Alberto violated the child everywhere until he himself collapsed with weariness.

One day Culafroy said:

"I'm going home, Berto."

"Going home? Well, see you this evening, Lou."

Why "See you this evening?" The phrase came out of Alberto's mouth so spontaneously that Culafroy took it for granted and replied:

"See you this evening, Berto."

Yet the day was over, they would not see each other until the following day, and Alberto knew it. He smiled foolishly at the thought that he had let slip a phrase that he had not meant. As for Culafroy, the meaning of this farewell remained hazy. The phrase had thrilled him, as do certain artless poems, the logic and grammar of which become apparent only after we have enjoyed their charm. Culafroy was thoroughly bewitched. It was washday at the slate house. On the drier in the garden, the hanging sheets formed a labyrinth where specters hovered. That would be the natural place for Alberto to wait. But at what time? He had mentioned no specific time. The wind shook the white sheets as the arm of an actress shakes a backdrop of painted canvas. Night thickened with its usual quietness and constructed a rigid architecture of broad planes, packed with shadows. Culafroy's stroll began just as the spherical, steaming moon rose in the sky. This was to be the scene of the drama. Would Alberto come to rob? He needed money, he said, "for his chick." He had a chick; hence he was a true cock. As for stealing, it was possible. He had once inquired about the furnishings in the slate house. Culafroy liked the idea. He hoped that Alberto would come for that too. The moon was rising into the sky with a solemnity calculated to impress sleepless humans. A thousand sounds that make up the silence of night pressed in about the child, like a tragic chorus, with the intensity of the music of brasses and the strangeness of houses of crime, and of prisons, too, where—oh, the horror of it—one never hears the rattle of a bunch of keys. Culafroy walked about barefoot, among the sheets. He was experiencing minutes as light as minuets, minutes composed of anxiety and tenderness. He even ventured a toe dance, but the sheets, which formed hanging partitions and corridors, the sheets, quiet and crafty as corpses, might have drawn together and imprisoned and smothered him, as the branches of certain trees in hot countries sometimes smother careless savages who lie down to rest in their shade. If he ceased to touch the ground, save by an illogical movement of his taut instep, this movement might have made him take off, leave the earth, might have launched him into worlds from which he would never return, for in space nothing could stop him. He placed the soles of his feet squarely on the ground so that they would hold him there more firmly. For he knew how to dance. He had plucked the following theme from a copy of *Screen Weekly:* "A little ballerina photographed in her ballet skirt, her arms curved gracefully above her head, her toe rooted to the floor, like a spearhead." And below the picture, the following caption: "Graceful Kitty Ruphlay, twelve years old." With an amazing sense of divination, this child, who had never seen a dancer, who had never seen a stage or any actor, understood the page-long article dealing with such matters as figures, entrechats, jetés-battus, tutus, toe-shoes, drops, footlights, and ballet. From the aspect of the word Nijinsky (the rise of the N, the drop of the loop of the j, the leap of the hook on the k and the fall of the y, graphic form of a name that seems to be drawing the artist's élan, with its bounds and rebounds on the boards, of the jumper who doesn't know which leg to come down on), he sensed the dancer's lightness, just as he will one day realize that Verlaine can only be the name of a poet-musician. He learned to dance by himself, just as he had learned to play the violin by himself. So he danced as he played. His every act was served by gestures necessitated not by the act itself, but by a choreography that transformed his life into a perpetual ballet. He quickly succeeded in dancing on his toes, and he did it everywhere: in the shed while gathering sticks of wood, in the little barn, under the cherry tree. . . . He would put aside his sabots and dance on the grass in black wool slippers, with his hands clinging to the low branches. He filled the countryside with a host of figurines who thought they were dancers in white tulle tutus, but who nonetheless remained a pale schoolboy in a black smock looking for mushrooms or dandelions. He was very much afraid of being discovered, especially by Alberto. "What would I say to him?" He thought of the form of suicide that might save him, and he decided upon hanging. Let us go back to that night. He was surprised and startled by the slightest movement of the branches, the slightest breath that was a bit dry. The moon struck ten. Then came aching anxiety. In his heart and throat the child discovered jealousy. He was now sure that Alberto would not come, that he would go and get drunk; and the idea of Alberto's betrayal was so acute that it established itself despotically in Culafroy's mind, to such a degree that he declared: "My despair is immense." Generally, when he was alone, he felt no need to utter his thoughts aloud, but today an inner sense of the tragic bade him observe an extraordinary protocol, and so he declared: "My despair is immense." He sniffled, but he did not cry. About him, the setting had ceased to appear marvelously unreal. Everything was exactly as it had been before: there were still the same white sheets hanging on wire lines which sagged beneath the weight, the same star-spangled sky, but their meaning had changed. The drama that was being enacted there had reached its phase of high pathos, the denouement: all that remained for the actor was to die. When I write that the meaning of the setting was no longer the same, I do not mean that for Culafroy—and later for Divine—the setting was never any different from what it would have been for anyone else, namely, wash drying on wire lines. He was well aware that he was a prisoner of sheets, but I beg of you to see the marvelous in this: a prisoner of familiar, though stiff sheets in the moonlight—unlike Ernestine, whom they would have reminded of brocade hangings or the halls of a marble palace, she who could not mount one step of a stairway without thinking of the word tier, and in the same circumstances, she would not have failed to feel profound despair and make the setting change attribution, to transform it into a white marble tomb, to magnify it, as it were, with her own sorrow, which was as lovely as a tomb, whereas for Culafroy nothing had moved, and this indifference of the setting better signified its hostility. Each thing, each object, was the result of a miracle, the accomplishing of which filled him with wonder. Likewise each gesture. He did not understand his room, nor the garden, nor the village. He understood nothing, not even that a stone was a stone, and this amazement in the face of what *is*—a setting which, by dint of being, ends by no longer being—left him the writhing prey of primitive, simple emotions: grief, joy, pride, shame. . . .

He fell asleep, like a drunken harlequin on the stage who sinks into his baggy sleeves and collapses on the grass beneath the violent light of the moon. The following day, he said nothing to Alberto. The fishing and the lolling in the rye at noon were what they were every day. That evening, the idea had crossed Alberto's mind of prowling about the slate house, with his hands in his pockets, whistling as he walked (He had a remarkable way of whistling with metallic stridency, and his virtuosity was not the least of his charms. This whistling was magical. It bewitched the girls. The boys, aware of his power, envied him. Perhaps he charmed the snakes.), but he did not come, for the town was hostile to him, especially if, like an evil angel, he went there at night. He slept.

They continued making love in the midst of the snakes. Divine remembers this. She thinks it was the loveliest period of her life.

Harriet Daimler

THE WOMAN THING

"Macdonald, can I turn on the light now?"
"Absolutely not."
He hunted for her body and found it by following the descent of the mattress to the precipice where she had to be.

"Then you turn it on, please," she let him pat her wet thighs and her dry belly and then graduate up to her breasts.
"Sleep!"

"I can't sleep. I must talk to you."

"Does a tropical disease prevent you from hearing your voice in the dark?"

"That's just it," she detached him from the nipple stuck between his irregular teeth. "I can feel me reabsorbing my voice. I want you to hear it."

"Attention is a child of darkness," Macdonald mumbled into his yawn.

"You'll go to sleep." Martha sat up on her side of the bed collapsing his in a landslide. "I know you'll go to sleep. You always do when I talk seriously."

"I go to sleep," her ingratitude woke him sharply, "after elevating my love to an ecstasy of pleasure for seventeen hours. Does that seem abrupt?" he labored to regain his own pinnacle.

"But we're always either sleeping or fucking," she moaned. "I can never talk seriously."

"Martha," he asked in fatalistic calm, "is this going to be the same as last week's conversation?"

"With variations."

"Then just rattle off the variation without the rest. I swear, I haven't managed to forget one consonant."

"If you won't turn on the light, can I open the curtain? It might still be day," the girl bargained.

"Keep your revolting facts of nature to yourself," he said, pinning her to the bed. "You Americans, no timing. Just this appalling accuracy. Clock where your cocks should be."

"Cunts," she beggared.

"A detail that wouldn't give nerves to a poet."

"You're not a poet, you're a doctor."

"I've forbidden you to use that word in this bed," he snapped at her, shutting his eyes at the unforgivable trespass.

"Why did you stop being a doctor?"

"I couldn't stand the image of myself, tall, slender, humorous eyes, vital hair, a nervous intensity, quick competent movements— and then that long white coat, so obscenely attractive, women got sick at the sight of me."

"Do you ever think of all those sick neglected patients?"

"People have a right to be sick," he said darkly.

"Also a right to be cured."

"Absolutely not."

"That's nonsense and you know it."

"I know that you're trying to keep me awake," Macdonald lifted the arm from her flattened body and scratched his eyes open, "when you've got my complex glandular system alerted, you'll sneak into that monumentally meaningless conversation of yours, the whole serious thing, variations and theme."

"Even if I had nothing else to say," Martha extracted her body from the tangle of damp, tobacco-stained, wine-stained, yogurt-, coffee-, and come-stained sheets, "I'd still say nonsense."

"Congratulations."

"Nonsense."

He listened to her bare feet pressing cigarette butts on the tile floor. "If people are healthy, they're healthy," he delivered himself of a quotation no one would ever quote, "and if they're sick they're sick, disgusting egomaniacs, all their ingenious little diseases that it takes generations to cultivate. Fuck them."

"What about being hit by cars?" she fought for the masses.

"Each man to his own bad habits," Macdonald reached above his head and squeezed forty watts of electricity into his eyes. "I frankly prefer livers decomposed by excessive drink, and insanity caused by sleeping all night and struggling to stay awake all day. Martha, there's enough light in the room. If you touch that curtain and one sliver of day falls across my exhausted form, I will consider your death a suicide."

She took a chance and pulled back the curtain. Had the window been wide enough to frame an adult skull or the curtains full enough to form one fold, her gesture would have achieved significance. Squinting one eye she tried to focus it through the architect's esoteric joke. "It's a glorious day. I think there's sun somewhere, but of course not in Paris."

"Of course not," Macdonald reached for the Gauloises, "you want to turn tourist agents into prophets."

"It's that wall, Mac," Martha stayed sentinel at the rampart through which the enemy could not be spotted until he'd shot the pinks of her eyes, "the whole world could be raging with peace and we'd just see the wall. Why," she turned her imploring naked search on him, "now why would the French build a hotel against a wall and then put a microscopic vaginal slit in all the rooms facing the wall when so many painters are screaming for commissions?"

"When this hotel opened, little one, daylight was recognized as vulgar and ill-flattering to fair complexions," he stared back at her, "and how wise were our ancestors is confirmed by your revolting appearance."

"Then why did you become a doctor?"

"Have I missed my cue," Macdonald apologized to his fellow players, "or did I just have a monotonous chat with myself about walls?"

"Well, why? Did you love humanity?"

"Never," his laugh turned into a nicotine addict's hackle, "humanity, those nauseous gases that solidified into you."

"But why?"

"Who can fathom nature?"

"No, the other why."

"Come back to bed," he said, "I can see you too clearly at this distance."

"I look like hell?"

"The enamel is cracking a bit," he admitted. "You look like the Mona Lisa that didn't get returned to the Louvre."

She rushed her face to the piece of mirror over the sink. "You're right," her fingers forcing the cracks to fuse and disappear. "I must put on all fresh powder."

"Women," he marveled, "how with the mysterious and subtle changes of your delicate inner life and metabolism you create life's only calendar."

"Also I'll have to make some more black for my eyes."

"Oh, Christ," he moaned, "you're going to smoke all the concierges out of their electric eyes."

"Well, I can't go around like this," she glared at him out of yesterday's ruined mask.

"Get back into bed."

"Why did you become a doctor?"

"So I could study my body," he relented, "without everyone getting suspicious. I was always mad for my body."

"Is that all?" She stood leaning over the bed looking for the opening, and then finding the corner where the blanket appeared to be in contact with mattress, crawled in.

"Oh no, my precious Penelope, also to study female parts. I

reasoned that if I could memorize all my vitals and then progress onto females', I'd make a fortune giving frigid American ladies, who sometimes came to our modest but picturesque village, orgasms. At the time I chose that livelihood," his words were aimless but his fingers on her cunt sure, "like most of my ignorant Scots neighbors, I thought that all frigid American ladies were rich. You, of course," he released a torrent of accusing smoke in her direction, "are only one of the examples confirming that a youth should not be left to choose his own destiny."

"Macdonald."

"The voice I hear is not of my present love but speaks like a specter out of last week, and the week before that week."

"Macdonald are you the only man who can make me come?"

"I wouldn't be surprised. I've always had rotten luck with my successes."

"Then it must be because we have a profound relationship."

"It must be."

"See," she pulled the burning cigarette out of his mouth, "see, you're going to sleep with a cigarette and the light and window and everything. We must have this discussion."

"Discussions," he groaned, "couldn't you write down your thoughts, leaving wide margins on either side of the paper for me to bluepencil in my corrections."

"Why were you the only man to make me come?"

"Because I'm clever. Because I have an iron and tireless prick."

"Nonsense."

"That phrase keeps recurring."

She increased the agony of the bedsprings and turned to him. "I think I was ready. I used to believe it was your great skill or my great love that made me come, but I've been reconsidering. I'd become less neurotic in Europe, any man could have done it."

"Why my sweet," he reached gently for her hand, "and have I been the last to try? I never dared to ask or to hope."

"Well, practically."

"Practically? You equivocate, have there been impractical results?"

"No one else can," she said bluntly.

"And the thing you wish to know is if this is a curse or a blessing? You are wondering if it will be necessary for you to throw your body on the burning pyre in the unfortunate calamity of my demise preceding yours."

"Yes, that's what I'm wondering."

"I can see your dilemma," he picked up another cracked mirror that fate had deposited on the bedside chair-table-crate and studied his ravaged teeth, "and when you allow for the modern savagery of inhumation, I marvel at how you maintain a calm. Then you don't really maintain, do you?"

"Badly."

"You would like me to assure that you will be the first of us to go? Is that what's haunting our idyllic relationship?"

"Do we have a relationship, Macdonald?"

"I knew it was a mistake to use that word." He spat on the insolent mirror, "I forgot about all the books you've been reading. Would you tweeze my eyebrows, Martha?"

"Do we have anything Macdonald?"

"Sure, all kinds of things." He carefully replaced the gilt mirror, and just as carefully separated her golden thighs. "Among which I sadly cannot include money."

"Macdonald, speak seriously to me, are we together because we love each other?"

"Is this famous discussion of yours an elaborate plot to make me impotent? Because that question would require a serious answer," he warmed his hands at the barricade, "if it made any sense at all."

"It makes great sense," she held him out, "it's the only thing that does make sense. Why are we here together in this bed?"

"Whereas the other answer would have to be too serious, this one is too obvious."

"Just to fuck, Macdonald, is that all?"

"You'll weep at that preposition when you hit sixty."

"But why each other? Why for three years each other?"

"We pretend to enjoy it."

"Is pretense everything?"

"I'm not prepared to deal with everything, just fucking."

"And will we want each other tomorrow, Macdonald?"

"Don't be impatient sweet. Let's wait and ignore that question tomorrow."

"But it makes everything so tenuous," she wept, "it makes every day so arbitrary, and then so identical."

"You want a reason bigger than either of us, my little one?"

"I want an answer."

"I can't give it to you." He wrestled with her hand that fell away like a sloppy drunk from the solid support of his offered pole.

"Thank you," she said grimly, "you can continue sleeping now."

"I have no reasons."

"You made that clear."

"I think reasons are so unreasonable."

"Love would be a reason," she shrieked.

"Is that a reason to love? Just to be neat and have a reason?"

"It would be the other way round."

"My suspicions are so strong as to be convictions."

"Hate would be a reason."

"So would geography, economy, chemistry, philosophy, or sodomy. So pick any one, or even two that satisfy you. I won't turn state's evidence."

"I'm a woman," she insisted into his calm face. The man next door put down *France-Soir*.

"If you're a woman," Macdonald surrendered on her desert-dry cunt, "why don't you go to work like all the other women and give me some pocket money and peace, then I'll be strong and beat you."

"That wouldn't mean anything."

"It might hurt, I'm bigger than I look."

"If you'd beat me out of jealousy or lust . . ."

"Bring me my strap, I'll try."

"Oh Macdonald, it's so weak our being together. It's as if once three years ago we got into bed and neither of us has had the energy to get out since."

"You exaggerate darling, we get out at least seven times a week. Ask any garçon at the Deux Magots."

"What's that?"

"It's a cathedral on St. Germain des Prés, across from the other Cathedral St. Germain des Prés, not far from that other Cathedral St. Sulpice."

"I think," she jumped out of bed in a flare of intensity, "that people should be together because they can't be apart."

"Like in prisons and mental institutions?" he suggested.

"I mean there should be an urgency, an inevitability, a decision that makes them be together."

"Tension is a good word."

"Yes tension, attraction, love."

"I hope my secretary is getting this all down."

"It's so easy to be cynical," she said contemptuously, reaching for another cigarette and lighting it slowly and attentively, letting the sulphur fumes burn away and inhaling the clean heat. He watched her carefully and approved.

"I want a man who needs me as a woman."

"You read that somewhere," he accused.

"A man who will accept being accepted as a man."

"You've been sneaking copies of *Reader's Digest* out of the library, naughty girl."

"Shut up," she hammered at him, "I'm not a child anymore playing fuck. Let's play fuck. We're too old for running bases so let's play fuck."

"Sure," he enthusiastically brought out his equipment, "get back into the bed."

"Macdonald, I want to commit myself."

He pulled his body back against the Greek pillar that the hotel outrageously disguised as a pillow. "It sounds very dangerous."

"And I must commit myself to someone."

"My toenails are a sight," he complained, "pedicure me."

"I want to say to someone, I accept you, and have him say back to me, I accept you. Simple but difficult."

"That one you overheard on a bus of sightseeing goldfish."

"What do you know about buses," she shrieked hopelessly, "when have you ever been on a bus?"

"Is that what you've been getting at for all these weeks," he sighed, "you feel I'm not enough of an adventurer, an explorer, a hunter. You want to lie on this bed thinking all day of ways to comfort me while I transfer like a madman from buses to métros to taxis and stagger home to you bulging with brutal worldliness to grind my knee into your cunt. And then you want to say that's my troubled man grinding his knee into my healing cunt."

"You're twisting it," her voice flew like a wild horse around the room looking for something unbroken.

"You want the serenity of abuse," he pursued, "you're afraid I'm not sufficiently amused by you. You want to be beaten into my digestive system."

"No, no, no."

"Figuratively of course," Macdonald calmed her, "none of us have that much energy left."

"We won't talk any more," her voice quivered.

"Don't boss me around," Macdonald continued. "I'm no pervert. Just because you can't be dependent is no reason to become independent. I feel like talking."

"Shut up, please shut your stupid mouth." She threaded the thick cord through the hole punched in the top of the tin sardine can and silently began to manufacture eye shadow.

"All right, when I get my second breath in three years we can talk some more."

"We shall never discuss anything again," she poured in the olive oil and lit the wick watching the black smoke rise. With priestly precision she erected a shed of tin over the smoke to catch the soot.

"Good."

"You're too disgustingly negative."

"And not at all positive."

"You leave so much out," she stood still but her rage trembled.

"Don't I."

"You leave responsibility and family and faith out."

"Completely."

"You leave the world out."

"I knew I overlooked something."

"And you and me out."

"What carelessness."

"Macdonald why you and me?" she exploded. "It goes back to why you and me."

"We happened in the same world that I left out."

"So did everybody else."

"But we're accident prone, we met."

"Thanks," she bent her head over the small smoking furnace.

"Your tears will excite me into surrendering myself," he warned. "I'll say that I'm your man and you my woman and apart we have no existence till death do us in and give us eternal life together."

"I never knew beauty," her two tears dried in long slate exclamation points on her chalk cheeks, "until I heard your words."

"Words," he said contemptuously, "incantations, you want to make a dedication out of fucking and use your body as a living altar."

"What else does a girl dream of," she demanded, "during her painful Brooklyn adolescence."

"You want me to prove that I'm better than you, so that you can really soar when you prove that I'm not."

"What could be easier."

"You have to be sure it's God's prick you stick on your pike-staff."

"You and your miserable balls."

"Get into this bed and shut your blasphemous mouth," he commanded.

"Never!"

He wrenched her on the bed in one graceless hurdle. "Put your woman's magic hand around my cock and make me feel good all over like that nauseous child in that nauseous book about that nauseous uncle."

"I wouldn't touch your filthy prick."

"When are you going to stop listening to your own words. Haven't I taught you that. You're revolting when you're serious, your entire Jewish ancestry comes squatting all over your face."

"You haven't taught me anything, except that a man and a woman can mean something together and we don't."

"I'll worry about your education after I fuck you."

"Don't come near me."

"How authentic, I have to rape you."

"You twist and vulgarize everything," she pounded his oncoming chest, "fucking should be a unity, where two people become one . . ."

"And you hate me so much you're unwilling to become me. Look darling, don't ever get confused about where I end and you begin," in infuriating calm he lit a cigarette. "I don't. That may be the clue to your reluctant orgasm. Good title. Maybe none of your former heroes made the distinction and you didn't want to be an old spoilsport and point it out to them just when they were having the best time."

"Can I only be satisfied by someone I despise?"

"I mean that you come with me because I leave you alone to enjoy yourself."

"That's masturbation," the scandal thickened her alarm.

"With an audience! Can you feel yourself turning indigo and going blind?" he squashed out the three hundred and twenty-fourth cigarette of the week. "Come, your great mind has stimulated my great cock."

It turned into a very serious session, no memorable jokes or clever ideas. He just stayed on top of her, embracing her buttocks to get her pressed against him and opening her cunt with his broad stiff staff. He got the head of his cock into the center of her sex, and stayed on it, rubbed on it, without mercy. She pressed her insides against it, revealing all her girlish secrets. He just ignored her the first time she came, persisting in deep indifferent thrusts. Her spread legs pulled together and locked him to her, and her perspiring body got ready for the second time. It was all very serious, Macdonald had lost his sense of humor.

He fucked her until she was a hot river, until he could feel her not knowing or caring who or what that thing inside of her was, just plunging it up and down inside of her with lavish fascism. Then he forgot her and let his body turn into an enormous prick that went where it wanted to go as fast and as deep and as hard as it could.

Her first words, when she could see that there was someone else in the world, were, "I'm so hungry and there's nothing to eat."

The American Express

Gregory Corso

*J*oel had entered a war that was new and shining.
A war that was an adventure.

And the fighting was to be a youthful heroic game to be played with exuberance and joy, without fear.

The old soldier could not understand Joel's zest. "Woe," he would say, "woe to the sinful nation, to a people laden with iniquity!"

"History, life! has been made rich! by war," sang Joel.

The old man grabbed him by the collar. "The armies of a people scattered and peeled, and a nation meted out and trodden down—"

Captain Blaze rode up to the two men. "Joel! Go to the battlefield and tell General Eatsun Smacknight's men are sacking and looting the town—tell him we need reinforcements! Hurry, make haste!"

"Yes sir!" And Joel jumped on his horse and was off.

At the start of the battle between the two armies led by Eatsun and Smacknight thousands of men wearing bright colorful uniforms stood facing each other at a distance of an encompassed smooth green field. The sun shone on the scene as though it were watching nothing else in all the world. The two armies were perfectly aligned, levied, flanked, and prepared to fight. They were men made for the occasion. They had no other thought or purpose but to charge, enter, clash, and overcome the enemy.

The two generals faced each other with their vast armies. They raised their arms; the lowering of them would signal the start of the onslaught.

Joel thundered urgency on a magnificent black horse. He reached the battlefield and brought his horse to a screaming halt before General Eatsun. "Sir! The enemy is spreading disorder and terror in town—they are sacking and looting, women and children are being slaughtered—"

"The battle will prove decisive here!" roared the general.

"But Captain Blaze said they will move north—they will come from behind—"

"You tell Captain Blaze to evacuate!"

"Yes sir!" And Joel pulled the reins of his horse, the horse stood up and turned in a wonderfully graceful fashion, and Joel was off.

The signaling arms went down, the onslaught was on.

Five of Smacknight's men were in hot pursuit of Joel.

Along the embankment of the river sat Thimble and Mr. D with binoculars, watching all.

The horsemen of both sides charged across the field like a rising music, and behind them the footmen screamed animal cries as they

ran sword-arms raised and swinging, and the banner carriers at the lead raced into each other and in immediate succession the entire horde interlocked into a riotous knot of death—heads fell, hands fell, hearts were pierced, necks were broken, ax rang on ax, and sword resounded on sword—the swiftness, and the fierceness, helmet-tumblings, and horses neighing, falling—knit upon knit until the whole violently chaotic spool was so hideously strange that it affected Nature to such an extent that all the trees in the vicinity went insane.

The five horsemen were catching up with Joel. He was not too far away from the besieged town—he held the neck of his horse and galloped mercilessly, occasionally turning to see the progress of his pursuers.

The townspeople were evacuating. The manager of the American Express and staff packed everything they could possibly carry and left. Hinderov immediately came out of the basement with a bucket of black paint and a brush.

"Victory!" he cried as he crossed out the AMERICAN from the windows and put, in its place, HINDEROV. And so it was that the American Express became the Hinderov Express. Bronskier jumped with joy—"Hinderov, you've won! It's all yours!" And, fate of fates, a bullet of war touched Bronskier's face—Albie hurried in horror to his father's side—Bronskier was dead.

Albie held his father in his arms. "Hear! O Great Queen of arms, whose favor my father won, as you defend the sire, defend the son. When on Hinderov's cause the banded powers of war he left, and sought the American Express, peace was his charge; received with peaceful show, he went a legate, but returned a foe—"Albie rose and walked toward Hinderov with murder in his eyes. Hinderov backed away. "What's wrong with you? Are you crazy? What are you doing—" And Hinderov backed away, and Albie came on.

"You fool! You dare to threaten me!" croaked Hinderov.

"You are the enemy of man, Hinderov—"

At that moment a sergeant rode up to them. "What regiment do you guys belong to?"

Hinderov sighed relief. "I know nothing about army arrangements, sergeant, but I would like to join a regiment—"

"Go east," ordered the sergeant, "the operations of our troops there have caused the enemy to break through—they are occupying positions within the territories of our land! Have you a horse?"

"No, sir—"

Albie stood sadly by the body of his father; he would have to bury him.

"And you!" called the sergeant; "have you any orders?"

"No—"

"What are you doing?"

"I will bury my father—"

Joel reached Captain Blaze and told him what General Eatsun had ordered.

"Damned Eatsun!" cursed the wearied, battle-worn captain; "he's ever bringing fresh orders, has he any idea where his military garrisons are held up? It's a queer business—nothing seems to come from the regimental staff; what are these telephones for? Not once have they called—what kind of staff is it that doesn't telephone its orders to the battalion? I do not have to adhere to Eatsun's orders, dammit!"

Joel, exhausted by his mission, sat down by the old soldier. The old soldier smiled and handed Joel a hot cup of coffee. Surrounding them were burning houses, and dying men, and dead men, and screaming women and crying babies—

"It's hell—" said Joel.

The old soldier shook a finger at Joel. "So long as a man is in this world he is midway between hell and heaven; hell is yet to be seen, m'boy—"

A wounded soldier grappling his shot stomach fell in terrible agony before Joel.

"But this is not what I thought it would be!" cried Joel, dropping his cup of coffee.

"Watch him," said the old soldier, "watch the carbon leave him. It's carbon that separates the living from the dead—it'll soon leave him—watch—"

"The poor man!"

"The thing about carbon," continued the old man, "is that it makes a basis for life in its ability to form, with other chemicals, extremely complex molecules—"

The dying soldier raised a death-reaching hand into life for help. . . . Joel knelt beside him and rested the poor man's head on his lap. Joel wished he were on his horse, moving fast. Everything seemed

alive and exciting when he moved. Suddenly a machine-gun assault mowed down Captain Blaze and the group of strategists surrounding him. The machine-gun unit fired for almost an hour on the trapped regiment. After the bloody engagement, Captain Blaze's men, who were decisively outnumbered, fled in confusion and panic.

Joel jumped up and raced to his horse.

"Take me!" cried the old soldier, "I haven't a horse—please take me!"

"Hurry!"

And the old soldier with desperate agility climbed on the horse—and Joel, with bullets whizzing all about, thundered off, the old soldier embracing his small waist.

Joel returned to the battlefield. Night was falling. In the sky crows dipped and climbed—the battle was over.

Generals Eatsun and Smacknight and their armies lay where they had fallen.

"The cords of death compassed me about, the cords of hell encompassed me, the snares of death forestalled me: therefore He sent out His arrows, and many lightnings, and discomfited them. I will pursue mine enemies, and catch them, neither will I turn until I have consumed them. I will smite them that they shall not be able to rise. Thou hath girded me with strength unto this war, and Thou shalt put mine enemies to flight; I will beat them small as dust before the faces of the wind, as the mire of the streets I will enfeeble them—"

Mr. D and Thimble were captured by the enemy. They were simply walking along the highway expounding theories about the battle that they had earlier witnessed when a band of Smacknight's soldiers engulfed them. They were brought to the enemy camp, and there they were both tied to a pole in a big tent.

"Well, lord love a duck, are they going to shoot us or eat us—" wondered Thimble.

Mr. D made a wry face as he tried to ease the tightness of the rope around his wrists—"Stupid birdbrains! Don't even know how to tie a man up!"

"Smacknight definitely lost that encounter today," stated Thimble. They both sat back to back with the pole in between.

"Seems like they're winning as far as we're concerned. How we gonna get out of here!"

"Here comes someone now—"

It was a big blackhaired man dressed in jangling armor, followed by four soldiers.

The soldiers put a little stool before the two tied men, and the big man sat on it, smiling, his teeth gleaming, his long black mustache cringing—and he rested his fat hands on his widened knees and leaned into Mr. D and Thimble—"Dogs! Swine! Spies!"

The two men said nothing.

"Do you deny you are spies!"

"We were taking a stroll," said Thimble.

"You were spying!"

"Can you loosen these ropes somewhat," asked Mr. D, still preoccupied with the bungled binding.

"Shut up!" the big man shouted. "I'll do the talking! Dogs! Lice! You are both guilty of spying; the penalty for spying is death. You will both be shot immediately!" And the big man jangling with silver and swords strutted out of the tent.

"Well, D, this looks like it—"

The four soldiers gathered about them and cut them free.

"Not so, Thimble! They're not going to get Mr. D!" And Mr. D, a tall thin humble-looking man, transformed into a fury of a man. He swung at the soldier closest to him with all his might and the soldier fell back into the other three. Thimble quickly picked up the stool and swung it blindly in all directions, and it connected with two soldiers. The other two soldiers drew their swords but Mr. D was on top of them with a heavy plank of wood and he brought it down upon their helmeted heads—it was done rapidly, in a matter of seconds, and the four soldiers lay still at their feet.

Mr. D picked up a sword and slashed the back of the tent. He and Thimble hurried out. It was night, and they ran like the wind into it.

After they were in the clear Thimble suggested they inform Eatsun's forces of the enemy's position but Mr. D advised against it, stating that both forces were obviously implements of death, and so meant them no good.

Joel assumed command of the army. He sat breathlessly before the battlefield. The battle had ceased but would shortly be resumed.

BOOM!

Joel raced into the muddy attack swinging swords and knives, shooting rifles and stens, flinging grenades and flares; and everybody dispersed in his path, and he skipped through the dispersion like a happy girl.

Tanks loomed before him; he threw tankbomb after tankbomb, and the tanks became all afire—

He shot the burning men teeming out of the burning tanks like a hard cold man.

The battle was over; he walked over the dead like an old market woman.

GREGORY CORSO

The American Express *is Gregory Corso's only novel, practically his only effort at prose writing. His name became known around the world for his poetry, and his outrageous fellowship with Allen Ginsberg, Jack Kerouac, and the other Beats who took their passionate, privately religious position against moderation, adjustment, objectivity, and all those proper patterns of behavior that allow what they feel to be an unacceptable world to function. Gregory, who has read his poems (particularly the outspoken* Bomb) *in most of the capitals of the world, became an expert victim of The American Expresses of the world. His wild and hilarious view of this venerable institution is the core of his novel. Gregory Corso was born in New York some thirty odd years ago, was something of a street urchin, spent time both in jail and Harvard University, New Jersey and New Delhi, and brings all of his experience into every word he writes.*

POBLACHT NA H EIREANN.

THE PROVISIONAL GOVERNMENT

OF THE

IRISH REPUBLIC

TO THE PEOPLE OF IRELAND.

IRISHMEN AND IRISHWOMEN : In the name of God and of the dead generations from which she receives her old tradition of nationhood, Ireland, through us, summons her children to her flag and strikes for her freedom.

Having organised and trained her manhood through her secret revolutionary organisation, the Irish Republican Brotherhood, and through her open military organisations, the Irish Volunteers and the Irish Citizen Army, having patiently perfected her discipline, having resolutely waited for the right moment to reveal itself, she now seizes that moment, and, supported by her exiled children in America and by gallant allies in Europe, but relying in the first on her own strength, she strikes in full confidence of victory.

We declare the right of the people of Ireland to the ownership of Ireland, and to the unfettered control of Irish destinies, to be sovereign and indefeasible. The long usurpation of that right by a foreign people and government has not extinguished the right, nor can it ever be extinguished except by the destruction of the Irish people. In every generation the Irish people have asserted their right to national freedom and sovereignty : six times during the past three hundred years they have asserted it in arms. Standing on that fundamental right and again asserting it in arms in the face of the world, we hereby proclaim the Irish Republic as a Sovereign Independent State, and we pledge our lives and the lives of our comrades-in-arms to the cause of its freedom, of its welfare, and of its exaltation among the nations.

The Irish Republic is entitled to, and hereby claims, the allegiance of every Irishman and Irishwoman. The Republic guarantees religious and civil liberty, equal rights and equal opportunities to all its citizens, and declares its resolve to pursue the happiness and prosperity of the whole nation and of all its parts, cherishing all the children of the nation equally, and oblivious of the differences carefully fostered by an alien government, which have divided a minority from the majority in the past.

Until our arms have brought the opportune moment for the establishment of a permanent National Government, representative of the whole people of Ireland and elected by the suffrages of all her men and women, the Provisional Government, hereby constituted, will administer the civil and military affairs of the Republic in trust for the people.

We place the cause of the Irish Republic under the protection of the Most High God, Whose blessing we invoke upon our arms, and we pray that no one who serves that cause will dishonour it by cowardice, inhumanity, or rapine. In this supreme hour the Irish nation must, by its valour and discipline and by the readiness of its children to sacrifice themselves for the common good, prove itself worthy of the august destiny to which it is called.

Signed on Behalf of the Provisional Government,

THOMAS J. CLARKE.

SEAN Mac DIARMADA. THOMAS MacDONAGH.

P. H. PEARSE. EAMONN CEANNT,

JAMES CONNOLLY. JOSEPH PLUNKETT

The
BLACK DIARIES
of Roger Casement

Maurice Girodias
& Peter Singleton-Gates

"Casement is home, Ireland is content," is the title of an article in The London Observer *dated February 28, 1965.*

Roger Casement was hanged as a traitor to Britain by Mr. Asquith's war cabinet in August, 1916. He was not a traitor, as he had freely repudiated his allegiance to Britain to become one of the leaders of the Irish nationalist movement. He was not only executed by a country which had treated his own as a colony for centuries, after a trial which stands out as a mockery of justice—he was also dishonored as a man, and as a political leader, when copies of his private diaries were deliberately circulated, under instructions from the British government, to reveal his homosexual obsessions.

When England returned his tortured skeleton to his countrymen, without any proper rehabilitation, without even one word of explanation, she only added insult to injury. By meekly accepting the action, the Irish themselves betrayed their self-consciousness, their distrust of this doubtful Irish saint. Ireland "was content" with very little.

I first read about Casement in 1957, and I was so fascinated by his incredible life story that I searched for more information on the subject. I found that there existed an abundance of biographies, invariably prejudiced, but in opposite ways.

The English biographers were always careful to honor Casement's career as a British diplomat, and to praise his single-handed action in the Congo, and later in South America, thanks to which it had been possible to introduce some measure of humanity in the earlier forms of colonialism. By embracing the Irish nationalist faith in 1913, and, later by going to Germany to raise an Irish brigade among British prisoners of war, Casement had unfortunately revealed himself as a foul traitor, as a cad, a crank, and it was not surprising to find that he had been a pervert all that time—was the conclusion of the British commentators.

As to the Irish writers, they were motivated by several simple facts: Casement had become a valuable figure in the Irish nationalist mythology. He died a Catholic, and in heroic style. The accusations of homosexuality preferred against him were incompatible with that sort of background; they were intolerable: therefore they were unfounded. Nobody knows exactly where the notion originated that Casement's diaries had been tampered with by the British secret service to alter their contents, but during the last forty years the issue has become one of remarkable public and political importance. The successive British governments have tried to hush it out of existence, but their secretive attitude, their refusal to let the famous diaries be examined for authentication, appeared as an admission of guilt.

I became convinced, by studying those various reports of Casement's story, that, although the original diaries had apparently been destroyed, and although the copies circulated by the British secret service in 1916 to smear Casement's character had been withdrawn as soon as that result had been achieved, there still existed at least one copy of the diaries somewhere in the world. I searched for it and finally found it in the possession of a retired London journalist, Peter Singleton-Gates.

I became convinced that the diaries, as reproduced in the typed copy that bears on the front page "New Scotland Yard, August 1916, REX v. CASEMENT," were authentic. That did not alter my opinion as to the use which had been made of the diaries by the British authorities, in 1916, to influence the hyper-respectable Victorian society of the time, and thus to discourage all who wanted to obtain a reprieve from the Home Secretary and save Casement's life after he had been sentenced to death. Such had been their tactics, before Casement, to discredit Parnell.

But the fact that Casement was a confessed homosexual should not have been balanced against his invaluable services, first to the cause of African and Indian populations, and later to the cause of Ireland.

It seems that there was a good deal of hypocrisy—social hypocrisy added to political convenience—in the attitude of both parties. The Irish nationalists were clamoring for a revision of the trial, but not very sincerely so, as they were at heart convinced that Casement was the superlative pederast his diaries revealed him to be—and that the diaries were authentic. And the British conservatives made the best possible use of the Irish unavowed wish for secrecy to ignore the real issue—which was, and still is, the full rehabilitation of Casement by those who took his life. But to clear Casement would be to admit that he had been officially murdered rather than legally tried and executed. To this day the Casement "mystery" is covered up under official declarations made by both sides, to the effect that the less said about the painful incident, the better for the preservation of Anglo-Irish relations. So Casement is really condemned to everlasting ignominy, the victim of a new, posthumous conspiracy.

To me, indeed, Casement is a hero. He was politically confused, emotionally unbalanced, maudlin when depressed and absurdly naive when in his best form; but he was exceptionally generous, he had extraordinary courage and a simple human wisdom which sprang from his natural goodness. He was a knot of confusions, religious, sexual, political, and professional, but that did not prevent him from sacrificing everything to the causes in which he believed.

I therefore decided to do what I could for my hero, and persuaded Singleton-Gates to contribute the diaries and his knowledge of the case to a large survey of Casement's life and times, which was eventually published in 1959, simultaneously in Paris, London, and New York. The book was never reviewed, which does not surprise me, but its effect was immediate: the British Home Secretary admitted that Casement's diaries were still in existence, and they were publicly displayed. A very limited number of self-appointed experts, both British and Irish, were authorized to study them; the former declared that they were convinced that the diaries were authentic and the latter that they were gross forgeries. Thus the balance of confusion was neatly preserved.

The secretive return of Casement's bones to Ireland by decision of the Labor cabinet of the day, the discreet state funerals in Dublin with a few words of homage spoken in Gaelic by Eamon de Valera, such is the uncomfortable conclusion of that long, pathetic, unlikely story.

But is it really?

When Casement retired from the British consular service in 1911, he was not long in associating with the various cultural and political movements which were trying to obtain Home Rule for Ireland.

The nationalist movement in Ireland was represented by John Redmond's party, and Redmond was at heart pro-British, and his ambitions did not go further than a travesty of independence. To break the progress toward Home Rule, the British conservatives sent to Ulster two men, Edward Carson and F.E. Smith, two lawyers who appealed to the pro-British sentiments of the Ulster counties to create an opposition inside Ireland against the national movement of independence.

Thus were created the conditions of an internal conflict between the Ulster Protestant minority of the North and the Catholic majority of the South. Carson and Smith were not long in starting an armed militia in Ulster, and the nationalists retaliated by founding the Irish Volunteers, in 1913. Roger Casement was one of the leaders of that new body.

When war broke out, he was sent to New York by his colleagues to raise funds for the Volunteers. There he met John Devoy and the other chiefs of the rather confused Irish movement. They decided to send Casement to Germany to secure help for the cause and, after many adventures, he finally arrived in the Wilhelmstrasse where he was received with full honors. Thus Casement was persuaded to raise the Irish legion in P.O.W. camps in Germany, which was meant to fight for the liberation of Ireland after the war.

His efforts were pitiful, and he never could gather more than

53 men for that venture. But he saw clearly that his good faith was being abused by the Germans. A virtual prisoner, disowned by his own friends in Dublin and in New York he led a miserable life in Germany until he heard of the preparations made for an armed rebellion, in 1916. He managed to return secretly to Ireland in a desperate effort to stop the Easter Rising, which he considered to be a mad and hopeless enterprise. He was caught immediately on landing from a German submarine and was sent to London. His trial for high treason, with his own private political foe, F. E. Smith, acting as prosecutor for the Crown, appears as a sinister travesty of justice. But Casement's last words, in the form of an address to the court which had just sentenced him to death, give an altogether different dimension to this tragedy of errors.

My Lord Chief Justice, as I wish to reach a much wider audience than I see before me here, I intended to read all that I propose to say. What I shall read now is something I wrote more than twenty days ago. I may say, my Lord, at once, that I protest against the jurisdiction of this court in my case on this charge, and the argument that I am now going to read is addressed not to this court, but to my own countrymen.

There is an objection, possibly not good in law, but surely good on moral grounds, against the application to me here of this old English statute, 565 years old, that seeks to deprive an Irishman today of life and honor, not for "adhering to the King's enemies," but for adhering to his own people.

When this statute was passed in 1351, what was the state of men's minds of the question of a far higher allegiance—that of a man to God and His kingdom? The law of that day did not permit a man to forsake his church or deny his God save with his life. The "heretic" then had the same doom as the "traitor."

Today a man may forswear God and His heavenly kingdom without fear or penalty, all earlier statutes having gone the way of Nero's edicts against the Christians, but that constitutional phantom, "the king," can still dig up from the dungeons and torture chambers of the Dark Ages a law that takes a man's life and limb for an exercise of conscience.

If true religion rests on love, it is equally true that loyalty rests on love. The law I am charged under has no parentage in love and claims the allegiance of today on the ignorance and blindness of the past.

I am being tried, in truth, not by my peers of the live present, but by the peers of the dead past; not by the civilization of the twentieth century, but by the brutality of the fourteenth; not even by a statute framed in the language of an enemy land—so antiquated is the law that must be sought today to slay an Irishman, whose offense is that he puts Ireland first.

Loyalty is a sentiment, not a law. It rests on love, not on restraint. The Government of Ireland by England rests on restraint and not on law; and since it demands no love it can evoke no loyalty.

But this statute is more absurd even than it is antiquated; and if it is potent to hang one Irishman, it is still more potent to gibbet all Englishmen.

Edward III was king not only of the realm of England, but also of the realm of France, and he was not king of Ireland. Yet his dead hand today may pull the noose around the Irishman's neck whose sovereign he was not, but it can strain no strand around the Frenchman's throat whose sovereign he was. For centuries the successors of Edward III claimed to be kings of France, and quartered the arms of France on their royal shield down to the Union with Ireland on 1st January, 1801. Throughout these hundreds of years these "kings of France" were constantly at war with their realm of France and their French subjects, who should have gone from birth to death with an obvious fear of treason before their eyes. But did they? Did the "kings of France" resident here at Windsor or in the Tower of London hang, draw and quarter as a traitor every Frenchman for 400 years who fell into their hands with arms in his hand? On the contrary, they received embassies of these traitors, presents from these traitors, even knighthood itself at the hands of these traitors, feasted with them, titled with them, fought with them—but did not assassinate them by law. Judicial assassination today is reserved only for one race of the king's subjects, for Irishmen; for those who cannot forget their allegiance to the realm of Ireland.

The kings of England as such had no rights in Ireland up to the time of Henry VIII, save such as rested on compact and mutual obligation entered between them and certain princes, chiefs, and lords of

Ireland. This form of legal right, such as it was, gave no king of England lawful power to impeach an Irishman for high treason under this statute of King Edward III of England until an Irish Act, known as Poyning's Law, the 10th of Henry VII, was passed in 1494 at Drogheda, by the Parliament of the Pale in Ireland, and enacted as law in part of Ireland. But if by Poyning's Law an Irishman of the Pale could be indicted for high treason under this act, he could be indicted only in one way and before one tribunal—by the laws of the realm of Ireland and in Ireland. The very Law of Poyning's, which, I believe, applies this statute of Edward III to Ireland, enacted also for the Irishman's defense "all those laws by which England claims her liberty." And what is the fundamental charter of an Englishman's liberty? That he shall be tried by his peers. With all respect I assert this court is to me, an Irishman, not a jury of my peers to try me in this vital issue, for it is patent to every man of conscience that I have a right, an indefeasible right, if tried at all, under this statute of high treason, to be tried in Ireland, before an Irish court and by an Irish jury. This court, this jury, the public opinion of this country, England, cannot but be prejudiced in varying degree against me, most of all in time of war. I did not land in England; I landed in Ireland. It was to Ireland I came; to Ireland I wanted to come; and the last place I desired to land in was England. But for the Attorney General of England there is only "England"—there is no Ireland, there is only the law of England—no right of Ireland; the liberty of Ireland and of Irishmen is to be judged by the power of England. Yet for me, the Irish outlaw, there is a land of Ireland, a right of Ireland, and a charter for all Irishmen to appeal to, in the last resort, a charter that even the very statutes of England itself cannot deprive us of—nay, more, a charter that Englishmen themselves assert as the fundamental bond of law that connects the two kingdoms. This charge of high treason involves a moral responsibility, as the very terms of the indictment against myself recite, inasmuch as I committed the acts I am charged with, to the "evil example of others in the like case." What was this "evil example" I set to others in the "like case," and who were these others? The "evil example" charged is that I asserted the rights of my own country, and the "others" I appealed to to aid my endeavor were my own countrymen. The example was given not to Englishmen, but to Irishmen, and the "like case" can never arise in England, but only in Ireland. To Englishmen I set no evil example, for I made no appeal to them. I asked no Englishman to help me. I asked Irishmen to fight for their rights. The "evil example" was only to other Irishmen who might come after me, and in "like case" seek to do as I did. How, then, since neither my example nor my appeal were addressed to Englishmen, can I be rightfully tried by them?

If I did wrong in making that appeal to Irishmen to join with me in an effort to fight for Ireland, it is by Irishmen, and by them alone, I can be rightfully judged. From this court and its jurisdiction I appeal to those I am alleged to have wronged, and to those I am alleged to have injured by my "evil example," and claim that they alone are competent to decide my guilt or my innocence. If they find me guilty, the statute may affix the penalty, but the statute does not override or annul my right to seek judgment at their hands.

This is so fundamental a right, so natural a right, so obvious a right that it is clear the Crown were aware of it when they brought me by force and by stealth from Ireland to this country. It was not I who landed in England, but the Crown who dragged me here, away from my own country to which I had turned with a price upon my head, away from my own countrymen whose loyalty is not in doubt, and safe from the judgment of my peers whose judgment I do not shrink from. I admit no other judgment but theirs. I accept no verdict save at their hands. I assert from this dock that I am being tried here, not because it is just, but because it is unjust. Place me before a jury of my own countrymen, be it Protestant or Catholic, Unionist or Nationalist, Sinn Féineach or Orangemen, and I shall accept the verdict and bow to the statute and all its penalties. But I shall accept no meaner finding against me than that of those whose loyalty I endanger by my example and to whom alone I made appeal. If they adjudge me guilty, then guilty I am. It is not I who am afraid of their verdict; it is the Crown. If this be not so, why fear the test? I fear it not. I demand it as my right.

That, my Lord, is the condemnation of English rule, of English-made law, of English government in Ireland, that it dare not rest on the will of the Irish people, but it exists in defiance of their will—that it is a rule derived not from right, but from conquest. Conquest, my Lord, gives no title, and if it exists over the body, it fails over the mind. It can exert no empire over men's reason and judgment and affections; and it is from this law of conquest without title to the reason, judgment, and affection of my own countrymen that I appeal.

My Lord, I beg to say a few more words. As I say, that was my opinion arrived at many days ago while I was a prisoner. I have no hesitation in reaffirming it here, and I hope that the gentlemen of the press who did not hear me yesterday may have heard me distinctly today. I wish my words to go much beyond this court.

I would add that the generous expression of sympathy extended me from many quarters, particularly from America, have touched me very much. In that country, as in my own, I am sure my motives are understood and not misjudged—for the achievement of their liberties has been an abiding inspiration to Irishmen and to all men elsewhere rightly struggling to be free in like cause.

My Lord Chief Justice, if I may continue, I am not called upon, I conceive, to say anything in answer to the enquiry your Lordship has addressed to me why sentence should not be passed upon me. Since I do not admit any verdict in this court, I cannot, my Lord, admit the fitness of the sentence that of necessity must follow it from this court. I hope I shall be acquitted of presumption if I say that the court I see before me now is not this High Court of Justice of England, but a far greater, a far higher, far older assemblage of justices —that of the people of Ireland. Since in the acts which have led to this trial it was the people of Ireland I sought to serve—and them alone—I leave my judgment and my sentence in their hands.

Let me pass from myself and my own fate to a far more pressing, as it is a far more urgent, theme—not the fate of the individual Irishman who may have tried and failed, but the claims and the fate of the country that has not failed. Ireland has outlived the failure of all her hopes—and yet she still hopes. Ireland has seen her sons— aye, and her daughters too—suffer from generation to generation always from the same cause, meeting always the same fate, and always at the hands of the same power; and always a fresh generation has passed on to withstand the same oppression. For if English authority be omnipotent—a power, as Mr. Gladstone phrased it, that reaches to the very ends of the earth—Irish hope exceeds the dimensions of that power, excels its authority, and renews with each generation the claims of the last. The cause that begets this indomitable persistency, the faculty of preserving through centuries of misery the remembrance of lost liberty, this surely is the noblest cause men ever strove for, ever lived for, ever died for. If this be the case I stand here today indicted for, and convicted of sustaining, then I stand in a goodly company and a right noble succession.

My counsel has referred to the Ulster Volunteer movement, and I will not touch at length upon that ground save only to say this, that neither I nor any of the leaders of the Irish Volunteers who were founded in Dublin in November, 1913, had quarrel with the Ulster Volunteers as such, who were born a year earlier. Our movement was not directed against them, but against the men who misused and misdirected the courage, the sincerity, and the local patriotism of the men of the north of Ireland. On the contrary, we welcomed the coming of the Ulster Volunteers, even while we deprecated the aims and intentions of those Englishmen who sought to pervert to an English party use—to the mean purposes of their own bid for place and power in England—the armed activities of simple Irishmen. We aimed at winning the Ulster Volunteers to the cause of a united Ireland. We aimed at uniting all Irishmen in a natural and national bond of cohesion based on mutual self-respect. Our hope was a natural one, and if left to ourselves, not hard to accomplish. If external influences of disintegration would but leave us alone, we were sure that nature itself must bring us together. It was not we, the Irish Volunteers, who broke the law, but a British party. The Government had permitted the Ulster Volunteers to be armed by Englishmen, to threaten not merely an English party in its hold on office, but to threaten that party through the lives and blood of Irishmen. The battle was to be fought in Ireland in order that the political "outs" of today should be the "ins" of tomorrow in Great Britain. A law designed for the benefit of Ireland was to be met, not on the floor of Parliament, where the fight had indeed been won, but on the field of battle much nearer home, where the armies would be composed of Irishmen slaying each other for the same English party again; and the British Navy would be the chartered "transports" that were to bring to our shores a numerous assemblage of military and ex-military experts in the congenial and profitable business of holding down subject populations abroad. Our choice lay in submitting to foreign lawlessness or resisting it, and we did not hesitate to choose. But while the lawbreakers had armed their would-be agents openly, and had been permitted to arm them openly, we were met within a few days of the founding of our movement, that aimed at uniting Ireland from within, by Government action from without directed against our obtaining any arms at all. The manifesto of the Irish Volunteers, promulgated at a public meeting in Dublin on the 25th November, 1913, stated with sincerity the aims of the organization as I have outlined them. If the aims contained in that manifesto were a threat to the unity of the British Empire, then so much the worse for the Empire. An Empire that can only be held together by one section of its governing population perpetually holding down and sowing dissension among a smaller but none the less governing section, must have some canker at its heart, some ruin at its root. The Government that permitted the arming of those whose leaders declared that Irish national unity was a thing that should be opposed by force of arms, within nine days of the issue of our manifesto of good will to Irishmen of every creed and class, took steps to nullify our efforts by prohibiting the import of all arms into Ireland as if it had been a hostile and blockaded coast. And this proclamation of the 4th December, 1913, known as the Arms Proclamation, was itself based on an illegal interpretation of the law, as the Chief Secretary has now publicly confessed. The proclamation was met by the loyalists of Great Britain with an act of still more lawless defiance —an act of widespread gun-running into Ulster that was denounced by the Lord Chancellor of England as "grossly illegal and utterly unconstitutional." How did the Irish Volunteers meet the incitements of civil war that were uttered by the party of law and order in England when they saw the prospect of deriving political profit to themselves from bloodshed among Irishmen?

I can answer for my own acts and speeches. While one English party was responsible for preaching a doctrine of hatred designed to bring about civil war in Ireland, the other, and that the party in power, took no active steps to restrain a propaganda that found its advocates in the Army, Navy, and Privy Council—in the Houses of Parliament and in the State Church—a propaganda the methods of whose expression were so "grossly illegal and utterly unconstitutional" that even the Lord Chancellor of England could find only words and no repressive action to apply to them. Since lawlessness sat in high places in England and laughed at the law as at the custodians of the law, what wonder was it that Irishmen should refuse to accept the verbal protestations of an English Lord Chancellor as a sufficient safeguard for their lives and their liberties? I know not how all my colleagues on the Volunteer Committee in Dublin reviewed the growing menace, but those with whom I was in closest co-operation redoubled, in face of these threats from without, our efforts to unite all Irishmen from within. Our appeals were made to Protestant and Unionist as much almost as to Catholic and Nationalist Irishmen. We hoped that by the exhibition of affection and good will on our part toward our political opponents in Ireland we should yet succeed in winning them from the side of an English party whose sole interest in our country lay in its oppression in the past, and in the present in its degradation to the mean and narrow needs of their political animosities. It is true that they based their actions, so they averred, on "fears for the Empire," and on a very diffuse loyalty that took in all the peoples of the Empire, save only the Irish. That blessed word "Empire" that bears so paradoxical a resemblance to charity! For if charity begins at home, "Empire" begins in other men's homes, and both may cover a multitude of sins. I for one was determined that Ireland was much more to me than "Empire," and that if charity begins at home, so must loyalty. Since arms were so necessary to make our organization a reality, and to give to the minds of Irishmen menaced with the most outrageous threats, a sense of security, it was our bounden duty to get arms before all else. I decided with this end in view to go to America, with surely a better right to appeal to Irishmen there for help in an hour of great national trial than those envoys of "Empire" could assert for their week-end descents upon Ireland, or their appeals to Germany. If, as the right honorable gentleman, the present Attorney General, asserted in a speech at Manchester, Nationalists would neither fight for Home Rule nor pay for it, it was our duty to show him that we knew how to do both. Within a few weeks of my arrival in the States the fund that had been opened to secure arms for the Volunteers of Ireland amounted to many thousands of pounds. In every case the money subscribed, whether it came from the purse of the wealthy man or the still readier pocket of the poor man, was Irish gold.

Then came the war. As Mr. Birrell said in his evidence recently laid before the Commission of Enquiry into the causes of the late rebellion in Ireland: "The war upset all our calculations." It upset mine no less than Mr. Birrell's, and put an end to my mission of peaceful effort in America. War between Great Britain and Germany meant, as I believed, ruin for all the hopes we had founded on the enrollment of the Irish Volunteers. A constitutional movement in

Ireland is never very far from a breach of the constitution, as the Loyalists of Ulster had been so eager to show us. The cause is not far to seek. A constitution to be maintained intact must be the achievement and the pride of the people themselves; must rest on their own free will and on their own determination to sustain it, instead of being something resident in another land whose chief representative is an armed force—armed not to protect the population but to hold it down. We had seen the working of the Irish Constitution in the refusal of the army of occupation at the Curragh to obey the orders of the Crown. And now that we were told the first duty of an Irishman was to enter that army, in return for a promissory note, payable after death—a scrap of paper that might or might not be redeemed, I felt over there in America that my first duty was to keep Irishmen at home in the only army that could safeguard our national existence. If small nationalities were to be the pawns in this game of embattled giants, I saw no reason why Ireland should shed her blood in any cause but her own, and if that be treason beyond the seas I am not ashamed to avow it or to answer for it here with my life. And when we had the doctrine of Unionist loyalty at last—"Mausers and Kaisers and any King you like," and I have heard that at Hamburg, not far from Limburg-on-the-Lahn—I felt I needed no other warrant than that these words conveyed to go forth and do likewise. The difference between us was that the Unionist champions chose a path they felt would lead to the Woolsack; while I went a road I knew must lead to the dock. And the event proves we were both right. The difference between us was that my "treason" was based on a ruthless sincerity that forced me to attempt in time and season to carry out in action what I said in word—whereas their treason lay in verbal incitements that they knew need never be made good in their bodies. And so, I am prouder to stand here today in the traitor's dock to answer this impeachment than to fill the place of my right honorable accusers.

(*At this point, the Attorney General rose from his seat, and declaring: "Change places with him? Nothing doing," left the courtroom. Casement resumed:*)

We have been told, we have been asked to hope, that after this war Ireland will get Home Rule, as a reward for the life blood shed in a cause which whoever else its success may benefit can surely not benefit Ireland. And what will Home Rule be in return for what its vague promise has taken and still hopes to take away from Ireland?

It is not necessary to climb the painful stairs of Irish history—that treadmill of a nation whose labors are as vain for her own uplifting as the convict's exertions are for his redemption—to review the long list of British promises made only to be broken—of Irish hopes raised only to be dashed to the ground. Home Rule when it comes, if come it does, will find an Ireland drained of all that is vital to its very existence—unless it be that unquenchable hope we build on the graves of the dead. We are told that if Irishmen go by the thousand to die, not for Ireland, but for Flanders, for Belgium, for a patch of sand on the deserts of Mesopotamia, or a rocky trench on the heights of Gallipoli, they are winning self-government for Ireland. But if they dare to lay down their lives on their native soil, if they dare to dream even that freedom can be won only at home by men resolved to fight for it there, then they are traitors to their country, and their dream and their deaths alike are phases of a dishonorable fantasy. But history is not so recorded in other lands. In Ireland alone in this twentieth century is loyalty held to be a crime. If loyalty be something less than love and more than law, then we have had enough of such loyalty for Ireland or Irishmen. If we are to be indicted as criminals, to be shot as murderers, to be imprisoned as convicts because our offense is that we love Ireland more than we value our lives, then I know not what virtue resides in any offer of self-government held out to brave men on such terms. Self-government is our right, a thing born in us at birth; a thing no more to be doled out to us or withheld from us by another people than the right to life itself—than the right to feel the sun or smell the flowers, or to love our kind. It is only from the convict these things are withheld for crime committed and proven—and Ireland that has wronged no man, that has injured no land, that has sought no dominion over others—Ireland is treated today among the nations of the world as if she was a convicted criminal. If it be treason to fight against such an unnatural fate as this, then I am proud to be a rebel, and shall cling to my "rebellion" with the last drop of my blood. If there be no right of rebellion against a state of things that no savage tribe would endure without resistance, then I am sure that it is better for men to fight and die without right than to live in such a state of right as this. Where all your rights become only an accumulated wrong; where men must beg with bated breath for leave to subsist in their own land, to think their own thoughts, to sing their own songs, to garner the fruits of their own labors—and even while they beg, to see things inexorably withdrawn from them —then surely it is a braver, a saner and a truer thing, to be a rebel in act and deed against such circumstances as these than tamely to accept it as the natural lot of men.

My Lord, I have done. Gentlemen of the jury, I wish to thank you for your verdict. I hope you will not take amiss what I said, or think that I made any imputation upon your truthfulness or your integrity when I spoke and said that this was not a trial by my peers. I maintain that I have a natural right to be tried in that natural jurisdiction, Ireland, my own country, and I would put it to you, how would you feel in the converse case, or rather how would all men here feel in the converse case, if an Englishman had landed here in England, and the Crown or the Government, for its own purposes, had conveyed him secretly from England to Ireland under a false name, committed him to prison under a false name, and brought him before a tribunal in Ireland under a statute which they knew involved a trial before an Irish jury? How would you feel yourselves as Englishmen if that man was to be submitted to trial by jury in a land inflamed against him and believing him to be a criminal, when his only crime was that he had cared for England more than for Ireland?